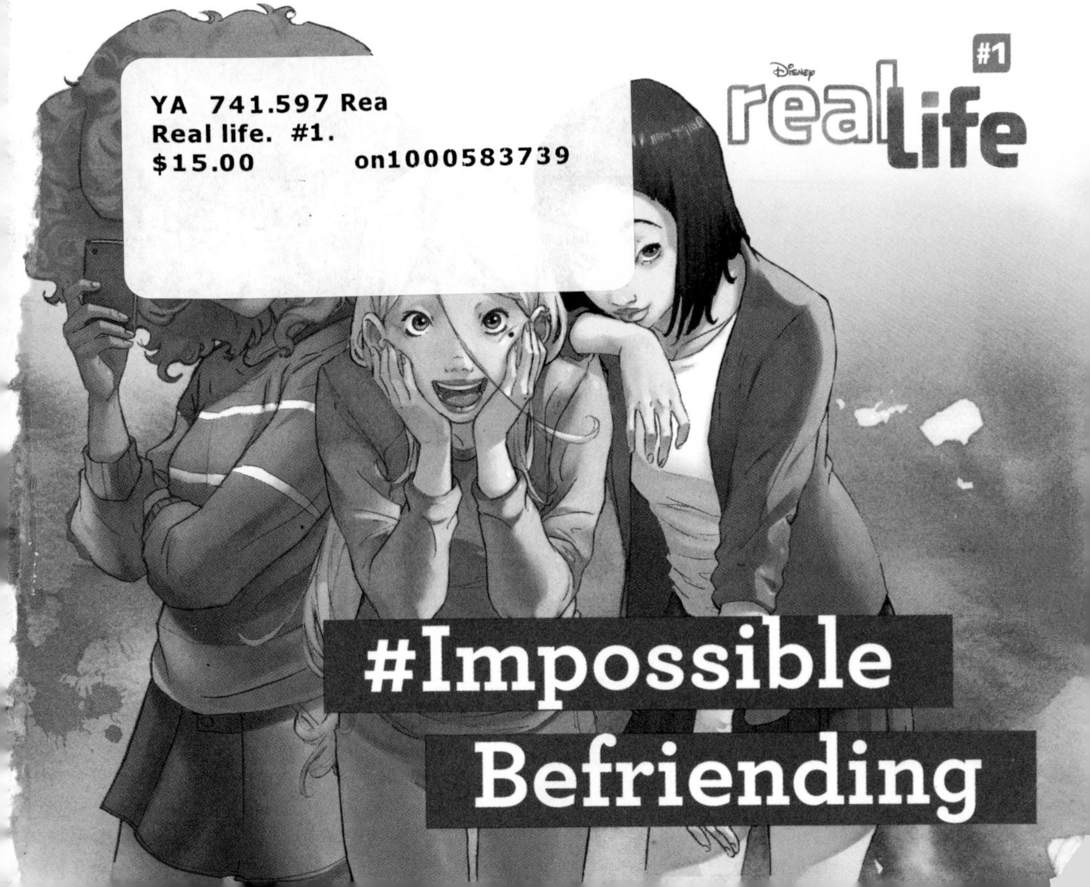
Disney
#1
real life
#Impossible
Befriending

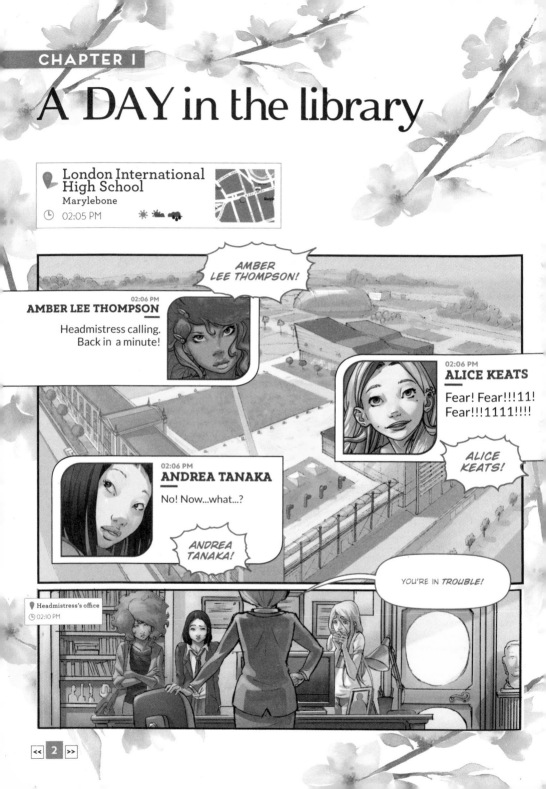

CHAPTER 1

A DAY in the library

London International High School
Marylebone
02:05 PM

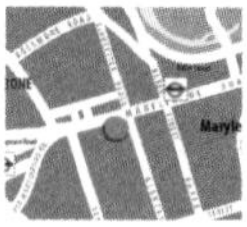

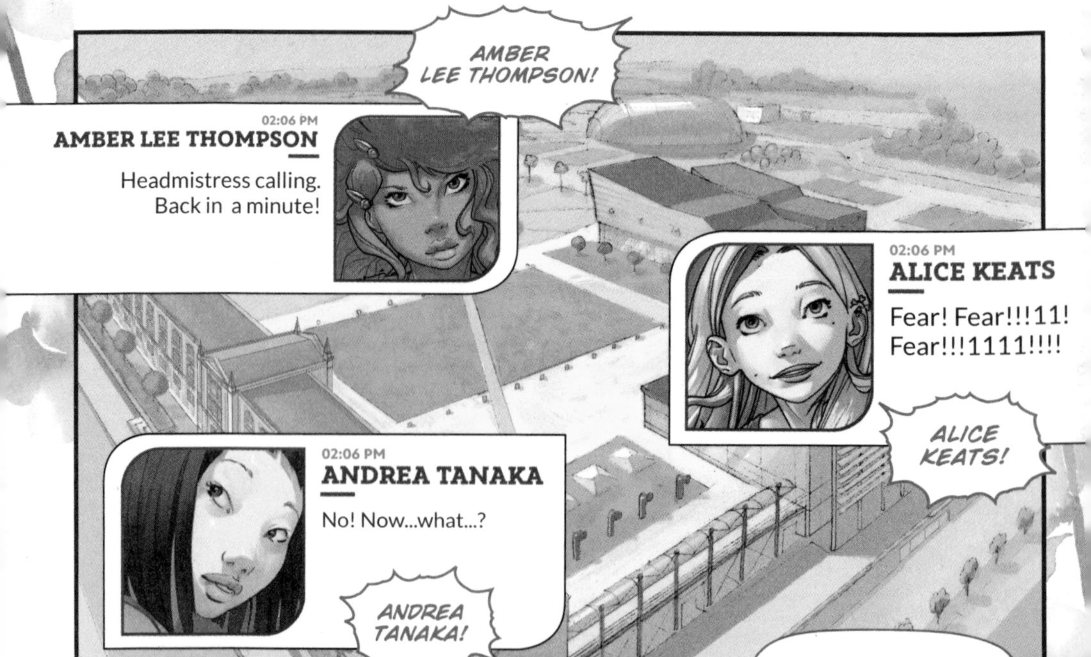
AMBER LEE THOMPSON!
02:06 PM
AMBER LEE THOMPSON
Headmistress calling. Back in a minute!
02:06 PM
ALICE KEATS
Fear! Fear!!!11! Fear!!!1111!!!!
ALICE KEATS!
02:06 PM
ANDREA TANAKA
No! Now...what...?
ANDREA TANAKA!

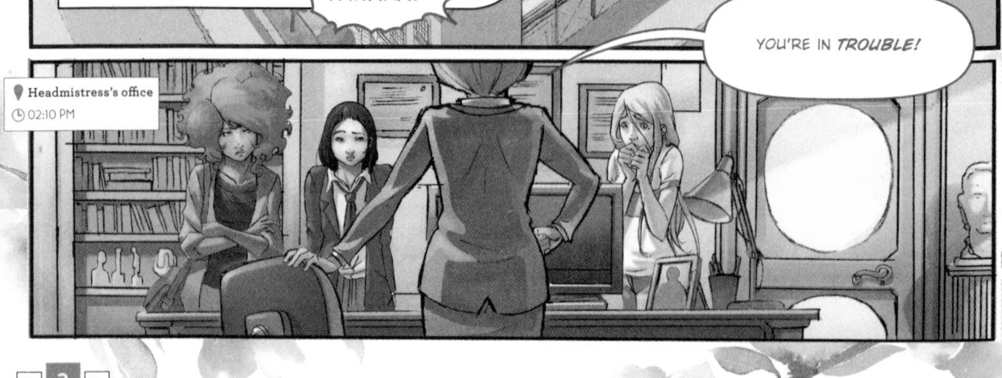
YOU'RE IN TROUBLE!
Headmistress's office
02:10 PM

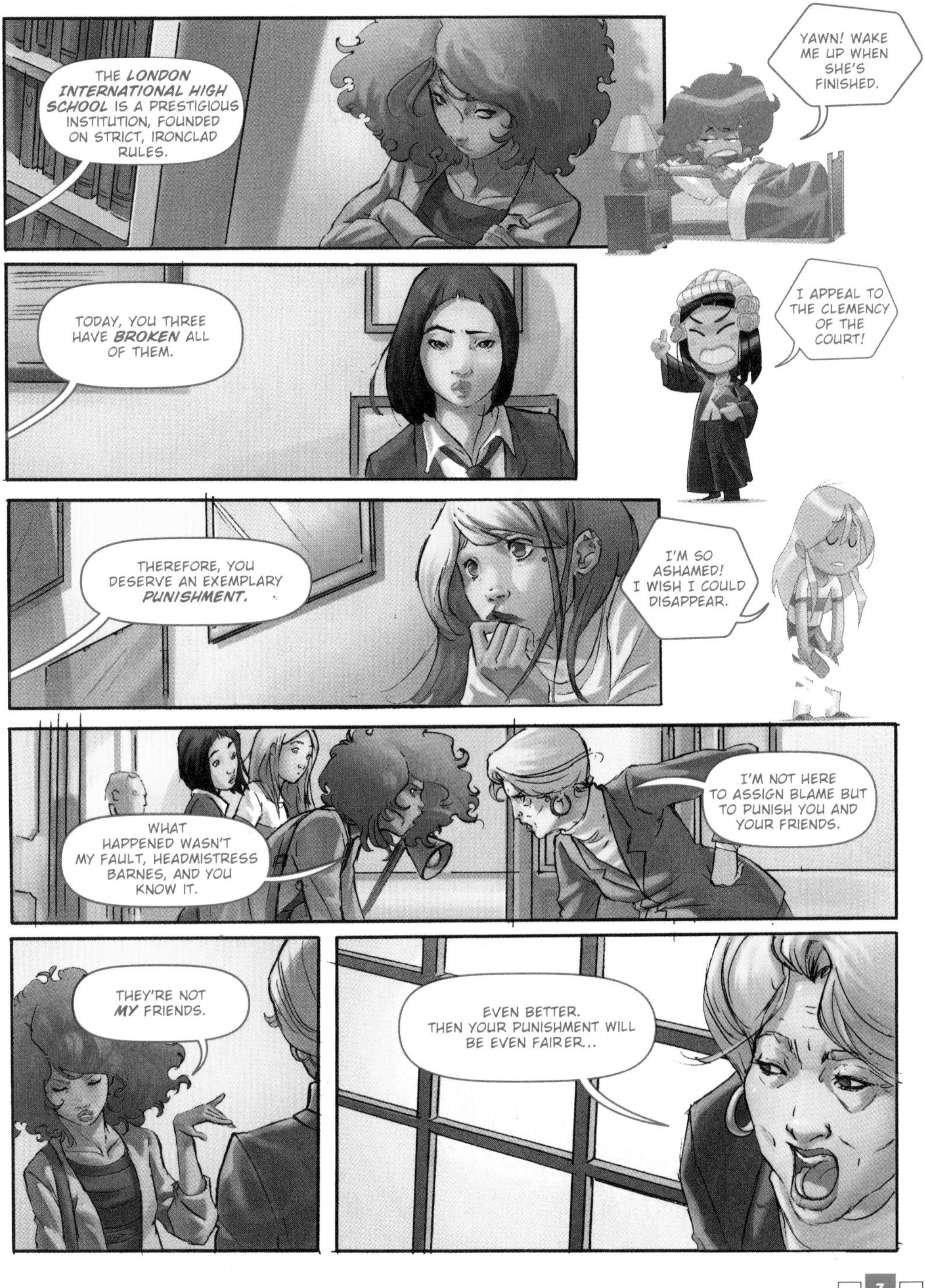
THE LONDON INTERNATIONAL HIGH SCHOOL IS A PRESTIGIOUS INSTITUTION, FOUNDED ON STRICT, IRONCLAD RULES.
YAWN! WAKE ME UP WHEN SHE'S FINISHED.
TODAY, YOU THREE HAVE BROKEN ALL OF THEM.
I APPEAL TO THE CLEMENCY OF THE COURT!
THEREFORE, YOU DESERVE AN EXEMPLARY PUNISHMENT.
I'M SO ASHAMED! I WISH I COULD DISAPPEAR.
WHAT HAPPENED WASN'T MY FAULT, HEADMISTRESS BARNES, AND YOU KNOW IT.
I'M NOT HERE TO ASSIGN BLAME BUT TO PUNISH YOU AND YOUR FRIENDS.
THEY'RE NOT MY FRIENDS.
EVEN BETTER. THEN YOUR PUNISHMENT WILL BE EVEN FAIRER...

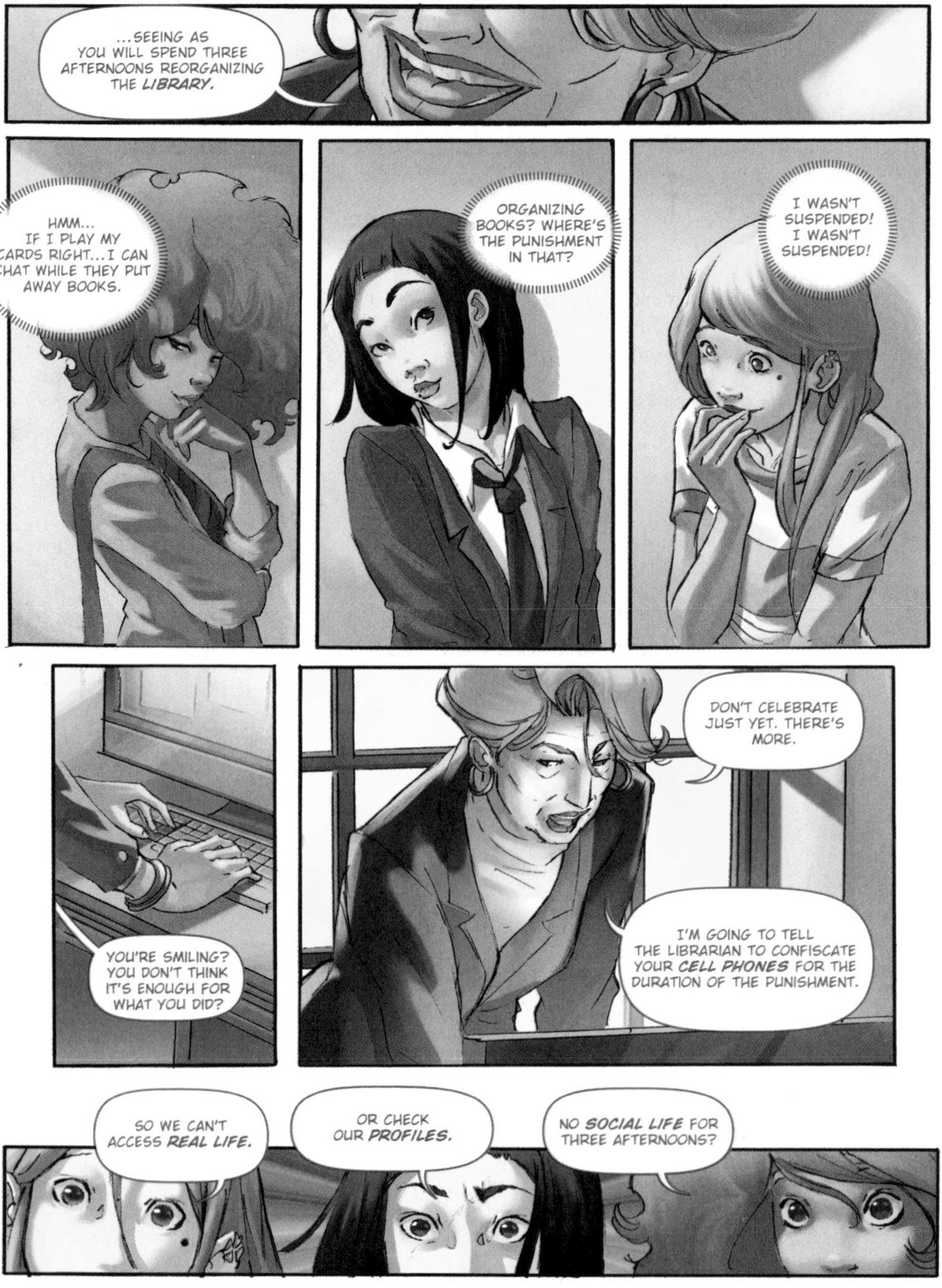
...SEEING AS YOU WILL SPEND THREE AFTERNOONS REORGANIZING THE *LIBRARY.*
HMM... IF I PLAY MY CARDS RIGHT...I CAN CHAT WHILE THEY PUT AWAY BOOKS.
ORGANIZING BOOKS? WHERE'S THE PUNISHMENT IN THAT?
I WASN'T SUSPENDED! I WASN'T SUSPENDED!
YOU'RE SMILING? YOU DON'T THINK IT'S ENOUGH FOR WHAT YOU DID?
DON'T CELEBRATE JUST YET. THERE'S MORE.
I'M GOING TO TELL THE LIBRARIAN TO CONFISCATE YOUR *CELL PHONES* FOR THE DURATION OF THE PUNISHMENT.
SO WE CAN'T ACCESS *REAL LIFE.*
OR CHECK OUR *PROFILES.*
NO *SOCIAL LIFE* FOR THREE AFTERNOONS?

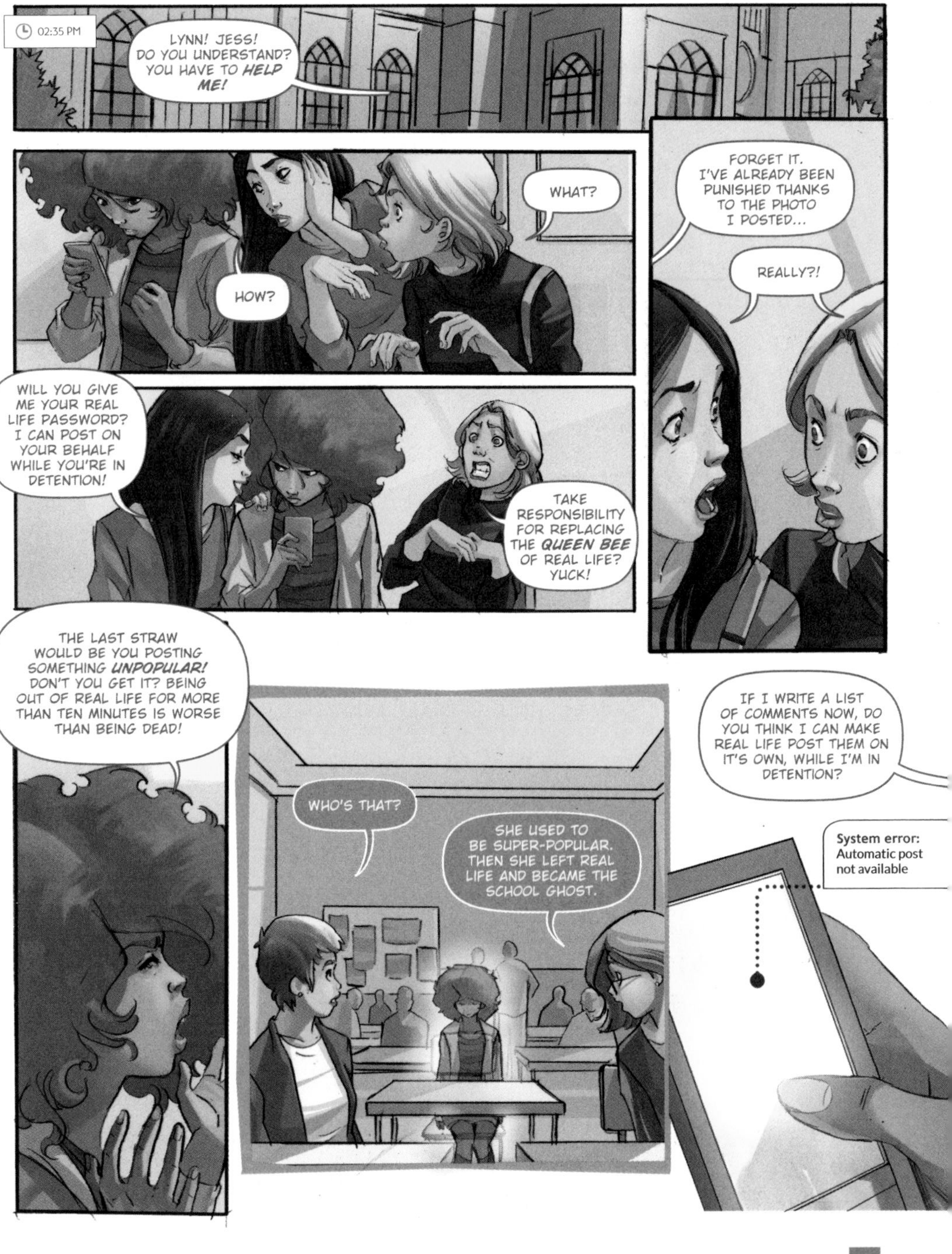
02:35 PM
LYNN! JESS! DO YOU UNDERSTAND? YOU HAVE TO HELP ME!
WHAT?
HOW?
FORGET IT. I'VE ALREADY BEEN PUNISHED THANKS TO THE PHOTO I POSTED...
REALLY?!
WILL YOU GIVE ME YOUR REAL LIFE PASSWORD? I CAN POST ON YOUR BEHALF WHILE YOU'RE IN DETENTION!
TAKE RESPONSIBILITY FOR REPLACING THE QUEEN BEE OF REAL LIFE? YUCK!
THE LAST STRAW WOULD BE YOU POSTING SOMETHING UNPOPULAR! DON'T YOU GET IT? BEING OUT OF REAL LIFE FOR MORE THAN TEN MINUTES IS WORSE THAN BEING DEAD!
WHO'S THAT?
SHE USED TO BE SUPER-POPULAR. THEN SHE LEFT REAL LIFE AND BECAME THE SCHOOL GHOST.
IF I WRITE A LIST OF COMMENTS NOW, DO YOU THINK I CAN MAKE REAL LIFE POST THEM ON IT'S OWN, WHILE I'M IN DETENTION?
System error: Automatic post not available

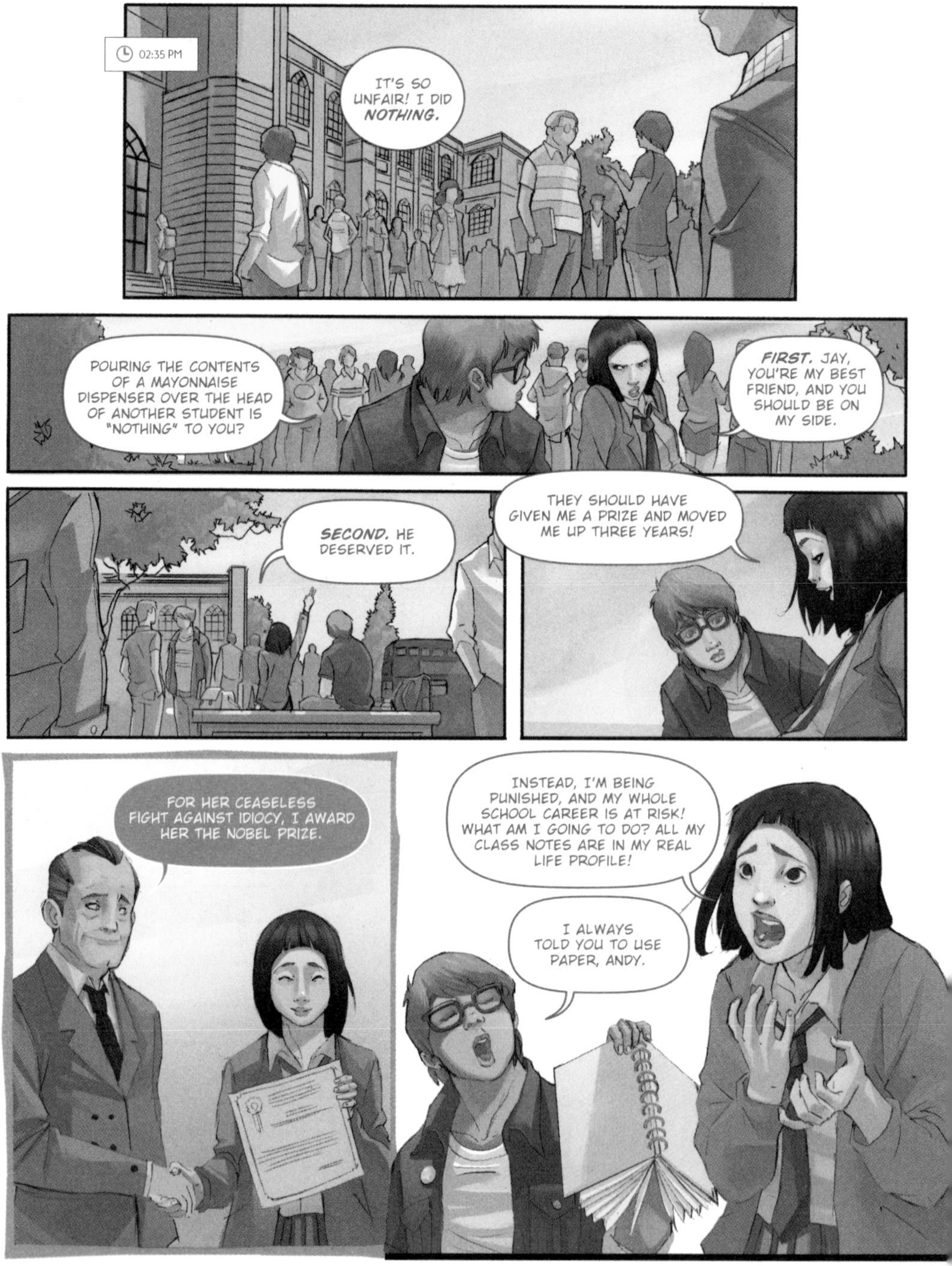
02:35 PM
IT'S SO UNFAIR! I DID *NOTHING.*
POURING THE CONTENTS OF A MAYONNAISE DISPENSER OVER THE HEAD OF ANOTHER STUDENT IS "NOTHING" TO YOU?
FIRST. JAY, YOU'RE MY BEST FRIEND, AND YOU SHOULD BE ON MY SIDE.
SECOND. HE DESERVED IT.
THEY SHOULD HAVE GIVEN ME A PRIZE AND MOVED ME UP THREE YEARS!
FOR HER CEASELESS FIGHT AGAINST IDIOCY, I AWARD HER THE NOBEL PRIZE.
INSTEAD, I'M BEING PUNISHED, AND MY WHOLE SCHOOL CAREER IS AT RISK! WHAT AM I GOING TO DO? ALL MY CLASS NOTES ARE IN MY REAL LIFE PROFILE!
I ALWAYS TOLD YOU TO USE PAPER, ANDY.

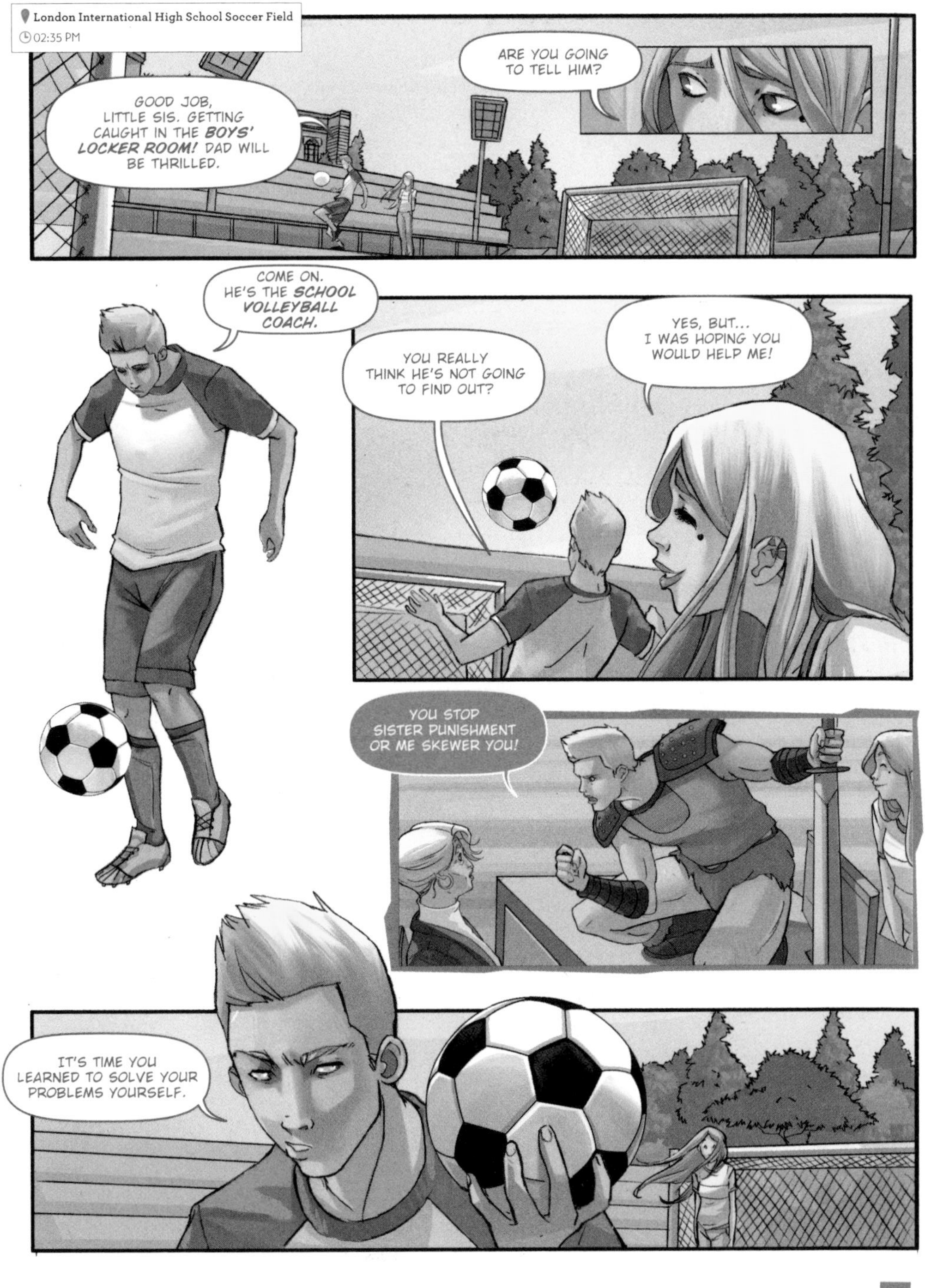
London International High School Soccer Field
02:35 PM
GOOD JOB, LITTLE SIS. GETTING CAUGHT IN THE **BOYS' LOCKER ROOM!** DAD WILL BE THRILLED.
ARE YOU GOING TO TELL HIM?
COME ON. HE'S THE **SCHOOL VOLLEYBALL COACH.**
YOU REALLY THINK HE'S NOT GOING TO FIND OUT?
YES, BUT... I WAS HOPING YOU WOULD HELP ME!
YOU STOP SISTER PUNISHMENT OR ME SKEWER YOU!
IT'S TIME YOU LEARNED TO SOLVE YOUR PROBLEMS YOURSELF.

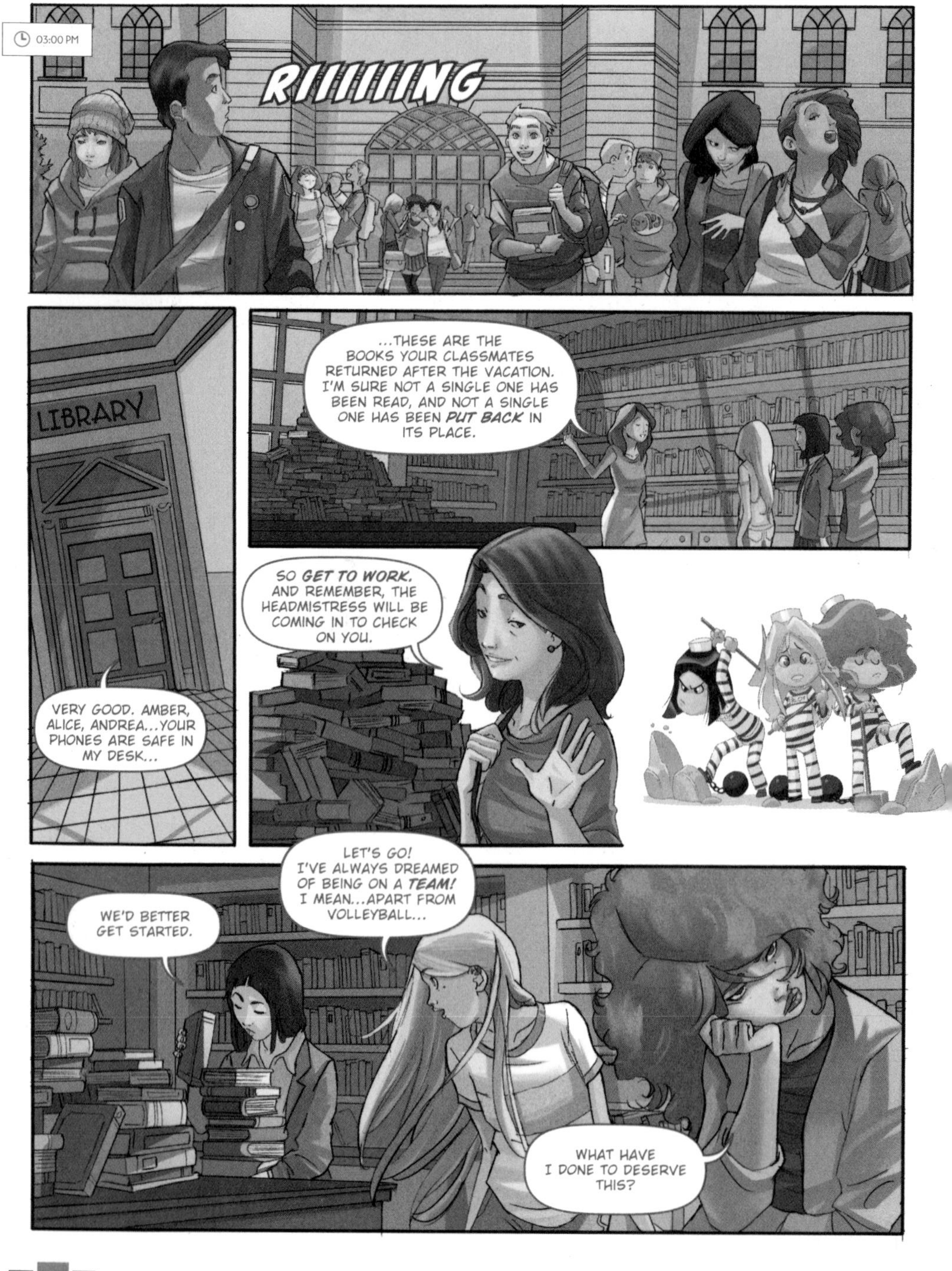
03:00 PM
RIIIIIING
VERY GOOD. AMBER, ALICE, ANDREA...YOUR PHONES ARE SAFE IN MY DESK...
LIBRARY
...THESE ARE THE BOOKS YOUR CLASSMATES RETURNED AFTER THE VACATION. I'M SURE NOT A SINGLE ONE HAS BEEN READ, AND NOT A SINGLE ONE HAS BEEN PUT BACK IN ITS PLACE.
SO GET TO WORK. AND REMEMBER, THE HEADMISTRESS WILL BE COMING IN TO CHECK ON YOU.
WE'D BETTER GET STARTED.
LET'S GO! I'VE ALWAYS DREAMED OF BEING ON A TEAM! I MEAN...APART FROM VOLLEYBALL...
WHAT HAVE I DONE TO DESERVE THIS?

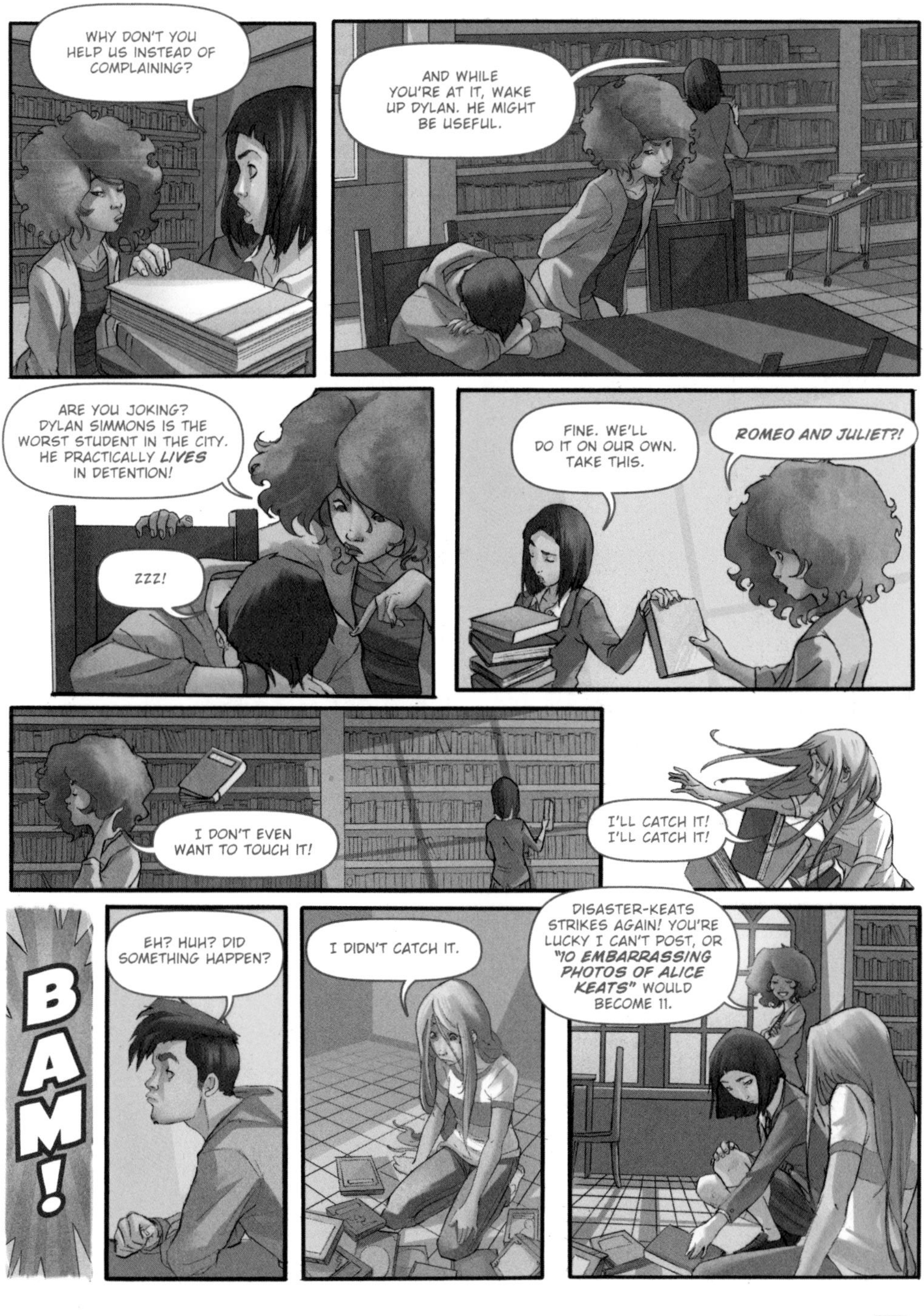
WHY DON'T YOU HELP US INSTEAD OF COMPLAINING?
AND WHILE YOU'RE AT IT, WAKE UP DYLAN. HE MIGHT BE USEFUL.
ARE YOU JOKING? DYLAN SIMMONS IS THE WORST STUDENT IN THE CITY. HE PRACTICALLY LIVES IN DETENTION!
ZZZ!
FINE. WE'LL DO IT ON OUR OWN. TAKE THIS.
ROMEO AND JULIET?!
I DON'T EVEN WANT TO TOUCH IT!
I'LL CATCH IT! I'LL CATCH IT!
BAM!
EH? HUH? DID SOMETHING HAPPEN?
I DIDN'T CATCH IT.
DISASTER-KEATS STRIKES AGAIN! YOU'RE LUCKY I CAN'T POST, OR "10 EMBARRASSING PHOTOS OF ALICE KEATS" WOULD BECOME 11.

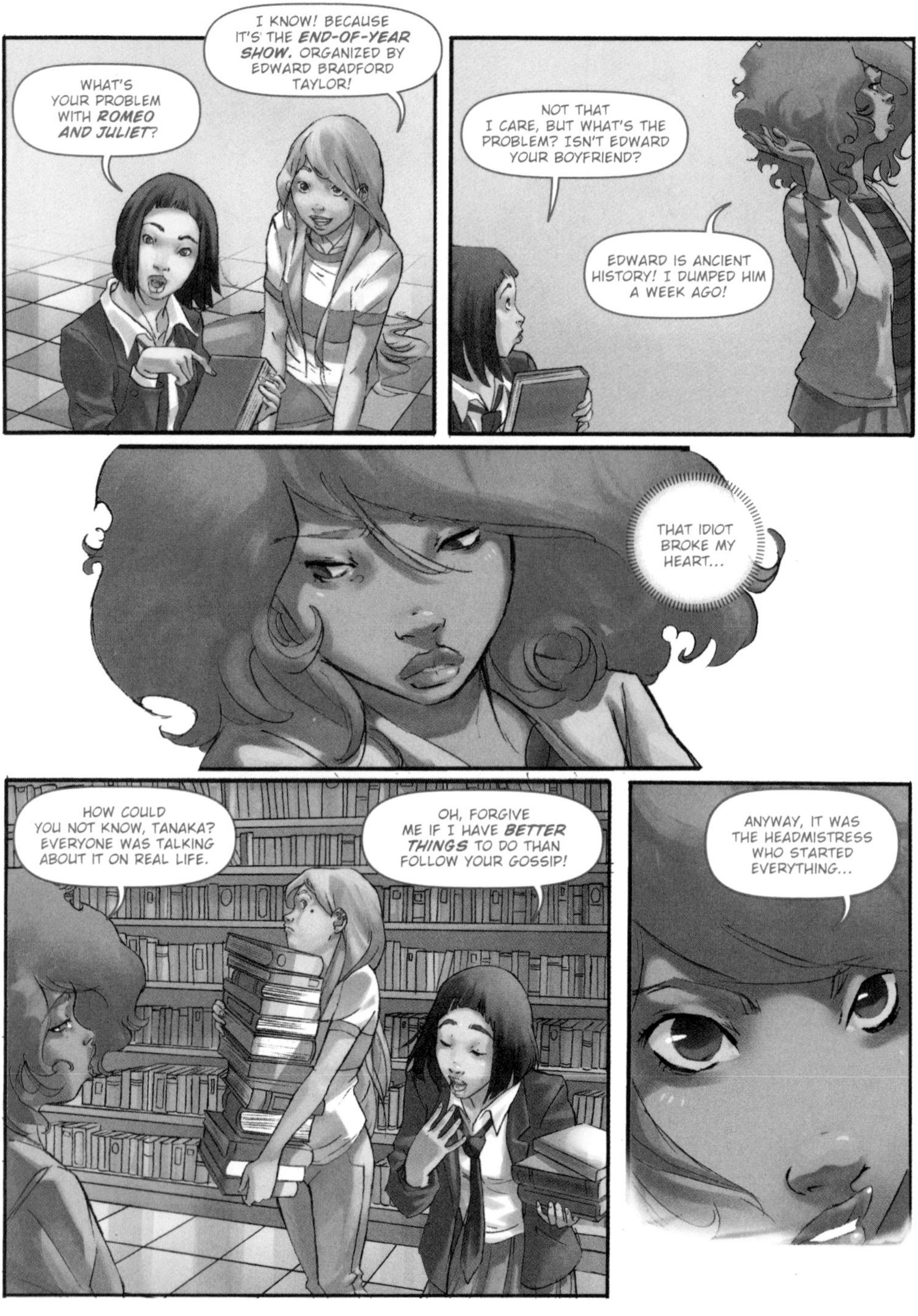
WHAT'S YOUR PROBLEM WITH *ROMEO AND JULIET*?
I KNOW! BECAUSE IT'S THE **END-OF-YEAR SHOW.** ORGANIZED BY EDWARD BRADFORD TAYLOR!
NOT THAT I CARE, BUT WHAT'S THE PROBLEM? ISN'T EDWARD YOUR BOYFRIEND?
EDWARD IS ANCIENT HISTORY! I DUMPED HIM A WEEK AGO!
THAT IDIOT BROKE MY HEART...
HOW COULD YOU NOT KNOW, TANAKA? EVERYONE WAS TALKING ABOUT IT ON REAL LIFE.
OH, FORGIVE ME IF I HAVE ***BETTER THINGS*** TO DO THAN FOLLOW YOUR GOSSIP!
ANYWAY, IT WAS THE HEADMISTRESS WHO STARTED EVERYTHING...

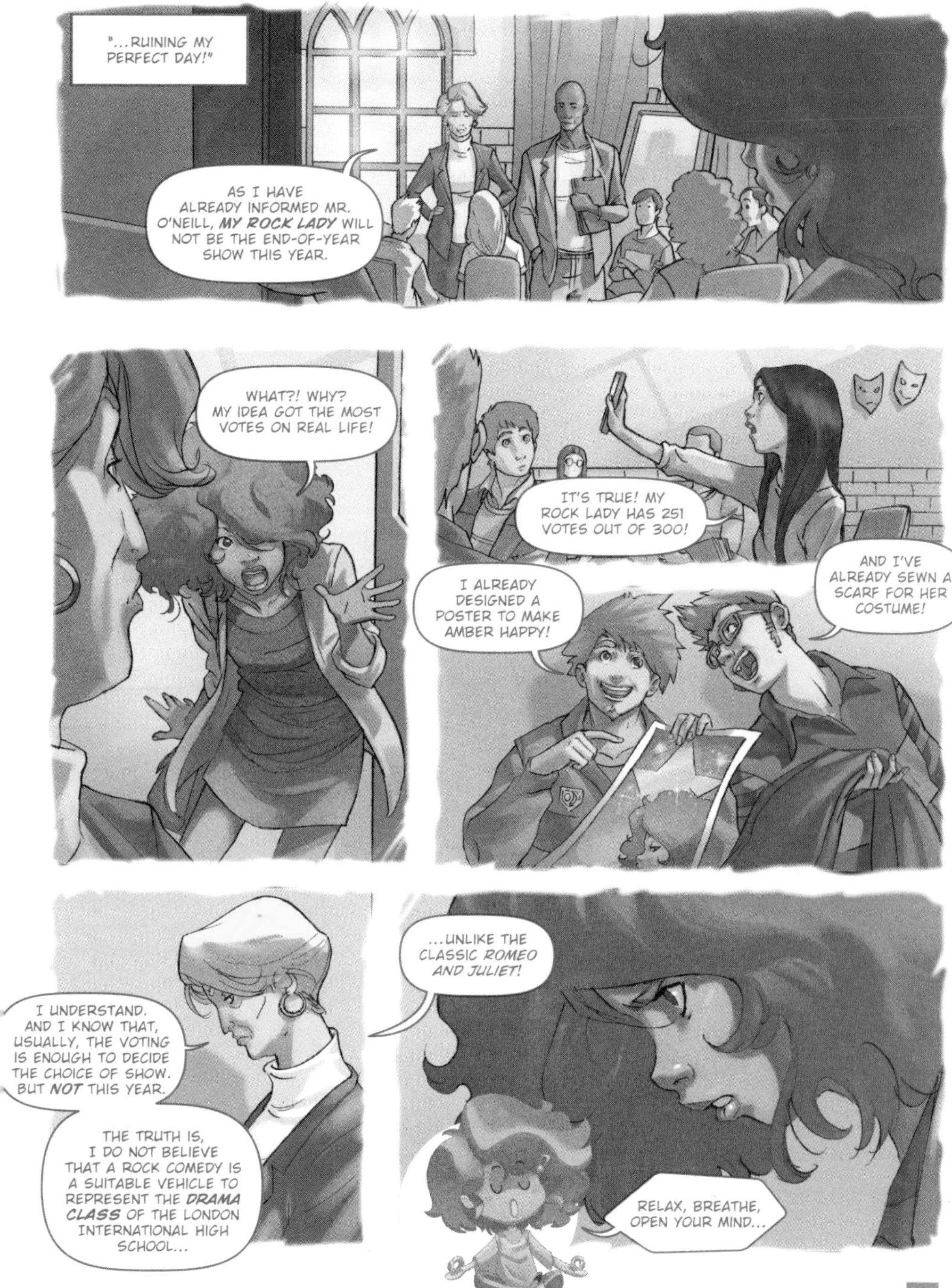
"...RUINING MY PERFECT DAY!"
AS I HAVE ALREADY INFORMED MR. O'NEILL, ***MY ROCK LADY*** WILL NOT BE THE END-OF-YEAR SHOW THIS YEAR.
WHAT?! WHY? MY IDEA GOT THE MOST VOTES ON REAL LIFE!
IT'S TRUE! MY ROCK LADY HAS 251 VOTES OUT OF 300!
I ALREADY DESIGNED A POSTER TO MAKE AMBER HAPPY!
AND I'VE ALREADY SEWN A SCARF FOR HER COSTUME!
I UNDERSTAND. AND I KNOW THAT, USUALLY, THE VOTING IS ENOUGH TO DECIDE THE CHOICE OF SHOW. BUT ***NOT*** THIS YEAR.
THE TRUTH IS, I DO NOT BELIEVE THAT A ROCK COMEDY IS A SUITABLE VEHICLE TO REPRESENT THE ***DRAMA CLASS*** OF THE LONDON INTERNATIONAL HIGH SCHOOL...
...UNLIKE THE CLASSIC *ROMEO AND JULIET*!
RELAX, BREATHE, OPEN YOUR MIND...

ROMEO AND JULIET? EDWARD'S IDEA?! COULD YOU BE MORE *UNORIGINAL*?

AY 11:35 PM

E THE SCHOOLPLAY

MY ROCK LADY

THE LEOPAR

EAST SIDE S

RATS

AND *MY ROCK LADY* CRUSHED IT.

HEADMISTRESS... YOU CAN'T DO THIS!

SHE ALREADY HAS.

MY SHOW IS MUCH BETTER THAN YOURS, EDWARD, AND YOU KNOW IT!

WHAT I KNOW IS THAT *MY* SHOW WILL BE THE ONE ON STAGE.

IT'S NOT FAIR.

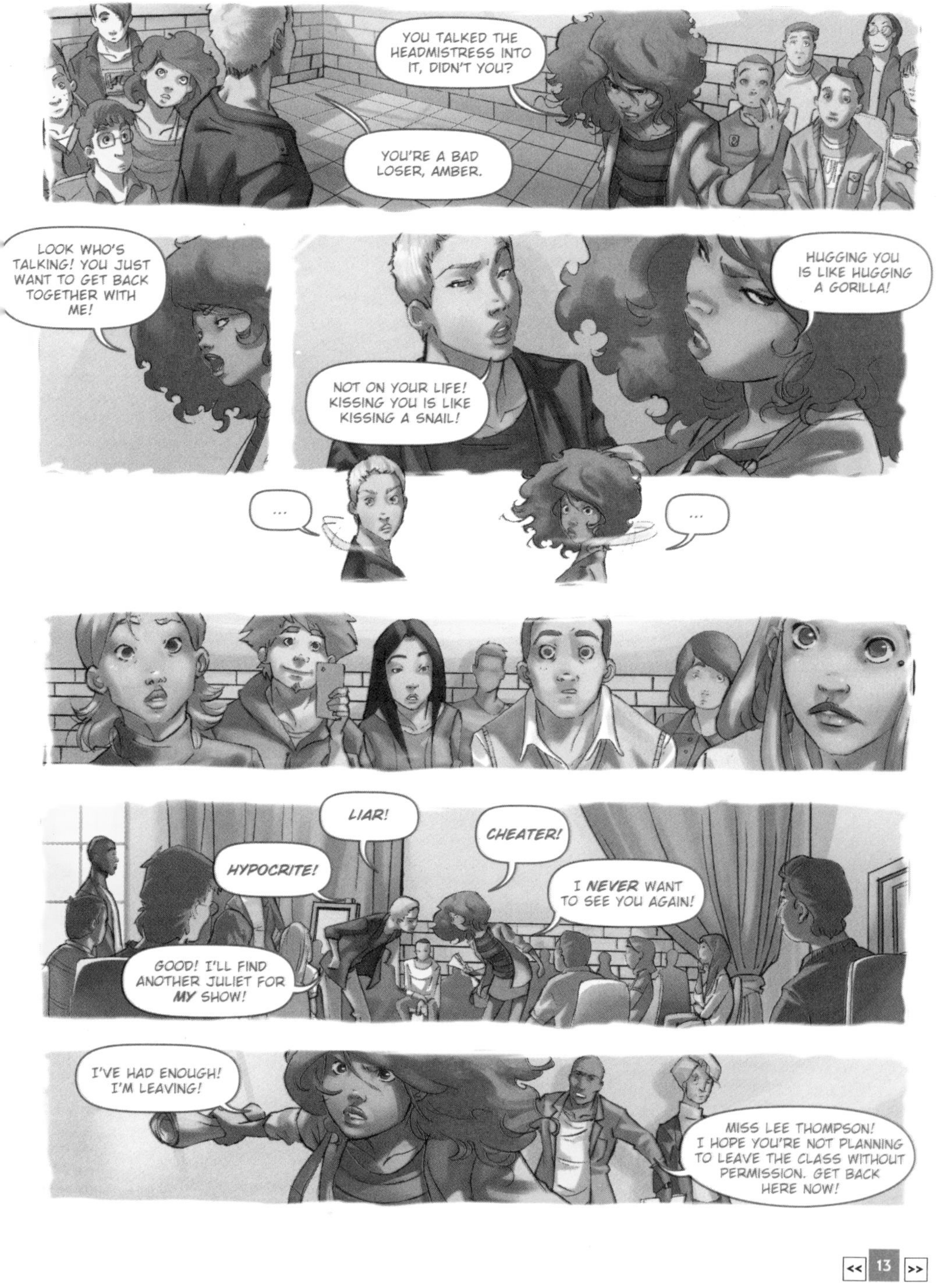
YOU TALKED THE HEADMISTRESS INTO IT, DIDN'T YOU?
YOU'RE A BAD LOSER, AMBER.
LOOK WHO'S TALKING! YOU JUST WANT TO GET BACK TOGETHER WITH ME!
HUGGING YOU IS LIKE HUGGING A GORILLA!
NOT ON YOUR LIFE! KISSING YOU IS LIKE KISSING A SNAIL!
...
...
LIAR!
CHEATER!
HYPOCRITE!
I NEVER WANT TO SEE YOU AGAIN!
GOOD! I'LL FIND ANOTHER JULIET FOR MY SHOW!
I'VE HAD ENOUGH! I'M LEAVING!
MISS LEE THOMPSON! I HOPE YOU'RE NOT PLANNING TO LEAVE THE CLASS WITHOUT PERMISSION. GET BACK HERE NOW!

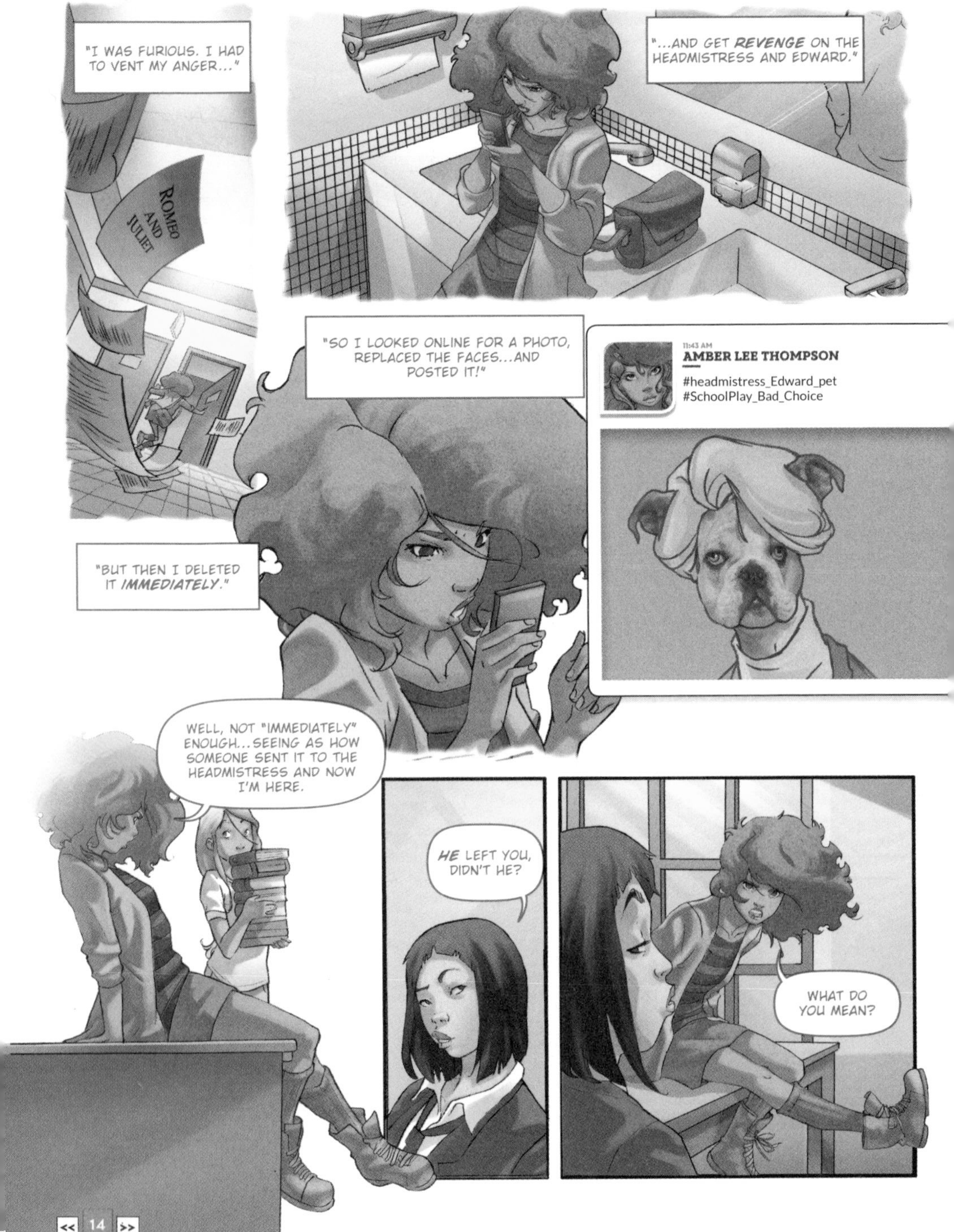
"I WAS FURIOUS. I HAD TO VENT MY ANGER..."
ROMEO AND JULIET
"...AND GET REVENGE ON THE HEADMISTRESS AND EDWARD."
"SO I LOOKED ONLINE FOR A PHOTO, REPLACED THE FACES...AND POSTED IT!"
11:43 AM
AMBER LEE THOMPSON
#headmistress_Edward_pet
#SchoolPlay_Bad_Choice
"BUT THEN I DELETED IT IMMEDIATELY."
WELL, NOT "IMMEDIATELY" ENOUGH...SEEING AS HOW SOMEONE SENT IT TO THE HEADMISTRESS AND NOW I'M HERE.
HE LEFT YOU, DIDN'T HE?
WHAT DO YOU MEAN?

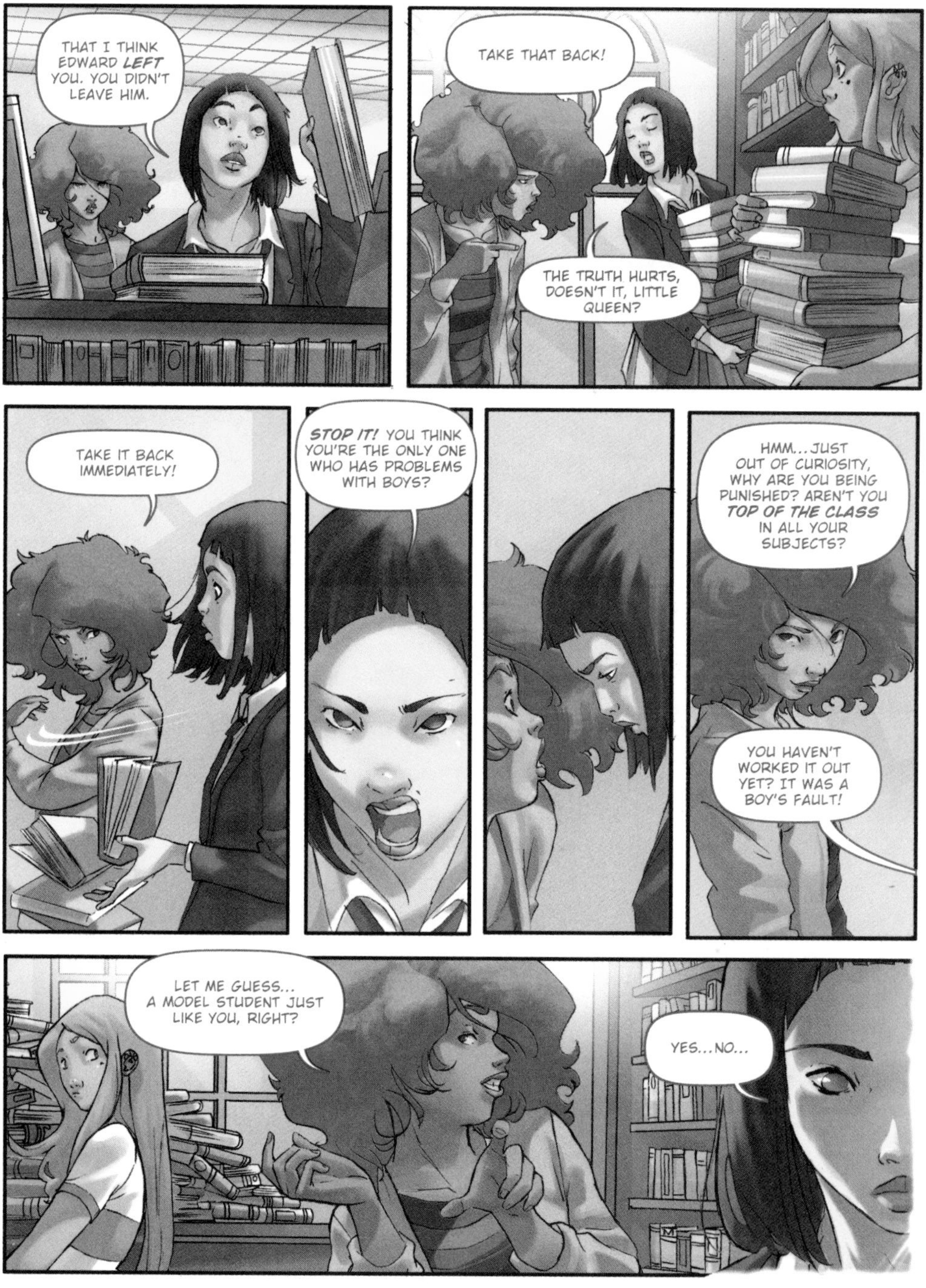
THAT I THINK EDWARD **LEFT** YOU. YOU DIDN'T LEAVE HIM.
TAKE THAT BACK!
THE TRUTH HURTS, DOESN'T IT, LITTLE QUEEN?
TAKE IT BACK IMMEDIATELY!
STOP IT! YOU THINK YOU'RE THE ONLY ONE WHO HAS PROBLEMS WITH BOYS?
HMM... JUST OUT OF CURIOSITY, WHY ARE YOU BEING PUNISHED? AREN'T YOU **TOP OF THE CLASS** IN ALL YOUR SUBJECTS?
YOU HAVEN'T WORKED IT OUT YET? IT WAS A BOY'S FAULT!
LET ME GUESS... A MODEL STUDENT JUST LIKE YOU, RIGHT?
YES... NO...

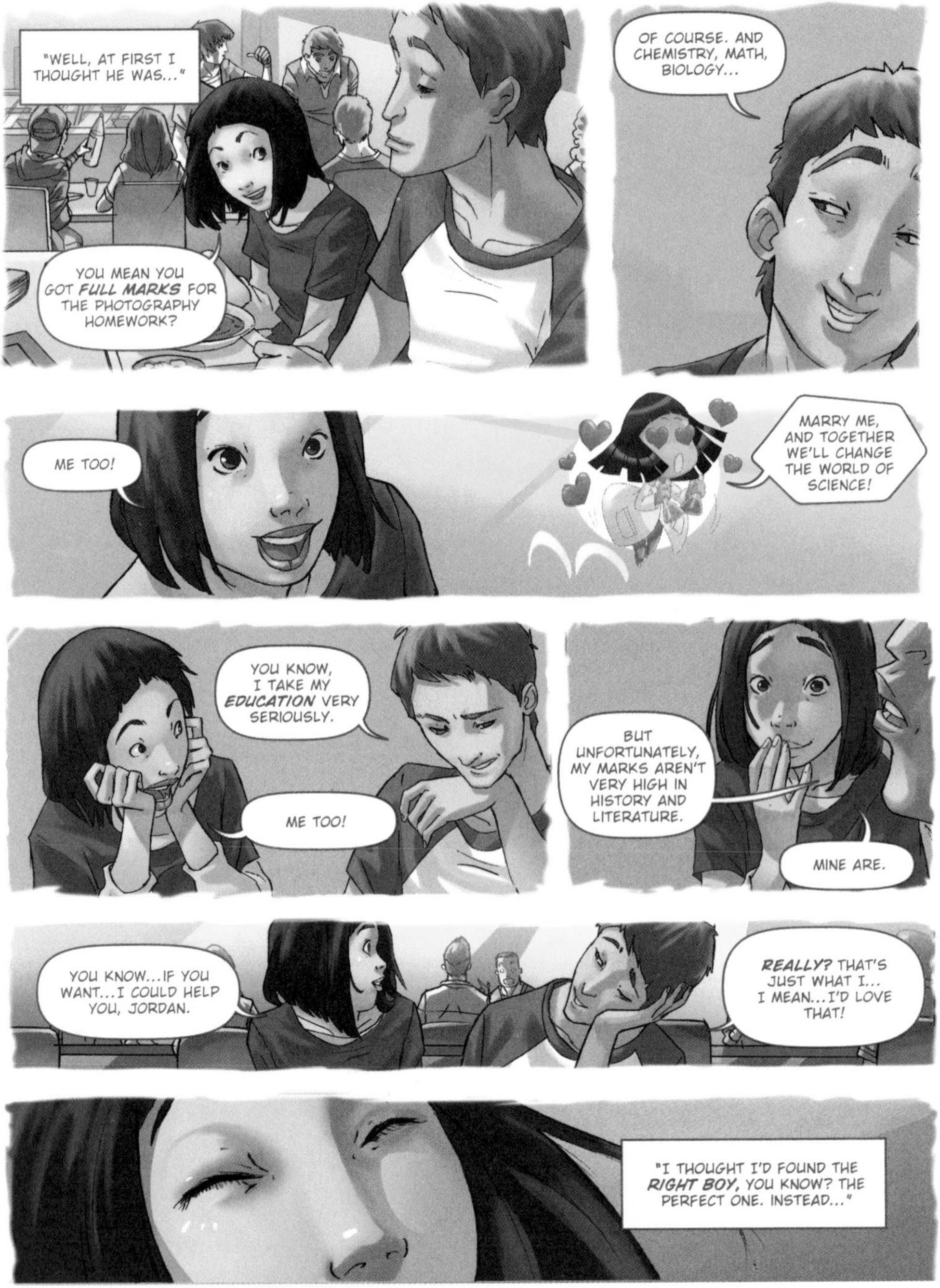
"WELL, AT FIRST I THOUGHT HE WAS..."
YOU MEAN YOU GOT FULL MARKS FOR THE PHOTOGRAPHY HOMEWORK?
OF COURSE. AND CHEMISTRY, MATH, BIOLOGY...
ME TOO!
MARRY ME, AND TOGETHER WE'LL CHANGE THE WORLD OF SCIENCE!
YOU KNOW, I TAKE MY EDUCATION VERY SERIOUSLY.
ME TOO!
BUT UNFORTUNATELY, MY MARKS AREN'T VERY HIGH IN HISTORY AND LITERATURE.
MINE ARE.
YOU KNOW...IF YOU WANT...I COULD HELP YOU, JORDAN.
REALLY? THAT'S JUST WHAT I... I MEAN...I'D LOVE THAT!
"I THOUGHT I'D FOUND THE RIGHT BOY, YOU KNOW? THE PERFECT ONE. INSTEAD..."

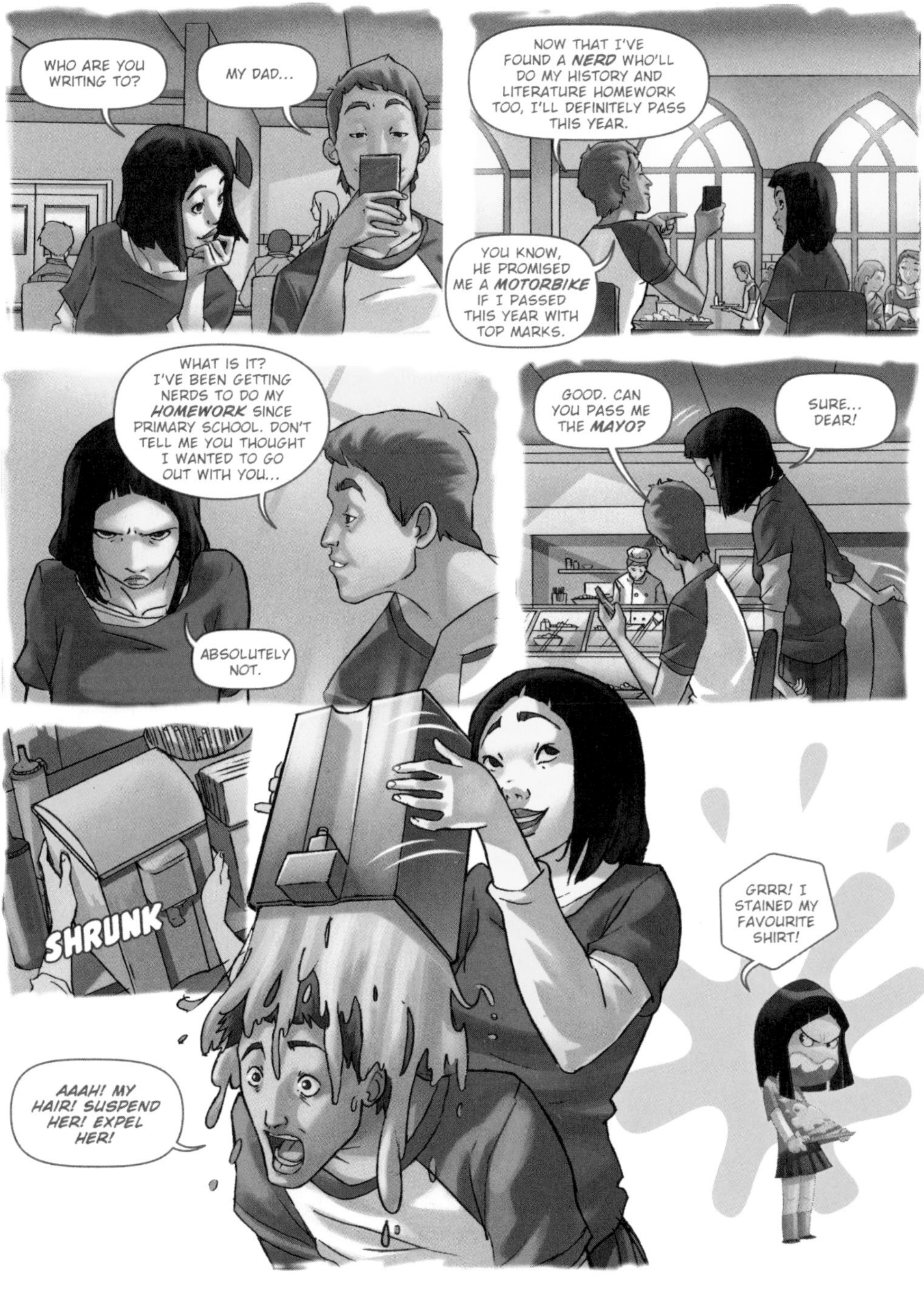
WHO ARE YOU WRITING TO?
MY DAD...
NOW THAT I'VE FOUND A NERD WHO'LL DO MY HISTORY AND LITERATURE HOMEWORK TOO, I'LL DEFINITELY PASS THIS YEAR.
YOU KNOW, HE PROMISED ME A MOTORBIKE IF I PASSED THIS YEAR WITH TOP MARKS.
WHAT IS IT? I'VE BEEN GETTING NERDS TO DO MY HOMEWORK SINCE PRIMARY SCHOOL. DON'T TELL ME YOU THOUGHT I WANTED TO GO OUT WITH YOU...
ABSOLUTELY NOT.
GOOD. CAN YOU PASS ME THE MAYO?
SURE... DEAR!
SHRUNK
AAAH! MY HAIR! SUSPEND HER! EXPEL HER!
GRRR! I STAINED MY FAVOURITE SHIRT!

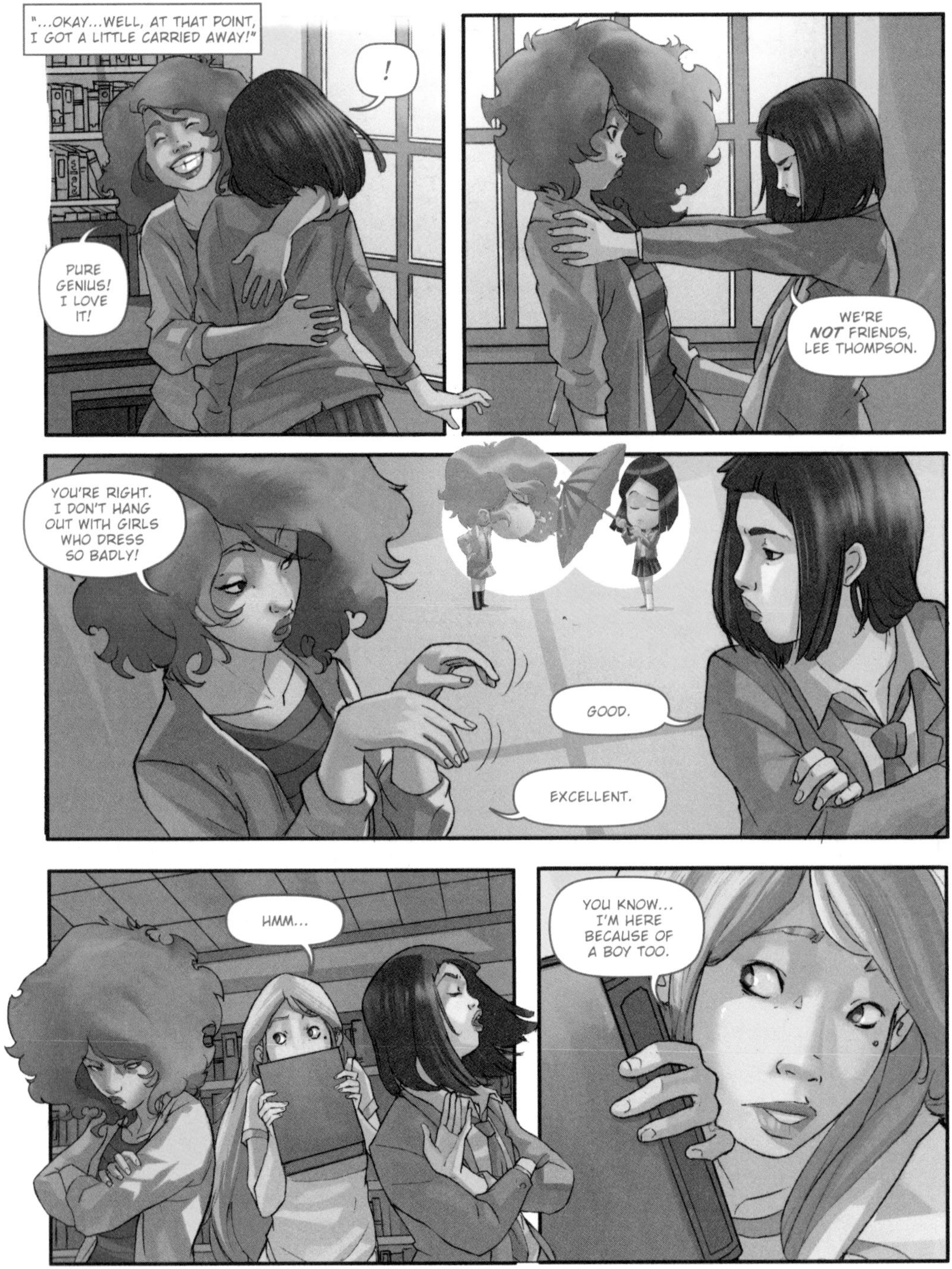
"...OKAY...WELL, AT THAT POINT, I GOT A LITTLE CARRIED AWAY!"
!
PURE GENIUS! I LOVE IT!
WE'RE **NOT** FRIENDS, LEE THOMPSON.
YOU'RE RIGHT. I DON'T HANG OUT WITH GIRLS WHO DRESS SO BADLY!
GOOD.
EXCELLENT.
HMM...
YOU KNOW... I'M HERE BECAUSE OF A BOY TOO.

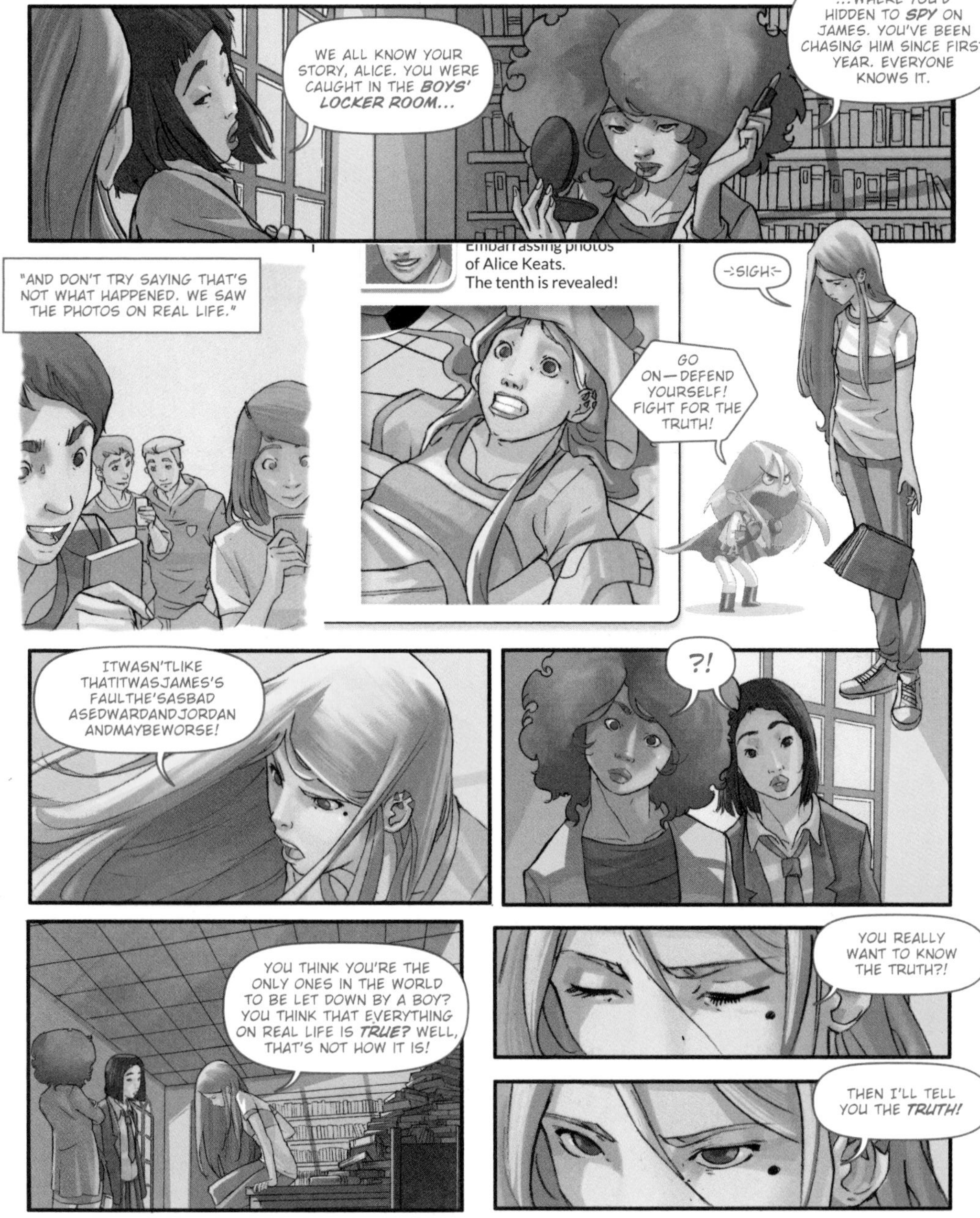
WE ALL KNOW YOUR STORY, ALICE. YOU WERE CAUGHT IN THE BOYS' LOCKER ROOM...
...WHERE YOU'D HIDDEN TO SPY ON JAMES. YOU'VE BEEN CHASING HIM SINCE FIRST YEAR. EVERYONE KNOWS IT.
"AND DON'T TRY SAYING THAT'S NOT WHAT HAPPENED. WE SAW THE PHOTOS ON REAL LIFE."
of Alice Keats.
The tenth is revealed!
SIGH
GO ON—DEFEND YOURSELF! FIGHT FOR THE TRUTH!
ITWASN'TLIKE THATITWASJAMES'S FAULTHE'SASBAD ASEDWARDANDJORDAN ANDMAYBEWORSE!
?!
YOU THINK YOU'RE THE ONLY ONES IN THE WORLD TO BE LET DOWN BY A BOY? YOU THINK THAT EVERYTHING ON REAL LIFE IS TRUE? WELL, THAT'S NOT HOW IT IS!
YOU REALLY WANT TO KNOW THE TRUTH?!
THEN I'LL TELL YOU THE TRUTH!

END OF CHAPTER 1

CHAPTER 2

DREAMING a perfect boy

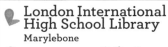

London International High School Library
Marylebone
03:45 PM

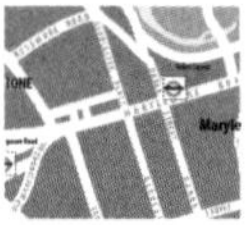

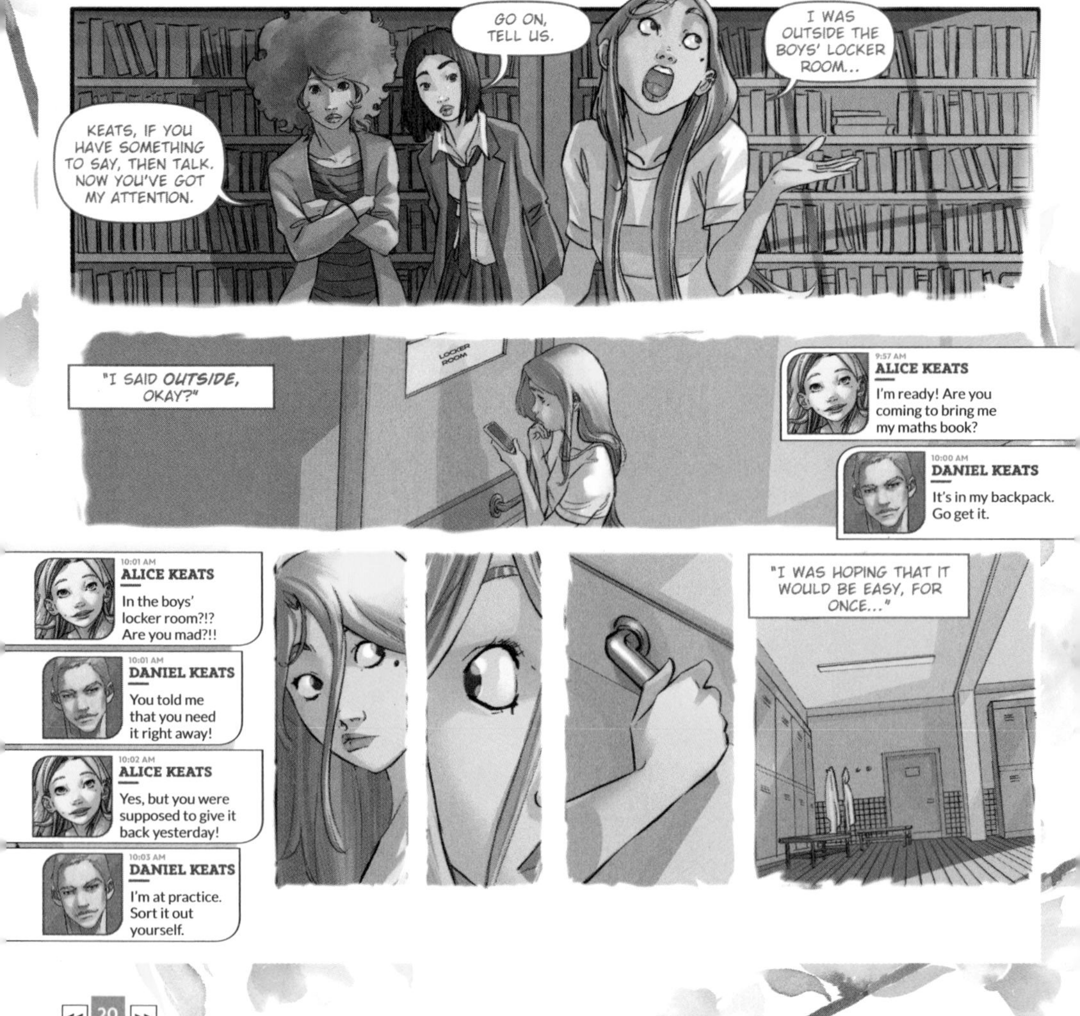
KEATS, IF YOU HAVE SOMETHING TO SAY, THEN TALK. NOW YOU'VE GOT MY ATTENTION.
GO ON, TELL US.
I WAS OUTSIDE THE BOYS' LOCKER ROOM...
"I SAID *OUTSIDE*, OKAY?"
LOCKER ROOM
9:57 AM
ALICE KEATS
I'm ready! Are you coming to bring me my maths book?
10:00 AM
DANIEL KEATS
It's in my backpack. Go get it.
10:01 AM
ALICE KEATS
In the boys' locker room?!? Are you mad?!!
10:01 AM
DANIEL KEATS
You told me that you need it right away!
10:02 AM
ALICE KEATS
Yes, but you were supposed to give it back yesterday!
10:03 AM
DANIEL KEATS
I'm at practice. Sort it out yourself.
"I WAS HOPING THAT IT WOULD BE EASY, FOR ONCE..."

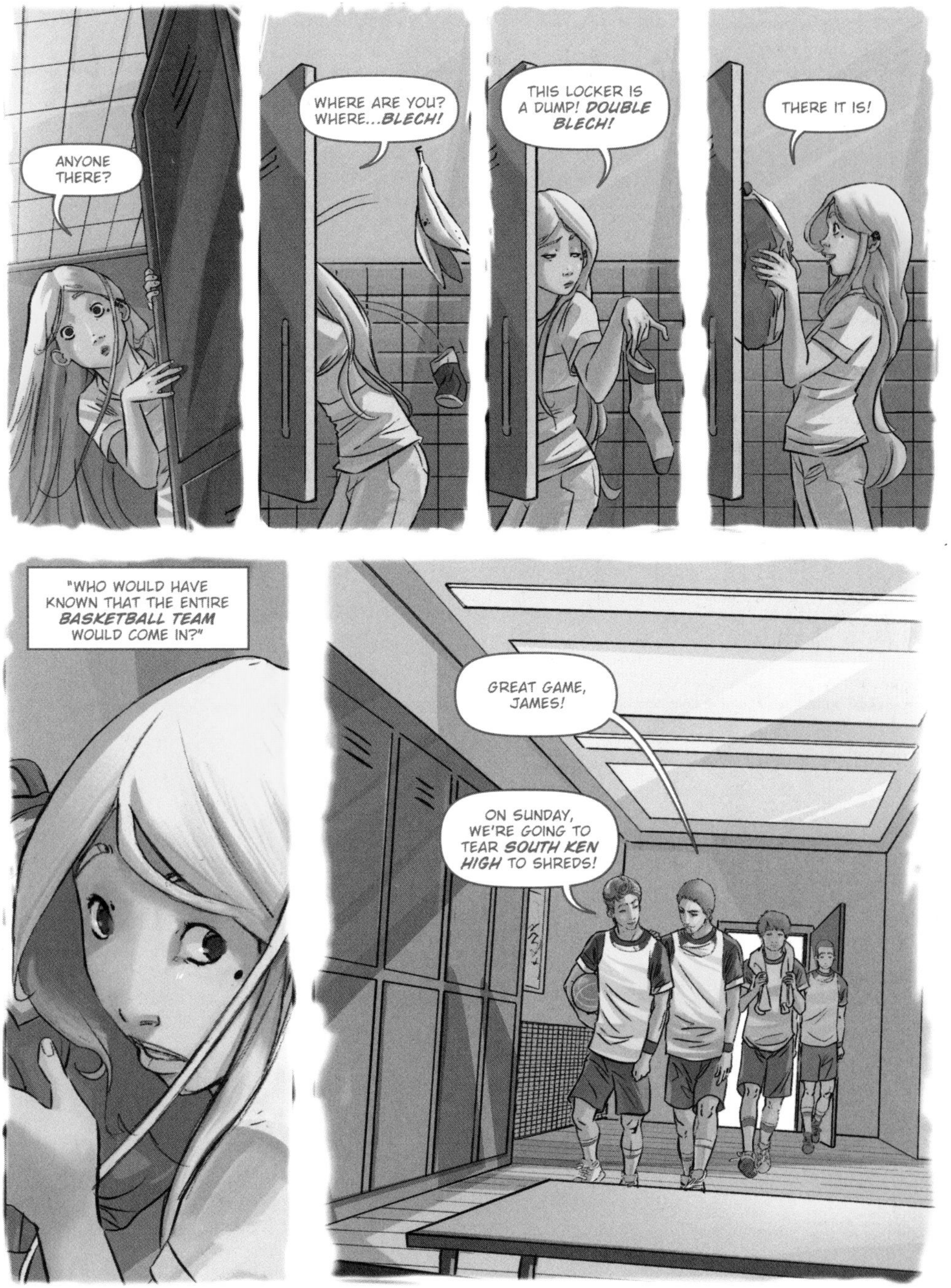
ANYONE THERE?
WHERE ARE YOU? WHERE...BLECH!
THIS LOCKER IS A DUMP! DOUBLE BLECH!
THERE IT IS!
"WHO WOULD HAVE KNOWN THAT THE ENTIRE BASKETBALL TEAM WOULD COME IN?"
GREAT GAME, JAMES!
ON SUNDAY, WE'RE GOING TO TEAR SOUTH KEN HIGH TO SHREDS!

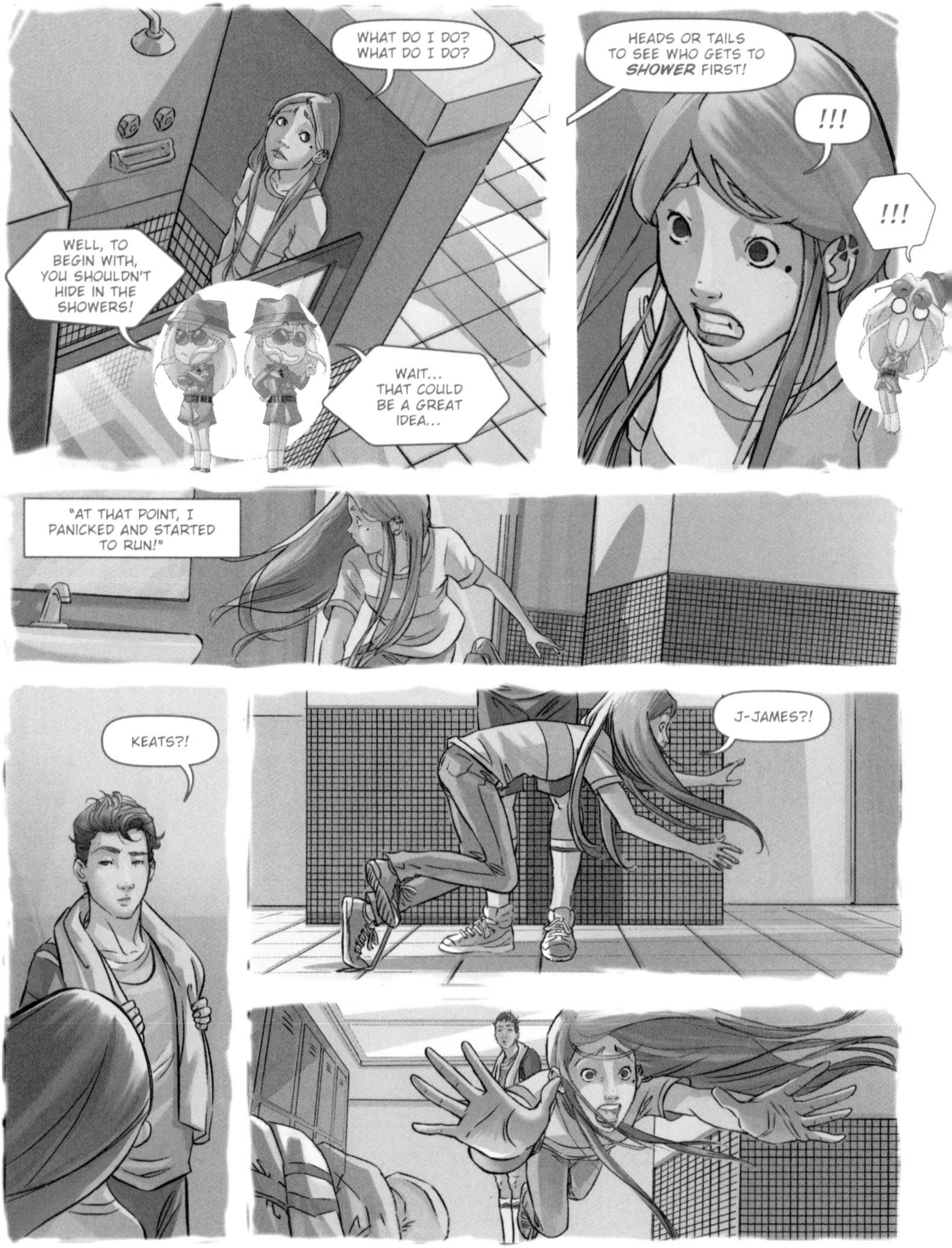
WHAT DO I DO? WHAT DO I DO?
WELL, TO BEGIN WITH, YOU SHOULDN'T HIDE IN THE SHOWERS!
WAIT... THAT COULD BE A GREAT IDEA...
HEADS OR TAILS TO SEE WHO GETS TO SHOWER FIRST!
!!!
!!!
"AT THAT POINT, I PANICKED AND STARTED TO RUN!"
KEATS?!
J-JAMES?!

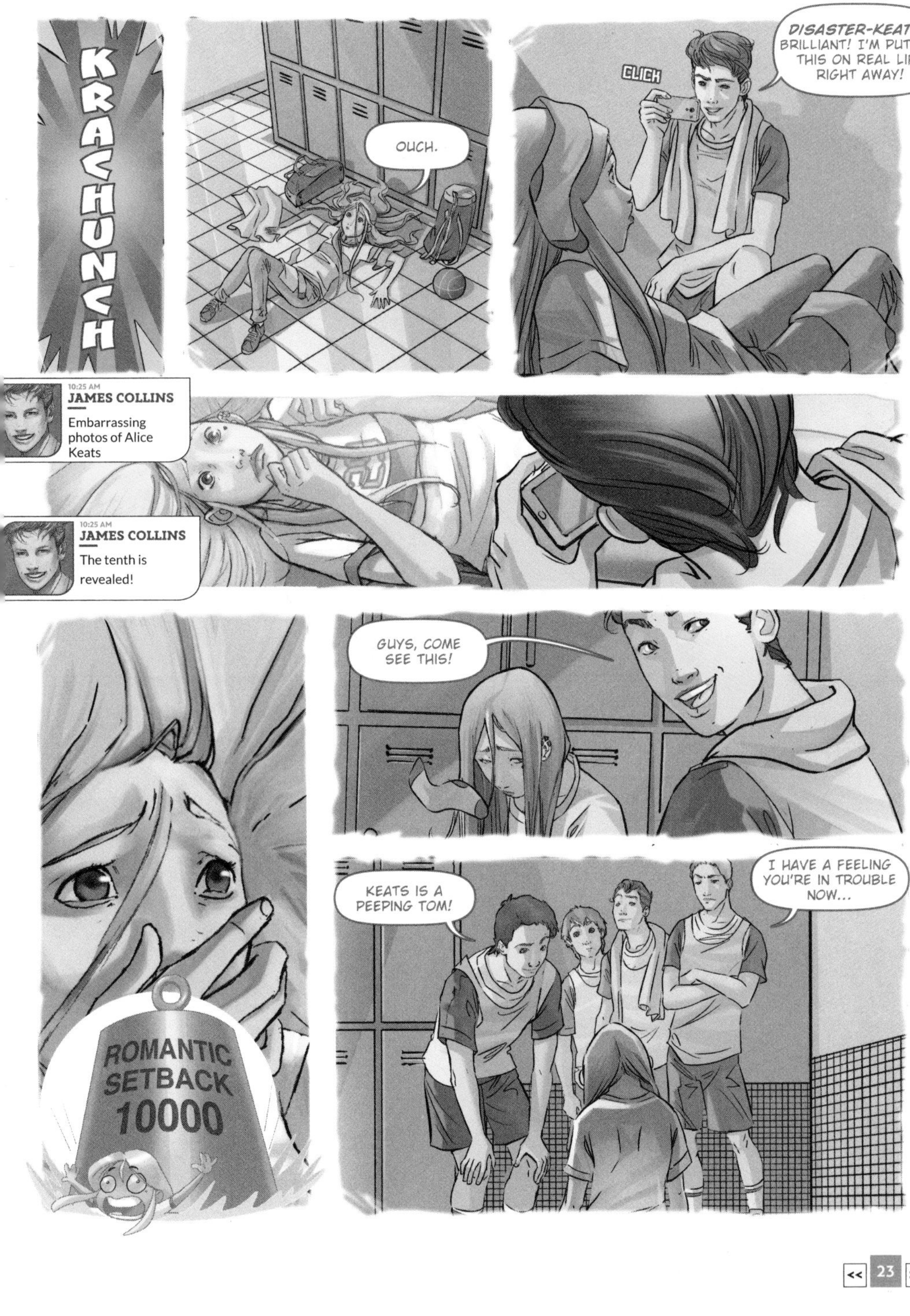
KRACHUNCH
OUCH.
CLICK
DISASTER-KEATS! BRILLIANT! I'M PUTTING THIS ON REAL LIFE RIGHT AWAY!
10:25 AM
JAMES COLLINS
Embarrassing photos of Alice Keats
10:25 AM
JAMES COLLINS
The tenth is revealed!
ROMANTIC SETBACK 10000
GUYS, COME SEE THIS!
KEATS IS A PEEPING TOM!
I HAVE A FEELING YOU'RE IN TROUBLE NOW...

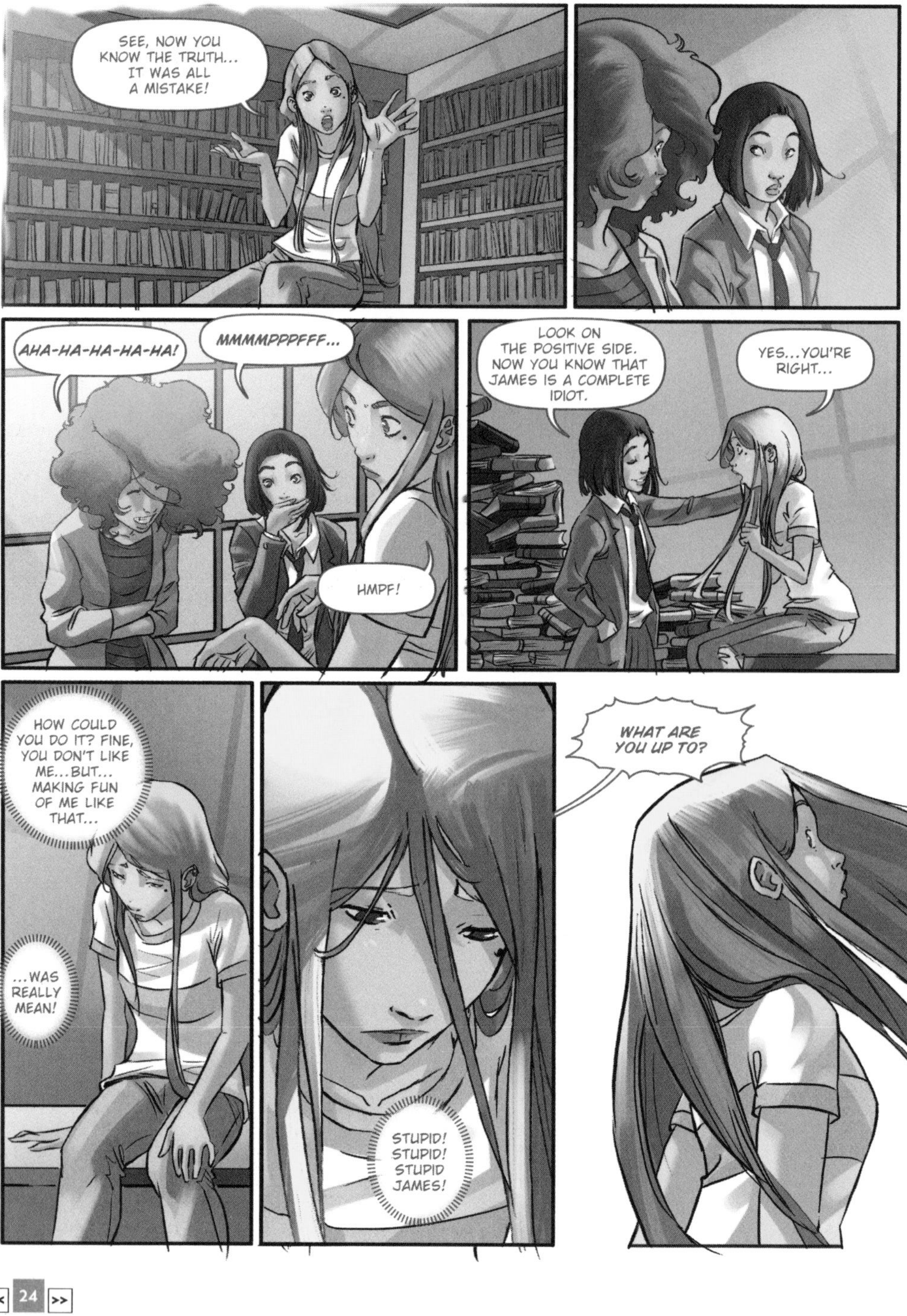
SEE, NOW YOU KNOW THE TRUTH... IT WAS ALL A MISTAKE!
AHA-HA-HA-HA-HA!
MMMMPPPFFF...
HMPF!
LOOK ON THE POSITIVE SIDE. NOW YOU KNOW THAT JAMES IS A COMPLETE IDIOT.
YES...YOU'RE RIGHT...
HOW COULD YOU DO IT? FINE, YOU DON'T LIKE ME...BUT... MAKING FUN OF ME LIKE THAT...
...WAS REALLY MEAN!
STUPID! STUPID! STUPID JAMES!
WHAT ARE YOU UP TO?

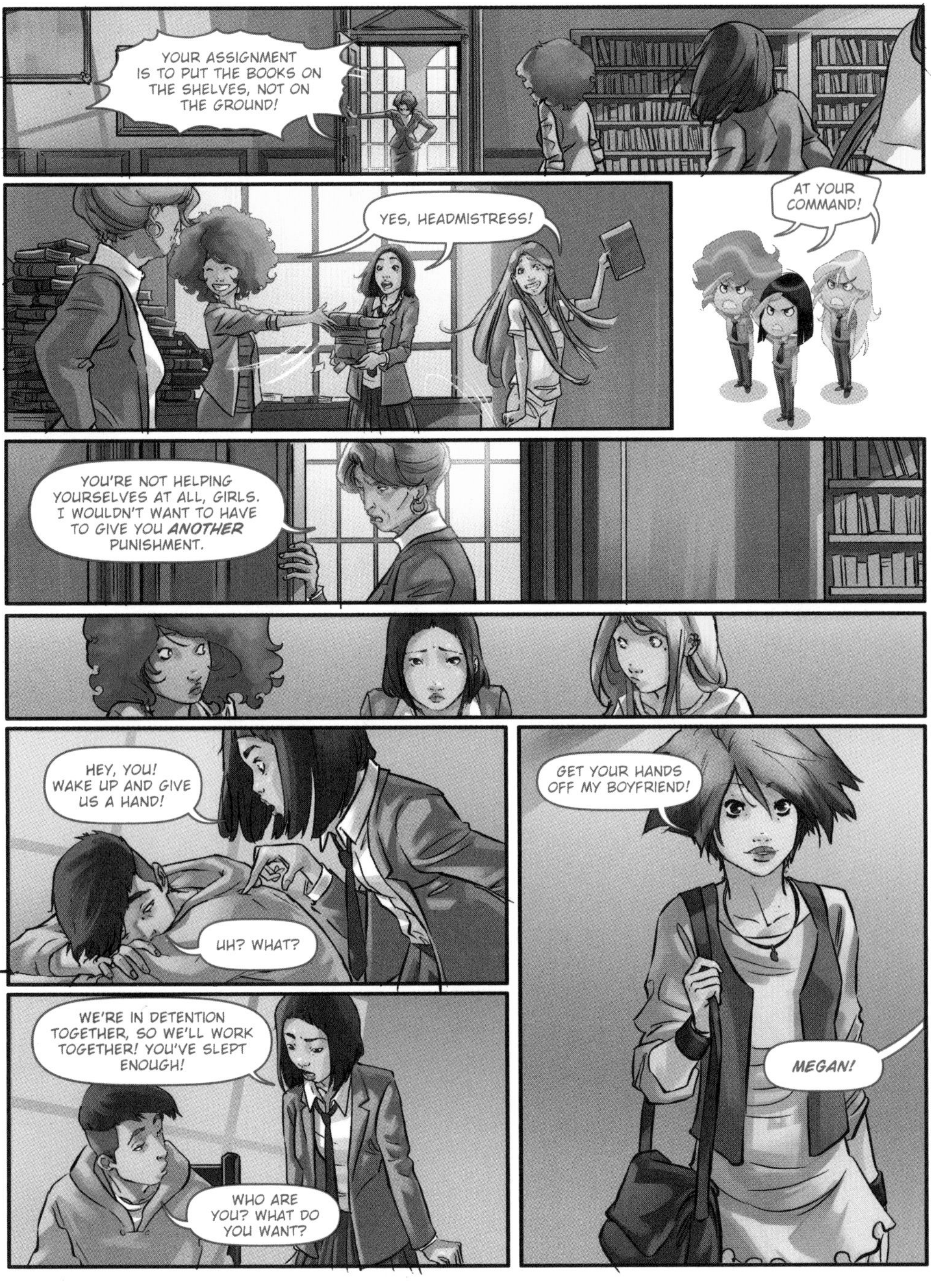
YOUR ASSIGNMENT IS TO PUT THE BOOKS ON THE SHELVES, NOT ON THE GROUND!
YES, HEADMISTRESS!
AT YOUR COMMAND!
YOU'RE NOT HELPING YOURSELVES AT ALL, GIRLS. I WOULDN'T WANT TO HAVE TO GIVE YOU **ANOTHER** PUNISHMENT.
HEY, YOU! WAKE UP AND GIVE US A HAND!
UH? WHAT?
WE'RE IN DETENTION TOGETHER, SO WE'LL WORK TOGETHER! YOU'VE SLEPT ENOUGH!
WHO ARE YOU? WHAT DO YOU WANT?
GET YOUR HANDS OFF MY BOYFRIEND!
MEGAN!

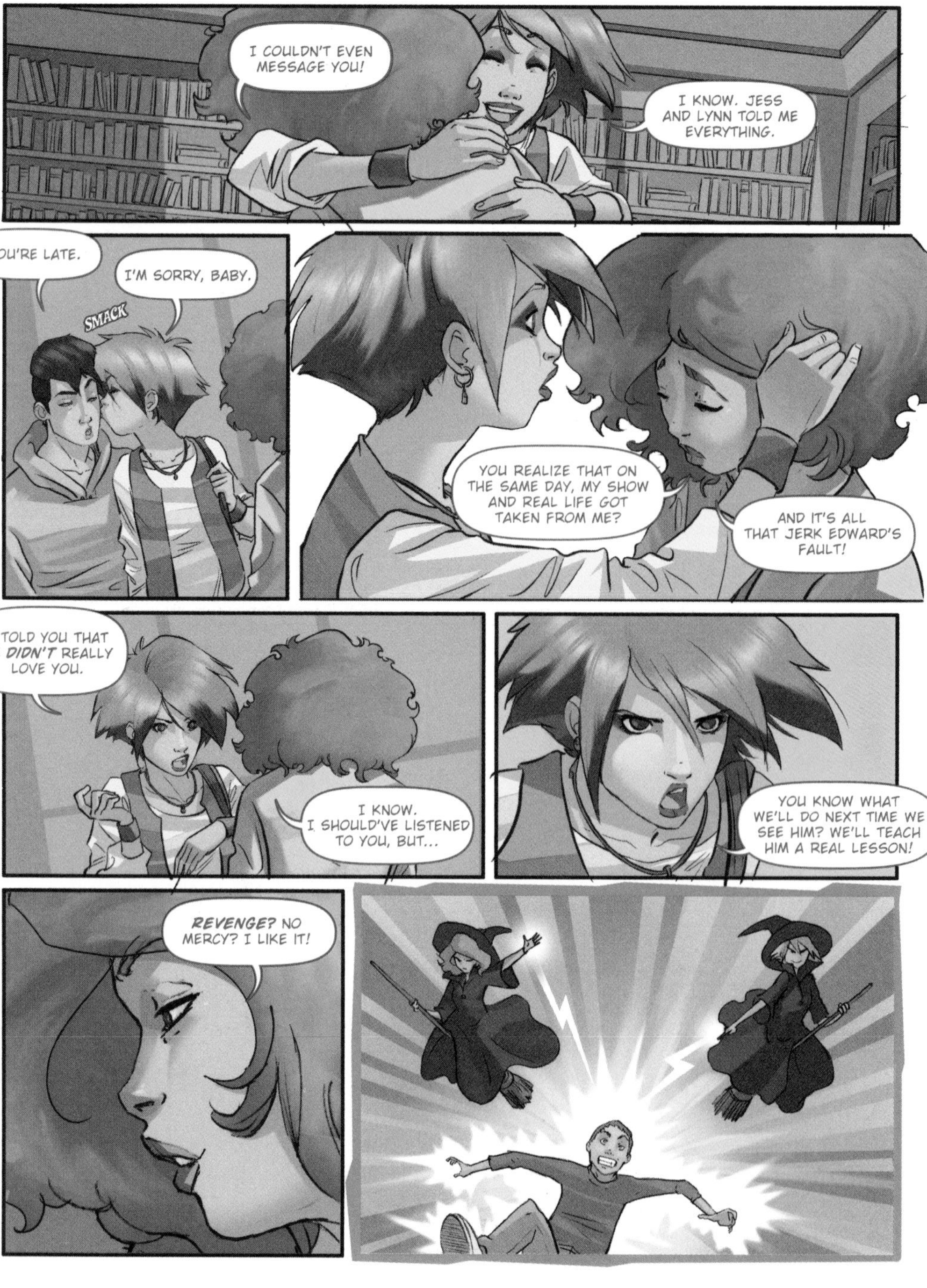
I COULDN'T EVEN MESSAGE YOU!
I KNOW. JESS AND LYNN TOLD ME EVERYTHING.
YOU'RE LATE.
I'M SORRY, BABY.
SMACK
YOU REALIZE THAT ON THE SAME DAY, MY SHOW AND REAL LIFE GOT TAKEN FROM ME?
AND IT'S ALL THAT JERK EDWARD'S FAULT!
I TOLD YOU THAT HE *DIDN'T* REALLY LOVE YOU.
I KNOW. I SHOULD'VE LISTENED TO YOU, BUT...
YOU KNOW WHAT WE'LL DO NEXT TIME WE SEE HIM? WE'LL TEACH HIM A REAL LESSON!
REVENGE? NO MERCY? I LIKE IT!

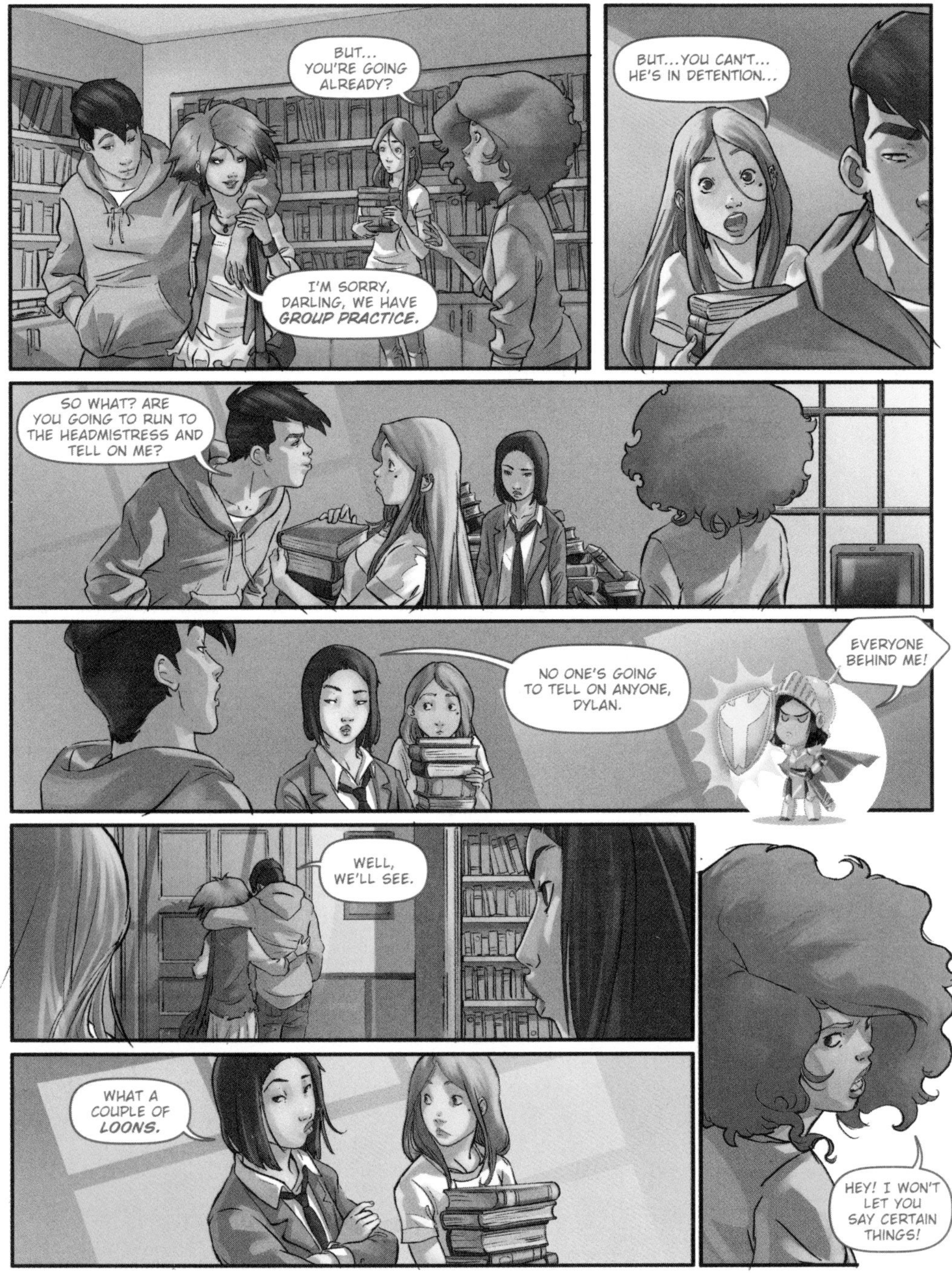
BUT... YOU'RE GOING ALREADY?
I'M SORRY, DARLING, WE HAVE **GROUP PRACTICE.**
BUT...YOU CAN'T... HE'S IN DETENTION...
SO WHAT? ARE YOU GOING TO RUN TO THE HEADMISTRESS AND TELL ON ME?
NO ONE'S GOING TO TELL ON ANYONE, DYLAN.
EVERYONE BEHIND ME!
WELL, WE'LL SEE.
WHAT A COUPLE OF **LOONS.**
HEY! I WON'T LET YOU SAY CERTAIN THINGS!

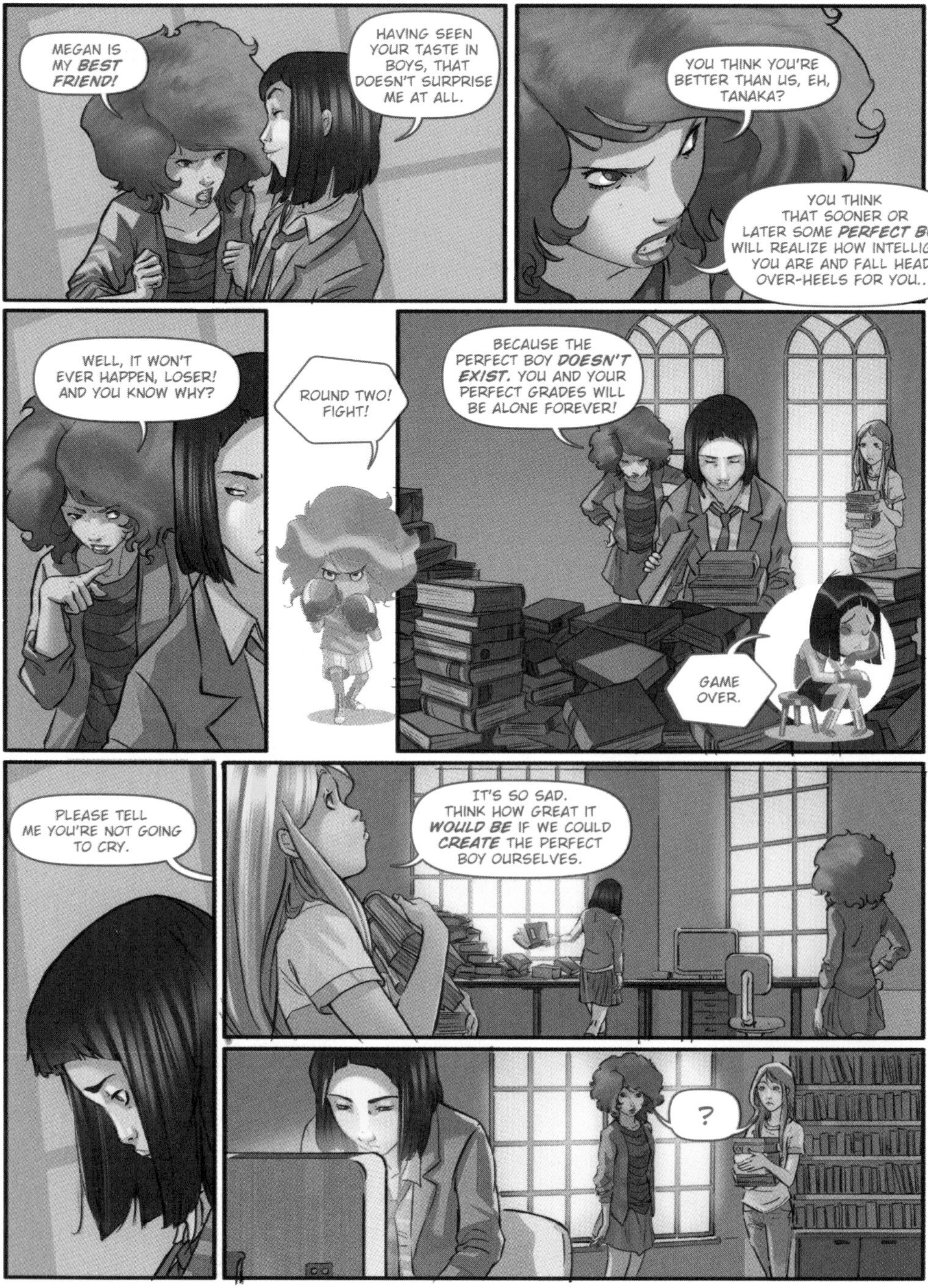
MEGAN IS MY BEST FRIEND!
HAVING SEEN YOUR TASTE IN BOYS, THAT DOESN'T SURPRISE ME AT ALL.
YOU THINK YOU'RE BETTER THAN US, EH, TANAKA?
YOU THINK THAT SOONER OR LATER SOME PERFECT BOY WILL REALIZE HOW INTELLIGENT YOU ARE AND FALL HEAD-OVER-HEELS FOR YOU...
WELL, IT WON'T EVER HAPPEN, LOSER! AND YOU KNOW WHY?
ROUND TWO! FIGHT!
BECAUSE THE PERFECT BOY DOESN'T EXIST. YOU AND YOUR PERFECT GRADES WILL BE ALONE FOREVER!
GAME OVER.
PLEASE TELL ME YOU'RE NOT GOING TO CRY.
IT'S SO SAD. THINK HOW GREAT IT WOULD BE IF WE COULD CREATE THE PERFECT BOY OURSELVES.
?

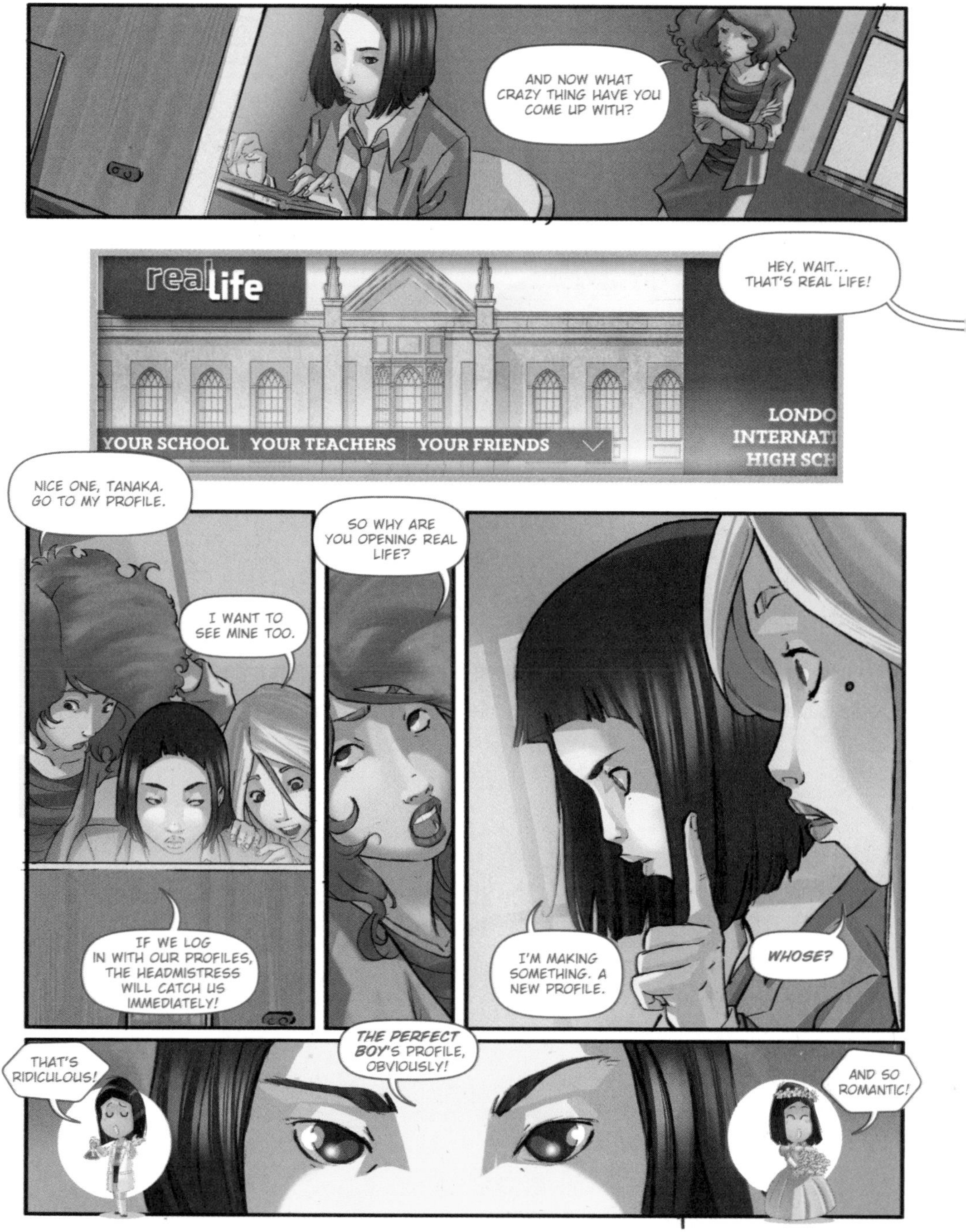
AND NOW WHAT CRAZY THING HAVE YOU COME UP WITH?
real life
YOUR SCHOOL
YOUR TEACHERS
YOUR FRIENDS
LONDO
INTERNATI
HIGH SCH
HEY, WAIT... THAT'S REAL LIFE!
NICE ONE, TANAKA. GO TO MY PROFILE.
I WANT TO SEE MINE TOO.
SO WHY ARE YOU OPENING REAL LIFE?
IF WE LOG IN WITH OUR PROFILES, THE HEADMISTRESS WILL CATCH US IMMEDIATELY!
I'M MAKING SOMETHING. A NEW PROFILE.
WHOSE?
THAT'S RIDICULOUS!
THE PERFECT BOY'S PROFILE, OBVIOUSLY!
AND SO ROMANTIC!

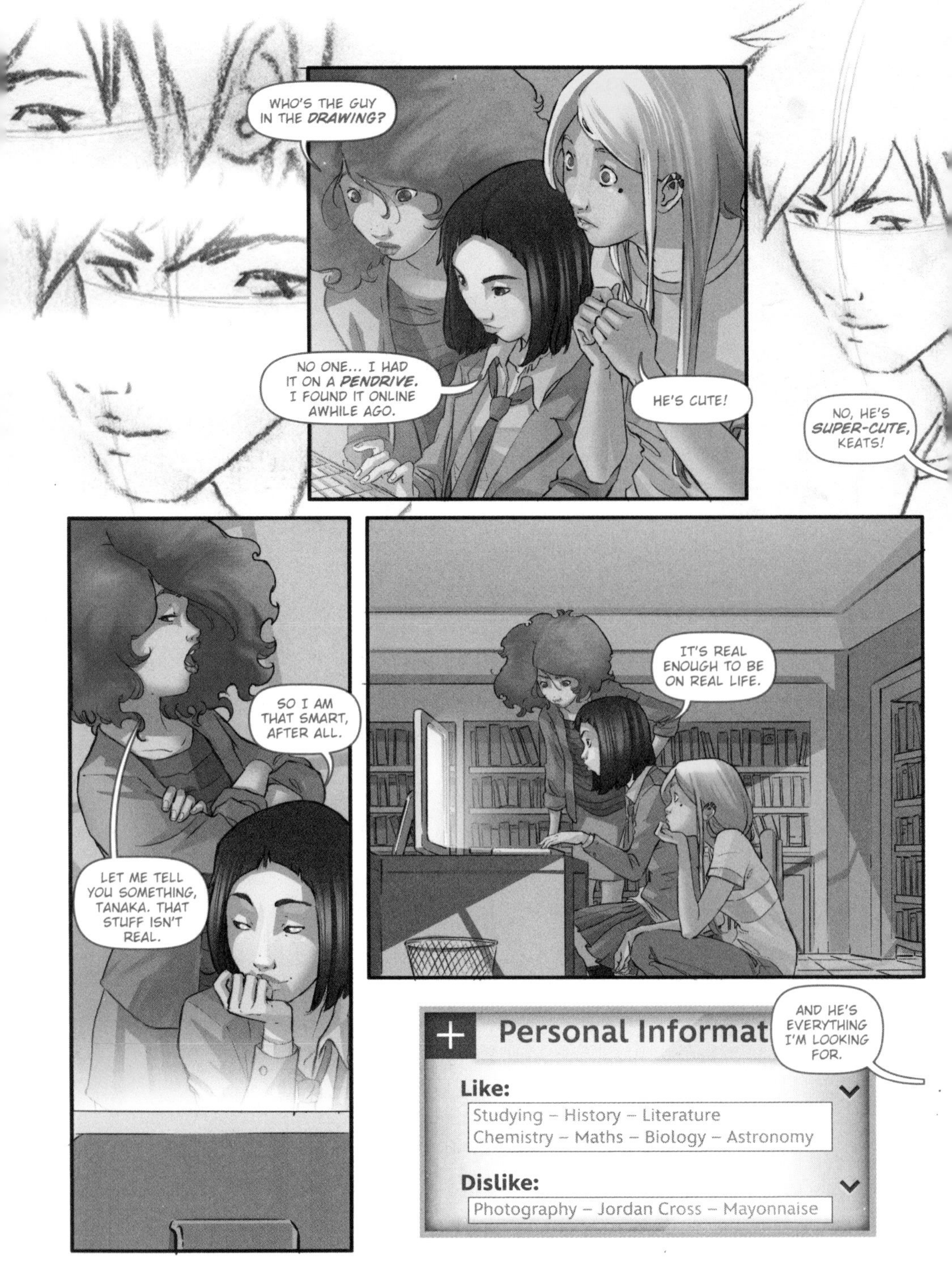
WHO'S THE GUY IN THE DRAWING?
NO ONE... I HAD IT ON A PENDRIVE. I FOUND IT ONLINE AWHILE AGO.
HE'S CUTE!
NO, HE'S SUPER-CUTE, KEATS!
SO I AM THAT SMART, AFTER ALL.
LET ME TELL YOU SOMETHING, TANAKA. THAT STUFF ISN'T REAL.
IT'S REAL ENOUGH TO BE ON REAL LIFE.
Personal Informat
AND HE'S EVERYTHING I'M LOOKING FOR.
Like:
Studying – History – Literature
Chemistry – Maths – Biology – Astronomy
Dislike:
Photography – Jordan Cross – Mayonnaise

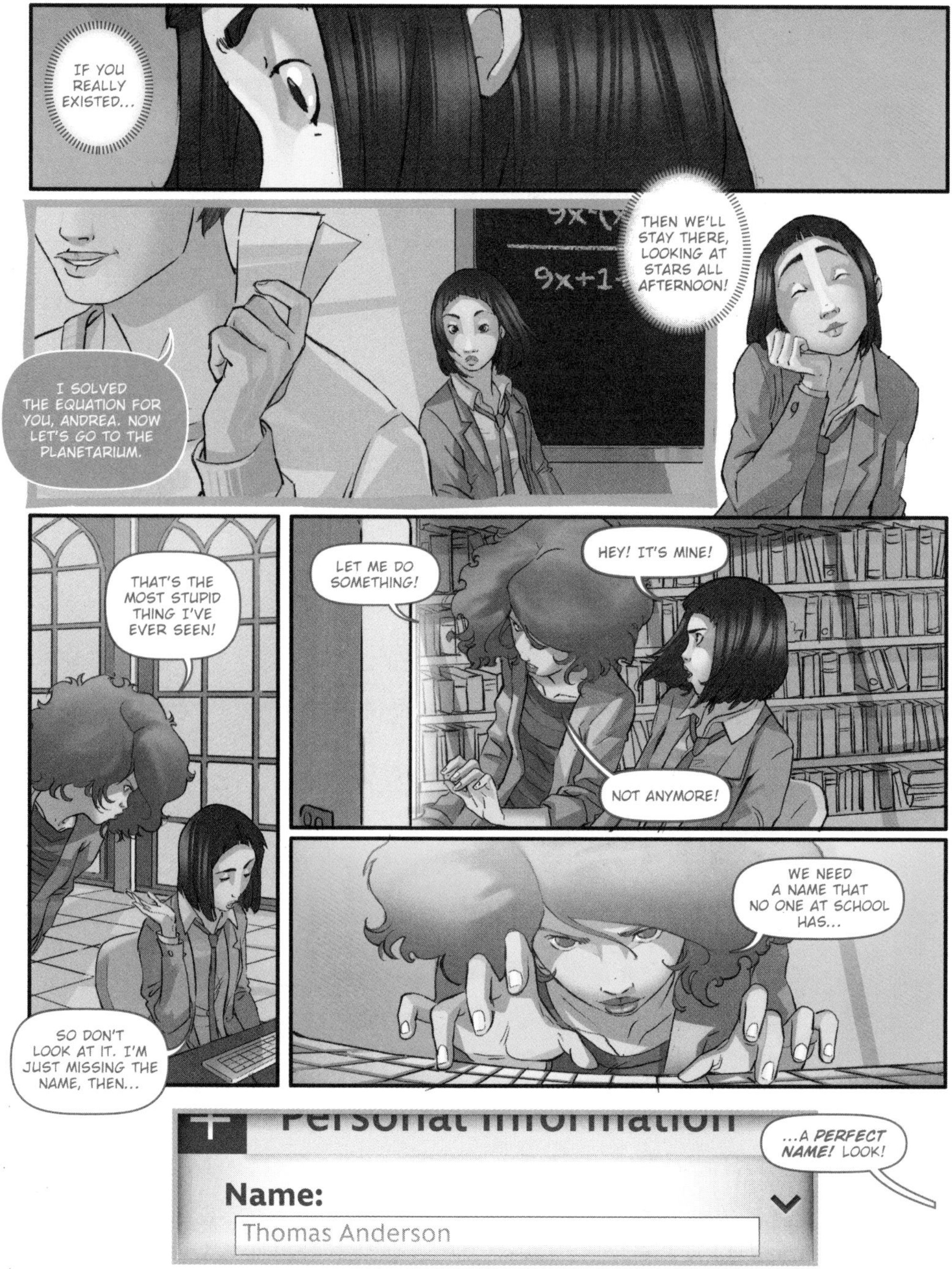
IF YOU REALLY EXISTED...
I SOLVED THE EQUATION FOR YOU, ANDREA. NOW LET'S GO TO THE PLANETARIUM.
THEN WE'LL STAY THERE, LOOKING AT STARS ALL AFTERNOON!
THAT'S THE MOST STUPID THING I'VE EVER SEEN!
SO DON'T LOOK AT IT. I'M JUST MISSING THE NAME, THEN...
LET ME DO SOMETHING!
HEY! IT'S MINE!
NOT ANYMORE!
WE NEED A NAME THAT NO ONE AT SCHOOL HAS...
Personal Information
Name:
Thomas Anderson
...A PERFECT NAME! LOOK!

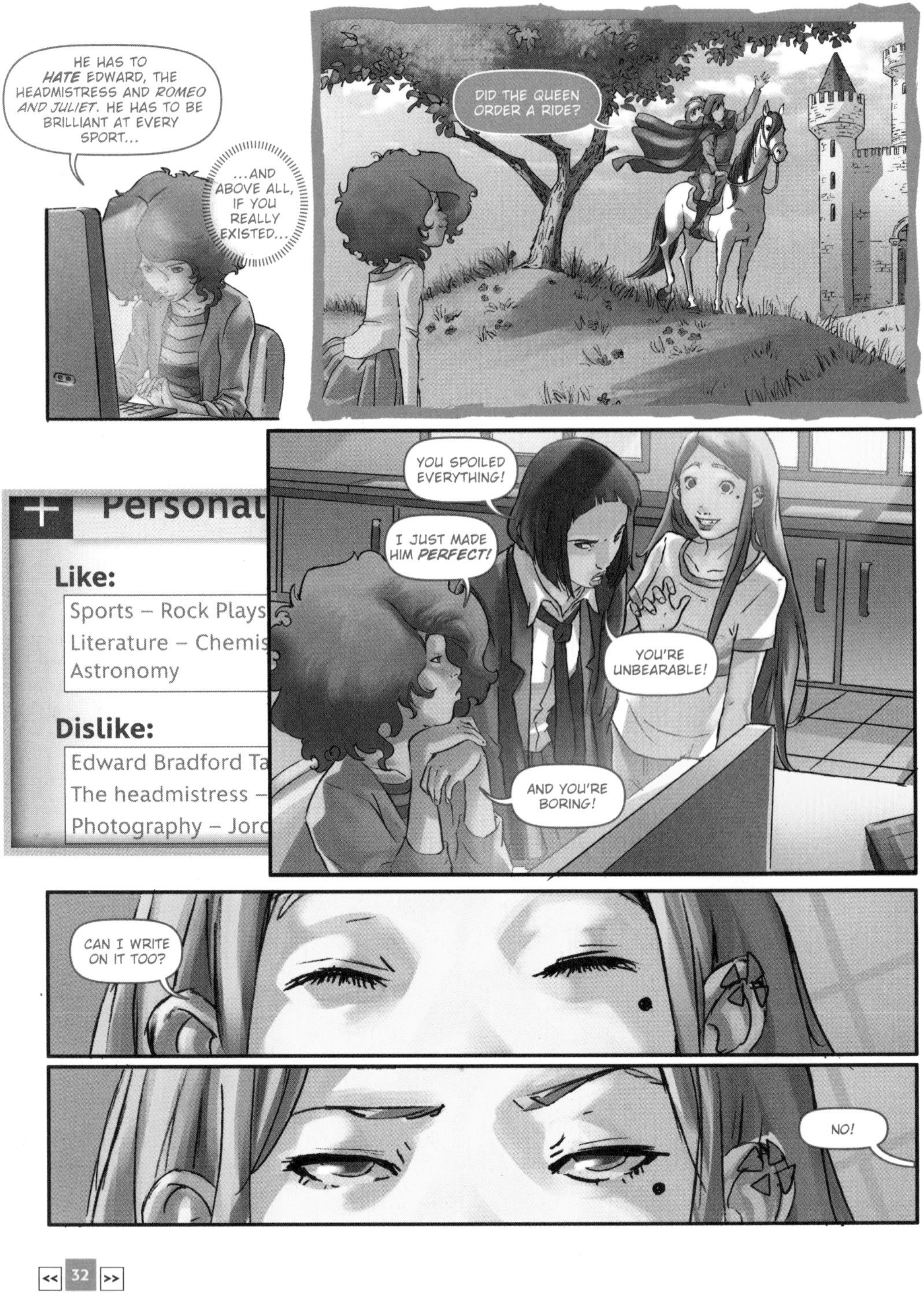

HE HAS TO HATE EDWARD, THE HEADMISTRESS AND ROMEO AND JULIET. HE HAS TO BE BRILLIANT AT EVERY SPORT...
...AND ABOVE ALL, IF YOU REALLY EXISTED...
DID THE QUEEN ORDER A RIDE?
Personal
Like:
Sports – Rock Plays
Literature – Chemis
Astronomy
Dislike:
Edward Bradford Ta
The headmistress –
Photography – Jord
YOU SPOILED EVERYTHING!
I JUST MADE HIM PERFECT!
YOU'RE UNBEARABLE!
AND YOU'RE BORING!
CAN I WRITE ON IT TOO?
NO!

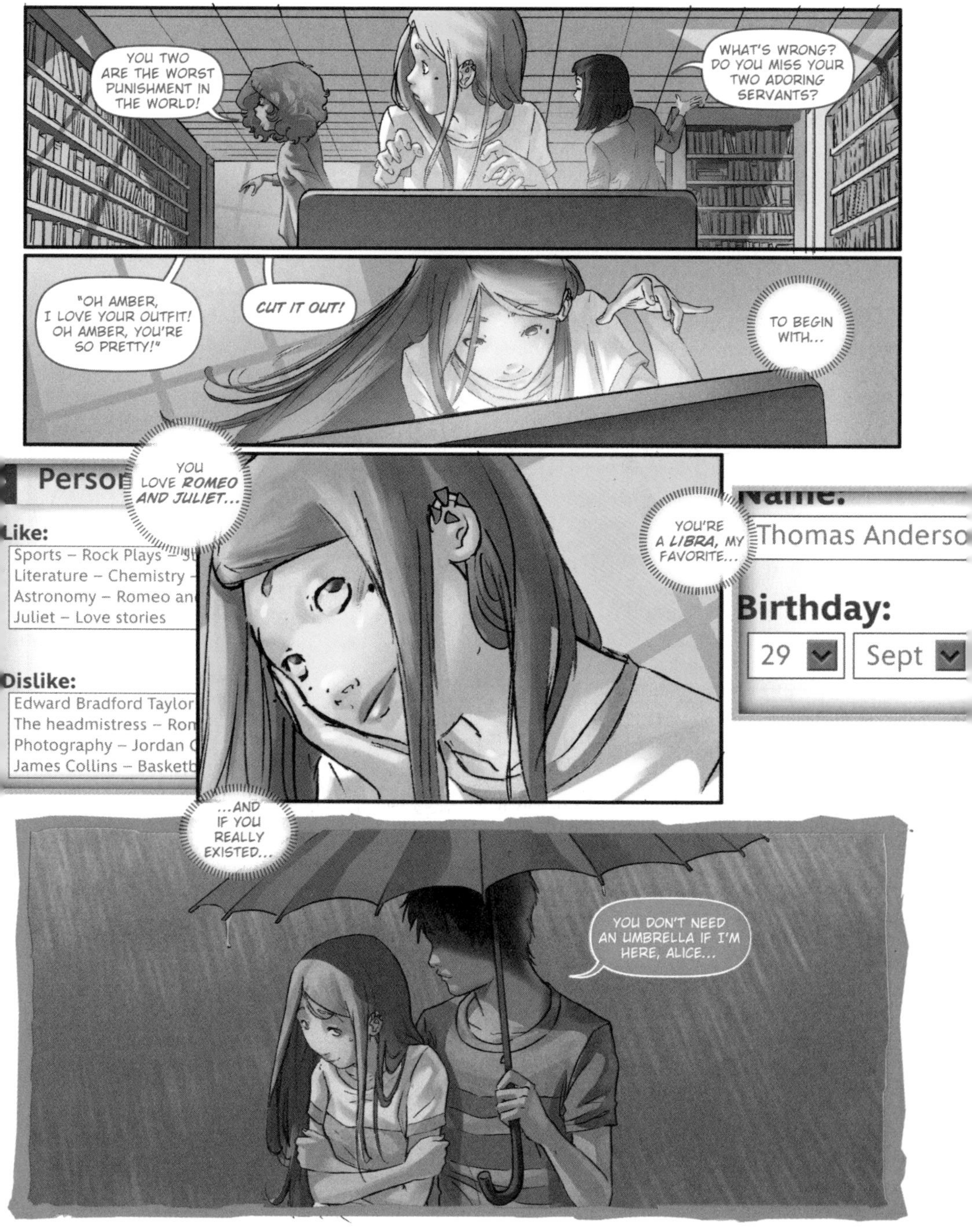

YOU TWO ARE THE WORST PUNISHMENT IN THE WORLD!
WHAT'S WRONG? DO YOU MISS YOUR TWO ADORING SERVANTS?
"OH AMBER, I LOVE YOUR OUTFIT! OH AMBER, YOU'RE SO PRETTY!"
CUT IT OUT!
TO BEGIN WITH...
Person
Like:
Sports – Rock Plays
Literature – Chemistry
Astronomy – Romeo and
Juliet – Love stories
Dislike:
Edward Bradford Taylor
The headmistress – Ro
Photography – Jordan
James Collins – Basketb
YOU LOVE ROMEO AND JULIET...
YOU'RE A LIBRA, MY FAVORITE...
Name:
Thomas Anderso
Birthday:
29
Sept
...AND IF YOU REALLY EXISTED...
YOU DON'T NEED AN UMBRELLA IF I'M HERE, ALICE...

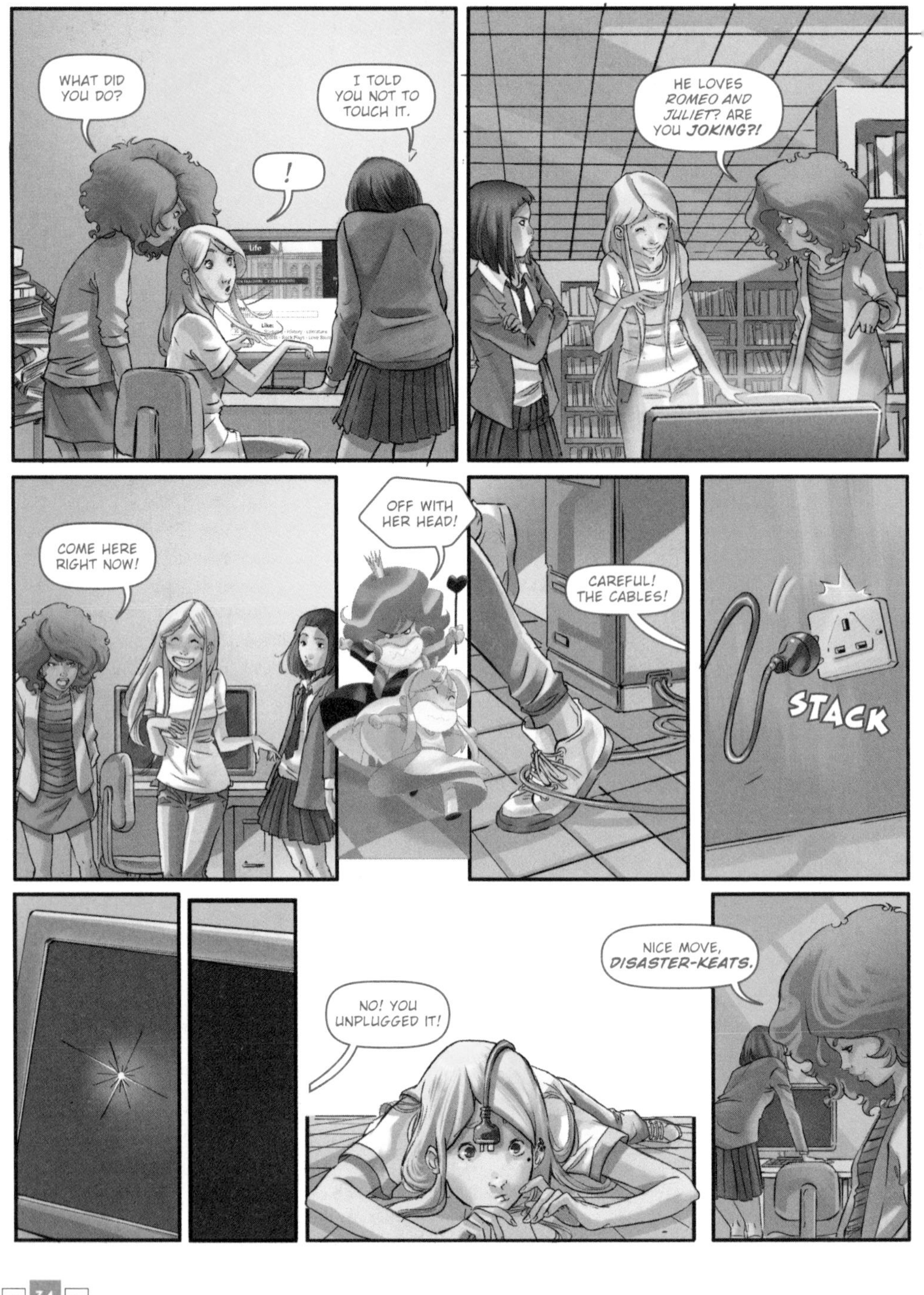
WHAT DID YOU DO?
I TOLD YOU NOT TO TOUCH IT.
!
HE LOVES *ROMEO AND JULIET*? ARE YOU **JOKING?!**
COME HERE RIGHT NOW!
OFF WITH HER HEAD!
CAREFUL! THE CABLES!
STACK
NO! YOU UNPLUGGED IT!
NICE MOVE, **DISASTER-KEATS.**

PUT THE CABLES BACK.

D-DONE...

THERE'S NOTHING WE CAN DO. IT DIDN'T SAVE THE *DATA*.

THOMAS ANDERSON NO LONGER *EXISTS*.

MIGHT AS WELL TURN IT OFF, THEN.

BEEP

BUT...WE COULD ALWAYS REWRITE IT, COULDN'T WE?

IN YOUR DREAMS! THE TORTURE IS *OVER*... AT LEAST FOR TODAY!

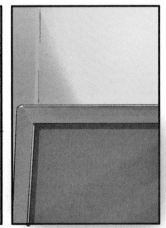

BYE, LOSERS!

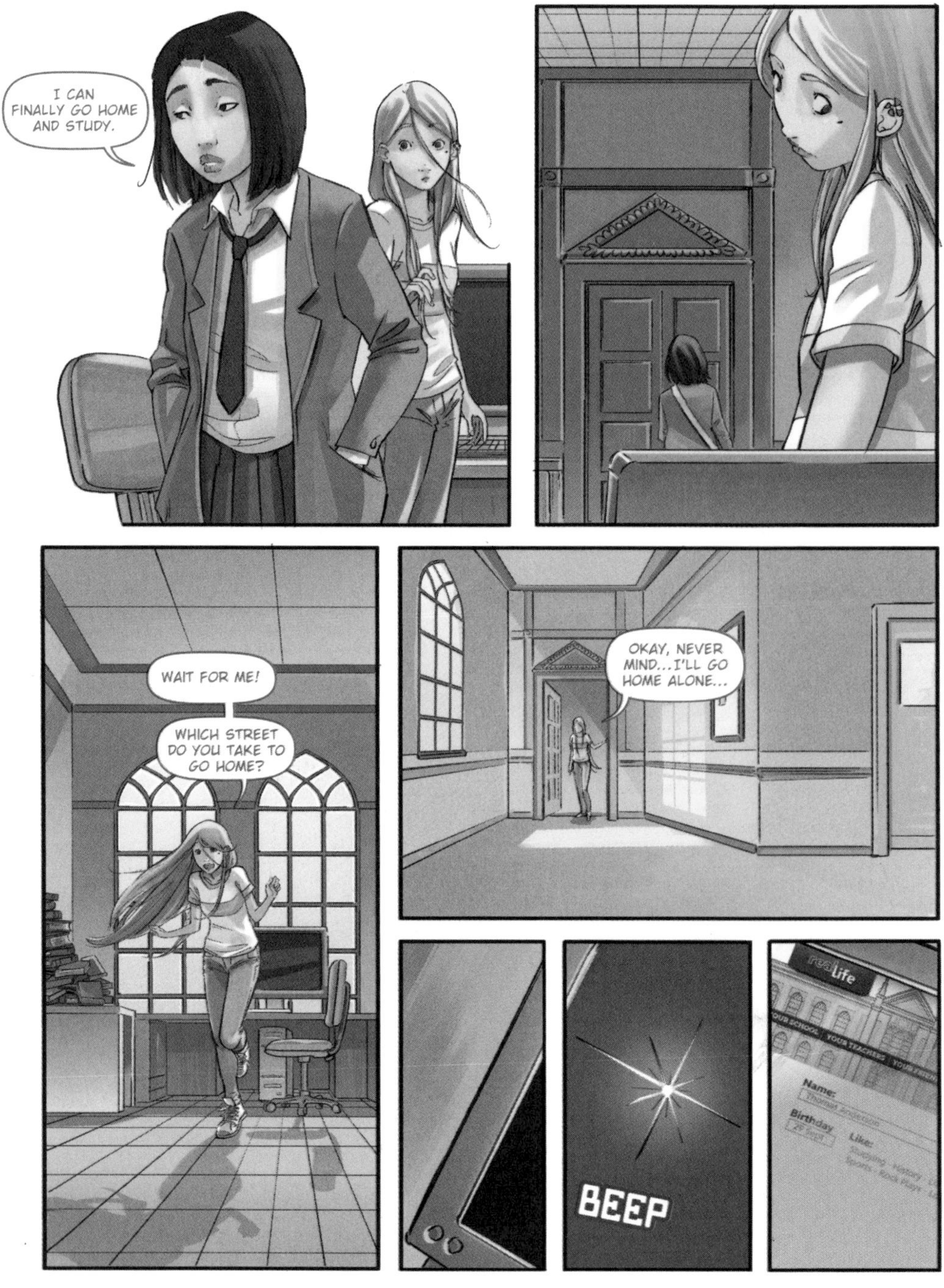
I CAN FINALLY GO HOME AND STUDY.
WAIT FOR ME!
WHICH STREET DO YOU TAKE TO GO HOME?
OKAY, NEVER MIND...I'LL GO HOME ALONE...
BEEP
Name:
Birthday
Like:

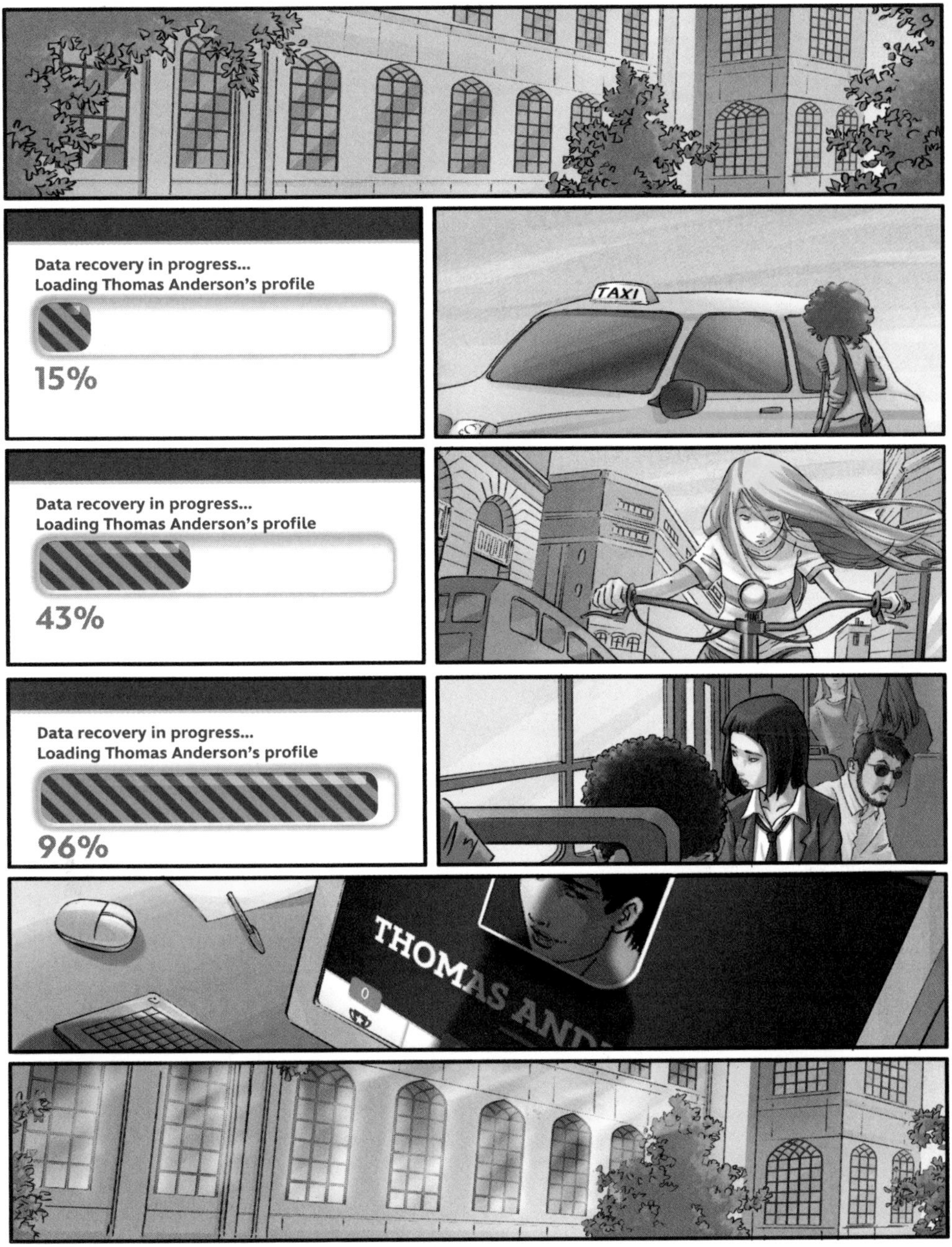
Data recovery in progress...
Loading Thomas Anderson's profile
15%
TAXI
Data recovery in progress...
Loading Thomas Anderson's profile
43%
Data recovery in progress...
Loading Thomas Anderson's profile
96%
THOMAS AND

END OF CHAPTER 2

CHAPTER 3

A NEW SCHOOLMATE

London International High School
Marylebone
08:25 AM

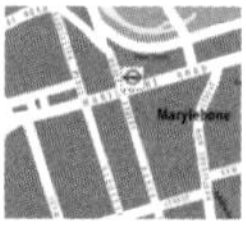

Marylebone

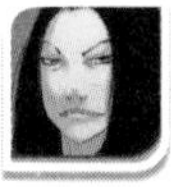

08:27 AM
LYNN JAVINS
#library_burned_down

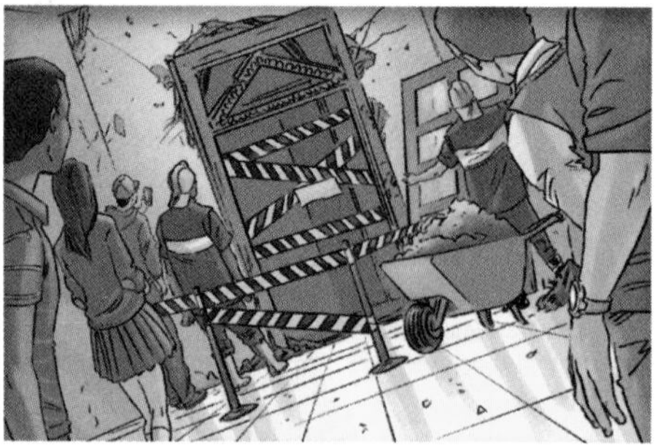

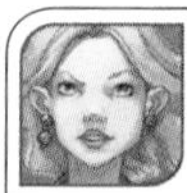

08:28 AM
JESS BAGLEY
What? I'll be right there!

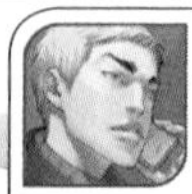

08:35 AM
EDWARD BRADFORD TAYLOR
Best Monday of the year!

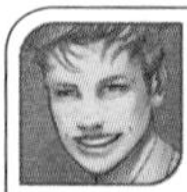

08:42 AM
JAMES COLLINS
I'm going to take a photo of myself in front of it. Who's coming?

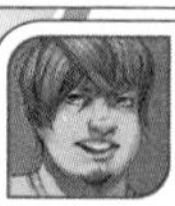

08:51 AM
BILL MARTIN
Good thing the dining hall didn't burn down! HAR HAR HAR

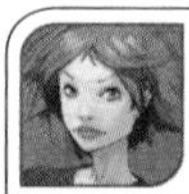

08:57 AM
MEGAN GARRITY
It happened on Friday?

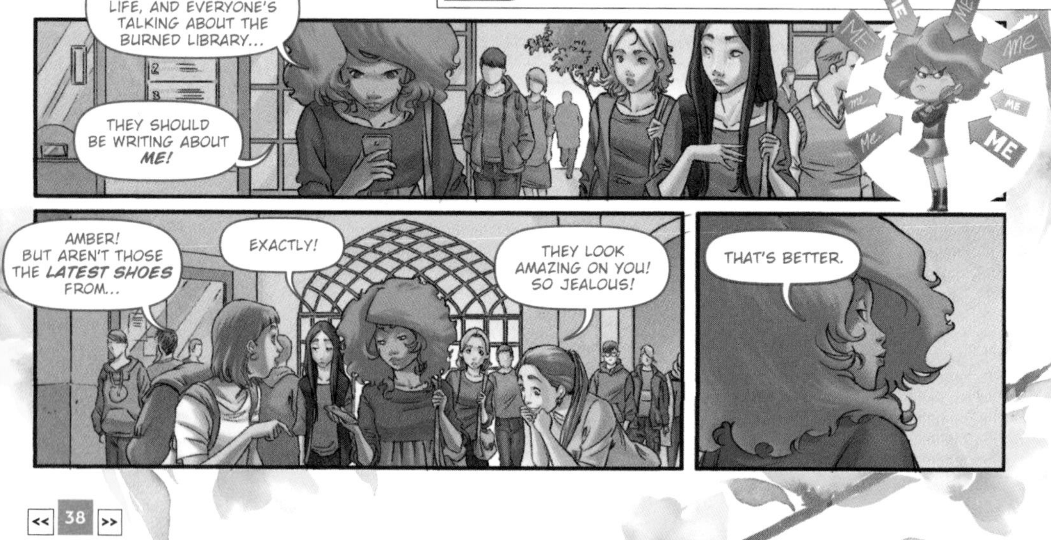

SO ANNOYING! I'M BACK ON REAL LIFE, AND EVERYONE'S TALKING ABOUT THE BURNED LIBRARY...
THEY SHOULD BE WRITING ABOUT *ME!*
ME
ME
ME
ME
ME
ME
ME
ME
AMBER! BUT AREN'T THOSE THE ***LATEST SHOES*** FROM...
EXACTLY!
THEY LOOK AMAZING ON YOU! SO JEALOUS!
THAT'S BETTER.

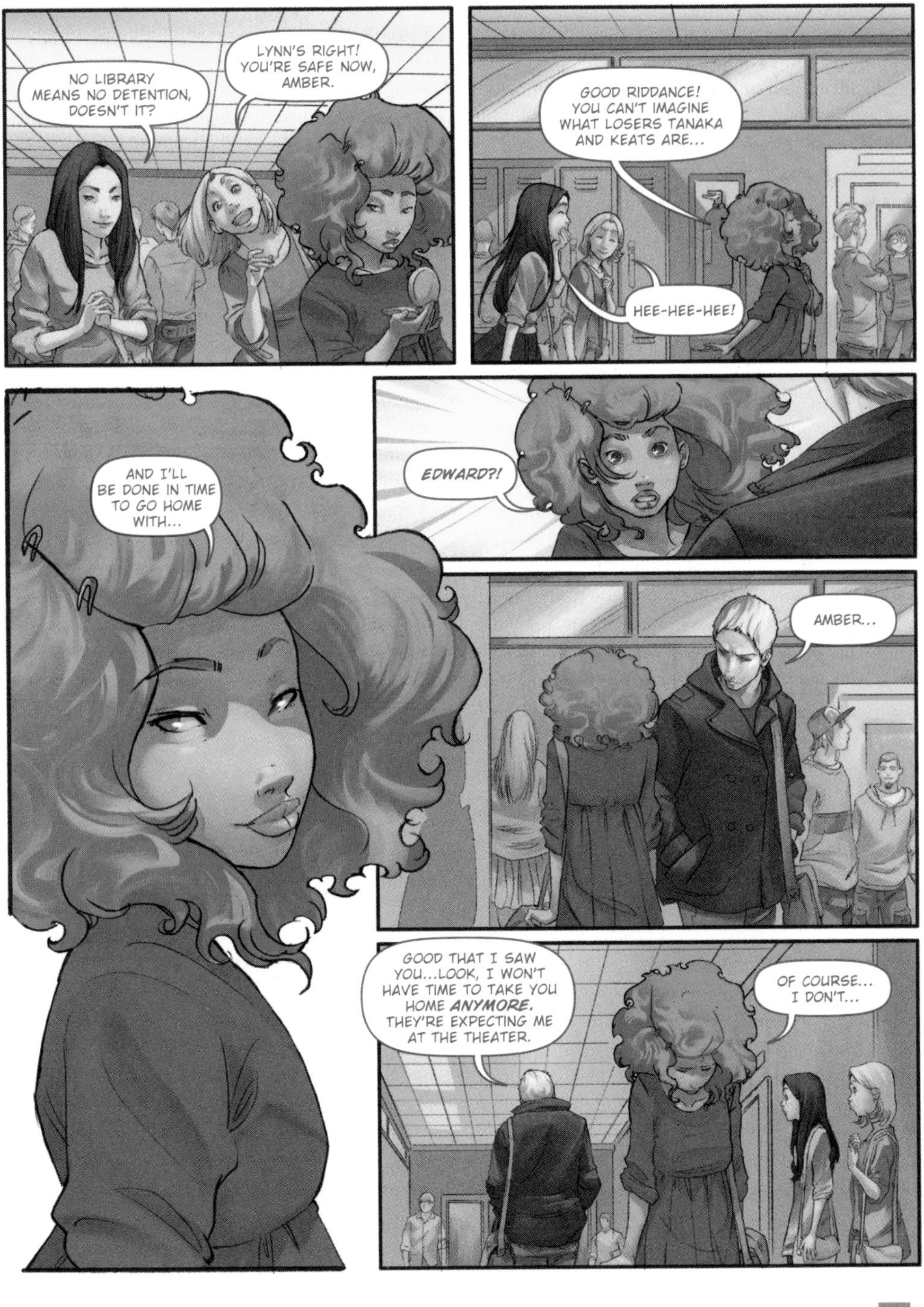
NO LIBRARY MEANS NO DETENTION, DOESN'T IT?
LYNN'S RIGHT! YOU'RE SAFE NOW, AMBER.
GOOD RIDDANCE! YOU CAN'T IMAGINE WHAT LOSERS TANAKA AND KEATS ARE...
HEE-HEE-HEE!
AND I'LL BE DONE IN TIME TO GO HOME WITH...
EDWARD?!
AMBER...
GOOD THAT I SAW YOU...LOOK, I WON'T HAVE TIME TO TAKE YOU HOME **ANYMORE.** THEY'RE EXPECTING ME AT THE THEATER.
OF COURSE... I DON'T...

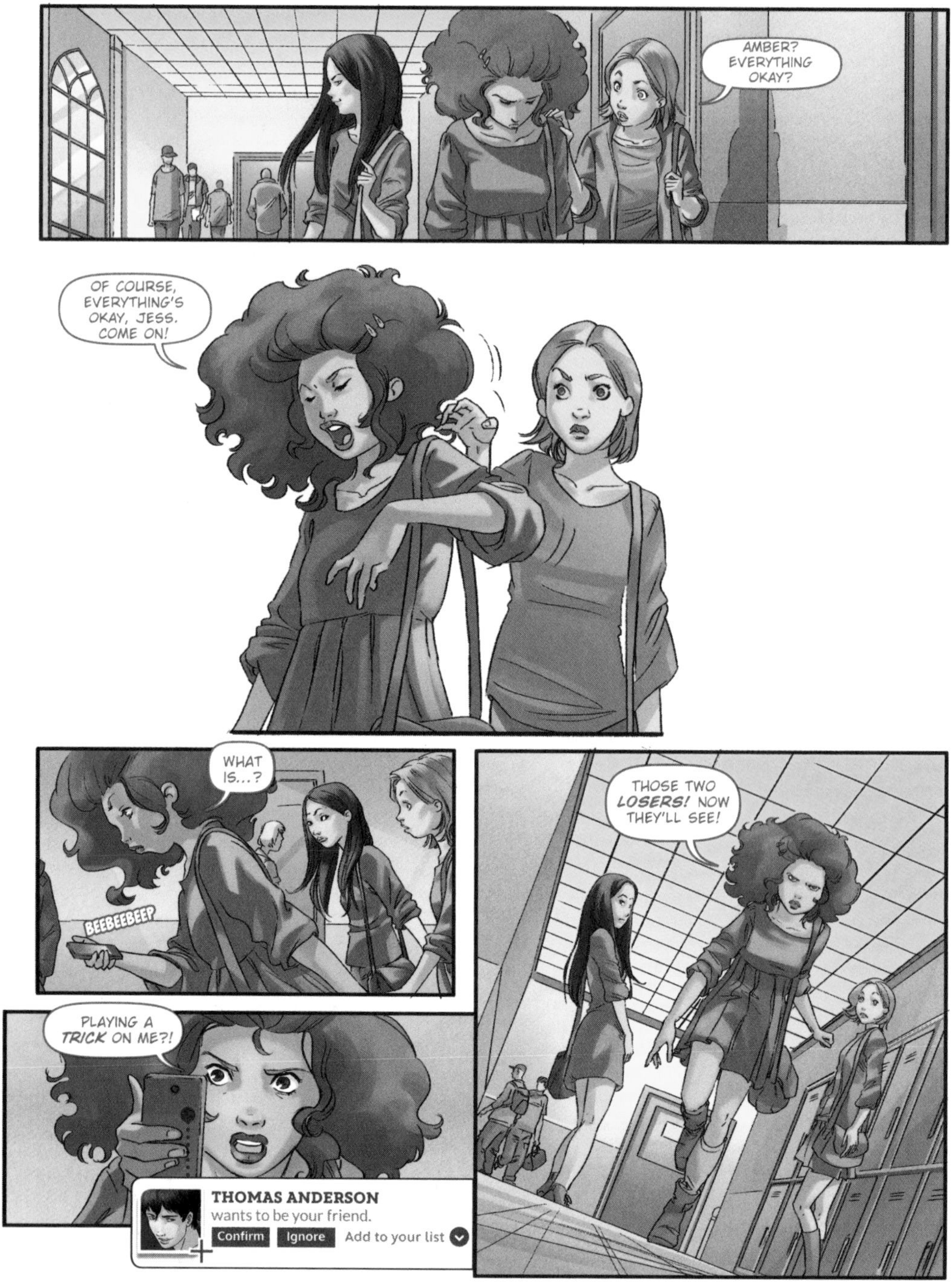

AMBER? EVERYTHING OKAY?
OF COURSE, EVERYTHING'S OKAY, JESS. COME ON!
WHAT IS...?
BEEBEEBEEP
PLAYING A *TRICK* ON ME?!
THOMAS ANDERSON
wants to be your friend.
Confirm
Ignore
Add to your list
THOSE TWO *LOSERS!* NOW THEY'LL SEE!

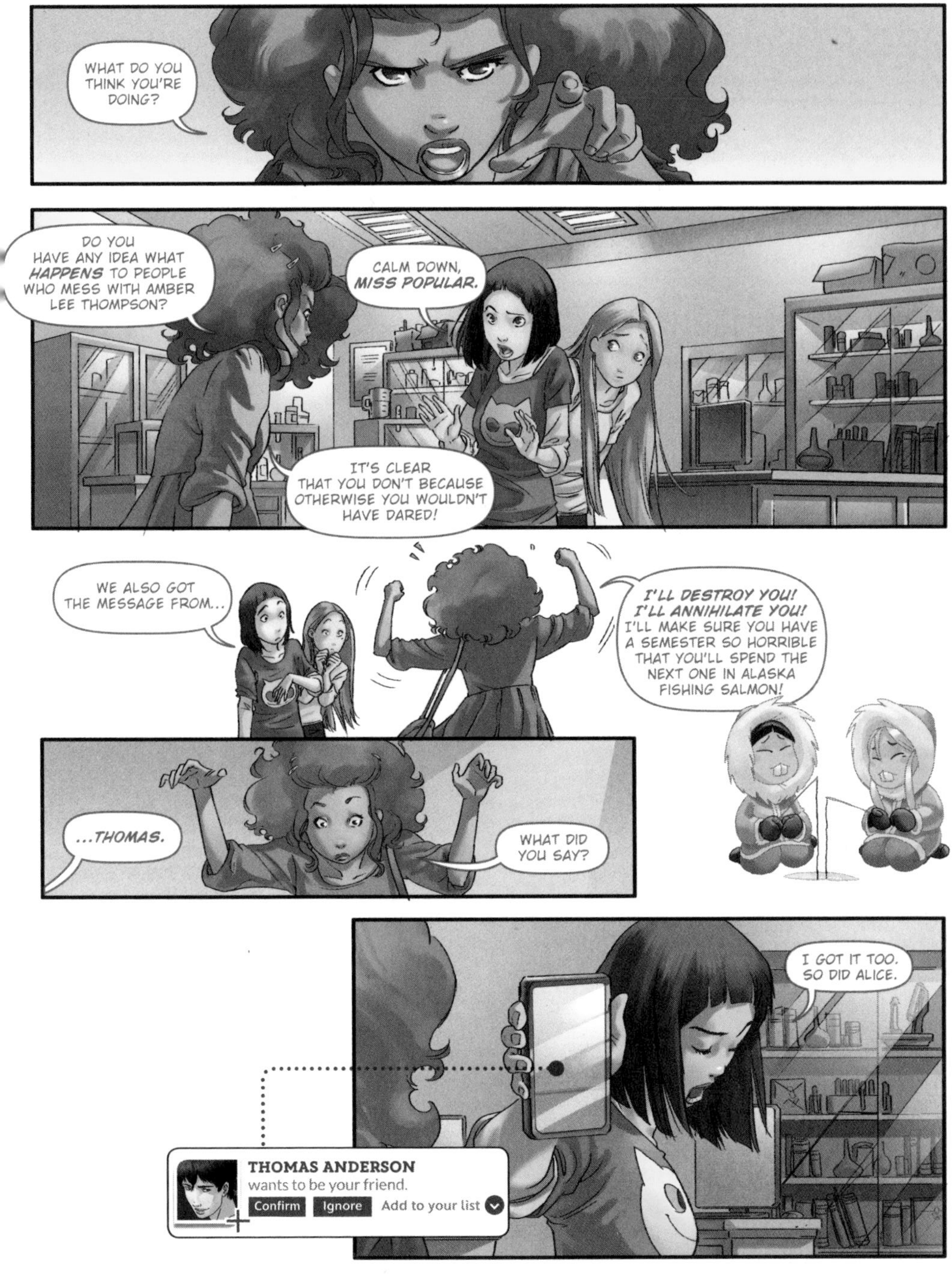
WHAT DO YOU THINK YOU'RE DOING?
DO YOU HAVE ANY IDEA WHAT HAPPENS TO PEOPLE WHO MESS WITH AMBER LEE THOMPSON?
CALM DOWN, MISS POPULAR.
IT'S CLEAR THAT YOU DON'T BECAUSE OTHERWISE YOU WOULDN'T HAVE DARED!
WE ALSO GOT THE MESSAGE FROM...
I'LL DESTROY YOU! I'LL ANNIHILATE YOU! I'LL MAKE SURE YOU HAVE A SEMESTER SO HORRIBLE THAT YOU'LL SPEND THE NEXT ONE IN ALASKA FISHING SALMON!
...THOMAS.
WHAT DID YOU SAY?
I GOT IT TOO. SO DID ALICE.
THOMAS ANDERSON
wants to be your friend.
Confirm
Ignore
Add to your list

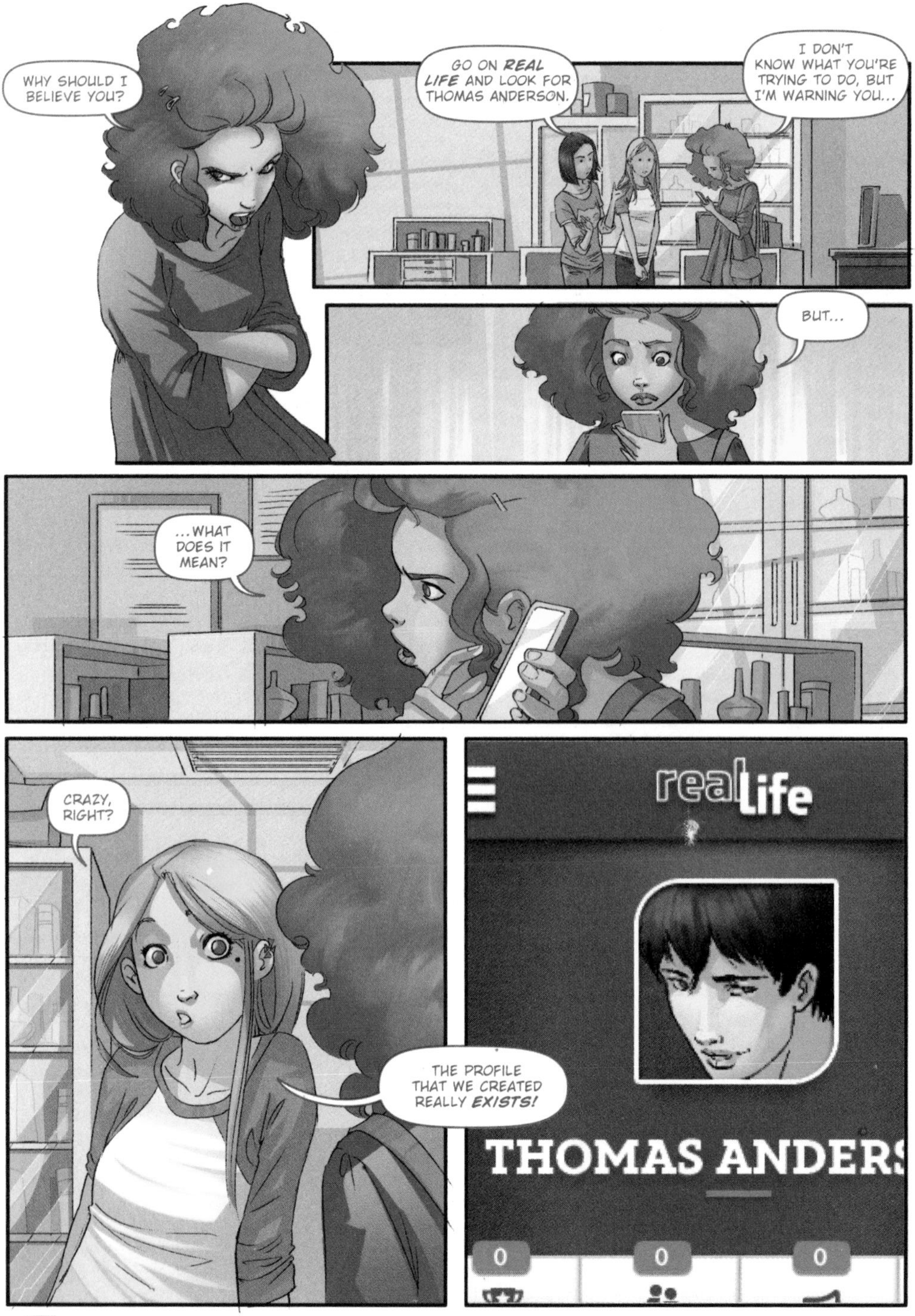
WHY SHOULD I BELIEVE YOU?
GO ON *REAL LIFE* AND LOOK FOR THOMAS ANDERSON.
I DON'T KNOW WHAT YOU'RE TRYING TO DO, BUT I'M WARNING YOU...
BUT...
...WHAT DOES IT MEAN?
CRAZY, RIGHT?
THE PROFILE THAT WE CREATED REALLY *EXISTS!*
real Life
THOMAS ANDERS
0
0
0

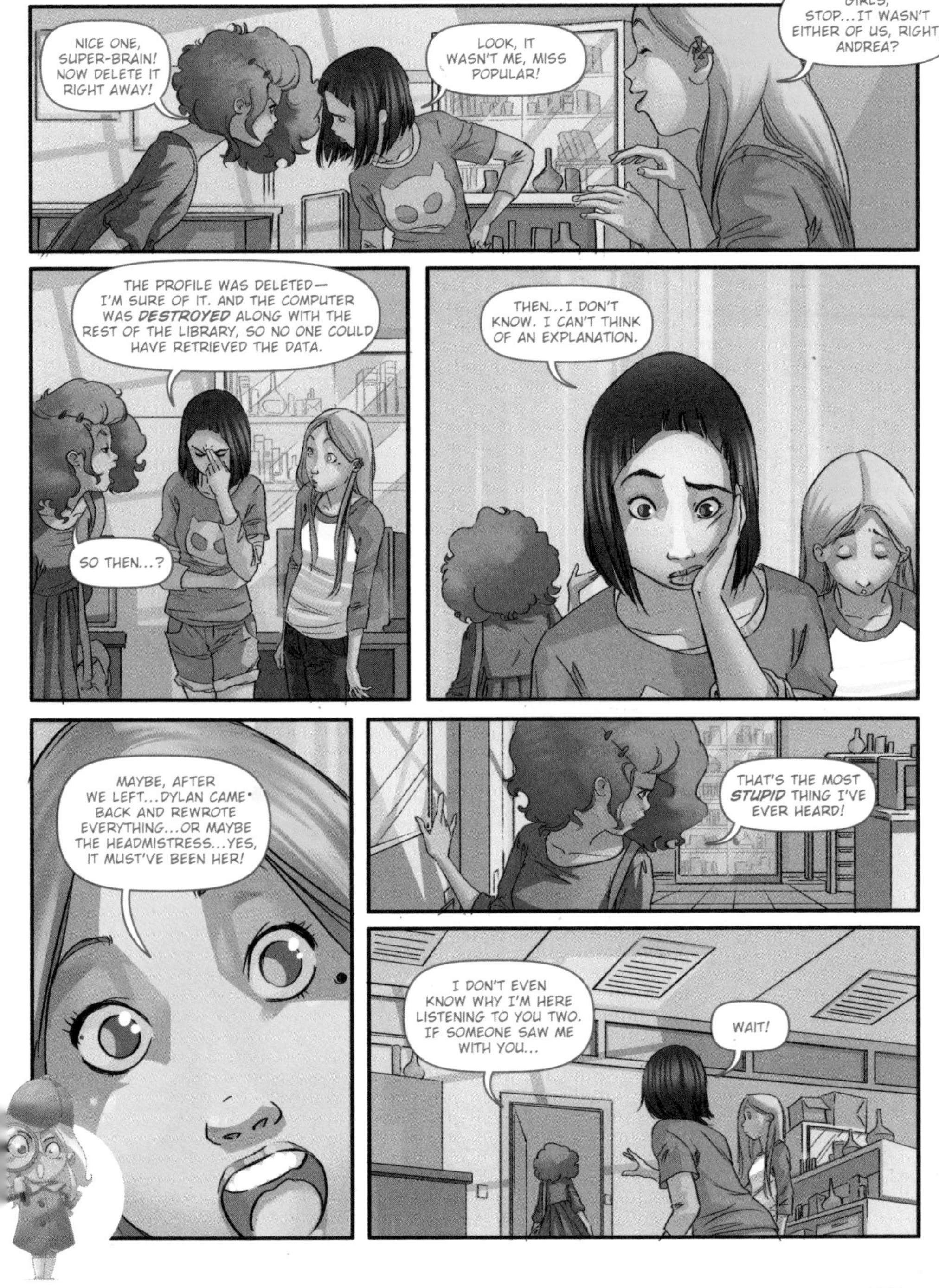
NICE ONE, SUPER-BRAIN! NOW DELETE IT RIGHT AWAY!
LOOK, IT WASN'T ME, MISS POPULAR!
GIRLS, STOP...IT WASN'T EITHER OF US, RIGHT, ANDREA?
THE PROFILE WAS DELETED—I'M SURE OF IT. AND THE COMPUTER WAS DESTROYED ALONG WITH THE REST OF THE LIBRARY, SO NO ONE COULD HAVE RETRIEVED THE DATA.
SO THEN...?
THEN...I DON'T KNOW. I CAN'T THINK OF AN EXPLANATION.
MAYBE, AFTER WE LEFT...DYLAN CAME BACK AND REWROTE EVERYTHING...OR MAYBE THE HEADMISTRESS...YES, IT MUST'VE BEEN HER!
THAT'S THE MOST STUPID THING I'VE EVER HEARD!
I DON'T EVEN KNOW WHY I'M HERE LISTENING TO YOU TWO. IF SOMEONE SAW ME WITH YOU...
WAIT!

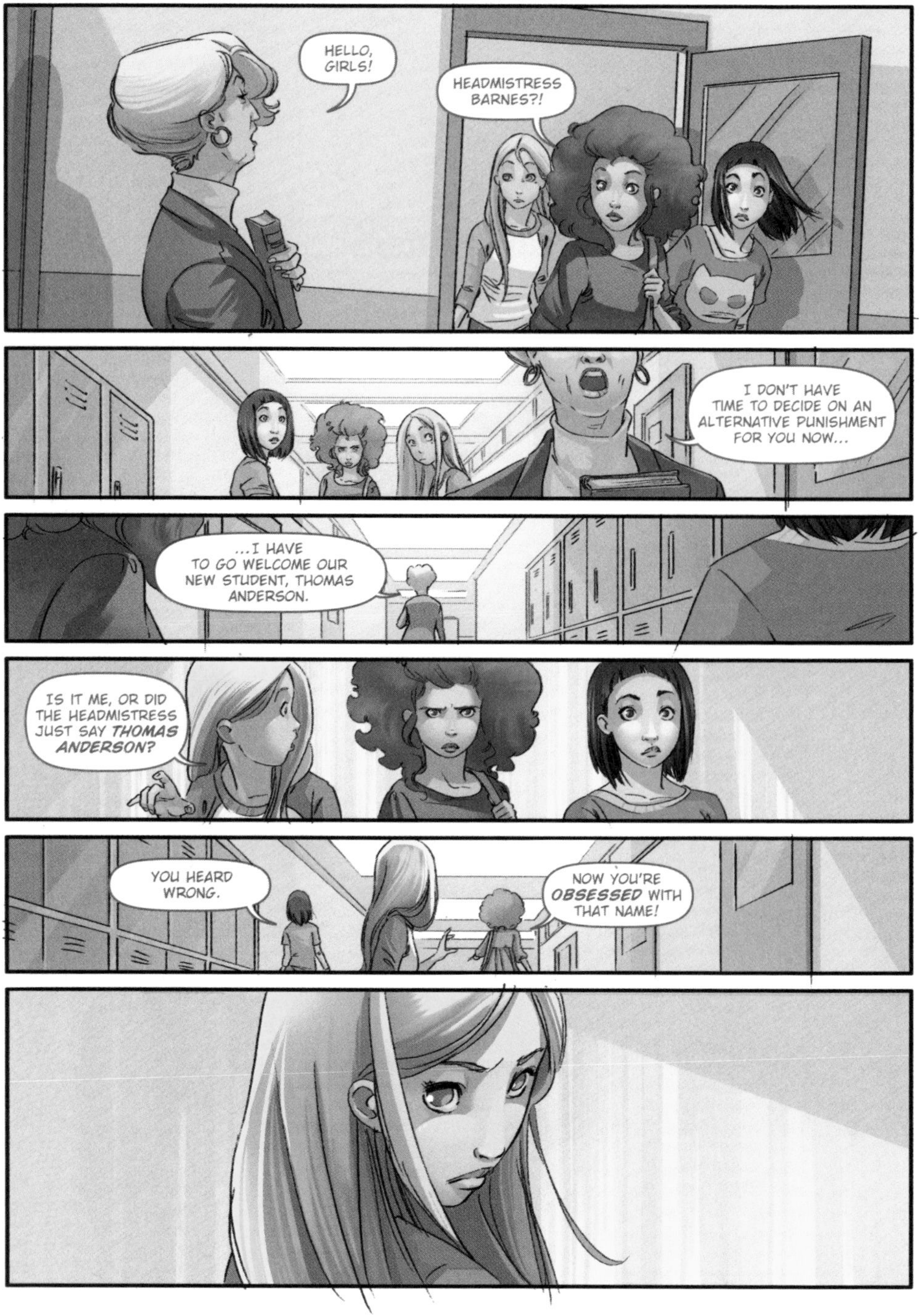
HELLO, GIRLS!
HEADMISTRESS BARNES?!
I DON'T HAVE TIME TO DECIDE ON AN ALTERNATIVE PUNISHMENT FOR YOU NOW...
...I HAVE TO GO WELCOME OUR NEW STUDENT, THOMAS ANDERSON.
IS IT ME, OR DID THE HEADMISTRESS JUST SAY *THOMAS ANDERSON?*
YOU HEARD WRONG.
NOW YOU'RE *OBSESSED* WITH THAT NAME!

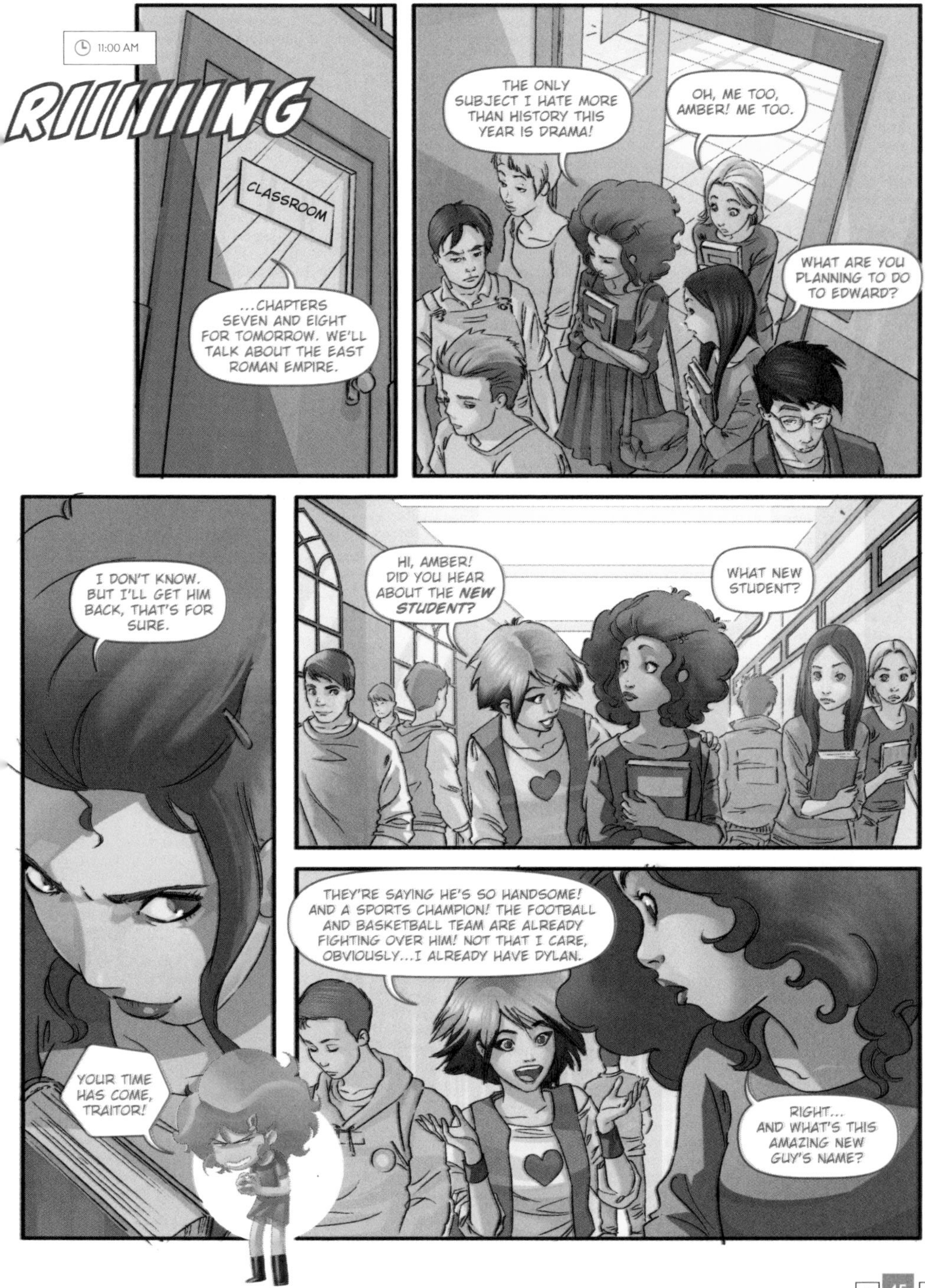
11:00 AM
RIIIIIING
CLASSROOM
...CHAPTERS SEVEN AND EIGHT FOR TOMORROW. WE'LL TALK ABOUT THE EAST ROMAN EMPIRE.
THE ONLY SUBJECT I HATE MORE THAN HISTORY THIS YEAR IS DRAMA!
OH, ME TOO, AMBER! ME TOO.
WHAT ARE YOU PLANNING TO DO TO EDWARD?
I DON'T KNOW. BUT I'LL GET HIM BACK, THAT'S FOR SURE.
HI, AMBER! DID YOU HEAR ABOUT THE ***NEW STUDENT?***
WHAT NEW STUDENT?
THEY'RE SAYING HE'S SO HANDSOME! AND A SPORTS CHAMPION! THE FOOTBALL AND BASKETBALL TEAM ARE ALREADY FIGHTING OVER HIM! NOT THAT I CARE, OBVIOUSLY...I ALREADY HAVE DYLAN.
YOUR TIME HAS COME, TRAITOR!
RIGHT... AND WHAT'S THIS AMAZING NEW GUY'S NAME?

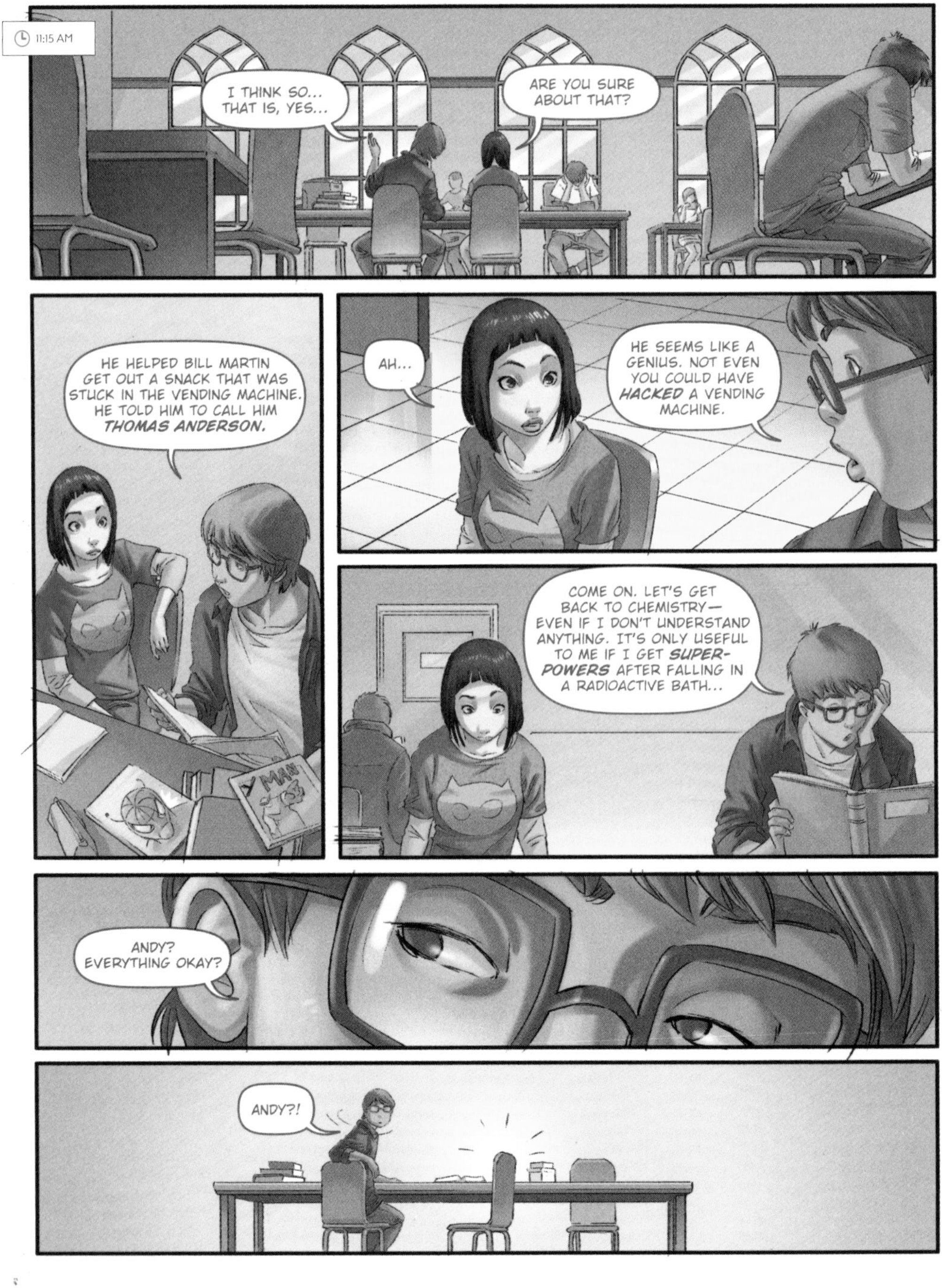
11:15 AM
I THINK SO... THAT IS, YES...
ARE YOU SURE ABOUT THAT?
HE HELPED BILL MARTIN GET OUT A SNACK THAT WAS STUCK IN THE VENDING MACHINE. HE TOLD HIM TO CALL HIM THOMAS ANDERSON.
AH...
HE SEEMS LIKE A GENIUS. NOT EVEN YOU COULD HAVE HACKED A VENDING MACHINE.
COME ON. LET'S GET BACK TO CHEMISTRY— EVEN IF I DON'T UNDERSTAND ANYTHING. IT'S ONLY USEFUL TO ME IF I GET SUPER-POWERS AFTER FALLING IN A RADIOACTIVE BATH...
ANDY? EVERYTHING OKAY?
ANDY?!

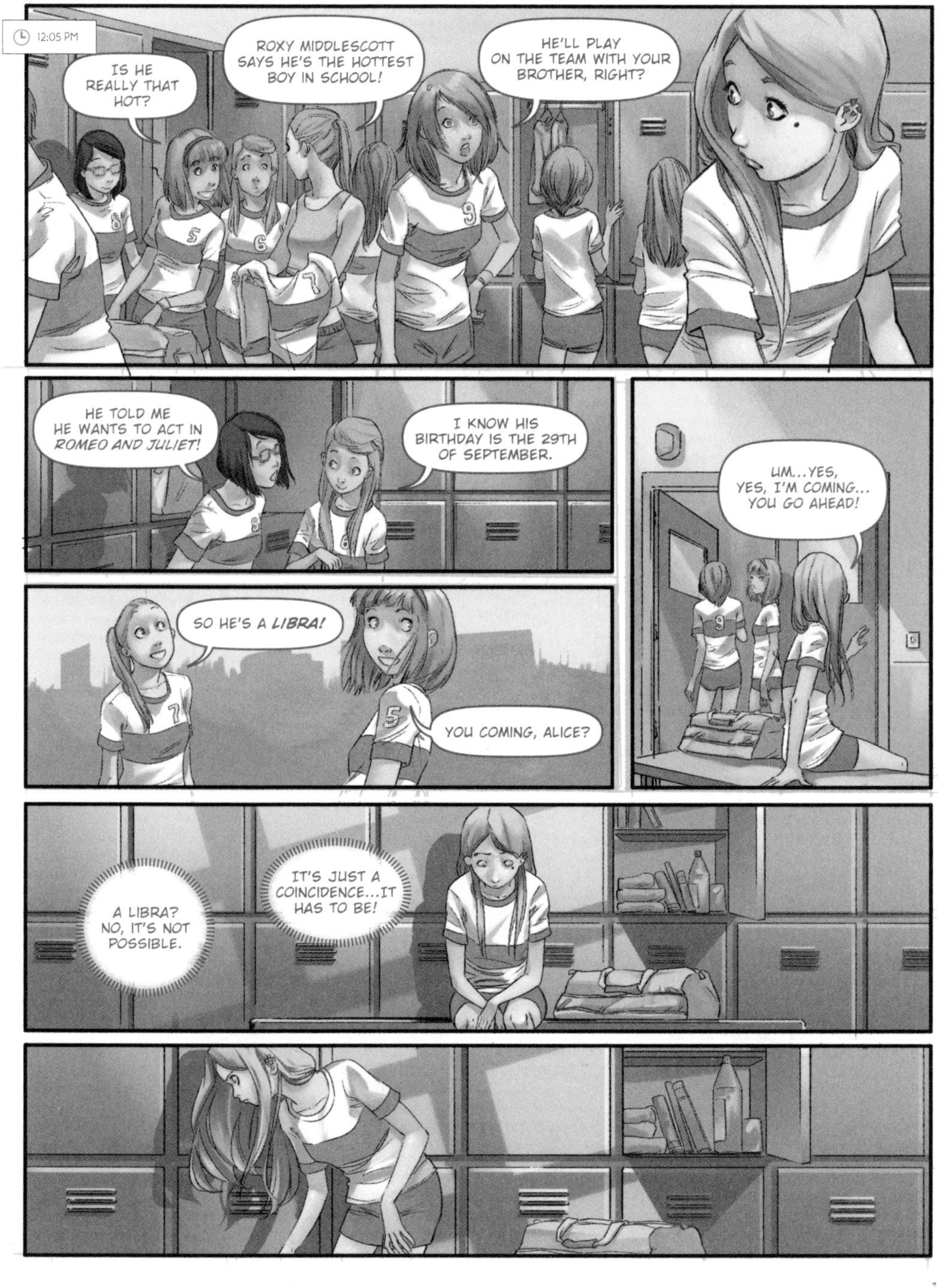
12:05 PM
IS HE REALLY THAT HOT?
ROXY MIDDLESCOTT SAYS HE'S THE HOTTEST BOY IN SCHOOL!
HE'LL PLAY ON THE TEAM WITH YOUR BROTHER, RIGHT?
HE TOLD ME HE WANTS TO ACT IN *ROMEO AND JULIET*!
I KNOW HIS BIRTHDAY IS THE 29TH OF SEPTEMBER.
UM...YES, YES, I'M COMING... YOU GO AHEAD!
SO HE'S A ***LIBRA!***
YOU COMING, ALICE?
A LIBRA? NO, IT'S NOT POSSIBLE.
IT'S JUST A COINCIDENCE...IT HAS TO BE!

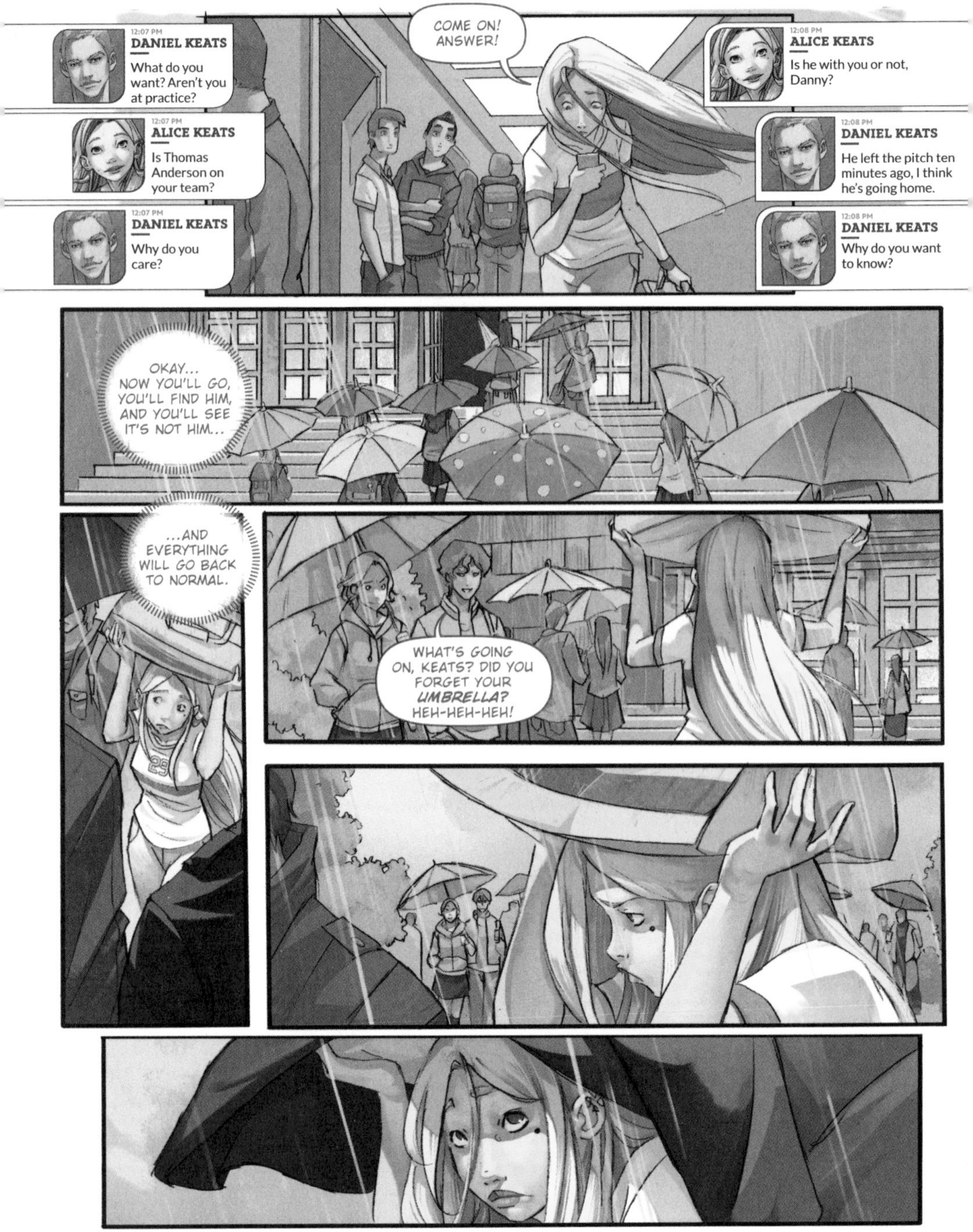
12:07 PM
DANIEL KEATS
What do you want? Aren't you at practice?
12:07 PM
ALICE KEATS
Is Thomas Anderson on your team?
12:07 PM
DANIEL KEATS
Why do you care?
COME ON! ANSWER!
12:08 PM
ALICE KEATS
Is he with you or not, Danny?
12:08 PM
DANIEL KEATS
He left the pitch ten minutes ago, I think he's going home.
12:08 PM
DANIEL KEATS
Why do you want to know?
OKAY... NOW YOU'LL GO, YOU'LL FIND HIM, AND YOU'LL SEE IT'S NOT HIM...
...AND EVERYTHING WILL GO BACK TO NORMAL.
WHAT'S GOING ON, KEATS? DID YOU FORGET YOUR *UMBRELLA?* HEH-HEH-HEH!

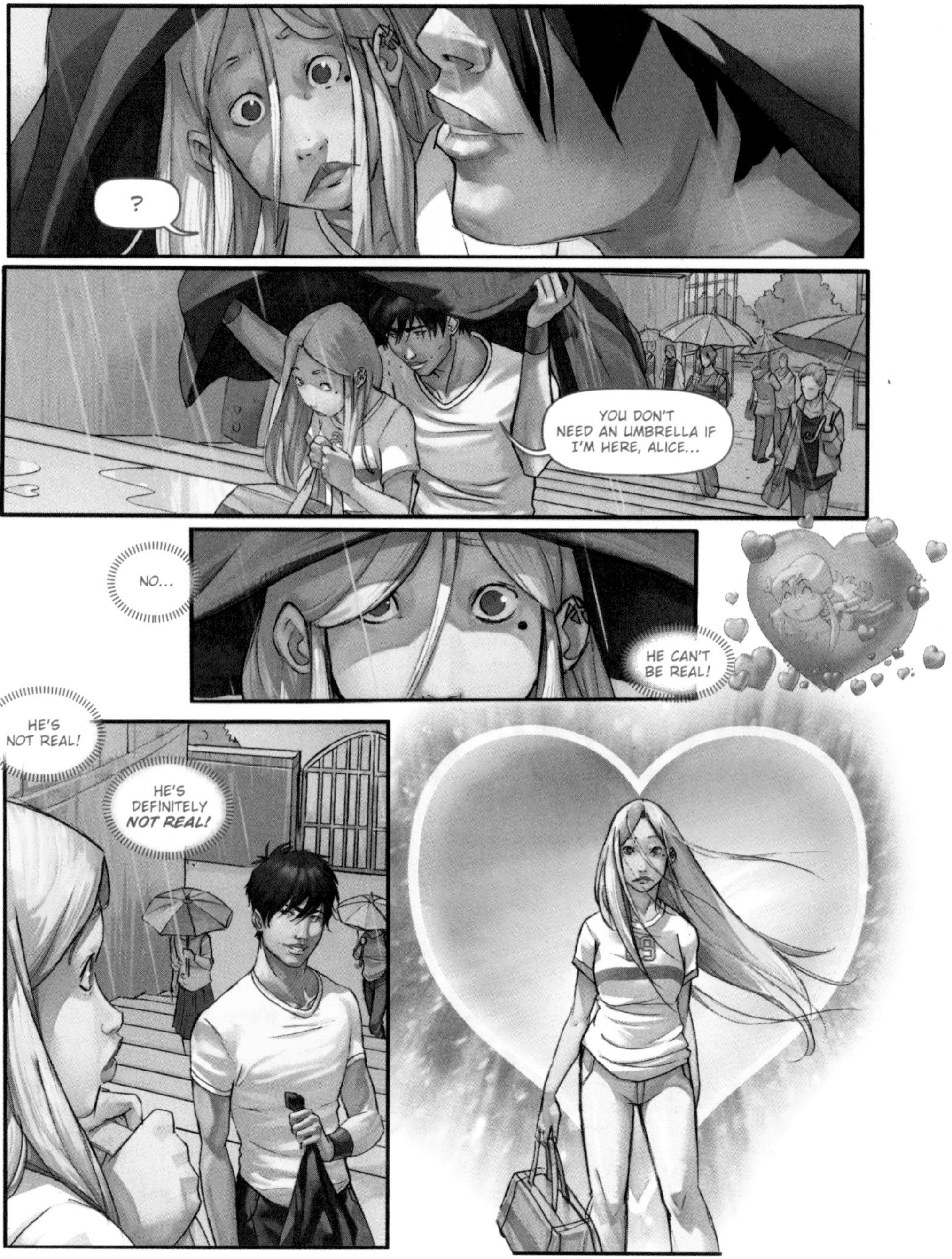

?
YOU DON'T NEED AN UMBRELLA IF I'M HERE, ALICE...
NO...
HE CAN'T BE REAL!
HE'S NOT REAL!
HE'S DEFINITELY NOT REAL!

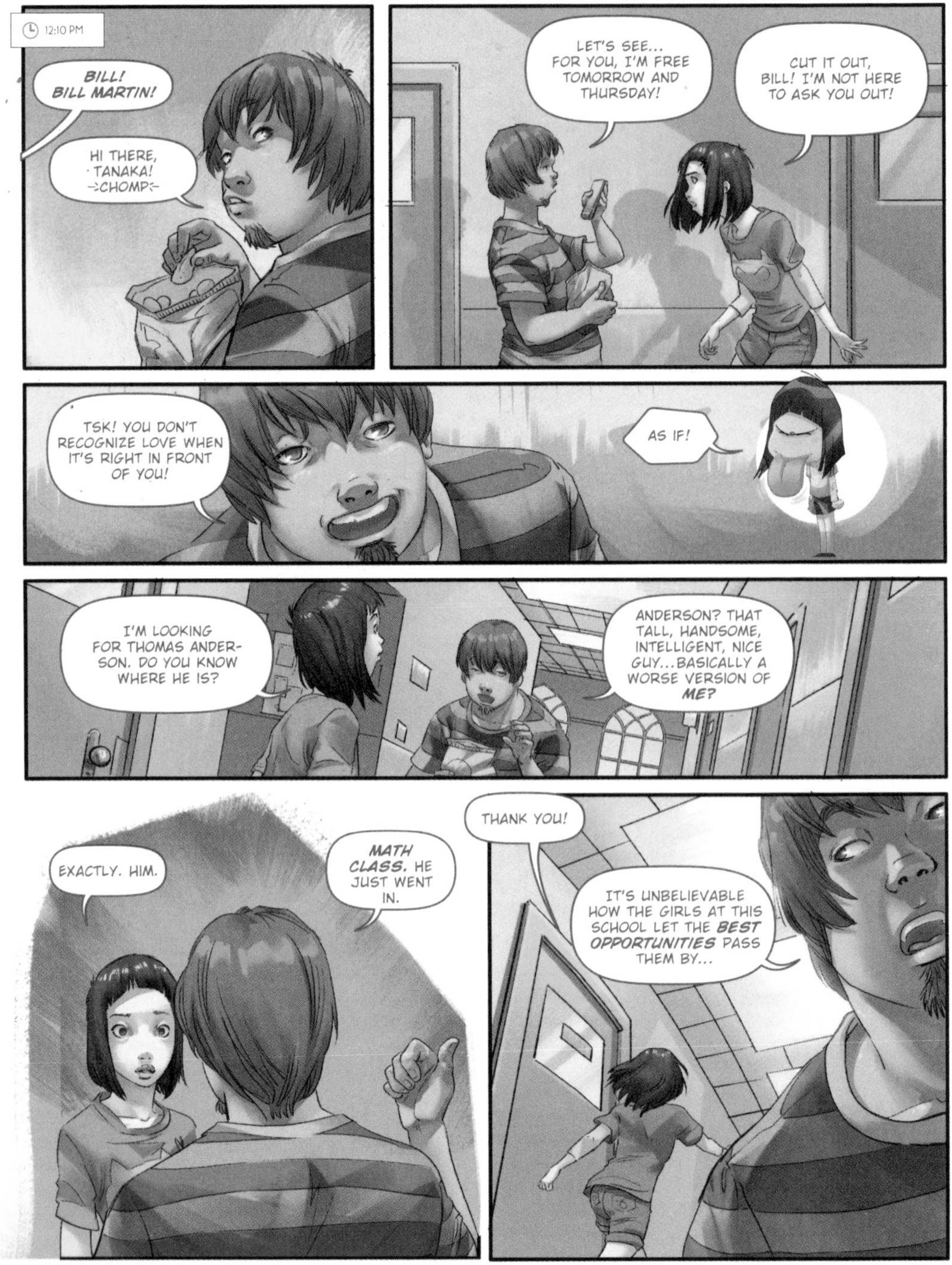
12:10 PM
BILL! BILL MARTIN!
HI THERE, TANAKA! CHOMP
LET'S SEE... FOR YOU, I'M FREE TOMORROW AND THURSDAY!
CUT IT OUT, BILL! I'M NOT HERE TO ASK YOU OUT!
TSK! YOU DON'T RECOGNIZE LOVE WHEN IT'S RIGHT IN FRONT OF YOU!
AS IF!
I'M LOOKING FOR THOMAS ANDER-SON. DO YOU KNOW WHERE HE IS?
ANDERSON? THAT TALL, HANDSOME, INTELLIGENT, NICE GUY...BASICALLY A WORSE VERSION OF ME?
EXACTLY. HIM.
MATH CLASS. HE JUST WENT IN.
THANK YOU!
IT'S UNBELIEVABLE HOW THE GIRLS AT THIS SCHOOL LET THE BEST OPPORTUNITIES PASS THEM BY...

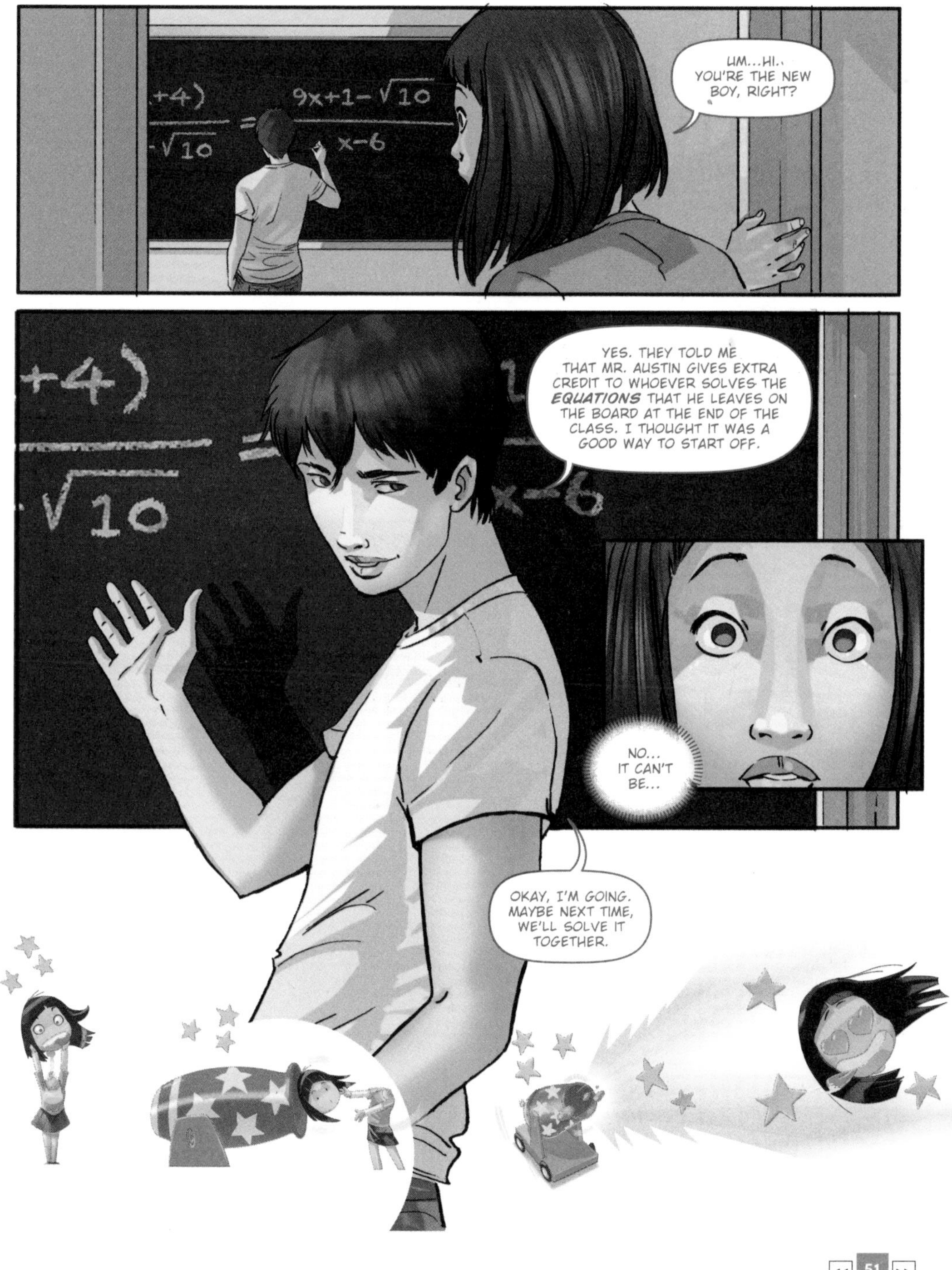
UM...HI.. YOU'RE THE NEW BOY, RIGHT?
YES. THEY TOLD ME THAT MR. AUSTIN GIVES EXTRA CREDIT TO WHOEVER SOLVES THE **EQUATIONS** THAT HE LEAVES ON THE BOARD AT THE END OF THE CLASS. I THOUGHT IT WAS A GOOD WAY TO START OFF.
NO... IT CAN'T BE...
OKAY, I'M GOING. MAYBE NEXT TIME, WE'LL SOLVE IT TOGETHER.

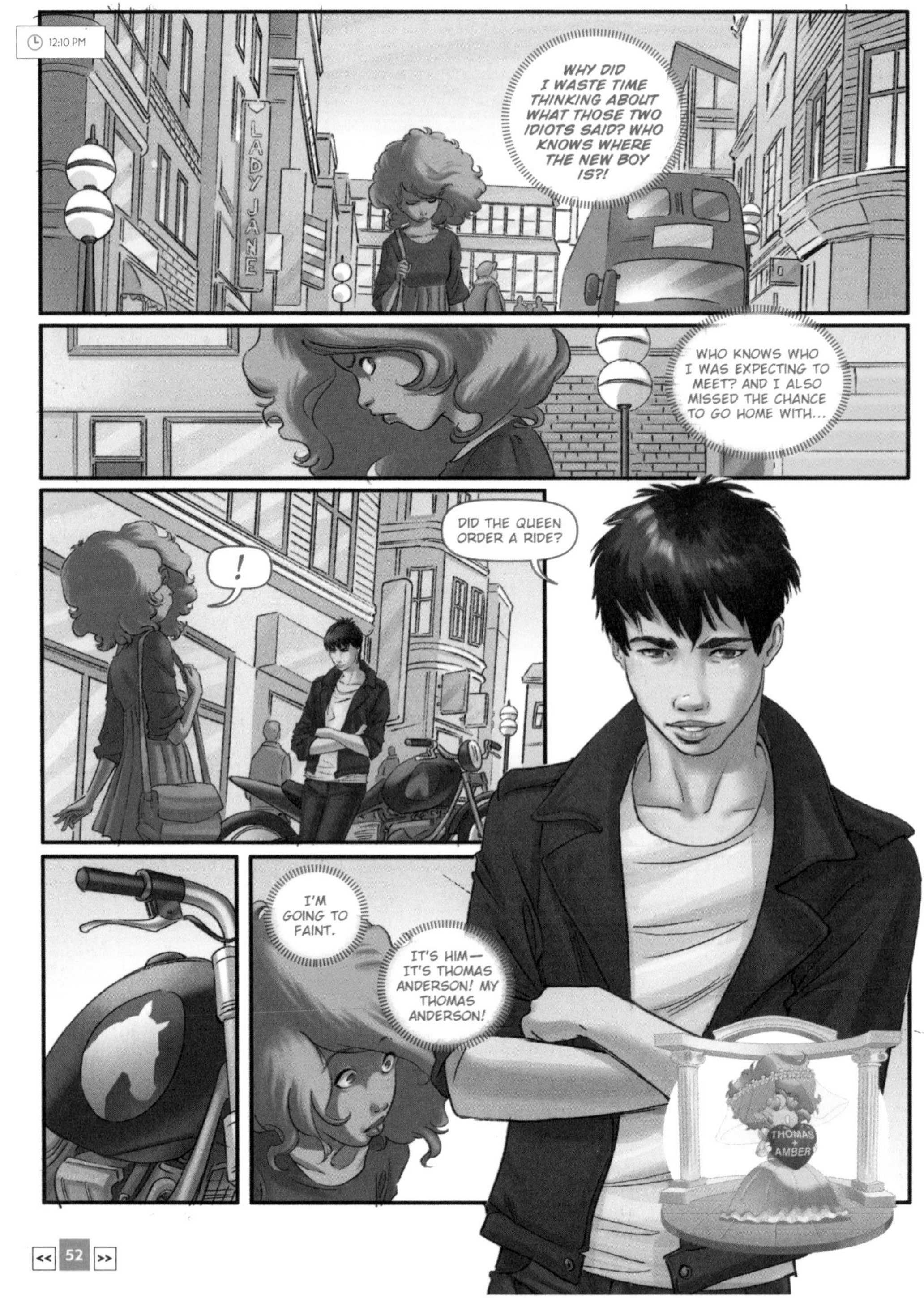

12:10 PM
WHY DID I WASTE TIME THINKING ABOUT WHAT THOSE TWO IDIOTS SAID? WHO KNOWS WHERE THE NEW BOY IS?!
LADY JANE
WHO KNOWS WHO I WAS EXPECTING TO MEET? AND I ALSO MISSED THE CHANCE TO GO HOME WITH...
!
DID THE QUEEN ORDER A RIDE?
I'M GOING TO FAINT.
IT'S HIM— IT'S THOMAS ANDERSON! MY THOMAS ANDERSON!
THOMAS + AMBER

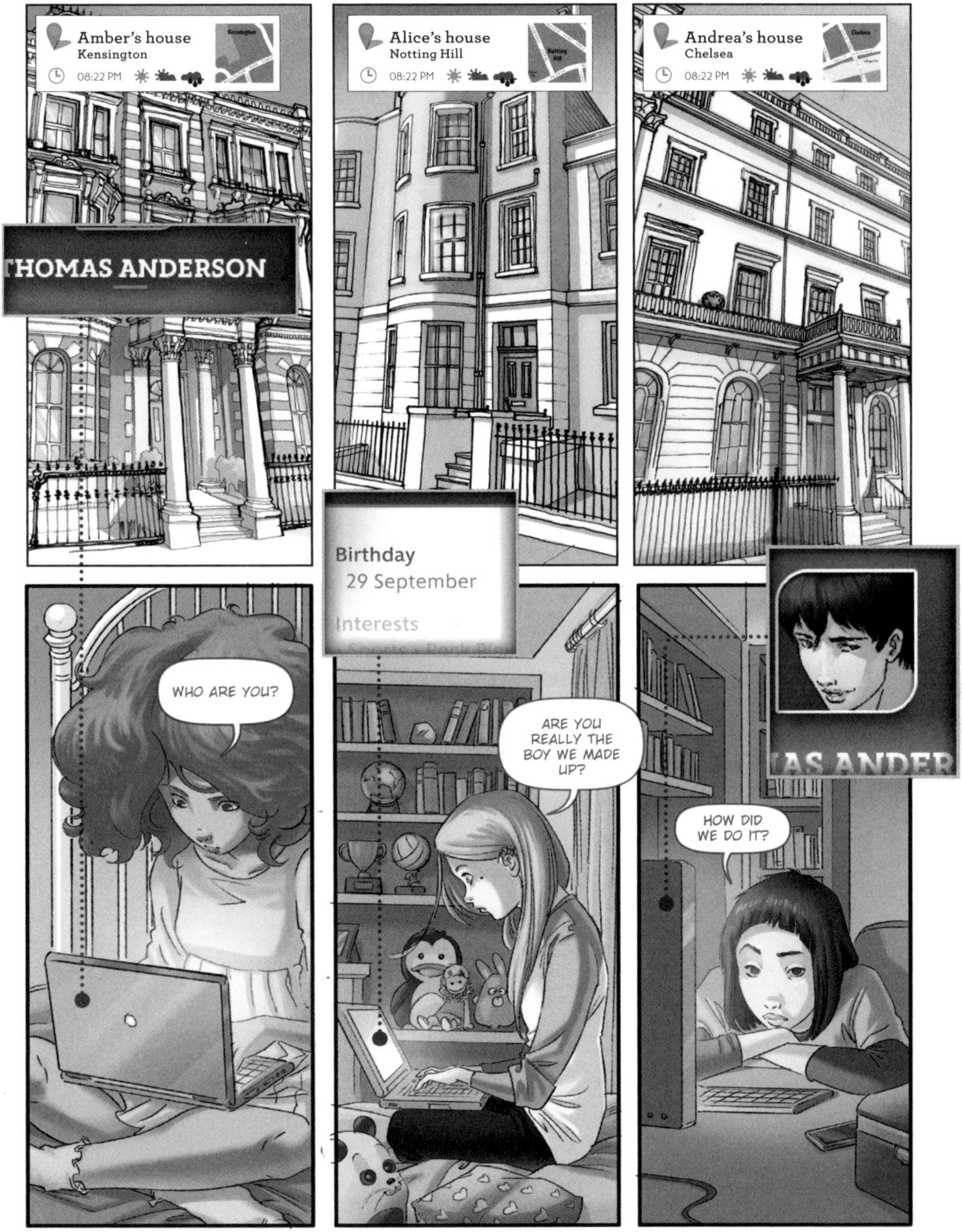
Amber's house
Kensington
08:22 PM
Alice's house
Notting Hill
08:22 PM
Andrea's house
Chelsea
08:22 PM
THOMAS ANDERSON
Birthday
29 September
Interests
WHO ARE YOU?
ARE YOU REALLY THE BOY WE MADE UP?
HOW DID WE DO IT?

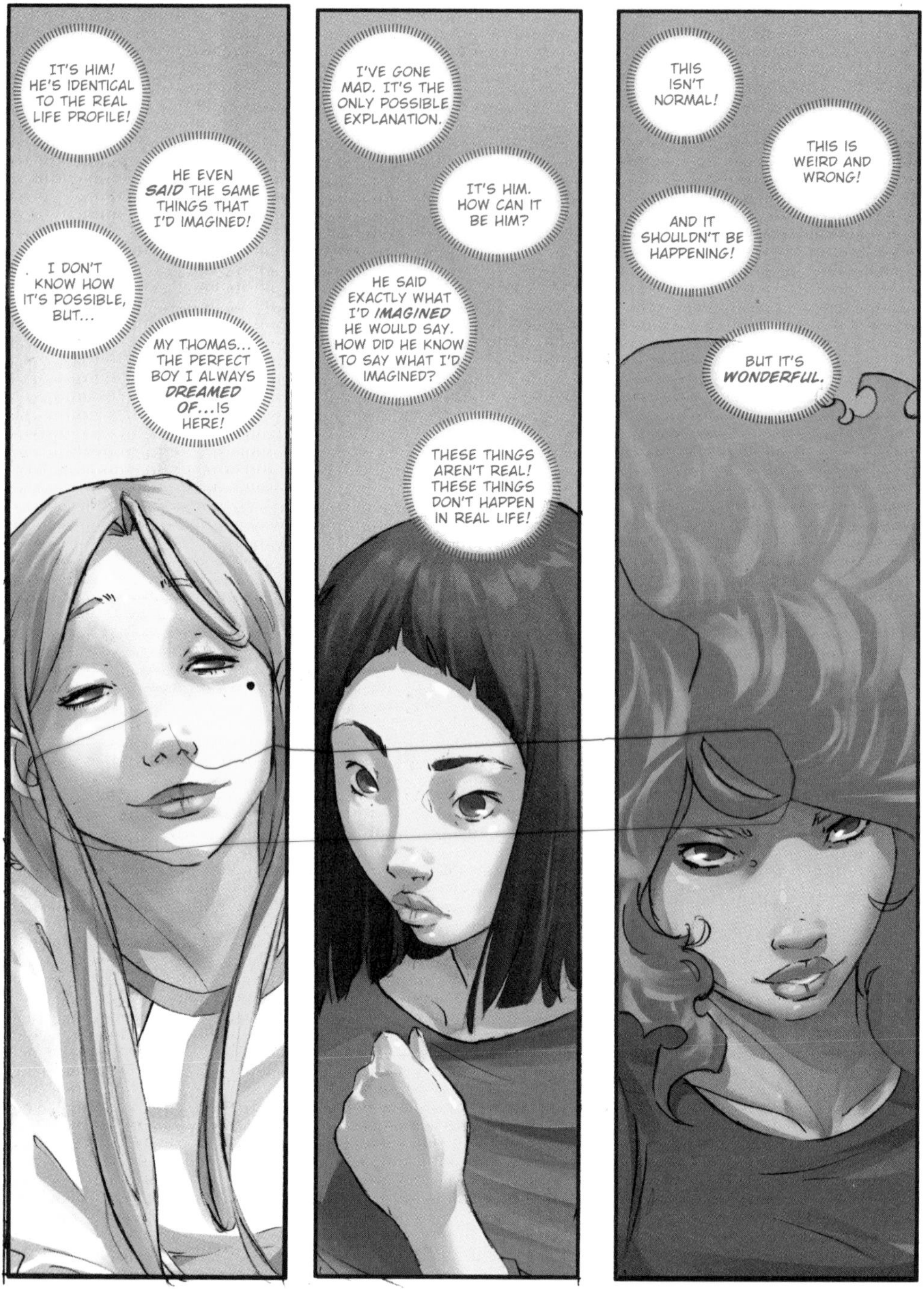

IT'S HIM! HE'S IDENTICAL TO THE REAL LIFE PROFILE!
HE EVEN *SAID* THE SAME THINGS THAT I'D IMAGINED!
I DON'T KNOW HOW IT'S POSSIBLE, BUT...
MY THOMAS... THE PERFECT BOY I ALWAYS *DREAMED OF...* IS HERE!
I'VE GONE MAD. IT'S THE ONLY POSSIBLE EXPLANATION.
IT'S HIM. HOW CAN IT BE HIM?
HE SAID EXACTLY WHAT I'D *IMAGINED* HE WOULD SAY. HOW DID HE KNOW TO SAY WHAT I'D IMAGINED?
THESE THINGS AREN'T REAL! THESE THINGS DON'T HAPPEN IN REAL LIFE!
THIS ISN'T NORMAL!
THIS IS WEIRD AND WRONG!
AND IT SHOULDN'T BE HAPPENING!
BUT IT'S *WONDERFUL.*

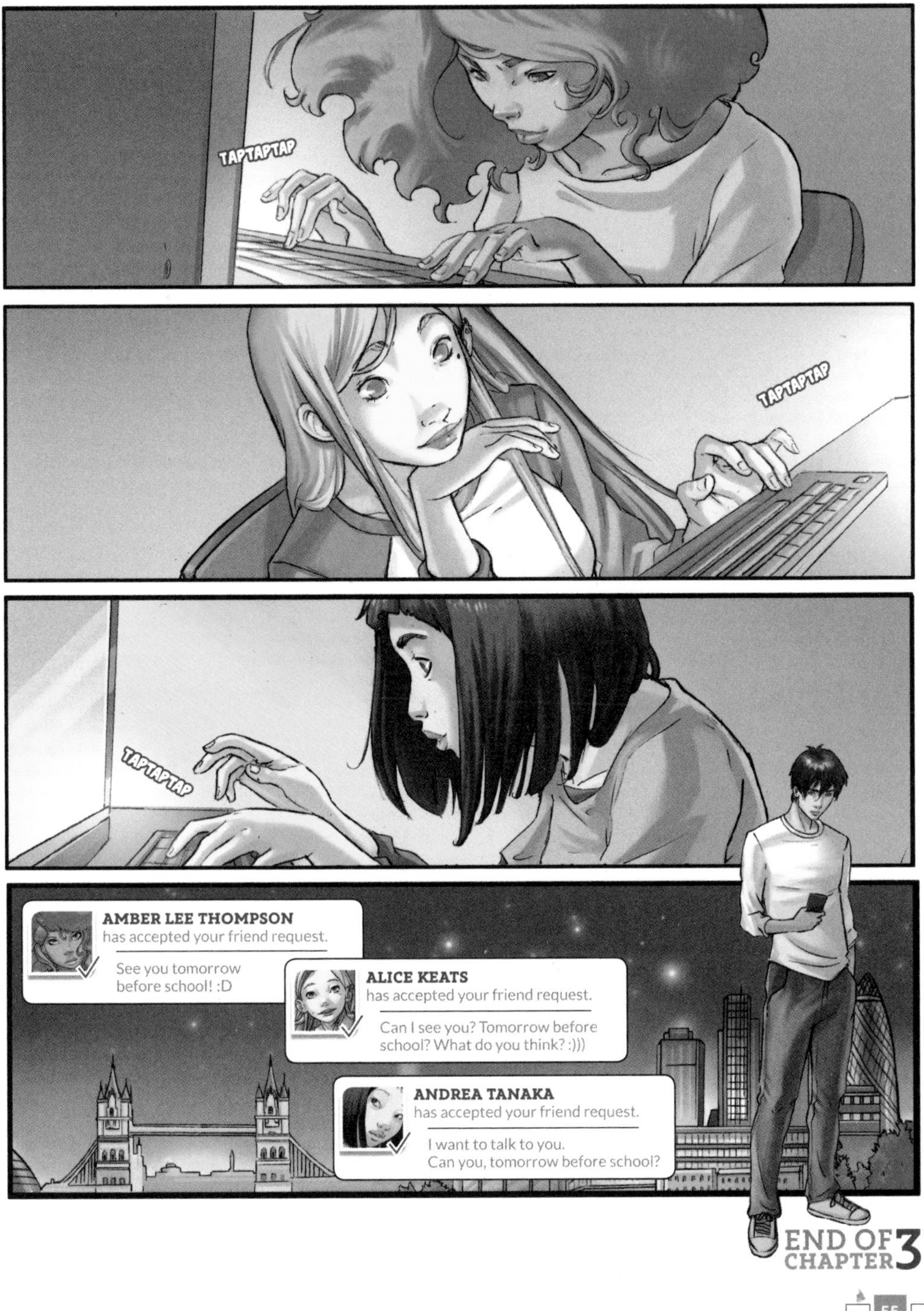
TAPTAPTAP
TAPTAPTAP
TAPTAPTAP
AMBER LEE THOMPSON
has accepted your friend request.
See you tomorrow before school! :D
ALICE KEATS
has accepted your friend request.
Can I see you? Tomorrow before school? What do you think? :)))
ANDREA TANAKA
has accepted your friend request.
I want to talk to you.
Can you, tomorrow before school?
END OF CHAPTER 3

Disney
realLife #1

#Impossible Befriending

Script: Alessandro Ferrari
Layout: Alberto Zanon
Cleanup: Elena Pianta and Alberto Zanon
Emotidolls: Andrea Scoppetta
Color: Massimo Rocca, Pierluigi Casolino, Andrea Scoppetta, Mario Perrotta, Slava Panarin, Giuseppe Fontana, Gianluca Barone
Watercolor backgrounds: Valeria Turati
Translation: Edizioni BD and Erin Brady
Lettering and Infographic: Edizioni BD

COVER
Layout and cleanup: Alberto Zanon
Color: Pierluigi Casolino

CONTRIBUTORS
Tomatofarm

Original project developed by Disney Publishing with the contribution of Barbara Baraldi, Paola Barbato, Micol Beltramini and Diana Tomatozombie

#2

#I'm Juliet

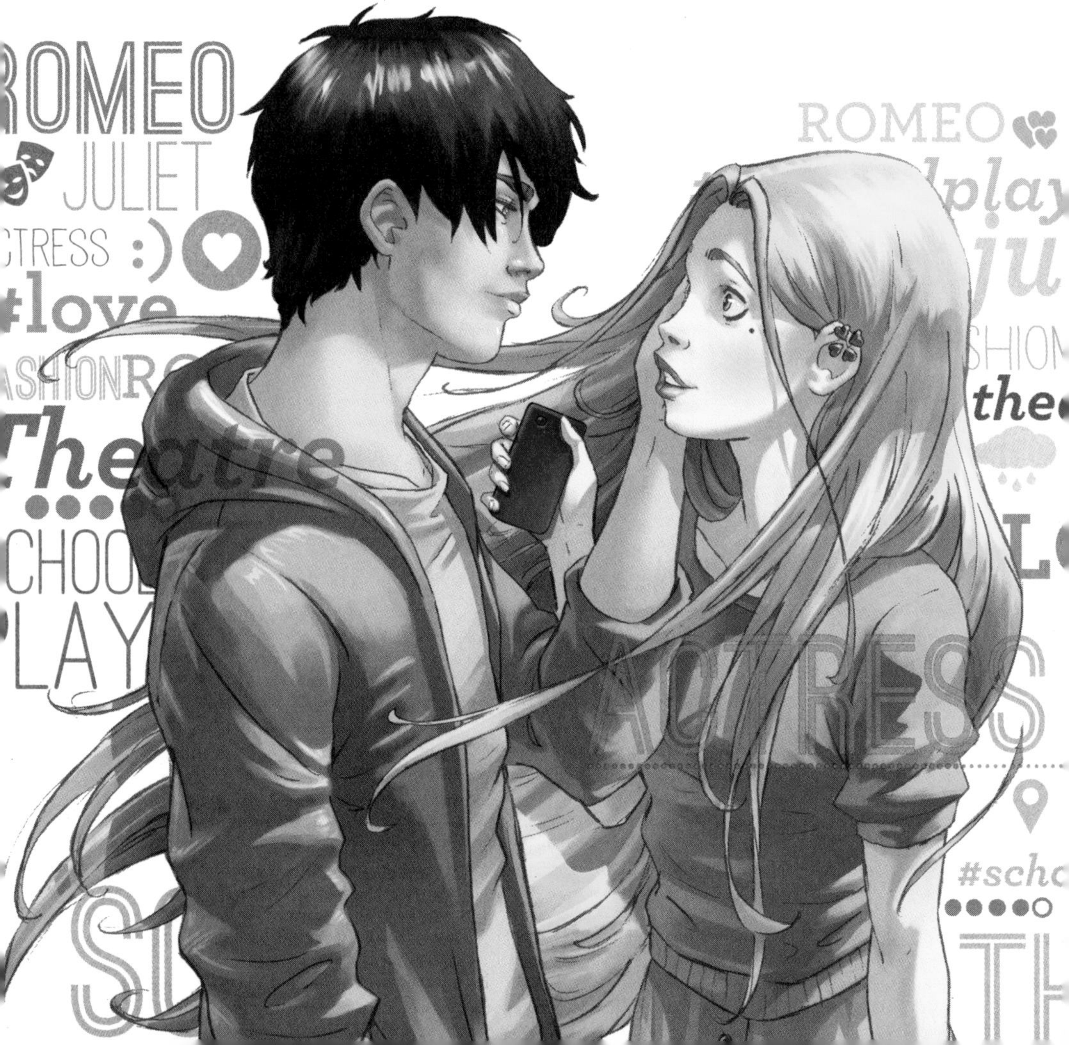

ROMEO
JULIET
Theatre
ROMEO
ACTRESS

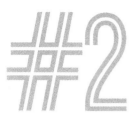

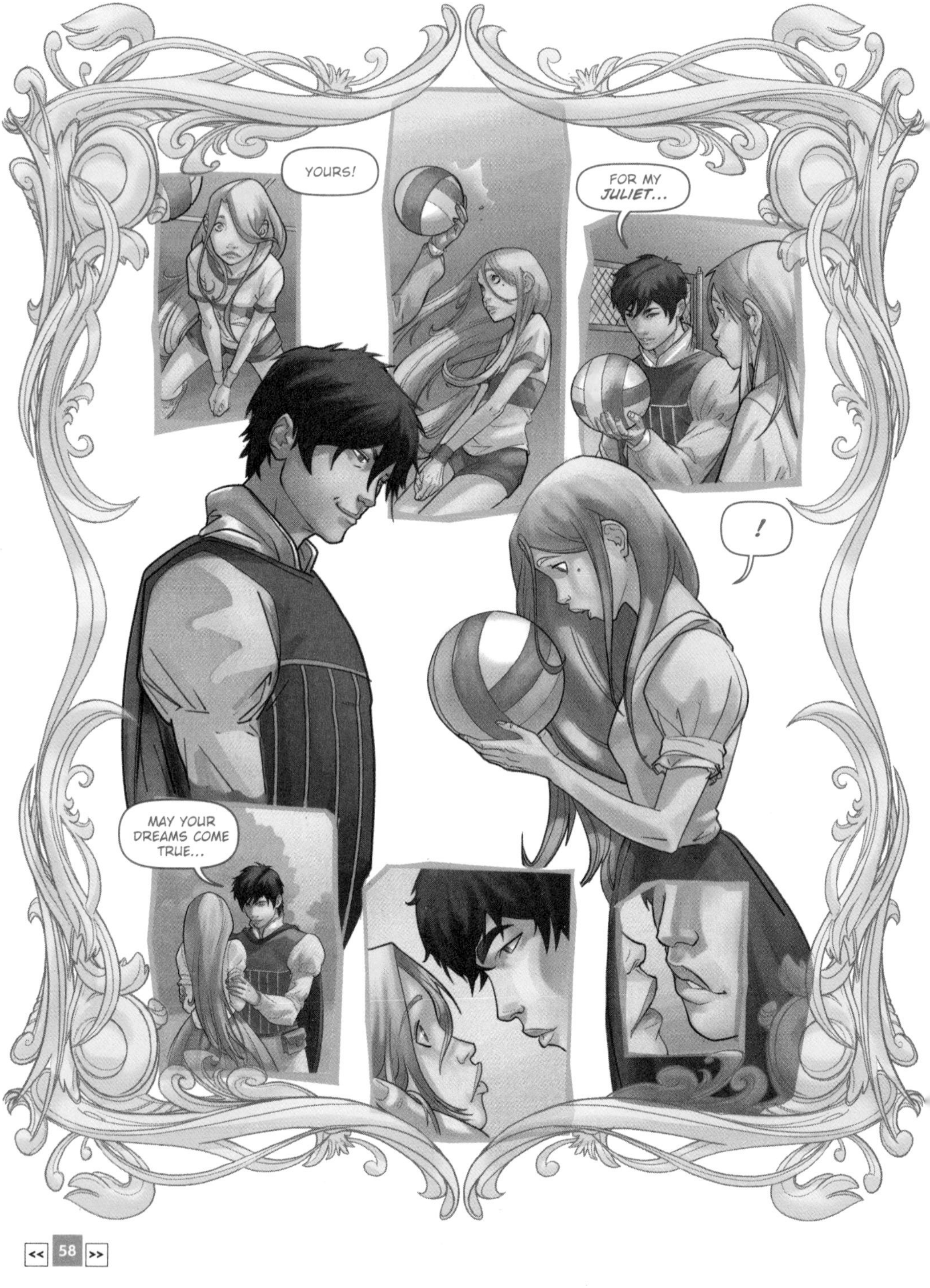
YOURS!
FOR MY JULIET...
!
MAY YOUR DREAMS COME TRUE...

CHAPTER 4

Big MATCH, Big CHOICE

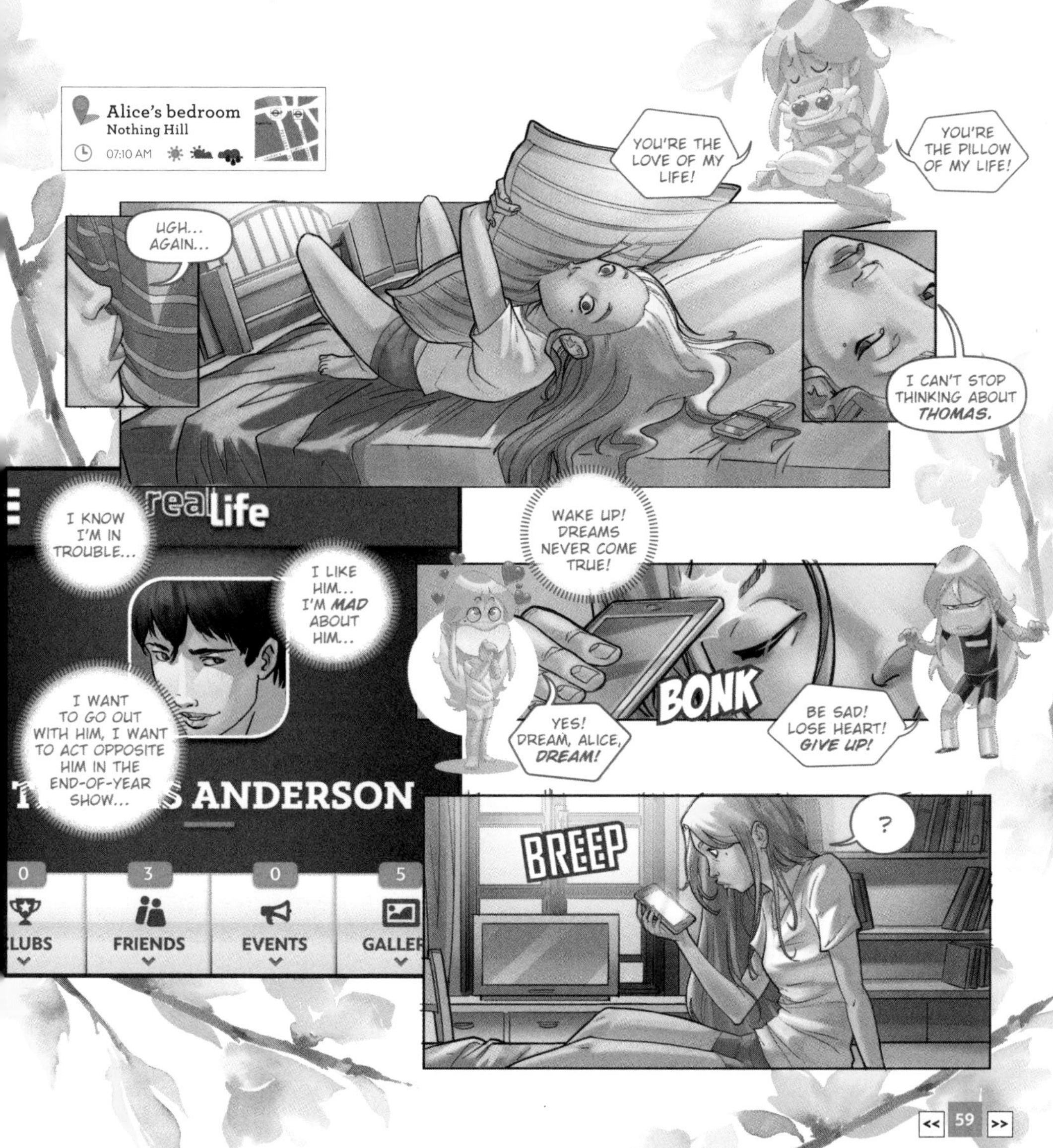

Alice's bedroom
Nothing Hill
07:10 AM
YOU'RE THE LOVE OF MY LIFE!
YOU'RE THE PILLOW OF MY LIFE!
UGH... AGAIN...
I CAN'T STOP THINKING ABOUT THOMAS.
realLife
I KNOW I'M IN TROUBLE...
I LIKE HIM... I'M MAD ABOUT HIM...
I WANT TO GO OUT WITH HIM, I WANT TO ACT OPPOSITE HIM IN THE END-OF-YEAR SHOW...
S ANDERSON
0 CLUBS
3 FRIENDS
0 EVENTS
5 GALLER
WAKE UP! DREAMS NEVER COME TRUE!
BONK
YES! DREAM, ALICE, DREAM!
BE SAD! LOSE HEART! GIVE UP!
BREEP
?

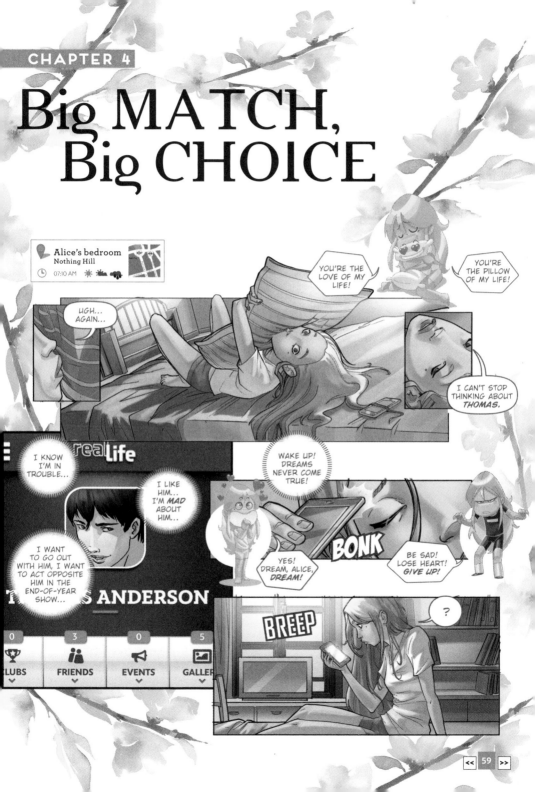

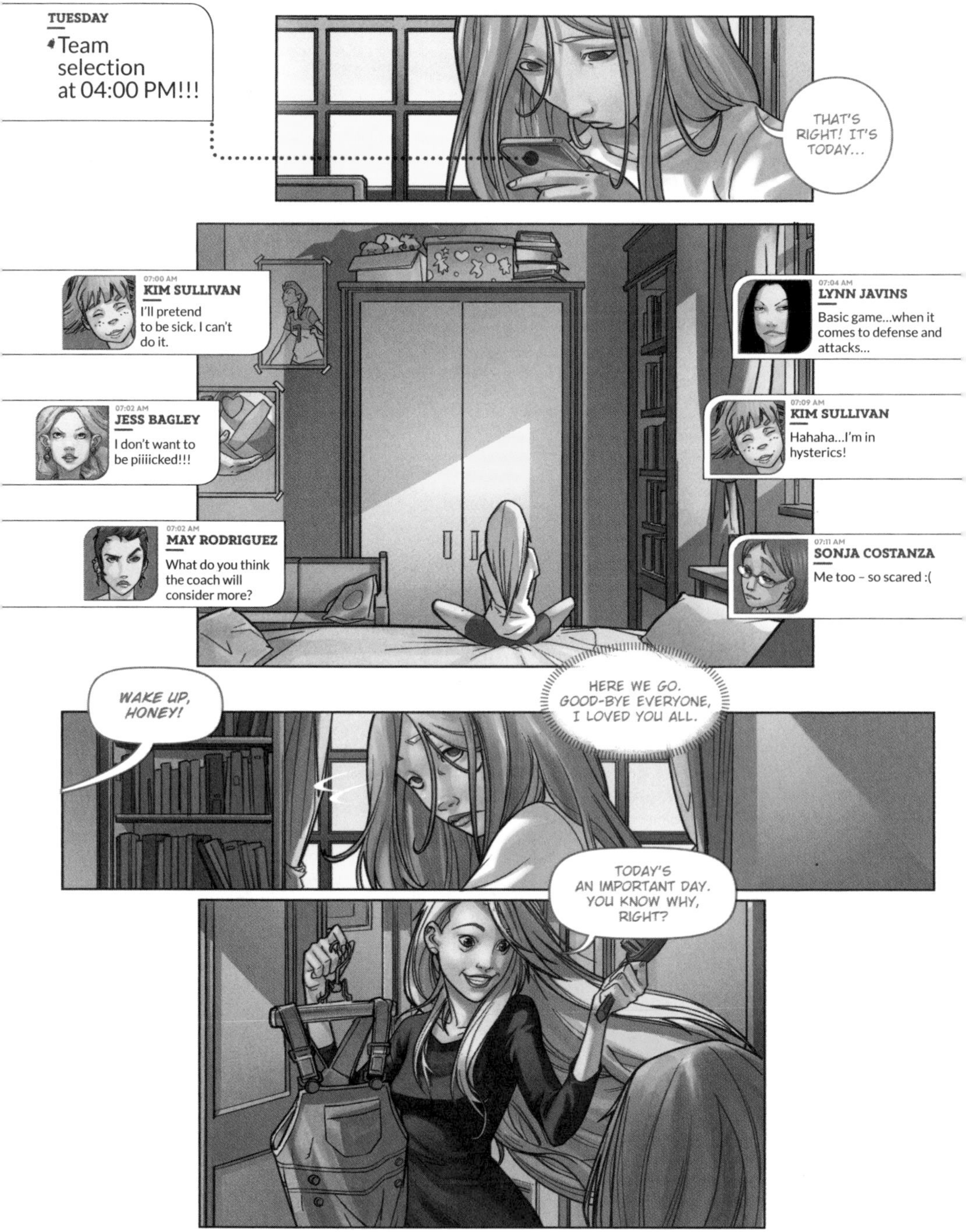

TUESDAY
Team selection at 04:00 PM!!!
THAT'S RIGHT! IT'S TODAY...
07:00 AM
KIM SULLIVAN
I'll pretend to be sick. I can't do it.
07:02 AM
JESS BAGLEY
I don't want to be piiiicked!!!
07:02 AM
MAY RODRIGUEZ
What do you think the coach will consider more?
07:04 AM
LYNN JAVINS
Basic game...when it comes to defense and attacks...
07:09 AM
KIM SULLIVAN
Hahaha...I'm in hysterics!
07:11 AM
SONJA COSTANZA
Me too – so scared :(
WAKE UP, HONEY!
HERE WE GO. GOOD-BYE EVERYONE, I LOVED YOU ALL.
TODAY'S AN IMPORTANT DAY. YOU KNOW WHY, RIGHT?

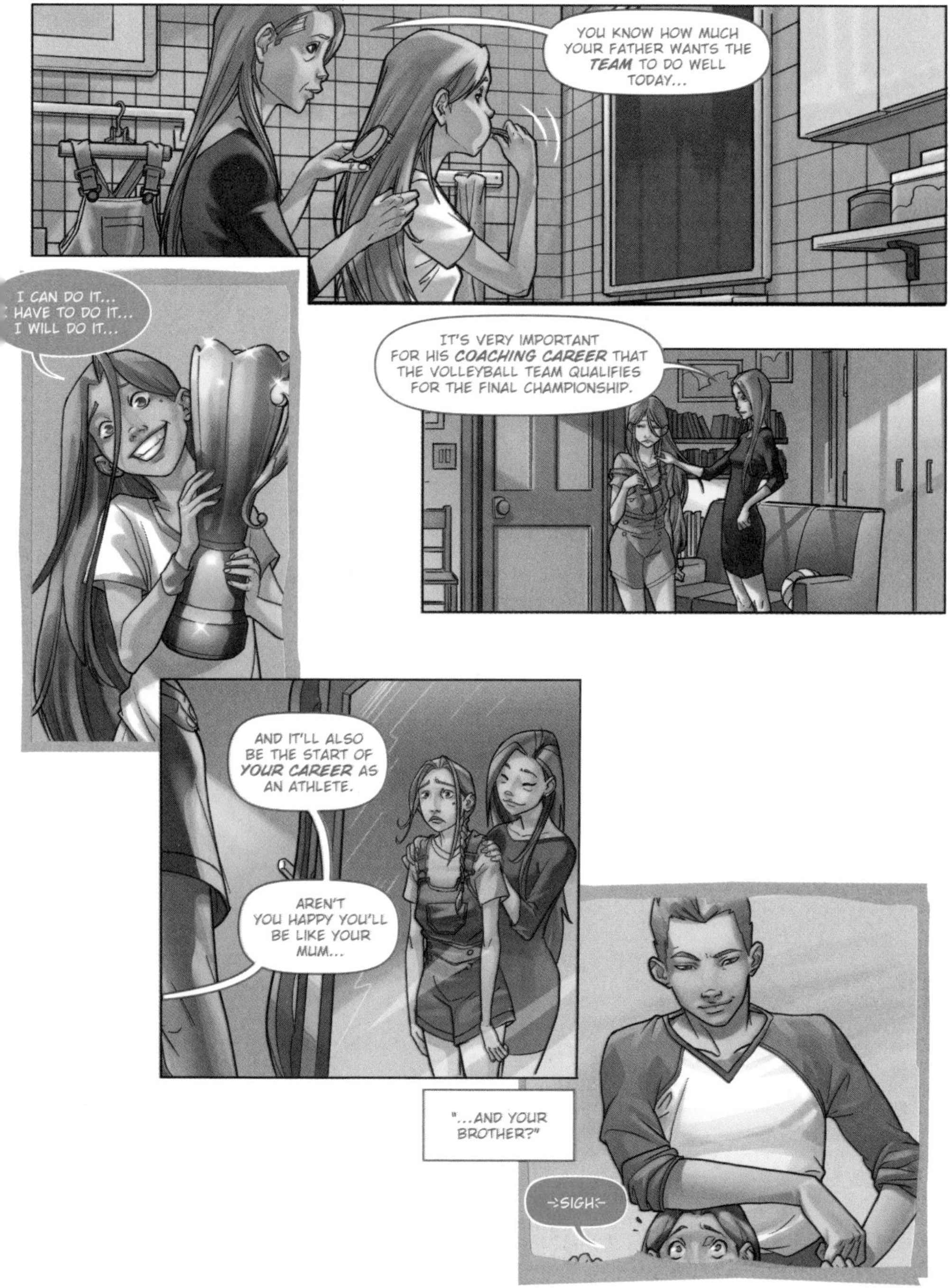
YOU KNOW HOW MUCH YOUR FATHER WANTS THE TEAM TO DO WELL TODAY...
I CAN DO IT... HAVE TO DO IT... I WILL DO IT...
IT'S VERY IMPORTANT FOR HIS COACHING CAREER THAT THE VOLLEYBALL TEAM QUALIFIES FOR THE FINAL CHAMPIONSHIP.
AND IT'LL ALSO BE THE START OF YOUR CAREER AS AN ATHLETE.
AREN'T YOU HAPPY YOU'LL BE LIKE YOUR MUM...
"...AND YOUR BROTHER?"
SIGH

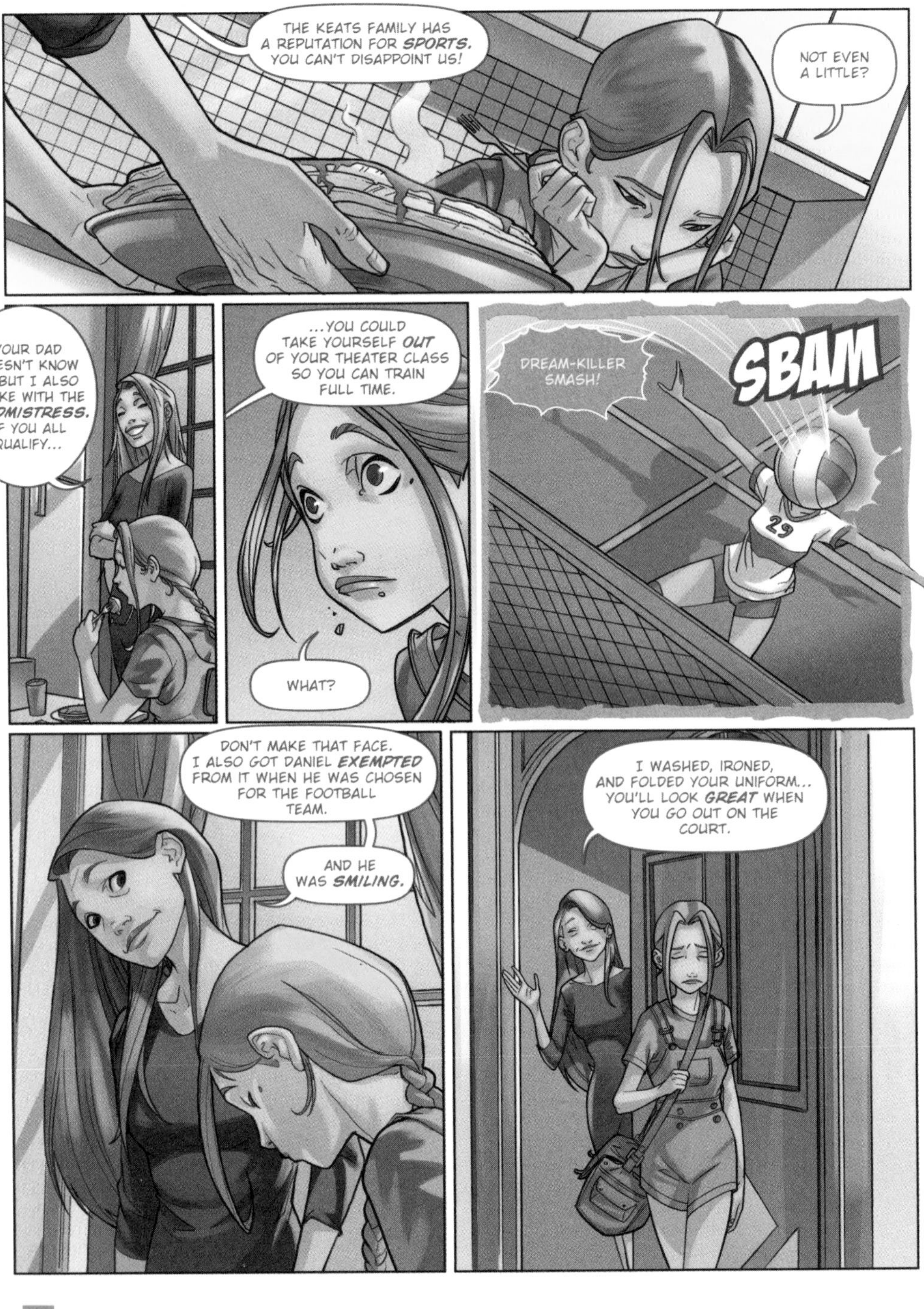
THE KEATS FAMILY HAS A REPUTATION FOR SPORTS. YOU CAN'T DISAPPOINT US!
NOT EVEN A LITTLE?
YOUR DAD DOESN'T KNOW IT, BUT I ALSO SPOKE WITH THE HEADMISTRESS. IF YOU ALL QUALIFY...
...YOU COULD TAKE YOURSELF OUT OF YOUR THEATER CLASS SO YOU CAN TRAIN FULL TIME.
WHAT?
DREAM-KILLER SMASH!
SBAM
29
DON'T MAKE THAT FACE. I ALSO GOT DANIEL EXEMPTED FROM IT WHEN HE WAS CHOSEN FOR THE FOOTBALL TEAM.
AND HE WAS SMILING.
I WASHED, IRONED, AND FOLDED YOUR UNIFORM... YOU'LL LOOK GREAT WHEN YOU GO OUT ON THE COURT.

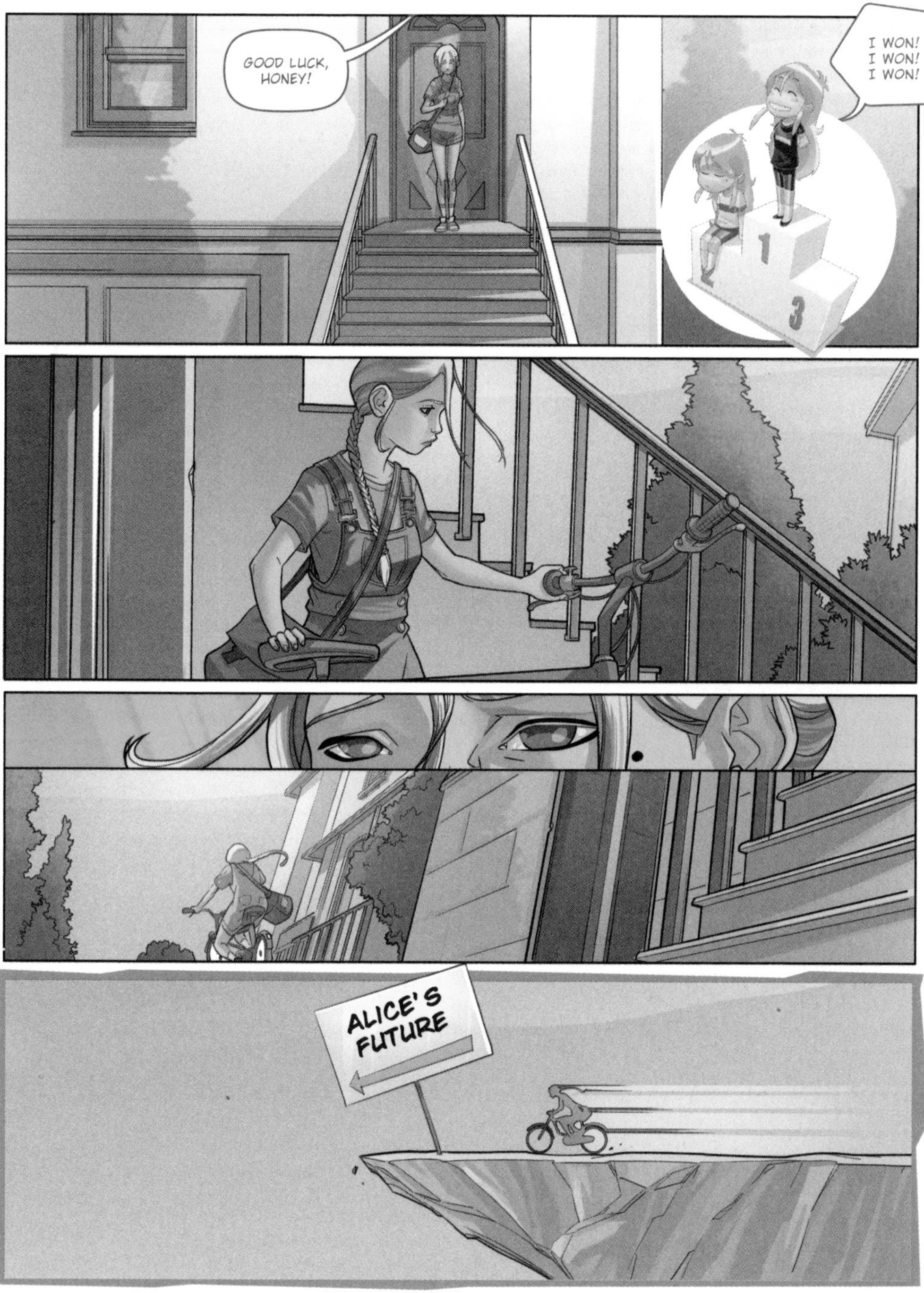
GOOD LUCK, HONEY!
I WON! I WON! I WON!
1
2
3
ALICE'S FUTURE

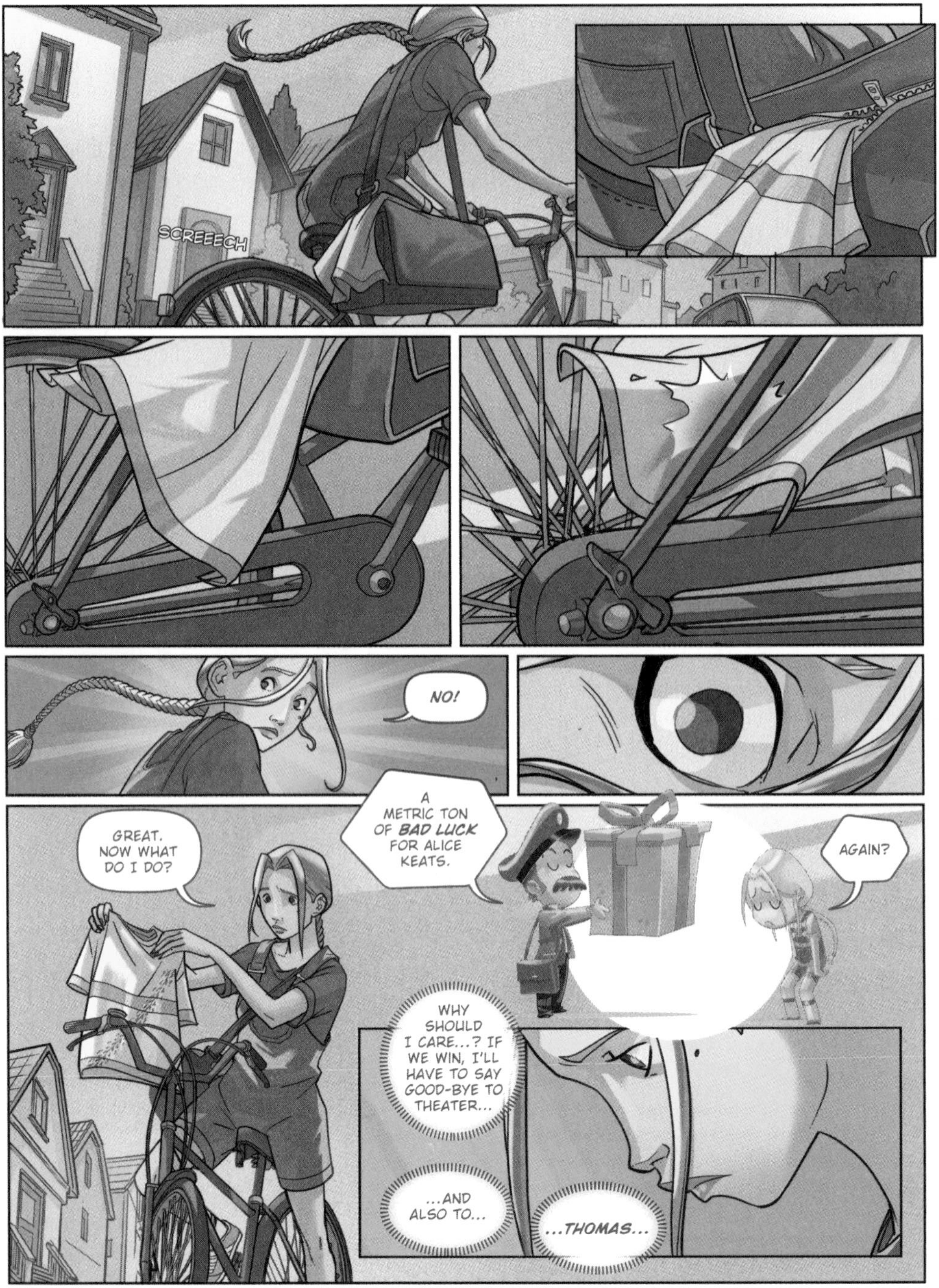
SCREEECH
NO!
GREAT. NOW WHAT DO I DO?
A METRIC TON OF BAD LUCK FOR ALICE KEATS.
AGAIN?
WHY SHOULD I CARE...? IF WE WIN, I'LL HAVE TO SAY GOOD-BYE TO THEATER...
...AND ALSO TO...
...THOMAS...

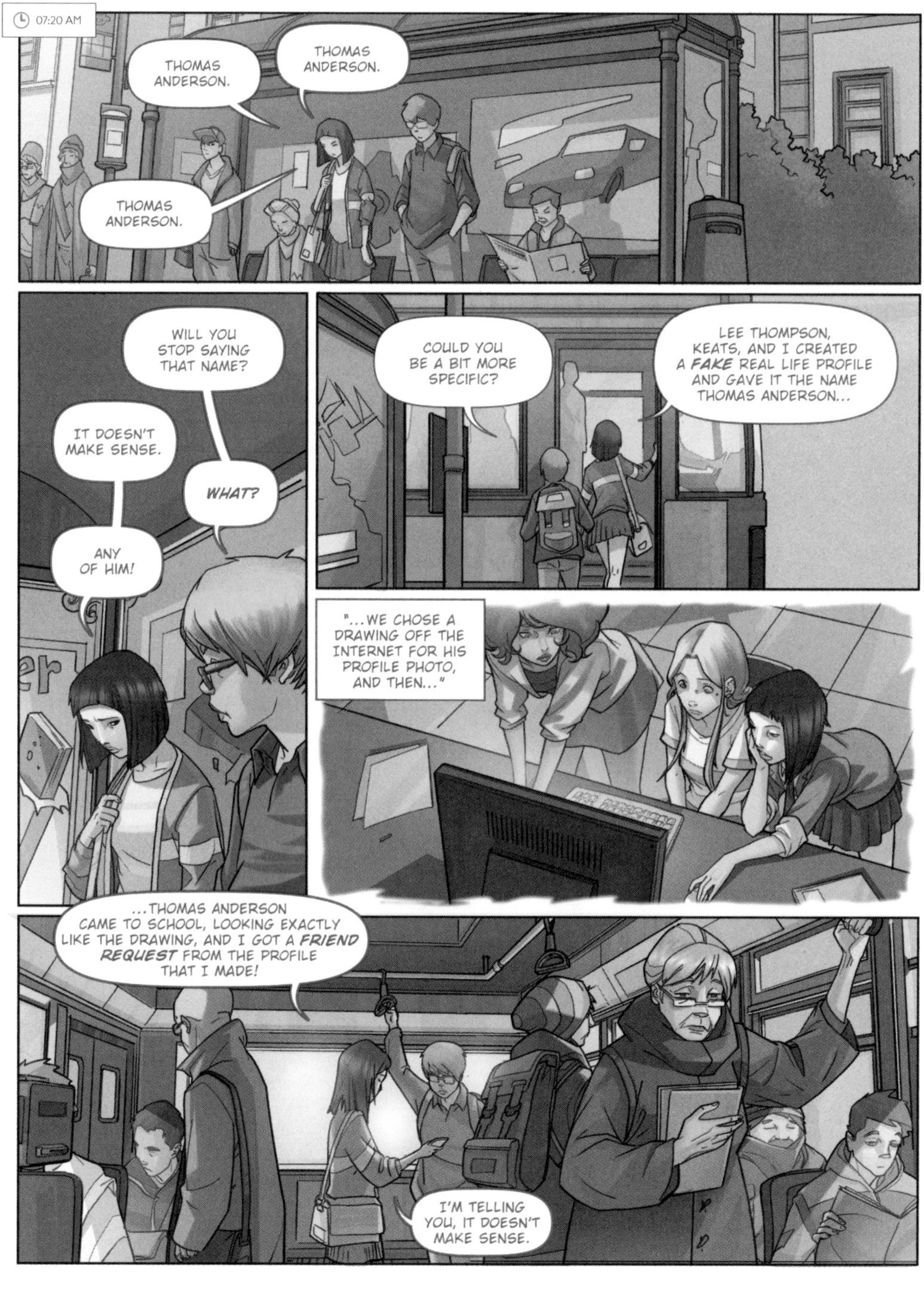
07:20 AM
THOMAS ANDERSON.
THOMAS ANDERSON.
THOMAS ANDERSON.
WILL YOU STOP SAYING THAT NAME?
IT DOESN'T MAKE SENSE.
WHAT?
ANY OF HIM!
COULD YOU BE A BIT MORE SPECIFIC?
LEE THOMPSON, KEATS, AND I CREATED A FAKE REAL LIFE PROFILE AND GAVE IT THE NAME THOMAS ANDERSON...
"...WE CHOSE A DRAWING OFF THE INTERNET FOR HIS PROFILE PHOTO, AND THEN..."
...THOMAS ANDERSON CAME TO SCHOOL, LOOKING EXACTLY LIKE THE DRAWING, AND I GOT A FRIEND REQUEST FROM THE PROFILE THAT I MADE!
I'M TELLING YOU, IT DOESN'T MAKE SENSE.

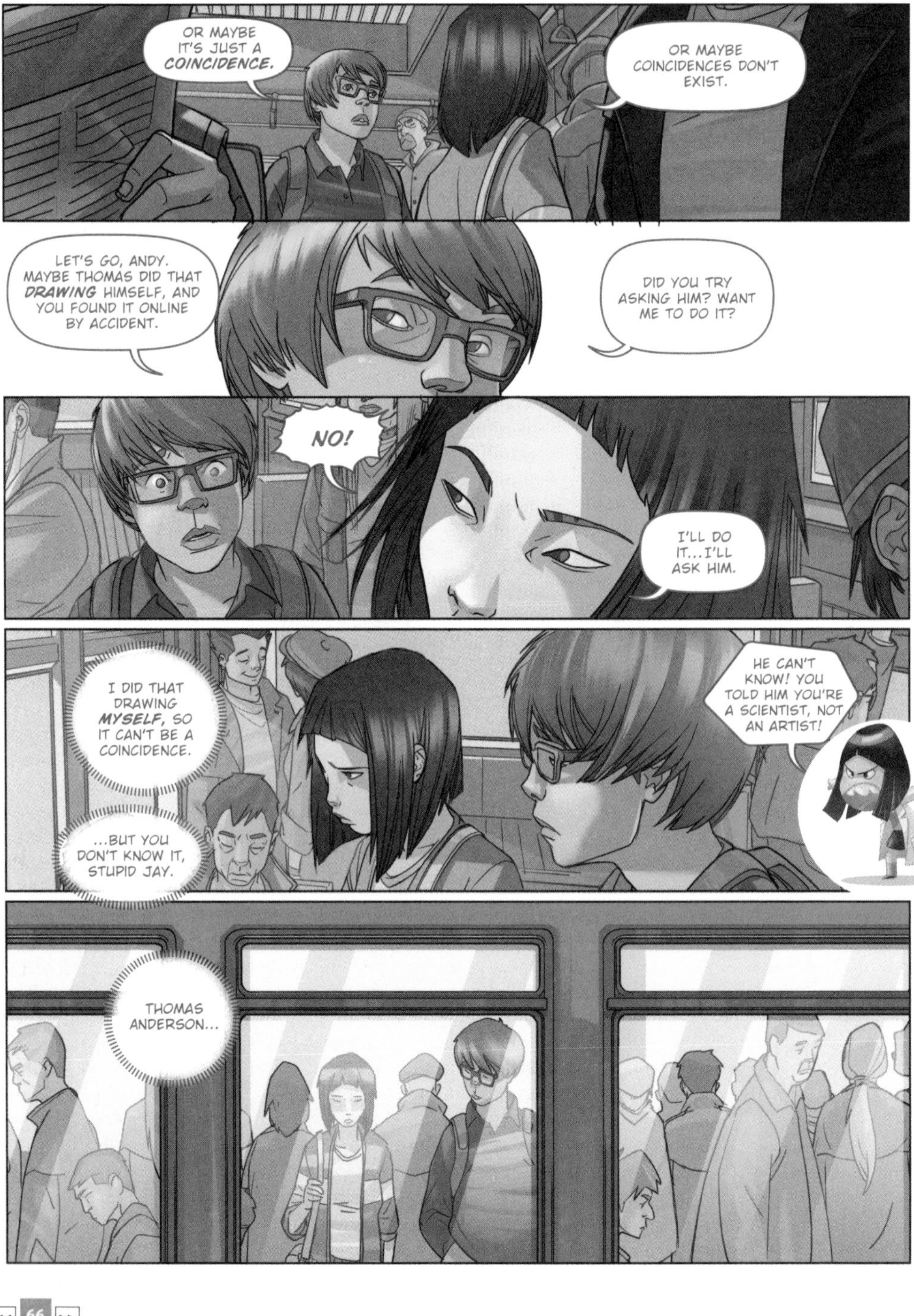
OR MAYBE IT'S JUST A COINCIDENCE.
OR MAYBE COINCIDENCES DON'T EXIST.
LET'S GO, ANDY. MAYBE THOMAS DID THAT DRAWING HIMSELF, AND YOU FOUND IT ONLINE BY ACCIDENT.
DID YOU TRY ASKING HIM? WANT ME TO DO IT?
NO!
I'LL DO IT... I'LL ASK HIM.
I DID THAT DRAWING MYSELF, SO IT CAN'T BE A COINCIDENCE.
...BUT YOU DON'T KNOW IT, STUPID JAY.
HE CAN'T KNOW! YOU TOLD HIM YOU'RE A SCIENTIST, NOT AN ARTIST!
THOMAS ANDERSON...

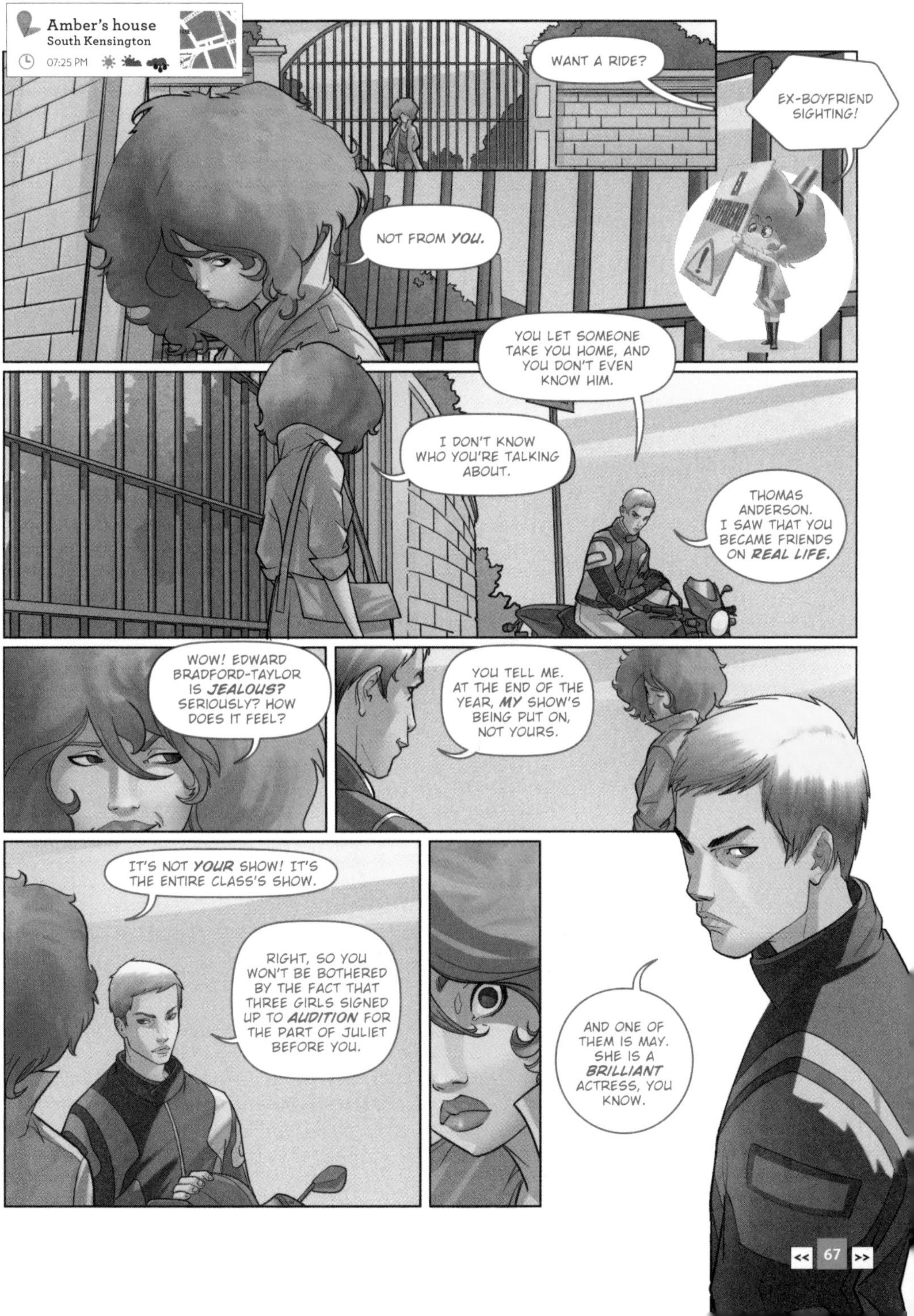
Amber's house
South Kensington
07:25 PM
WANT A RIDE?
EX-BOYFRIEND SIGHTING!
EX BOYFRIEND
NOT FROM YOU.
YOU LET SOMEONE TAKE YOU HOME, AND YOU DON'T EVEN KNOW HIM.
I DON'T KNOW WHO YOU'RE TALKING ABOUT.
THOMAS ANDERSON. I SAW THAT YOU BECAME FRIENDS ON REAL LIFE.
WOW! EDWARD BRADFORD-TAYLOR IS JEALOUS? SERIOUSLY? HOW DOES IT FEEL?
YOU TELL ME. AT THE END OF THE YEAR, MY SHOW'S BEING PUT ON, NOT YOURS.
IT'S NOT YOUR SHOW! IT'S THE ENTIRE CLASS'S SHOW.
RIGHT, SO YOU WON'T BE BOTHERED BY THE FACT THAT THREE GIRLS SIGNED UP TO AUDITION FOR THE PART OF JULIET BEFORE YOU.
AND ONE OF THEM IS MAY. SHE IS A BRILLIANT ACTRESS, YOU KNOW.

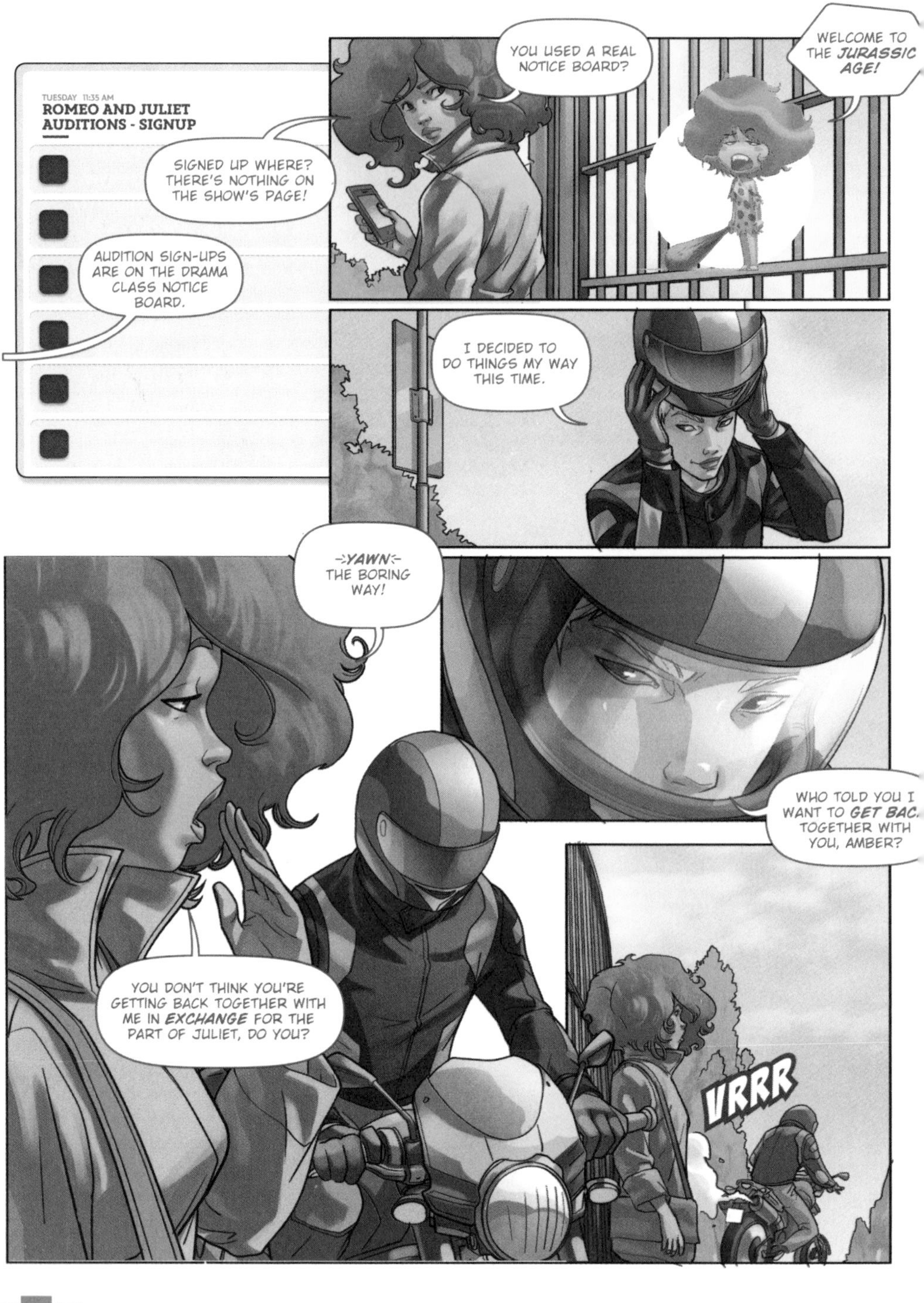
TUESDAY 11:35 AM
ROMEO AND JULIET AUDITIONS - SIGNUP
SIGNED UP WHERE? THERE'S NOTHING ON THE SHOW'S PAGE!
AUDITION SIGN-UPS ARE ON THE DRAMA CLASS NOTICE BOARD.
YOU USED A REAL NOTICE BOARD?
WELCOME TO THE *JURASSIC AGE!*
I DECIDED TO DO THINGS MY WAY THIS TIME.
-YAWN- THE BORING WAY!
YOU DON'T THINK YOU'RE GETTING BACK TOGETHER WITH ME IN *EXCHANGE* FOR THE PART OF JULIET, DO YOU?
WHO TOLD YOU I WANT TO *GET BAC* TOGETHER WITH YOU, AMBER?
VRRR

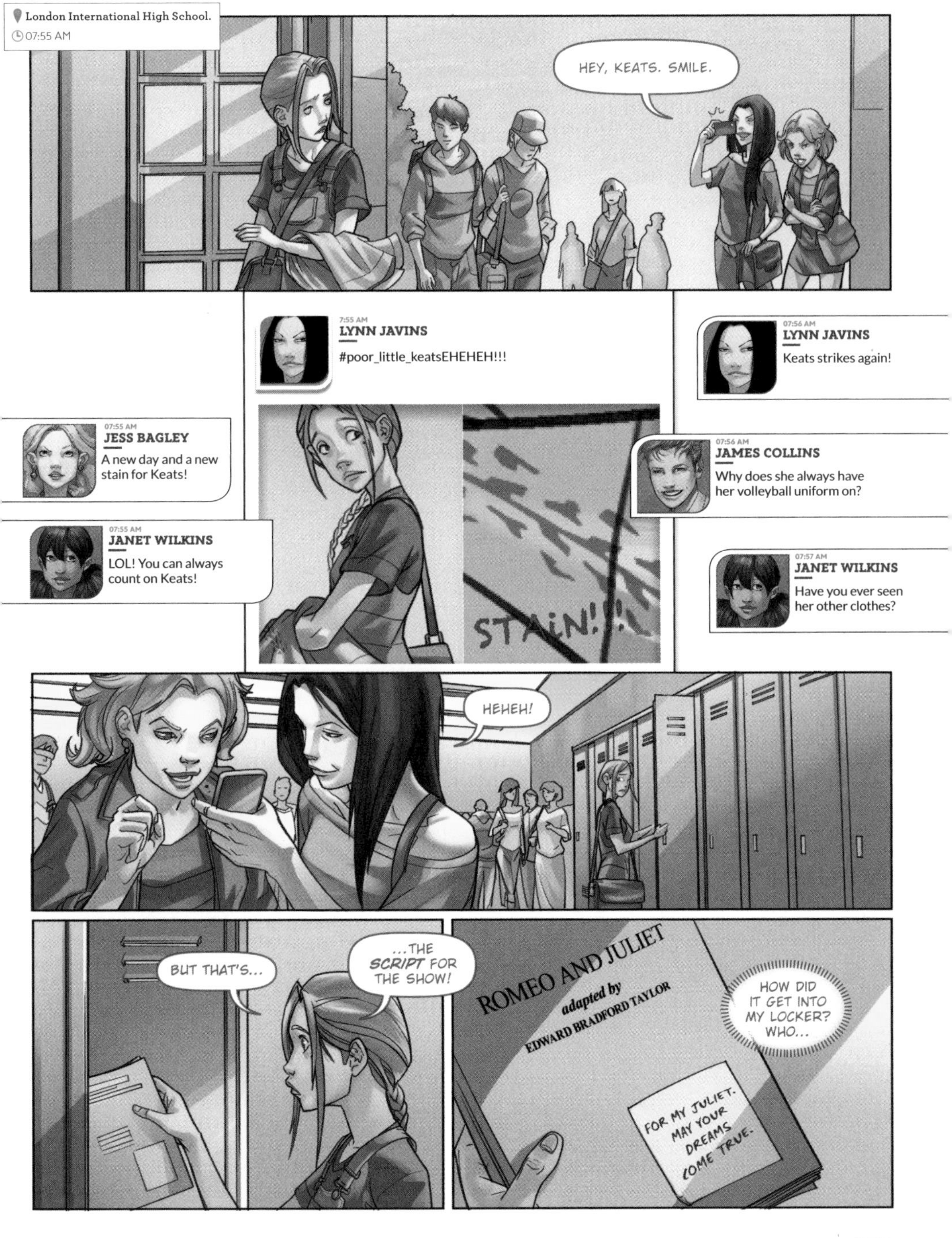
London International High School.
07:55 AM
HEY, KEATS. SMILE.
7:55 AM
LYNN JAVINS
#poor_little_keatsEHEHEH!!!
07:56 AM
LYNN JAVINS
Keats strikes again!
07:55 AM
JESS BAGLEY
A new day and a new stain for Keats!
07:56 AM
JAMES COLLINS
Why does she always have her volleyball uniform on?
07:55 AM
JANET WILKINS
LOL! You can always count on Keats!
07:57 AM
JANET WILKINS
Have you ever seen her other clothes?
STAIN!!!
HEHEH!
BUT THAT'S...
...THE SCRIPT FOR THE SHOW!
ROMEO AND JULIET
adapted by
EDWARD BRADFORD TAYLOR
HOW DID IT GET INTO MY LOCKER? WHO...
FOR MY JULIET. MAY YOUR DREAMS COME TRUE.

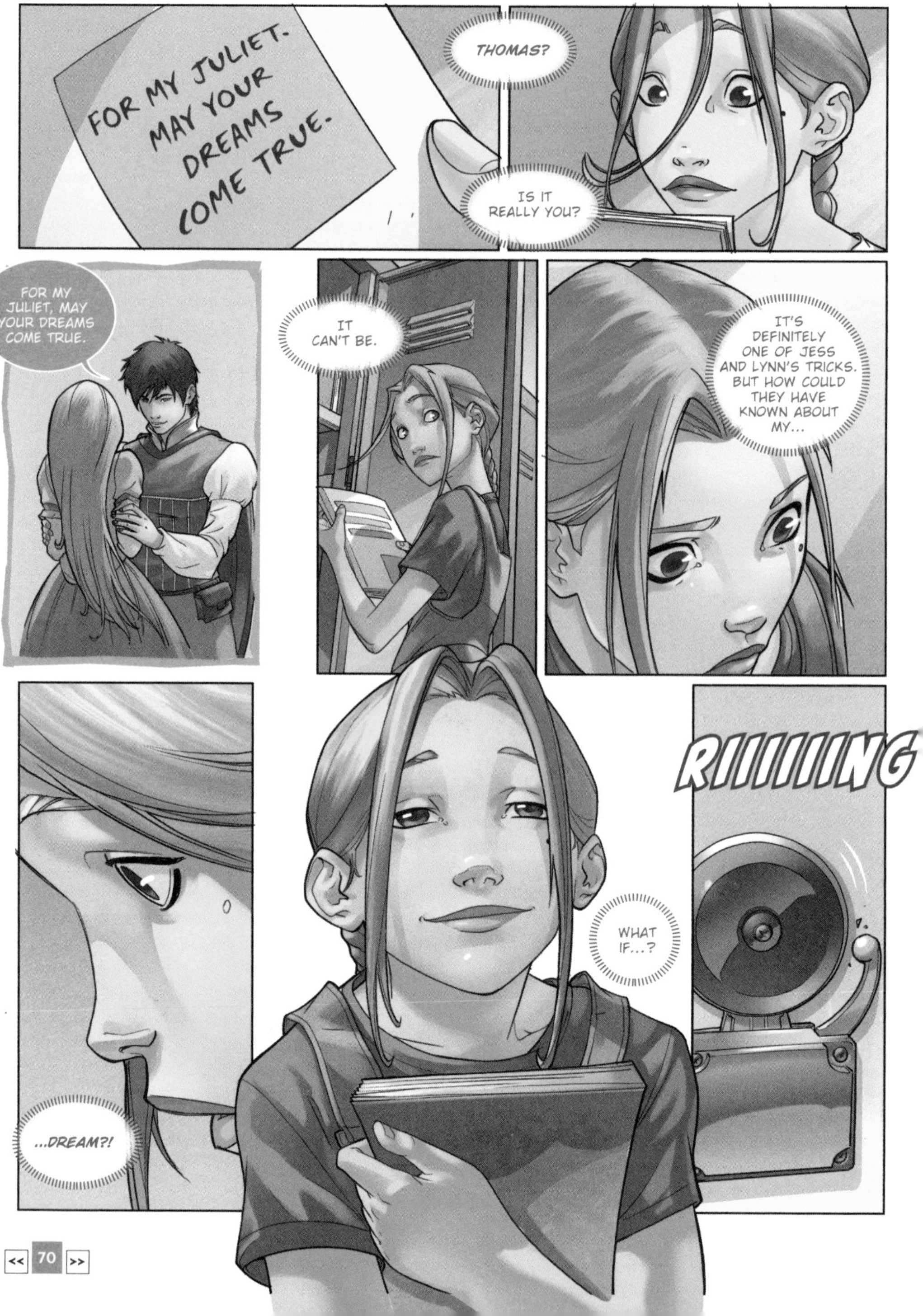

FOR MY JULIET. MAY YOUR DREAMS COME TRUE.
THOMAS?
IS IT REALLY YOU?
FOR MY JULIET, MAY YOUR DREAMS COME TRUE.
IT CAN'T BE.
IT'S DEFINITELY ONE OF JESS AND LYNN'S TRICKS. BUT HOW COULD THEY HAVE KNOWN ABOUT MY...
...DREAM?!
WHAT IF...?
RIIIIIING

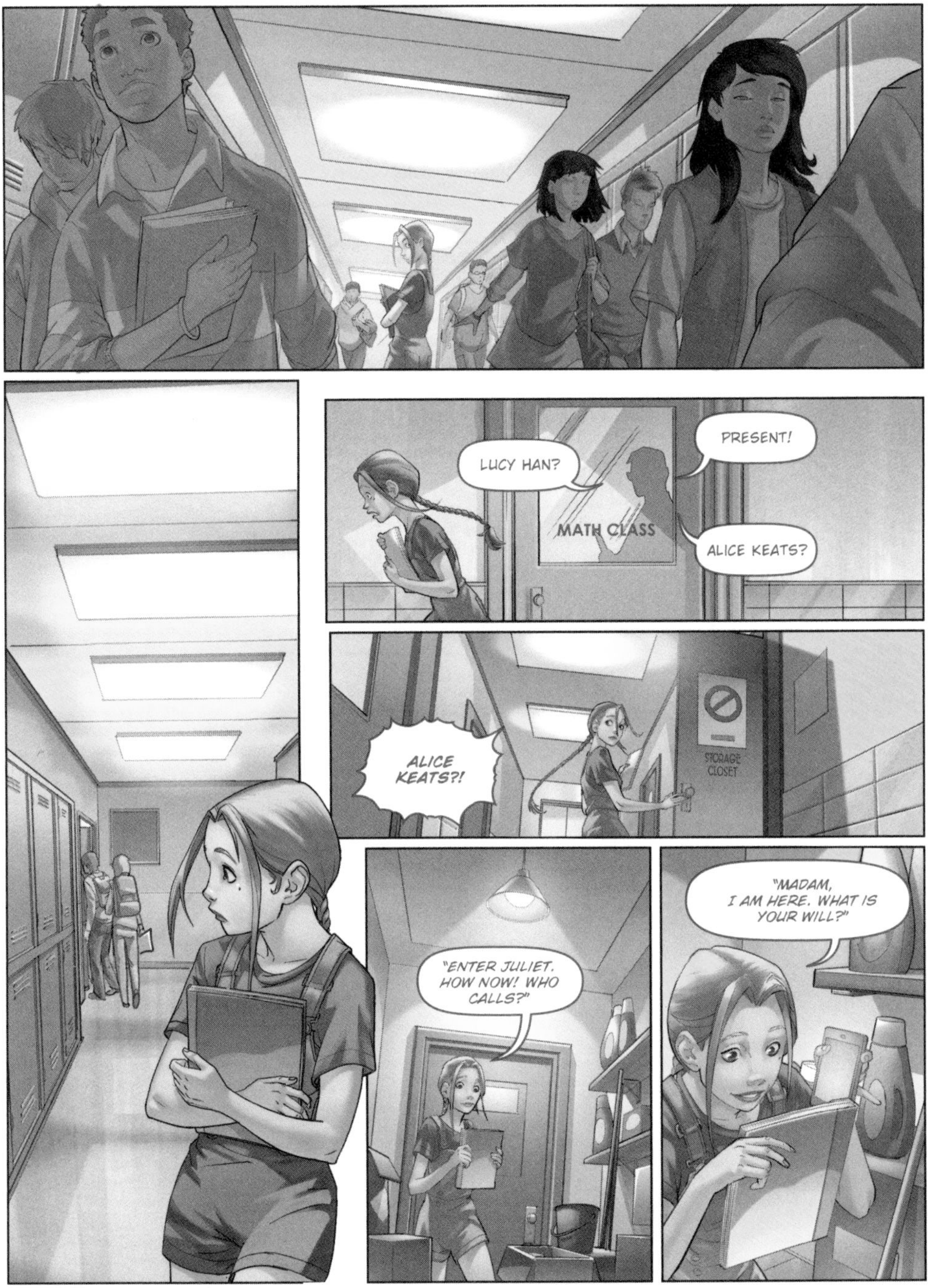
LUCY HAN?
PRESENT!
MATH CLASS
ALICE KEATS?
ALICE KEATS?!
STORAGE CLOSET
"ENTER JULIET. HOW NOW! WHO CALLS?"
"MADAM, I AM HERE. WHAT IS YOUR WILL?"

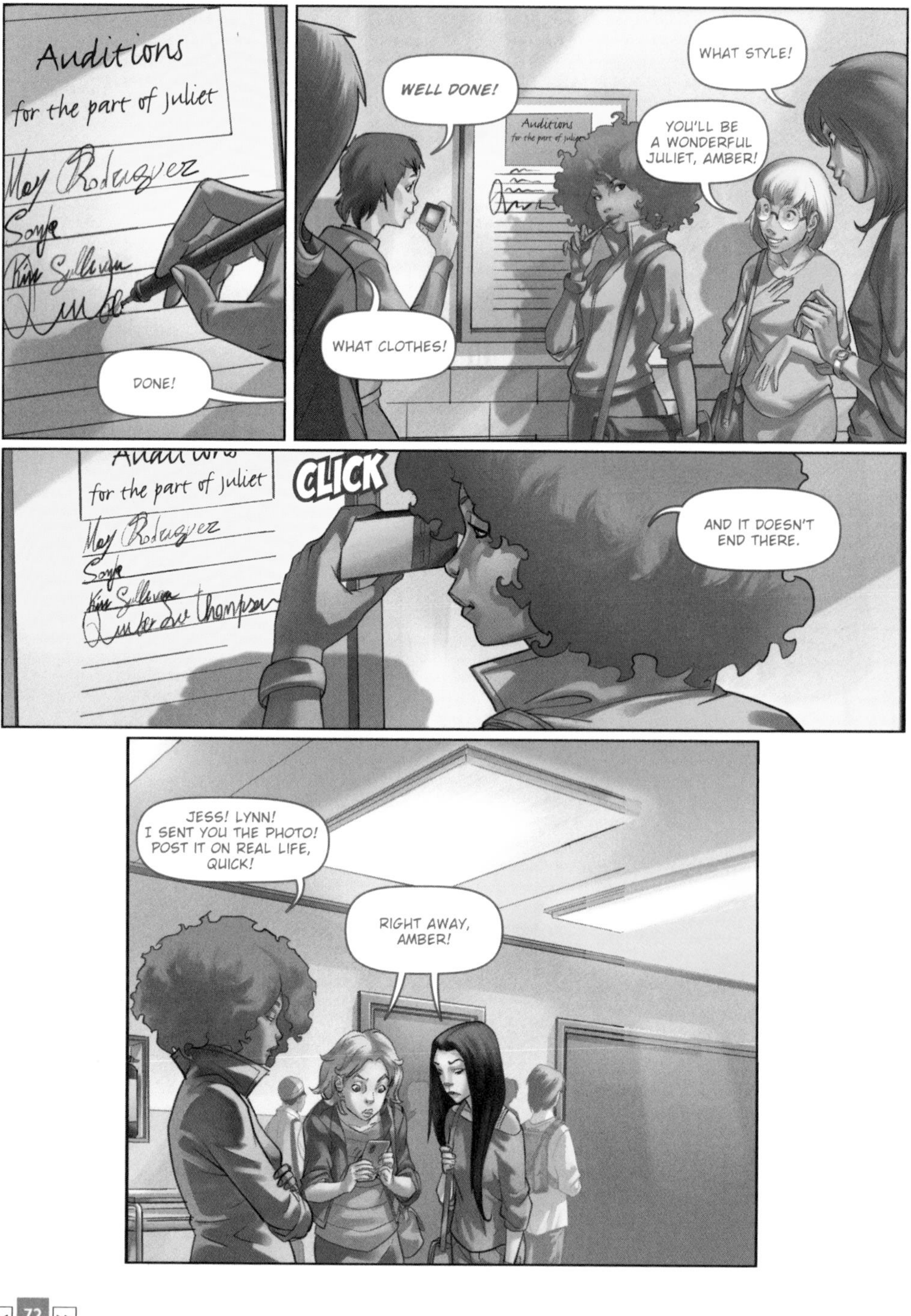

Auditions
for the part of Juliet
DONE!
WELL DONE!
WHAT CLOTHES!
WHAT STYLE!
YOU'LL BE A WONDERFUL JULIET, AMBER!
CLICK
AND IT DOESN'T END THERE.
JESS! LYNN! I SENT YOU THE PHOTO! POST IT ON REAL LIFE, QUICK!
RIGHT AWAY, AMBER!

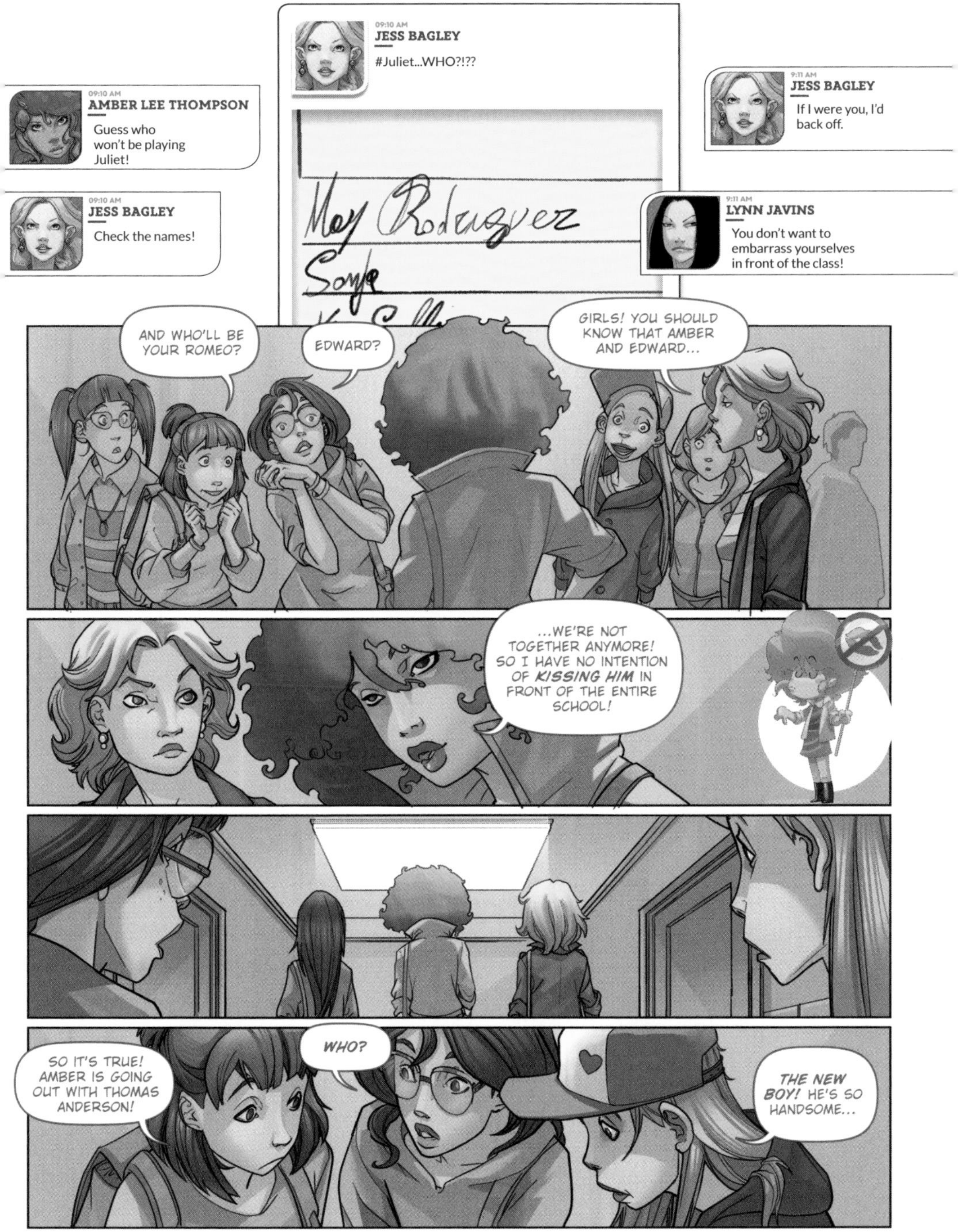
09:10 AM
AMBER LEE THOMPSON
Guess who won't be playing Juliet!
09:10 AM
JESS BAGLEY
#Juliet...WHO?!??
09:10 AM
JESS BAGLEY
Check the names!
9:11 AM
JESS BAGLEY
If I were you, I'd back off.
9:11 AM
LYNN JAVINS
You don't want to embarrass yourselves in front of the class!
AND WHO'LL BE YOUR ROMEO?
EDWARD?
GIRLS! YOU SHOULD KNOW THAT AMBER AND EDWARD...
...WE'RE NOT TOGETHER ANYMORE! SO I HAVE NO INTENTION OF KISSING HIM IN FRONT OF THE ENTIRE SCHOOL!
SO IT'S TRUE! AMBER IS GOING OUT WITH THOMAS ANDERSON!
WHO?
THE NEW BOY! HE'S SO HANDSOME...

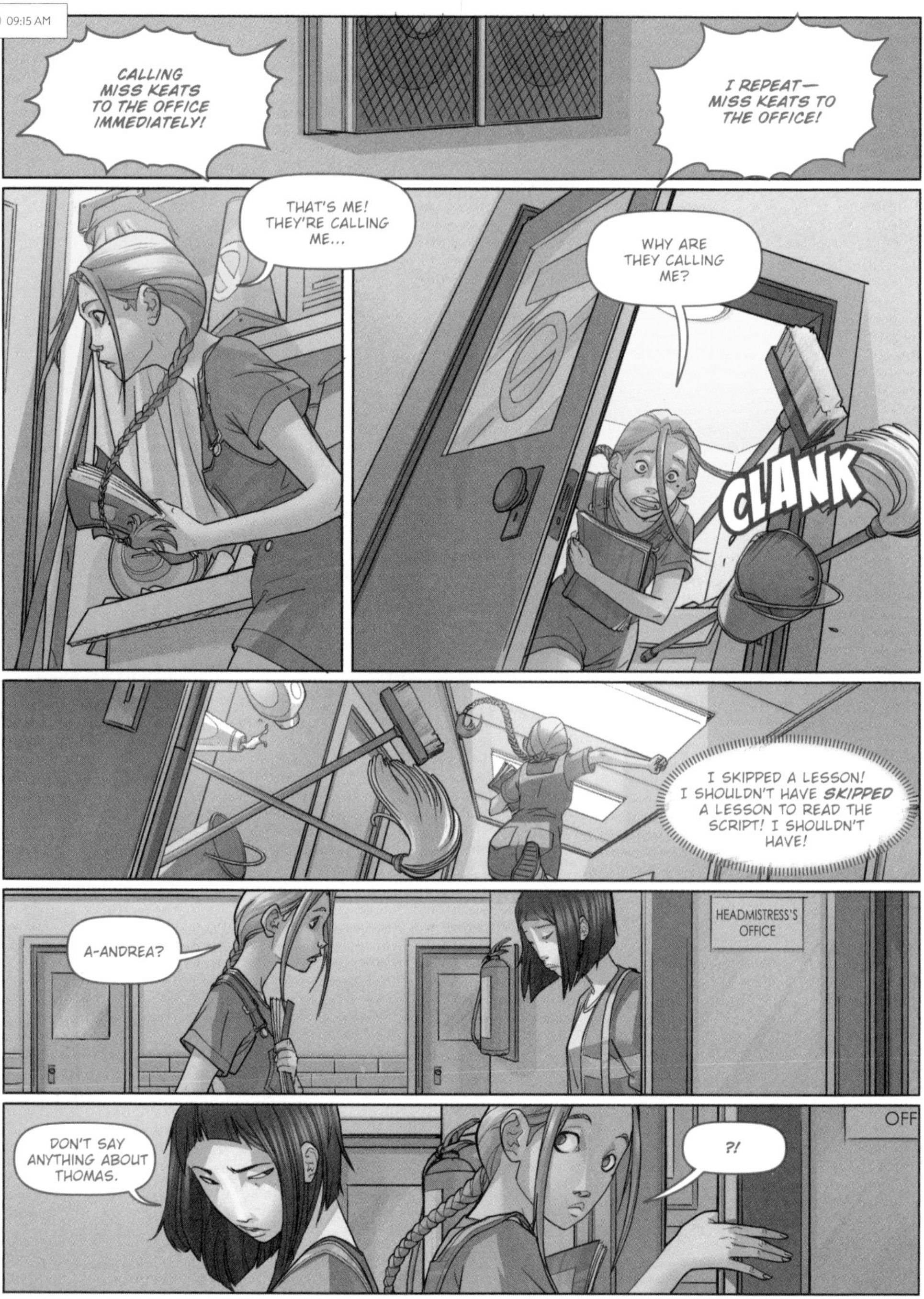
CALLING MISS KEATS TO THE OFFICE IMMEDIATELY!
I REPEAT— MISS KEATS TO THE OFFICE!
THAT'S ME! THEY'RE CALLING ME...
WHY ARE THEY CALLING ME?
CLANK
I SKIPPED A LESSON! I SHOULDN'T HAVE SKIPPED A LESSON TO READ THE SCRIPT! I SHOULDN'T HAVE!
A-ANDREA?
HEADMISTRESS'S OFFICE
DON'T SAY ANYTHING ABOUT THOMAS.
?!
OFF

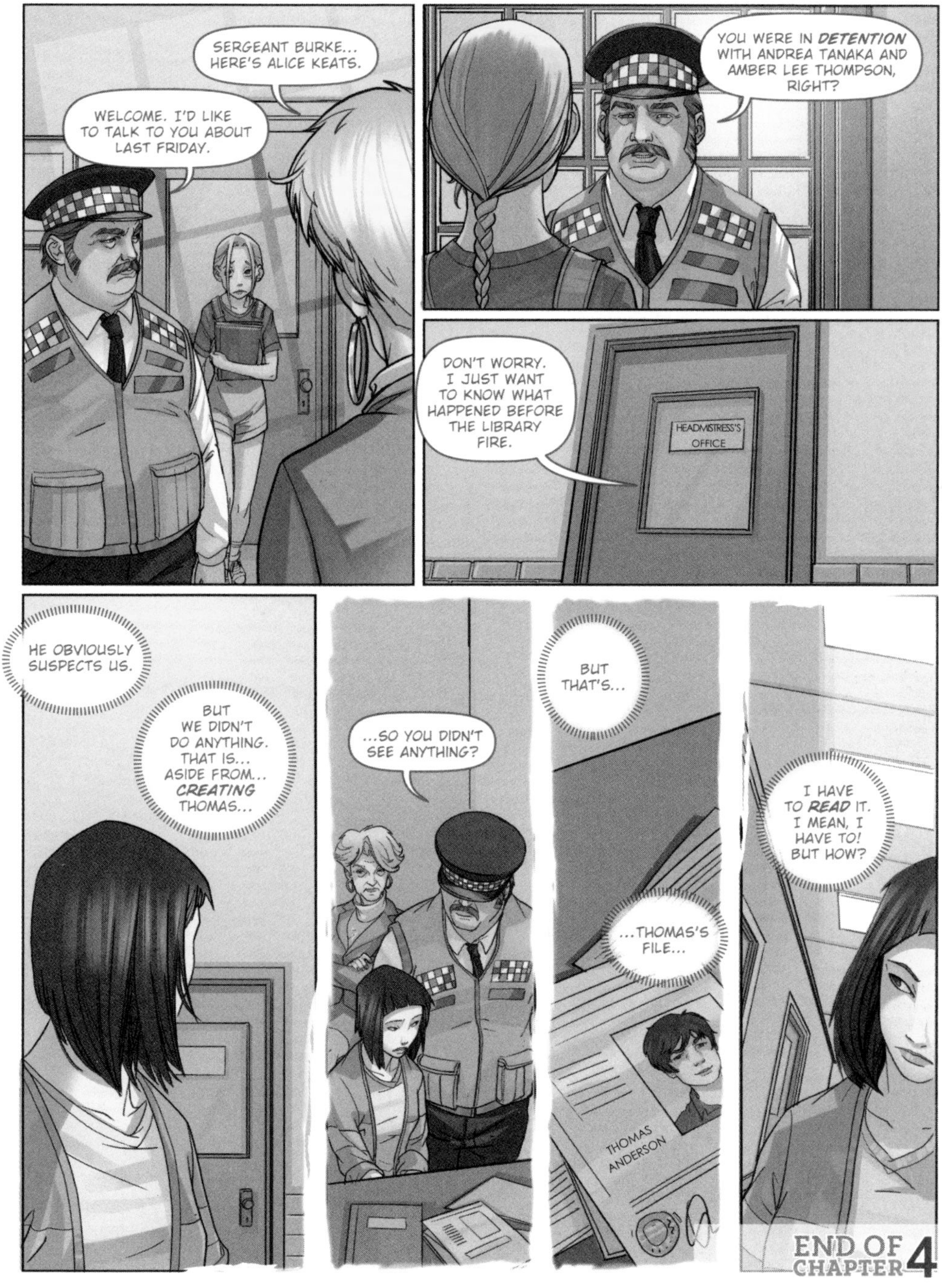
SERGEANT BURKE... HERE'S ALICE KEATS.
WELCOME. I'D LIKE TO TALK TO YOU ABOUT LAST FRIDAY.
YOU WERE IN DETENTION WITH ANDREA TANAKA AND AMBER LEE THOMPSON, RIGHT?
DON'T WORRY. I JUST WANT TO KNOW WHAT HAPPENED BEFORE THE LIBRARY FIRE.
HEADMISTRESS'S OFFICE
HE OBVIOUSLY SUSPECTS US.
BUT WE DIDN'T DO ANYTHING. THAT IS... ASIDE FROM... CREATING THOMAS...
...SO YOU DIDN'T SEE ANYTHING?
BUT THAT'S...
...THOMAS'S FILE...
THOMAS ANDERSON
I HAVE TO READ IT. I MEAN, I HAVE TO! BUT HOW?
END OF CHAPTER 4

CHAPTER 5

The VANISHING boy

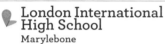

London International High School

Marylebone

ONE WEEK AGO. 05:45 PM

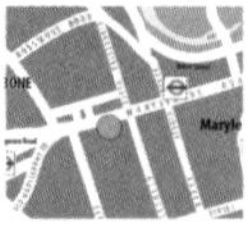

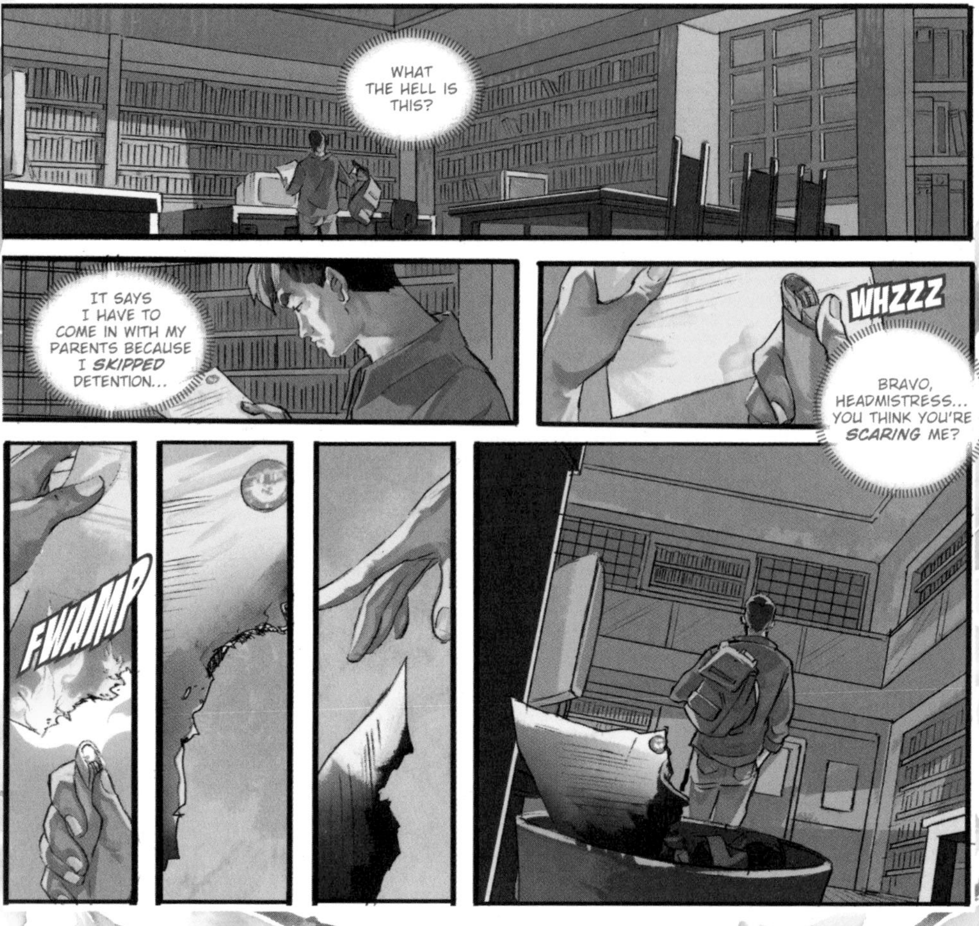
WHAT THE HELL IS THIS?
IT SAYS I HAVE TO COME IN WITH MY PARENTS BECAUSE I SKIPPED DETENTION...
WHZZZ
BRAVO, HEADMISTRESS... YOU THINK YOU'RE SCARING ME?
FWAMP

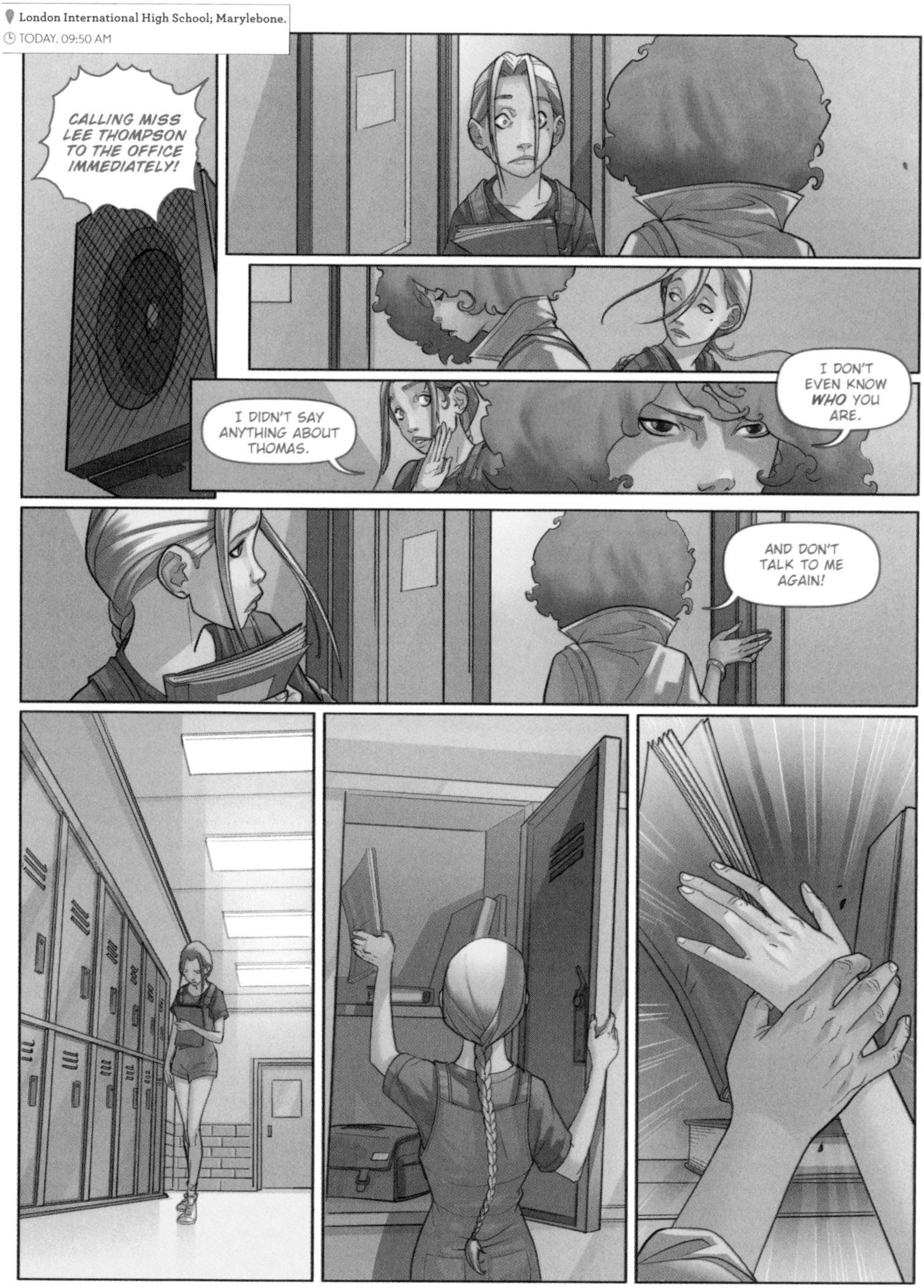
London International High School; Marylebone.
TODAY. 09:50 AM
CALLING MISS LEE THOMPSON TO THE OFFICE IMMEDIATELY!
I DIDN'T SAY ANYTHING ABOUT THOMAS.
I DON'T EVEN KNOW WHO YOU ARE.
AND DON'T TALK TO ME AGAIN!

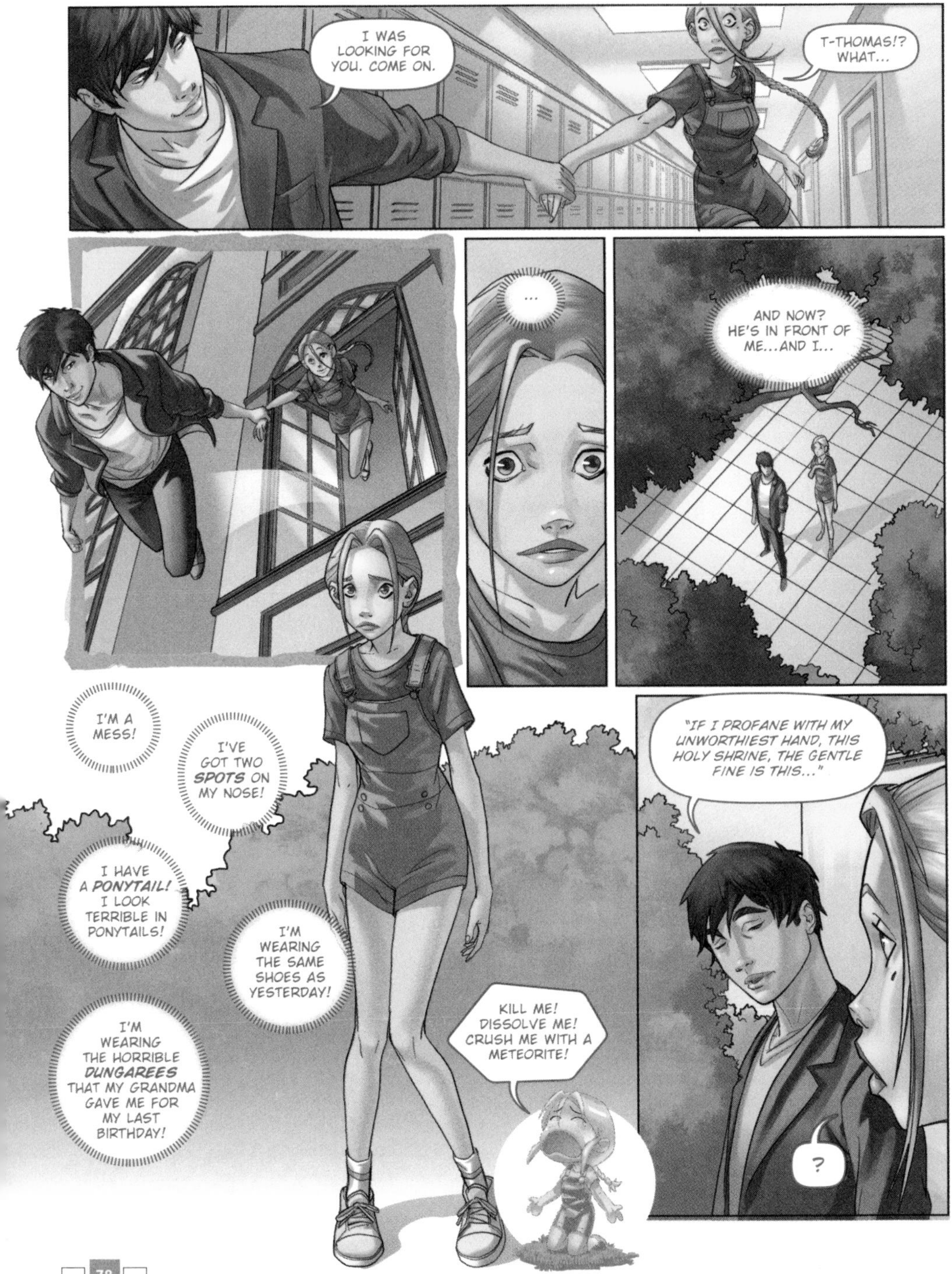
I WAS LOOKING FOR YOU. COME ON.
T-THOMAS!? WHAT...
...
AND NOW? HE'S IN FRONT OF ME...AND I...
I'M A MESS!
I'VE GOT TWO SPOTS ON MY NOSE!
I HAVE A PONYTAIL! I LOOK TERRIBLE IN PONYTAILS!
I'M WEARING THE SAME SHOES AS YESTERDAY!
I'M WEARING THE HORRIBLE DUNGAREES THAT MY GRANDMA GAVE ME FOR MY LAST BIRTHDAY!
KILL ME! DISSOLVE ME! CRUSH ME WITH A METEORITE!
"IF I PROFANE WITH MY UNWORTHIEST HAND, THIS HOLY SHRINE, THE GENTLE FINE IS THIS..."
?

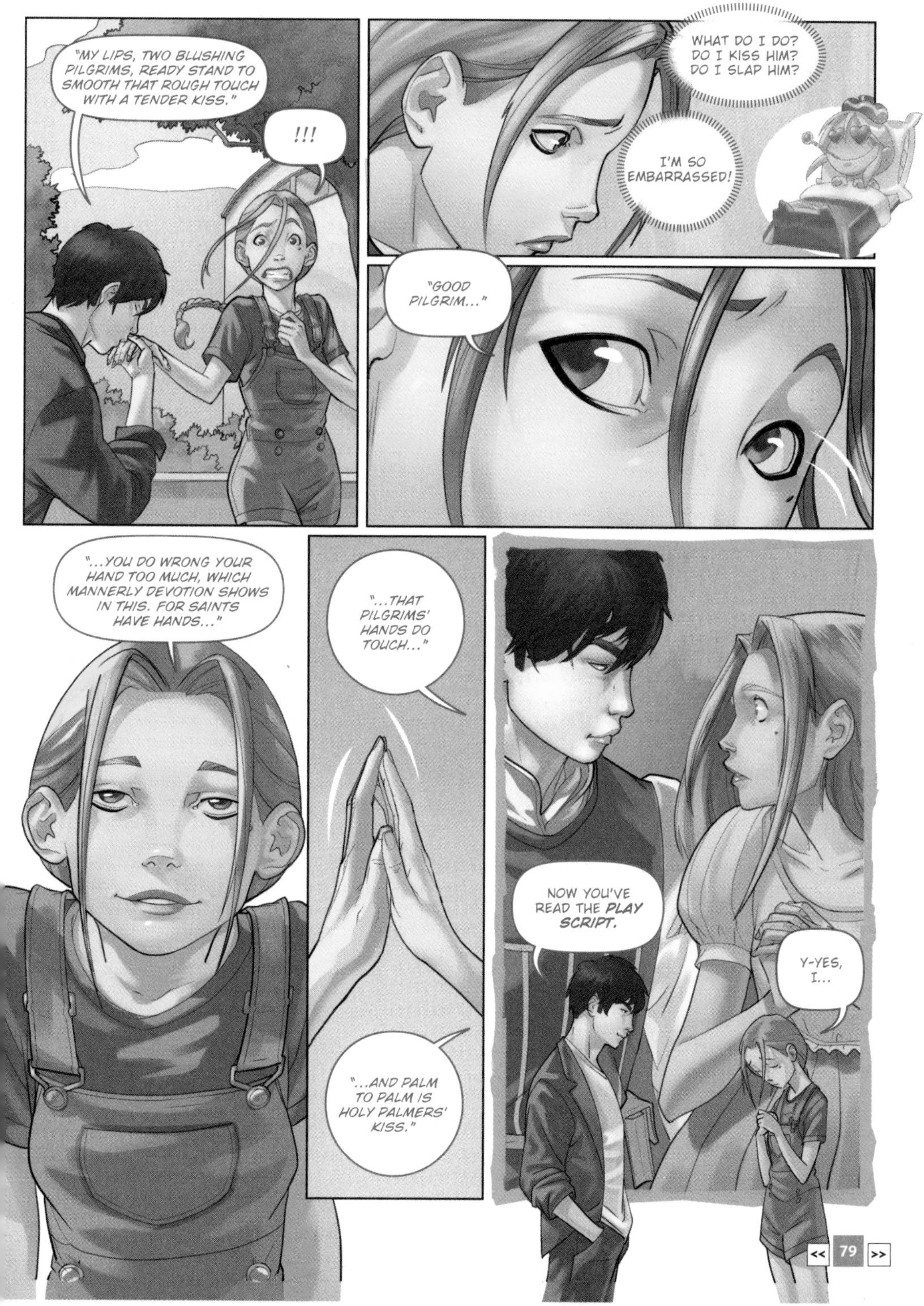
"MY LIPS, TWO BLUSHING PILGRIMS, READY STAND TO SMOOTH THAT ROUGH TOUCH WITH A TENDER KISS."
!!!
WHAT DO I DO? DO I KISS HIM? DO I SLAP HIM?
I'M SO EMBARRASSED!
"GOOD PILGRIM..."
"...YOU DO WRONG YOUR HAND TOO MUCH, WHICH MANNERLY DEVOTION SHOWS IN THIS. FOR SAINTS HAVE HANDS..."
"...THAT PILGRIMS' HANDS DO TOUCH..."
"...AND PALM TO PALM IS HOLY PALMERS' KISS."
NOW YOU'VE READ THE **PLAY SCRIPT.**
Y-YES, I...

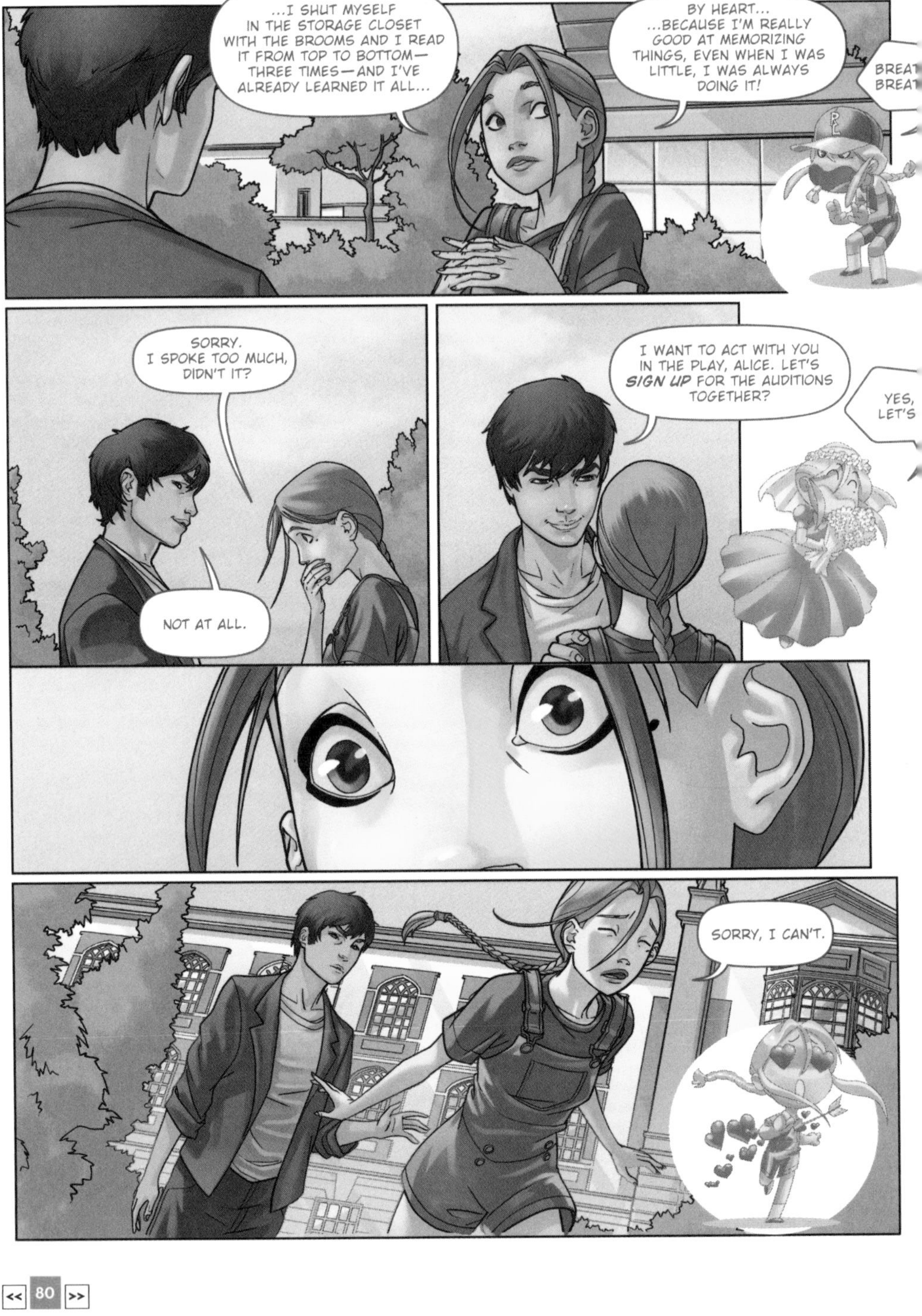
...I SHUT MYSELF IN THE STORAGE CLOSET WITH THE BROOMS AND I READ IT FROM TOP TO BOTTOM—THREE TIMES—AND I'VE ALREADY LEARNED IT ALL...
BY HEART... ...BECAUSE I'M REALLY GOOD AT MEMORIZING THINGS, EVEN WHEN I WAS LITTLE, I WAS ALWAYS DOING IT!
BREAT BREAT
SORRY. I SPOKE TOO MUCH, DIDN'T IT?
NOT AT ALL.
I WANT TO ACT WITH YOU IN THE PLAY, ALICE. LET'S **SIGN UP** FOR THE AUDITIONS TOGETHER?
YES, LET'S
SORRY, I CAN'T.

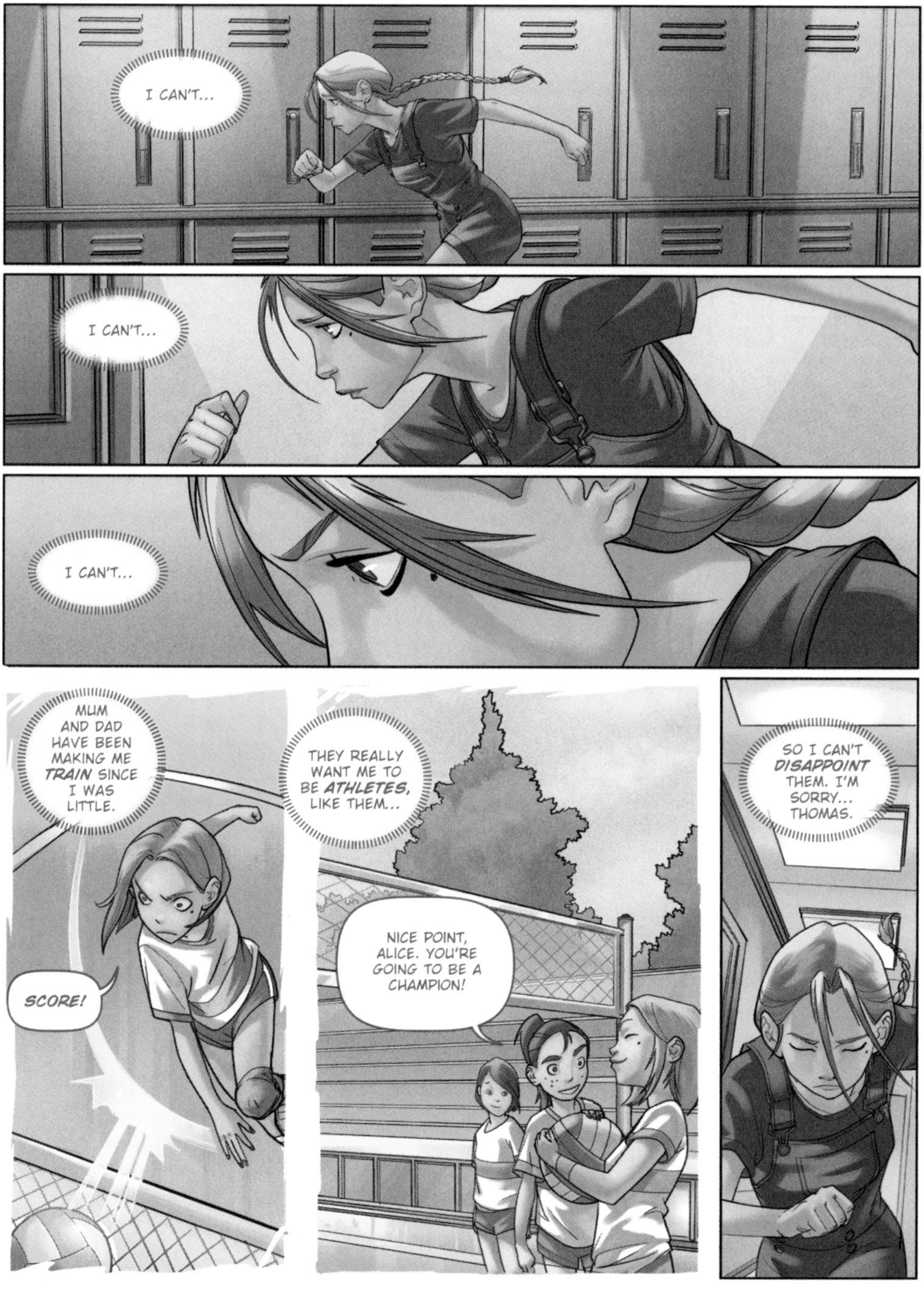

I CAN'T...
I CAN'T...
I CAN'T...
MUM AND DAD HAVE BEEN MAKING ME TRAIN SINCE I WAS LITTLE.
SCORE!
THEY REALLY WANT ME TO BE ATHLETES, LIKE THEM...
NICE POINT, ALICE. YOU'RE GOING TO BE A CHAMPION!
SO I CAN'T DISAPPOINT THEM. I'M SORRY... THOMAS.

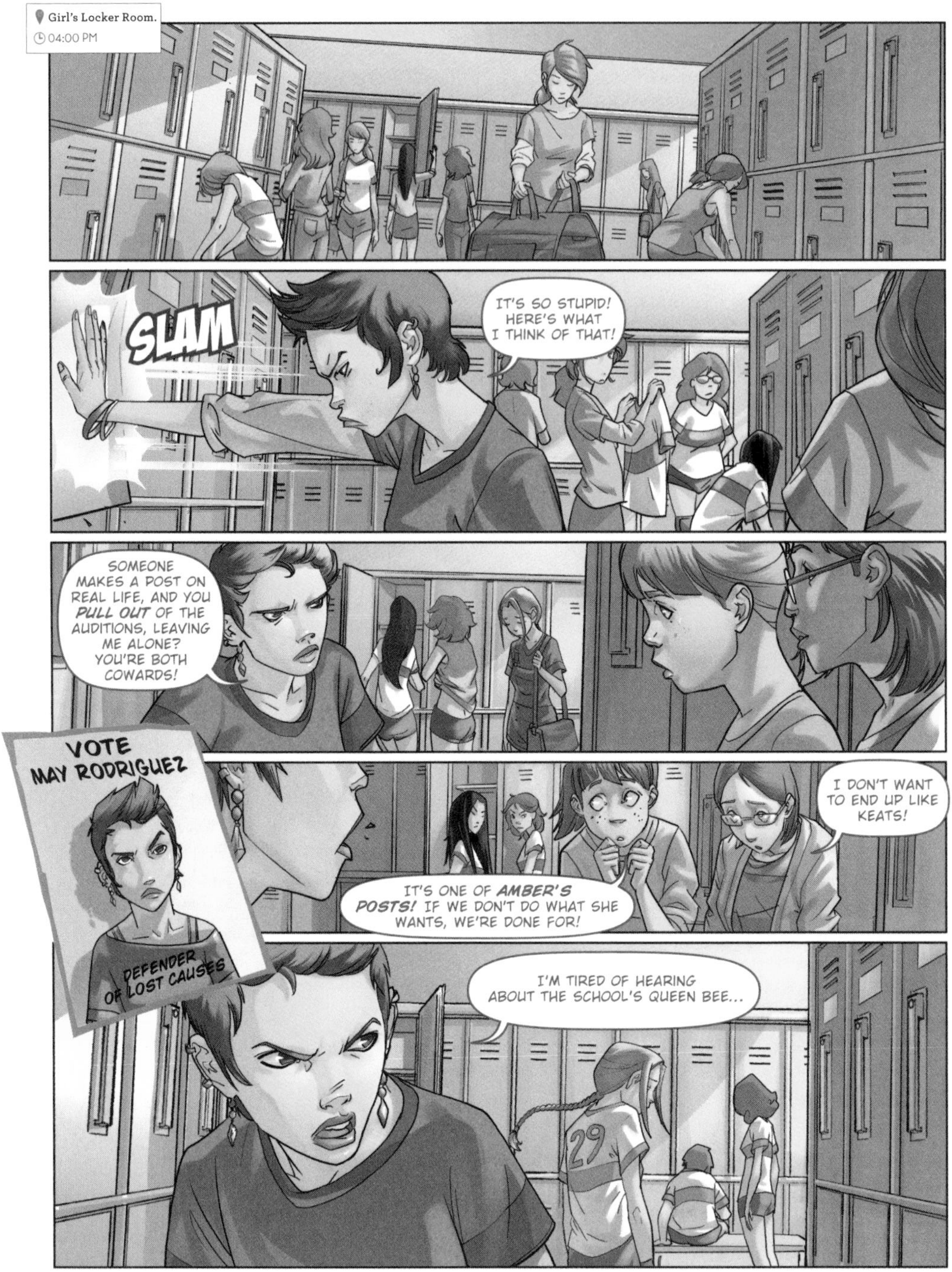
Girl's Locker Room.
04:00 PM
SLAM
IT'S SO STUPID! HERE'S WHAT I THINK OF THAT!
SOMEONE MAKES A POST ON REAL LIFE, AND YOU *PULL OUT* OF THE AUDITIONS, LEAVING ME ALONE? YOU'RE BOTH COWARDS!
VOTE MAY RODRIGUEZ
DEFENDER OF LOST CAUSES
I DON'T WANT TO END UP LIKE KEATS!
IT'S ONE OF *AMBER'S POSTS!* IF WE DON'T DO WHAT SHE WANTS, WE'RE DONE FOR!
I'M TIRED OF HEARING ABOUT THE SCHOOL'S QUEEN BEE...

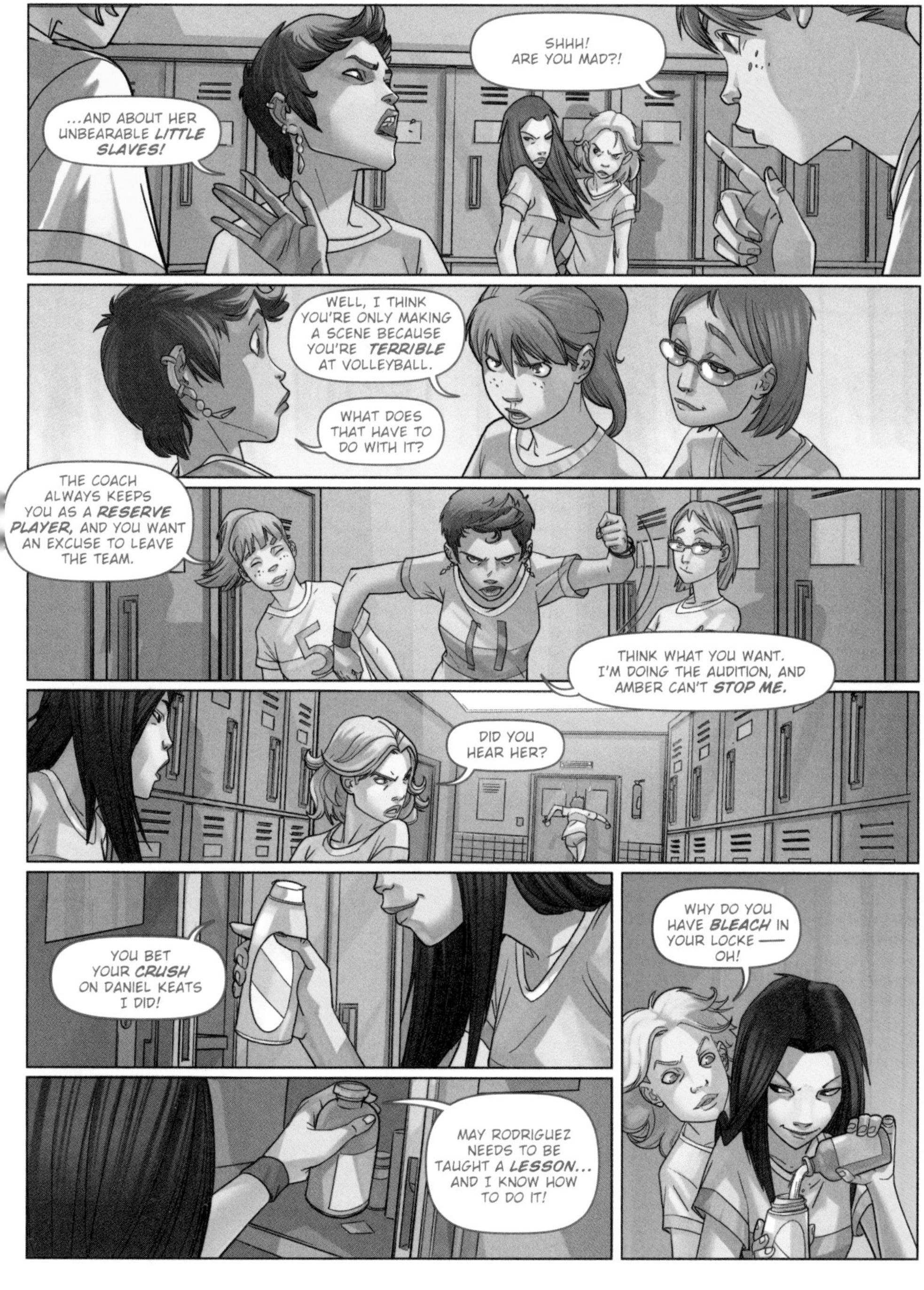
...AND ABOUT HER UNBEARABLE *LITTLE SLAVES!*
SHHH! ARE YOU MAD?!
WELL, I THINK YOU'RE ONLY MAKING A SCENE BECAUSE YOU'RE *TERRIBLE* AT VOLLEYBALL.
WHAT DOES THAT HAVE TO DO WITH IT?
THE COACH ALWAYS KEEPS YOU AS A *RESERVE PLAYER,* AND YOU WANT AN EXCUSE TO LEAVE THE TEAM.
THINK WHAT YOU WANT. I'M DOING THE AUDITION, AND AMBER CAN'T *STOP ME.*
DID YOU HEAR HER?
YOU BET YOUR *CRUSH* ON DANIEL KEATS I DID!
WHY DO YOU HAVE *BLEACH* IN YOUR LOCKE — OH!
MAY RODRIGUEZ NEEDS TO BE TAUGHT A *LESSON...* AND I KNOW HOW TO DO IT!

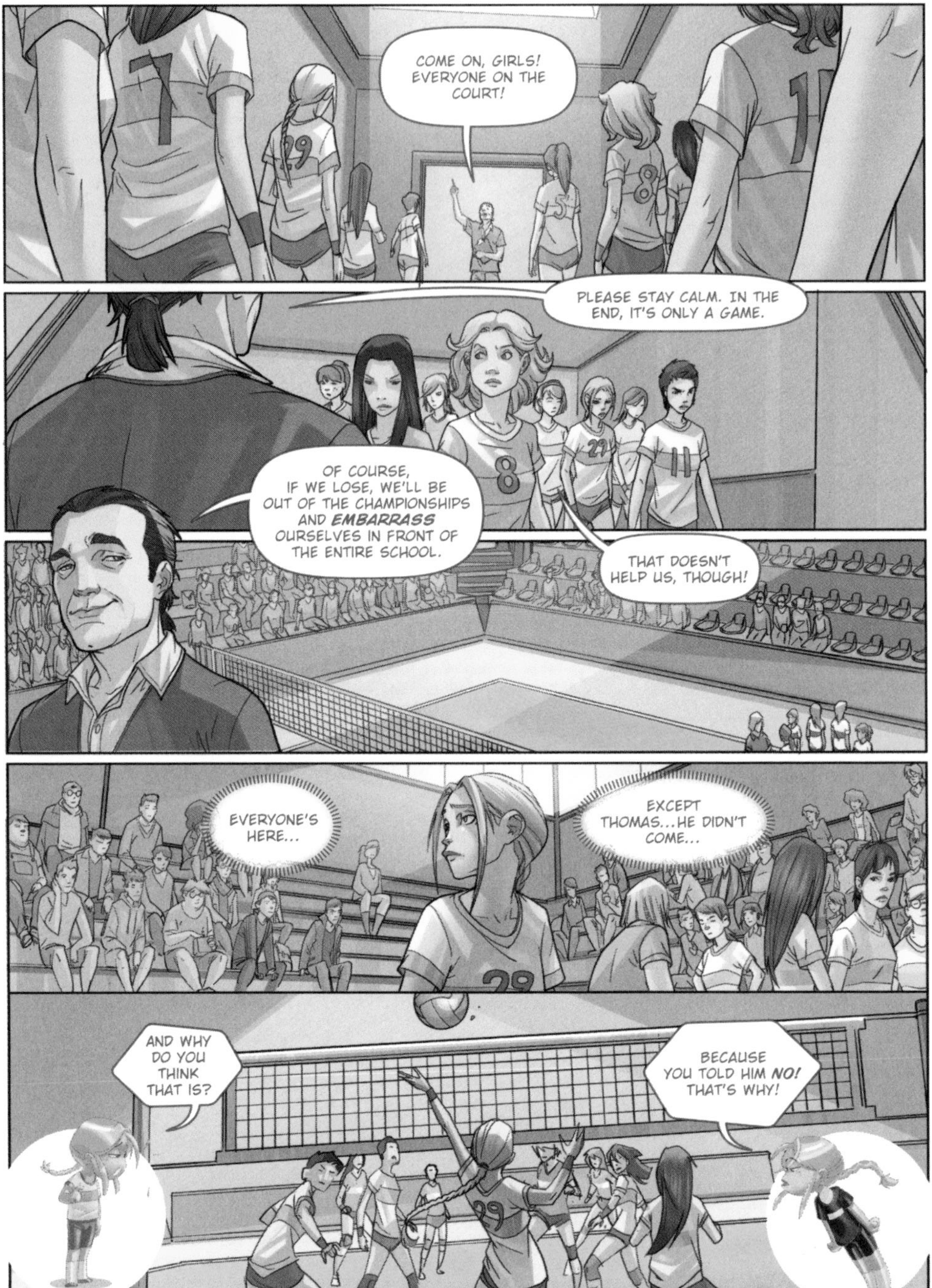
COME ON, GIRLS! EVERYONE ON THE COURT!
PLEASE STAY CALM. IN THE END, IT'S ONLY A GAME.
OF COURSE, IF WE LOSE, WE'LL BE OUT OF THE CHAMPIONSHIPS AND **EMBARRASS** OURSELVES IN FRONT OF THE ENTIRE SCHOOL.
THAT DOESN'T HELP US, THOUGH!
EVERYONE'S HERE...
EXCEPT THOMAS...HE DIDN'T COME...
AND WHY DO YOU THINK THAT IS?
BECAUSE YOU TOLD HIM **NO!** THAT'S WHY!

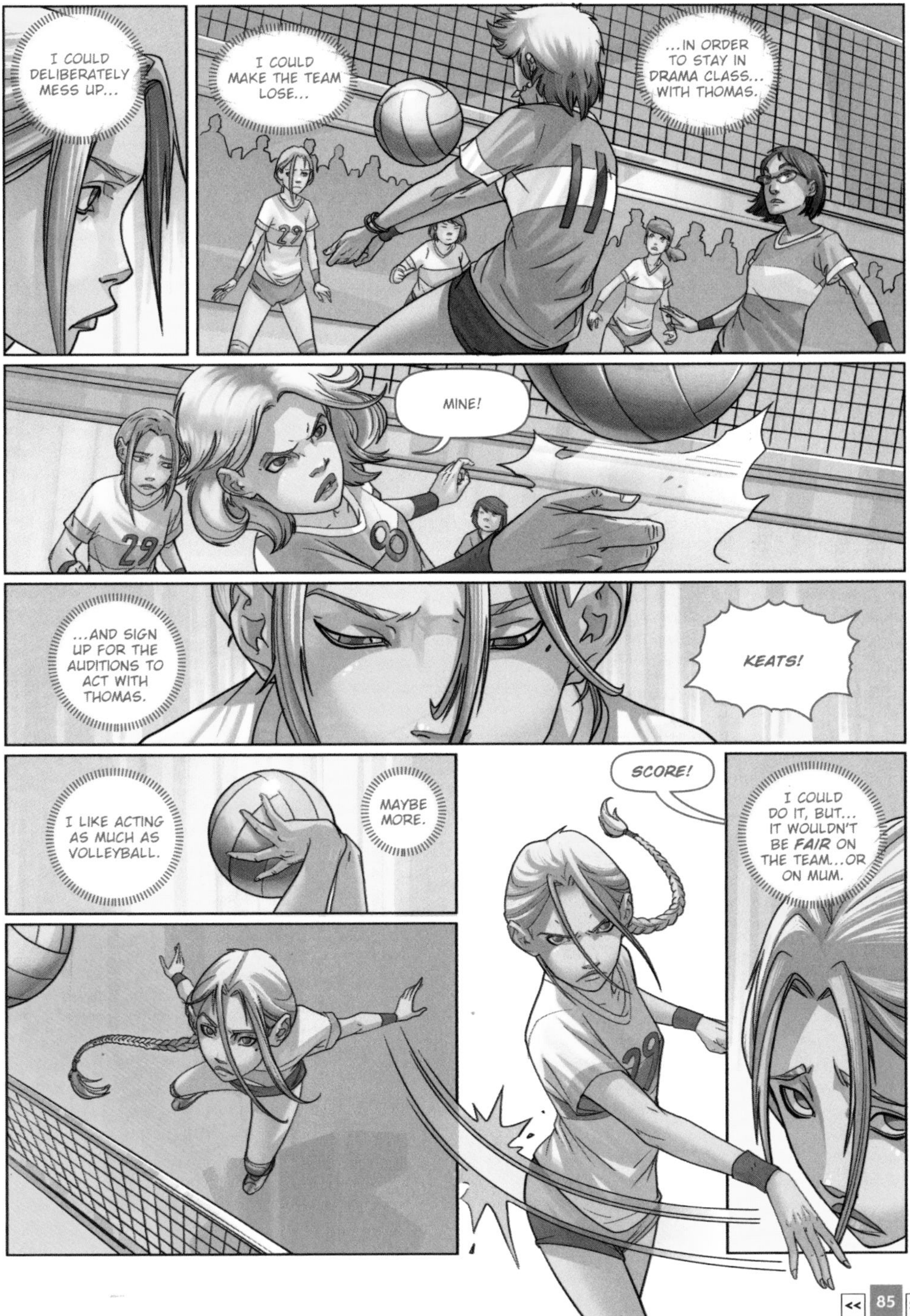
I COULD DELIBERATELY MESS UP...
I COULD MAKE THE TEAM LOSE...
...IN ORDER TO STAY IN DRAMA CLASS... WITH THOMAS.
MINE!
...AND SIGN UP FOR THE AUDITIONS TO ACT WITH THOMAS.
KEATS!
I LIKE ACTING AS MUCH AS VOLLEYBALL.
MAYBE MORE.
SCORE!
I COULD DO IT, BUT... IT WOULDN'T BE FAIR ON THE TEAM...OR ON MUM.

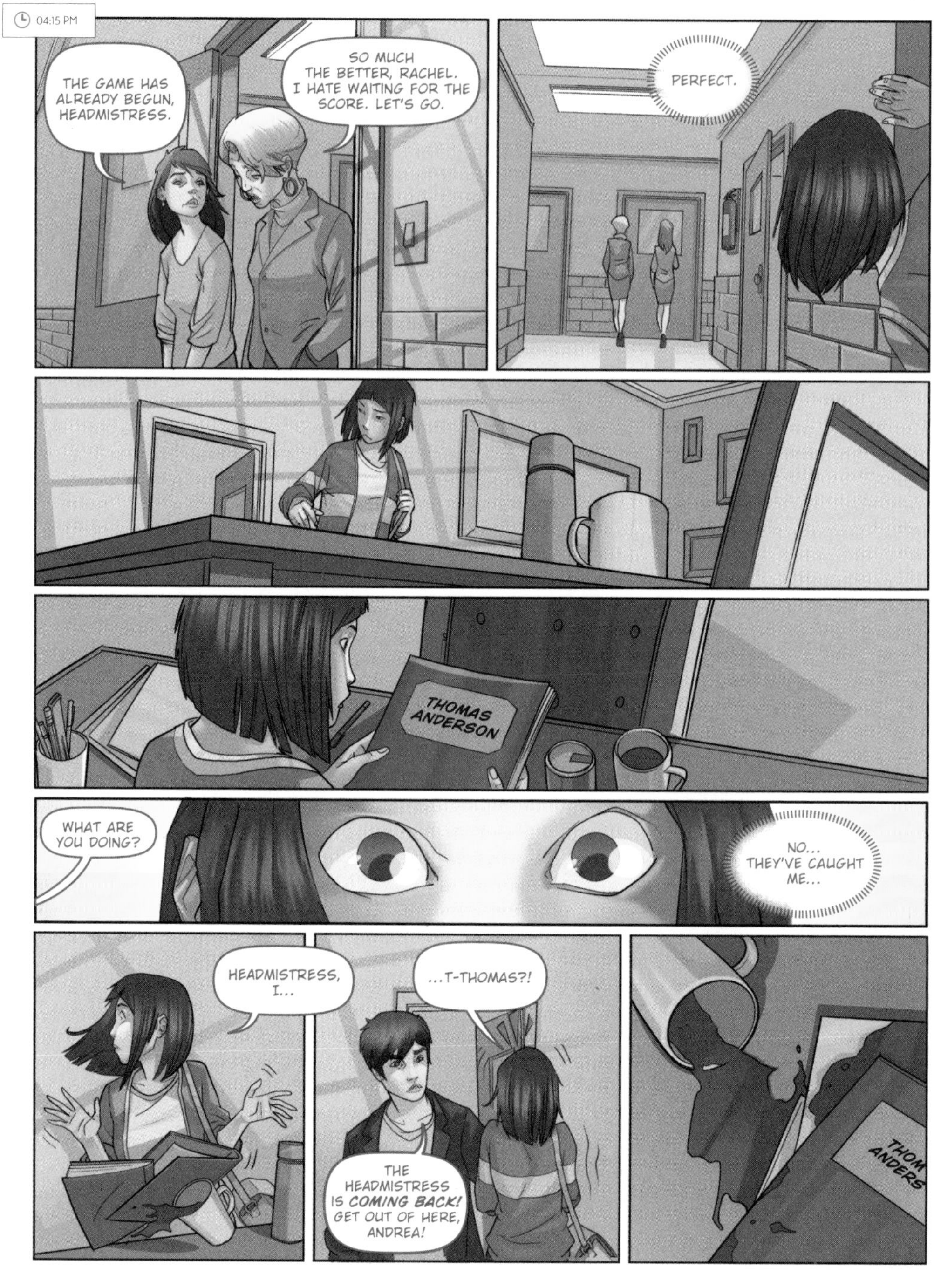
04:15 PM
THE GAME HAS ALREADY BEGUN, HEADMISTRESS.
SO MUCH THE BETTER, RACHEL. I HATE WAITING FOR THE SCORE. LET'S GO.
PERFECT.
THOMAS ANDERSON
WHAT ARE YOU DOING?
NO... THEY'VE CAUGHT ME...
HEADMISTRESS, I...
...T-THOMAS?!
THE HEADMISTRESS IS ***COMING BACK!*** GET OUT OF HERE, ANDREA!
THOM ANDERS

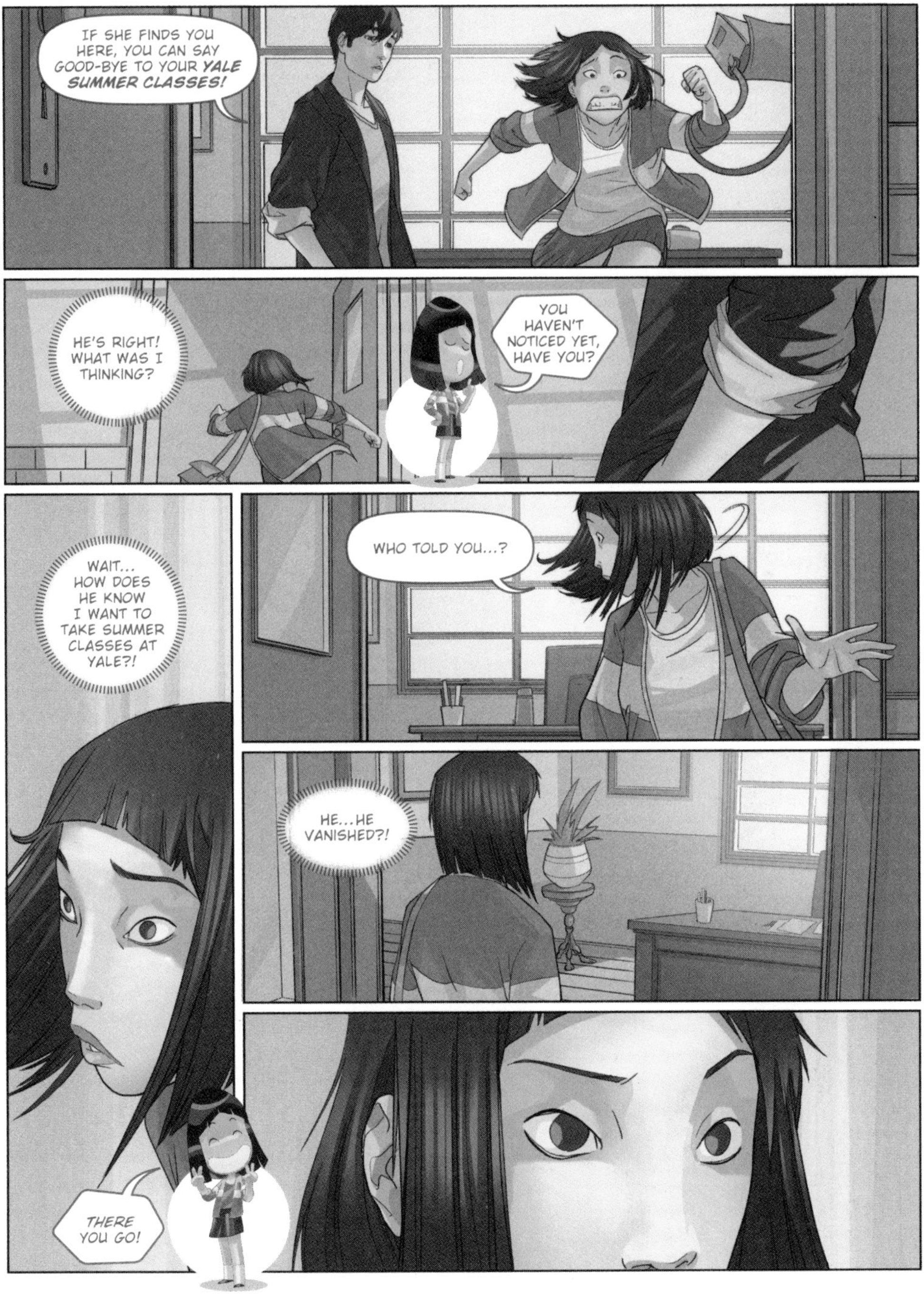
IF SHE FINDS YOU HERE, YOU CAN SAY GOOD-BYE TO YOUR YALE SUMMER CLASSES!
HE'S RIGHT! WHAT WAS I THINKING?
YOU HAVEN'T NOTICED YET, HAVE YOU?
WAIT... HOW DOES HE KNOW I WANT TO TAKE SUMMER CLASSES AT YALE?!
WHO TOLD YOU...?
HE...HE VANISHED?!
THERE YOU GO!

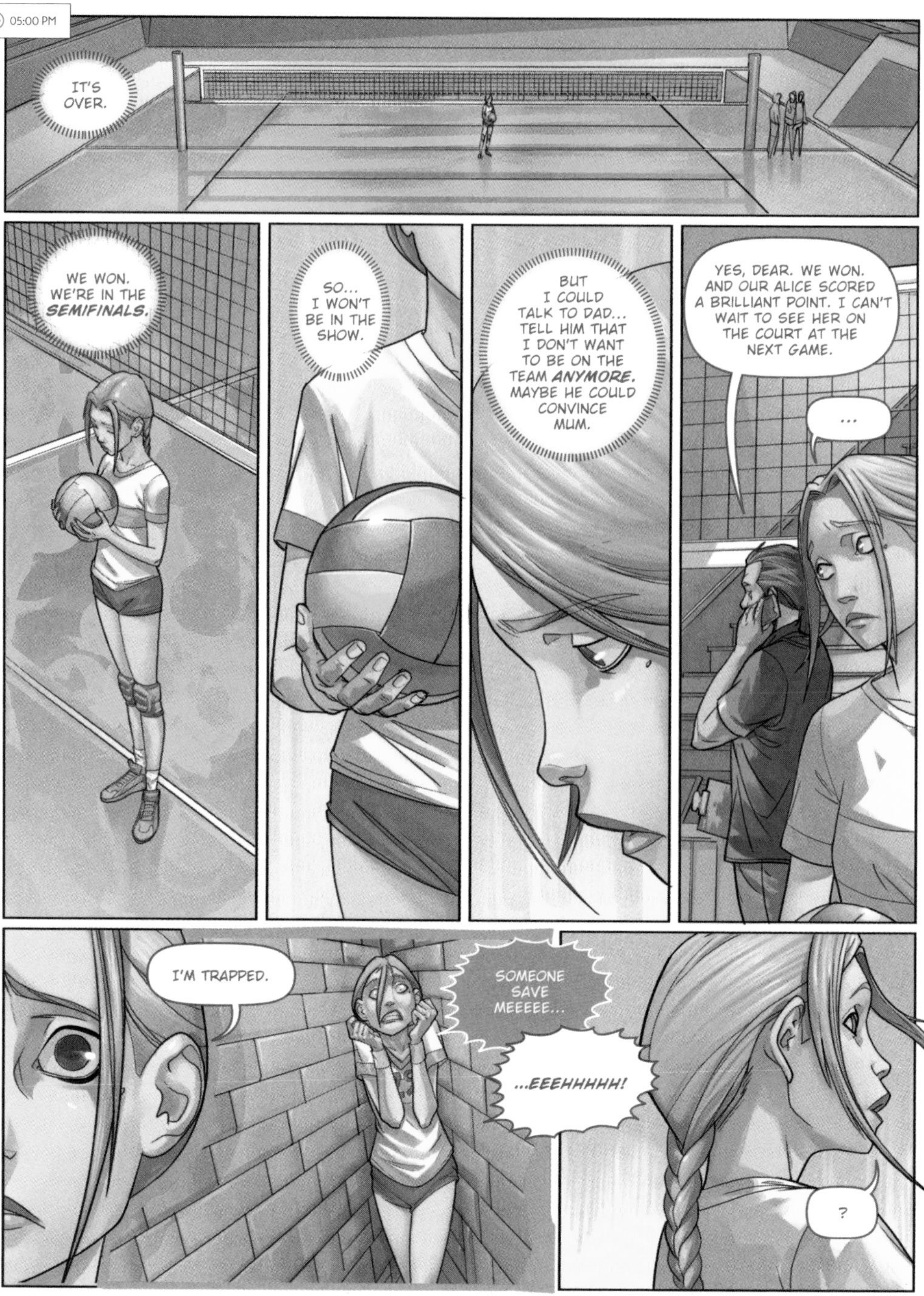
IT'S OVER.
WE WON. WE'RE IN THE SEMIFINALS.
SO... I WON'T BE IN THE SHOW.
BUT I COULD TALK TO DAD... TELL HIM THAT I DON'T WANT TO BE ON THE TEAM ANYMORE. MAYBE HE COULD CONVINCE MUM.
YES, DEAR. WE WON. AND OUR ALICE SCORED A BRILLIANT POINT. I CAN'T WAIT TO SEE HER ON THE COURT AT THE NEXT GAME.
...
I'M TRAPPED.
SOMEONE SAVE MEEEEE...
...EEEHHHHH!
?

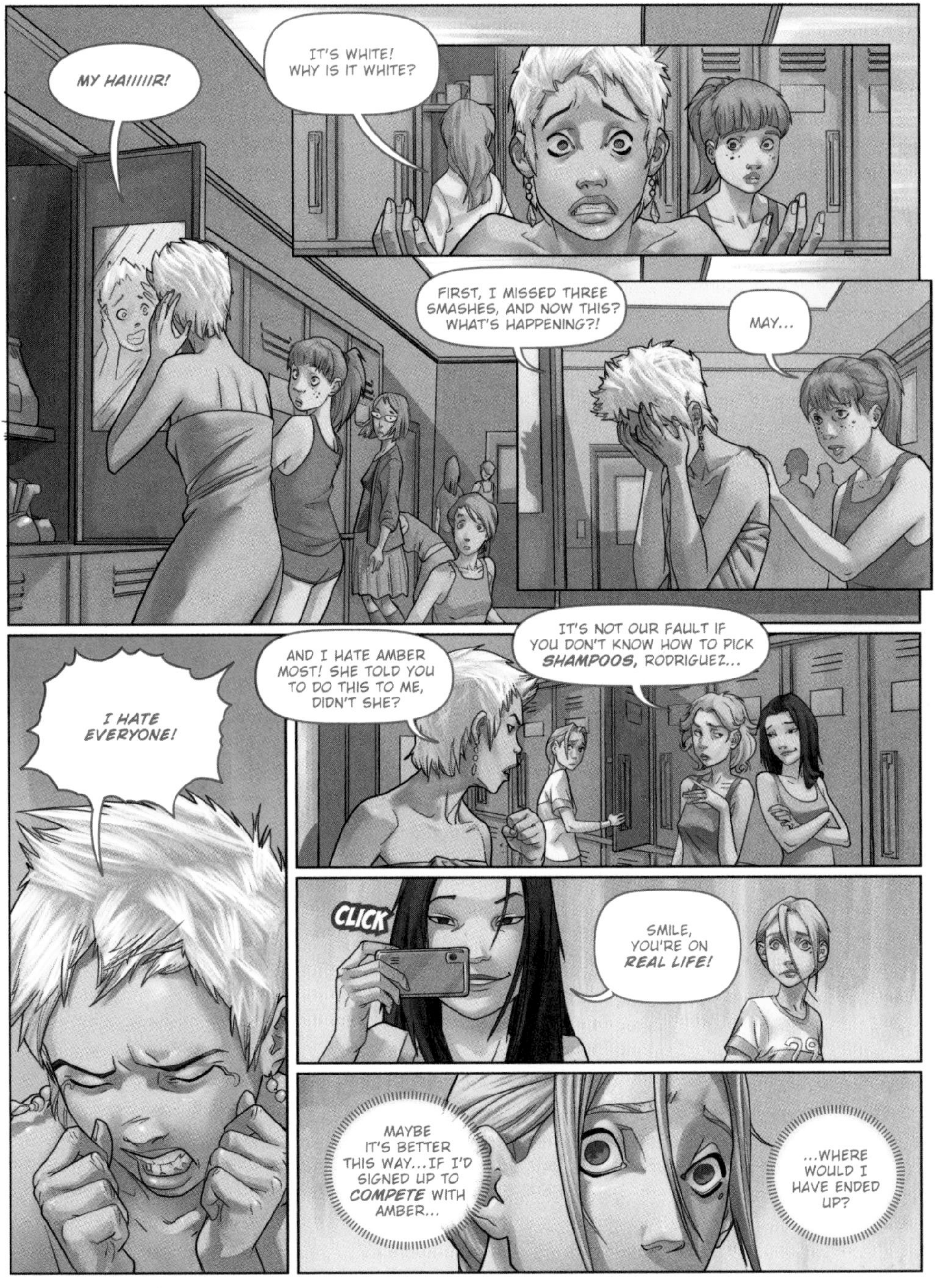
MY HAIIIIIR!
IT'S WHITE! WHY IS IT WHITE?
FIRST, I MISSED THREE SMASHES, AND NOW THIS? WHAT'S HAPPENING?!
MAY...
I HATE EVERYONE!
AND I HATE AMBER MOST! SHE TOLD YOU TO DO THIS TO ME, DIDN'T SHE?
IT'S NOT OUR FAULT IF YOU DON'T KNOW HOW TO PICK SHAMPOOS, RODRIGUEZ...
CLICK
SMILE, YOU'RE ON REAL LIFE!
MAYBE IT'S BETTER THIS WAY...IF I'D SIGNED UP TO COMPETE WITH AMBER...
...WHERE WOULD I HAVE ENDED UP?

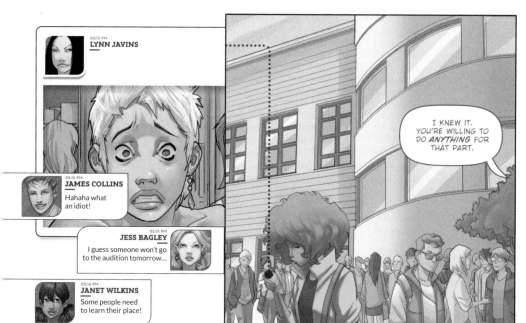

05:15 PM
LYNN JAVINS

05:15 PM
JAMES COLLINS
Hahaha what an idiot!

05:15 PM
JESS BAGLEY
I guess someone won't go to the audition tomorrow...

05:16 PM
JANET WILKINS
Some people need to learn their place!

I KNEW IT. YOU'RE WILLING TO DO *ANYTHING* FOR THAT PART.

YOU THINK IT WAS ME?

IT DOESN'T MATTER WHAT I THINK. IT'S WHAT *YOU* WANTED...

...AND AMBER LEE THOMPSON *ALWAYS* GETS WHAT SHE WANTS. AND THAT'S WHY I LIKE YOU.

BUT I DON'T LIKE *YOU* ANYMORE! GET IT INTO YOUR HEAD!

RIGHT. NOW YOU LIKE ANDERSON. BUT DOES HE KNOW *WHO* YOU REALLY ARE?

YOU DON'T KNOW ANYTHING ABOUT WHO I REALLY AM, EDWARD!

WHAT'S BOTHERING YOU IS THAT LYNN AND JESS DIDN'T ASK YOUR *PERMISSION*, ISN'T IT?

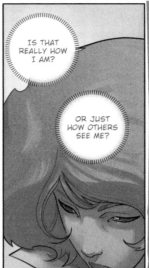

IS THAT REALLY HOW I AM?

OR JUST HOW OTHERS SEE ME?

MAKE WAY FOR QUEEN AMBER!

OOOH, AMBER—! YOU AAAARE THE QUEEN FOR USSSS!

WELL, HOW'S IT MY FAULT IF EVERYONE LOVES ME?

EVERYONE... BUT THOMAS...

NO. THAT'S *NOT THE WAY* I WANT TO WIN.

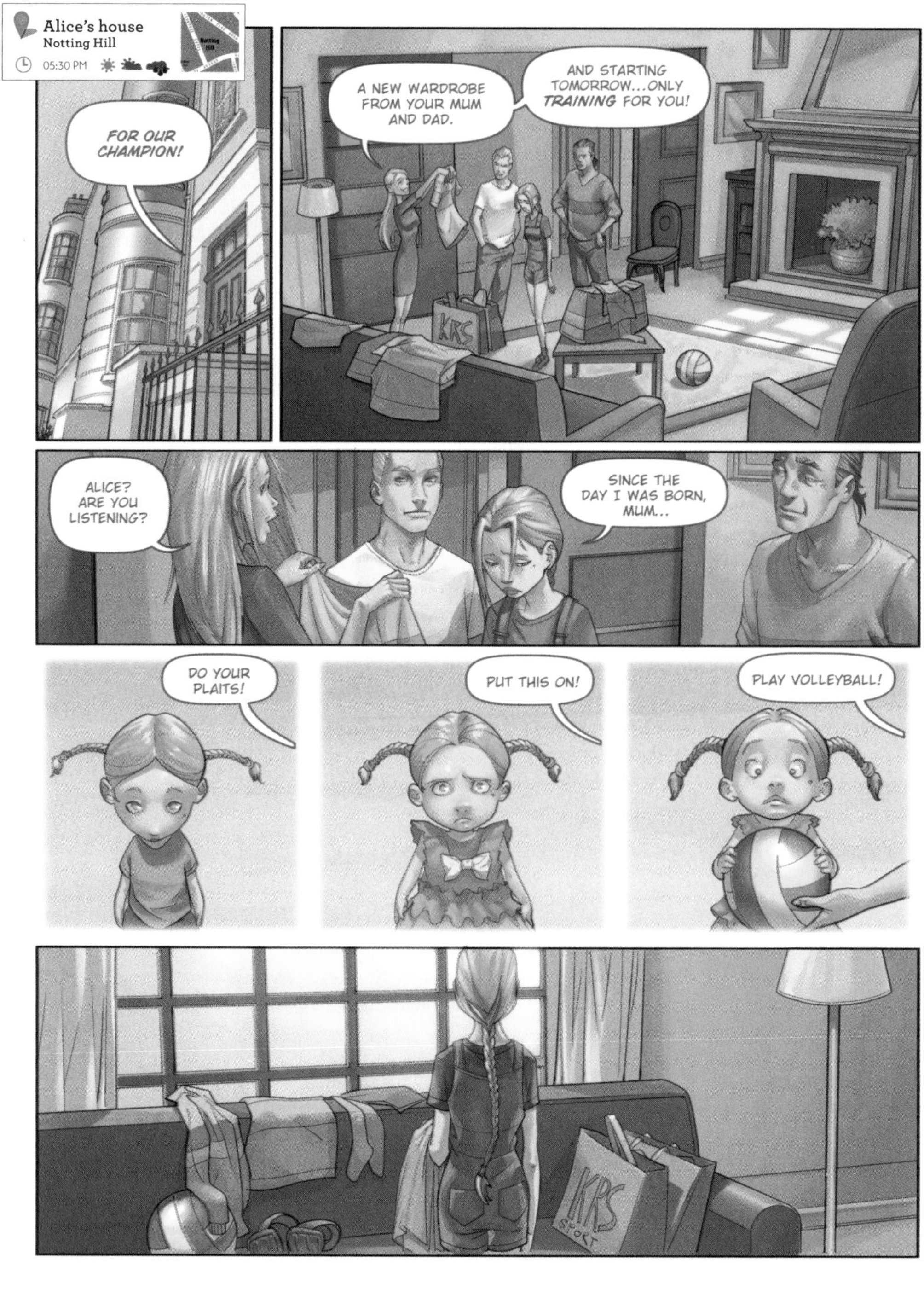

Alice's house
Notting Hill
05:30 PM
Notting Hill
FOR OUR CHAMPION!
A NEW WARDROBE FROM YOUR MUM AND DAD.
AND STARTING TOMORROW...ONLY TRAINING FOR YOU!
KRS
ALICE? ARE YOU LISTENING?
SINCE THE DAY I WAS BORN, MUM...
DO YOUR PLAITS!
PUT THIS ON!
PLAY VOLLEYBALL!
KRS SPORT

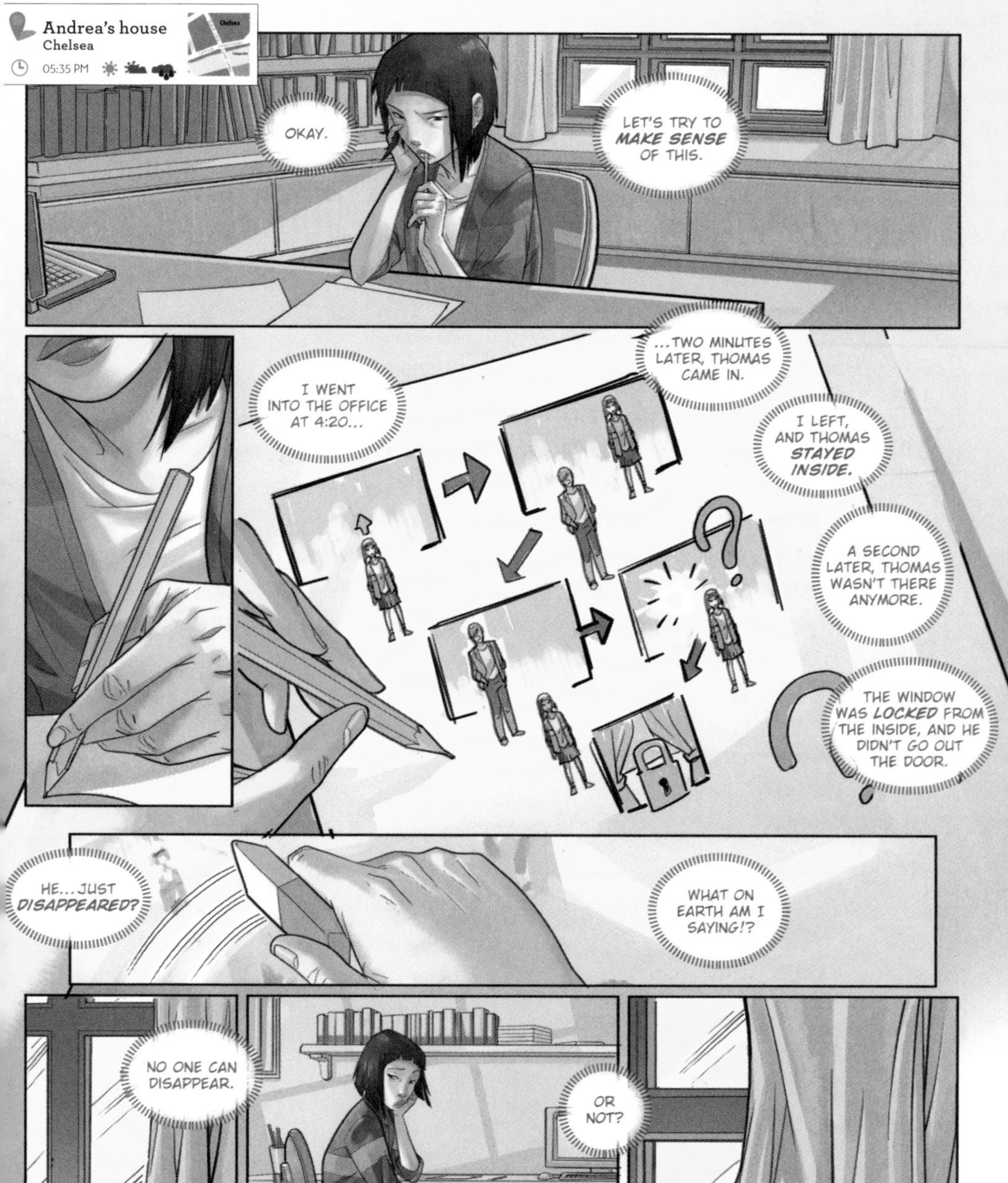
Andrea's house
Chelsea
05:35 PM
OKAY.
LET'S TRY TO MAKE SENSE OF THIS.
I WENT INTO THE OFFICE AT 4:20...
...TWO MINUTES LATER, THOMAS CAME IN.
I LEFT, AND THOMAS STAYED INSIDE.
A SECOND LATER, THOMAS WASN'T THERE ANYMORE.
THE WINDOW WAS LOCKED FROM THE INSIDE, AND HE DIDN'T GO OUT THE DOOR.
HE... JUST DISAPPEARED?
WHAT ON EARTH AM I SAYING!?
NO ONE CAN DISAPPEAR.
OR NOT?

END OF CHAPTER 5

CHAPTER 6

I KNOW who I AM

London International High School
Marylebone
11:30 AM

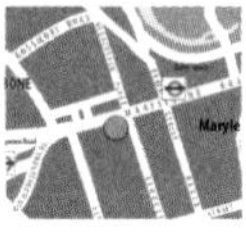

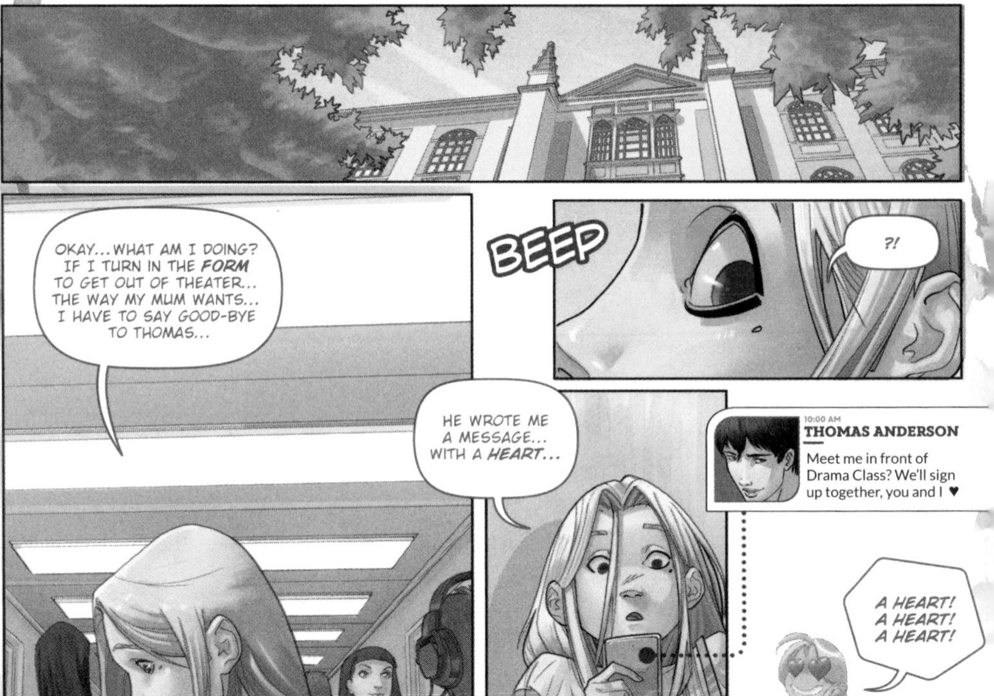
OKAY... WHAT AM I DOING? IF I TURN IN THE *FORM* TO GET OUT OF THEATER... THE WAY MY MUM WANTS... I HAVE TO SAY GOOD-BYE TO THOMAS...
BEEP
?!
HE WROTE ME A MESSAGE... WITH A *HEART*...
10:00 AM
THOMAS ANDERSON
Meet me in front of Drama Class? We'll sign up together, you and I ♥
A HEART! A HEART! A HEART!

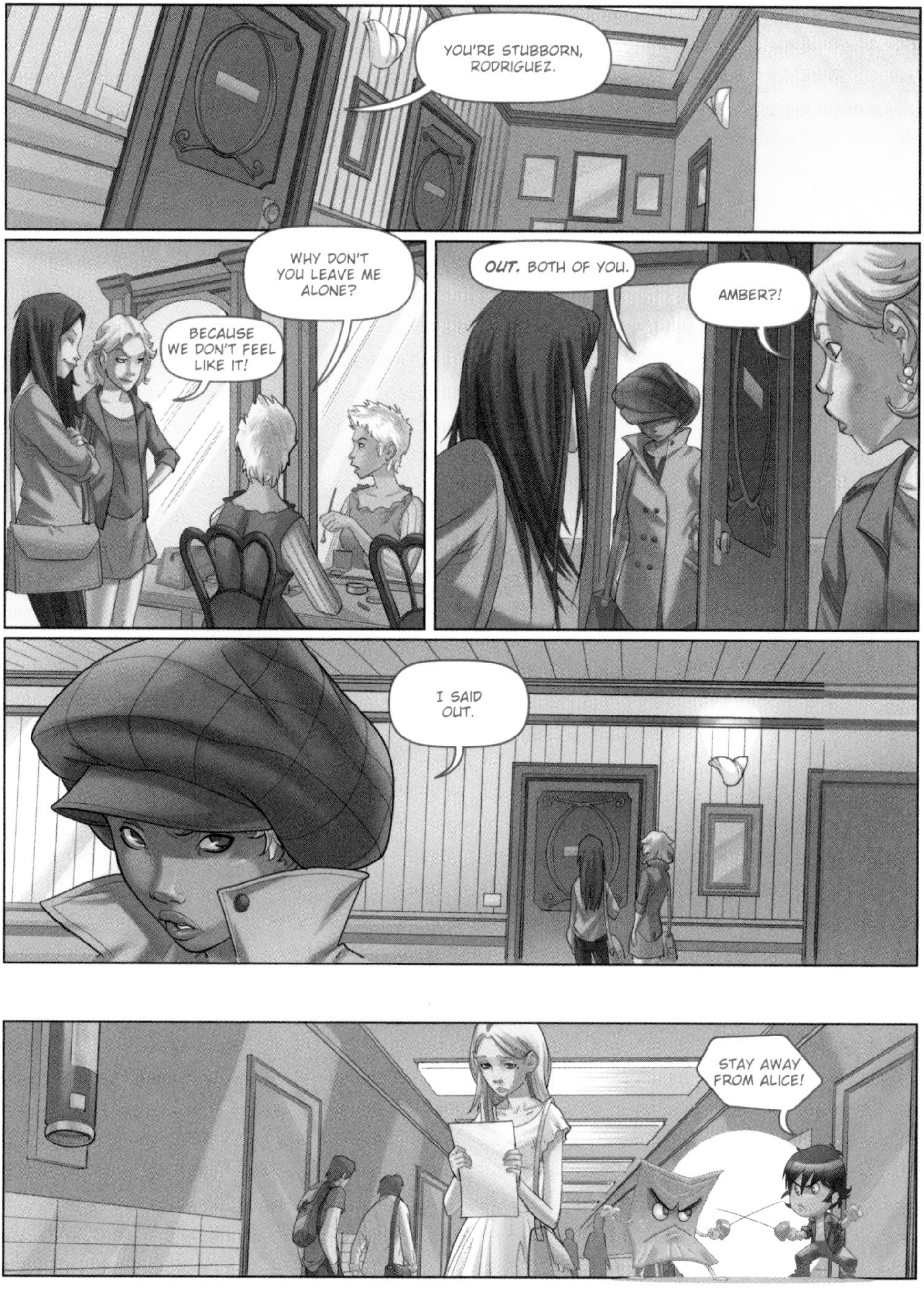
YOU'RE STUBBORN, RODRIGUEZ.
WHY DON'T YOU LEAVE ME ALONE?
BECAUSE WE DON'T FEEL LIKE IT!
OUT. BOTH OF YOU.
AMBER?!
I SAID OUT.
STAY AWAY FROM ALICE!

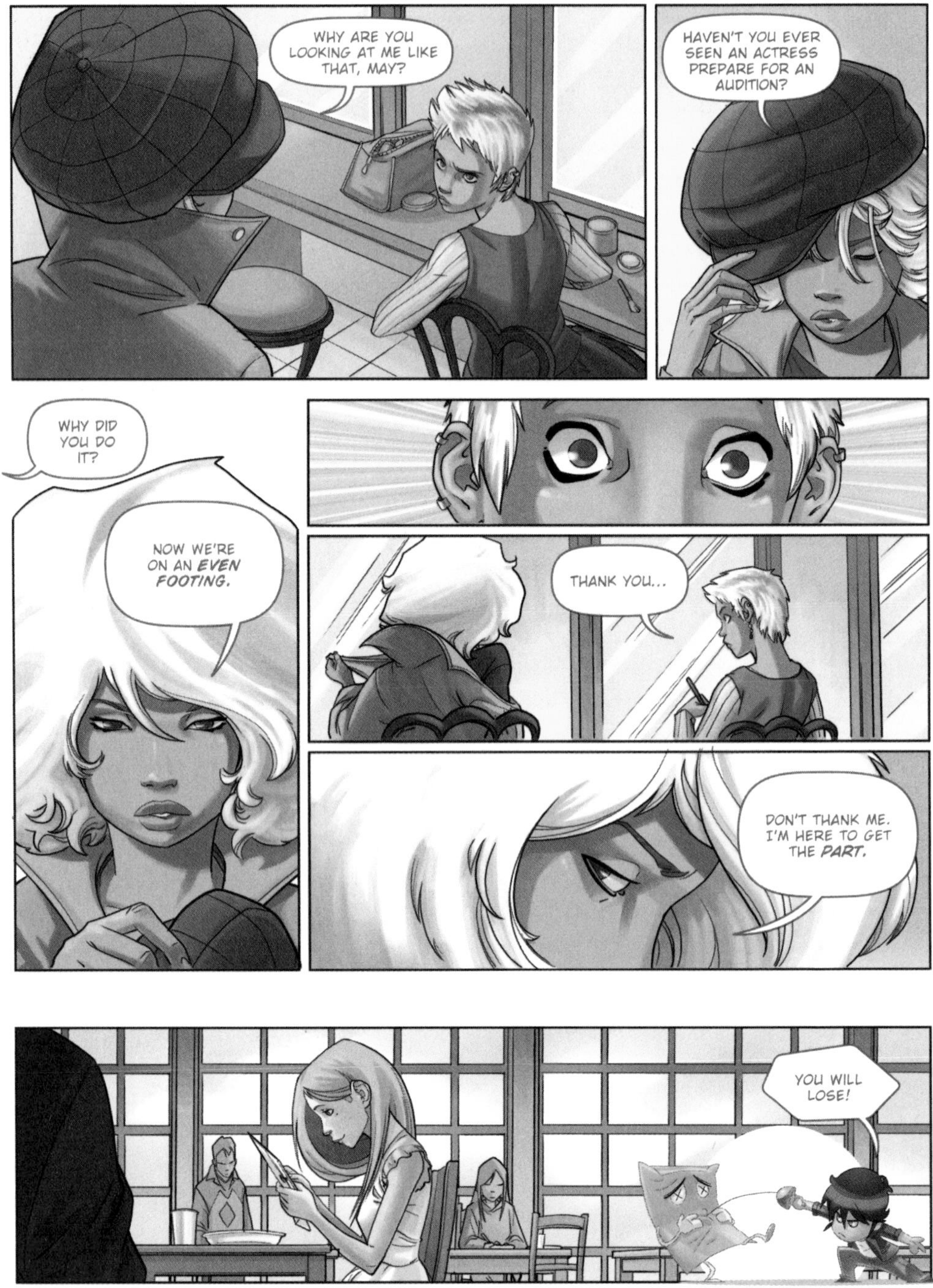
WHY ARE YOU LOOKING AT ME LIKE THAT, MAY?
HAVEN'T YOU EVER SEEN AN ACTRESS PREPARE FOR AN AUDITION?
WHY DID YOU DO IT?
NOW WE'RE ON AN *EVEN FOOTING.*
THANK YOU...
DON'T THANK ME. I'M HERE TO GET THE *PART.*
YOU WILL LOSE!

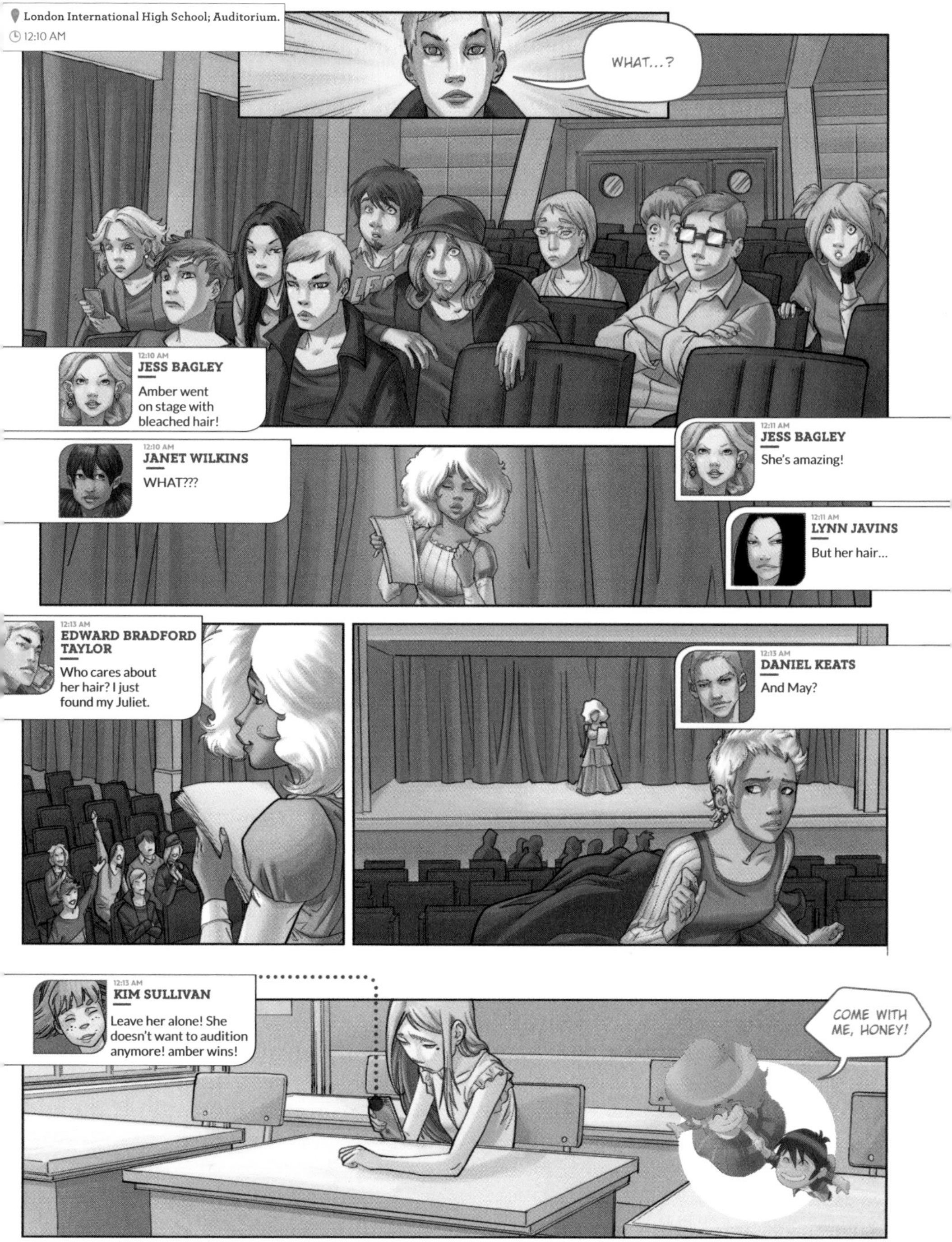
London International High School; Auditorium.
12:10 AM
WHAT...?
12:10 AM
JESS BAGLEY
Amber went on stage with bleached hair!
12:10 AM
JANET WILKINS
WHAT???
12:11 AM
JESS BAGLEY
She's amazing!
12:11 AM
LYNN JAVINS
But her hair...
12:13 AM
EDWARD BRADFORD TAYLOR
Who cares about her hair? I just found my Juliet.
12:13 AM
DANIEL KEATS
And May?
12:13 AM
KIM SULLIVAN
Leave her alone! She doesn't want to audition anymore! amber wins!
COME WITH ME, HONEY!

HOW DID YOU KNOW THAT MAY WOULD QUIT?

I DIDN'T KNOW.

YOU COULD HAVE LOST THE PART AND ENDED UP WITH *BLEACHED HAIR.*

OR I COULD HAVE GOTTEN THE PART AND USED A *WIG!*

IS THIS THE *REAL* AMBER?

MAYBE. WHY?

BECAUSE I LIKE HER.

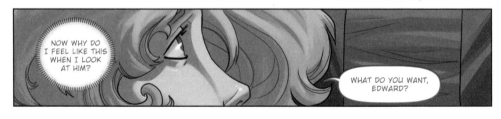

NOW WHY DO I FEEL LIKE THIS WHEN I LOOK AT HIM?

WHAT DO YOU WANT, EDWARD?

THE EVIL FORM TRIUMPHS!

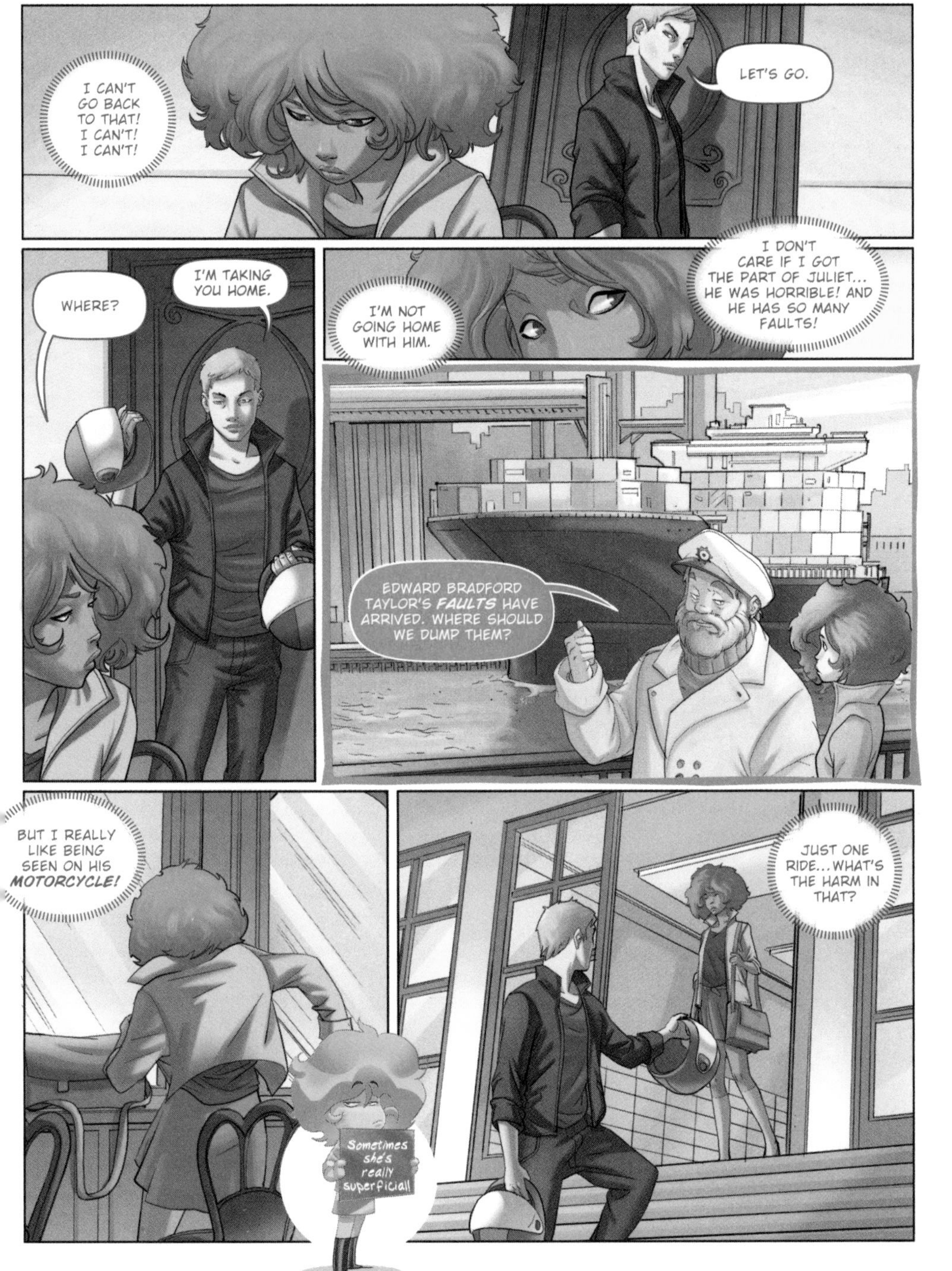

I CAN'T GO BACK TO THAT! I CAN'T! I CAN'T!
LET'S GO.
WHERE?
I'M TAKING YOU HOME.
I'M NOT GOING HOME WITH HIM.
I DON'T CARE IF I GOT THE PART OF JULIET... HE WAS HORRIBLE! AND HE HAS SO MANY FAULTS!
EDWARD BRADFORD TAYLOR'S **FAULTS** HAVE ARRIVED. WHERE SHOULD WE DUMP THEM?
BUT I REALLY LIKE BEING SEEN ON HIS **MOTORCYCLE!**
JUST ONE RIDE...WHAT'S THE HARM IN THAT?
Sometimes she's really superficial!

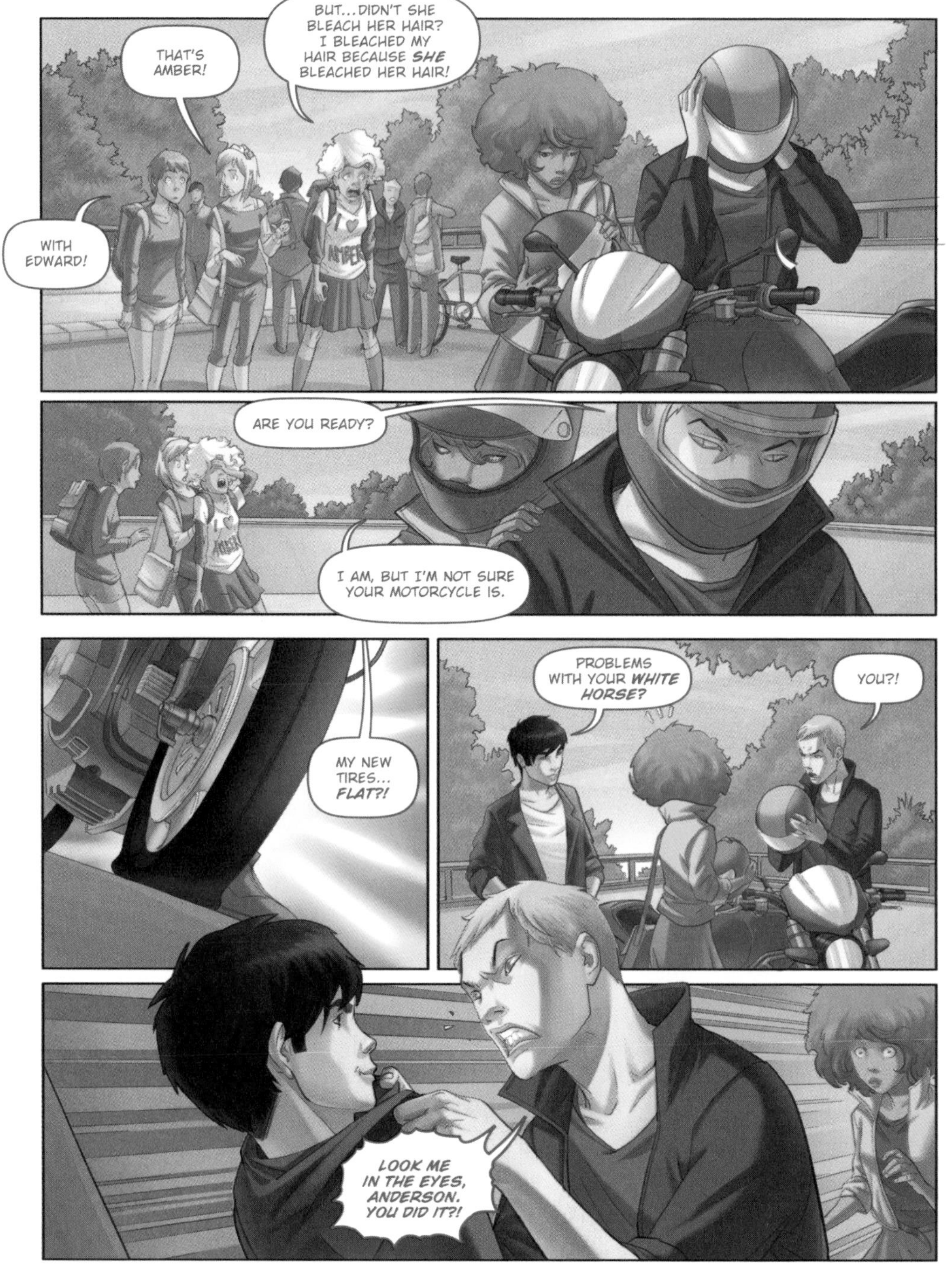
THAT'S AMBER!
BUT...DIDN'T SHE BLEACH HER HAIR? I BLEACHED MY HAIR BECAUSE SHE BLEACHED HER HAIR!
WITH EDWARD!
ARE YOU READY?
I AM, BUT I'M NOT SURE YOUR MOTORCYCLE IS.
MY NEW TIRES... FLAT?!
PROBLEMS WITH YOUR WHITE HORSE?
YOU?!
LOOK ME IN THE EYES, ANDERSON. YOU DID IT?!

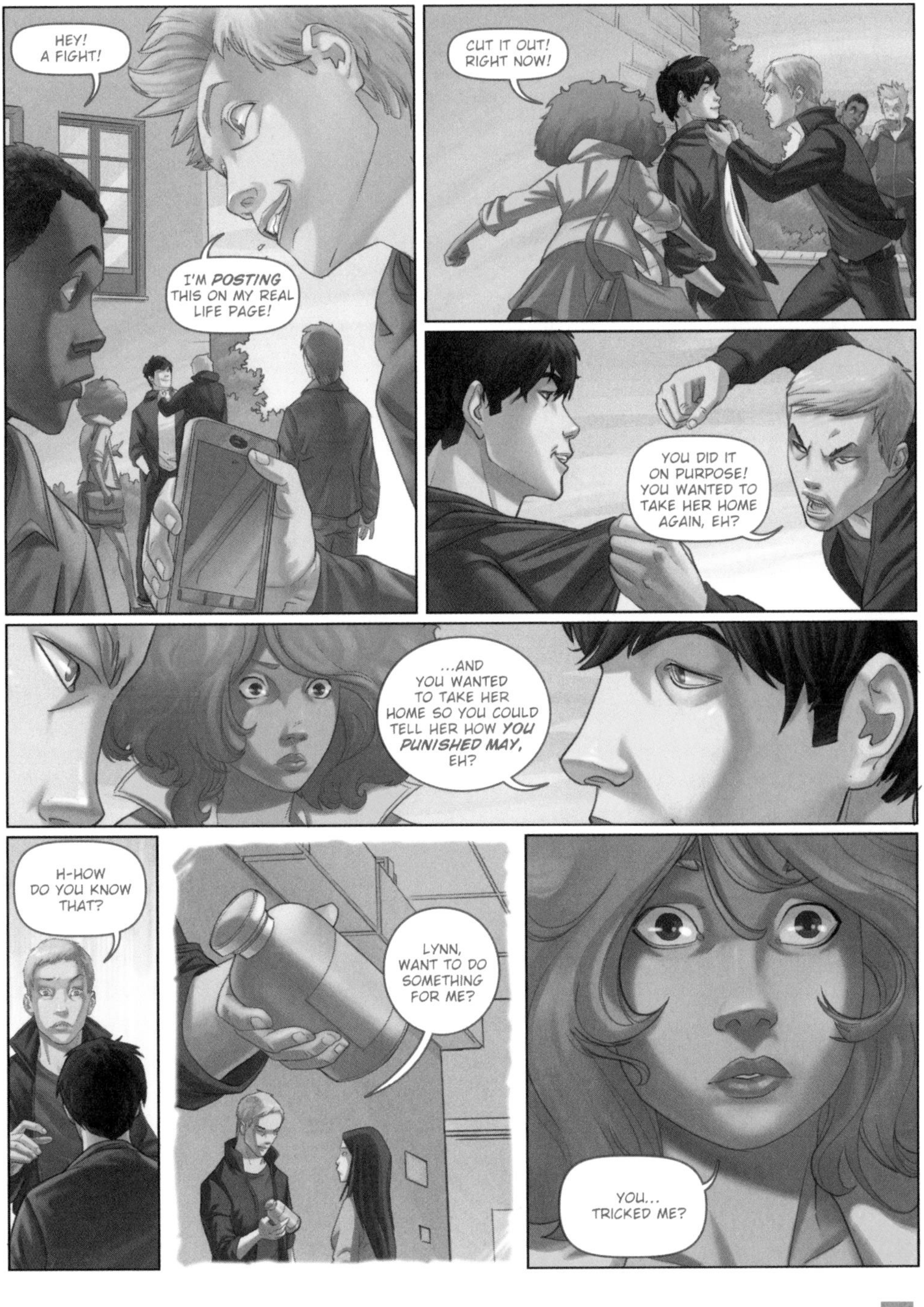
HEY!
A FIGHT!
I'M POSTING THIS ON MY REAL LIFE PAGE!
CUT IT OUT! RIGHT NOW!
YOU DID IT ON PURPOSE! YOU WANTED TO TAKE HER HOME AGAIN, EH?
...AND YOU WANTED TO TAKE HER HOME SO YOU COULD TELL HER HOW YOU PUNISHED MAY, EH?
H-HOW DO YOU KNOW THAT?
LYNN, WANT TO DO SOMETHING FOR ME?
YOU... TRICKED ME?

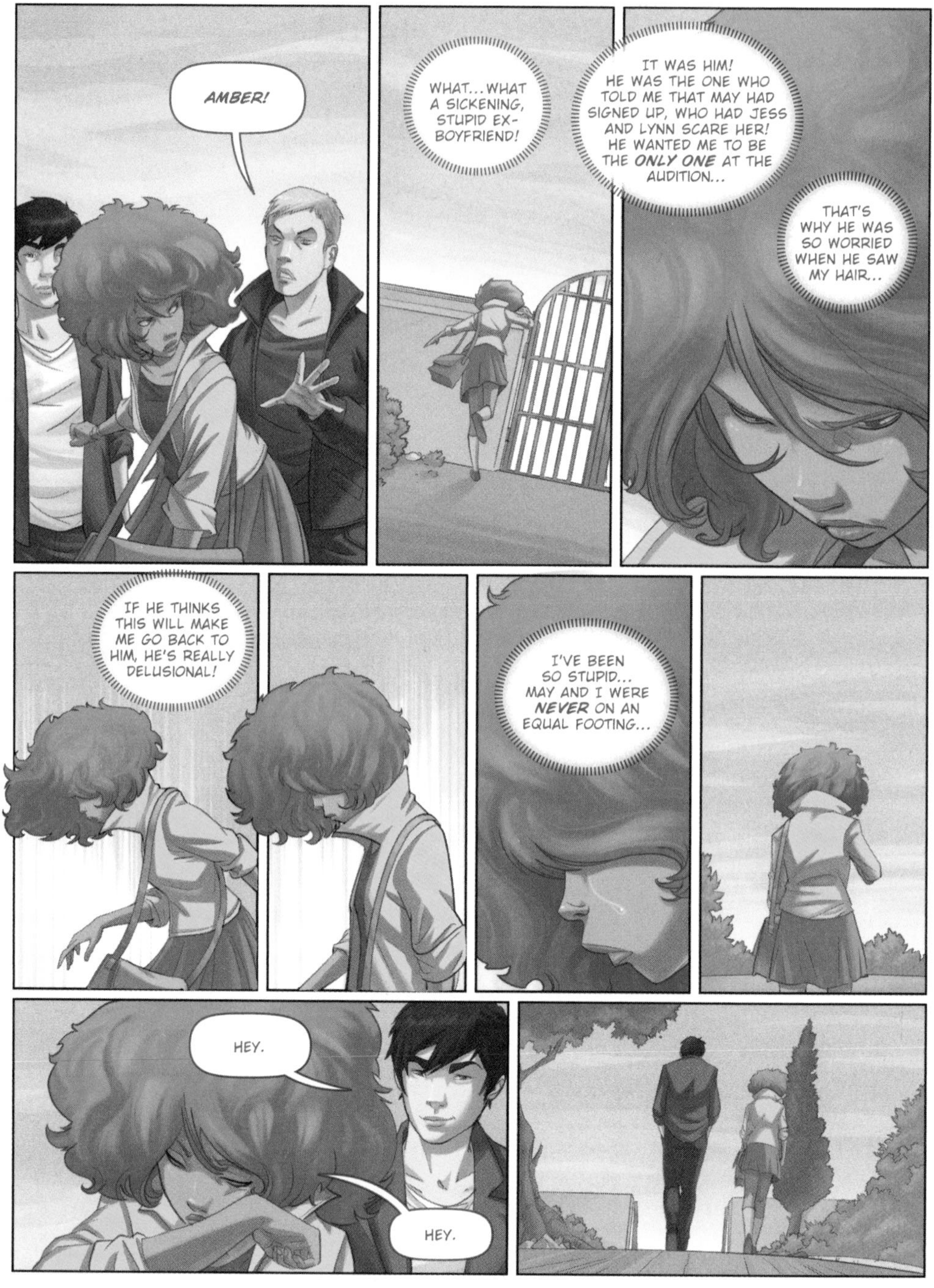
AMBER!
WHAT...WHAT A SICKENING, STUPID EX-BOYFRIEND!
IT WAS HIM! HE WAS THE ONE WHO TOLD ME THAT MAY HAD SIGNED UP, WHO HAD JESS AND LYNN SCARE HER! HE WANTED ME TO BE THE ONLY ONE AT THE AUDITION...
THAT'S WHY HE WAS SO WORRIED WHEN HE SAW MY HAIR...
IF HE THINKS THIS WILL MAKE ME GO BACK TO HIM, HE'S REALLY DELUSIONAL!
I'VE BEEN SO STUPID... MAY AND I WERE NEVER ON AN EQUAL FOOTING...
HEY.
HEY.

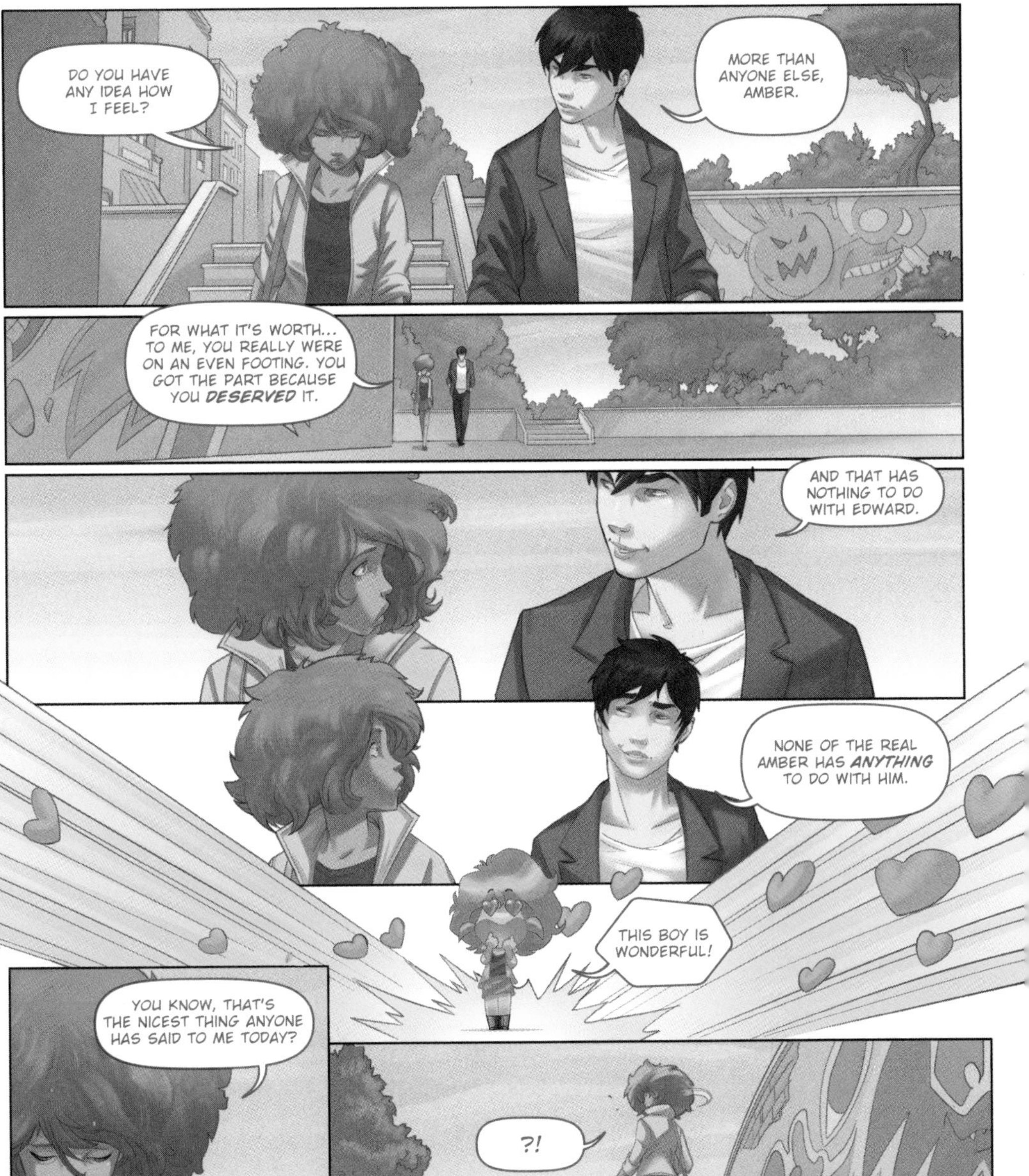
DO YOU HAVE ANY IDEA HOW I FEEL?
MORE THAN ANYONE ELSE, AMBER.
FOR WHAT IT'S WORTH... TO ME, YOU REALLY WERE ON AN EVEN FOOTING. YOU GOT THE PART BECAUSE YOU *DESERVED* IT.
AND THAT HAS NOTHING TO DO WITH EDWARD.
NONE OF THE REAL AMBER HAS *ANYTHING* TO DO WITH HIM.
THIS BOY IS WONDERFUL!
YOU KNOW, THAT'S THE NICEST THING ANYONE HAS SAID TO ME TODAY?
WHAT DO YOU THINK ABOUT — ?
?!

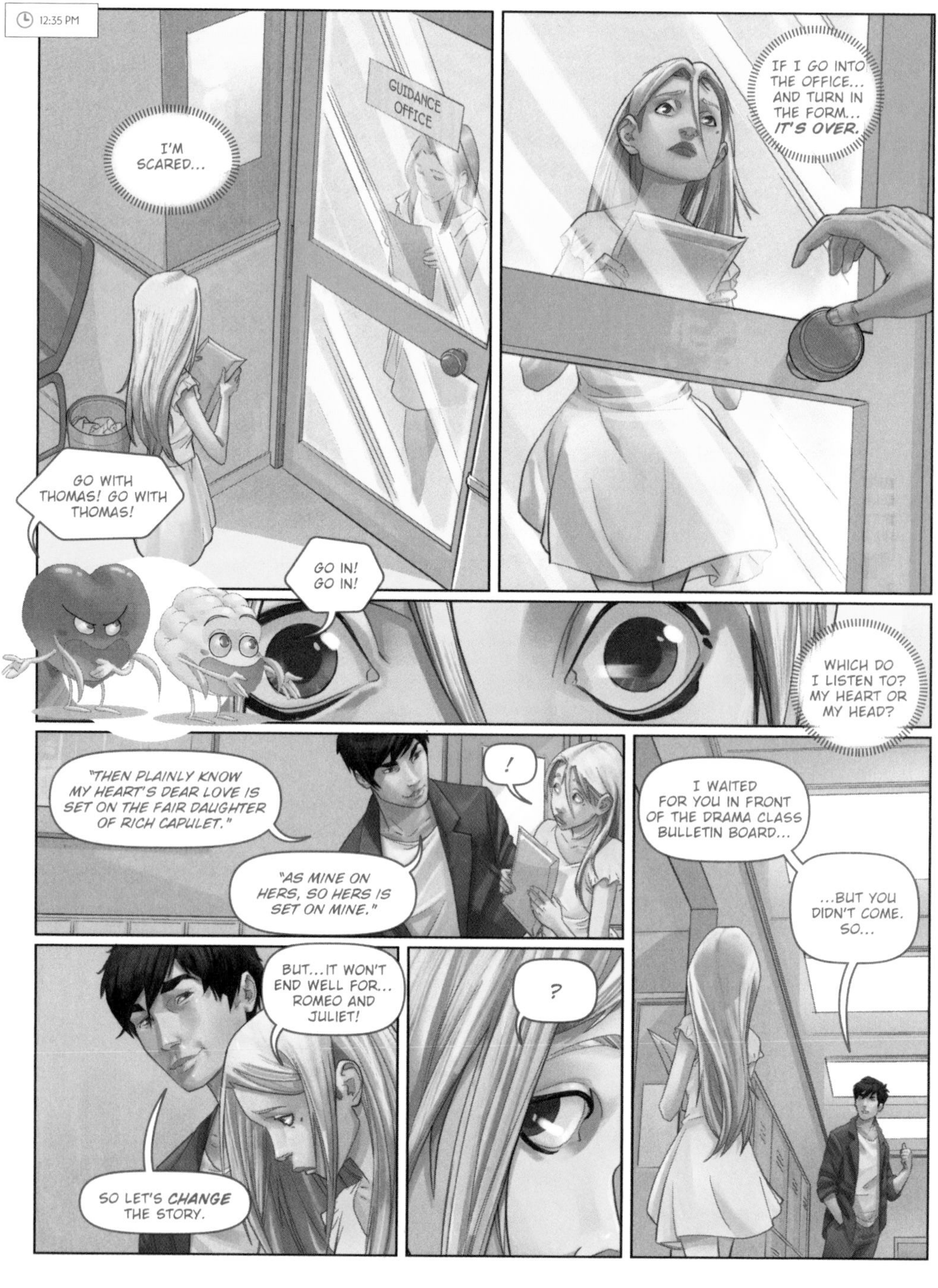
I'M SCARED...
IF I GO INTO THE OFFICE... AND TURN IN THE FORM... IT'S OVER.
GUIDANCE OFFICE
GO WITH THOMAS! GO WITH THOMAS!
GO IN! GO IN!
WHICH DO I LISTEN TO? MY HEART OR MY HEAD?
"THEN PLAINLY KNOW MY HEART'S DEAR LOVE IS SET ON THE FAIR DAUGHTER OF RICH CAPULET."
!
"AS MINE ON HERS, SO HERS IS SET ON MINE."
I WAITED FOR YOU IN FRONT OF THE DRAMA CLASS BULLETIN BOARD...
...BUT YOU DIDN'T COME. SO...
BUT...IT WON'T END WELL FOR... ROMEO AND JULIET!
?
SO LET'S CHANGE THE STORY.

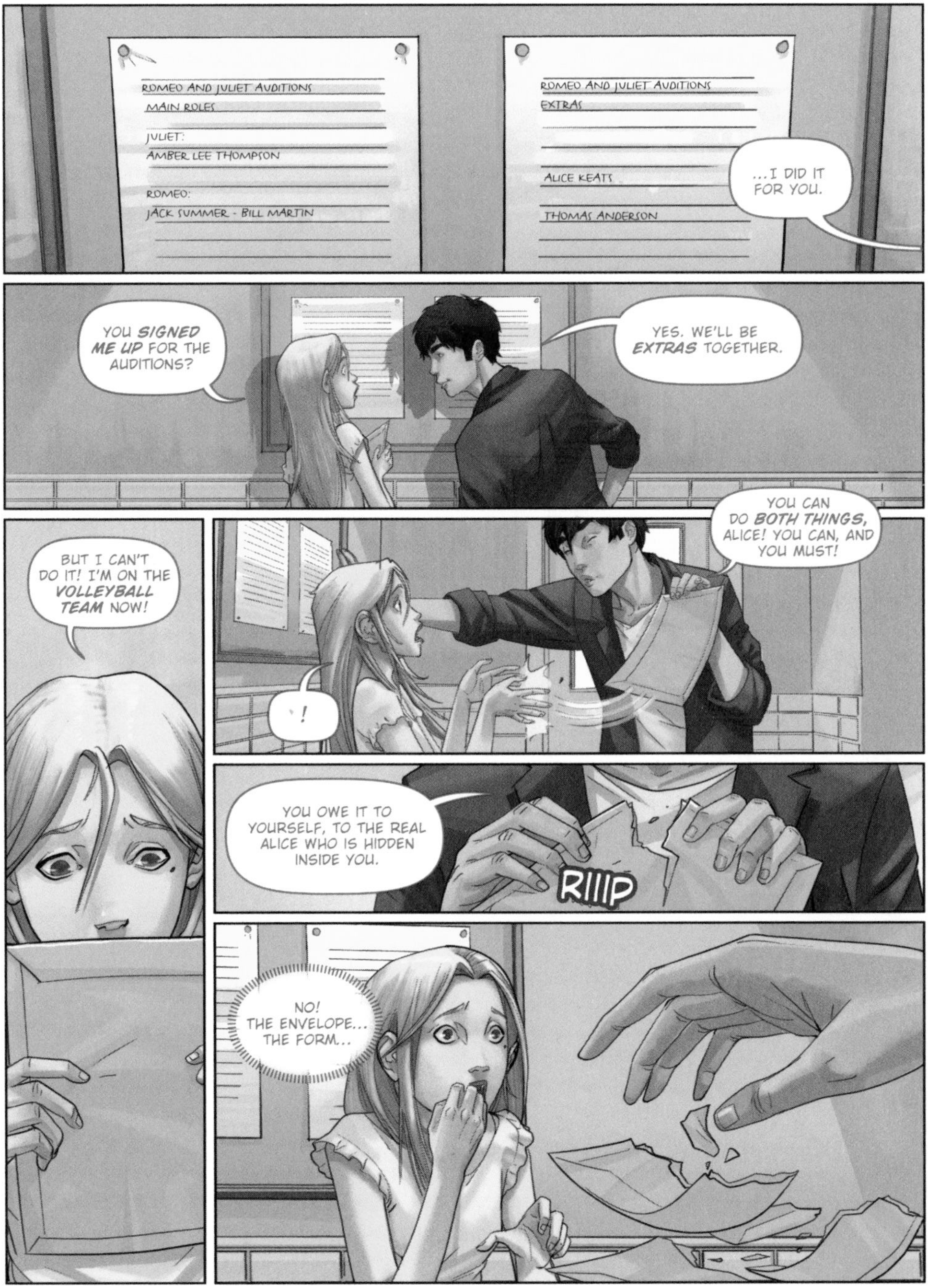
ROMEO AND JULIET AUDITIONS
MAIN ROLES
JULIET:
AMBER LEE THOMPSON
ROMEO:
JACK SUMMER - BILL MARTIN
ROMEO AND JULIET AUDITIONS
EXTRAS
ALICE KEATS
THOMAS ANDERSON
...I DID IT FOR YOU.
YOU SIGNED ME UP FOR THE AUDITIONS?
YES. WE'LL BE EXTRAS TOGETHER.
BUT I CAN'T DO IT! I'M ON THE VOLLEYBALL TEAM NOW!
YOU CAN DO BOTH THINGS, ALICE! YOU CAN, AND YOU MUST!
!
YOU OWE IT TO YOURSELF, TO THE REAL ALICE WHO IS HIDDEN INSIDE YOU.
RIIIP
NO! THE ENVELOPE... THE FORM...

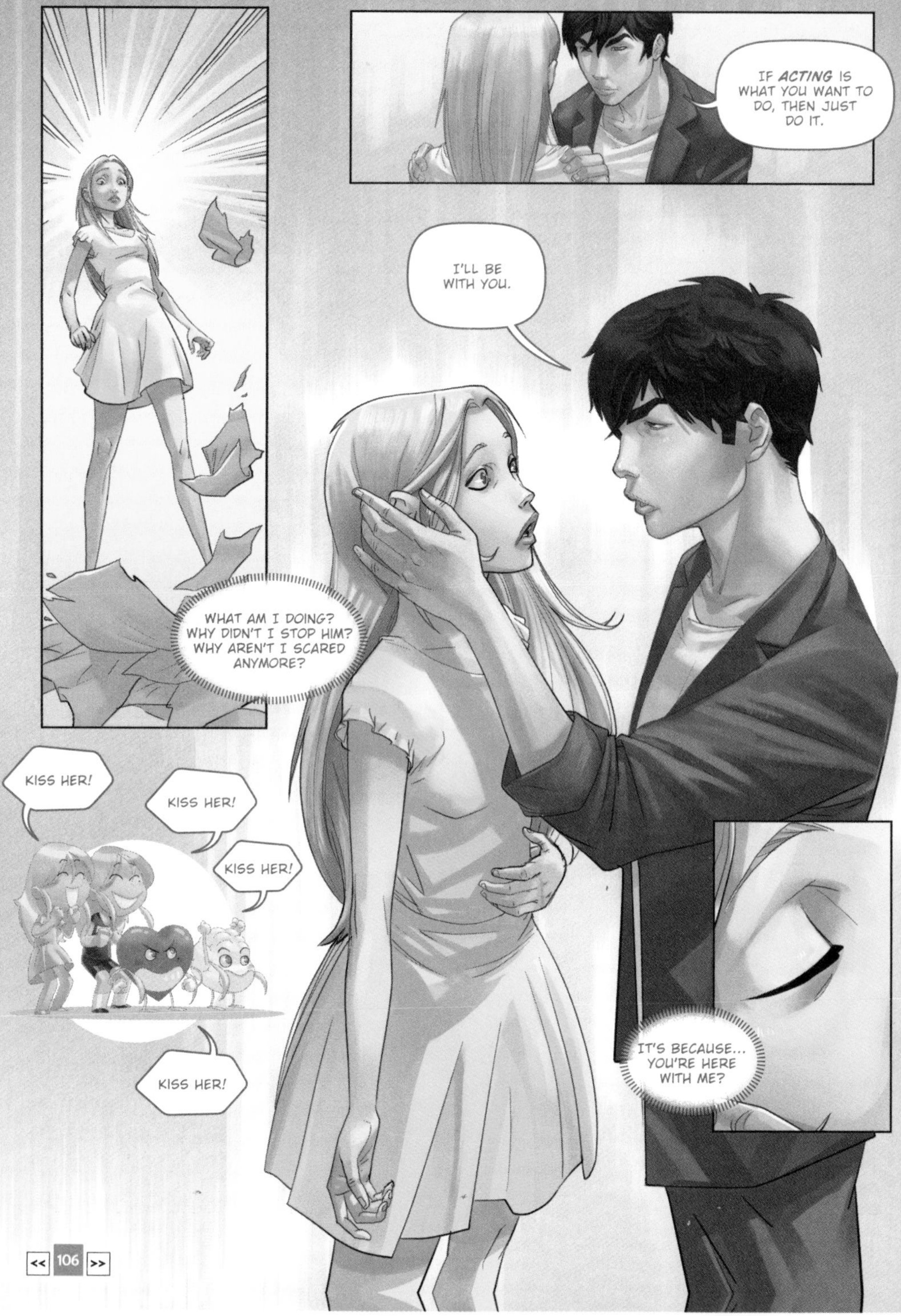
IF ACTING IS WHAT YOU WANT TO DO, THEN JUST DO IT.
I'LL BE WITH YOU.
WHAT AM I DOING? WHY DIDN'T I STOP HIM? WHY AREN'T I SCARED ANYMORE?
KISS HER!
KISS HER!
KISS HER!
KISS HER!
IT'S BECAUSE... YOU'RE HERE WITH ME?

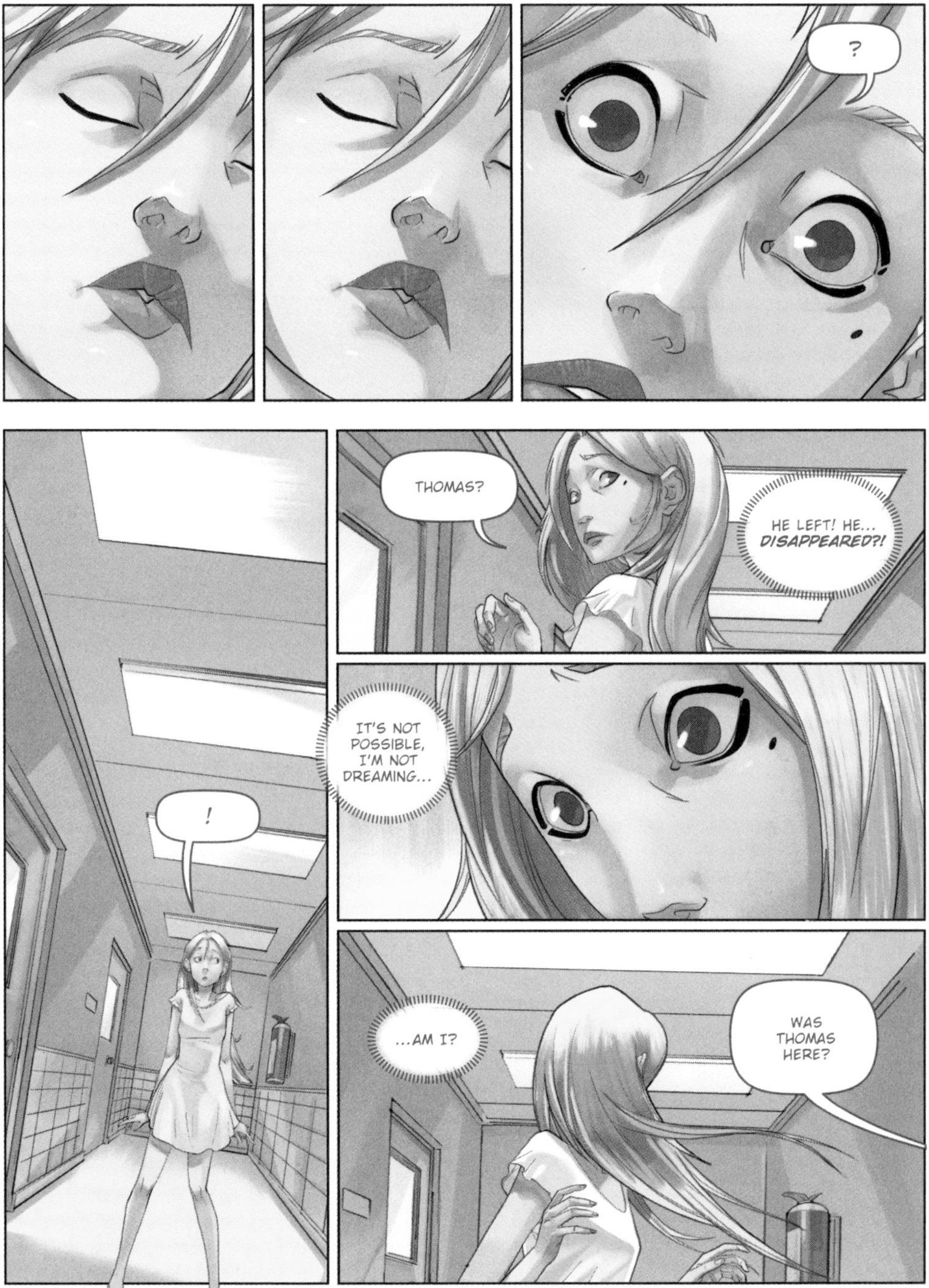
?
THOMAS?
HE LEFT! HE... DISAPPEARED?!
IT'S NOT POSSIBLE, I'M NOT DREAMING...
!
...AM I?
WAS THOMAS HERE?

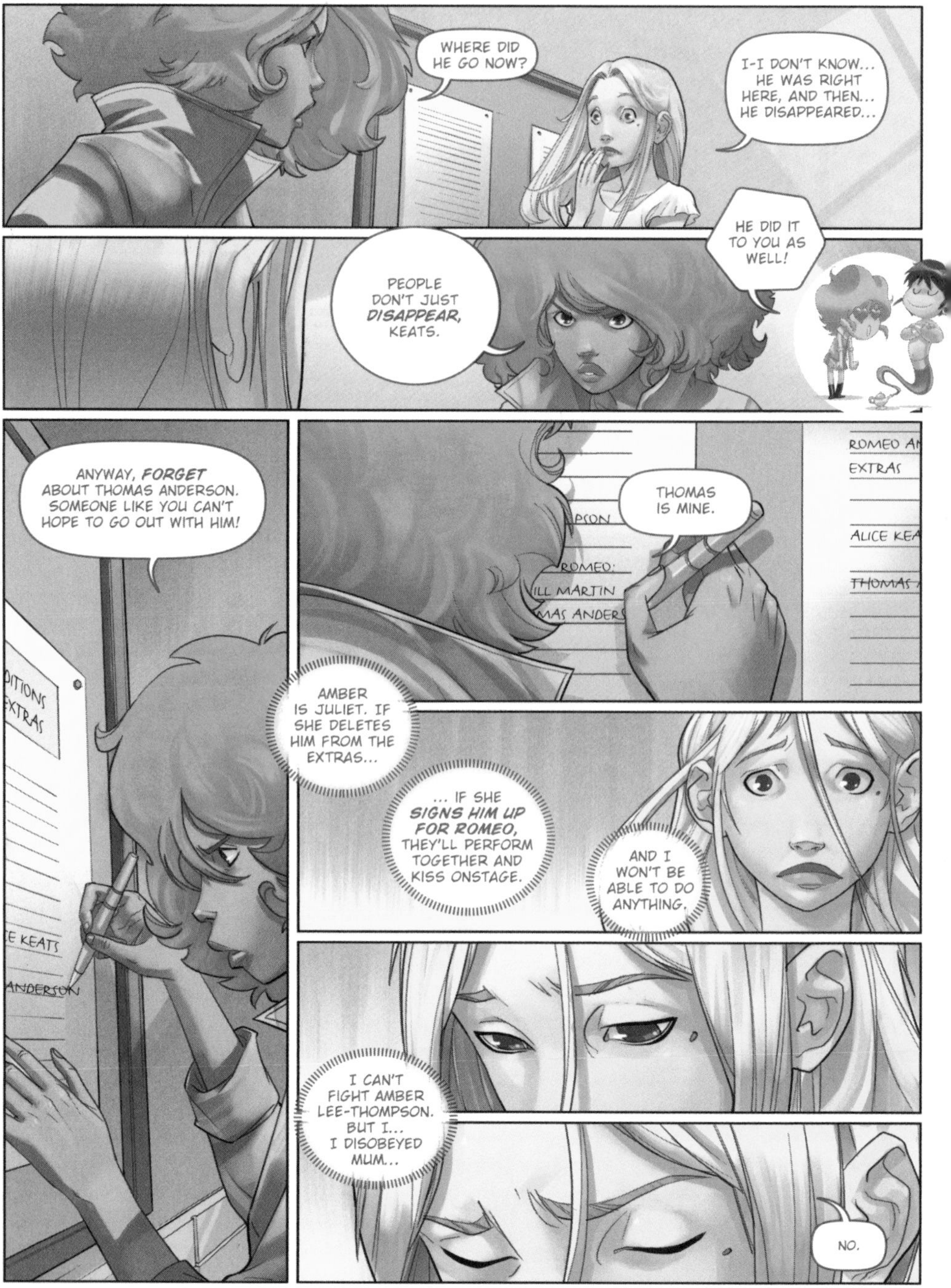
WHERE DID HE GO NOW?
I-I DON'T KNOW... HE WAS RIGHT HERE, AND THEN... HE DISAPPEARED...
PEOPLE DON'T JUST *DISAPPEAR,* KEATS.
HE DID IT TO YOU AS WELL!
ANYWAY, **FORGET** ABOUT THOMAS ANDERSON. SOMEONE LIKE YOU CAN'T HOPE TO GO OUT WITH HIM!
THOMAS IS MINE.
AMBER IS JULIET. IF SHE DELETES HIM FROM THE EXTRAS...
... IF SHE ***SIGNS HIM UP FOR ROMEO,*** THEY'LL PERFORM TOGETHER AND KISS ONSTAGE.
AND I WON'T BE ABLE TO DO ANYTHING.
I CAN'T FIGHT AMBER LEE-THOMPSON. BUT I... I DISOBEYED MUM...
NO.

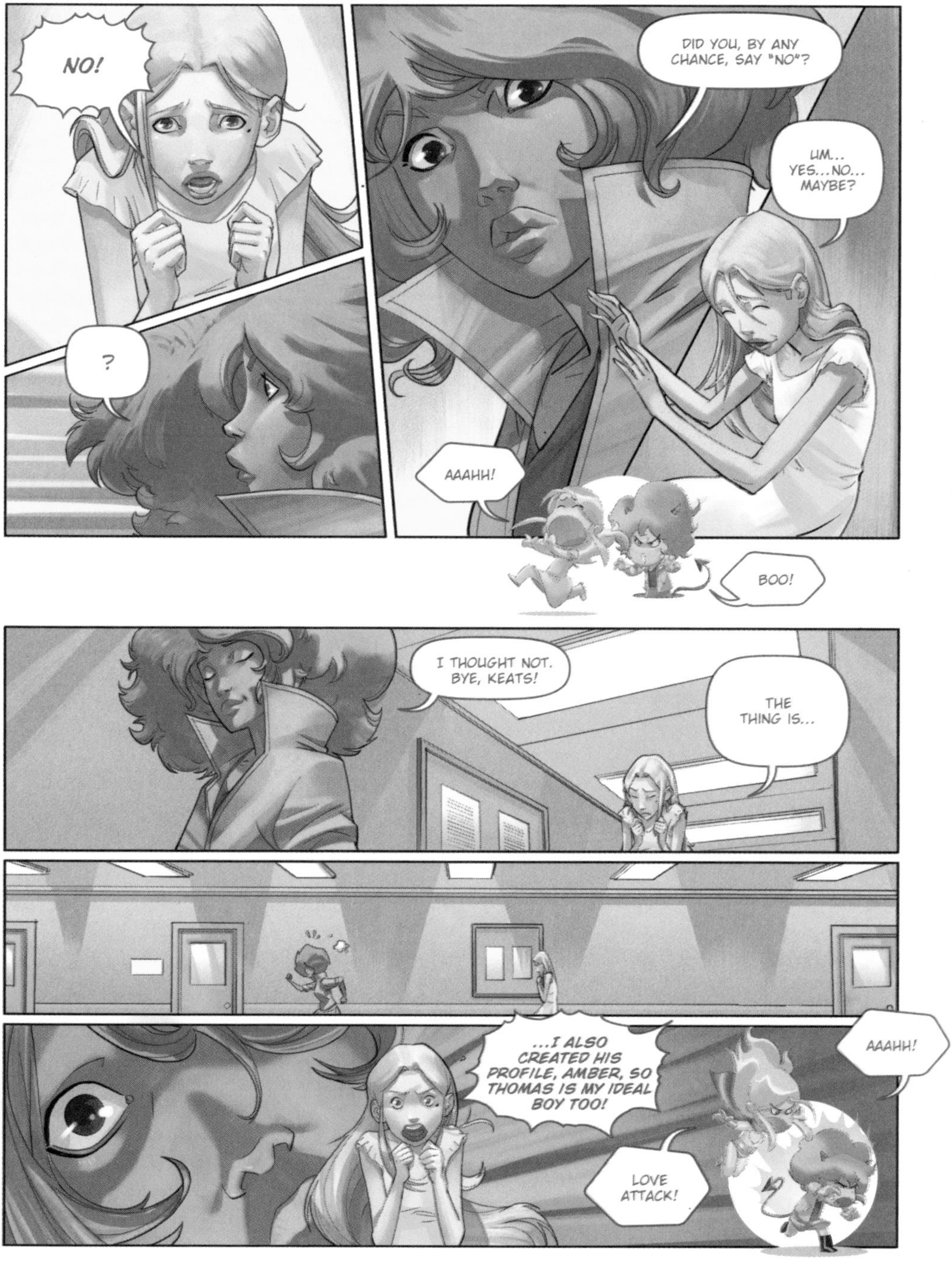
NO!
?
DID YOU, BY ANY CHANCE, SAY "NO"?
UM... YES...NO... MAYBE?
AAAHH!
BOO!
I THOUGHT NOT. BYE, KEATS!
THE THING IS...
...I ALSO CREATED HIS PROFILE, AMBER, SO THOMAS IS MY IDEAL BOY TOO!
AAAHH!
LOVE ATTACK!

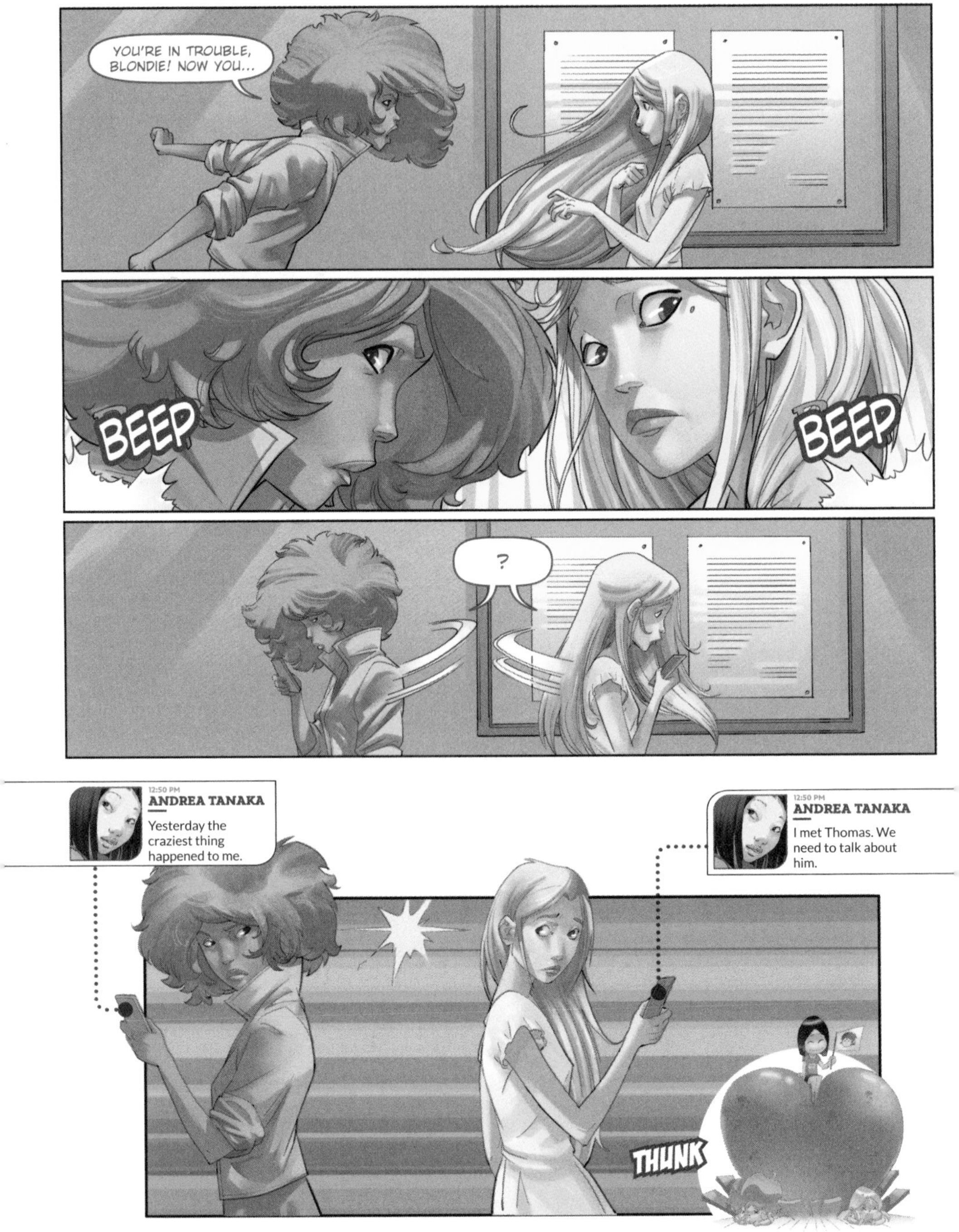
YOU'RE IN TROUBLE, BLONDIE! NOW YOU...
BEEP
BEEP
?
12:50 PM
ANDREA TANAKA
Yesterday the craziest thing happened to me.
12:50 PM
ANDREA TANAKA
I met Thomas. We need to talk about him.
THUNK

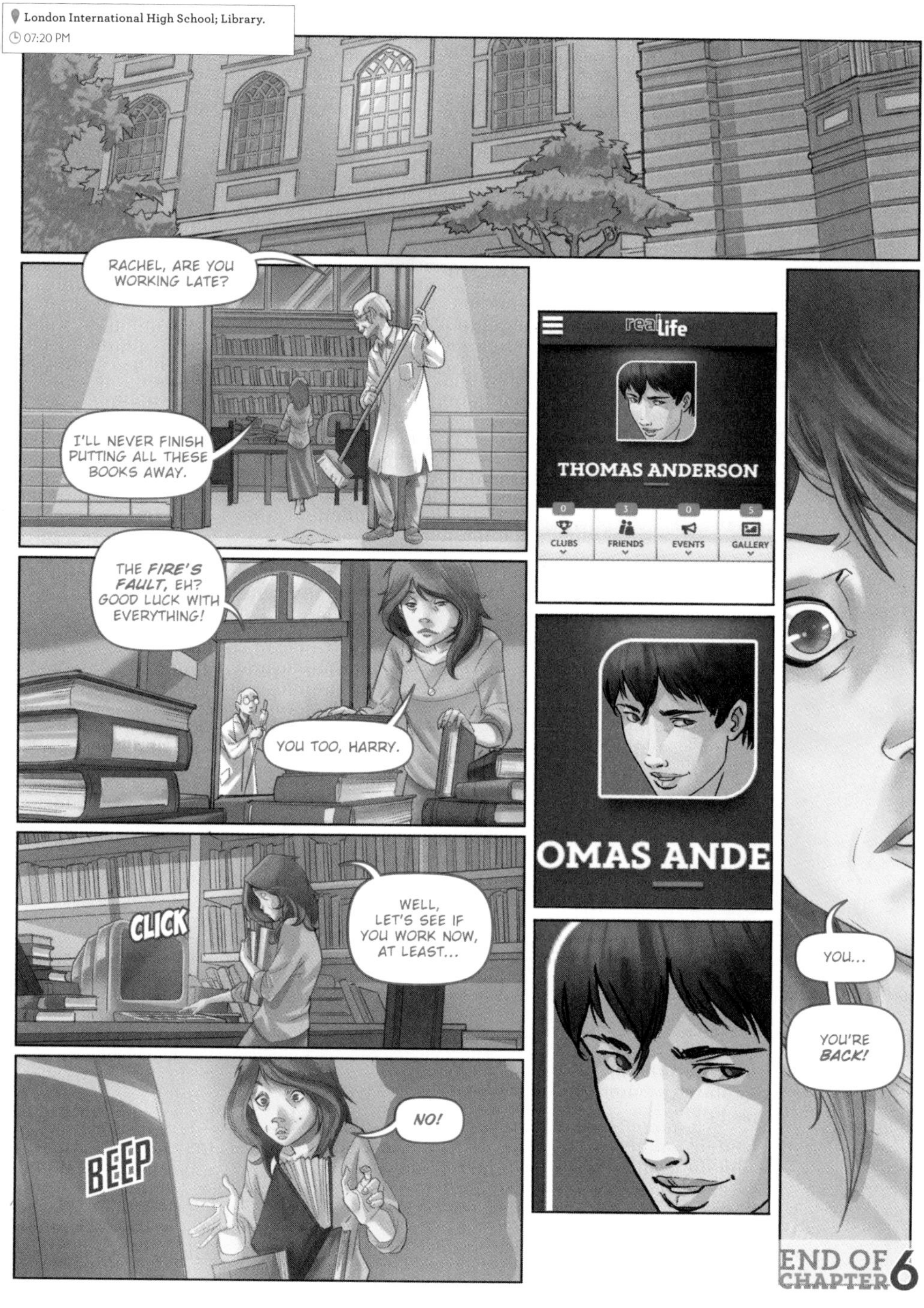
London International High School; Library.
07:20 PM
RACHEL, ARE YOU WORKING LATE?
I'LL NEVER FINISH PUTTING ALL THESE BOOKS AWAY.
THE *FIRE'S FAULT*, EH? GOOD LUCK WITH EVERYTHING!
YOU TOO, HARRY.
CLICK
WELL, LET'S SEE IF YOU WORK NOW, AT LEAST...
BEEP
NO!
realLife
THOMAS ANDERSON
0 CLUBS
3 FRIENDS
0 EVENTS
5 GALLERY
OMAS ANDE
YOU...
YOU'RE *BACK!*
END OF CHAPTER 6

Disney

reallife #2

#I'm Juliet

Script: Alessandro Ferrari
Layout: Alberto Zanon
Cleanup: Marco Failla
Emotidolls: Andrea Scoppetta
Color: Massimo Rocca, Pierluigi Casolino, Andrea Scoppetta, Mario Perrotta, Slava Panarin, Giuseppe Fontana, Gianluca Barone
Watercolor backgrounds: Valeria Turati
Translation: Edizioni BD and Erin Brady
Lettering and Infographic: Edizioni BD

COVER
Layout and cleanup: Alberto Zanon
Color: Massimo Rocca

CONTRIBUTORS
Tomatofarm

Original project developed by Disney Publishing with the contribution of Barbara Baraldi, Paola Barbato, Micol Beltramini and Diana Tomatozombie

#3

#Mission in Chinatown

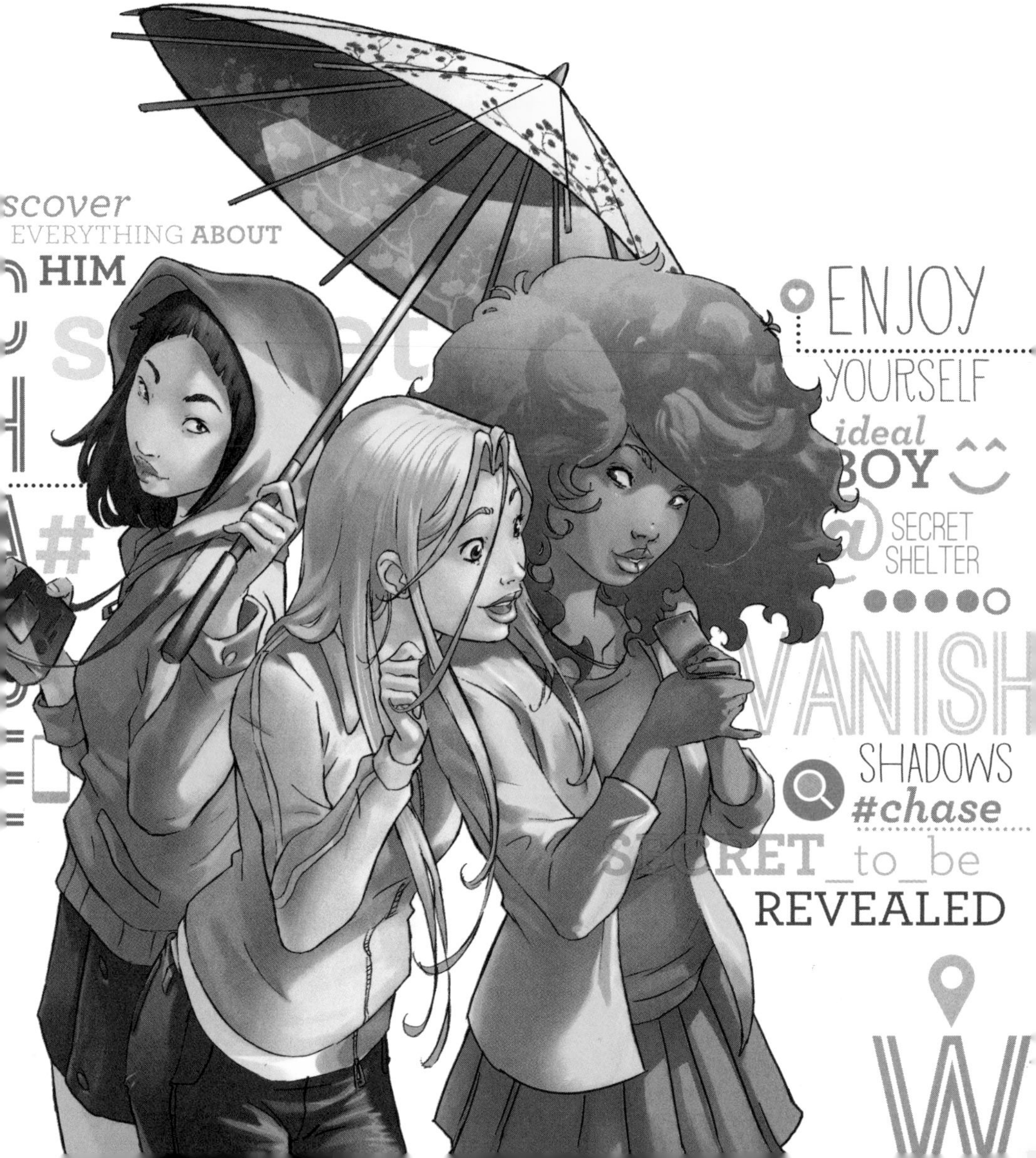
scover
EVERYTHING ABOUT
HIM
ENJOY
YOURSELF
ideal
BOY
SECRET
SHELTER
VANISH
SHADOWS
#chase
RET_to_be
REVEALED

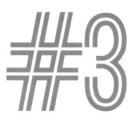

CHAPTER 7

A SECRET PLAN

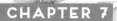

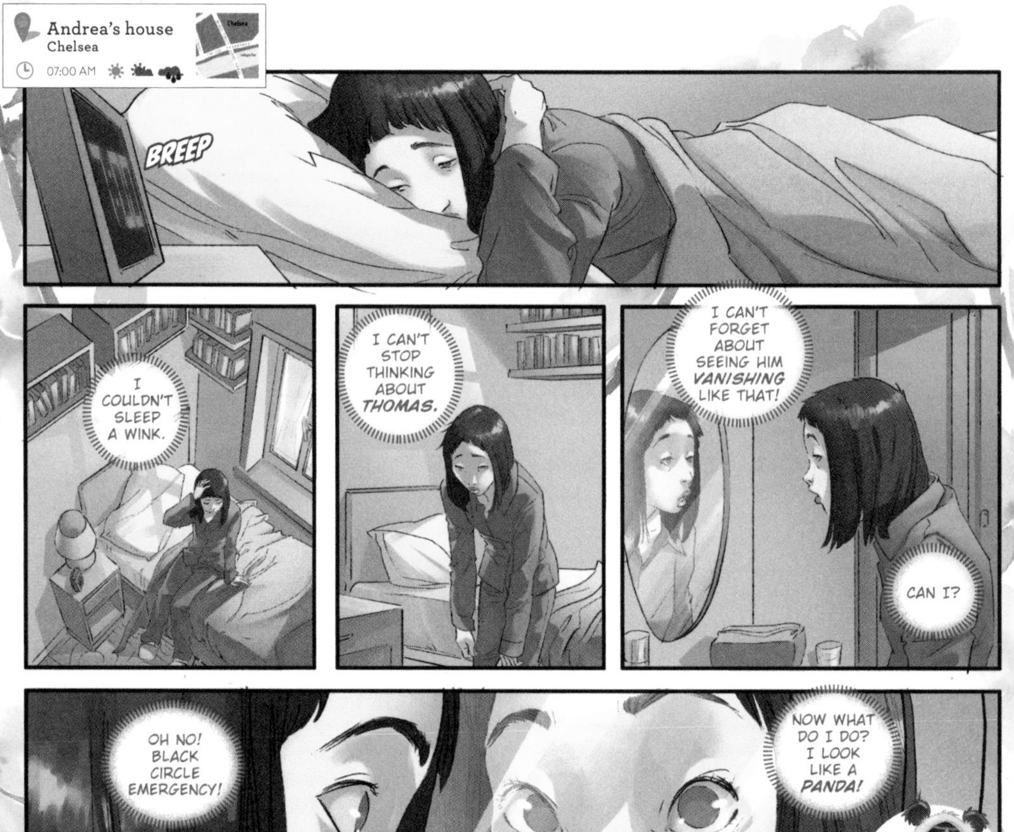
Andrea's house
Chelsea
07:00 AM
BREEP
I COULDN'T SLEEP A WINK.
I CAN'T STOP THINKING ABOUT THOMAS.
I CAN'T FORGET ABOUT SEEING HIM VANISHING LIKE THAT!
CAN I?
OH NO! BLACK CIRCLE EMERGENCY!
NOW WHAT DO I DO? I LOOK LIKE A PANDA!

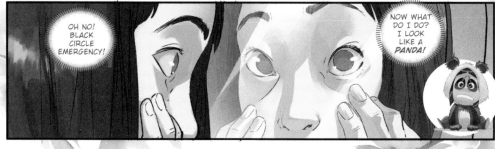

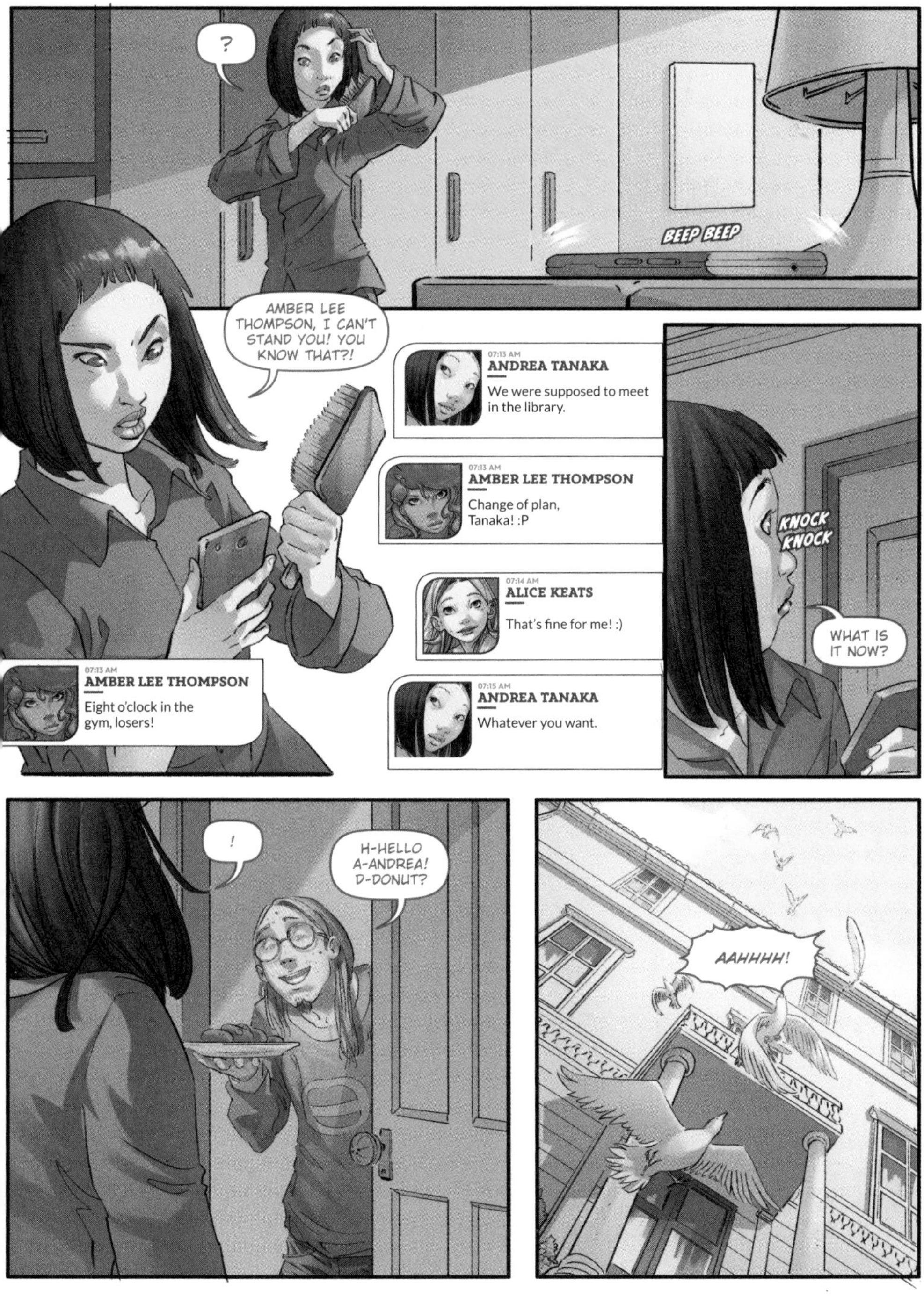
?
BEEP BEEP
AMBER LEE THOMPSON, I CAN'T STAND YOU! YOU KNOW THAT?!
07:13 AM
AMBER LEE THOMPSON
Eight o'clock in the gym, losers!
07:13 AM
ANDREA TANAKA
We were supposed to meet in the library.
07:13 AM
AMBER LEE THOMPSON
Change of plan, Tanaka! :P
07:14 AM
ALICE KEATS
That's fine for me! :)
07:15 AM
ANDREA TANAKA
Whatever you want.
KNOCK KNOCK
WHAT IS IT NOW?
!
H-HELLO A-ANDREA! D-DONUT?
AAHHHH!

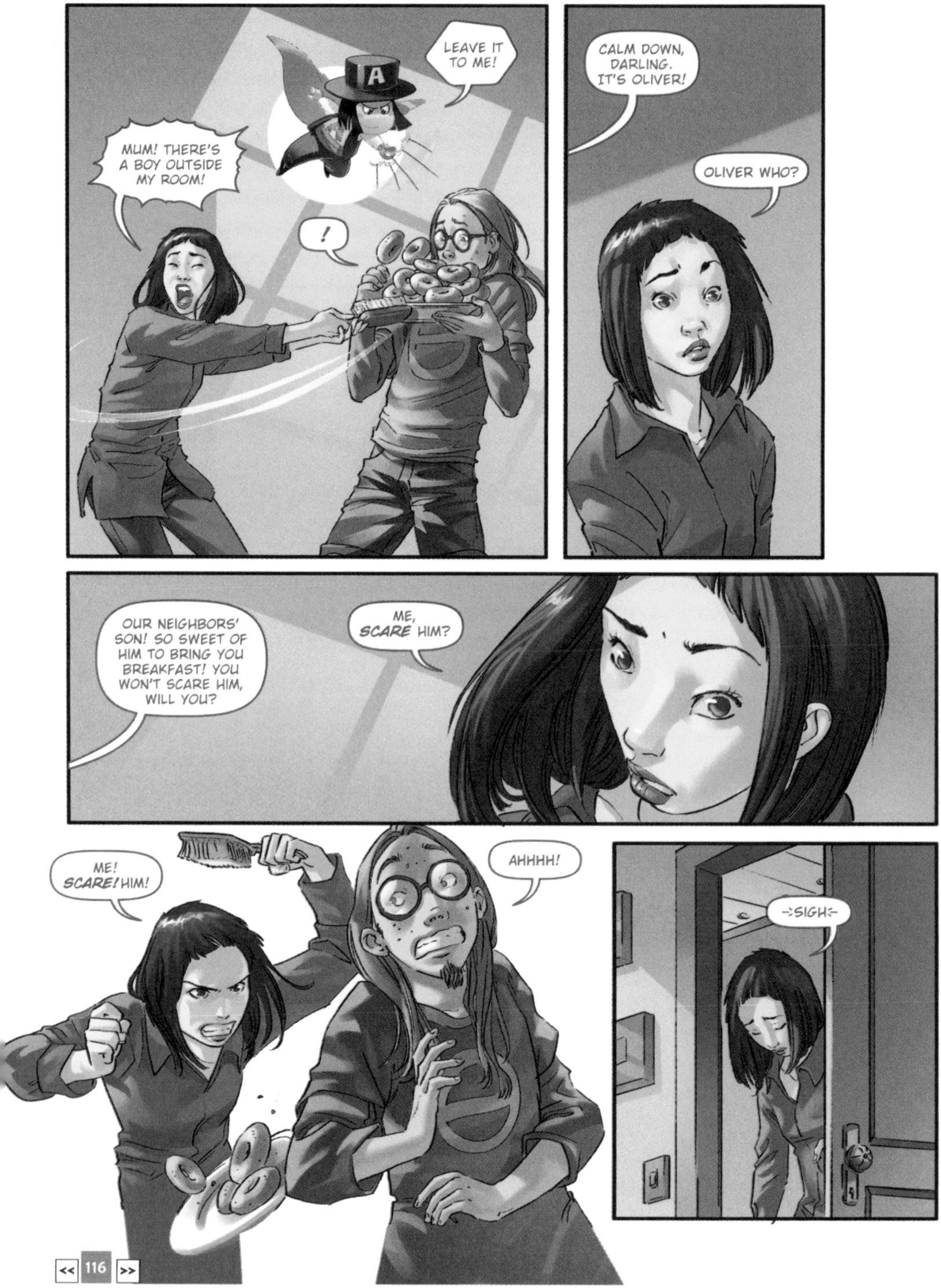
MUM! THERE'S A BOY OUTSIDE MY ROOM!
LEAVE IT TO ME!
A
!
CALM DOWN, DARLING. IT'S OLIVER!
OLIVER WHO?
OUR NEIGHBORS' SON! SO SWEET OF HIM TO BRING YOU BREAKFAST! YOU WON'T SCARE HIM, WILL YOU?
ME, SCARE HIM?
ME! SCARE! HIM!
AHHHH!
-SIGH-

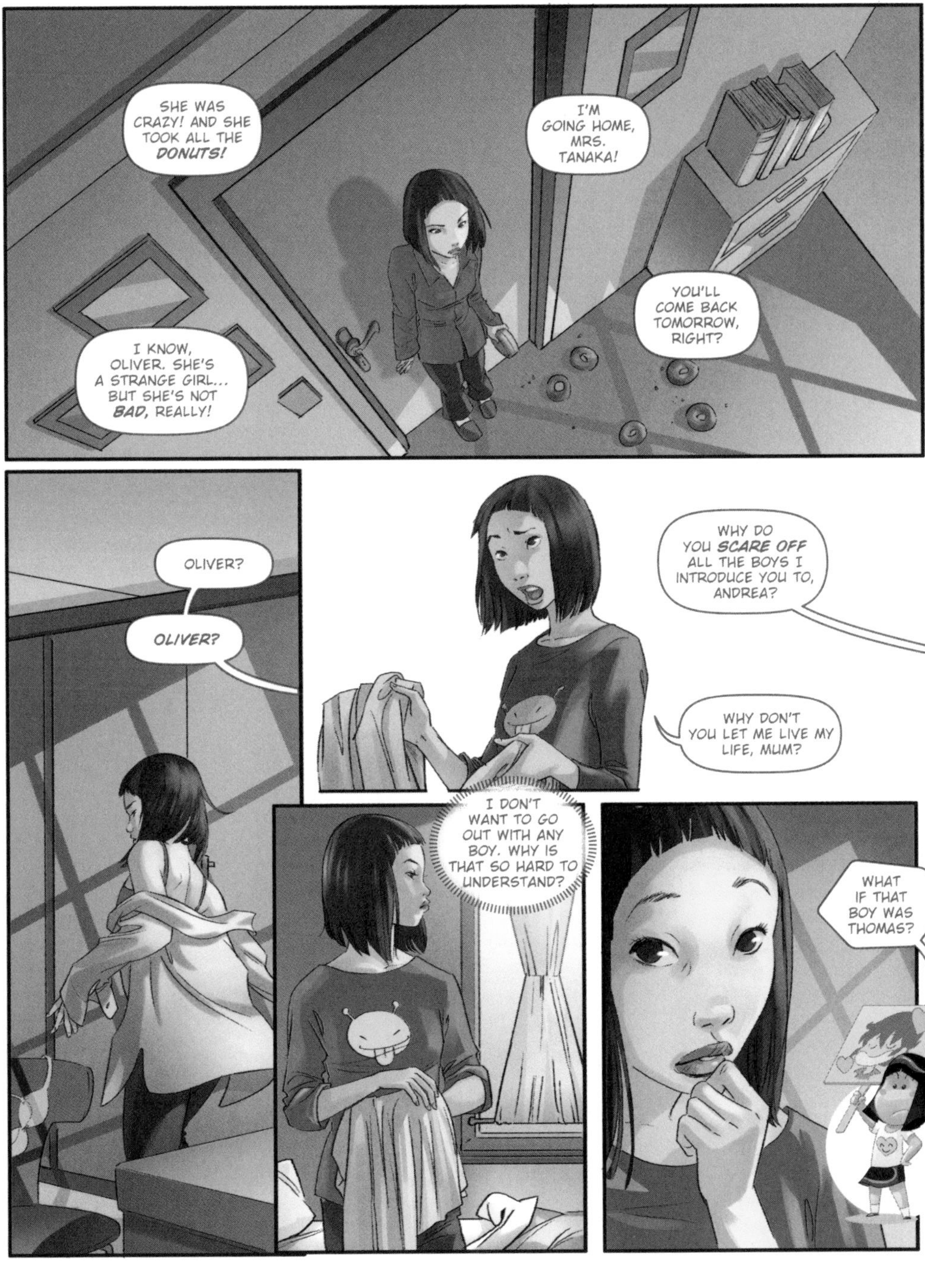
SHE WAS CRAZY! AND SHE TOOK ALL THE DONUTS!
I KNOW, OLIVER. SHE'S A STRANGE GIRL... BUT SHE'S NOT BAD, REALLY!
I'M GOING HOME, MRS. TANAKA!
YOU'LL COME BACK TOMORROW, RIGHT?
OLIVER?
OLIVER?
WHY DO YOU SCARE OFF ALL THE BOYS I INTRODUCE YOU TO, ANDREA?
WHY DON'T YOU LET ME LIVE MY LIFE, MUM?
I DON'T WANT TO GO OUT WITH ANY BOY. WHY IS THAT SO HARD TO UNDERSTAND?
WHAT IF THAT BOY WAS THOMAS?

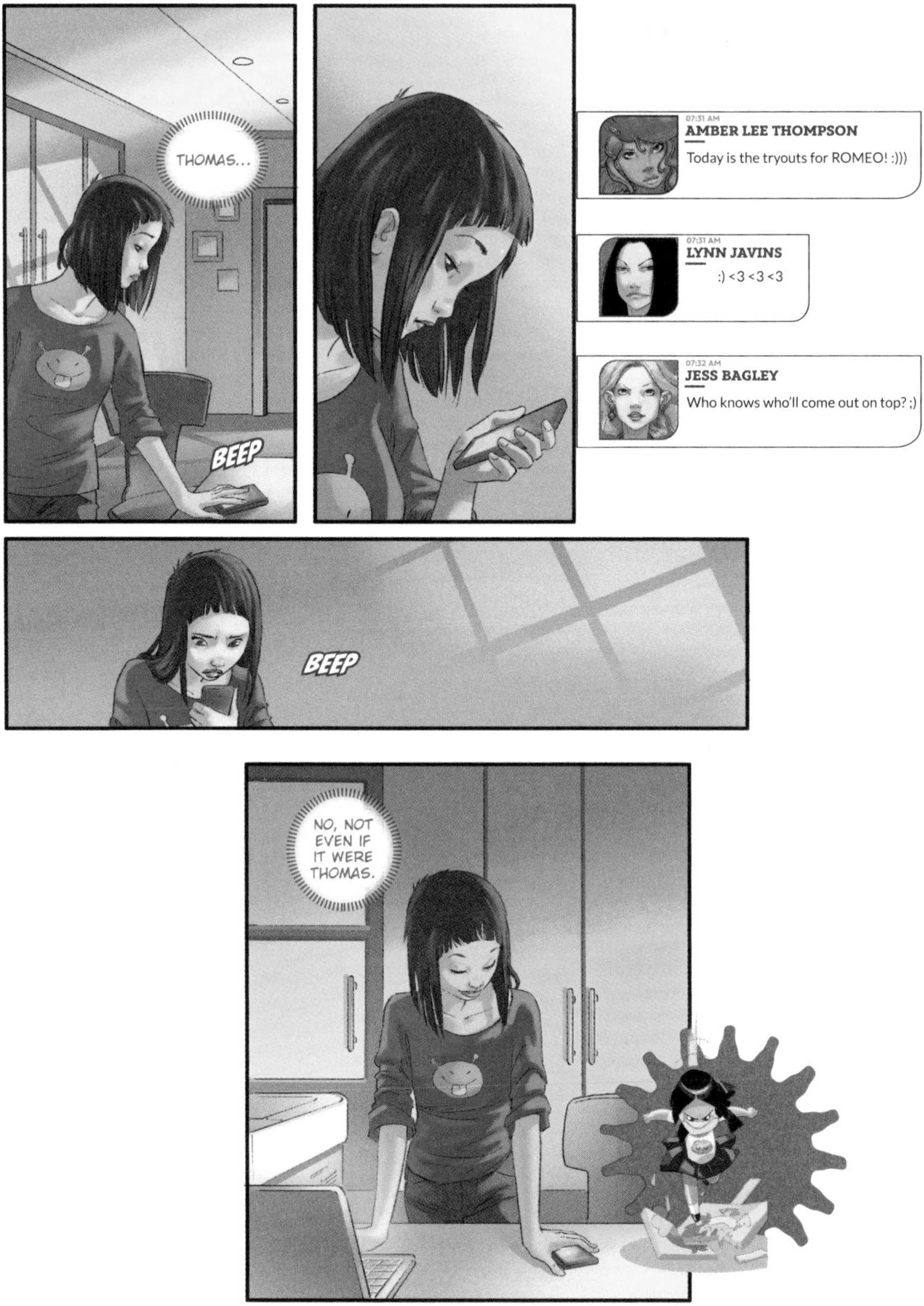
THOMAS...
BEEP
07:31 AM
AMBER LEE THOMPSON
Today is the tryouts for ROMEO! :)))
07:31 AM
LYNN JAVINS
:) <3 <3 <3
07:32 AM
JESS BAGLEY
Who knows who'll come out on top? ;)
BEEP
NO, NOT EVEN IF IT WERE THOMAS.

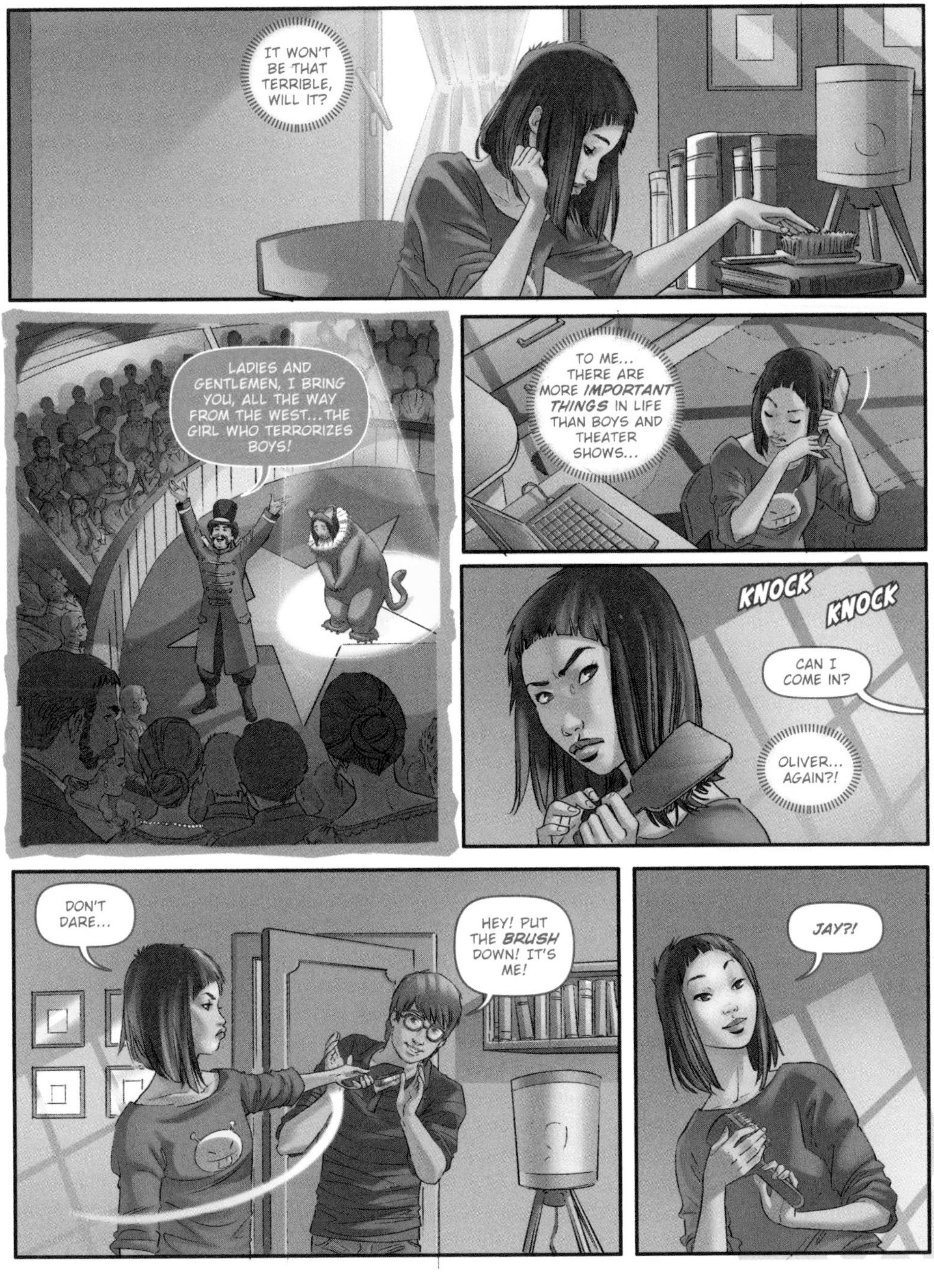
IT WON'T BE THAT TERRIBLE, WILL IT?
LADIES AND GENTLEMEN, I BRING YOU, ALL THE WAY FROM THE WEST...THE GIRL WHO TERRORIZES BOYS!
TO ME... THERE ARE MORE IMPORTANT THINGS IN LIFE THAN BOYS AND THEATER SHOWS...
KNOCK
KNOCK
CAN I COME IN?
OLIVER... AGAIN?!
DON'T DARE...
HEY! PUT THE BRUSH DOWN! IT'S ME!
JAY?!

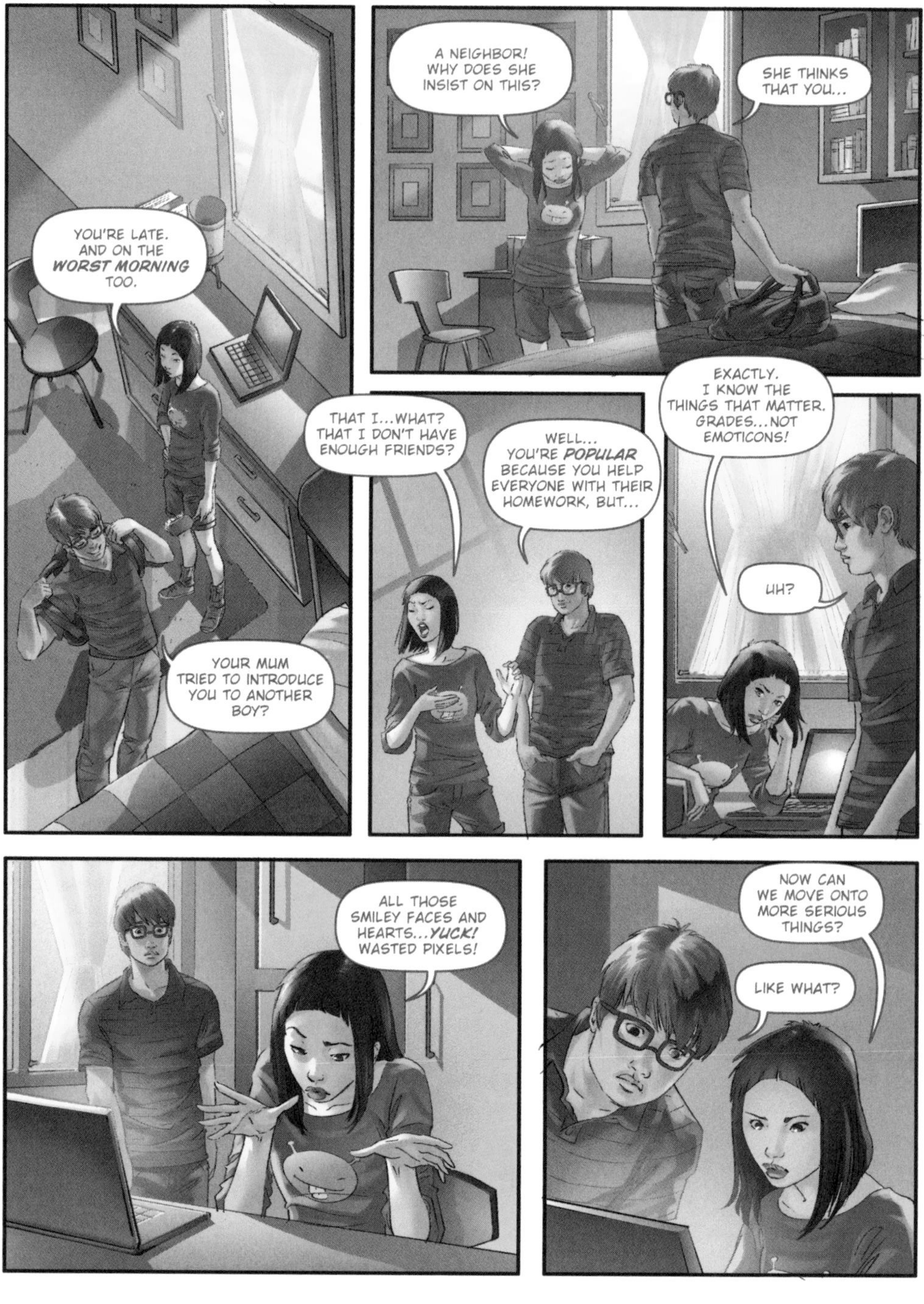
YOU'RE LATE. AND ON THE **WORST MORNING** TOO.
YOUR MUM TRIED TO INTRODUCE YOU TO ANOTHER BOY?
A NEIGHBOR! WHY DOES SHE INSIST ON THIS?
SHE THINKS THAT YOU...
THAT I...WHAT? THAT I DON'T HAVE ENOUGH FRIENDS?
WELL... YOU'RE **POPULAR** BECAUSE YOU HELP EVERYONE WITH THEIR HOMEWORK, BUT...
EXACTLY. I KNOW THE THINGS THAT MATTER. GRADES...NOT EMOTICONS!
UH?
ALL THOSE SMILEY FACES AND HEARTS...**YUCK!** WASTED PIXELS!
NOW CAN WE MOVE ONTO MORE SERIOUS THINGS?
LIKE WHAT?

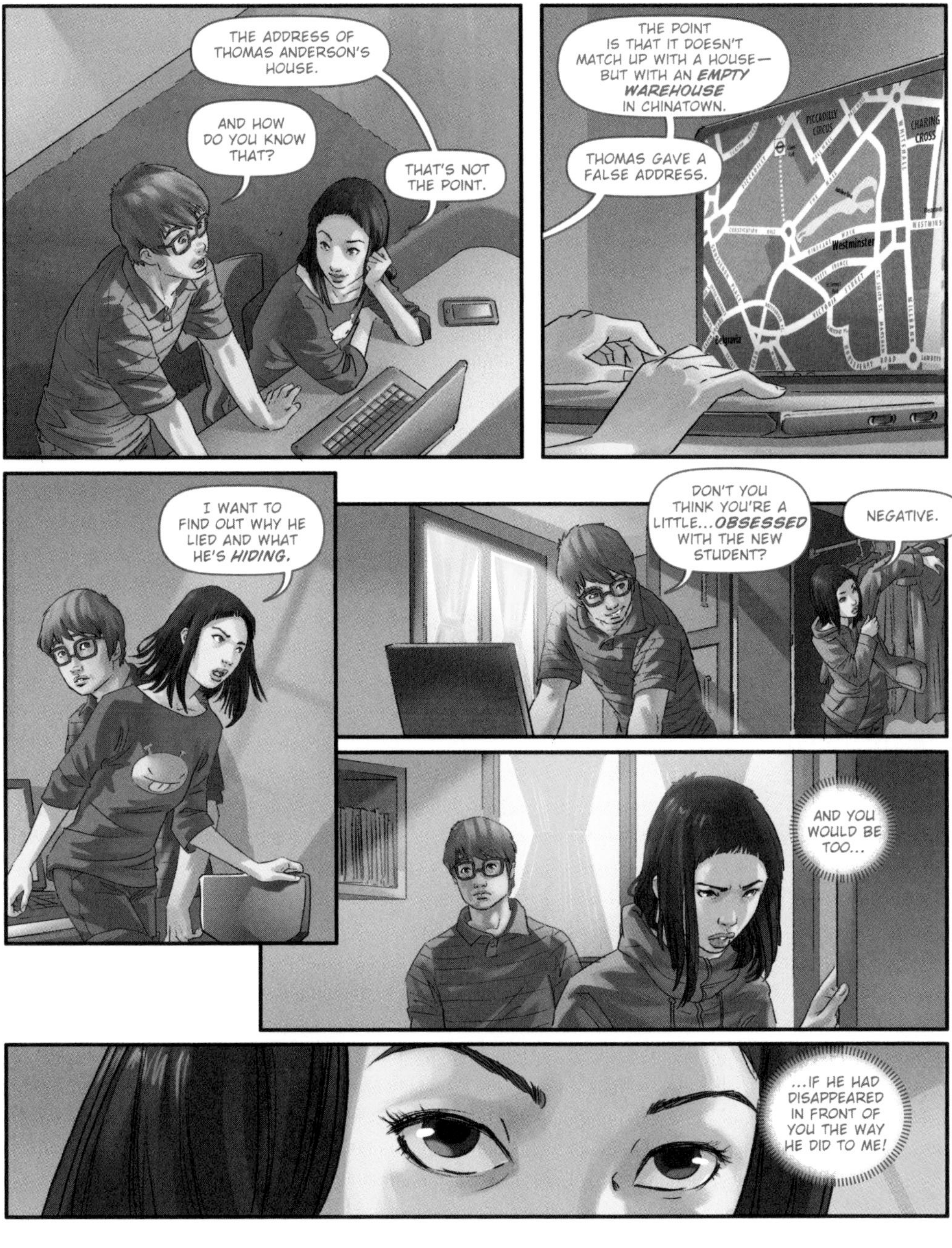
THE ADDRESS OF THOMAS ANDERSON'S HOUSE.
AND HOW DO YOU KNOW THAT?
THAT'S NOT THE POINT.
THE POINT IS THAT IT DOESN'T MATCH UP WITH A HOUSE— BUT WITH AN ***EMPTY WAREHOUSE*** IN CHINATOWN.
THOMAS GAVE A FALSE ADDRESS.
PICCADILLY CIRCUS
CHARING CROSS
Westminster
Belgravia
I WANT TO FIND OUT WHY HE LIED AND WHAT HE'S ***HIDING.***
DON'T YOU THINK YOU'RE A LITTLE...***OBSESSED*** WITH THE NEW STUDENT?
NEGATIVE.
AND YOU WOULD BE TOO...
...IF HE HAD DISAPPEARED IN FRONT OF YOU THE WAY HE DID TO ME!

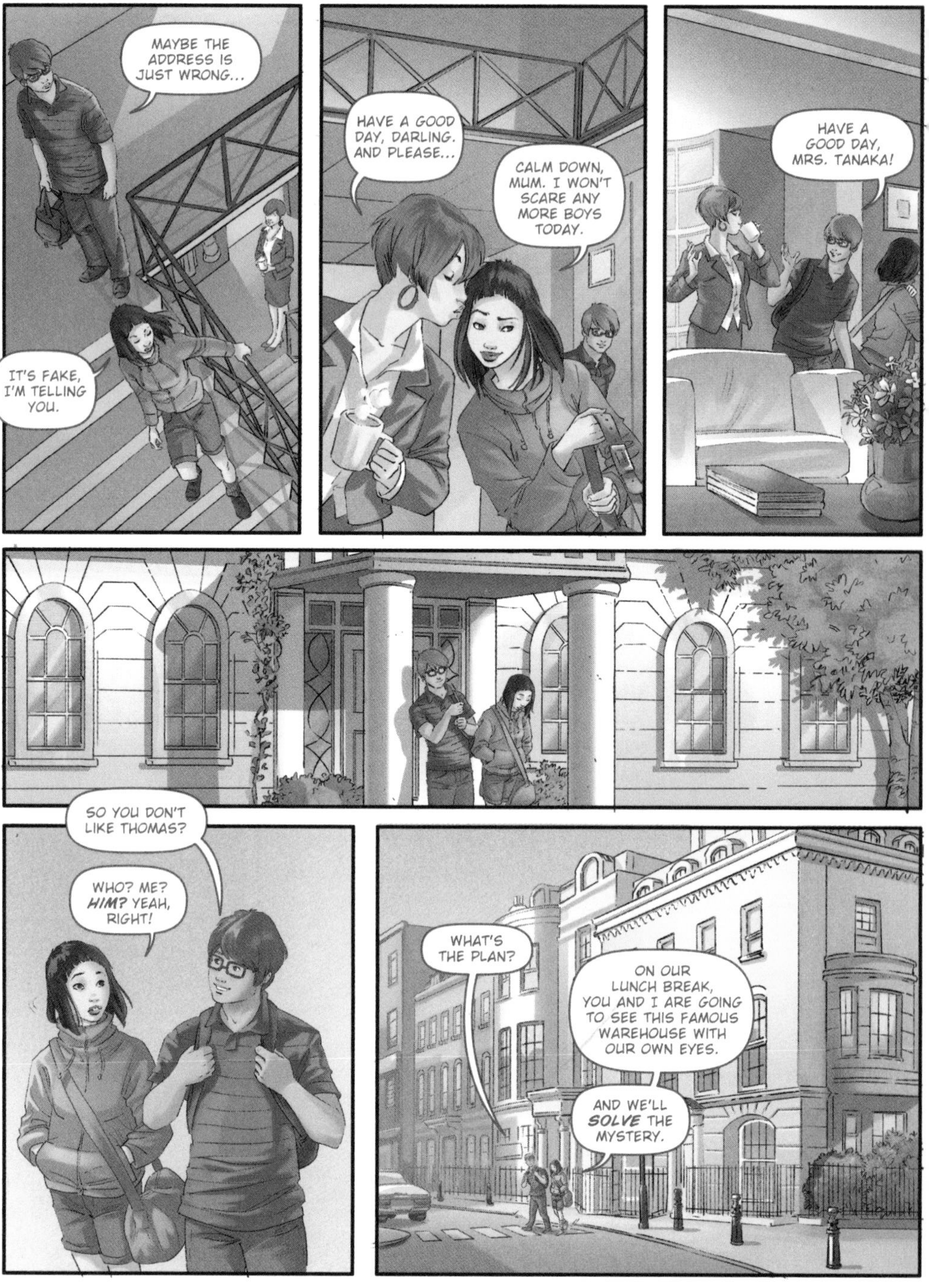
MAYBE THE ADDRESS IS JUST WRONG...
IT'S FAKE, I'M TELLING YOU.
HAVE A GOOD DAY, DARLING. AND PLEASE...
CALM DOWN, MUM. I WON'T SCARE ANY MORE BOYS TODAY.
HAVE A GOOD DAY, MRS. TANAKA!
SO YOU DON'T LIKE THOMAS?
WHO? ME? ***HIM?*** YEAH, RIGHT!
WHAT'S THE PLAN?
ON OUR LUNCH BREAK, YOU AND I ARE GOING TO SEE THIS FAMOUS WAREHOUSE WITH OUR OWN EYES.
AND WE'LL ***SOLVE*** THE MYSTERY.

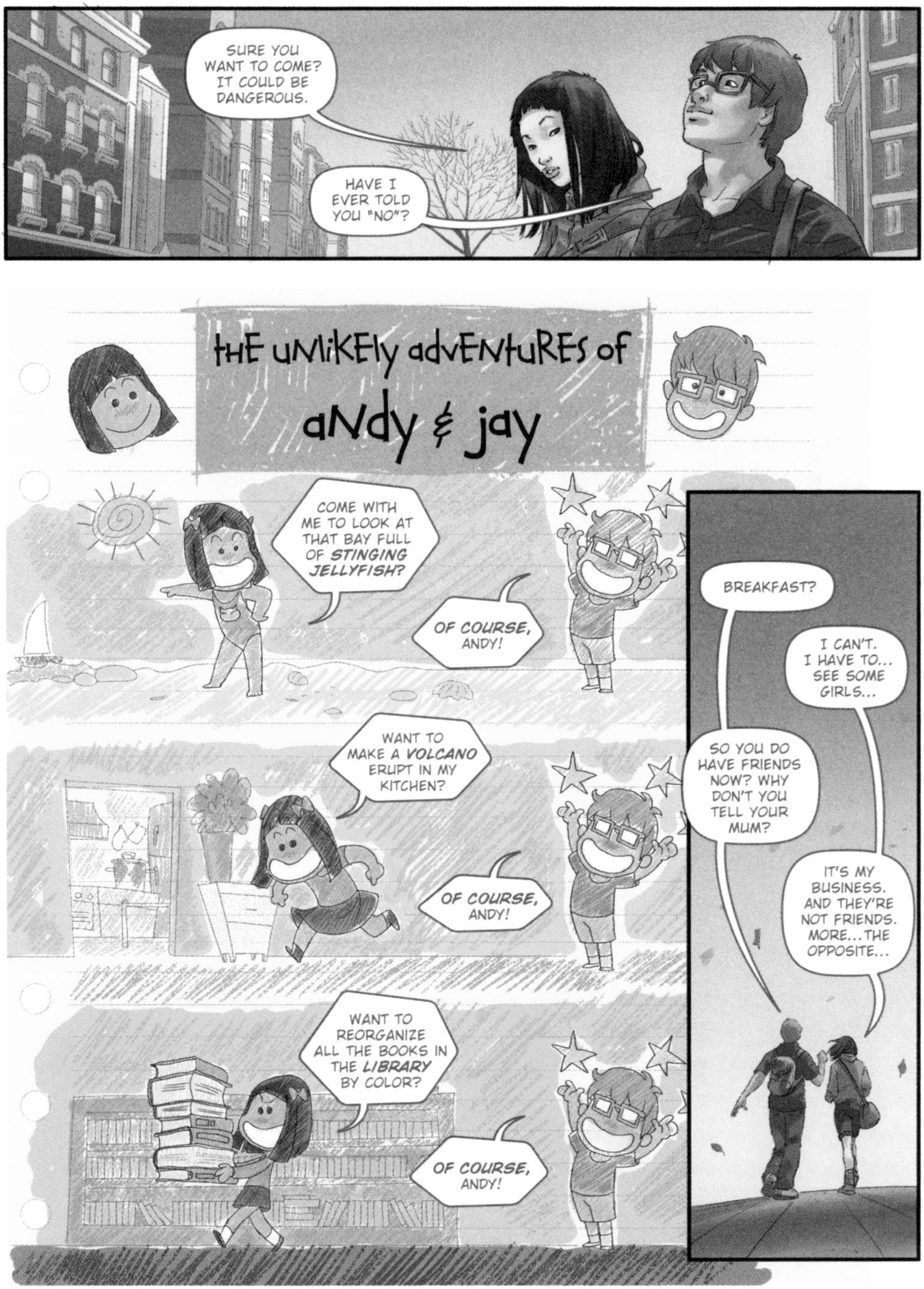
SURE YOU WANT TO COME? IT COULD BE DANGEROUS.
HAVE I EVER TOLD YOU "NO"?
THE UNLIKELY ADVENTURES OF ANDY & JAY
COME WITH ME TO LOOK AT THAT BAY FULL OF STINGING JELLYFISH?
OF COURSE, ANDY!
WANT TO MAKE A VOLCANO ERUPT IN MY KITCHEN?
OF COURSE, ANDY!
WANT TO REORGANIZE ALL THE BOOKS IN THE LIBRARY BY COLOR?
OF COURSE, ANDY!
BREAKFAST?
I CAN'T. I HAVE TO... SEE SOME GIRLS...
SO YOU DO HAVE FRIENDS NOW? WHY DON'T YOU TELL YOUR MUM?
IT'S MY BUSINESS. AND THEY'RE NOT FRIENDS. MORE...THE OPPOSITE...

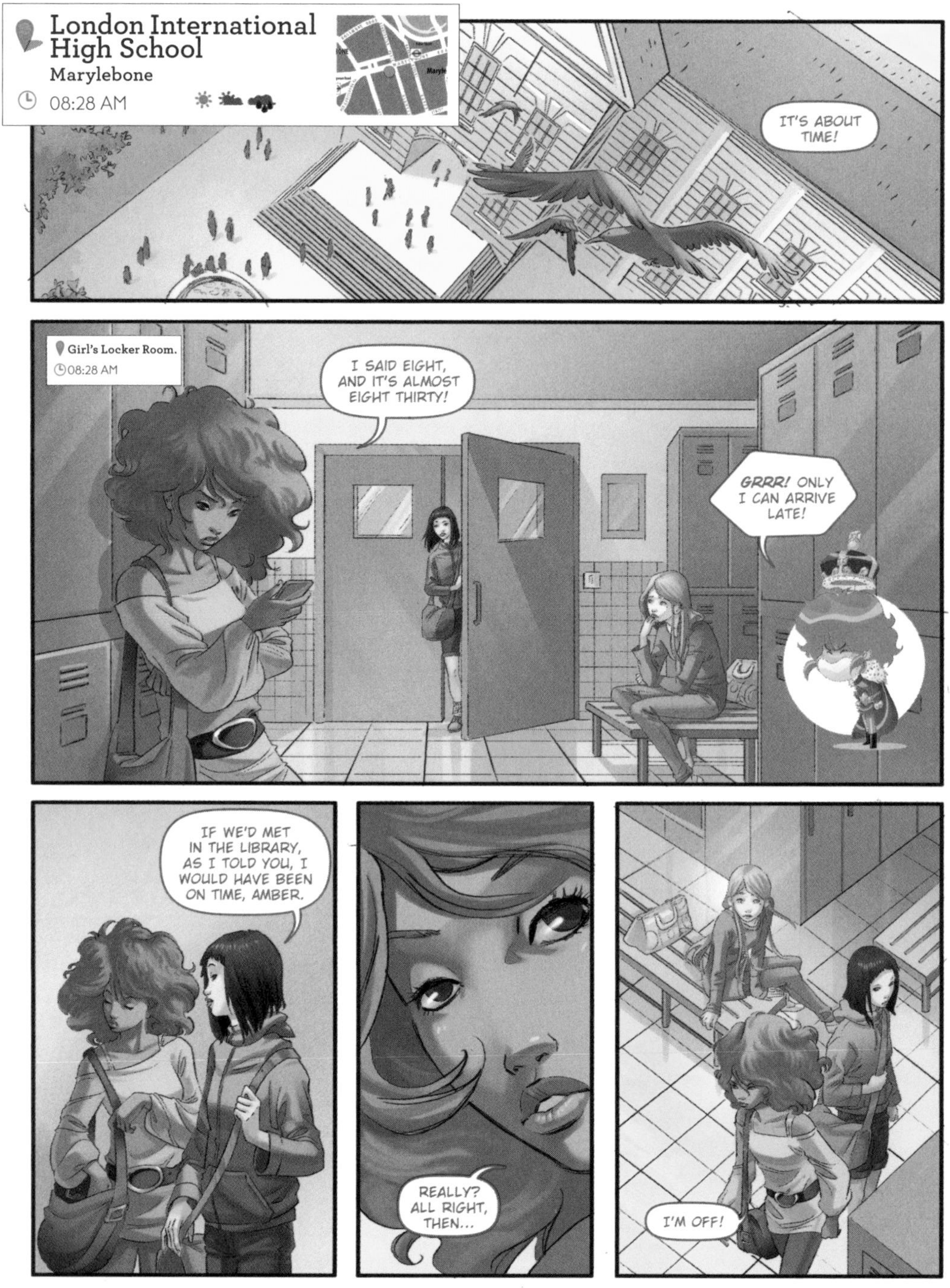
London International High School
Marylebone
08:28 AM
IT'S ABOUT TIME!
Girl's Locker Room.
08:28 AM
I SAID EIGHT, AND IT'S ALMOST EIGHT THIRTY!
GRRR! ONLY I CAN ARRIVE LATE!
IF WE'D MET IN THE LIBRARY, AS I TOLD YOU, I WOULD HAVE BEEN ON TIME, AMBER.
REALLY? ALL RIGHT, THEN...
I'M OFF!

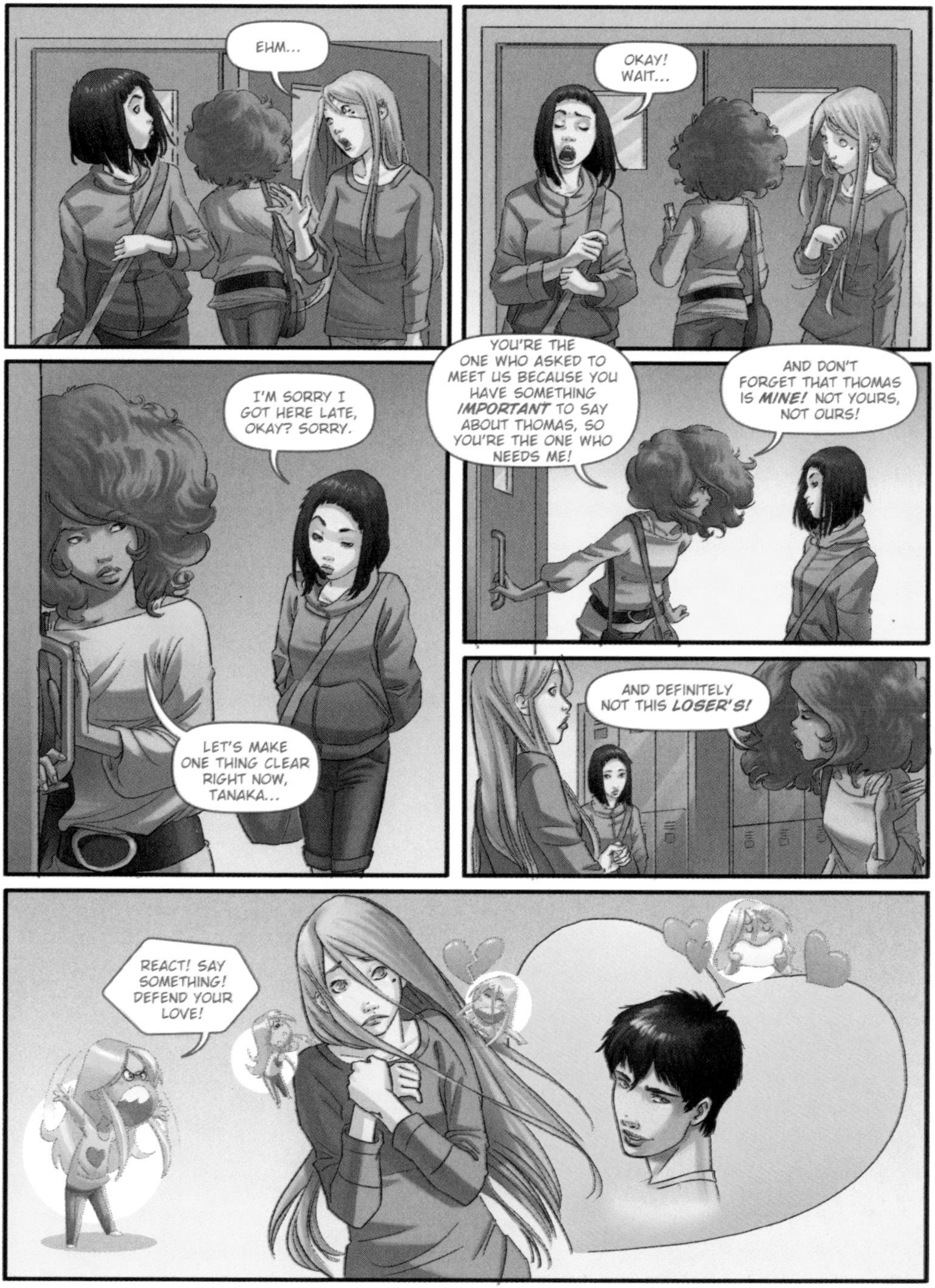
EHM...
OKAY! WAIT...
I'M SORRY I GOT HERE LATE, OKAY? SORRY.
LET'S MAKE ONE THING CLEAR RIGHT NOW, TANAKA...
YOU'RE THE ONE WHO ASKED TO MEET US BECAUSE YOU HAVE SOMETHING IMPORTANT TO SAY ABOUT THOMAS, SO YOU'RE THE ONE WHO NEEDS ME!
AND DON'T FORGET THAT THOMAS IS MINE! NOT YOURS, NOT OURS!
AND DEFINITELY NOT THIS LOSER'S!
REACT! SAY SOMETHING! DEFEND YOUR LOVE!

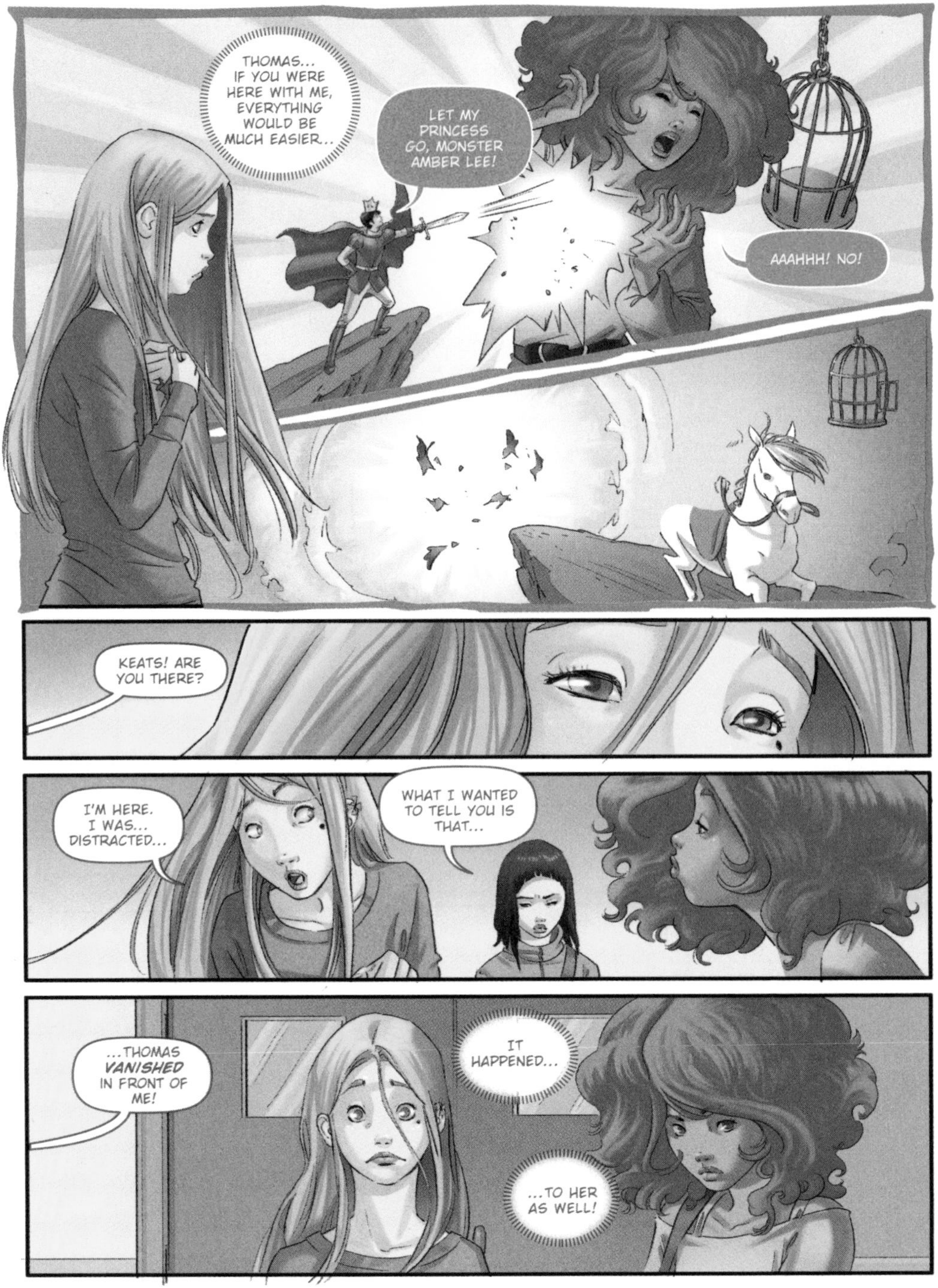
THOMAS... IF YOU WERE HERE WITH ME, EVERYTHING WOULD BE MUCH EASIER...
LET MY PRINCESS GO, MONSTER AMBER LEE!
AAAHHH! NO!
KEATS! ARE YOU THERE?
I'M HERE. I WAS... DISTRACTED...
WHAT I WANTED TO TELL YOU IS THAT...
...THOMAS VANISHED IN FRONT OF ME!
IT HAPPENED...
...TO HER AS WELL!

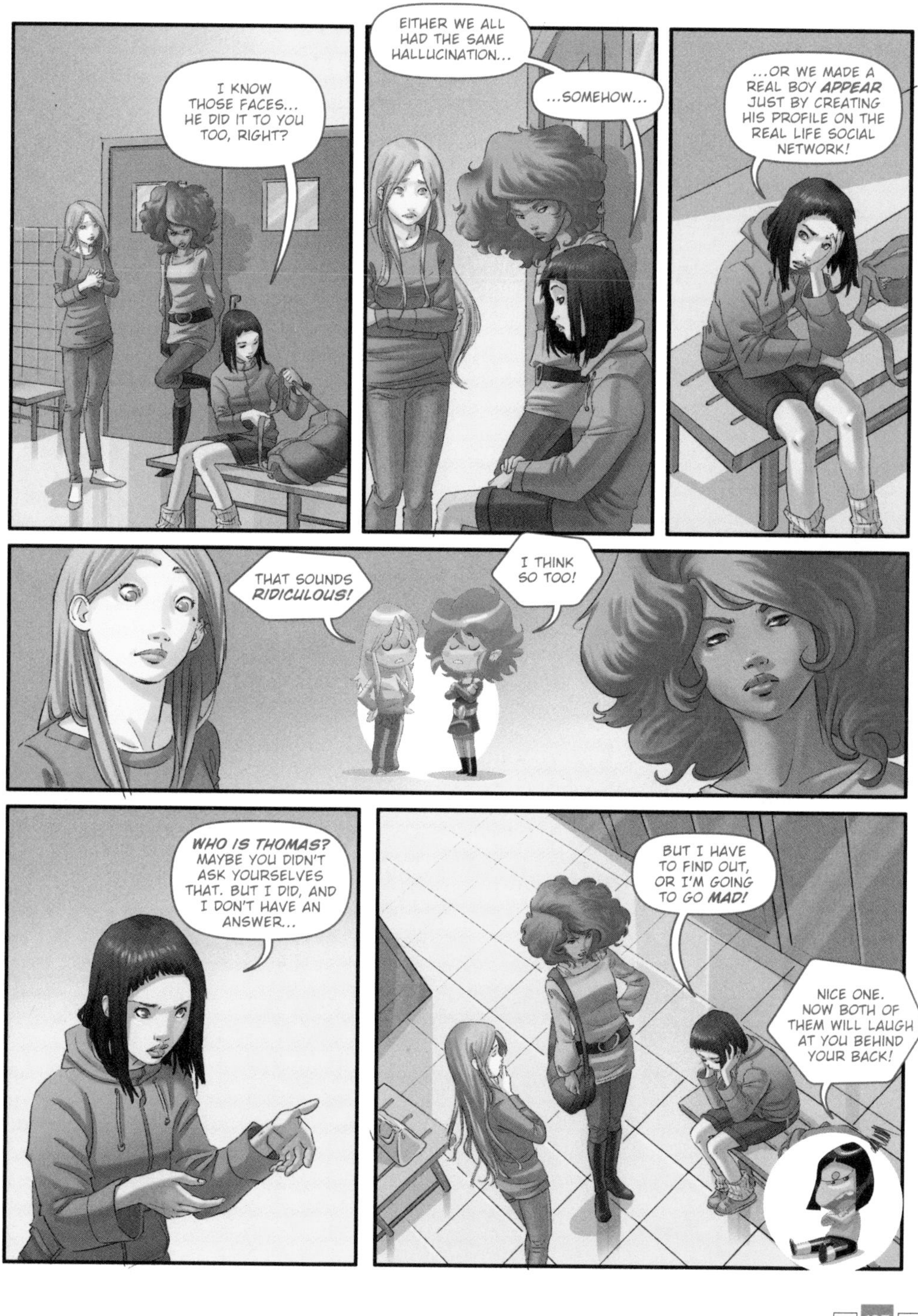
I KNOW THOSE FACES... HE DID IT TO YOU TOO, RIGHT?
EITHER WE ALL HAD THE SAME HALLUCINATION...
...SOMEHOW...
...OR WE MADE A REAL BOY APPEAR JUST BY CREATING HIS PROFILE ON THE REAL LIFE SOCIAL NETWORK!
THAT SOUNDS RIDICULOUS!
I THINK SO TOO!
WHO IS THOMAS? MAYBE YOU DIDN'T ASK YOURSELVES THAT. BUT I DID, AND I DON'T HAVE AN ANSWER...
BUT I HAVE TO FIND OUT, OR I'M GOING TO GO MAD!
NICE ONE. NOW BOTH OF THEM WILL LAUGH AT YOU BEHIND YOUR BACK!

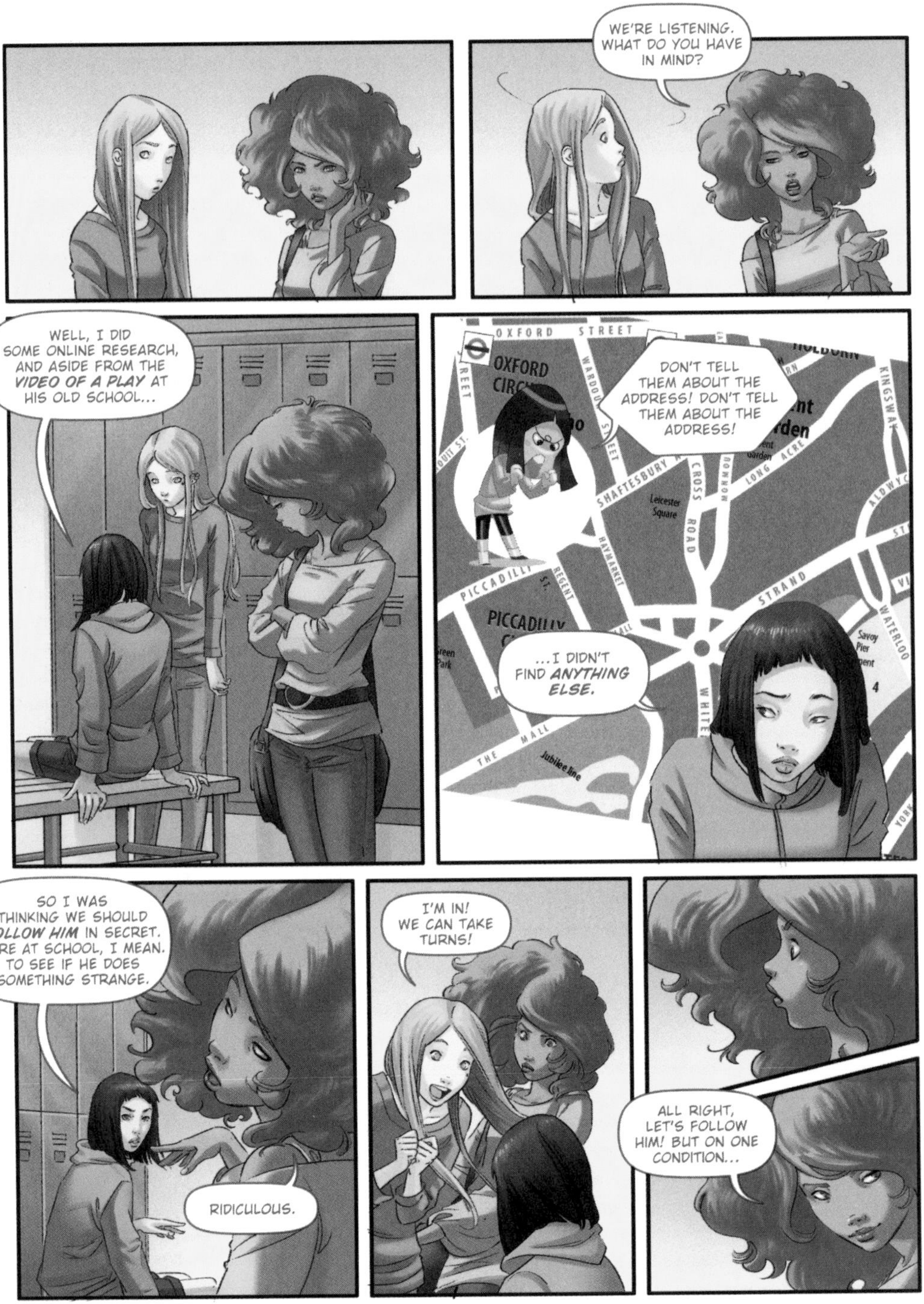

WE'RE LISTENING. WHAT DO YOU HAVE IN MIND?
WELL, I DID SOME ONLINE RESEARCH, AND ASIDE FROM THE **VIDEO OF A PLAY** AT HIS OLD SCHOOL...
OXFORD STREET
DON'T TELL THEM ABOUT THE ADDRESS! DON'T TELL THEM ABOUT THE ADDRESS!
SHAFTESBURY
Leicester Square
CROSS ROAD
LONG ACRE
HAYMARKET
PICCADILLY
REGENT
STRAND
WATERLOO
Savoy Pier
THE MALL
Jubilee line
...I DIDN'T FIND **ANYTHING ELSE.**
SO I WAS THINKING WE SHOULD **FOLLOW HIM** IN SECRET. HERE AT SCHOOL, I MEAN. TO SEE IF HE DOES SOMETHING STRANGE.
RIDICULOUS.
I'M IN! WE CAN TAKE TURNS!
ALL RIGHT, LET'S FOLLOW HIM! BUT ON ONE CONDITION...

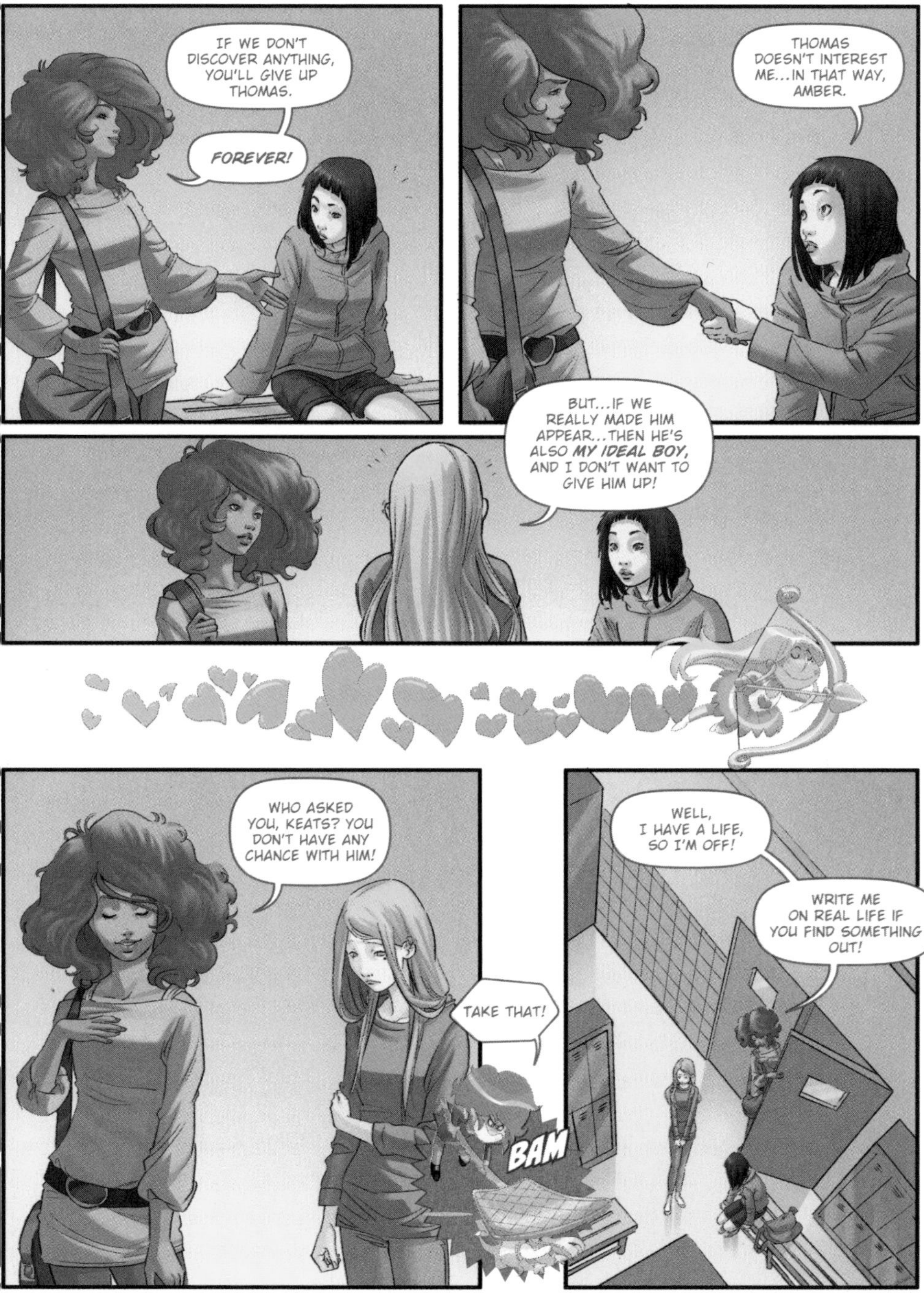
IF WE DON'T DISCOVER ANYTHING, YOU'LL GIVE UP THOMAS.
FOREVER!
THOMAS DOESN'T INTEREST ME...IN THAT WAY, AMBER.
BUT...IF WE REALLY MADE HIM APPEAR...THEN HE'S ALSO MY IDEAL BOY, AND I DON'T WANT TO GIVE HIM UP!
WHO ASKED YOU, KEATS? YOU DON'T HAVE ANY CHANCE WITH HIM!
TAKE THAT!
BAM
WELL, I HAVE A LIFE, SO I'M OFF!
WRITE ME ON REAL LIFE IF YOU FIND SOMETHING OUT!

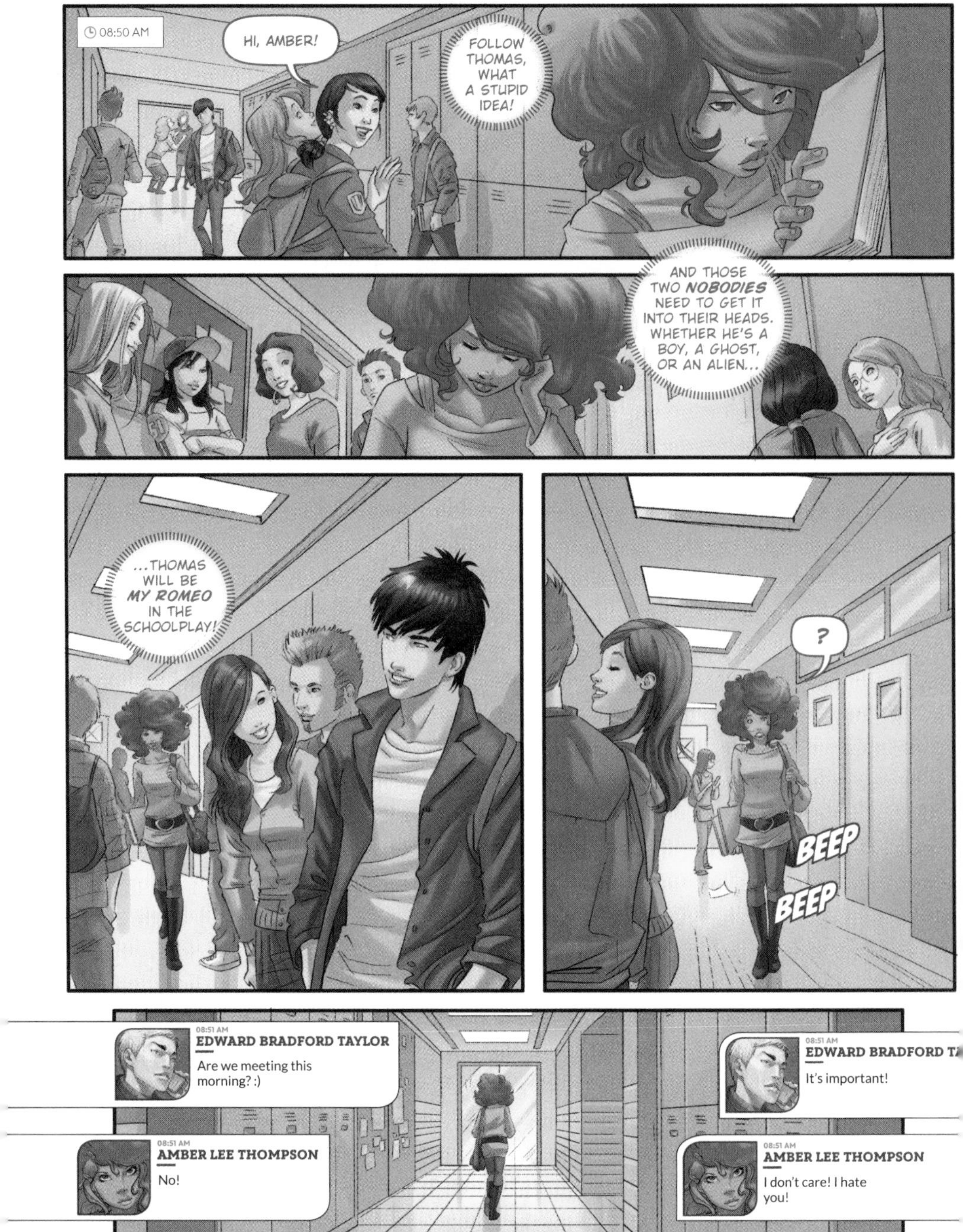
08:50 AM
HI, AMBER!
FOLLOW THOMAS, WHAT A STUPID IDEA!
AND THOSE TWO NOBODIES NEED TO GET IT INTO THEIR HEADS. WHETHER HE'S A BOY, A GHOST, OR AN ALIEN...
...THOMAS WILL BE MY ROMEO IN THE SCHOOLPLAY!
?
BEEP
BEEP
08:51 AM
EDWARD BRADFORD TAYLOR
Are we meeting this morning? :)
08:51 AM
EDWARD BRADFORD TA
It's important!
08:51 AM
AMBER LEE THOMPSON
No!
08:51 AM
AMBER LEE THOMPSON
I don't care! I hate you!

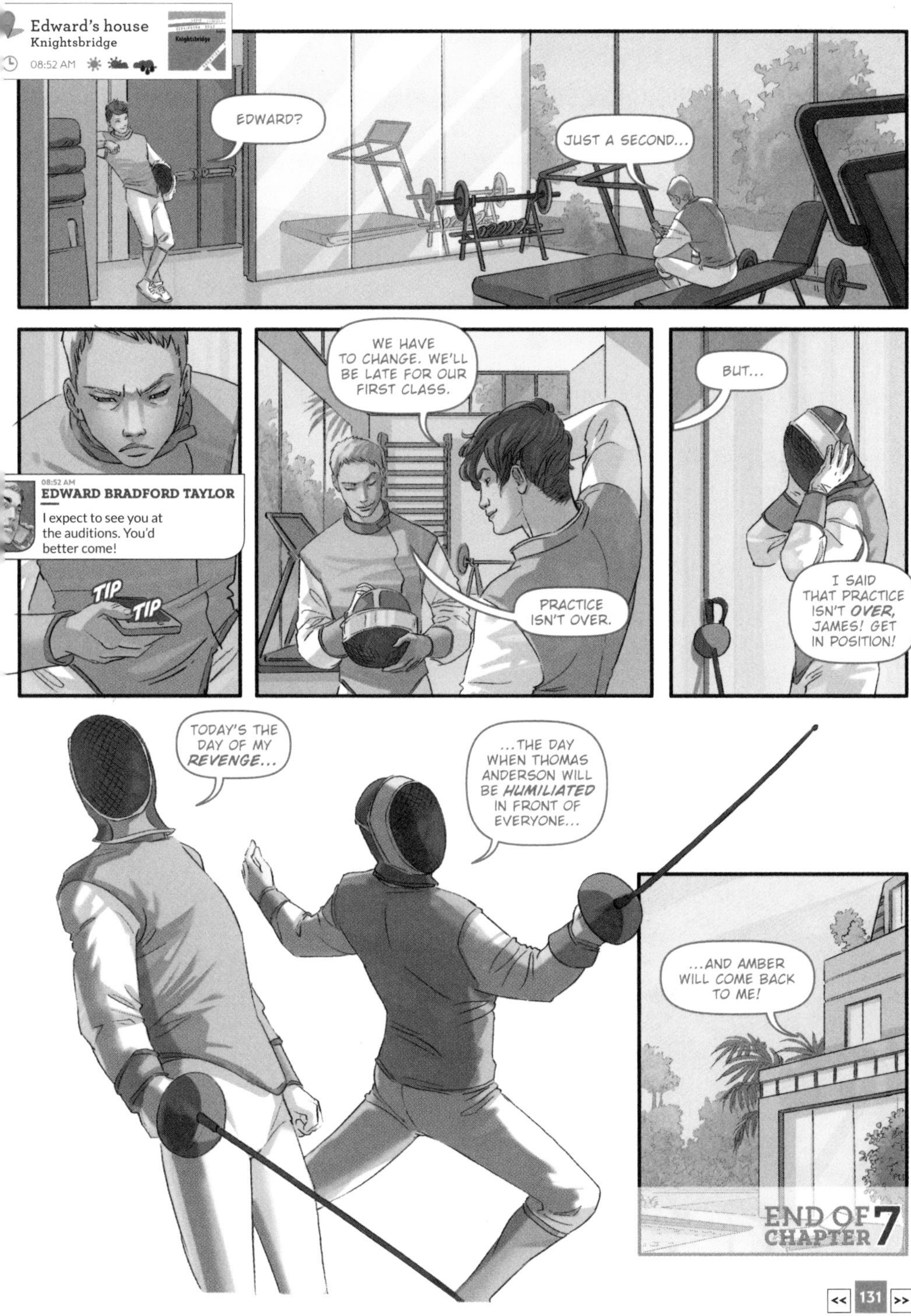

Edward's house
Knightsbridge
08:52 AM
Knightsbridge
EDWARD?
JUST A SECOND...
08:52 AM
EDWARD BRADFORD TAYLOR
I expect to see you at the auditions. You'd better come!
TIP
TIP
WE HAVE TO CHANGE. WE'LL BE LATE FOR OUR FIRST CLASS.
PRACTICE ISN'T OVER.
BUT...
I SAID THAT PRACTICE ISN'T OVER, JAMES! GET IN POSITION!
TODAY'S THE DAY OF MY REVENGE...
...THE DAY WHEN THOMAS ANDERSON WILL BE HUMILIATED IN FRONT OF EVERYONE...
...AND AMBER WILL COME BACK TO ME!
END OF CHAPTER 7

CHAPTER 8

MYSTERY out of town

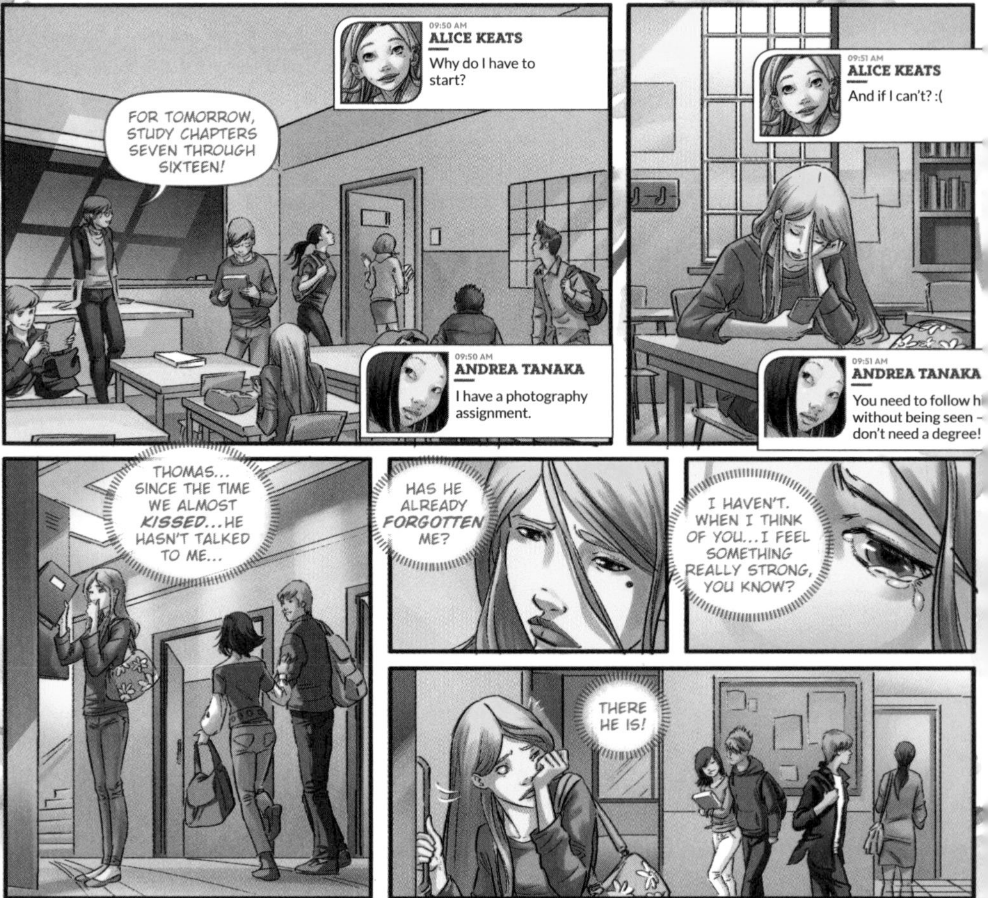

09:50 AM
ALICE KEATS
Why do I have to start?
FOR TOMORROW, STUDY CHAPTERS SEVEN THROUGH SIXTEEN!
09:50 AM
ANDREA TANAKA
I have a photography assignment.
09:51 AM
ALICE KEATS
And if I can't? :(
09:51 AM
ANDREA TANAKA
You need to follow h
without being seen –
don't need a degree!
THOMAS... SINCE THE TIME WE ALMOST KISSED...HE HASN'T TALKED TO ME...
HAS HE ALREADY FORGOTTEN ME?
I HAVEN'T. WHEN I THINK OF YOU...I FEEL SOMETHING REALLY STRONG, YOU KNOW?
THERE HE IS!

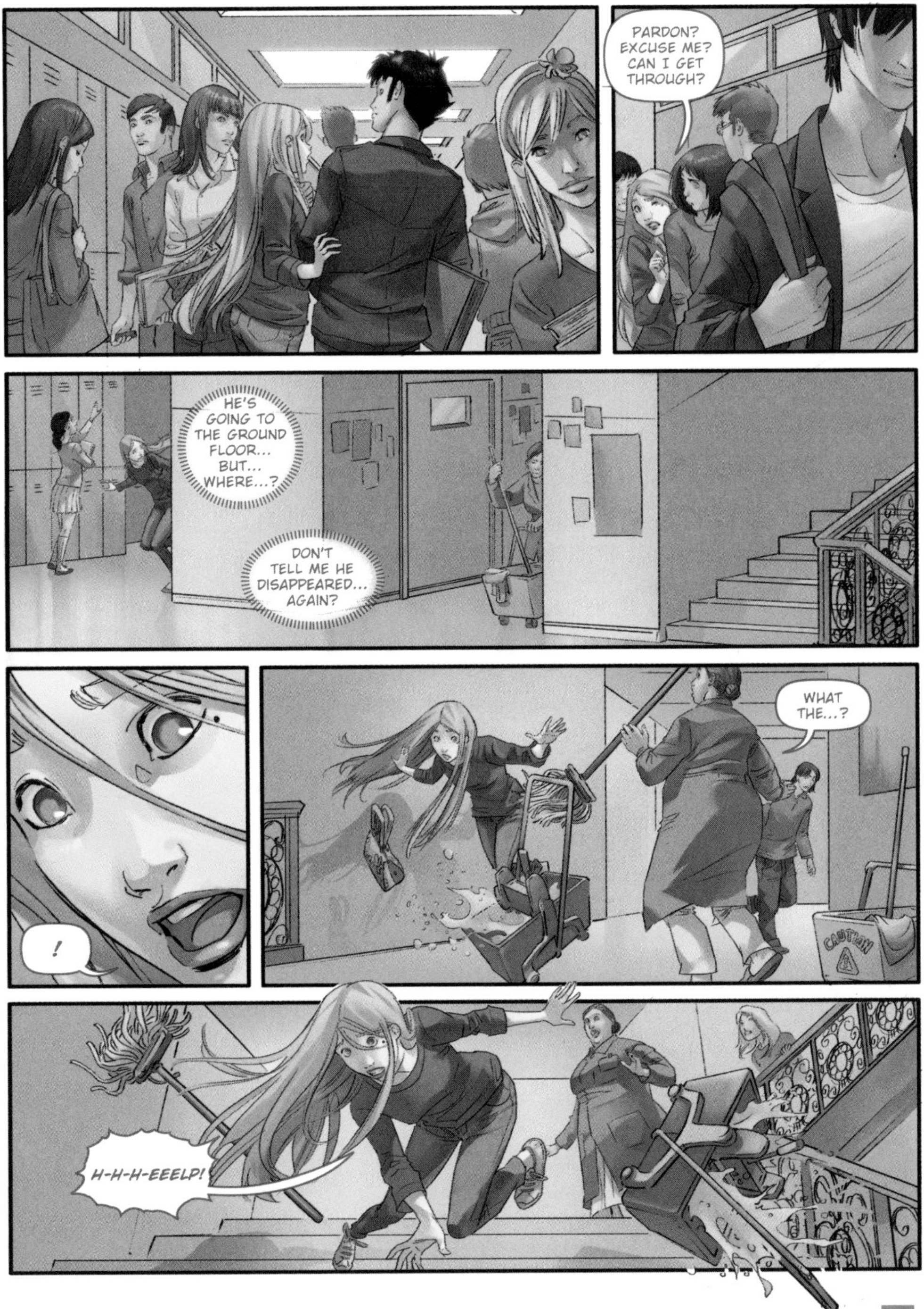
PARDON? EXCUSE ME? CAN I GET THROUGH?
HE'S GOING TO THE GROUND FLOOR... BUT... WHERE...?
DON'T TELL ME HE DISAPPEARED... AGAIN?
!
WHAT THE...?
CAUTION
H-H-H-EEELP!

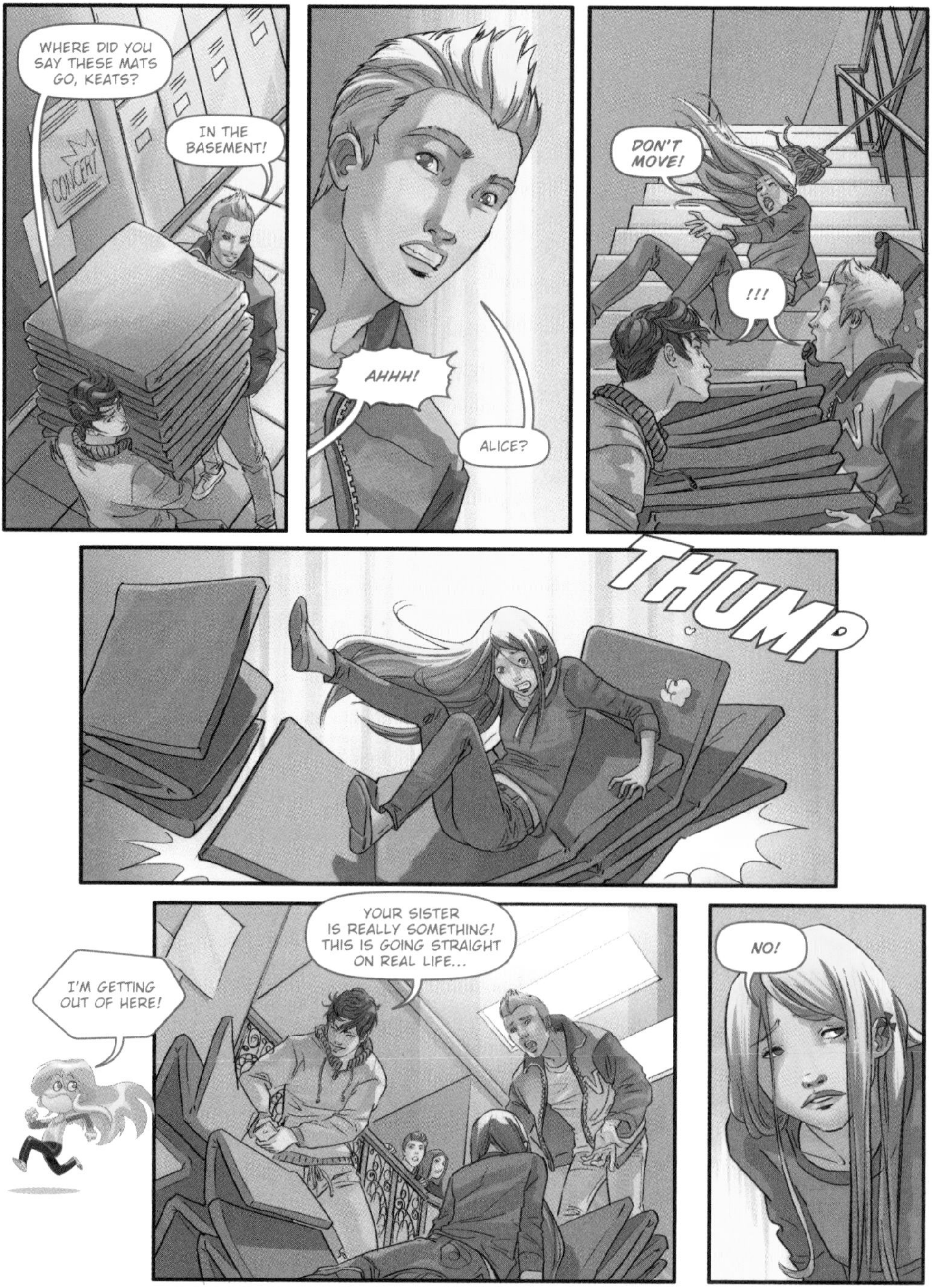
WHERE DID YOU SAY THESE MATS GO, KEATS?
IN THE BASEMENT!
CONCERT
AHHH!
ALICE?
DON'T MOVE!
!!!
THUMP
I'M GETTING OUT OF HERE!
YOUR SISTER IS REALLY SOMETHING! THIS IS GOING STRAIGHT ON REAL LIFE...
NO!

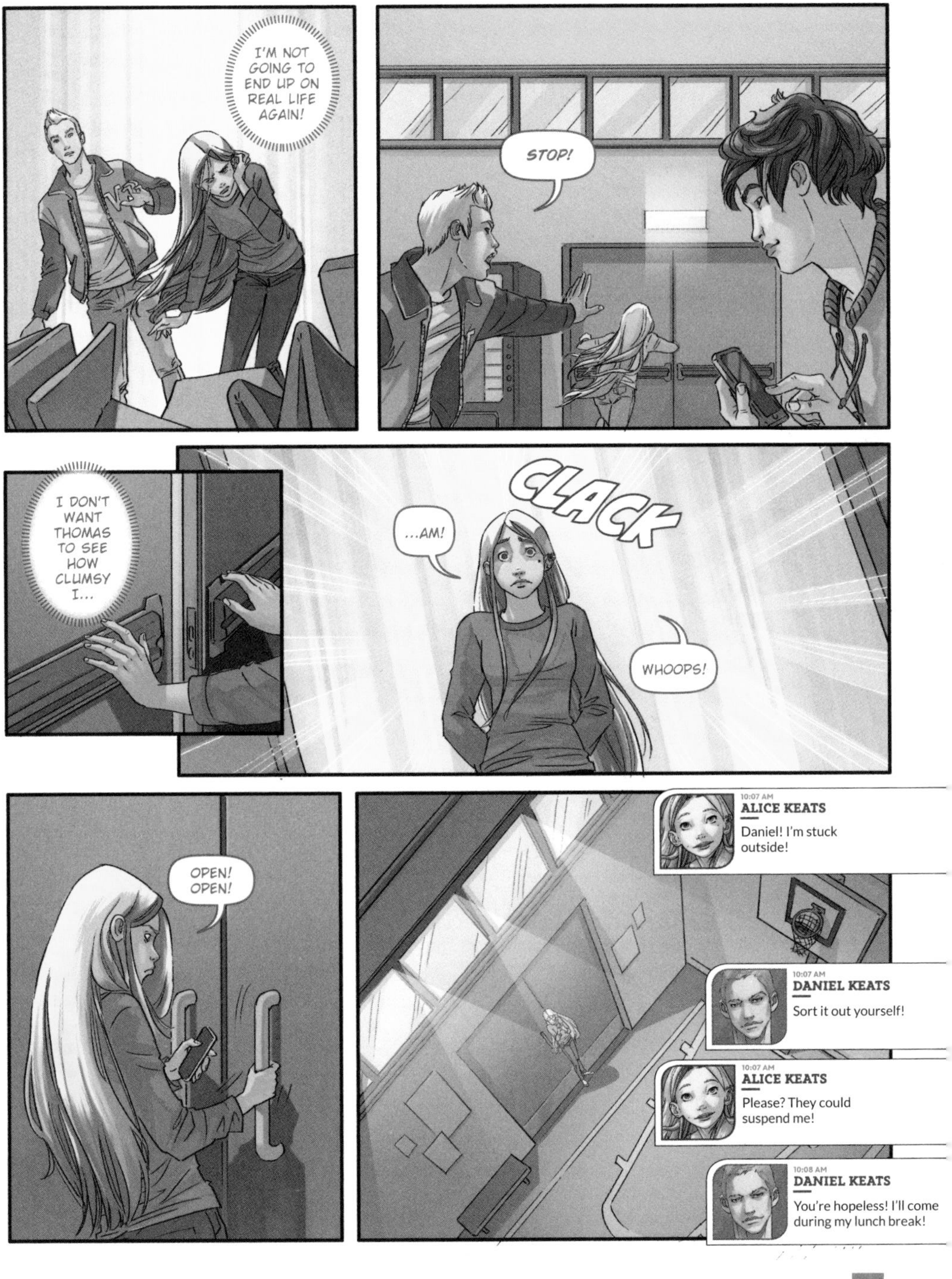
I'M NOT GOING TO END UP ON REAL LIFE AGAIN!
STOP!
I DON'T WANT THOMAS TO SEE HOW CLUMSY I...
CLACK
...AM!
WHOOPS!
OPEN! OPEN!
10:07 AM
ALICE KEATS
Daniel! I'm stuck outside!
10:07 AM
DANIEL KEATS
Sort it out yourself!
10:07 AM
ALICE KEATS
Please? They could suspend me!
10:08 AM
DANIEL KEATS
You're hopeless! I'll come during my lunch break!

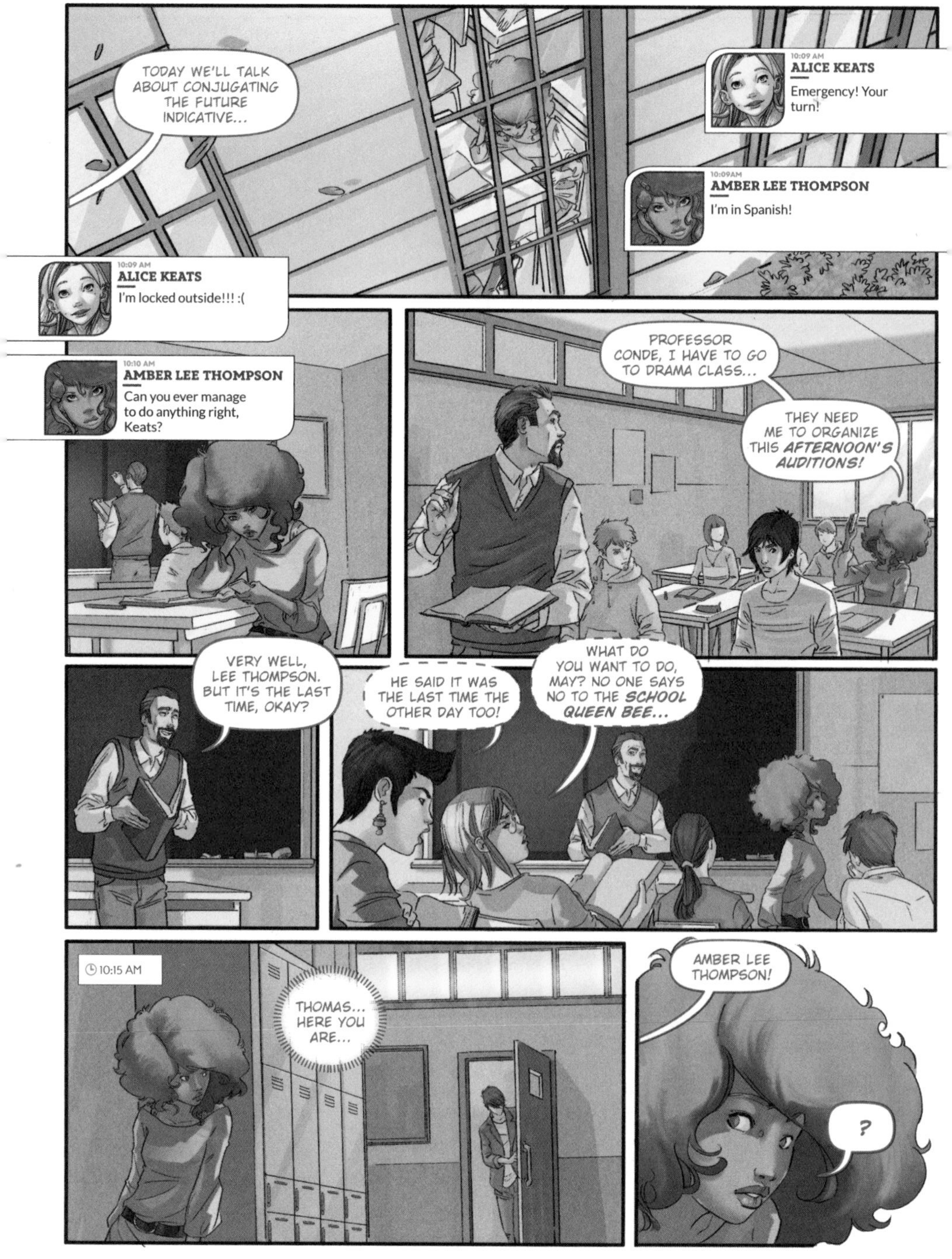
TODAY WE'LL TALK ABOUT CONJUGATING THE FUTURE INDICATIVE...
10:09 AM
ALICE KEATS
Emergency! Your turn!
10:09AM
AMBER LEE THOMPSON
I'm in Spanish!
10:09 AM
ALICE KEATS
I'm locked outside!!! :(
10:10 AM
AMBER LEE THOMPSON
Can you ever manage to do anything right, Keats?
PROFESSOR CONDE, I HAVE TO GO TO DRAMA CLASS...
THEY NEED ME TO ORGANIZE THIS AFTERNOON'S AUDITIONS!
VERY WELL, LEE THOMPSON. BUT IT'S THE LAST TIME, OKAY?
HE SAID IT WAS THE LAST TIME THE OTHER DAY TOO!
WHAT DO YOU WANT TO DO, MAY? NO ONE SAYS NO TO THE SCHOOL QUEEN BEE...
10:15 AM
THOMAS... HERE YOU ARE...
AMBER LEE THOMPSON!
?

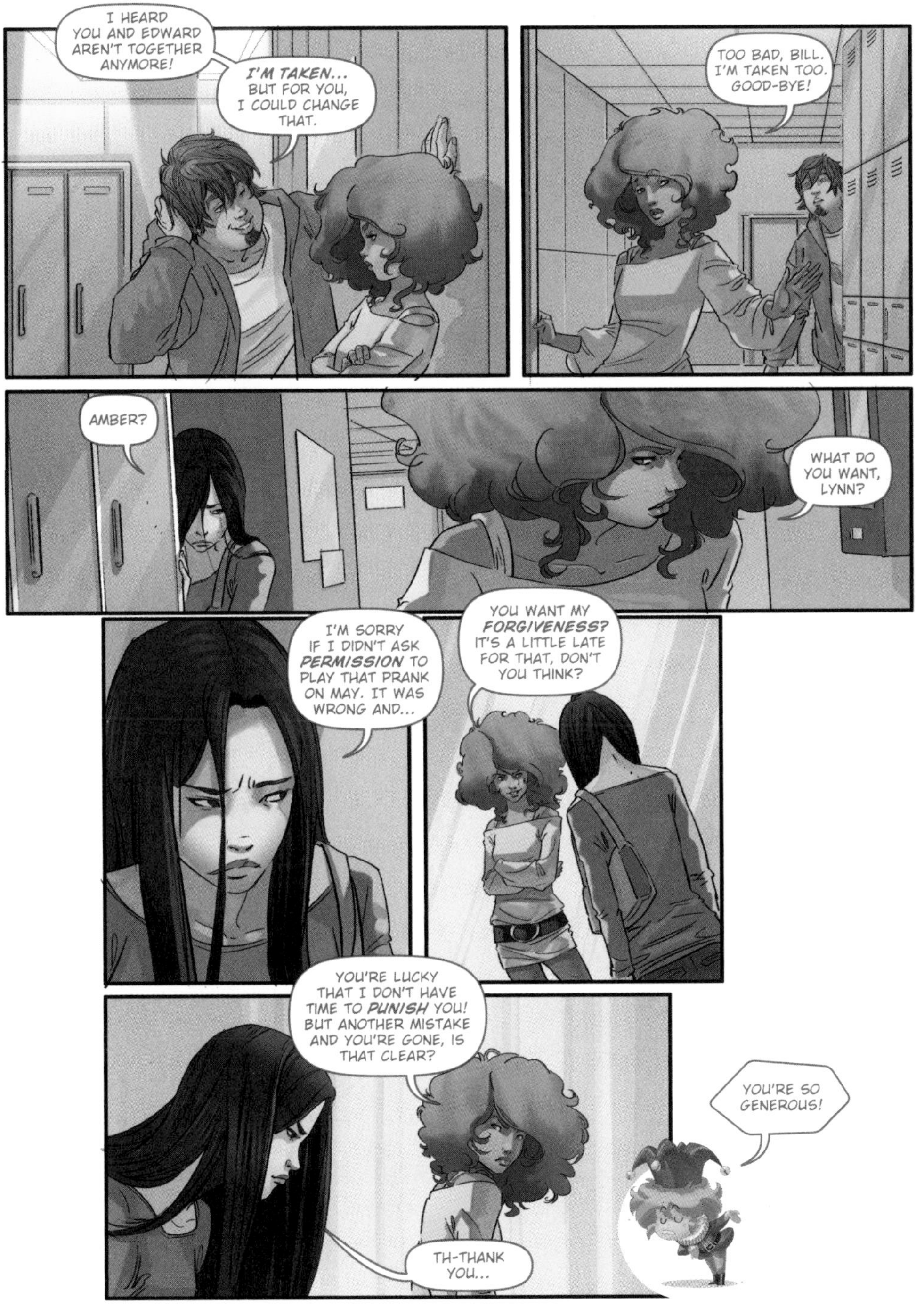
I HEARD YOU AND EDWARD AREN'T TOGETHER ANYMORE!
I'M TAKEN... BUT FOR YOU, I COULD CHANGE THAT.
TOO BAD, BILL. I'M TAKEN TOO. GOOD-BYE!
AMBER?
WHAT DO YOU WANT, LYNN?
I'M SORRY IF I DIDN'T ASK *PERMISSION* TO PLAY THAT PRANK ON MAY. IT WAS WRONG AND...
YOU WANT MY *FORGIVENESS?* IT'S A LITTLE LATE FOR THAT, DON'T YOU THINK?
YOU'RE LUCKY THAT I DON'T HAVE TIME TO *PUNISH* YOU! BUT ANOTHER MISTAKE AND YOU'RE GONE, IS THAT CLEAR?
TH-THANK YOU...
YOU'RE SO GENEROUS!

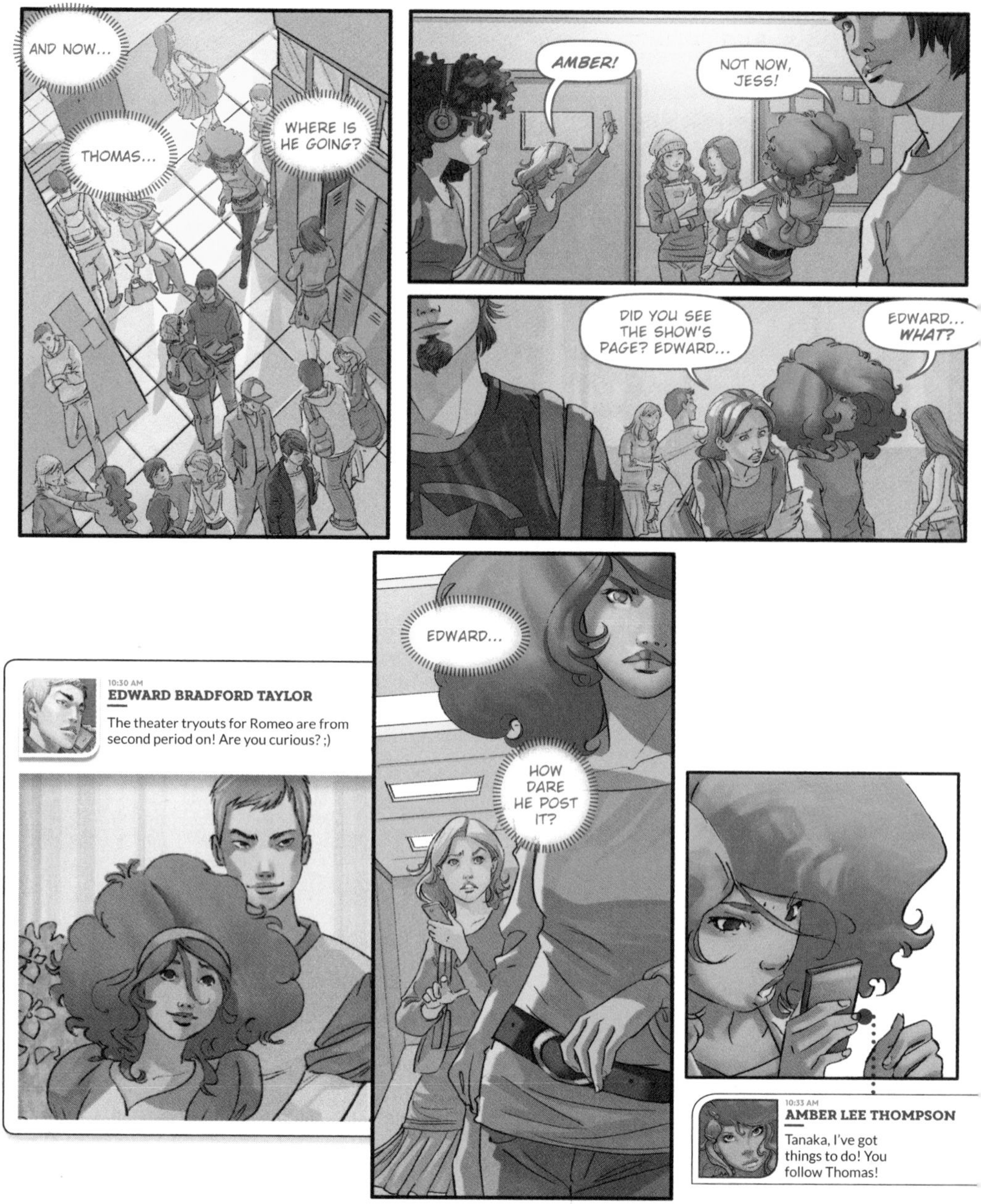
AND NOW...
THOMAS...
WHERE IS HE GOING?
AMBER!
NOT NOW, JESS!
DID YOU SEE THE SHOW'S PAGE? EDWARD...
EDWARD... WHAT?
EDWARD...
10:30 AM
EDWARD BRADFORD TAYLOR
The theater tryouts for Romeo are from second period on! Are you curious? ;)
HOW DARE HE POST IT?
10:33 AM
AMBER LEE THOMPSON
Tanaka, I've got things to do! You follow Thomas!

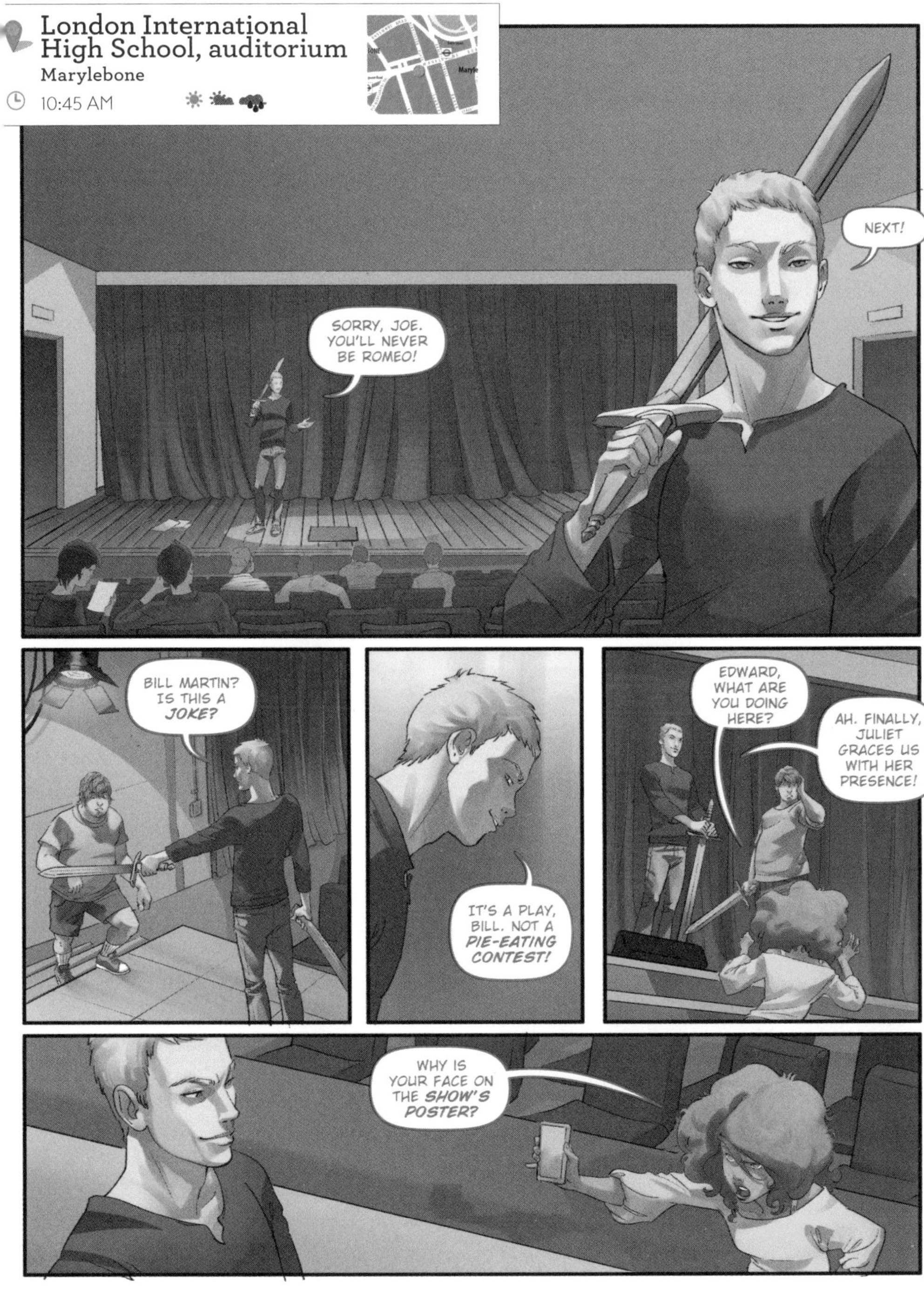
London International
High School, auditorium
Marylebone
10:45 AM
Marylebone
SORRY, JOE. YOU'LL NEVER BE ROMEO!
NEXT!
BILL MARTIN? IS THIS A *JOKE?*
IT'S A PLAY, BILL. NOT A *PIE-EATING CONTEST!*
EDWARD, WHAT ARE YOU DOING HERE?
AH. FINALLY, JULIET GRACES US WITH HER PRESENCE!
WHY IS YOUR FACE ON THE *SHOW'S POSTER?*

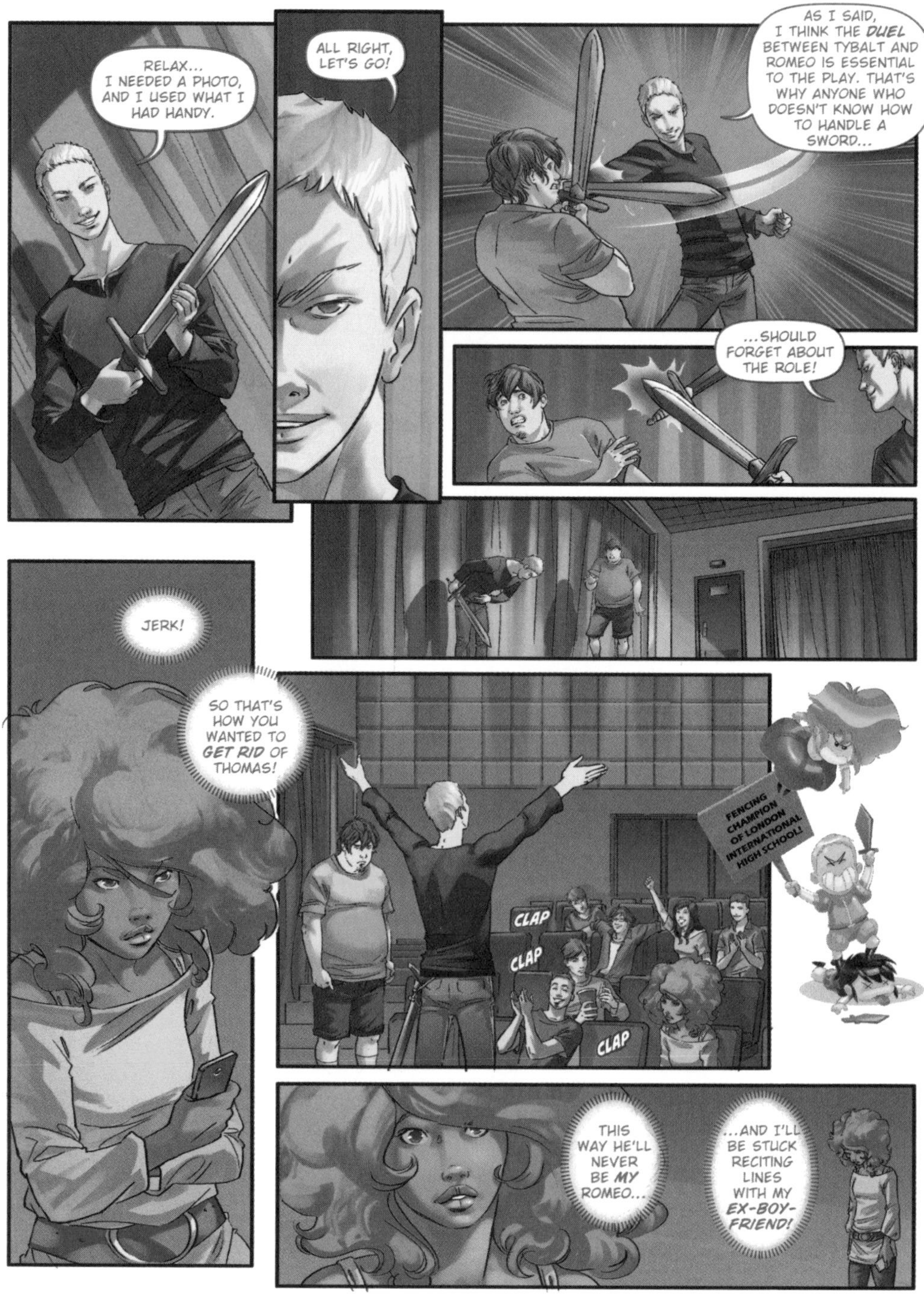
RELAX... I NEEDED A PHOTO, AND I USED WHAT I HAD HANDY.
ALL RIGHT, LET'S GO!
AS I SAID, I THINK THE DUEL BETWEEN TYBALT AND ROMEO IS ESSENTIAL TO THE PLAY. THAT'S WHY ANYONE WHO DOESN'T KNOW HOW TO HANDLE A SWORD...
...SHOULD FORGET ABOUT THE ROLE!
JERK!
SO THAT'S HOW YOU WANTED TO GET RID OF THOMAS!
FENCING CHAMPION OF LONDON INTERNATIONAL HIGH SCHOOL!
CLAP
CLAP
CLAP
THIS WAY HE'LL NEVER BE MY ROMEO...
...AND I'LL BE STUCK RECITING LINES WITH MY EX-BOY-FRIEND!

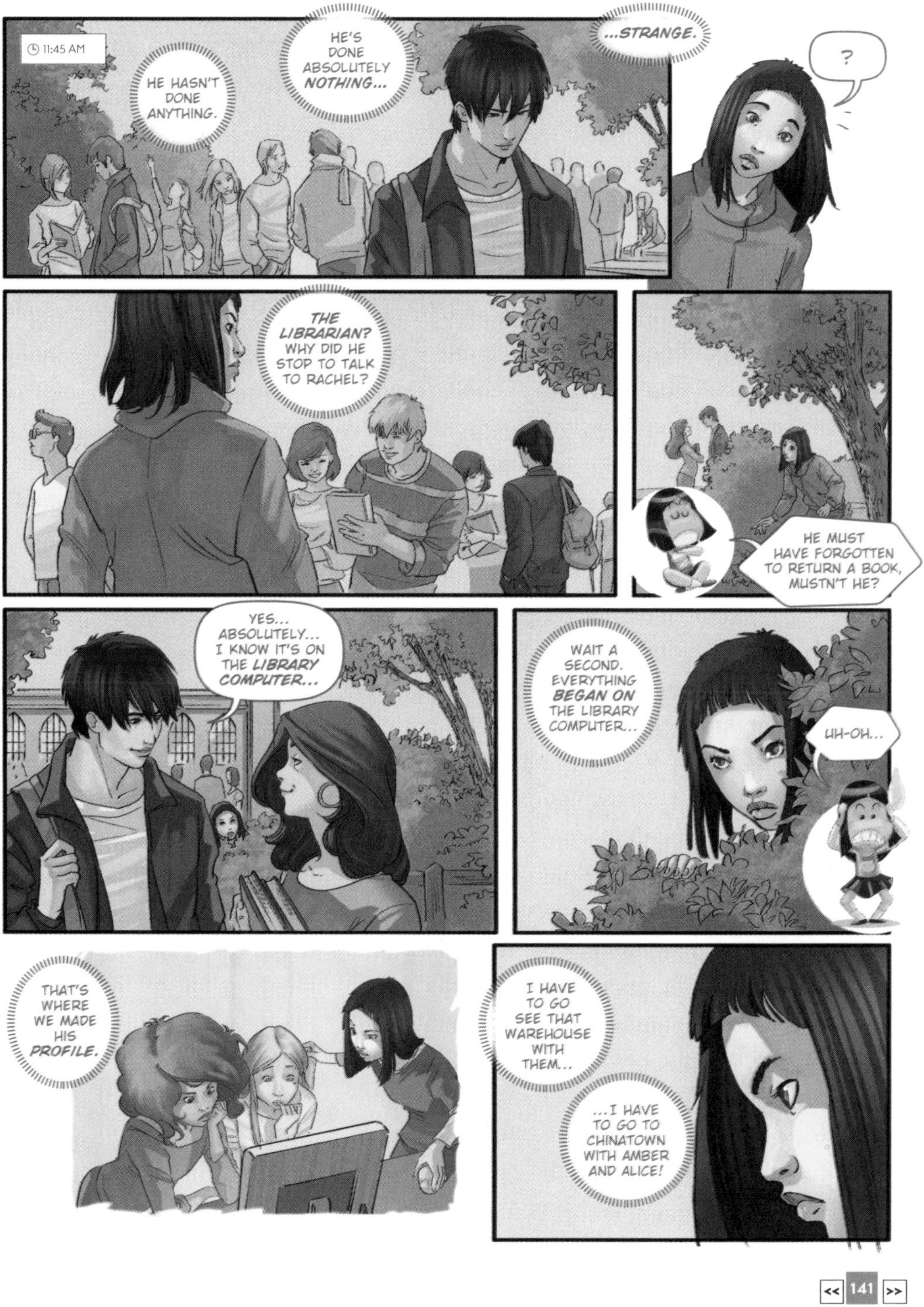
11:45 AM
HE HASN'T DONE ANYTHING.
HE'S DONE ABSOLUTELY NOTHING...
...STRANGE.
?
THE LIBRARIAN? WHY DID HE STOP TO TALK TO RACHEL?
HE MUST HAVE FORGOTTEN TO RETURN A BOOK, MUSTN'T HE?
YES... ABSOLUTELY... I KNOW IT'S ON THE LIBRARY COMPUTER...
WAIT A SECOND. EVERYTHING BEGAN ON THE LIBRARY COMPUTER...
UH-OH...
THAT'S WHERE WE MADE HIS PROFILE.
I HAVE TO GO SEE THAT WAREHOUSE WITH THEM...
...I HAVE TO GO TO CHINATOWN WITH AMBER AND ALICE!

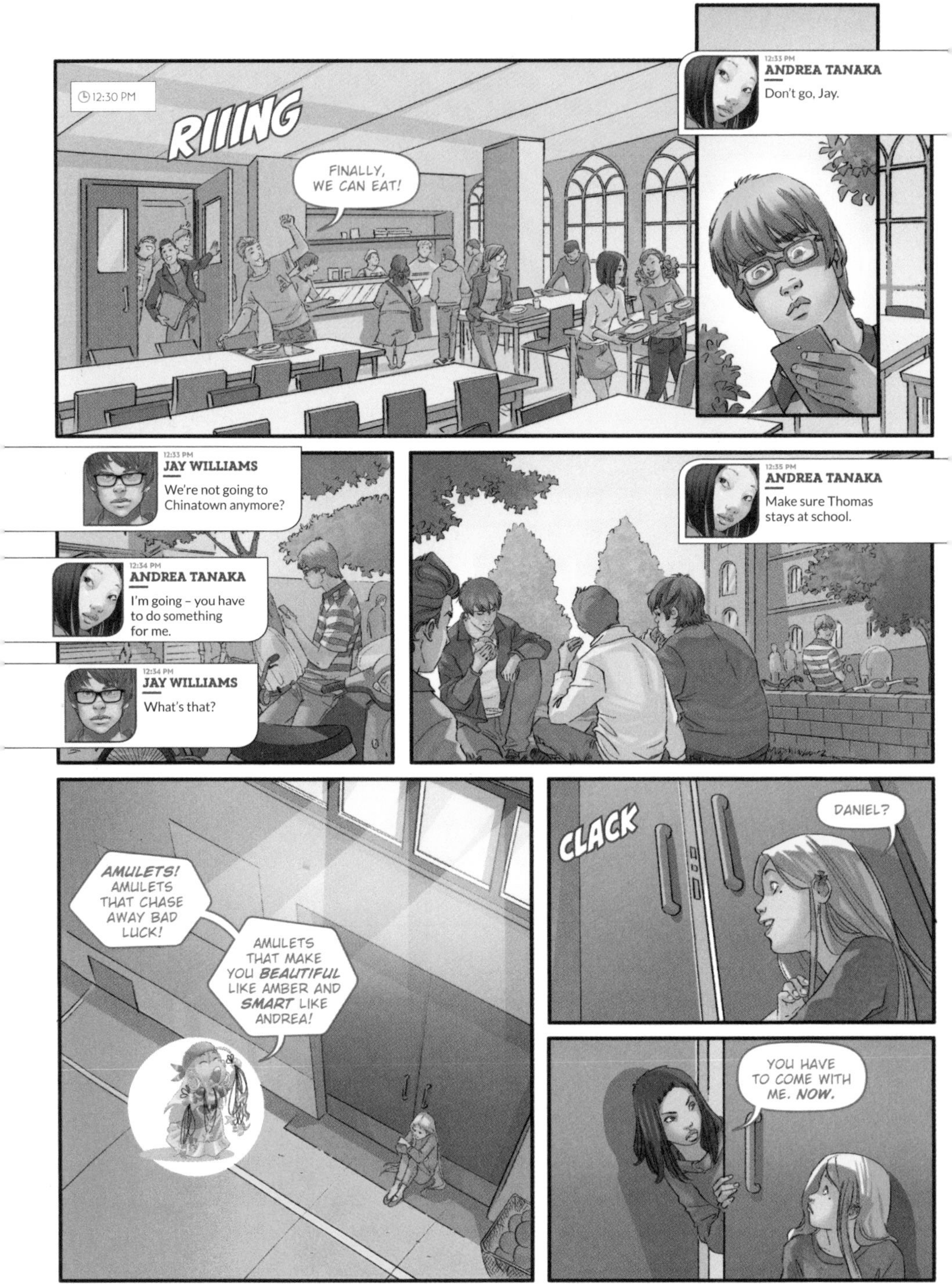
12:30 PM
RIIING
FINALLY, WE CAN EAT!
12:33 PM ANDREA TANAKA
Don't go, Jay.
12:33 PM JAY WILLIAMS
We're not going to Chinatown anymore?
12:34 PM ANDREA TANAKA
I'm going – you have to do something for me.
12:34 PM JAY WILLIAMS
What's that?
12:35 PM ANDREA TANAKA
Make sure Thomas stays at school.
AMULETS! AMULETS THAT CHASE AWAY BAD LUCK!
AMULETS THAT MAKE YOU BEAUTIFUL LIKE AMBER AND SMART LIKE ANDREA!
CLACK
DANIEL?
YOU HAVE TO COME WITH ME. NOW.

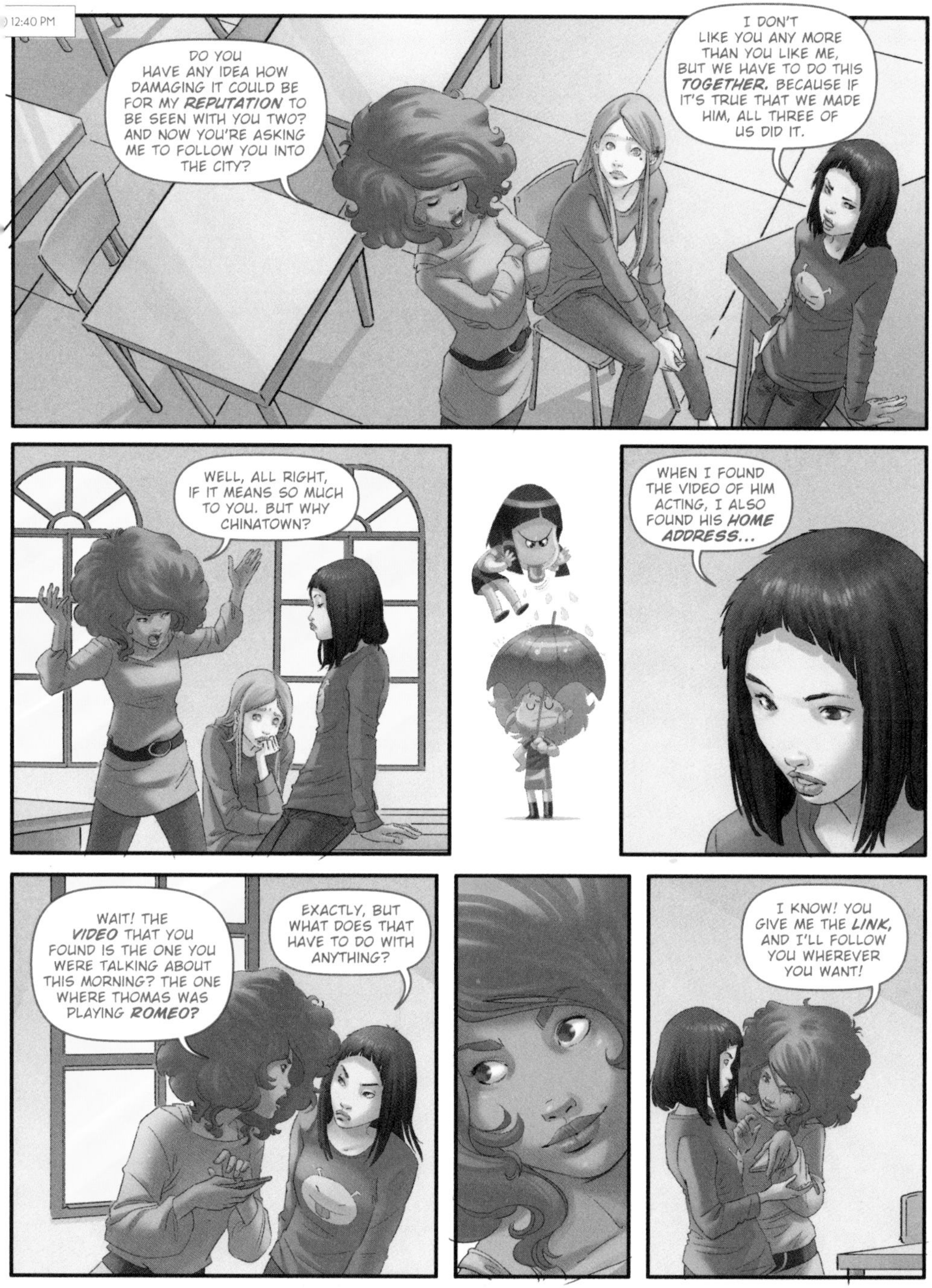

12:40 PM
DO YOU HAVE ANY IDEA HOW DAMAGING IT COULD BE FOR MY *REPUTATION* TO BE SEEN WITH YOU TWO? AND NOW YOU'RE ASKING ME TO FOLLOW YOU INTO THE CITY?
I DON'T LIKE YOU ANY MORE THAN YOU LIKE ME, BUT WE HAVE TO DO THIS *TOGETHER.* BECAUSE IF IT'S TRUE THAT WE MADE HIM, ALL THREE OF US DID IT.
WELL, ALL RIGHT, IF IT MEANS SO MUCH TO YOU. BUT WHY CHINATOWN?
WHEN I FOUND THE VIDEO OF HIM ACTING, I ALSO FOUND HIS *HOME ADDRESS...*
WAIT! THE *VIDEO* THAT YOU FOUND IS THE ONE YOU WERE TALKING ABOUT THIS MORNING? THE ONE WHERE THOMAS WAS PLAYING *ROMEO?*
EXACTLY, BUT WHAT DOES THAT HAVE TO DO WITH ANYTHING?
I KNOW! YOU GIVE ME THE *LINK,* AND I'LL FOLLOW YOU WHEREVER YOU WANT!

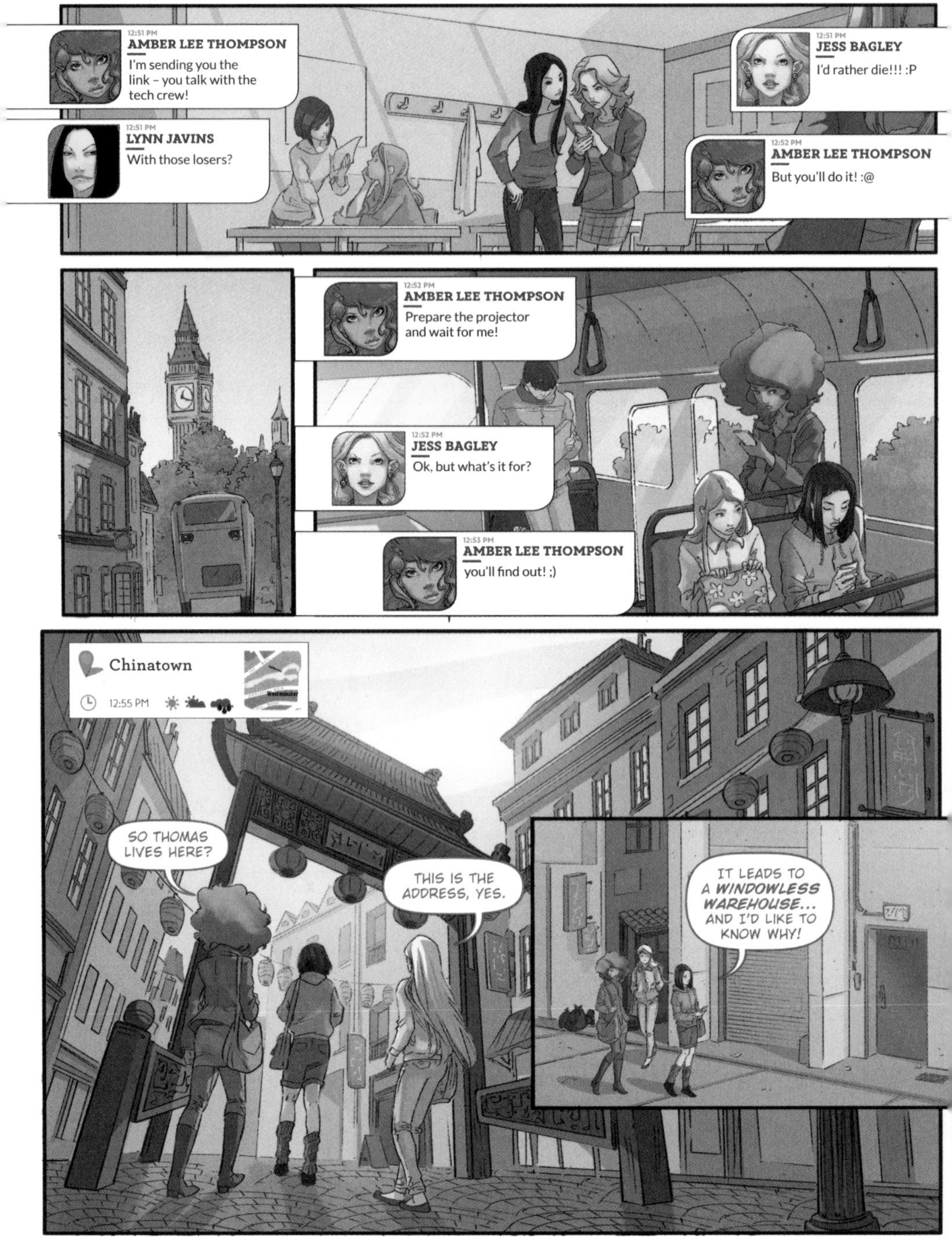
12:51 PM
AMBER LEE THOMPSON
I'm sending you the link – you talk with the tech crew!
12:51 PM
LYNN JAVINS
With those losers?
12:51 PM
JESS BAGLEY
I'd rather die!!! :P
12:52 PM
AMBER LEE THOMPSON
But you'll do it! :@
12:52 PM
AMBER LEE THOMPSON
Prepare the projector and wait for me!
12:52 PM
JESS BAGLEY
Ok, but what's it for?
12:53 PM
AMBER LEE THOMPSON
you'll find out! ;)
Chinatown
12:55 PM
SO THOMAS LIVES HERE?
THIS IS THE ADDRESS, YES.
IT LEADS TO A ***WINDOWLESS WAREHOUSE...*** AND I'D LIKE TO KNOW WHY!

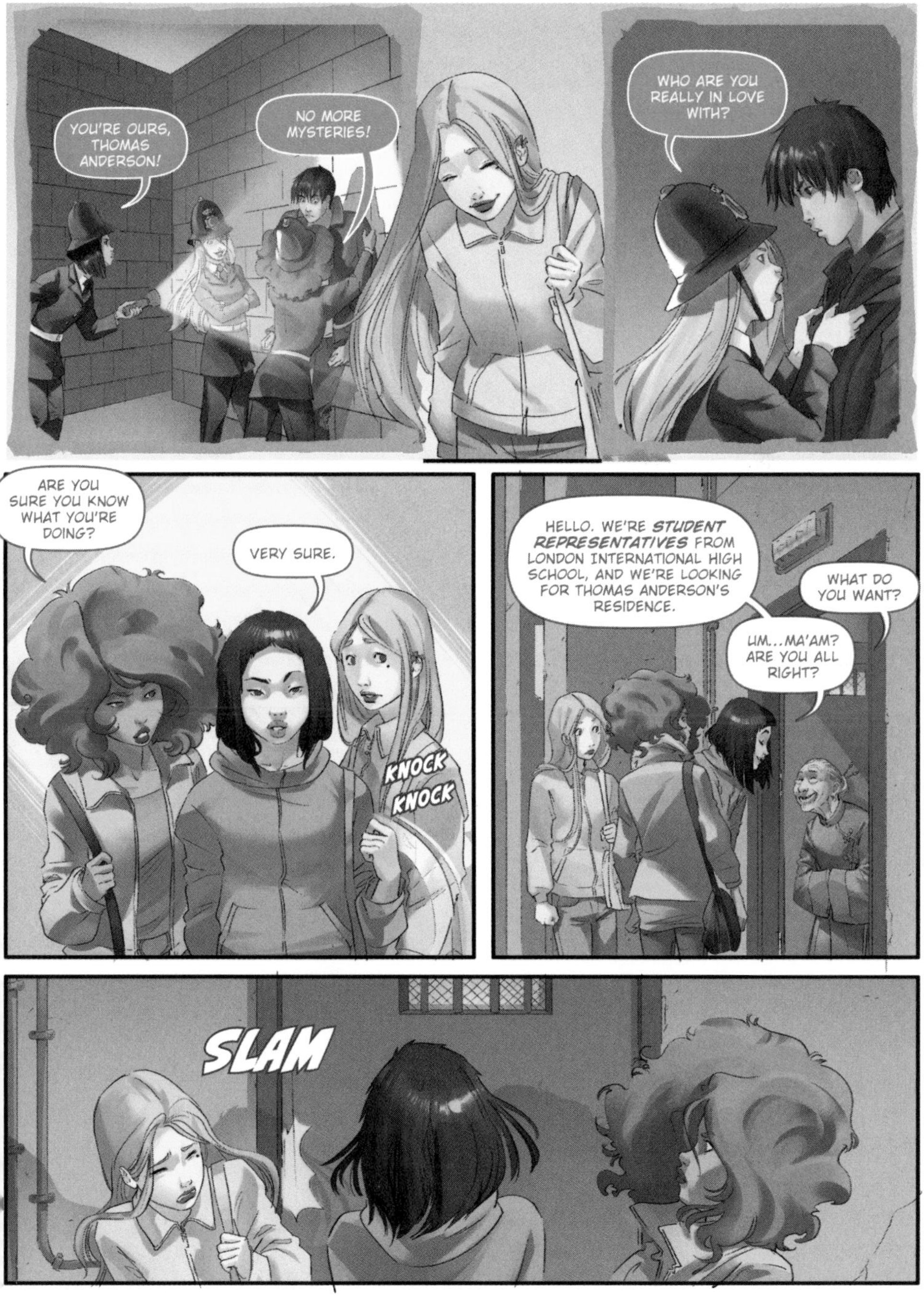

YOU'RE OURS, THOMAS ANDERSON!
NO MORE MYSTERIES!
WHO ARE YOU REALLY IN LOVE WITH?
ARE YOU SURE YOU KNOW WHAT YOU'RE DOING?
VERY SURE.
KNOCK
KNOCK
HELLO. WE'RE STUDENT REPRESENTATIVES FROM LONDON INTERNATIONAL HIGH SCHOOL, AND WE'RE LOOKING FOR THOMAS ANDERSON'S RESIDENCE.
WHAT DO YOU WANT?
UM...MA'AM? ARE YOU ALL RIGHT?
SLAM

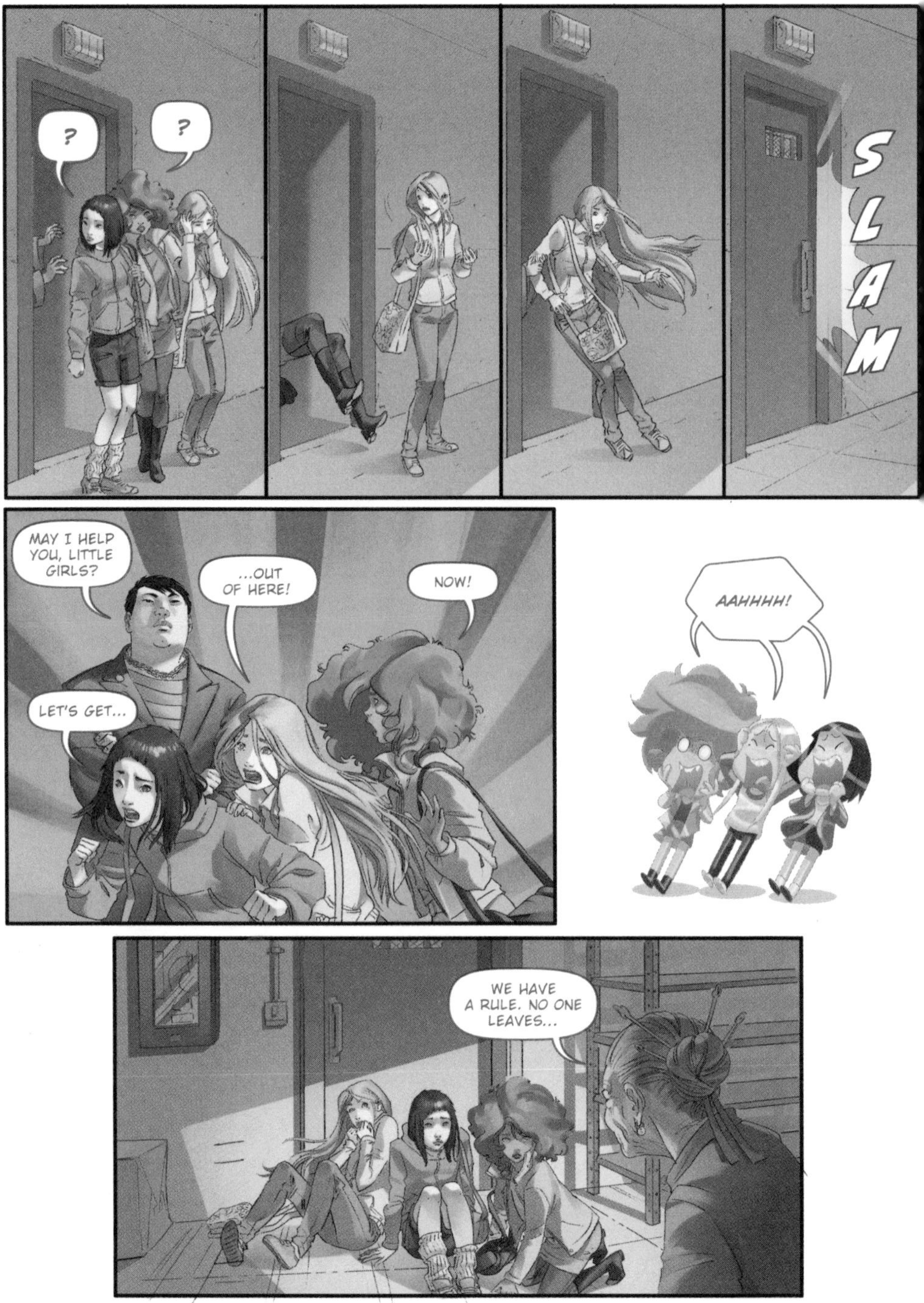
?
?
SLAM
MAY I HELP YOU, LITTLE GIRLS?
LET'S GET...
...OUT OF HERE!
NOW!
AAHHHH!
WE HAVE A RULE. NO ONE LEAVES...

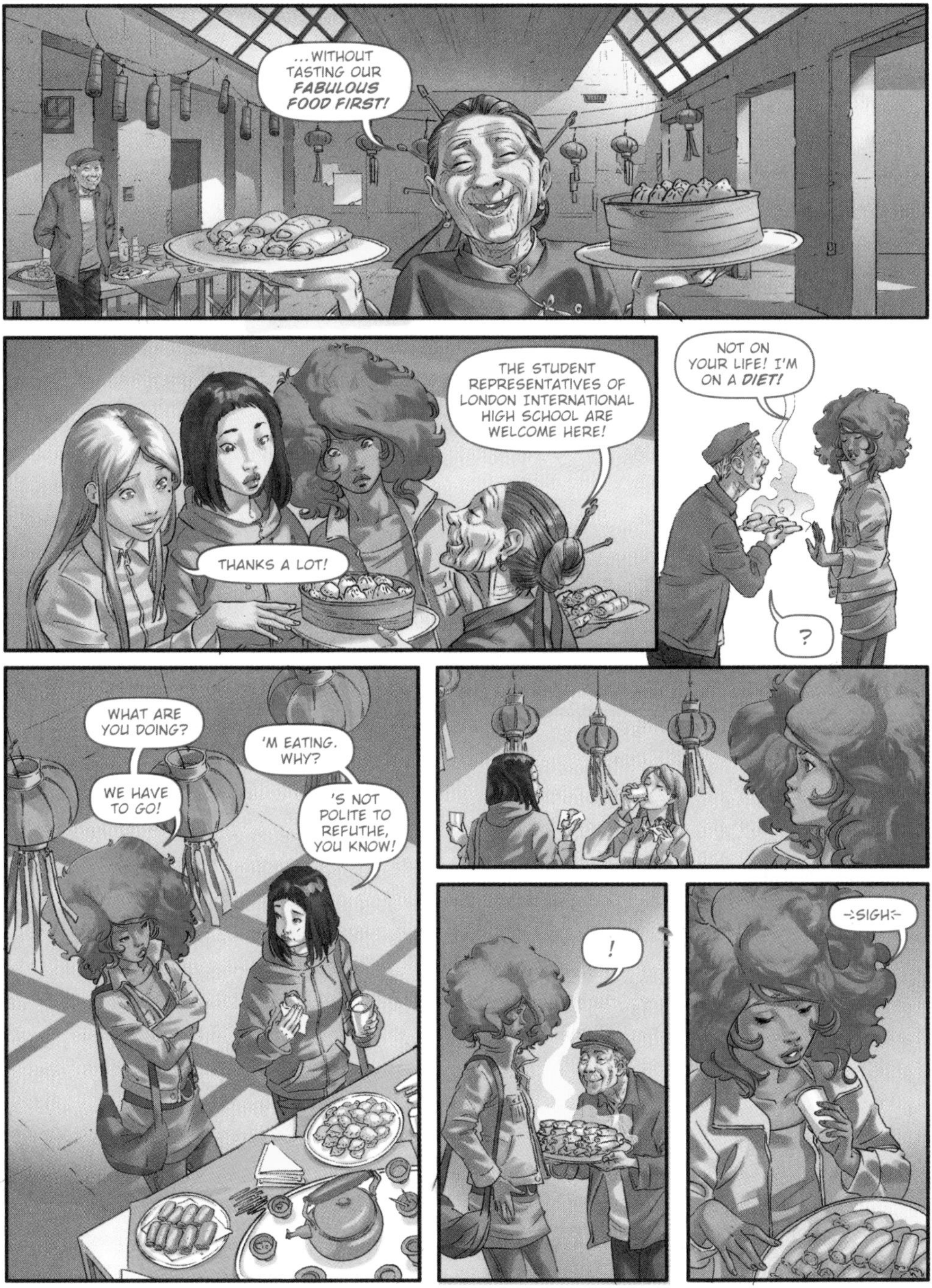
...WITHOUT TASTING OUR FABULOUS FOOD FIRST!
THE STUDENT REPRESENTATIVES OF LONDON INTERNATIONAL HIGH SCHOOL ARE WELCOME HERE!
THANKS A LOT!
NOT ON YOUR LIFE! I'M ON A DIET!
?
WHAT ARE YOU DOING?
WE HAVE TO GO!
'M EATING. WHY?
'S NOT POLITE TO REFUTHE, YOU KNOW!
!
-SIGH-

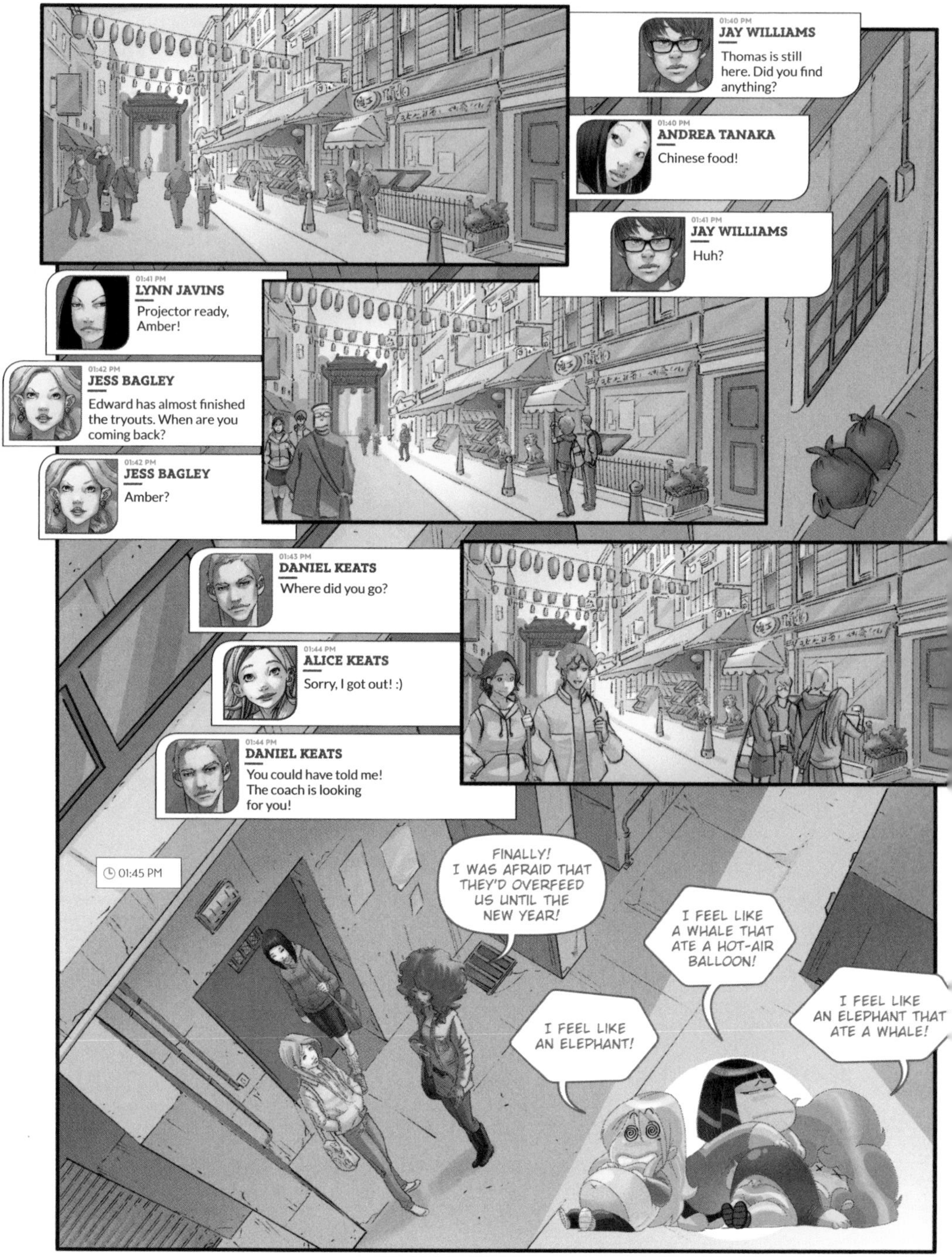

01:40 PM
JAY WILLIAMS
Thomas is still here. Did you find anything?
01:40 PM
ANDREA TANAKA
Chinese food!
01:41 PM
JAY WILLIAMS
Huh?
01:41 PM
LYNN JAVINS
Projector ready, Amber!
01:42 PM
JESS BAGLEY
Edward has almost finished the tryouts. When are you coming back?
01:42 PM
JESS BAGLEY
Amber?
01:43 PM
DANIEL KEATS
Where did you go?
01:44 PM
ALICE KEATS
Sorry, I got out! :)
01:44 PM
DANIEL KEATS
You could have told me! The coach is looking for you!
01:45 PM
FINALLY! I WAS AFRAID THAT THEY'D OVERFEED US UNTIL THE NEW YEAR!
I FEEL LIKE AN ELEPHANT!
I FEEL LIKE A WHALE THAT ATE A HOT-AIR BALLOON!
I FEEL LIKE AN ELEPHANT THAT ATE A WHALE!

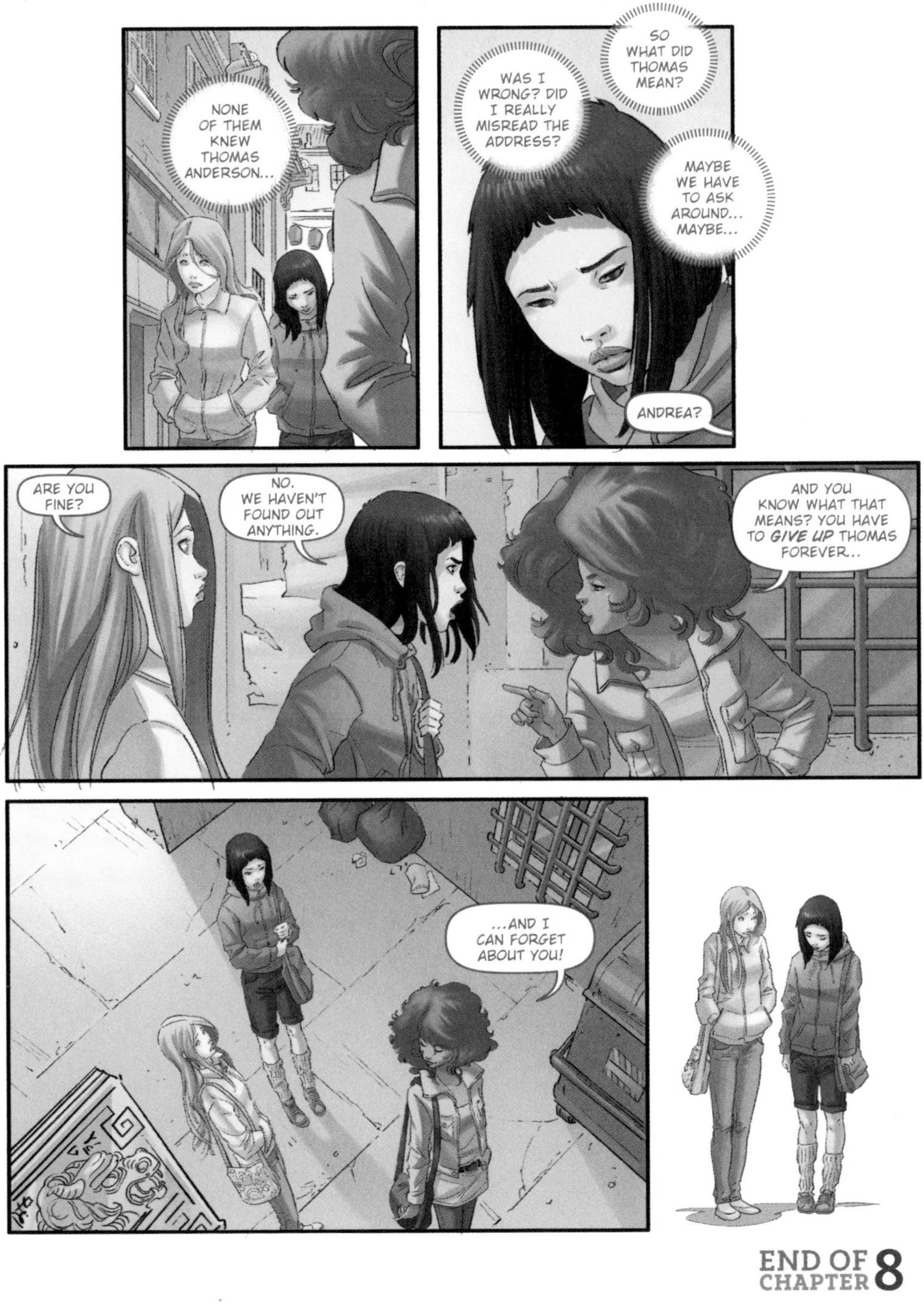
NONE OF THEM KNEW THOMAS ANDERSON...
WAS I WRONG? DID I REALLY MISREAD THE ADDRESS?
SO WHAT DID THOMAS MEAN?
MAYBE WE HAVE TO ASK AROUND... MAYBE...
ANDREA?
ARE YOU FINE?
NO. WE HAVEN'T FOUND OUT ANYTHING.
AND YOU KNOW WHAT THAT MEANS? YOU HAVE TO GIVE UP THOMAS FOREVER..
...AND I CAN FORGET ABOUT YOU!

END OF CHAPTER 8

CHAPTER 9

A new ROMEO

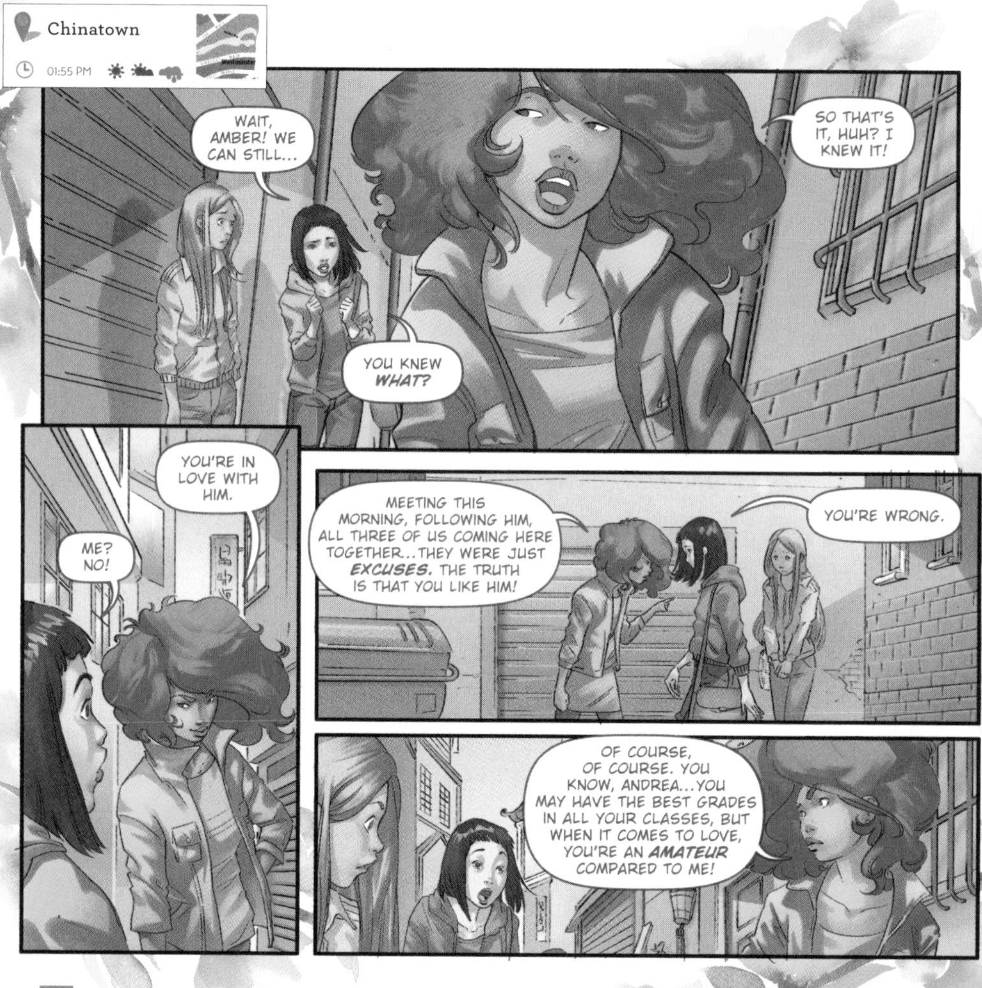

Chinatown
01:55 PM
WAIT, AMBER! WE CAN STILL...
SO THAT'S IT, HUH? I KNEW IT!
YOU KNEW WHAT?
YOU'RE IN LOVE WITH HIM.
ME? NO!
MEETING THIS MORNING, FOLLOWING HIM, ALL THREE OF US COMING HERE TOGETHER...THEY WERE JUST EXCUSES. THE TRUTH IS THAT YOU LIKE HIM!
YOU'RE WRONG.
OF COURSE, OF COURSE. YOU KNOW, ANDREA...YOU MAY HAVE THE BEST GRADES IN ALL YOUR CLASSES, BUT WHEN IT COMES TO LOVE, YOU'RE AN AMATEUR COMPARED TO ME!

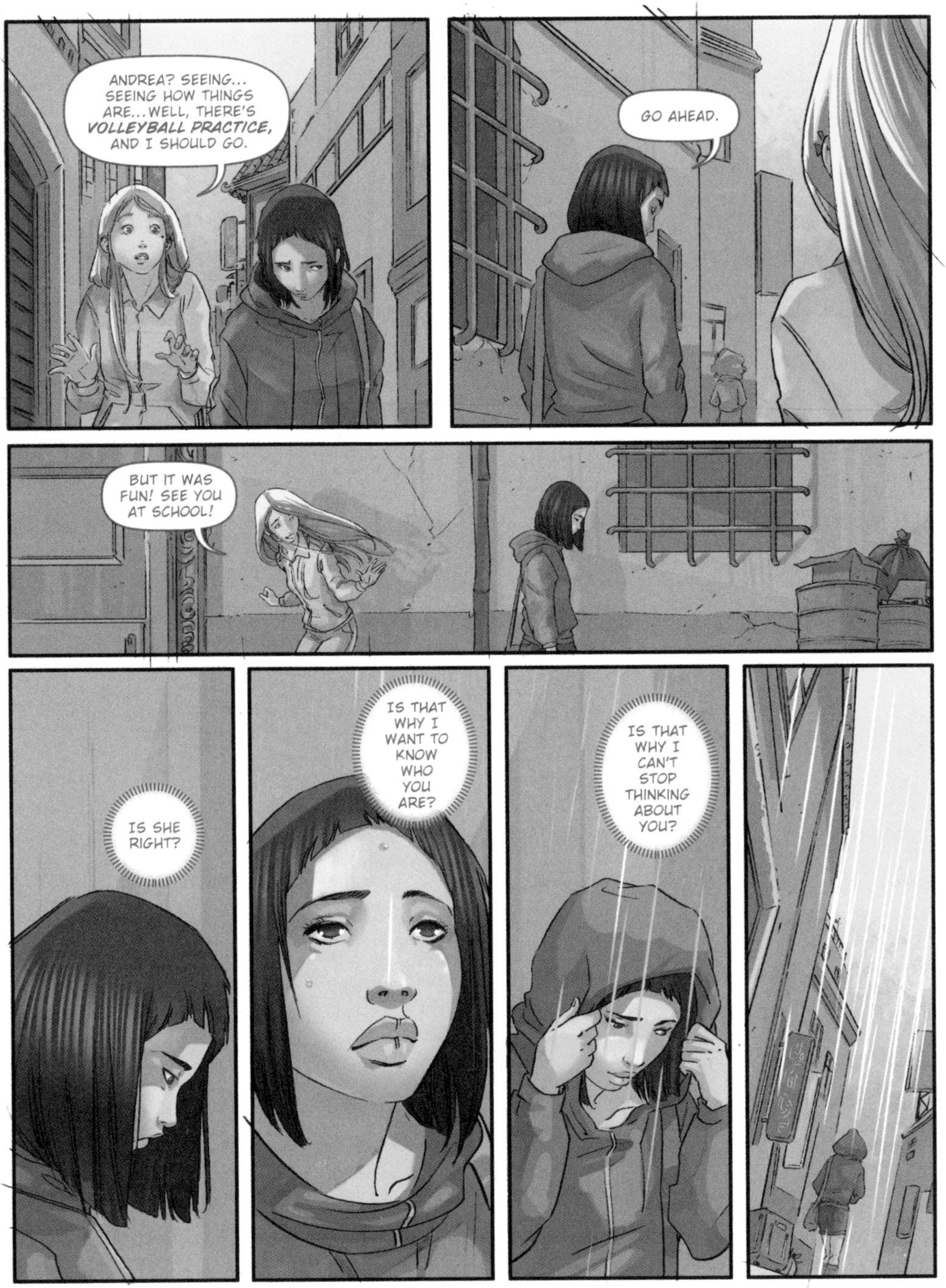
ANDREA? SEEING... SEEING HOW THINGS ARE...WELL, THERE'S ***VOLLEYBALL PRACTICE,*** AND I SHOULD GO.
GO AHEAD.
BUT IT WAS FUN! SEE YOU AT SCHOOL!
IS SHE RIGHT?
IS THAT WHY I WANT TO KNOW WHO YOU ARE?
IS THAT WHY I CAN'T STOP THINKING ABOUT YOU?

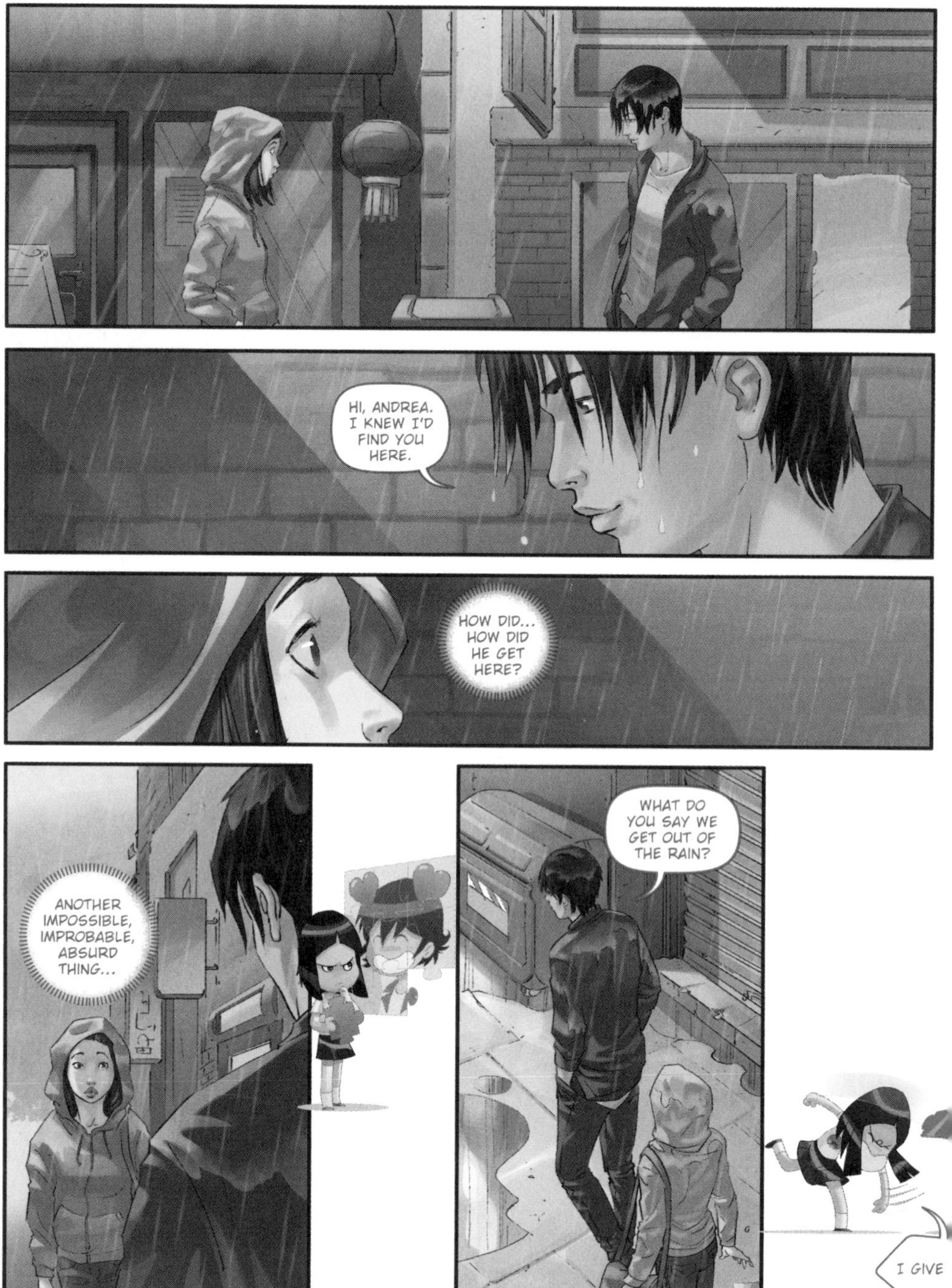
HI, ANDREA. I KNEW I'D FIND YOU HERE.
HOW DID... HOW DID HE GET HERE?
ANOTHER IMPOSSIBLE, IMPROBABLE, ABSURD THING...
WHAT DO YOU SAY WE GET OUT OF THE RAIN?
I GIVE

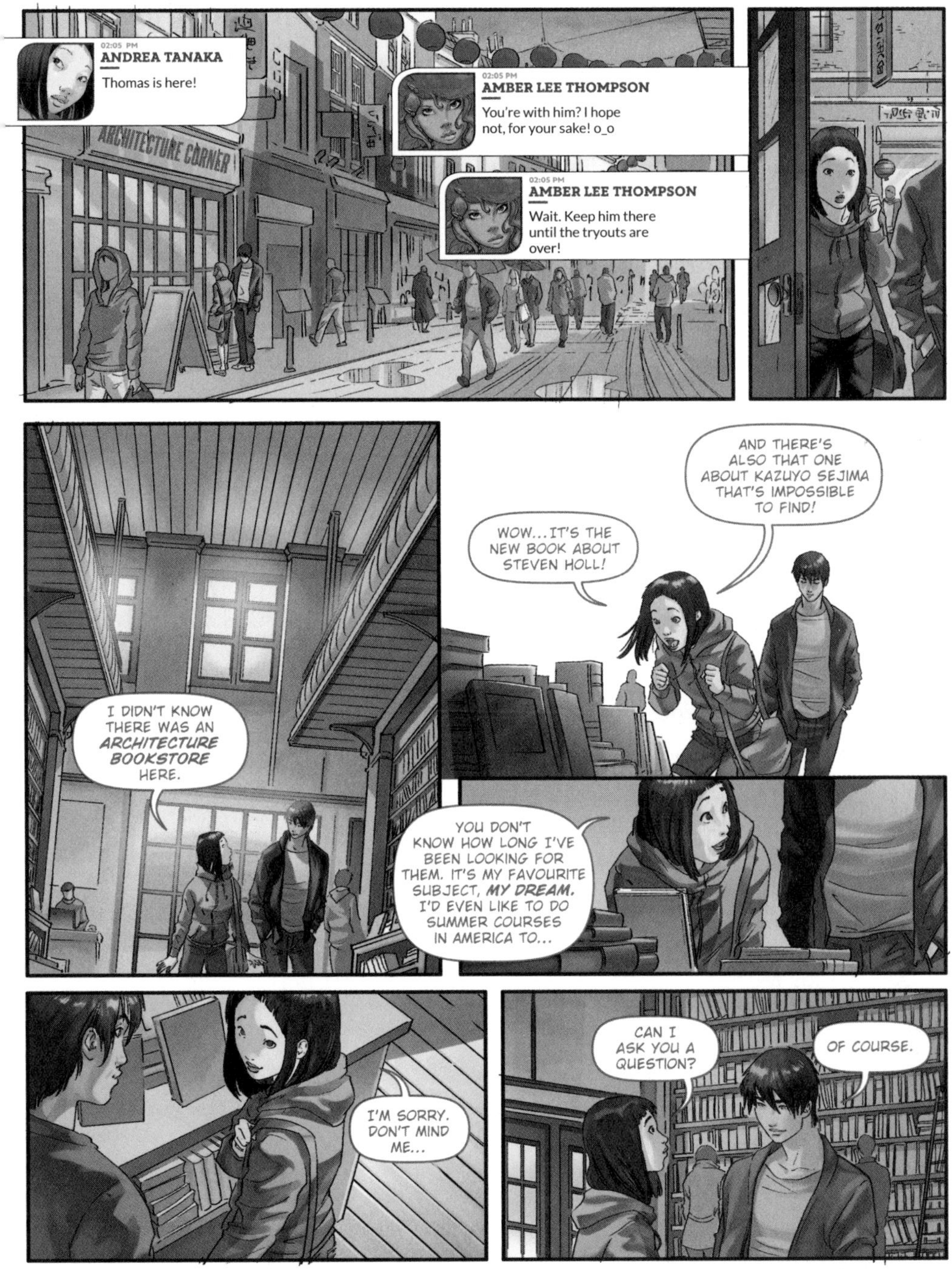
02:05 PM
ANDREA TANAKA
Thomas is here!
ARCHITECTURE CORNER
02:05 PM
AMBER LEE THOMPSON
You're with him? I hope not, for your sake! o_o
02:05 PM
AMBER LEE THOMPSON
Wait. Keep him there until the tryouts are over!
I DIDN'T KNOW THERE WAS AN ARCHITECTURE BOOKSTORE HERE.
WOW... IT'S THE NEW BOOK ABOUT STEVEN HOLL!
AND THERE'S ALSO THAT ONE ABOUT KAZUYO SEJIMA THAT'S IMPOSSIBLE TO FIND!
YOU DON'T KNOW HOW LONG I'VE BEEN LOOKING FOR THEM. IT'S MY FAVOURITE SUBJECT, MY DREAM. I'D EVEN LIKE TO DO SUMMER COURSES IN AMERICA TO...
I'M SORRY. DON'T MIND ME...
CAN I ASK YOU A QUESTION?
OF COURSE.

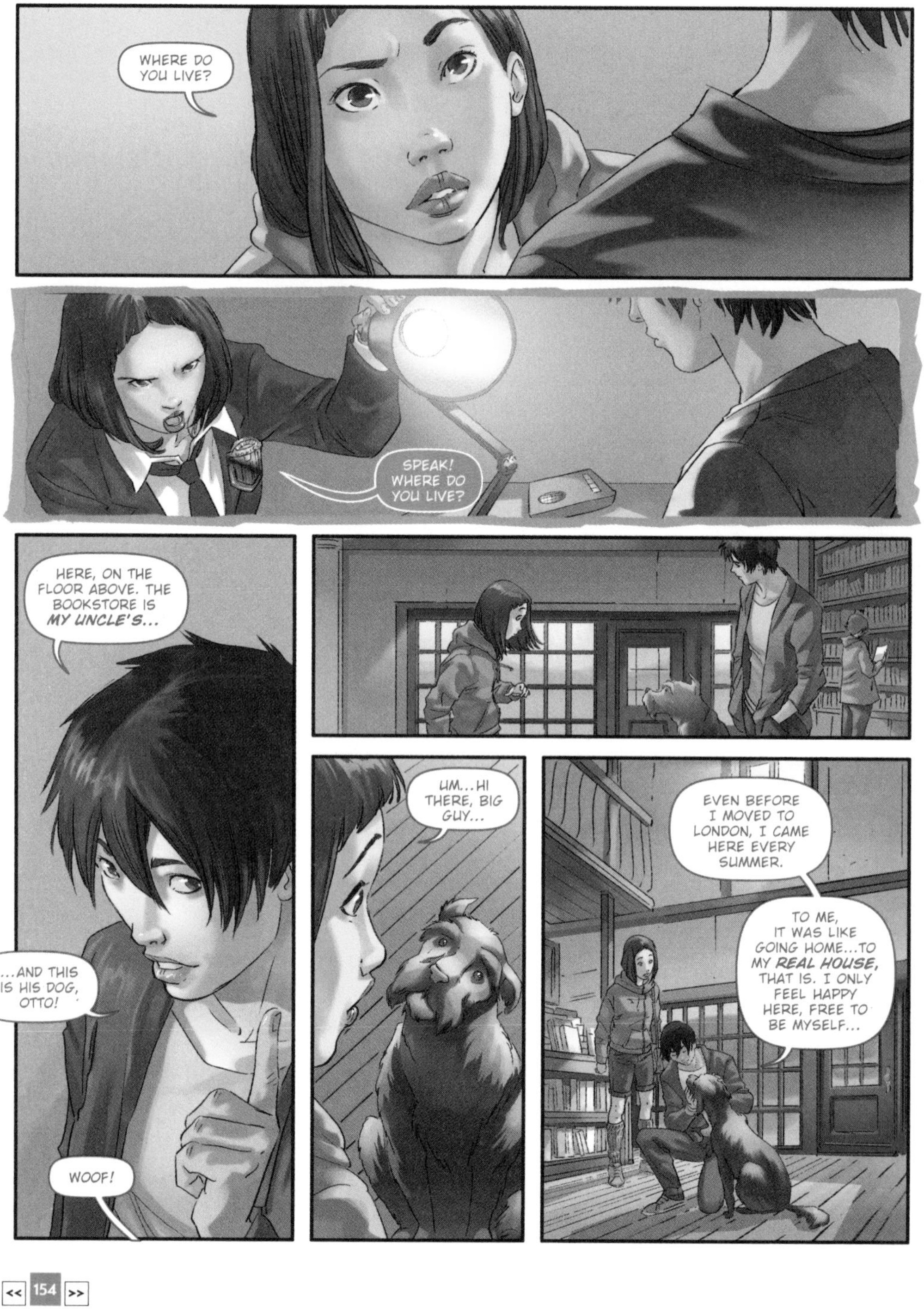
WHERE DO YOU LIVE?
SPEAK! WHERE DO YOU LIVE?
HERE, ON THE FLOOR ABOVE. THE BOOKSTORE IS *MY UNCLE'S...*
...AND THIS IS HIS DOG, OTTO!
WOOF!
UM...HI THERE, BIG GUY...
EVEN BEFORE I MOVED TO LONDON, I CAME HERE EVERY SUMMER.
TO ME, IT WAS LIKE GOING HOME...TO MY *REAL HOUSE,* THAT IS. I ONLY FEEL HAPPY HERE, FREE TO BE MYSELF...

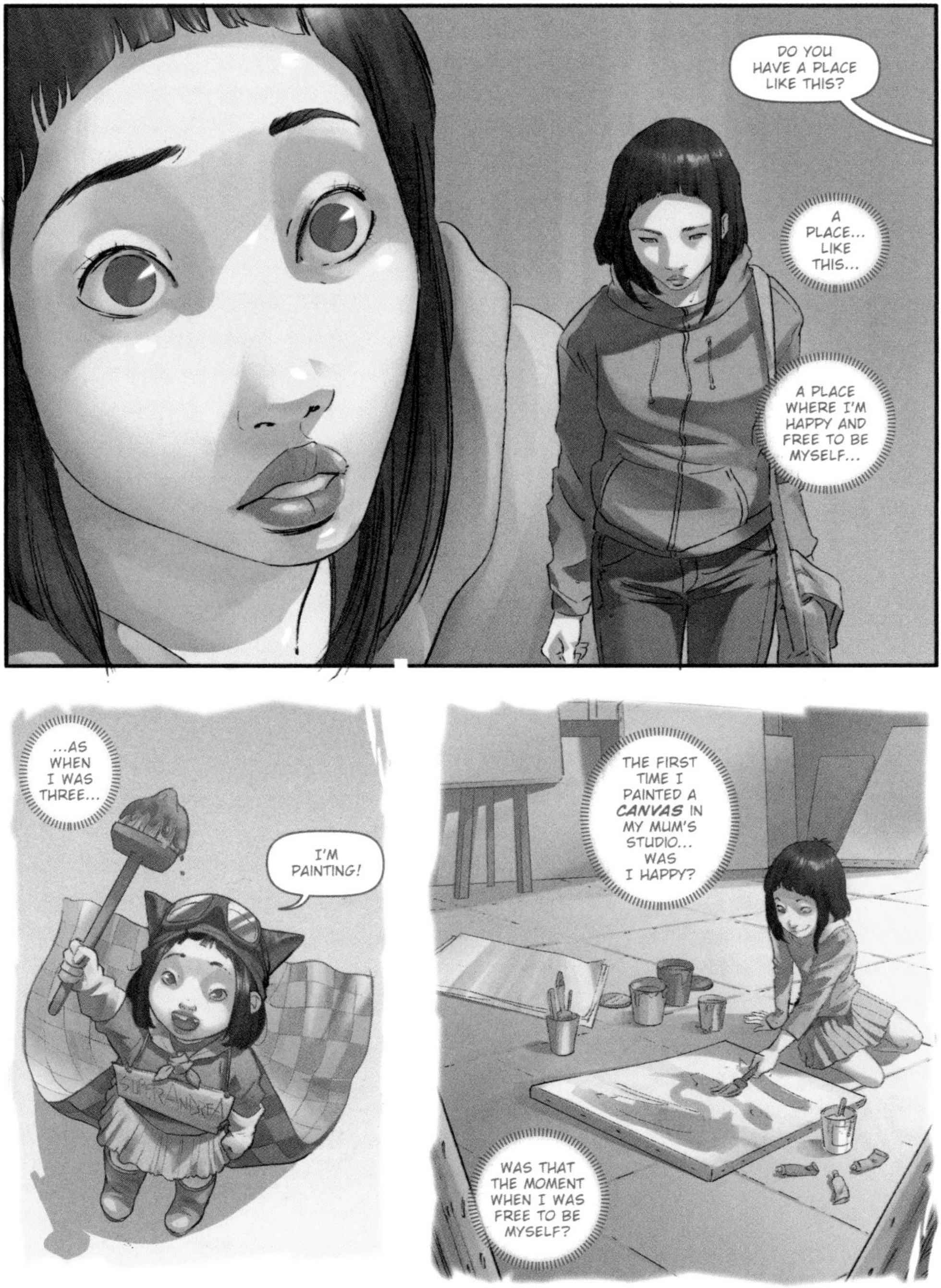
DO YOU HAVE A PLACE LIKE THIS?
A PLACE... LIKE THIS...
A PLACE WHERE I'M HAPPY AND FREE TO BE MYSELF...
...AS WHEN I WAS THREE...
I'M PAINTING!
THE FIRST TIME I PAINTED A CANVAS IN MY MUM'S STUDIO... WAS I HAPPY?
WAS THAT THE MOMENT WHEN I WAS FREE TO BE MYSELF?

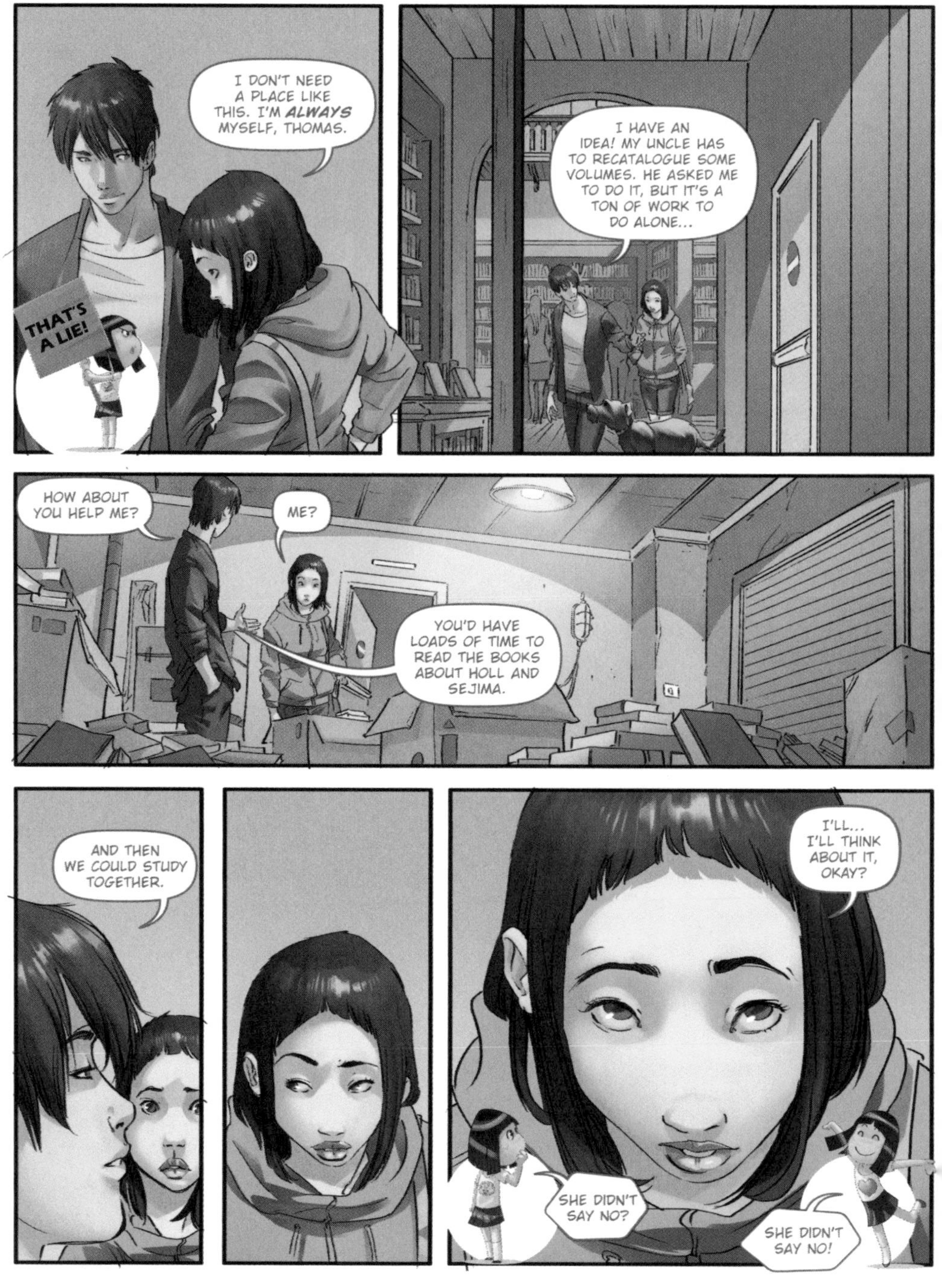
I DON'T NEED A PLACE LIKE THIS. I'M ALWAYS MYSELF, THOMAS.
THAT'S A LIE!
I HAVE AN IDEA! MY UNCLE HAS TO RECATALOGUE SOME VOLUMES. HE ASKED ME TO DO IT, BUT IT'S A TON OF WORK TO DO ALONE...
HOW ABOUT YOU HELP ME?
ME?
YOU'D HAVE LOADS OF TIME TO READ THE BOOKS ABOUT HOLL AND SEJIMA.
AND THEN WE COULD STUDY TOGETHER.
I'LL... I'LL THINK ABOUT IT, OKAY?
SHE DIDN'T SAY NO?
SHE DIDN'T SAY NO!

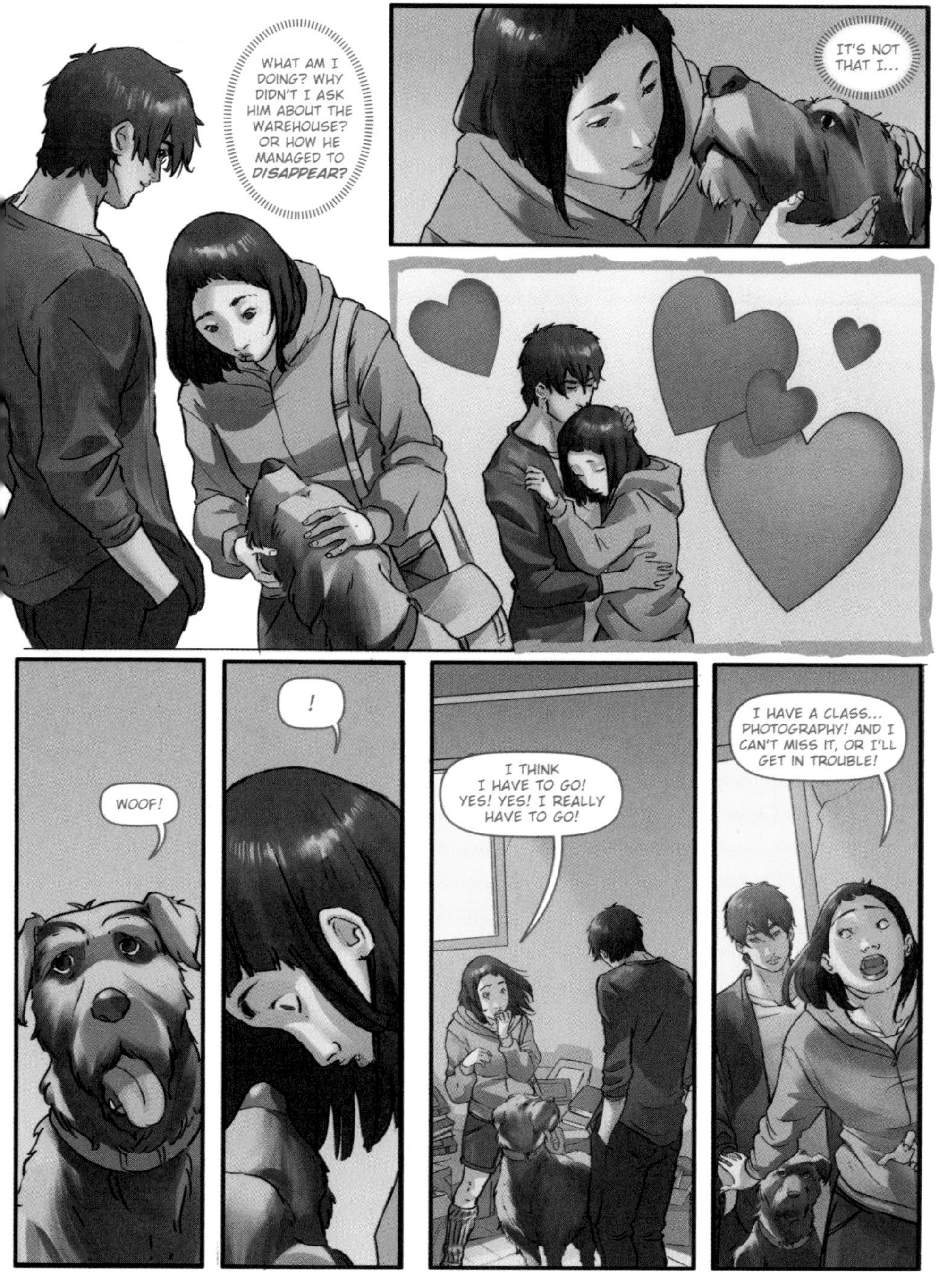
WHAT AM I DOING? WHY DIDN'T I ASK HIM ABOUT THE WAREHOUSE? OR HOW HE MANAGED TO *DISAPPEAR?*
IT'S NOT THAT I...
WOOF!
!
I THINK I HAVE TO GO! YES! YES! I REALLY HAVE TO GO!
I HAVE A CLASS... PHOTOGRAPHY! AND I CAN'T MISS IT, OR I'LL GET IN TROUBLE!

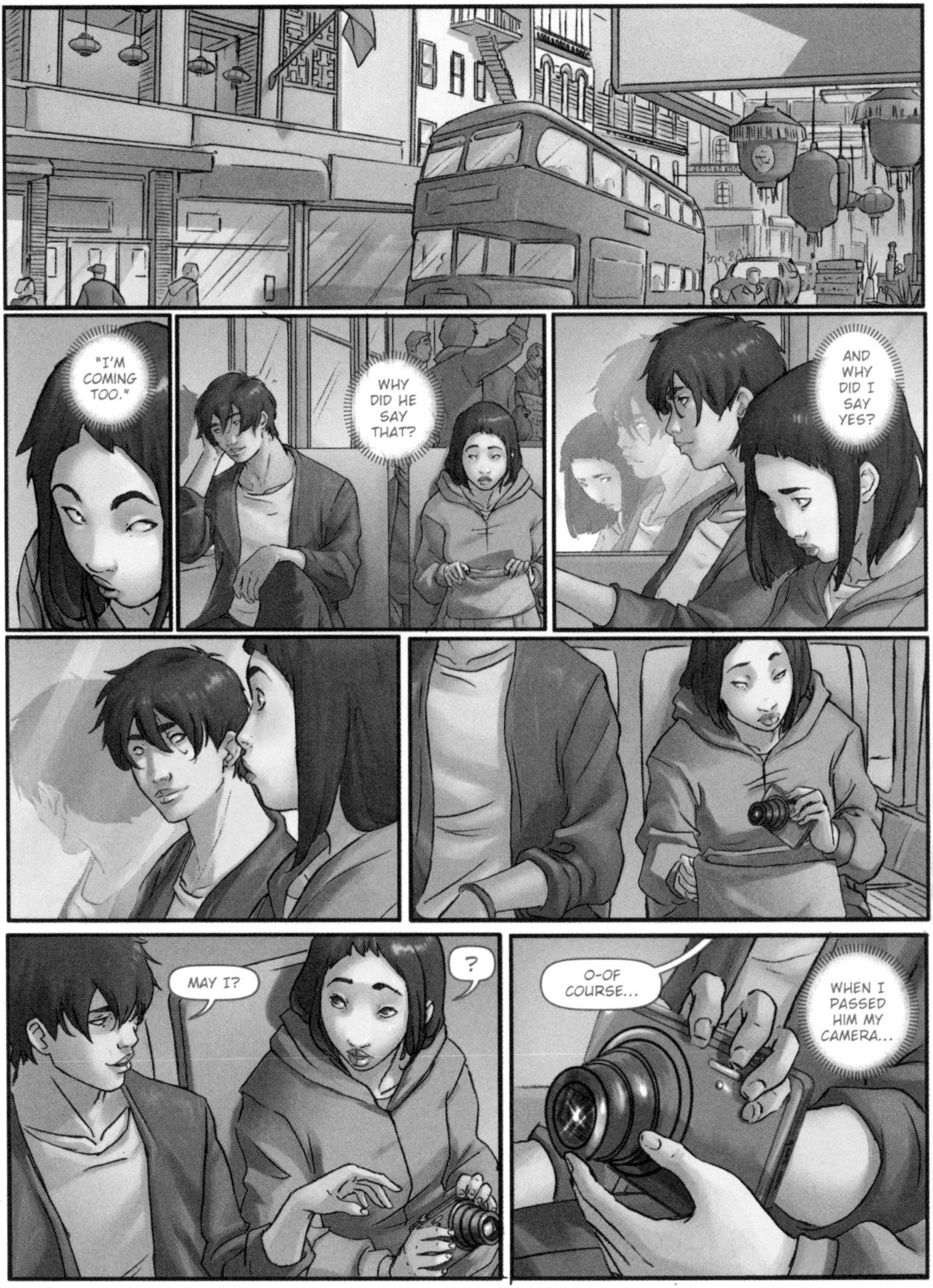
"I'M COMING TOO."
WHY DID HE SAY THAT?
AND WHY DID I SAY YES?
MAY I?
?
O-OF COURSE...
WHEN I PASSED HIM MY CAMERA...

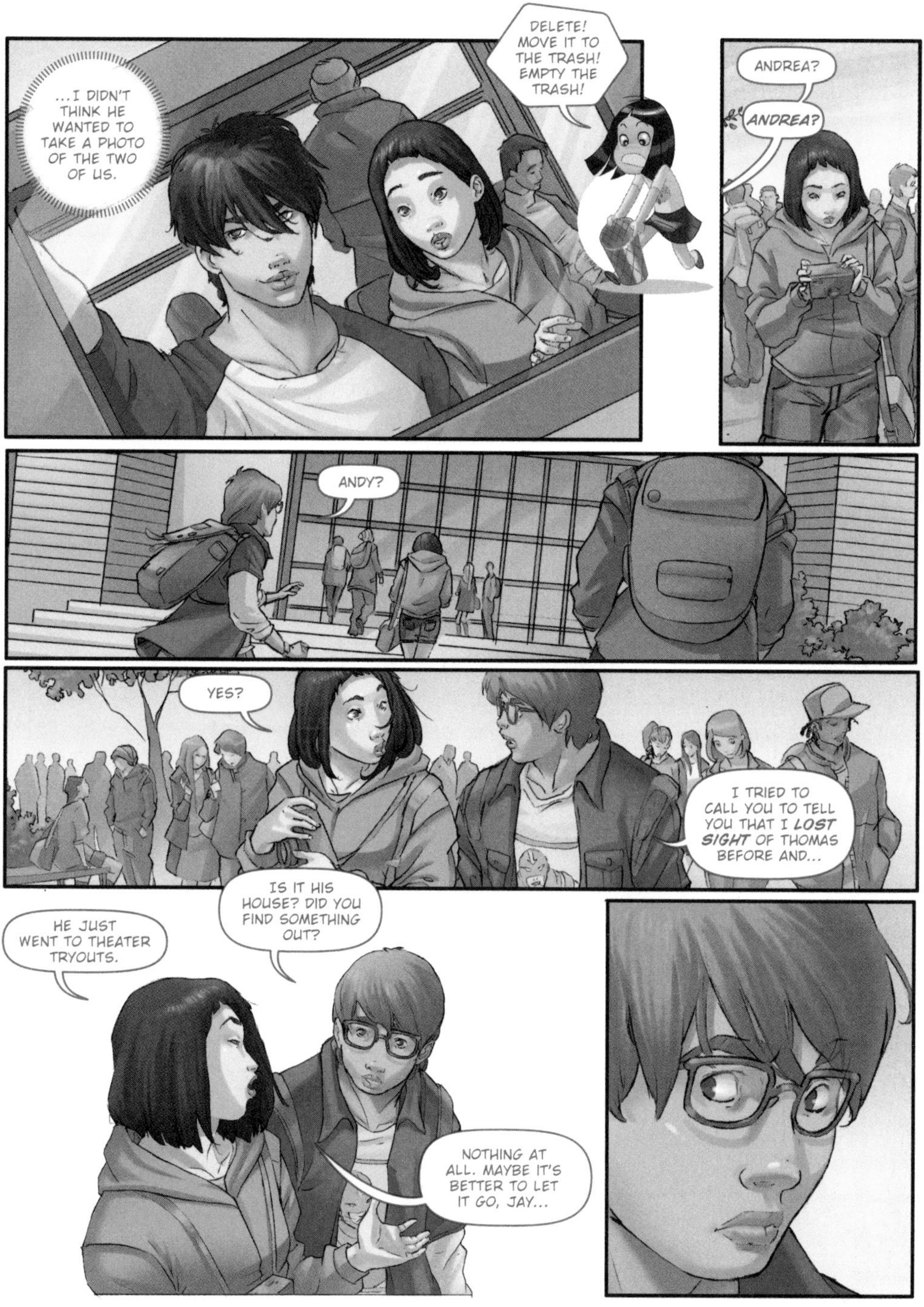
...I DIDN'T THINK HE WANTED TO TAKE A PHOTO OF THE TWO OF US.
DELETE! MOVE IT TO THE TRASH! EMPTY THE TRASH!
ANDREA?
ANDREA?
ANDY?
YES?
I TRIED TO CALL YOU TO TELL YOU THAT I LOST SIGHT OF THOMAS BEFORE AND...
IS IT HIS HOUSE? DID YOU FIND SOMETHING OUT?
HE JUST WENT TO THEATER TRYOUTS.
NOTHING AT ALL. MAYBE IT'S BETTER TO LET IT GO, JAY...

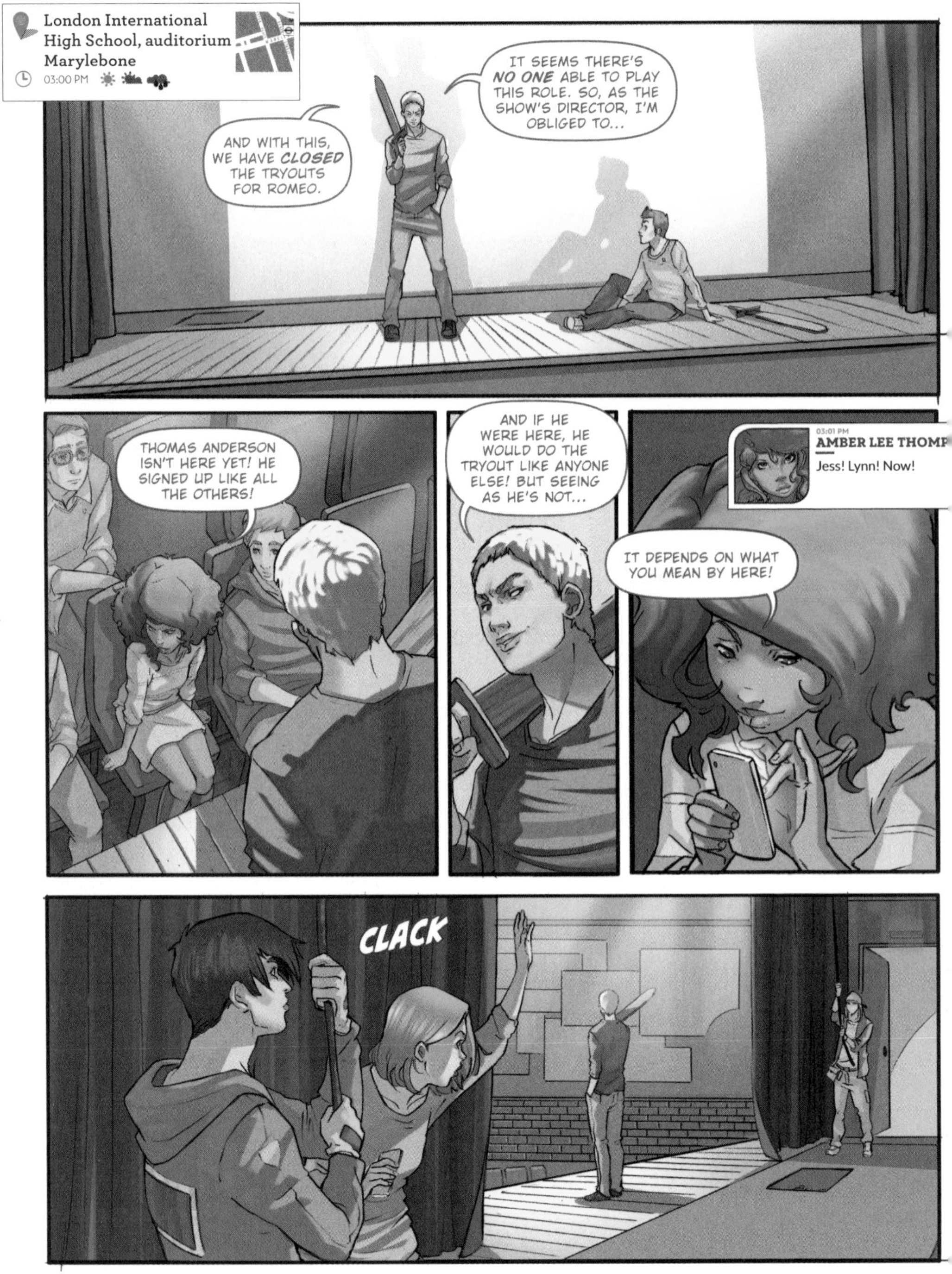

London International High School, auditorium
Marylebone
03:00 PM
IT SEEMS THERE'S NO ONE ABLE TO PLAY THIS ROLE. SO, AS THE SHOW'S DIRECTOR, I'M OBLIGED TO...
AND WITH THIS, WE HAVE CLOSED THE TRYOUTS FOR ROMEO.
THOMAS ANDERSON ISN'T HERE YET! HE SIGNED UP LIKE ALL THE OTHERS!
AND IF HE WERE HERE, HE WOULD DO THE TRYOUT LIKE ANYONE ELSE! BUT SEEING AS HE'S NOT...
03:01 PM
AMBER LEE THOMP
Jess! Lynn! Now!
IT DEPENDS ON WHAT YOU MEAN BY HERE!
CLACK

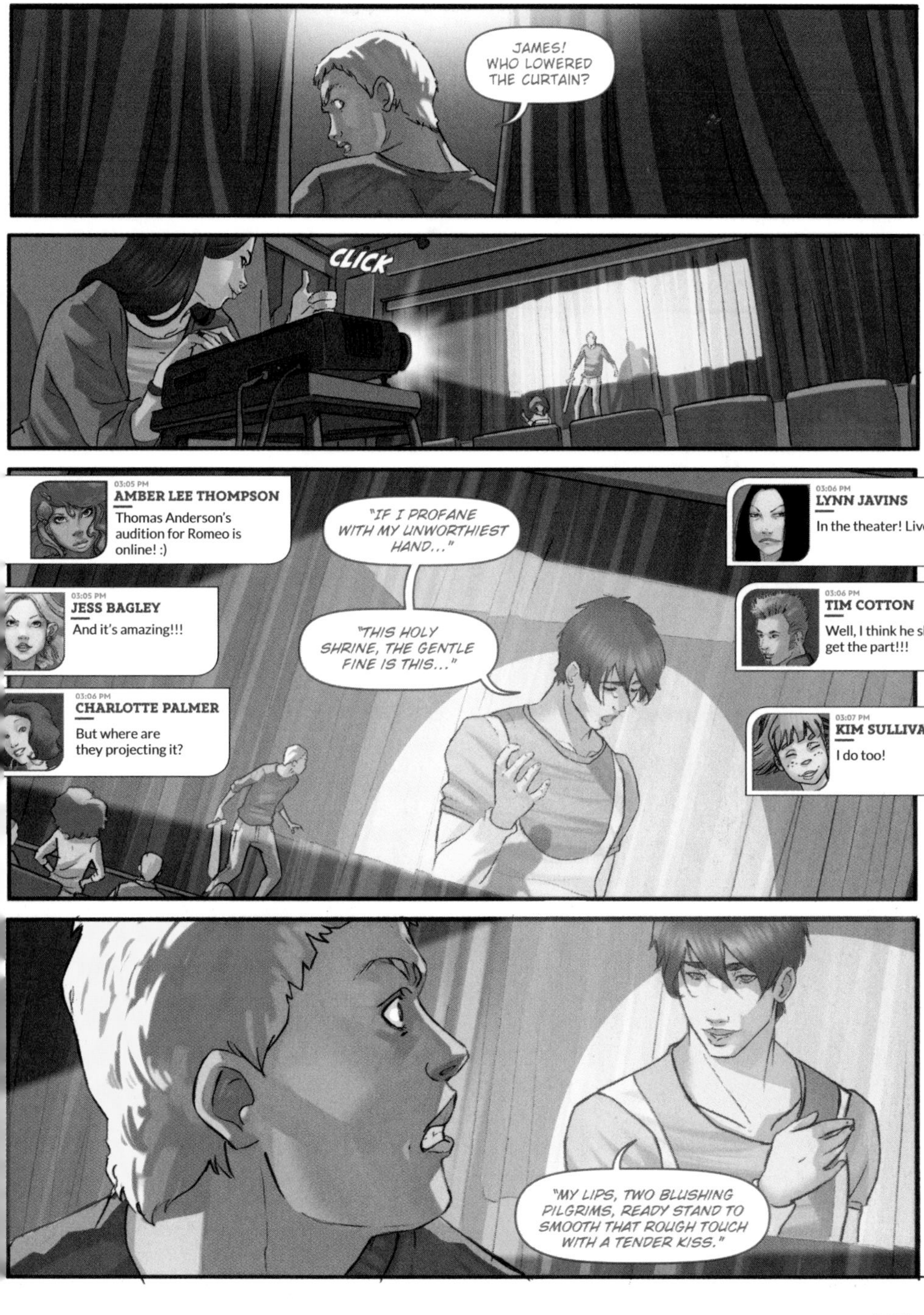
JAMES! WHO LOWERED THE CURTAIN?
CLICK
03:05 PM AMBER LEE THOMPSON Thomas Anderson's audition for Romeo is online! :)
"IF I PROFANE WITH MY UNWORTHIEST HAND..."
03:06 PM LYNN JAVINS In the theater! Live!
03:05 PM JESS BAGLEY And it's amazing!!!
"THIS HOLY SHRINE, THE GENTLE FINE IS THIS..."
03:06 PM TIM COTTON Well, I think he should get the part!!!
03:06 PM CHARLOTTE PALMER But where are they projecting it?
03:07 PM KIM SULLIVAN I do too!
"MY LIPS, TWO BLUSHING PILGRIMS, READY STAND TO SMOOTH THAT ROUGH TOUCH WITH A TENDER KISS."

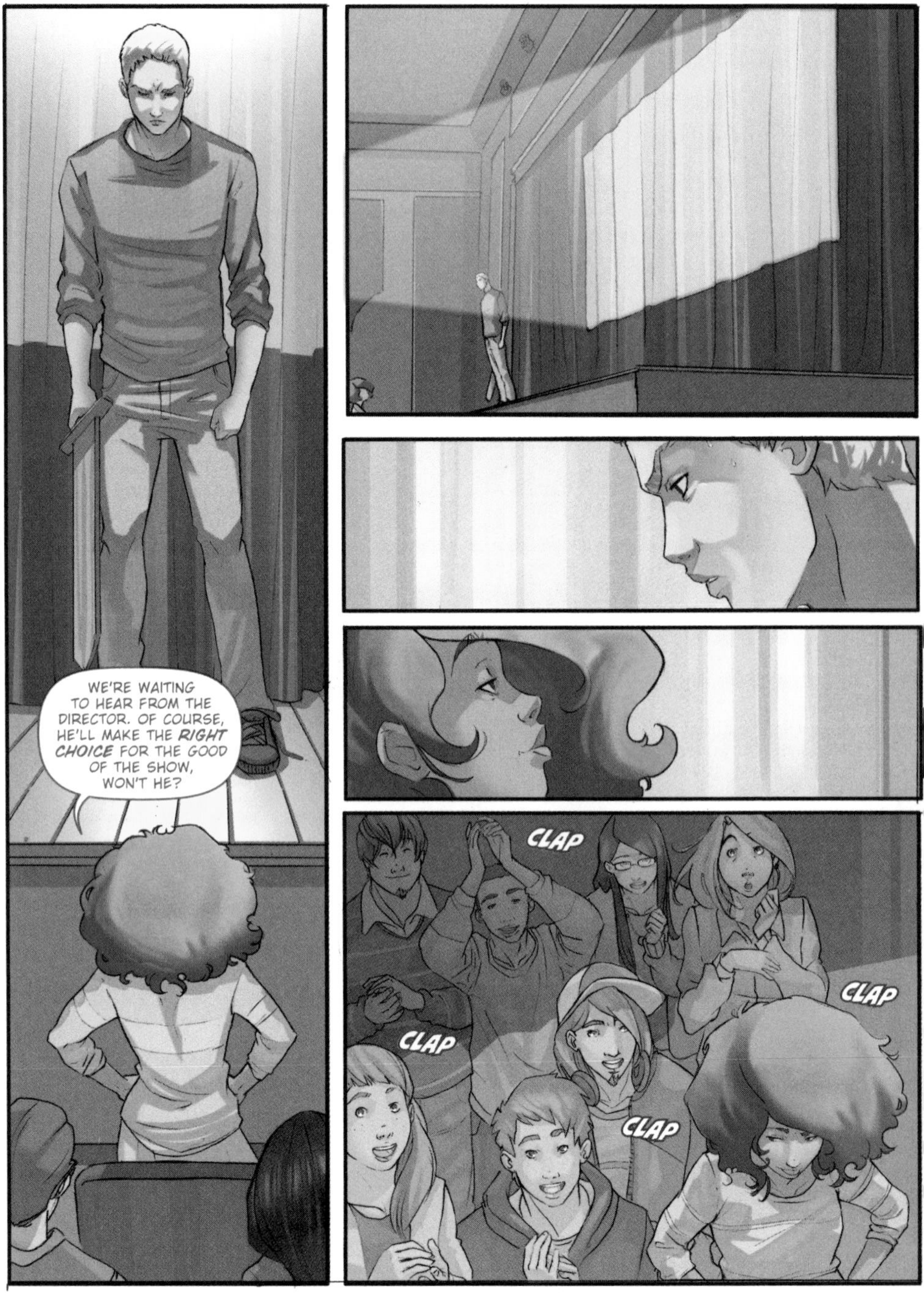
WE'RE WAITING TO HEAR FROM THE DIRECTOR. OF COURSE, HE'LL MAKE THE *RIGHT CHOICE* FOR THE GOOD OF THE SHOW, WON'T HE?
CLAP
CLAP
CLAP
CLAP

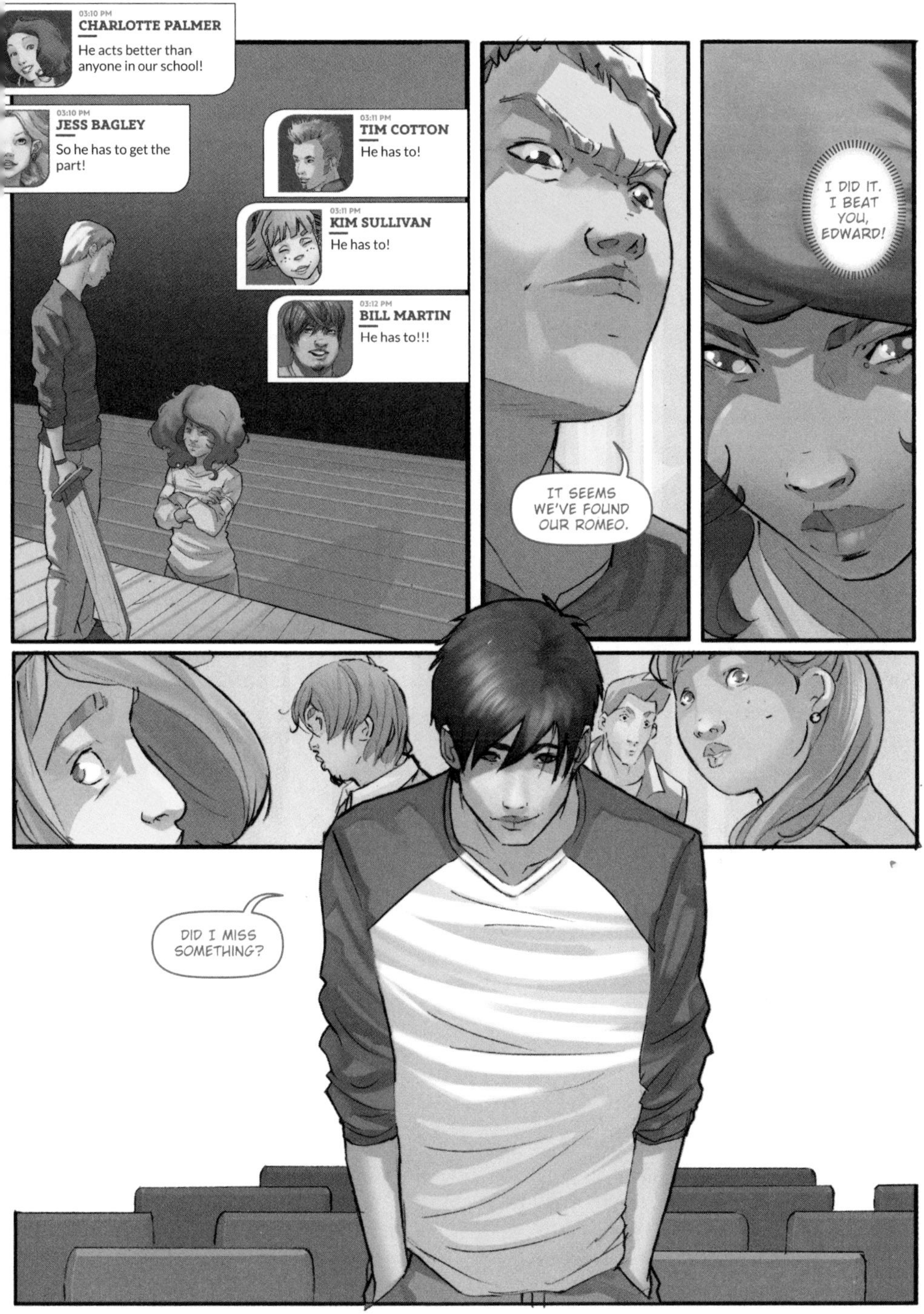
03:10 PM
CHARLOTTE PALMER
He acts better than anyone in our school!
03:10 PM
JESS BAGLEY
So he has to get the part!
03:11 PM
TIM COTTON
He has to!
03:11 PM
KIM SULLIVAN
He has to!
03:12 PM
BILL MARTIN
He has to!!!
IT SEEMS WE'VE FOUND OUR ROMEO.
I DID IT. I BEAT YOU, EDWARD!
DID I MISS SOMETHING?

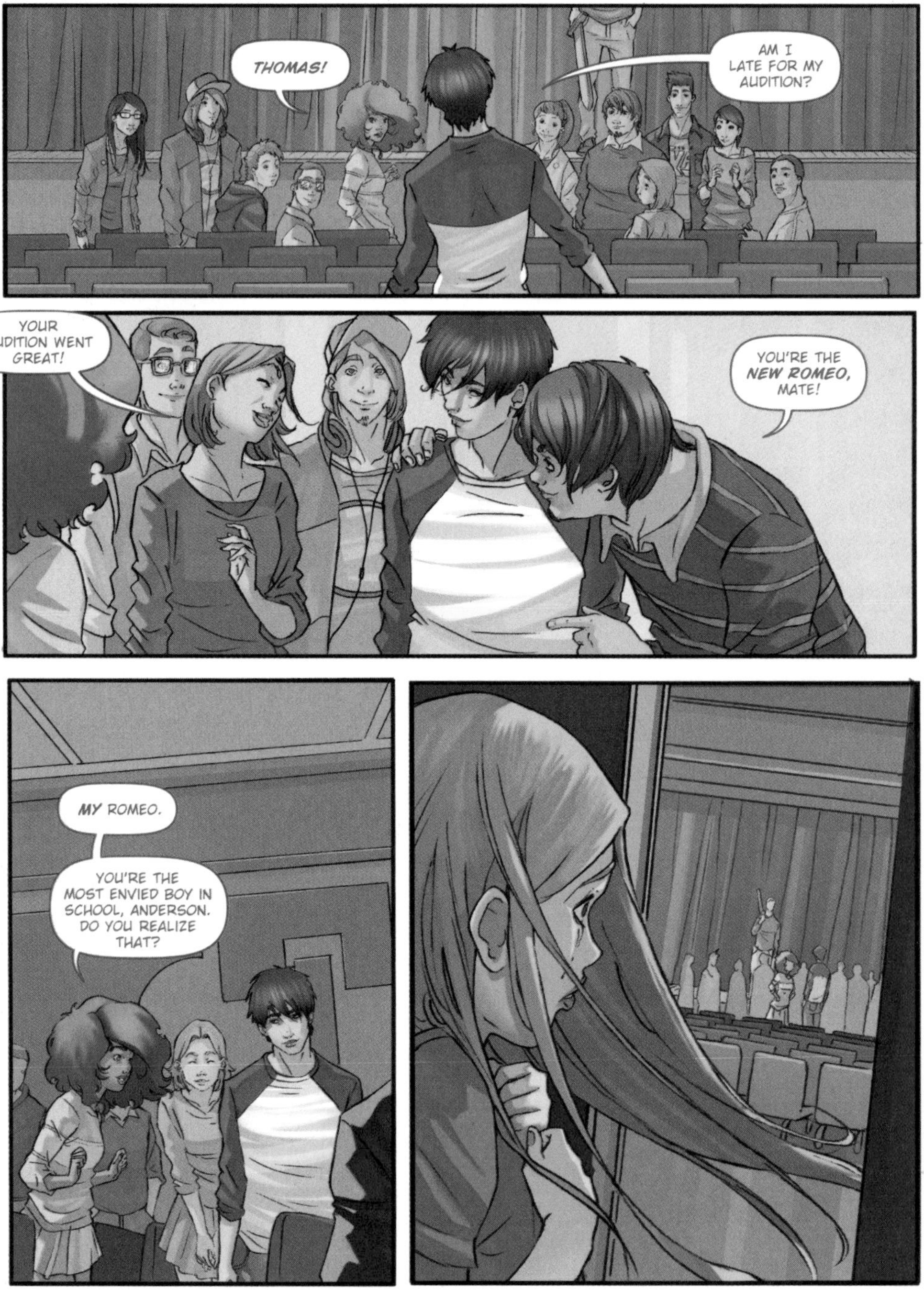
THOMAS!
AM I LATE FOR MY AUDITION?
YOUR AUDITION WENT GREAT!
YOU'RE THE NEW ROMEO, MATE!
MY ROMEO.
YOU'RE THE MOST ENVIED BOY IN SCHOOL, ANDERSON. DO YOU REALIZE THAT?

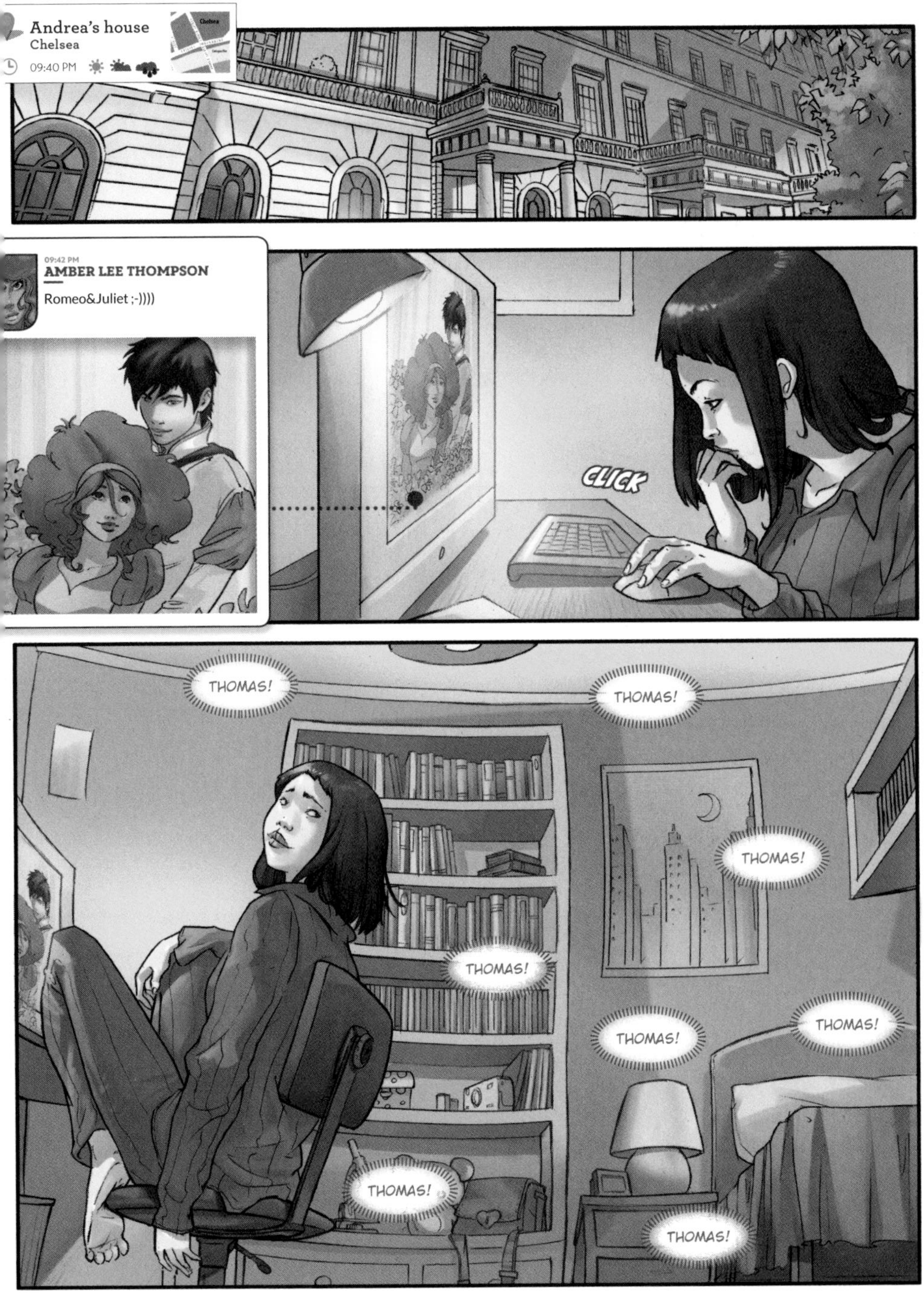
Andrea's house
Chelsea
09:40 PM
09:42 PM
AMBER LEE THOMPSON
Romeo&Juliet ;-))))
CLICK
THOMAS!
THOMAS!
THOMAS!
THOMAS!
THOMAS!
THOMAS!
THOMAS!
THOMAS!

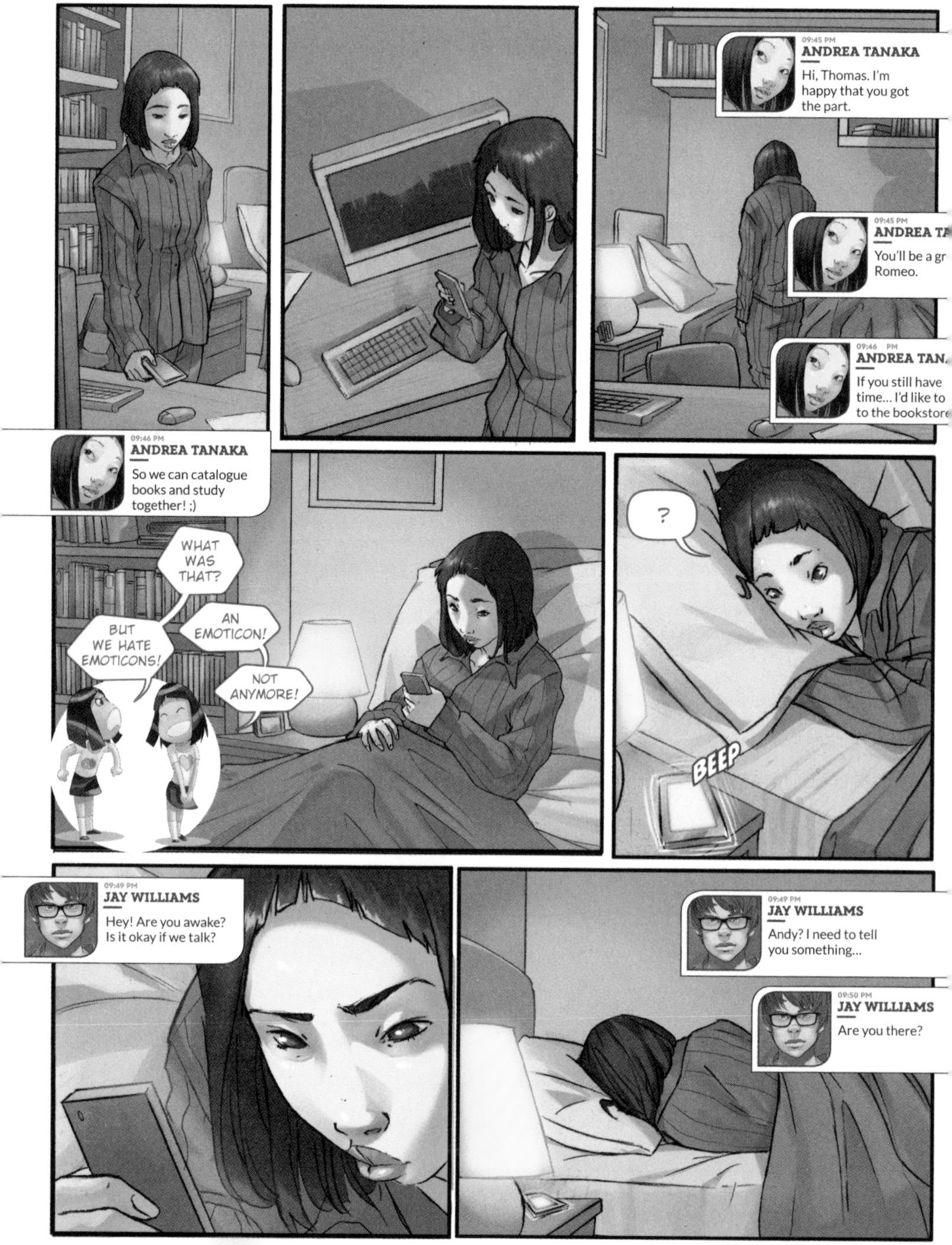
09:45 PM
ANDREA TANAKA
Hi, Thomas. I'm happy that you got the part.
09:45 PM
ANDREA TA
You'll be a gr
Romeo.
09:46 PM
ANDREA TAN
If you still have time... I'd like to
to the bookstore
09:46 PM
ANDREA TANAKA
So we can catalogue books and study together! ;)
WHAT WAS THAT?
AN EMOTICON!
BUT WE HATE EMOTICONS!
NOT ANYMORE!
?
BEEP
09:49 PM
JAY WILLIAMS
Hey! Are you awake? Is it okay if we talk?
09:49 PM
JAY WILLIAMS
Andy? I need to tell you something...
09:50 PM
JAY WILLIAMS
Are you there?

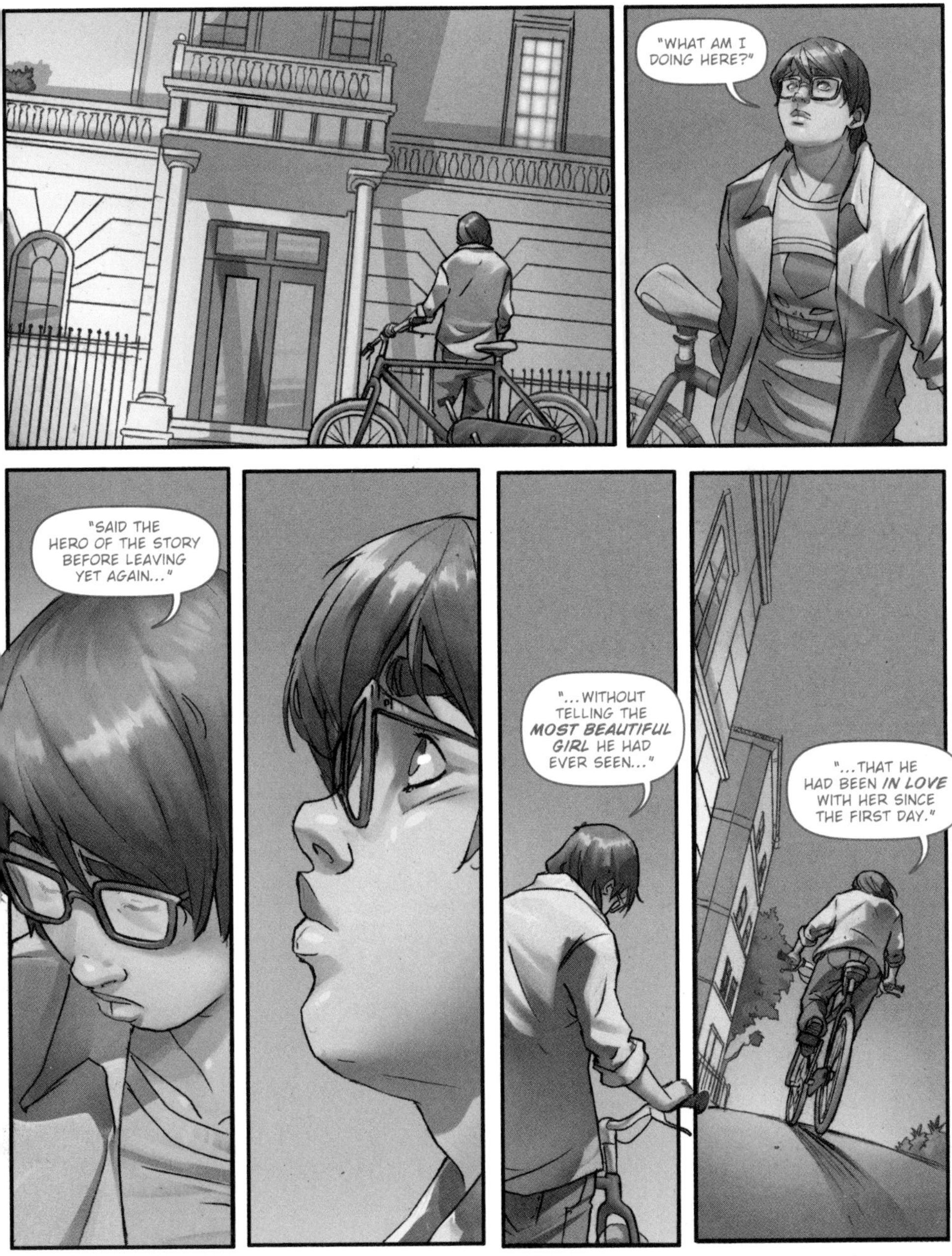
"WHAT AM I DOING HERE?"
"SAID THE HERO OF THE STORY BEFORE LEAVING YET AGAIN..."
"...WITHOUT TELLING THE **MOST BEAUTIFUL GIRL** HE HAD EVER SEEN..."
"...THAT HE HAD BEEN **IN LOVE** WITH HER SINCE THE FIRST DAY."

END OF CHAPTER 9

Disney **real** life #3

#Mission in Chinatown

Script: Alessandro Ferrari
Layout: Giada Perissinotto and Alberto Zanon
Cleanup: Elena Pianta and Alberto Zanon
Emotidolls: Andrea Scoppetta
Color: Massimo Rocca, Pierluigi Casolino, Andrea Scoppetta, Mario Perrotta, Slava Panarin, Giuseppe Fontana, Gianluca Barone
Watercolor backgrounds: Valeria Turati
Translation: Edizioni BD and Erin Brady
Lettering and Infographic: Edizioni BD

COVER
Layout and cleanup: Alberto Zanon
Color: Massimo Rocca

CONTRIBUTORS
Tomatofarm

Original project developed by Disney Publishing with the contribution of Barbara Baraldi, Paola Barbato, Micol Beltramini and Diana Tomatozombie

#4 #The Day I'll Kiss Him

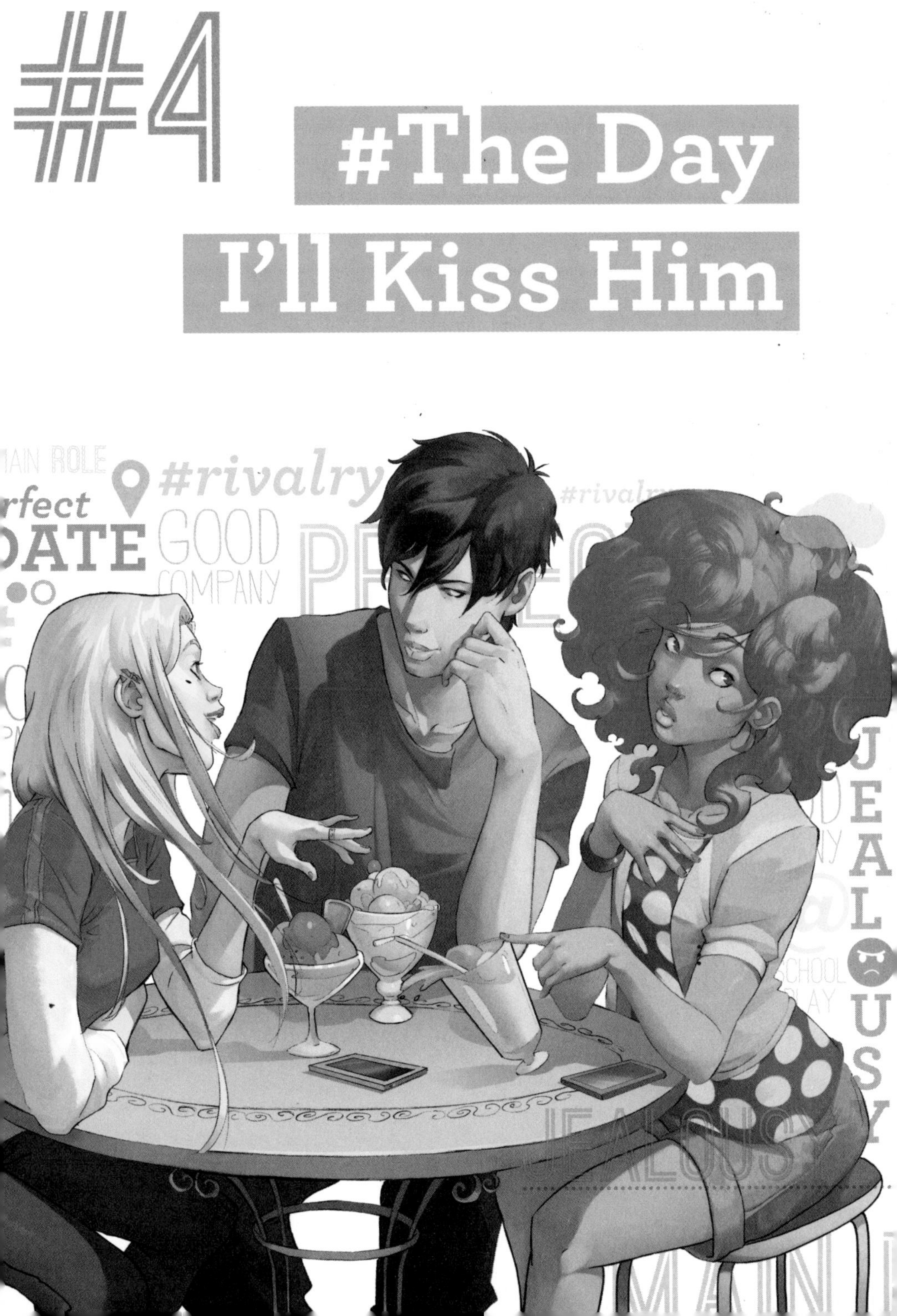
#rivalry
GOOD
COMPANY
#rival
SCHOOL
PLAY
JEALOUSY
JEALOUSY

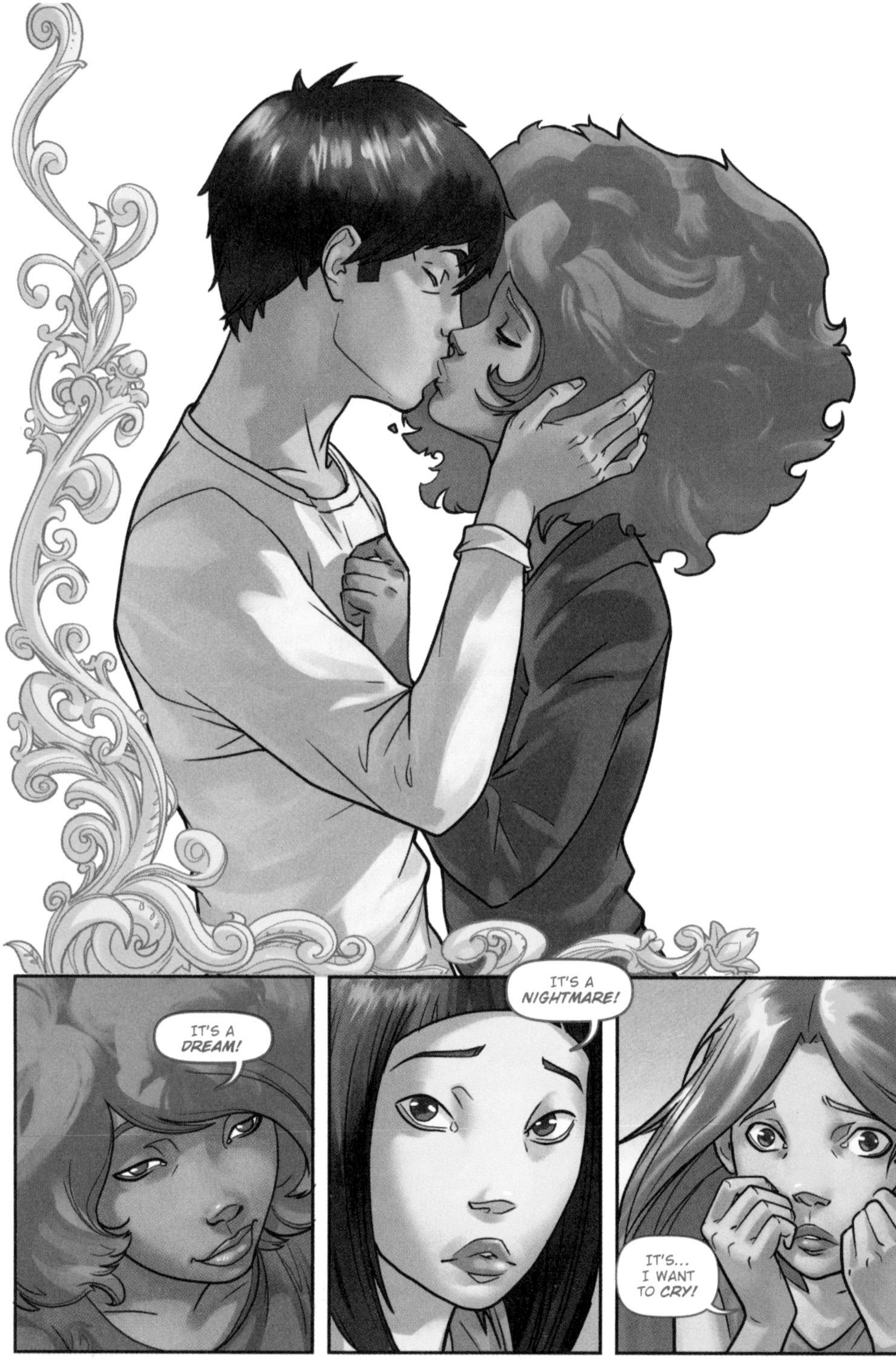
IT'S A DREAM!
IT'S A NIGHTMARE!
IT'S... I WANT TO CRY!

CHAPTER 10

ROMANTIC countdown

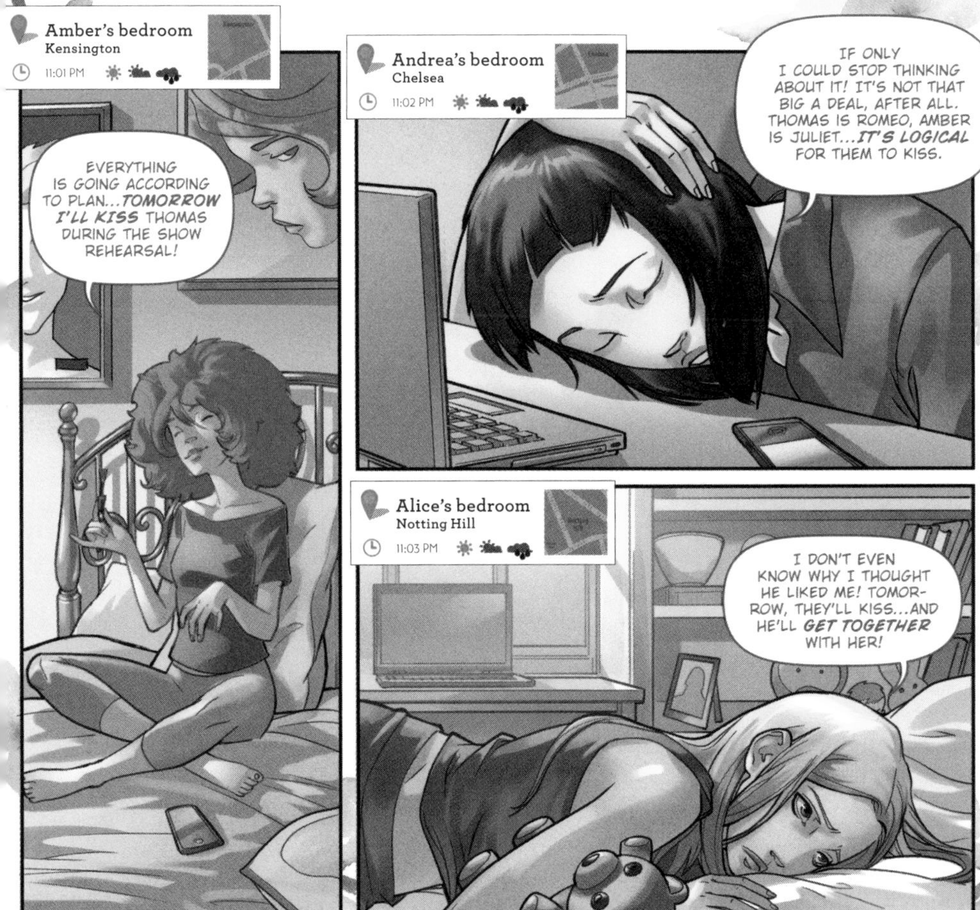
Amber's bedroom
Kensington
11:01 PM
EVERYTHING IS GOING ACCORDING TO PLAN... TOMORROW I'LL KISS THOMAS DURING THE SHOW REHEARSAL!
Andrea's bedroom
Chelsea
11:02 PM
IF ONLY I COULD STOP THINKING ABOUT IT! IT'S NOT THAT BIG A DEAL, AFTER ALL. THOMAS IS ROMEO, AMBER IS JULIET... IT'S LOGICAL FOR THEM TO KISS.
Alice's bedroom
Notting Hill
11:03 PM
I DON'T EVEN KNOW WHY I THOUGHT HE LIKED ME! TOMORROW, THEY'LL KISS... AND HE'LL GET TOGETHER WITH HER!

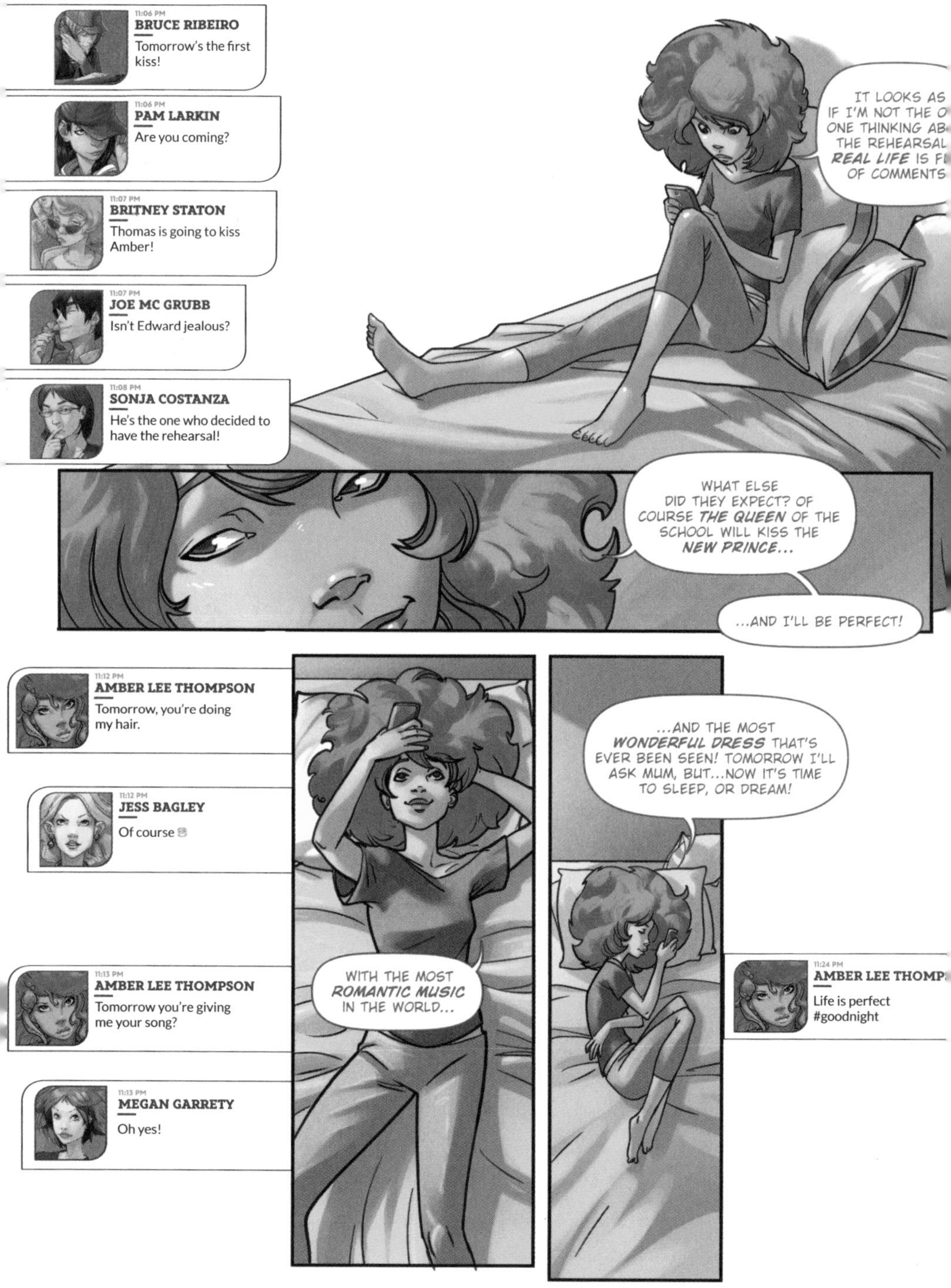
11:06 PM
BRUCE RIBEIRO
Tomorrow's the first kiss!
11:06 PM
PAM LARKIN
Are you coming?
11:07 PM
BRITNEY STATON
Thomas is going to kiss Amber!
11:07 PM
JOE MC GRUBB
Isn't Edward jealous?
11:08 PM
SONJA COSTANZA
He's the one who decided to have the rehearsal!
IT LOOKS AS IF I'M NOT THE O ONE THINKING AB THE REHEARSAL REAL LIFE IS F OF COMMENTS
WHAT ELSE DID THEY EXPECT? OF COURSE THE QUEEN OF THE SCHOOL WILL KISS THE NEW PRINCE...
...AND I'LL BE PERFECT!
11:12 PM
AMBER LEE THOMPSON
Tomorrow, you're doing my hair.
11:12 PM
JESS BAGLEY
Of course
11:13 PM
AMBER LEE THOMPSON
Tomorrow you're giving me your song?
11:13 PM
MEGAN GARRETY
Oh yes!
WITH THE MOST ROMANTIC MUSIC IN THE WORLD...
...AND THE MOST WONDERFUL DRESS THAT'S EVER BEEN SEEN! TOMORROW I'LL ASK MUM, BUT...NOW IT'S TIME TO SLEEP, OR DREAM!
11:24 PM
AMBER LEE THOMP
Life is perfect #goodnight

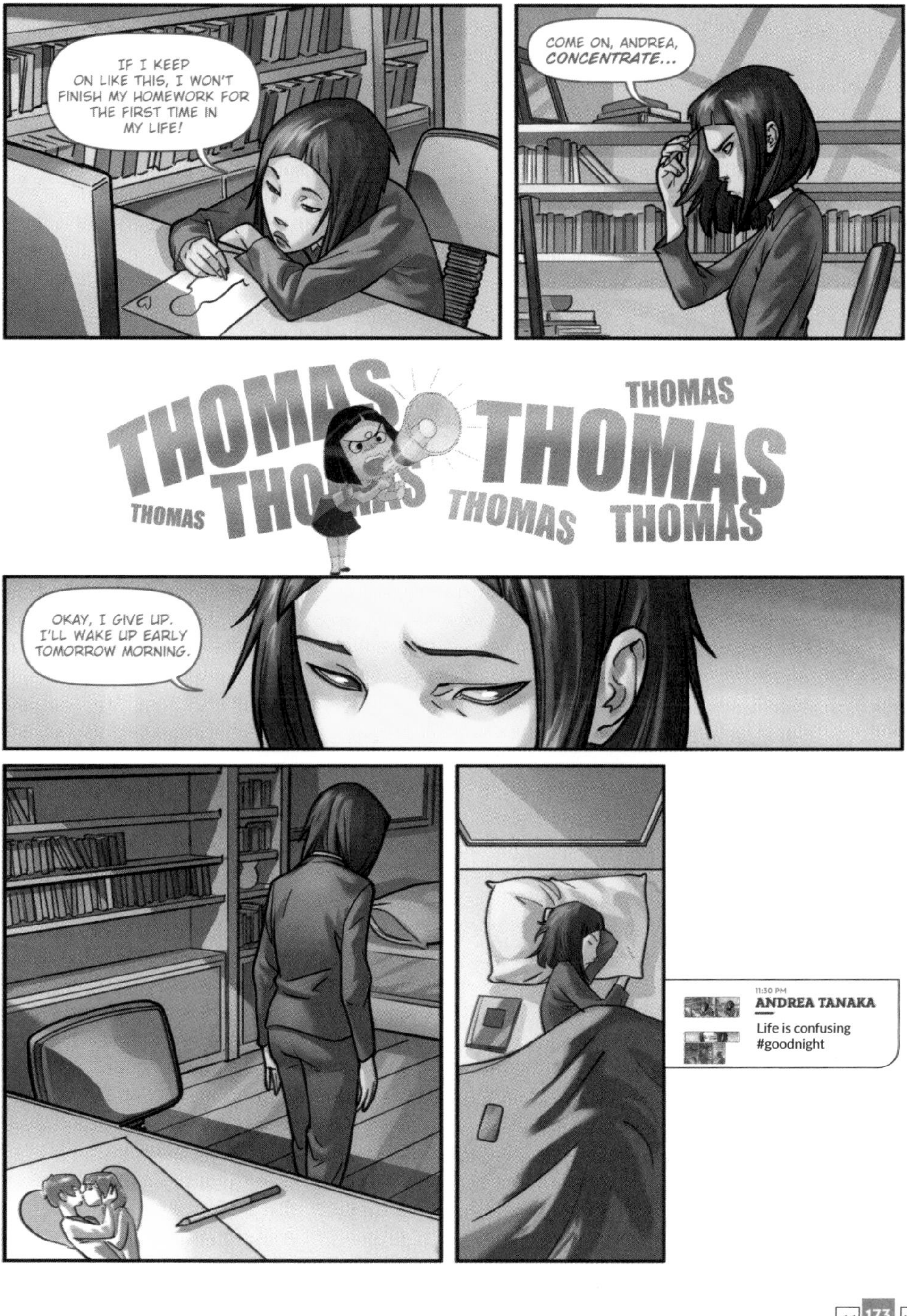
IF I KEEP ON LIKE THIS, I WON'T FINISH MY HOMEWORK FOR THE FIRST TIME IN MY LIFE!
COME ON, ANDREA, *CONCENTRATE...*
THOMAS THOMAS THOMAS THOMAS THOMAS THOMAS THOMAS THOMAS
OKAY, I GIVE UP. I'LL WAKE UP EARLY TOMORROW MORNING.
11:30 PM
ANDREA TANAKA
Life is confusing
#goodnight

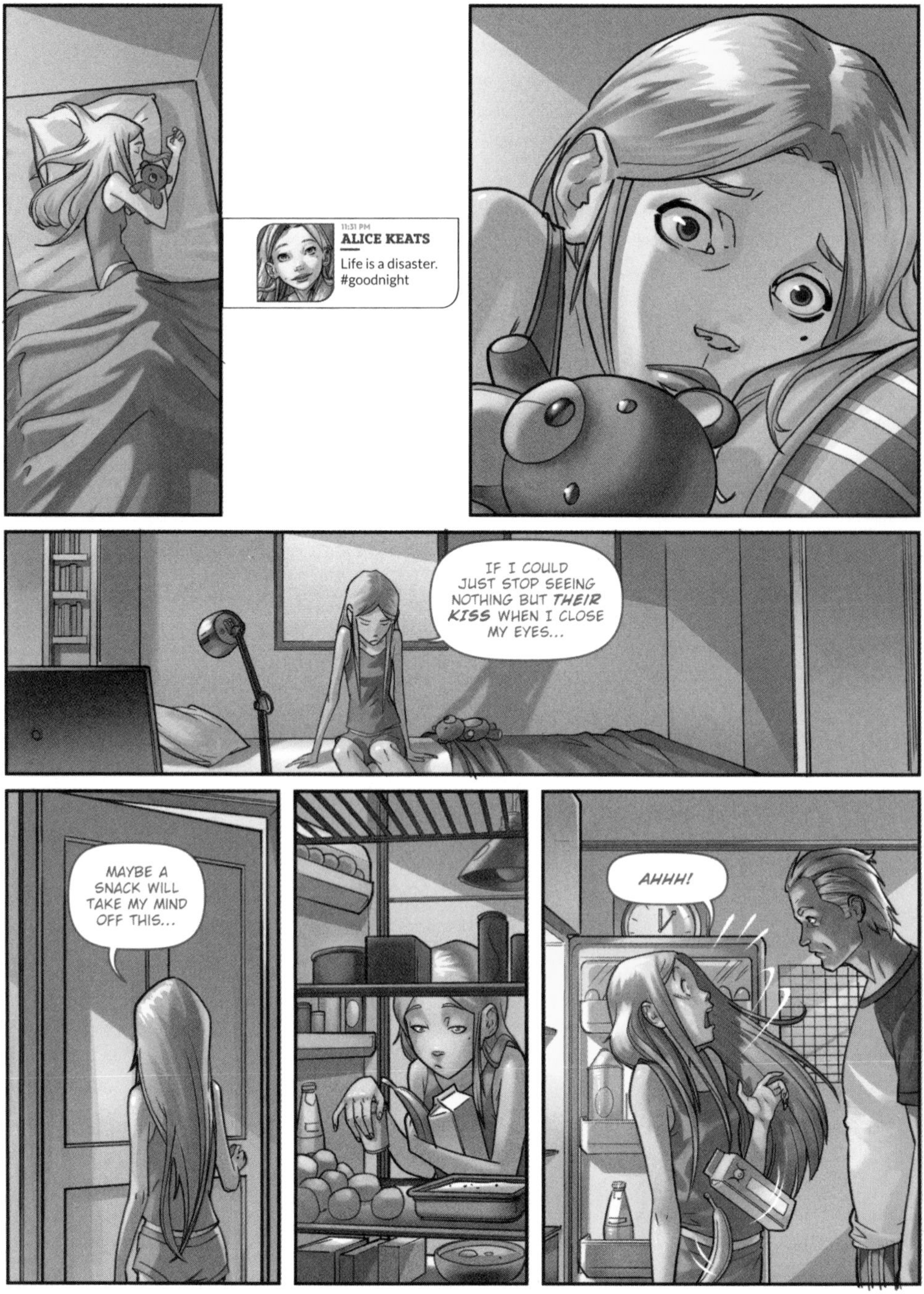
11:31 PM
ALICE KEATS
Life is a disaster. #goodnight
IF I COULD JUST STOP SEEING NOTHING BUT THEIR KISS WHEN I CLOSE MY EYES...
MAYBE A SNACK WILL TAKE MY MIND OFF THIS...
AHHH!

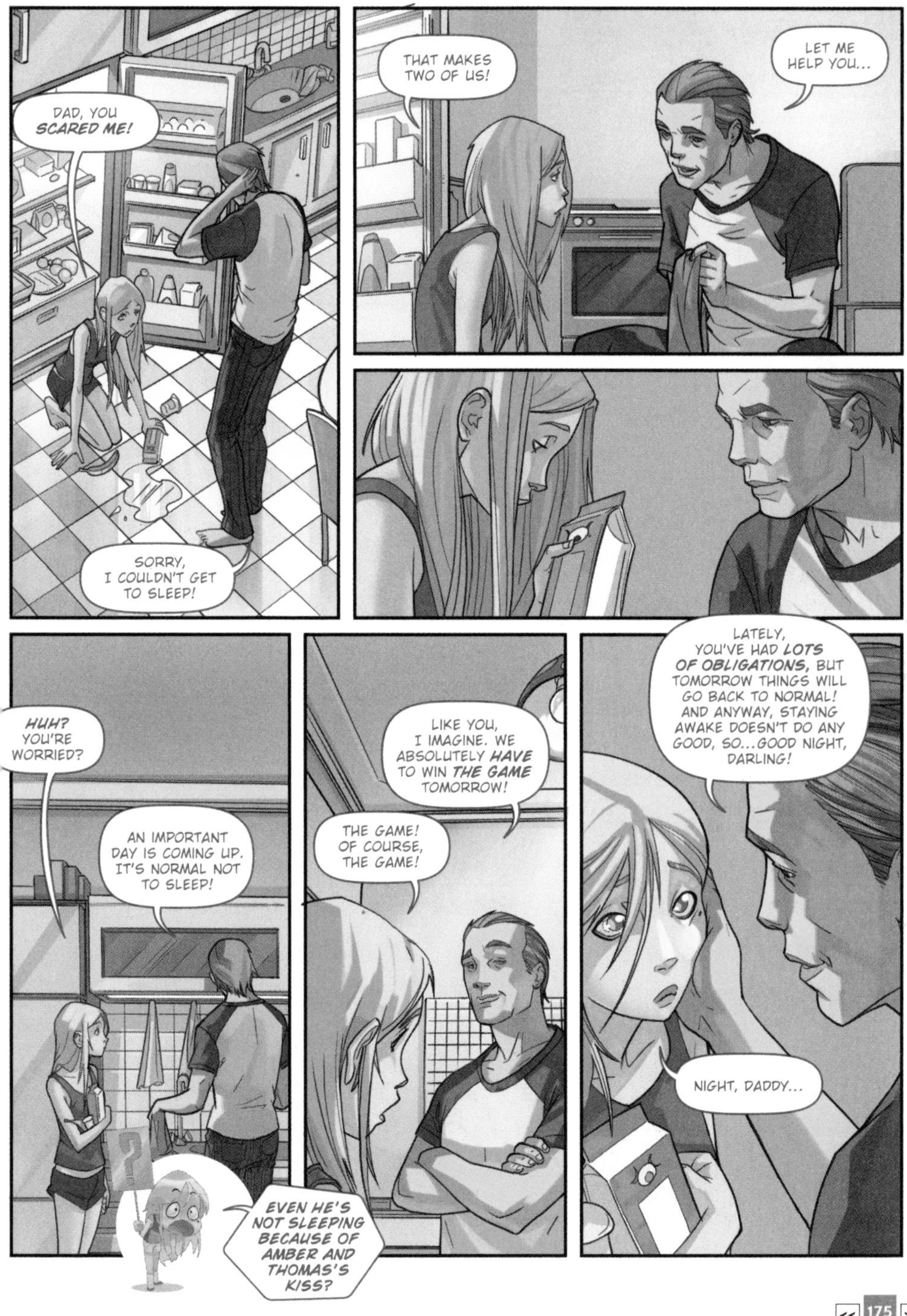

DAD, YOU SCARED ME!
SORRY, I COULDN'T GET TO SLEEP!
THAT MAKES TWO OF US!
LET ME HELP YOU...
HUH? YOU'RE WORRIED?
AN IMPORTANT DAY IS COMING UP. IT'S NORMAL NOT TO SLEEP!
EVEN HE'S NOT SLEEPING BECAUSE OF AMBER AND THOMAS'S KISS?
LIKE YOU, I IMAGINE. WE ABSOLUTELY HAVE TO WIN THE GAME TOMORROW!
THE GAME! OF COURSE, THE GAME!
LATELY, YOU'VE HAD LOTS OF OBLIGATIONS, BUT TOMORROW THINGS WILL GO BACK TO NORMAL! AND ANYWAY, STAYING AWAKE DOESN'T DO ANY GOOD, SO...GOOD NIGHT, DARLING!
NIGHT, DADDY...

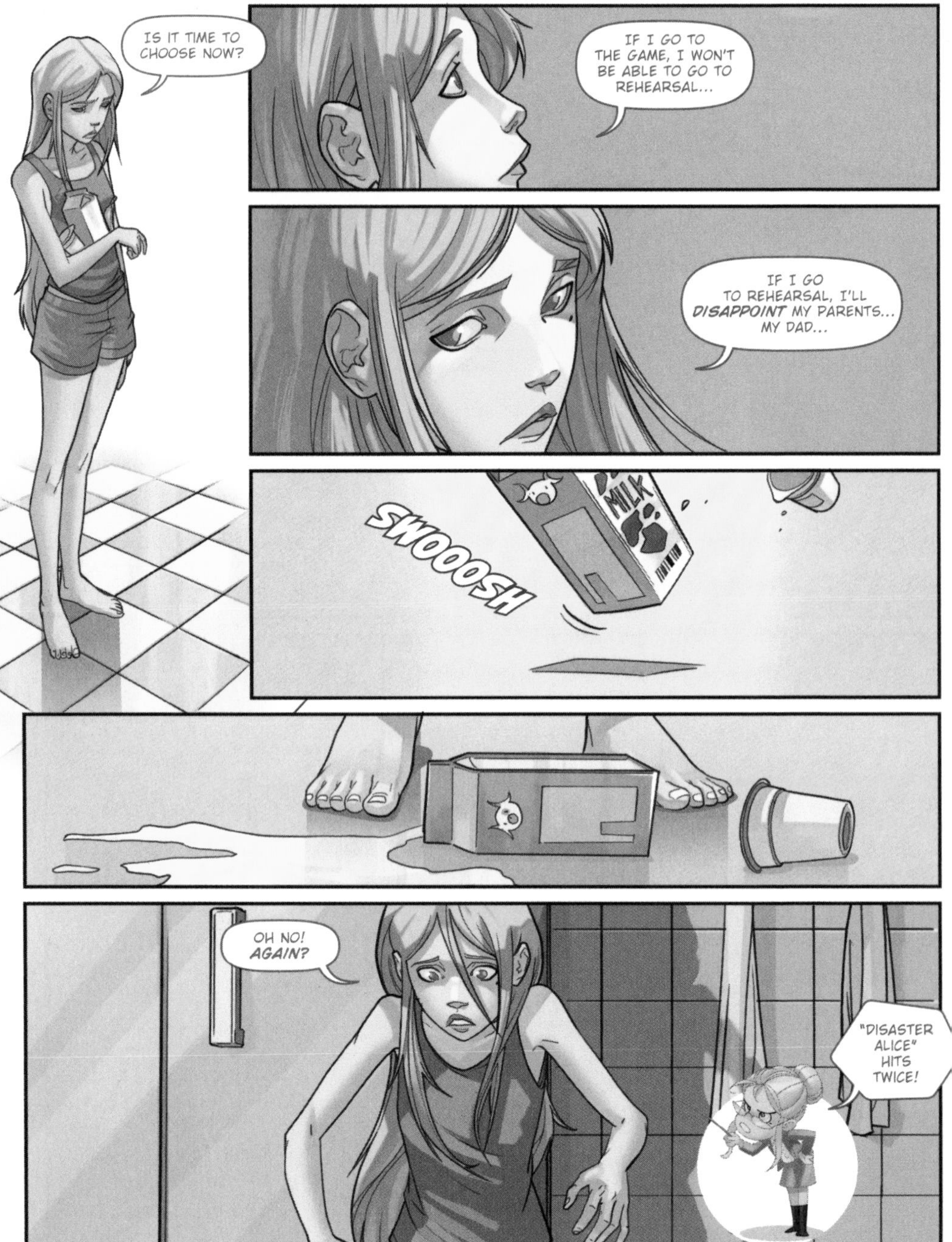
IS IT TIME TO CHOOSE NOW?
IF I GO TO THE GAME, I WON'T BE ABLE TO GO TO REHEARSAL...
IF I GO TO REHEARSAL, I'LL *DISAPPOINT* MY PARENTS... MY DAD...
MILK
SWOOOSH
OH NO! ***AGAIN?***
"DISASTER ALICE" HITS TWICE!

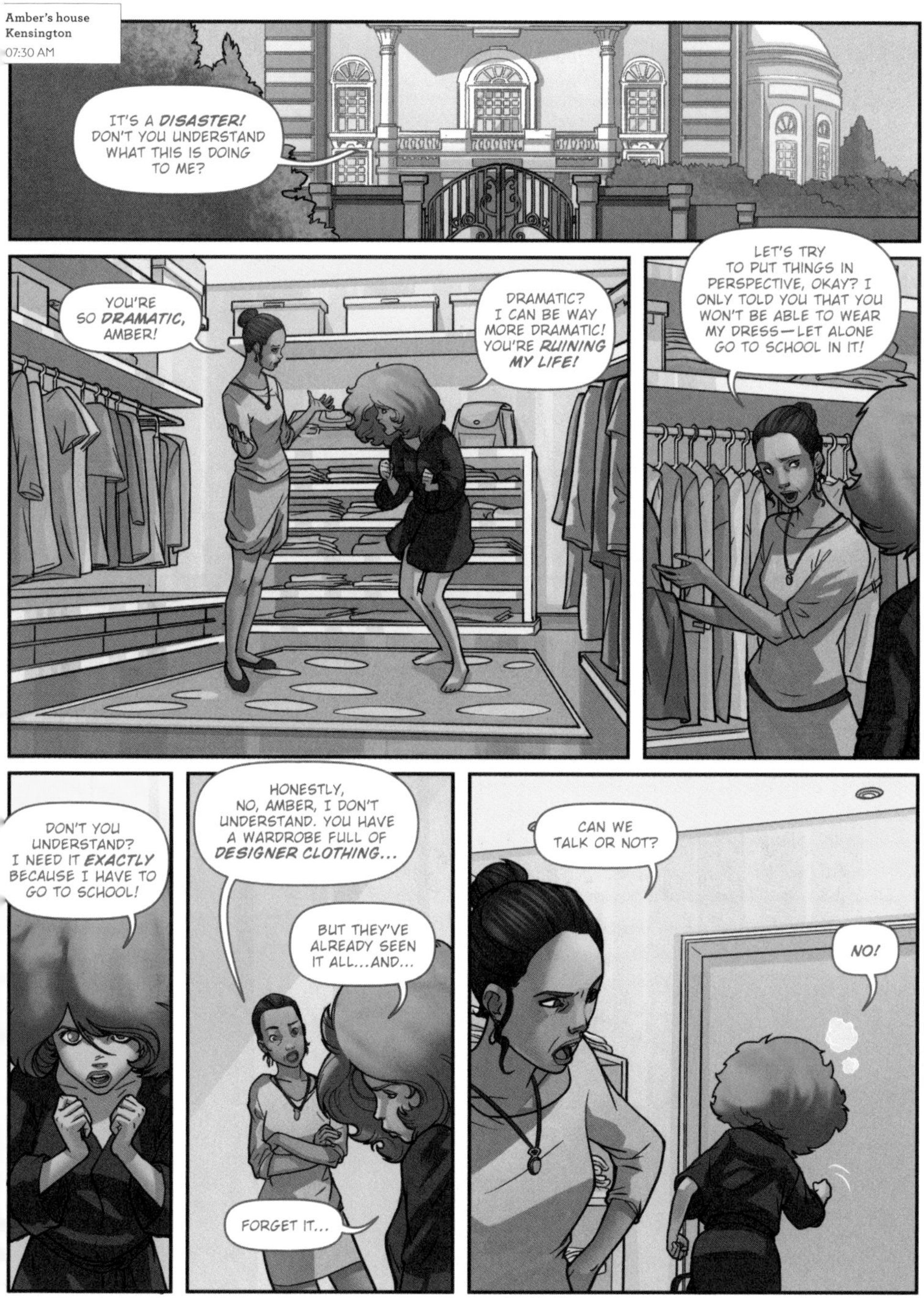
Amber's house
Kensington
07:30 AM
IT'S A DISASTER! DON'T YOU UNDERSTAND WHAT THIS IS DOING TO ME?
YOU'RE SO DRAMATIC, AMBER!
DRAMATIC? I CAN BE WAY MORE DRAMATIC! YOU'RE RUINING MY LIFE!
LET'S TRY TO PUT THINGS IN PERSPECTIVE, OKAY? I ONLY TOLD YOU THAT YOU WON'T BE ABLE TO WEAR MY DRESS—LET ALONE GO TO SCHOOL IN IT!
DON'T YOU UNDERSTAND? I NEED IT EXACTLY BECAUSE I HAVE TO GO TO SCHOOL!
HONESTLY, NO, AMBER, I DON'T UNDERSTAND. YOU HAVE A WARDROBE FULL OF DESIGNER CLOTHING...
BUT THEY'VE ALREADY SEEN IT ALL...AND...
FORGET IT...
CAN WE TALK OR NOT?
NO!

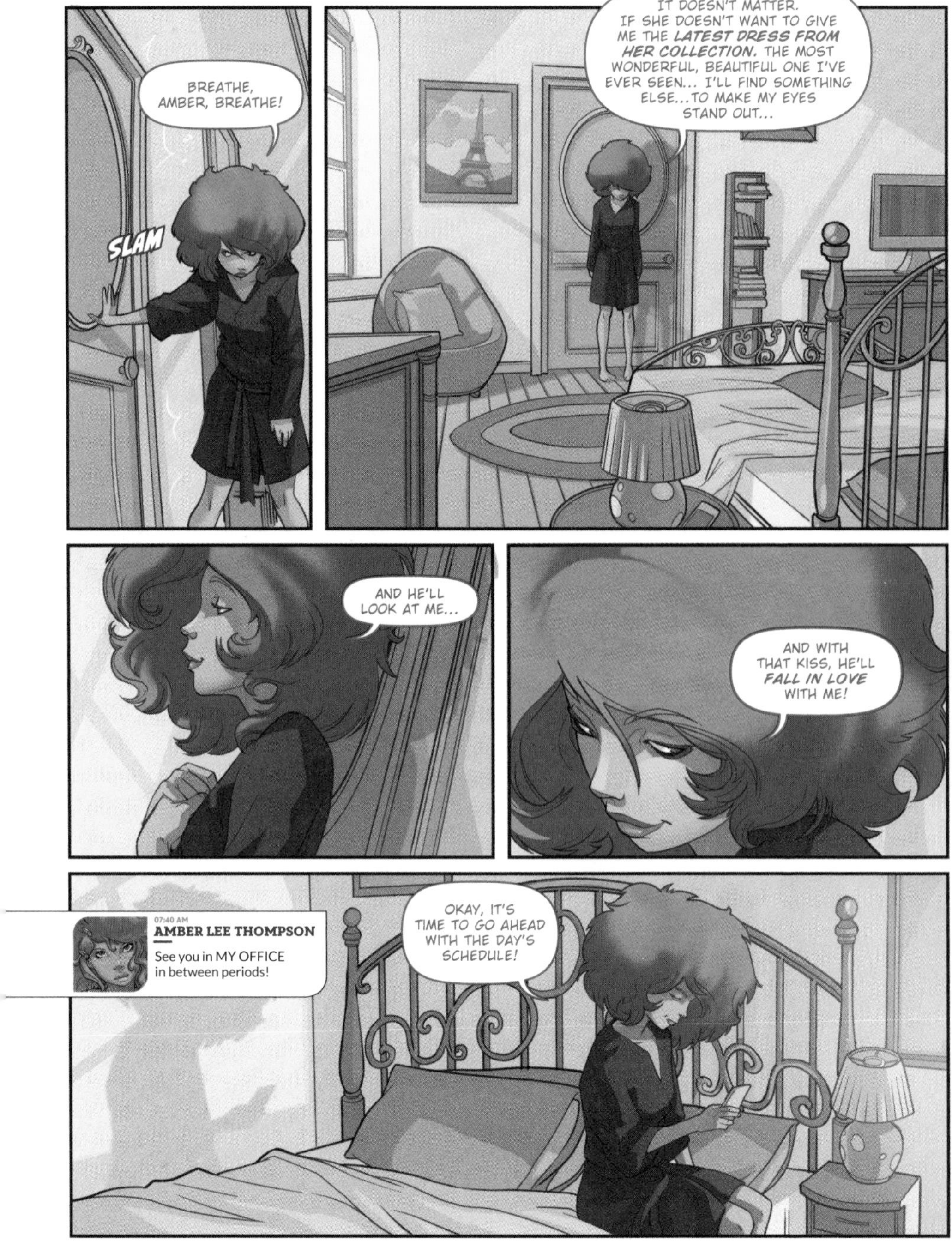
BREATHE, AMBER, BREATHE!
SLAM
IT DOESN'T MATTER. IF SHE DOESN'T WANT TO GIVE ME THE LATEST DRESS FROM HER COLLECTION. THE MOST WONDERFUL, BEAUTIFUL ONE I'VE EVER SEEN... I'LL FIND SOMETHING ELSE...TO MAKE MY EYES STAND OUT...
AND HE'LL LOOK AT ME...
AND WITH THAT KISS, HE'LL FALL IN LOVE WITH ME!
07:40 AM
AMBER LEE THOMPSON
See you in MY OFFICE in between periods!
OKAY, IT'S TIME TO GO AHEAD WITH THE DAY'S SCHEDULE!

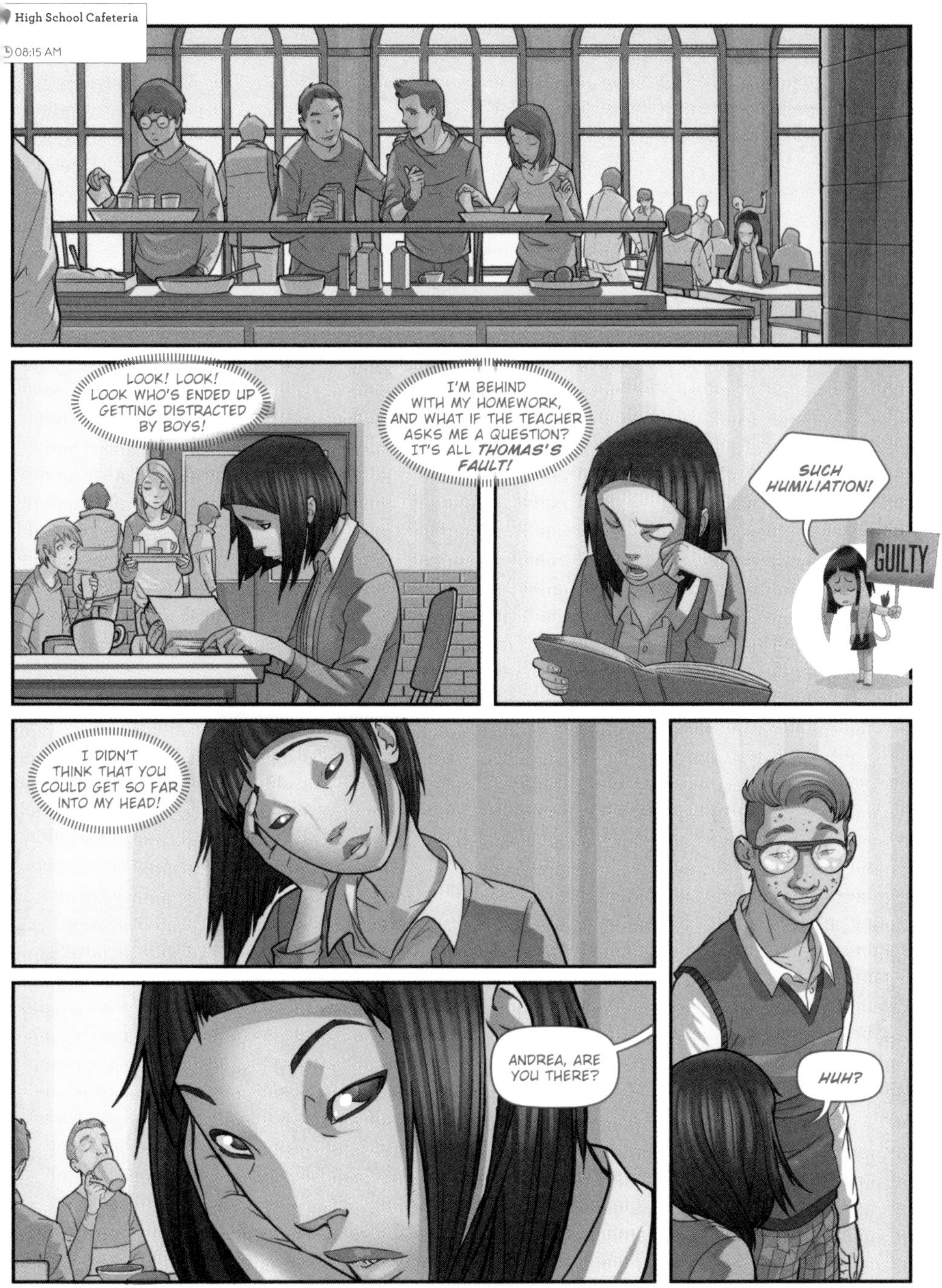
High School Cafeteria
08:15 AM
LOOK! LOOK! LOOK WHO'S ENDED UP GETTING DISTRACTED BY BOYS!
I'M BEHIND WITH MY HOMEWORK, AND WHAT IF THE TEACHER ASKS ME A QUESTION? IT'S ALL THOMAS'S FAULT!
SUCH HUMILIATION!
GUILTY
I DIDN'T THINK THAT YOU COULD GET SO FAR INTO MY HEAD!
ANDREA, ARE YOU THERE?
HUH?

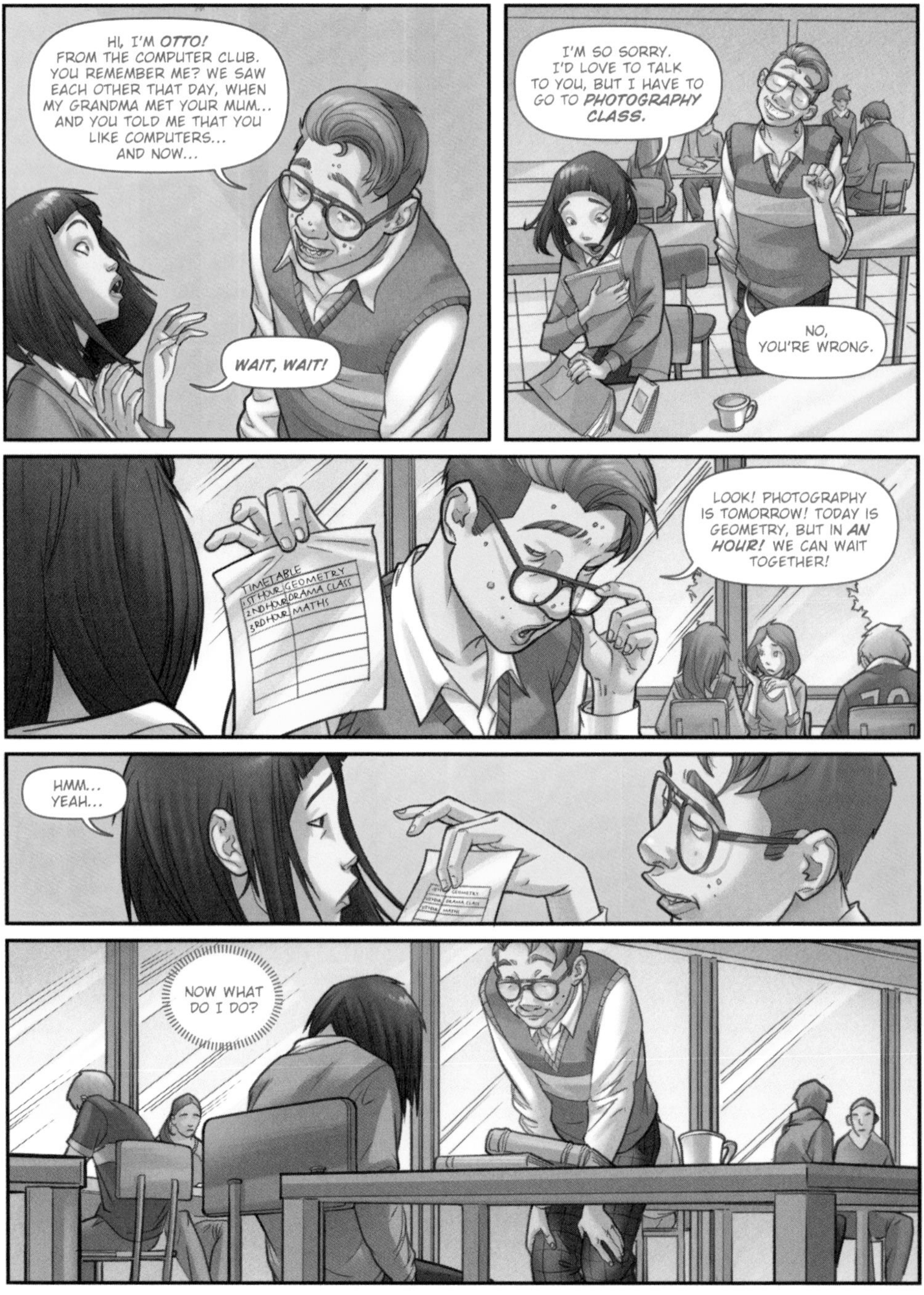
HI, I'M OTTO! FROM THE COMPUTER CLUB. YOU REMEMBER ME? WE SAW EACH OTHER THAT DAY, WHEN MY GRANDMA MET YOUR MUM... AND YOU TOLD ME THAT YOU LIKE COMPUTERS... AND NOW...
WAIT, WAIT!
I'M SO SORRY. I'D LOVE TO TALK TO YOU, BUT I HAVE TO GO TO PHOTOGRAPHY CLASS.
NO, YOU'RE WRONG.
TIMETABLE
1ST HOUR GEOMETRY
2ND HOUR DRAMA CLASS
3RD HOUR MATHS
LOOK! PHOTOGRAPHY IS TOMORROW! TODAY IS GEOMETRY, BUT IN AN HOUR! WE CAN WAIT TOGETHER!
HMM... YEAH...
NOW WHAT DO I DO?

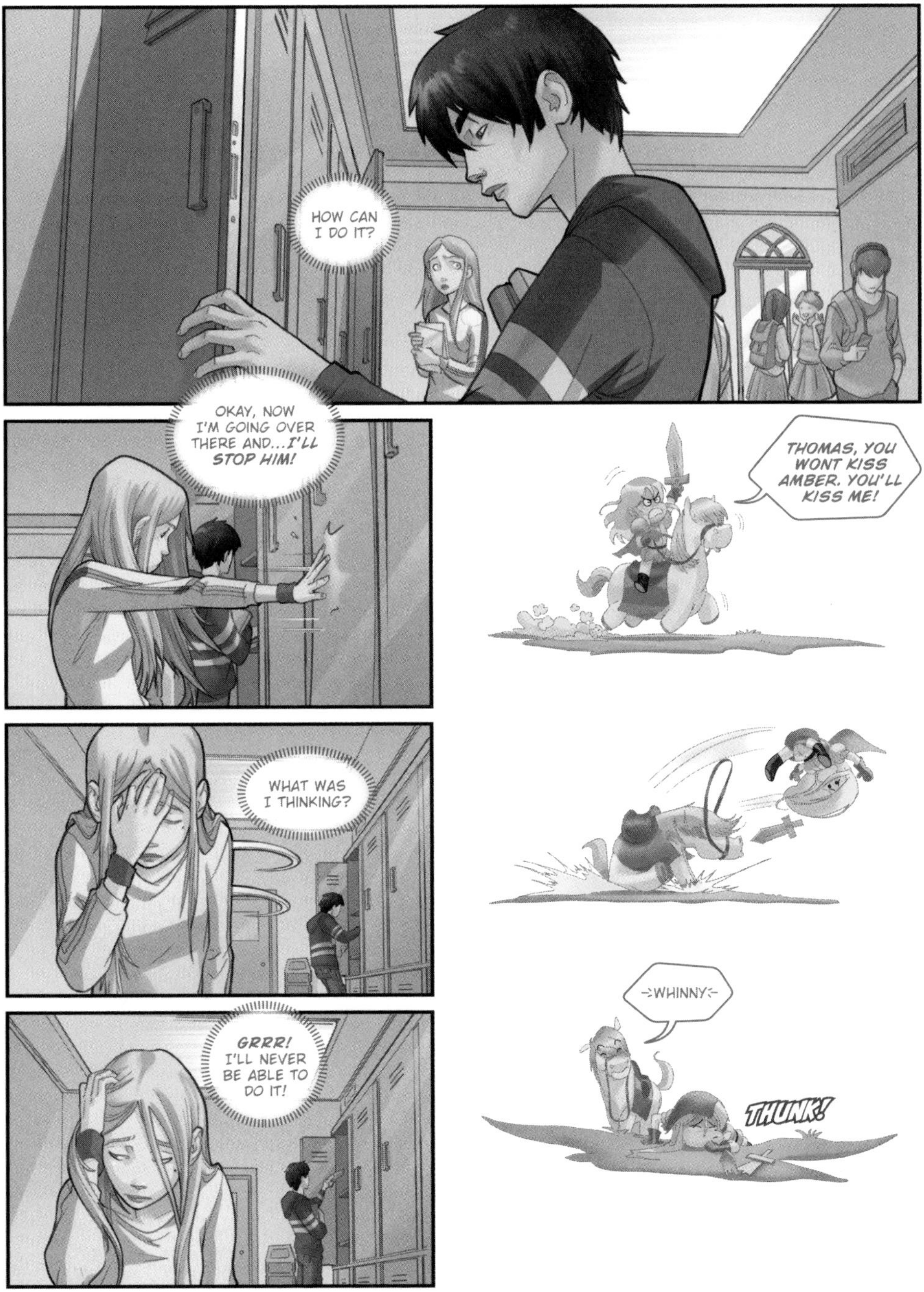
HOW CAN I DO IT?
OKAY, NOW I'M GOING OVER THERE AND... *I'LL STOP HIM!*
THOMAS, YOU WONT KISS AMBER. YOU'LL KISS ME!
WHAT WAS I THINKING?
-WHINNY-
GRRR! I'LL NEVER BE ABLE TO DO IT!
THUNK!

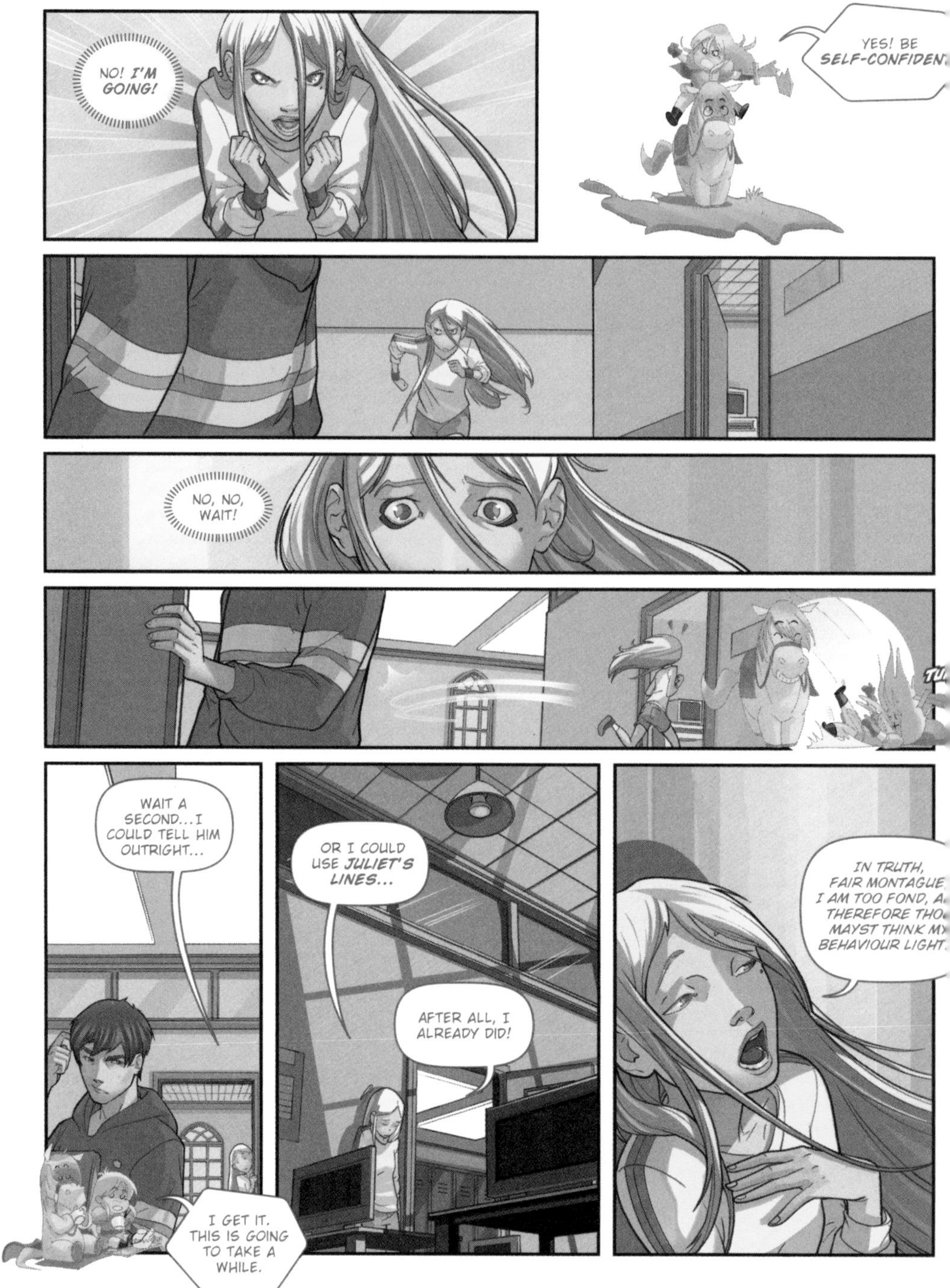

NO! I'M GOING!
YES! BE SELF-CONFIDEN
NO, NO, WAIT!
WAIT A SECOND...I COULD TELL HIM OUTRIGHT...
I GET IT. THIS IS GOING TO TAKE A WHILE.
OR I COULD USE JULIET'S LINES...
AFTER ALL, I ALREADY DID!
IN TRUTH, FAIR MONTAGUE, I AM TOO FOND, A THEREFORE THO MAYST THINK MY BEHAVIOUR LIGHT.

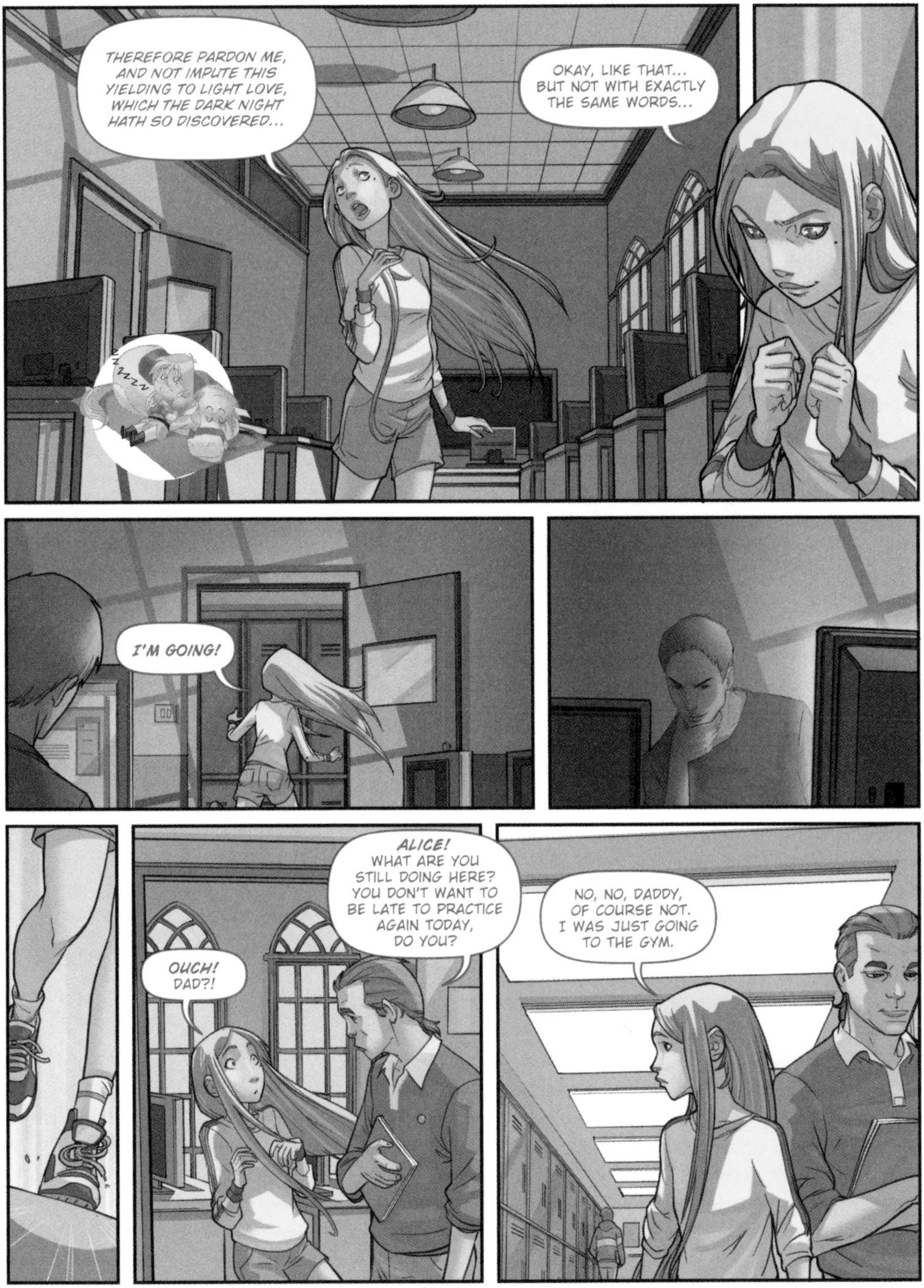
THEREFORE PARDON ME, AND NOT IMPUTE THIS YIELDING TO LIGHT LOVE, WHICH THE DARK NIGHT HATH SO DISCOVERED...
OKAY, LIKE THAT... BUT NOT WITH EXACTLY THE SAME WORDS...
I'M GOING!
OUCH! DAD?!
ALICE! WHAT ARE YOU STILL DOING HERE? YOU DON'T WANT TO BE LATE TO PRACTICE AGAIN TODAY, DO YOU?
NO, NO, DADDY, OF COURSE NOT. I WAS JUST GOING TO THE GYM.

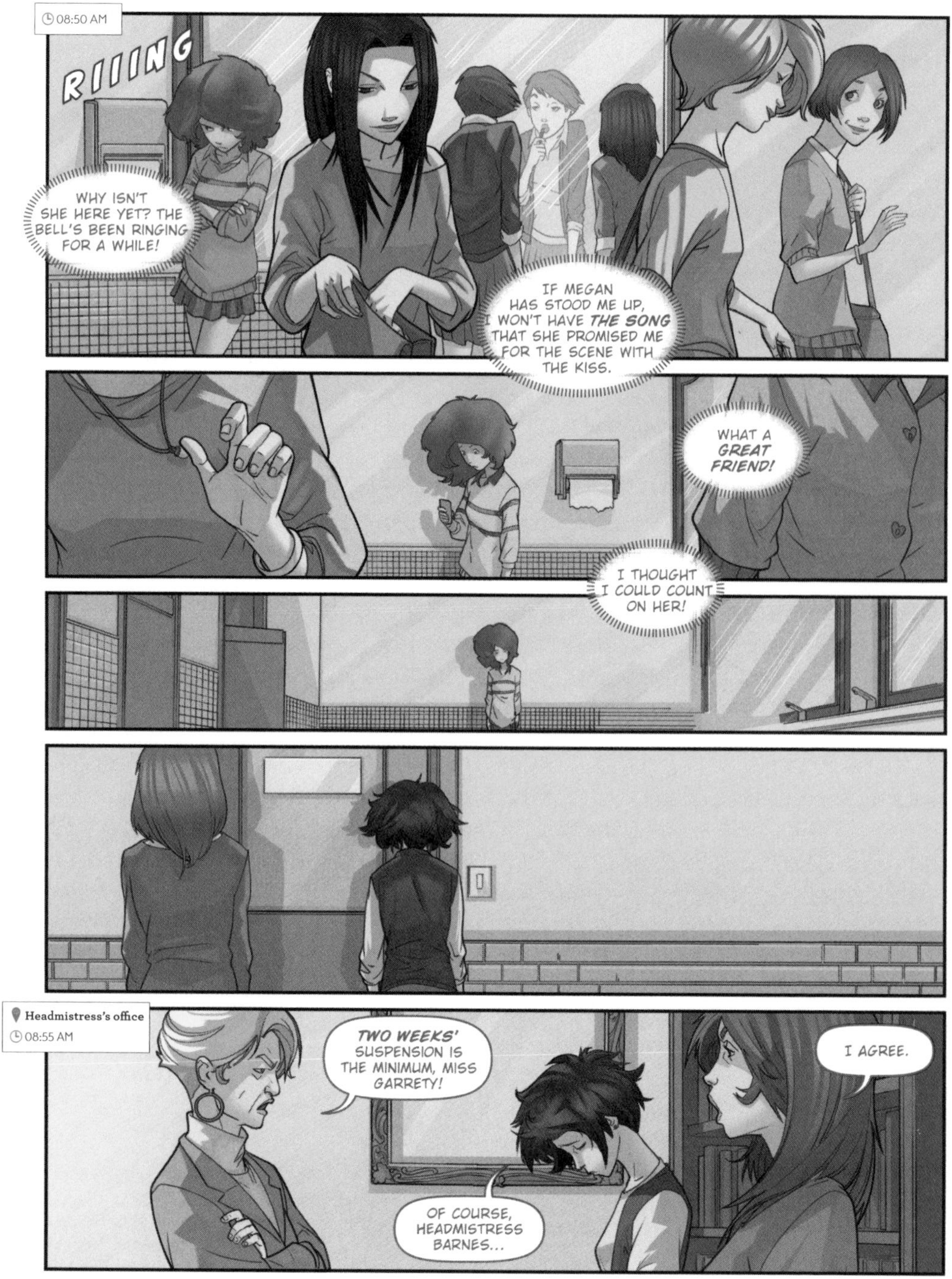
08:50 AM
RIIING
WHY ISN'T SHE HERE YET? THE BELL'S BEEN RINGING FOR A WHILE!
IF MEGAN HAS STOOD ME UP, I WON'T HAVE THE SONG THAT SHE PROMISED ME FOR THE SCENE WITH THE KISS.
WHAT A GREAT FRIEND!
I THOUGHT I COULD COUNT ON HER!
Headmistress's office
08:55 AM
TWO WEEKS' SUSPENSION IS THE MINIMUM, MISS GARRETY!
OF COURSE, HEADMISTRESS BARNES...
I AGREE.

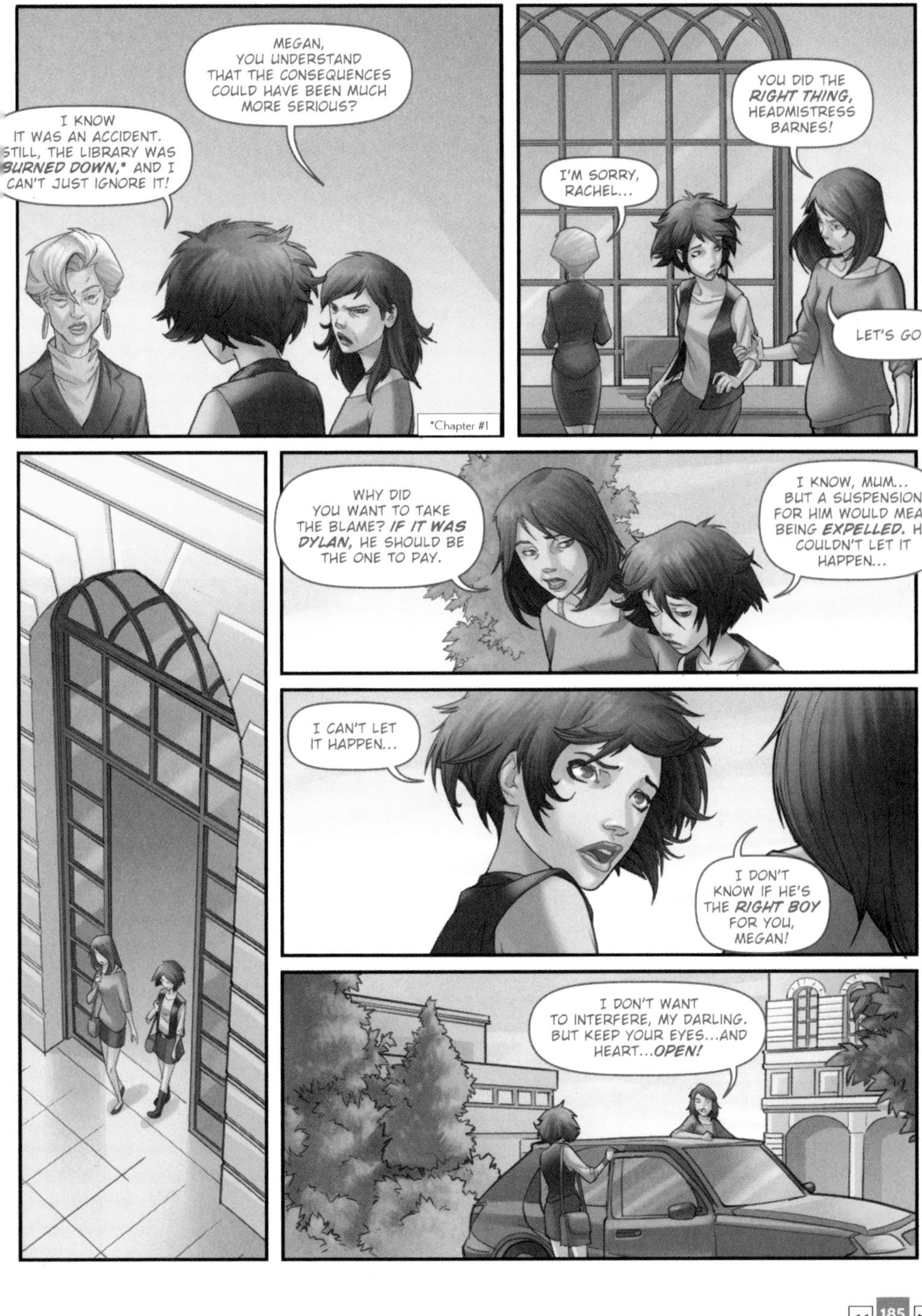

I KNOW IT WAS AN ACCIDENT. STILL, THE LIBRARY WAS BURNED DOWN,* AND I CAN'T JUST IGNORE IT!
MEGAN, YOU UNDERSTAND THAT THE CONSEQUENCES COULD HAVE BEEN MUCH MORE SERIOUS?
*Chapter #1
YOU DID THE RIGHT THING, HEADMISTRESS BARNES!
I'M SORRY, RACHEL...
LET'S GO!
WHY DID YOU WANT TO TAKE THE BLAME? IF IT WAS DYLAN, HE SHOULD BE THE ONE TO PAY.
I KNOW, MUM... BUT A SUSPENSION FOR HIM WOULD MEAN BEING EXPELLED. HE COULDN'T LET IT HAPPEN...
I CAN'T LET IT HAPPEN...
I DON'T KNOW IF HE'S THE RIGHT BOY FOR YOU, MEGAN!
I DON'T WANT TO INTERFERE, MY DARLING. BUT KEEP YOUR EYES...AND HEART...OPEN!

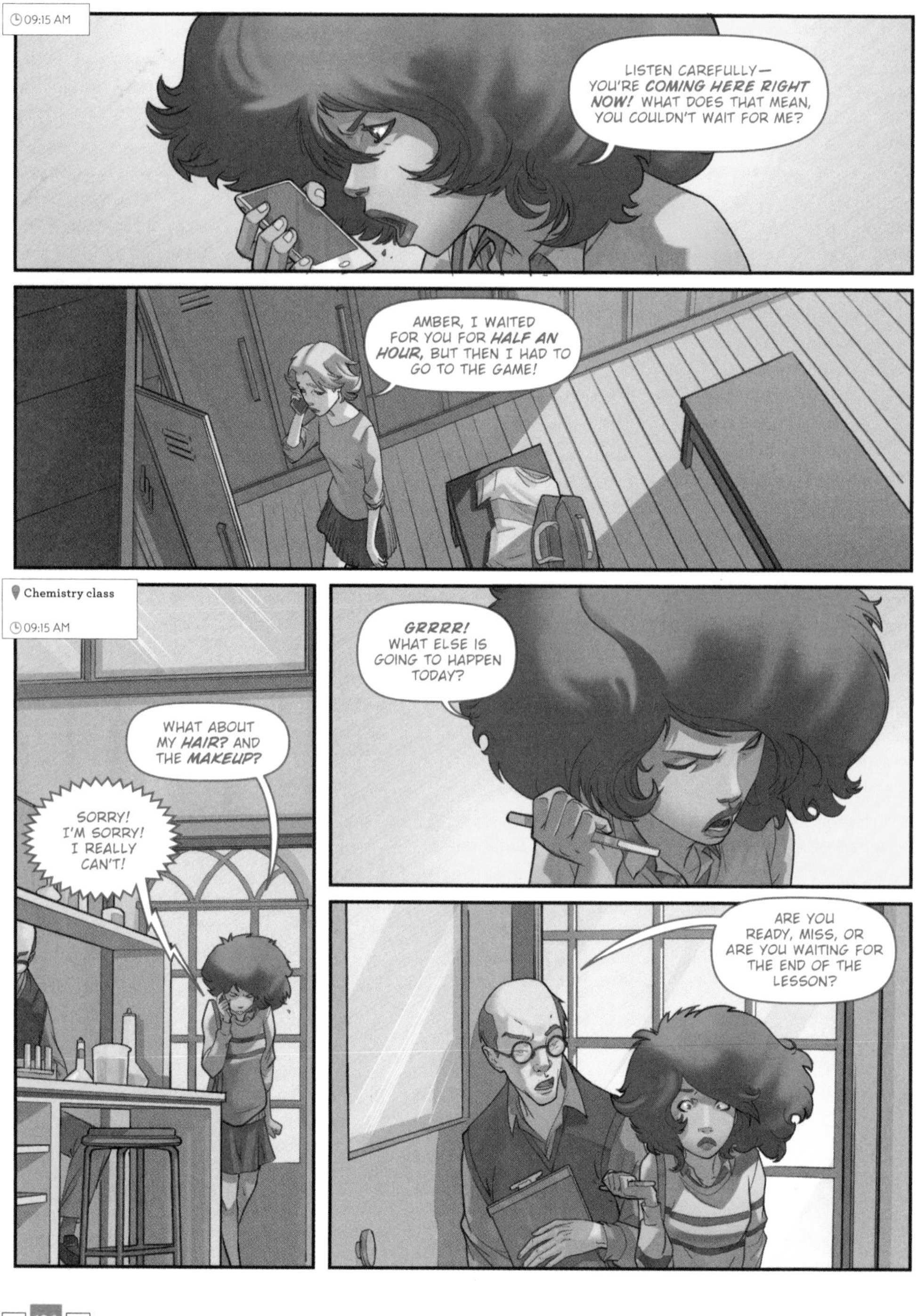
09:15 AM
LISTEN CAREFULLY— YOU'RE COMING HERE RIGHT NOW! WHAT DOES THAT MEAN, YOU COULDN'T WAIT FOR ME?
AMBER, I WAITED FOR YOU FOR HALF AN HOUR, BUT THEN I HAD TO GO TO THE GAME!
Chemistry class
09:15 AM
WHAT ABOUT MY HAIR? AND THE MAKEUP?
SORRY! I'M SORRY! I REALLY CAN'T!
GRRRR! WHAT ELSE IS GOING TO HAPPEN TODAY?
ARE YOU READY, MISS, OR ARE YOU WAITING FOR THE END OF THE LESSON?

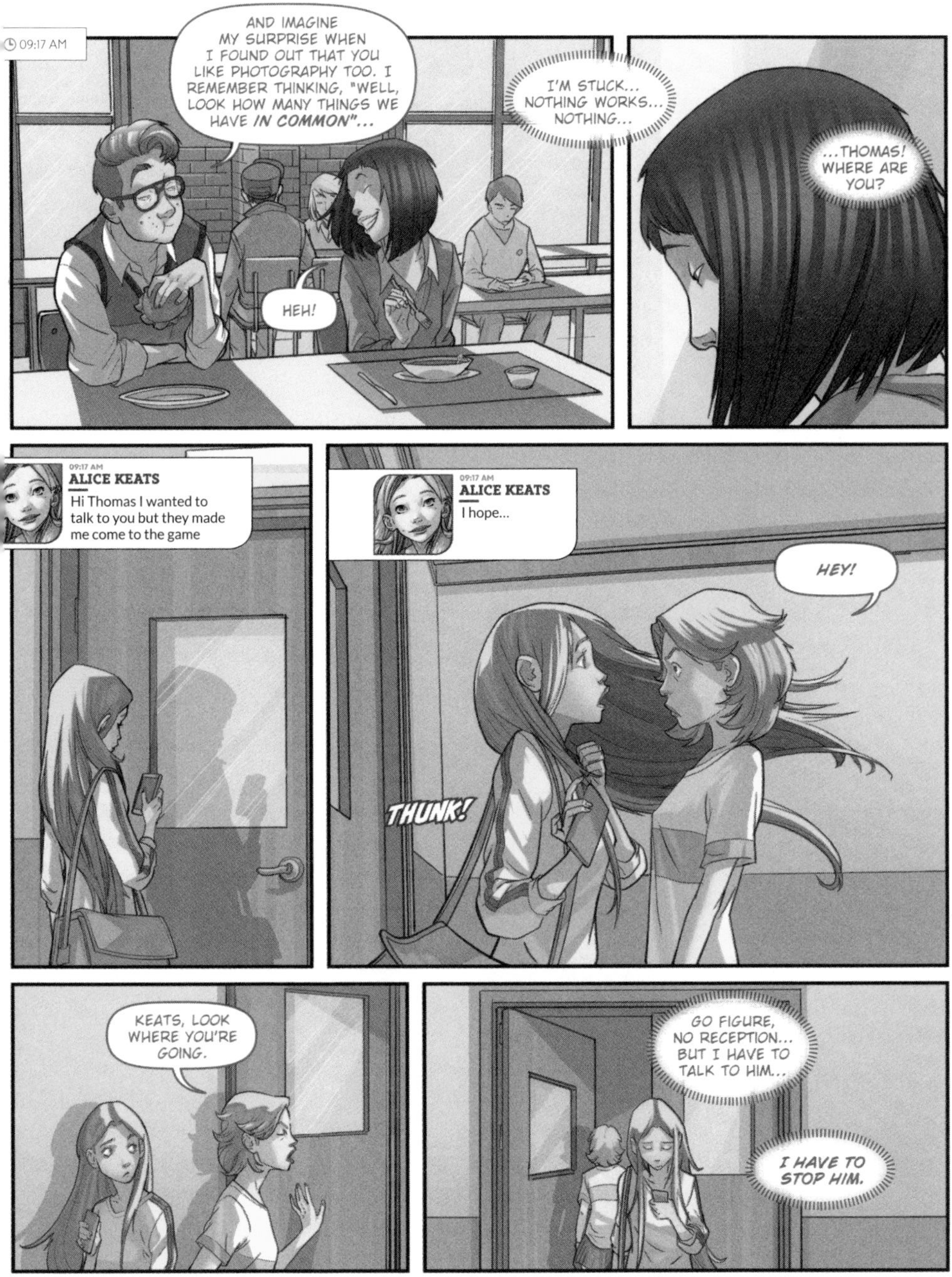
09:17 AM
AND IMAGINE MY SURPRISE WHEN I FOUND OUT THAT YOU LIKE PHOTOGRAPHY TOO. I REMEMBER THINKING, "WELL, LOOK HOW MANY THINGS WE HAVE *IN COMMON*"...
HEH!
I'M STUCK... NOTHING WORKS... NOTHING...
...THOMAS! WHERE ARE YOU?
09:17 AM
ALICE KEATS
Hi Thomas I wanted to talk to you but they made me come to the game
09:17 AM
ALICE KEATS
I hope...
HEY!
THUNK!
KEATS, LOOK WHERE YOU'RE GOING.
GO FIGURE, NO RECEPTION... BUT I HAVE TO TALK TO HIM...
I HAVE TO STOP HIM.

END OF CHAPTER 10

CHAPTER II

UPSIDE-down DAY

High School, Chemistry class

09:20 AM

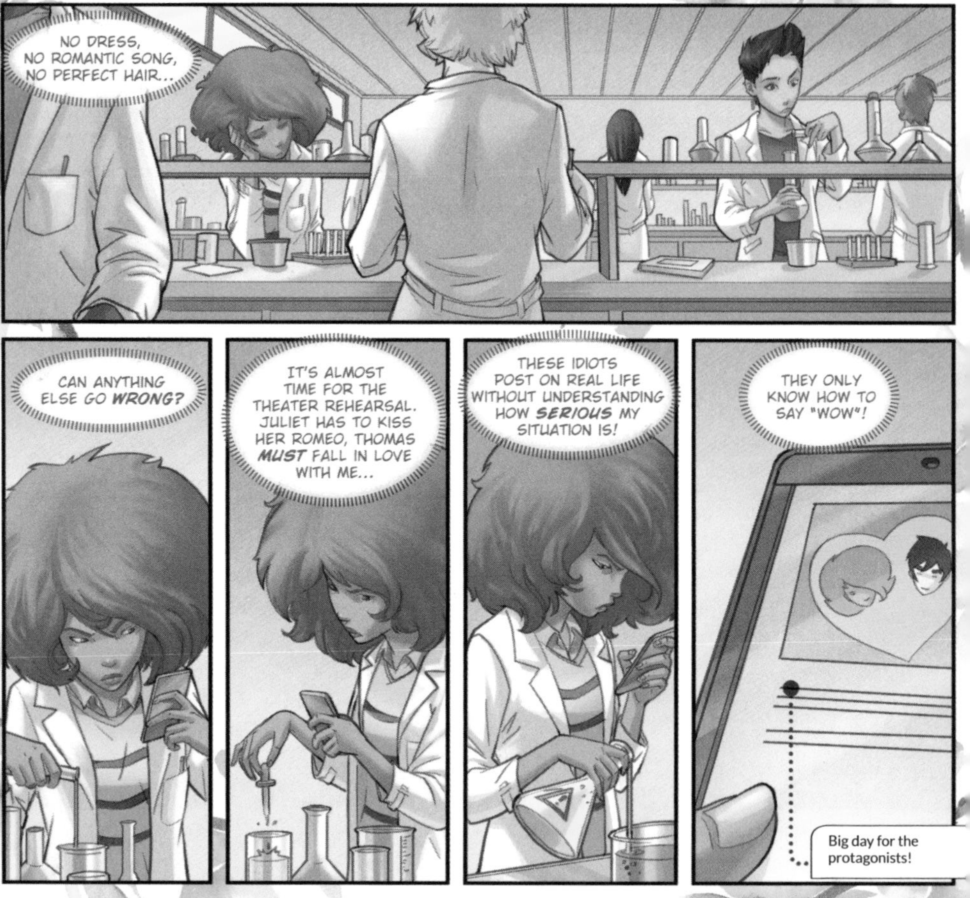
NO DRESS, NO ROMANTIC SONG, NO PERFECT HAIR...
CAN ANYTHING ELSE GO **WRONG?**
IT'S ALMOST TIME FOR THE THEATER REHEARSAL. JULIET HAS TO KISS HER ROMEO, THOMAS **MUST** FALL IN LOVE WITH ME...
THESE IDIOTS POST ON REAL LIFE WITHOUT UNDERSTANDING HOW **SERIOUS** MY SITUATION IS!
THEY ONLY KNOW HOW TO SAY "WOW"!
Big day for the protagonists!

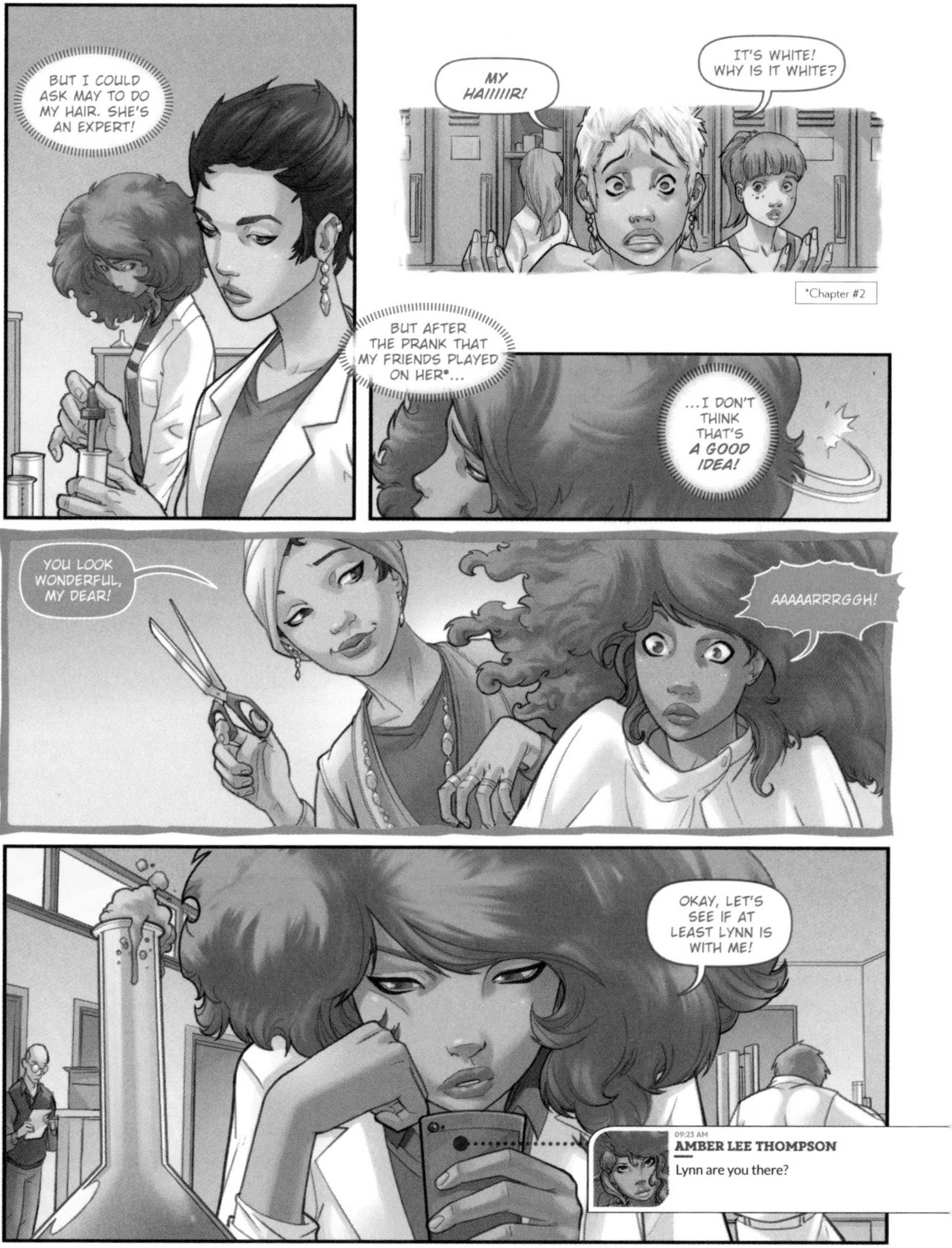
BUT I COULD ASK MAY TO DO MY HAIR. SHE'S AN EXPERT!
MY HAIIIIIR!
IT'S WHITE! WHY IS IT WHITE?
*Chapter #2
BUT AFTER THE PRANK THAT MY FRIENDS PLAYED ON HER*...
...I DON'T THINK THAT'S A GOOD IDEA!
YOU LOOK WONDERFUL, MY DEAR!
AAAAARRRGGH!
OKAY, LET'S SEE IF AT LEAST LYNN IS WITH ME!
09:23 AM
AMBER LEE THOMPSON
Lynn are you there?

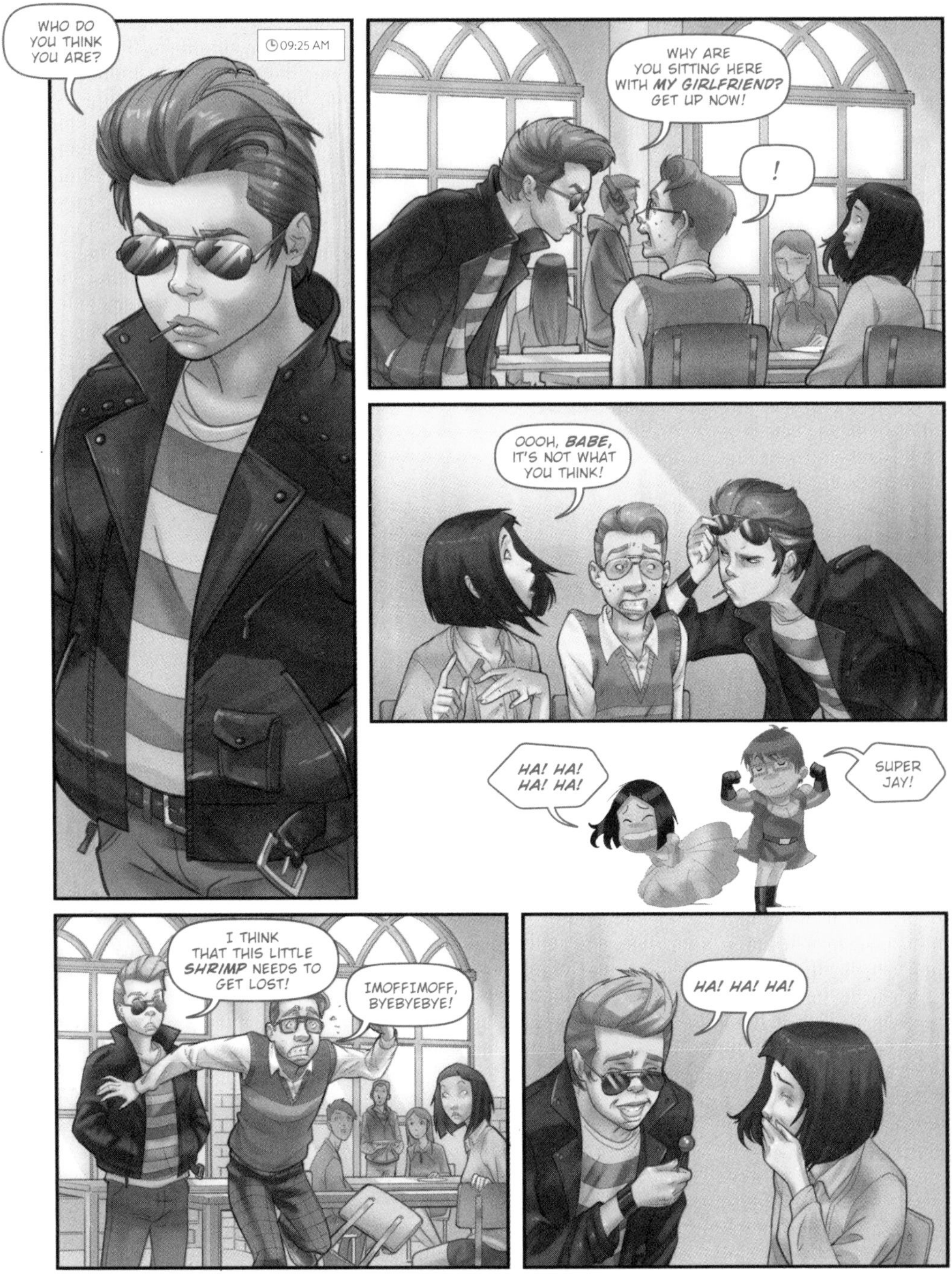
WHO DO YOU THINK YOU ARE?
09:25 AM
WHY ARE YOU SITTING HERE WITH MY GIRLFRIEND? GET UP NOW!
!
OOOH, BABE, IT'S NOT WHAT YOU THINK!
HA! HA! HA! HA!
SUPER JAY!
I THINK THAT THIS LITTLE SHRIMP NEEDS TO GET LOST!
IMOFFIMOFF, BYEBYEBYE!
HA! HA! HA!

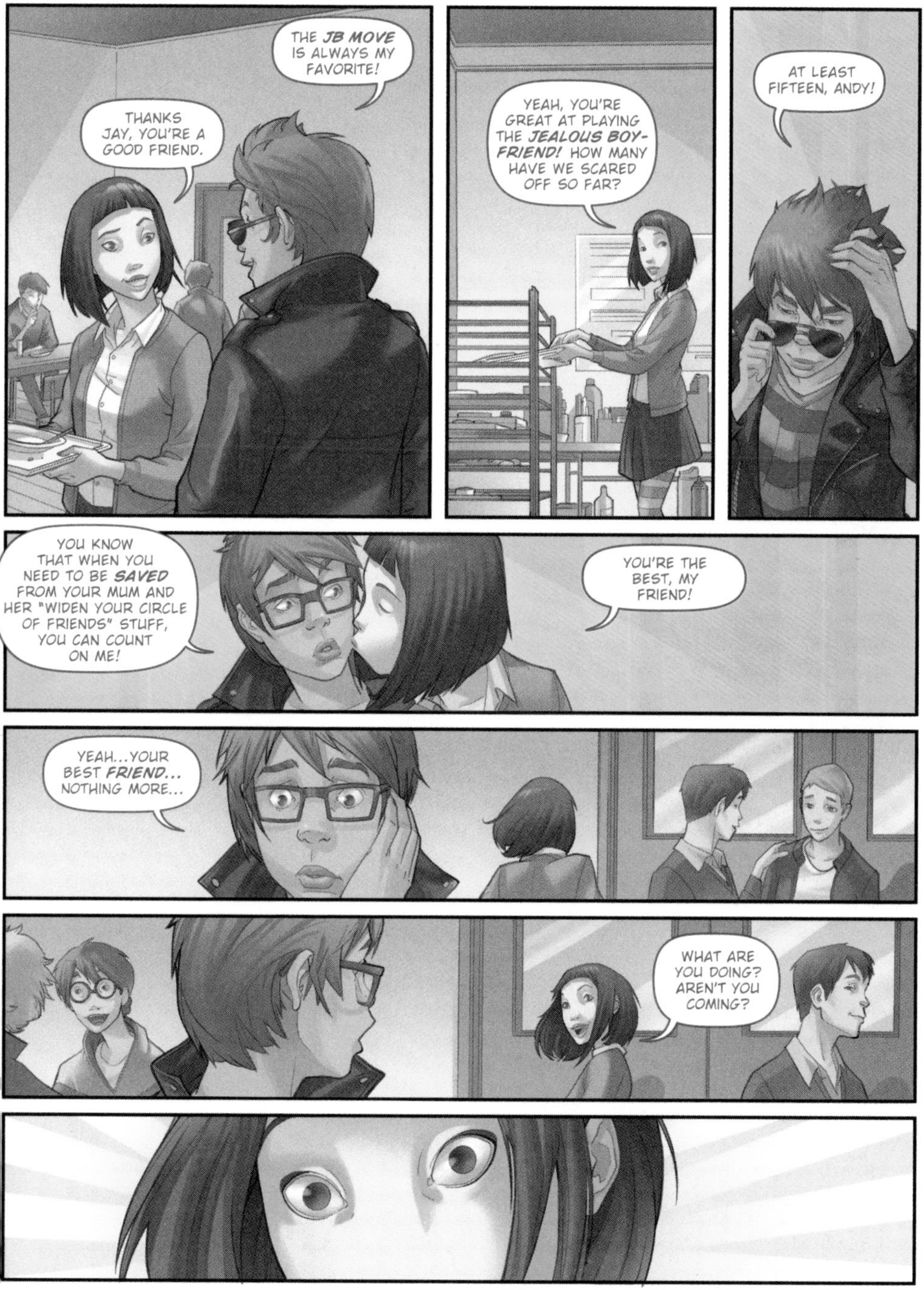
THE JB MOVE IS ALWAYS MY FAVORITE!
THANKS JAY, YOU'RE A GOOD FRIEND.
YEAH, YOU'RE GREAT AT PLAYING THE JEALOUS BOY-FRIEND! HOW MANY HAVE WE SCARED OFF SO FAR?
AT LEAST FIFTEEN, ANDY!
YOU KNOW THAT WHEN YOU NEED TO BE SAVED FROM YOUR MUM AND HER "WIDEN YOUR CIRCLE OF FRIENDS" STUFF, YOU CAN COUNT ON ME!
YOU'RE THE BEST, MY FRIEND!
YEAH...YOUR BEST FRIEND... NOTHING MORE...
WHAT ARE YOU DOING? AREN'T YOU COMING?

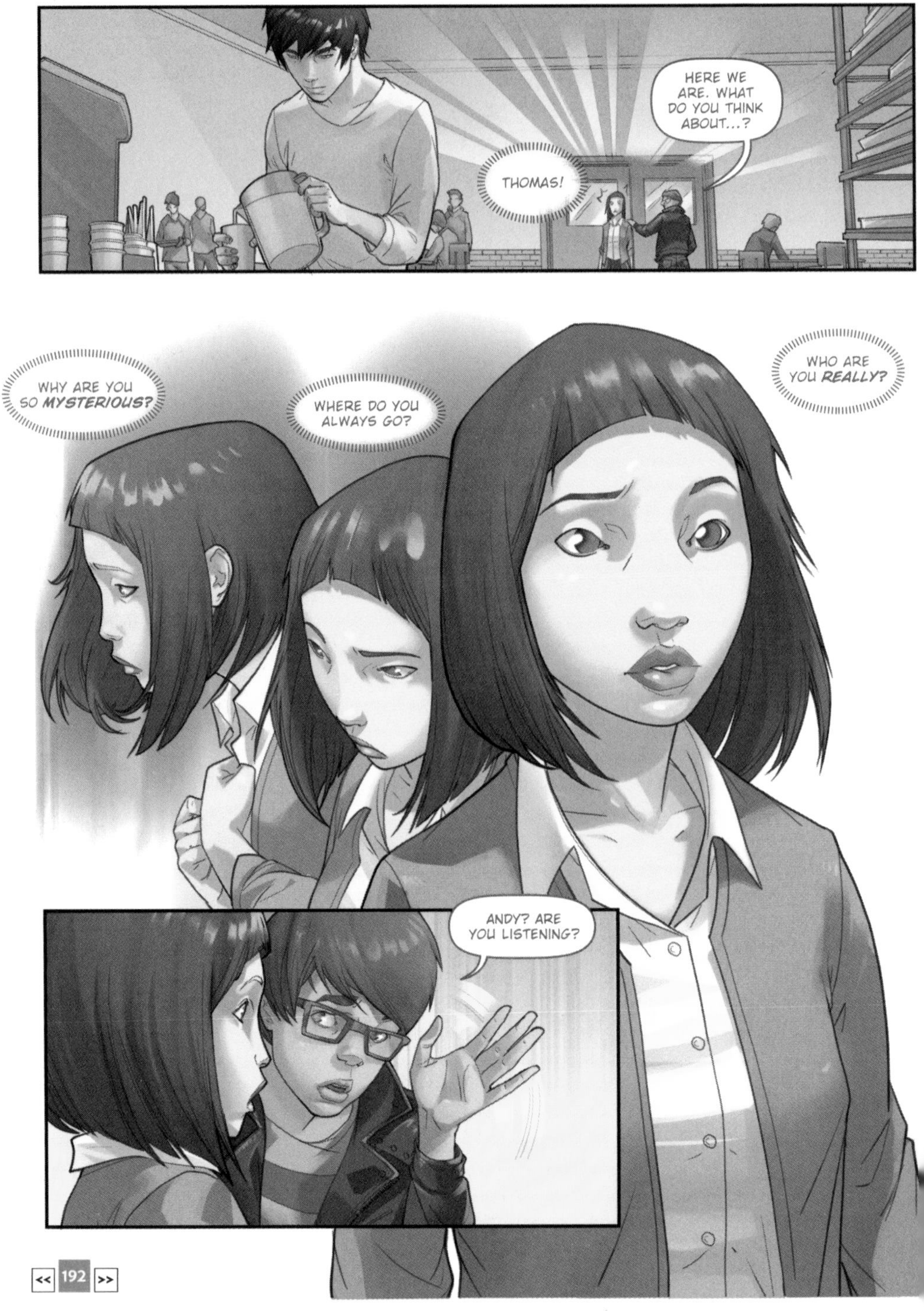
HERE WE ARE. WHAT DO YOU THINK ABOUT...?
THOMAS!
WHY ARE YOU SO MYSTERIOUS?
WHERE DO YOU ALWAYS GO?
WHO ARE YOU REALLY?
ANDY? ARE YOU LISTENING?

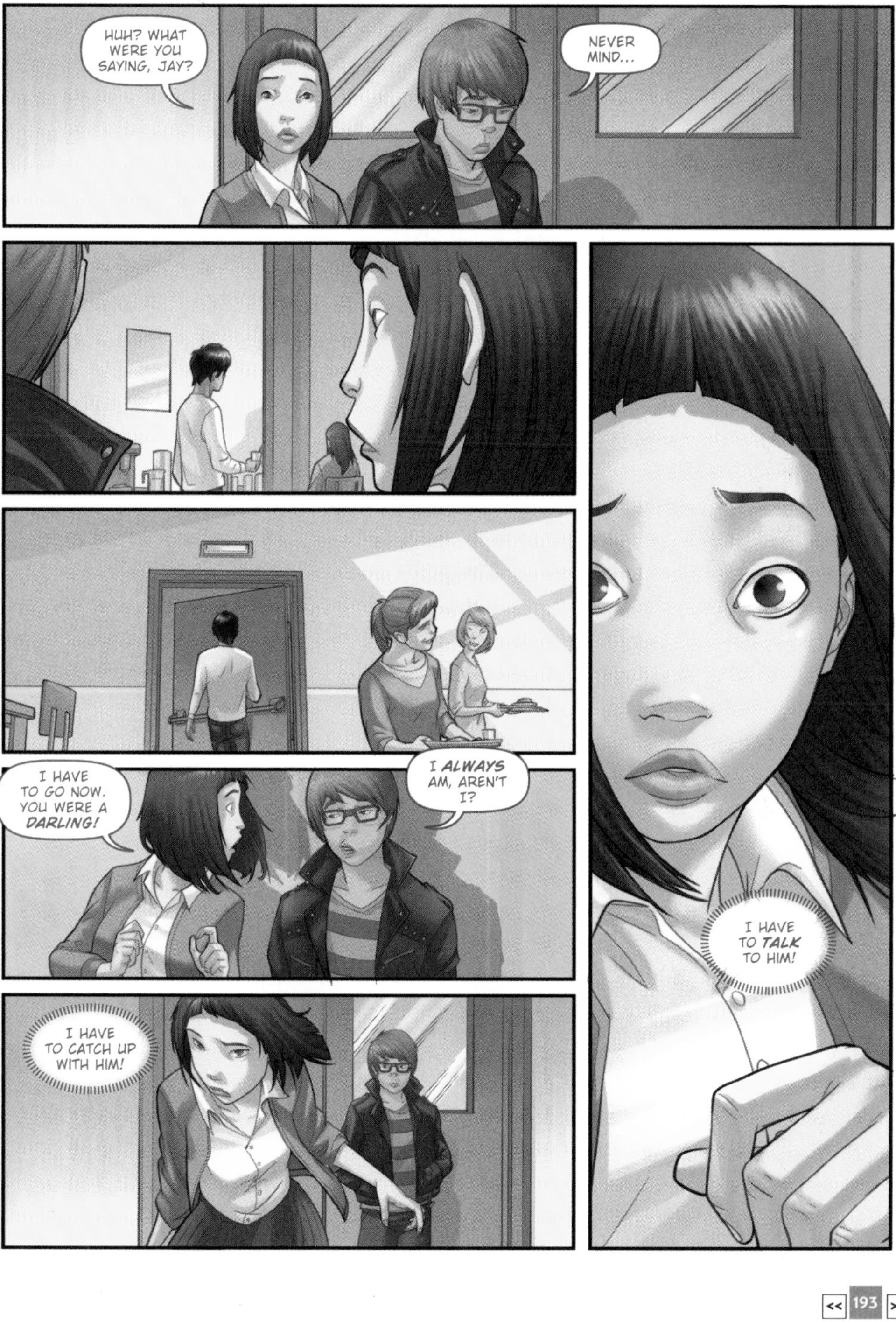
HUH? WHAT WERE YOU SAYING, JAY?
NEVER MIND...
I HAVE TO TALK TO HIM!
I HAVE TO GO NOW. YOU WERE A DARLING!
I ALWAYS AM, AREN'T I?
I HAVE TO CATCH UP WITH HIM!

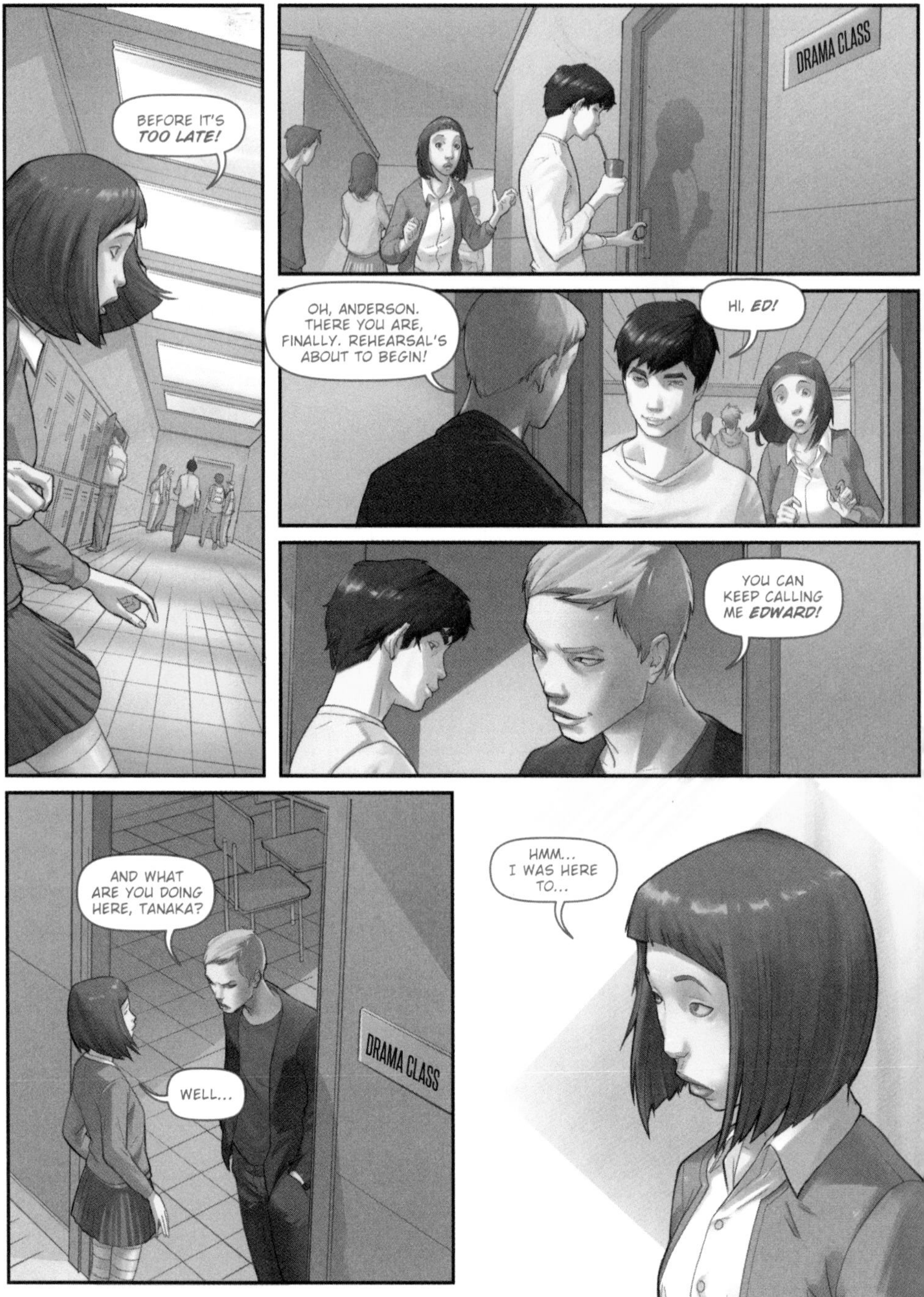
BEFORE IT'S *TOO LATE!*
DRAMA CLASS
OH, ANDERSON. THERE YOU ARE, FINALLY. REHEARSAL'S ABOUT TO BEGIN!
HI, *ED!*
YOU CAN KEEP CALLING ME *EDWARD!*
AND WHAT ARE YOU DOING HERE, TANAKA?
DRAMA CLASS
WELL...
HMM... I WAS HERE TO...

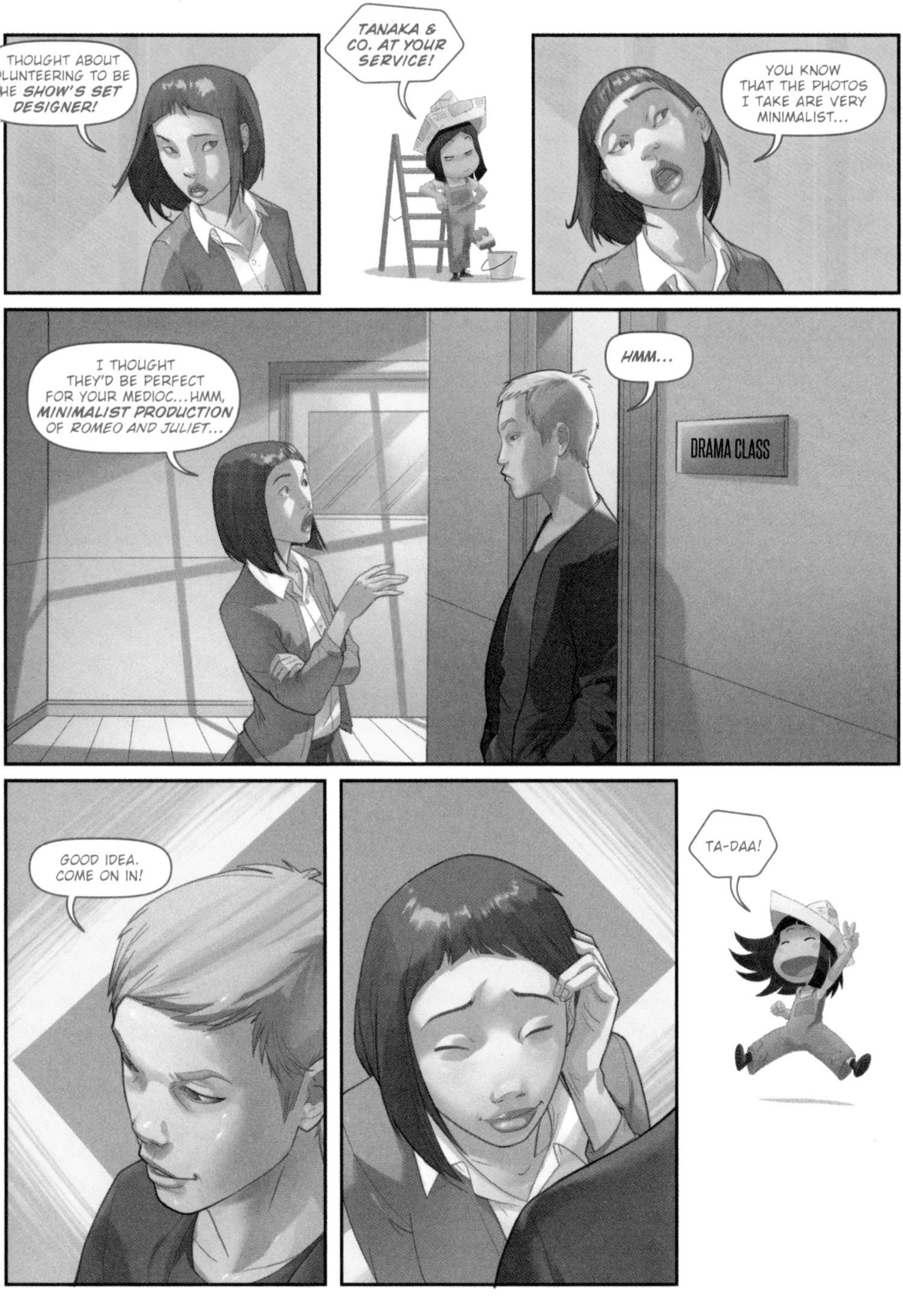

THOUGHT ABOUT
LUNTEERING TO BE
HE SHOW'S SET
DESIGNER!
TANAKA & CO. AT YOUR SERVICE!
YOU KNOW THAT THE PHOTOS I TAKE ARE VERY MINIMALIST...
I THOUGHT THEY'D BE PERFECT FOR YOUR MEDIOC...HMM, MINIMALIST PRODUCTION OF ROMEO AND JULIET...
HMM...
DRAMA CLASS
GOOD IDEA. COME ON IN!
TA-DAA!

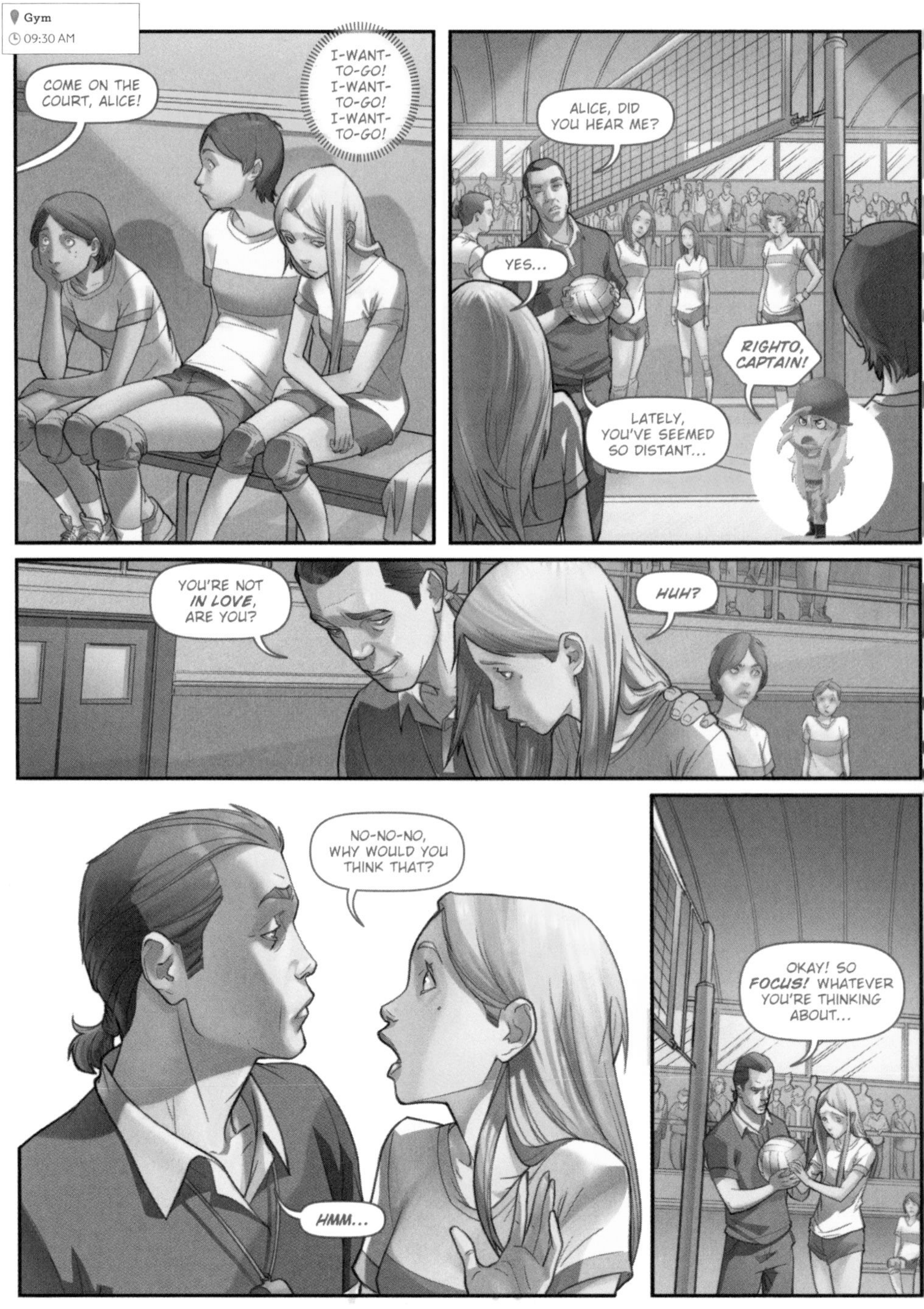
Gym
09:30 AM
COME ON THE COURT, ALICE!
I-WANT-TO-GO! I-WANT-TO-GO! I-WANT-TO-GO!
ALICE, DID YOU HEAR ME?
YES...
LATELY, YOU'VE SEEMED SO DISTANT...
RIGHTO, CAPTAIN!
YOU'RE NOT IN LOVE, ARE YOU?
HUH?
NO-NO-NO, WHY WOULD YOU THINK THAT?
HMM...
OKAY! SO FOCUS! WHATEVER YOU'RE THINKING ABOUT...

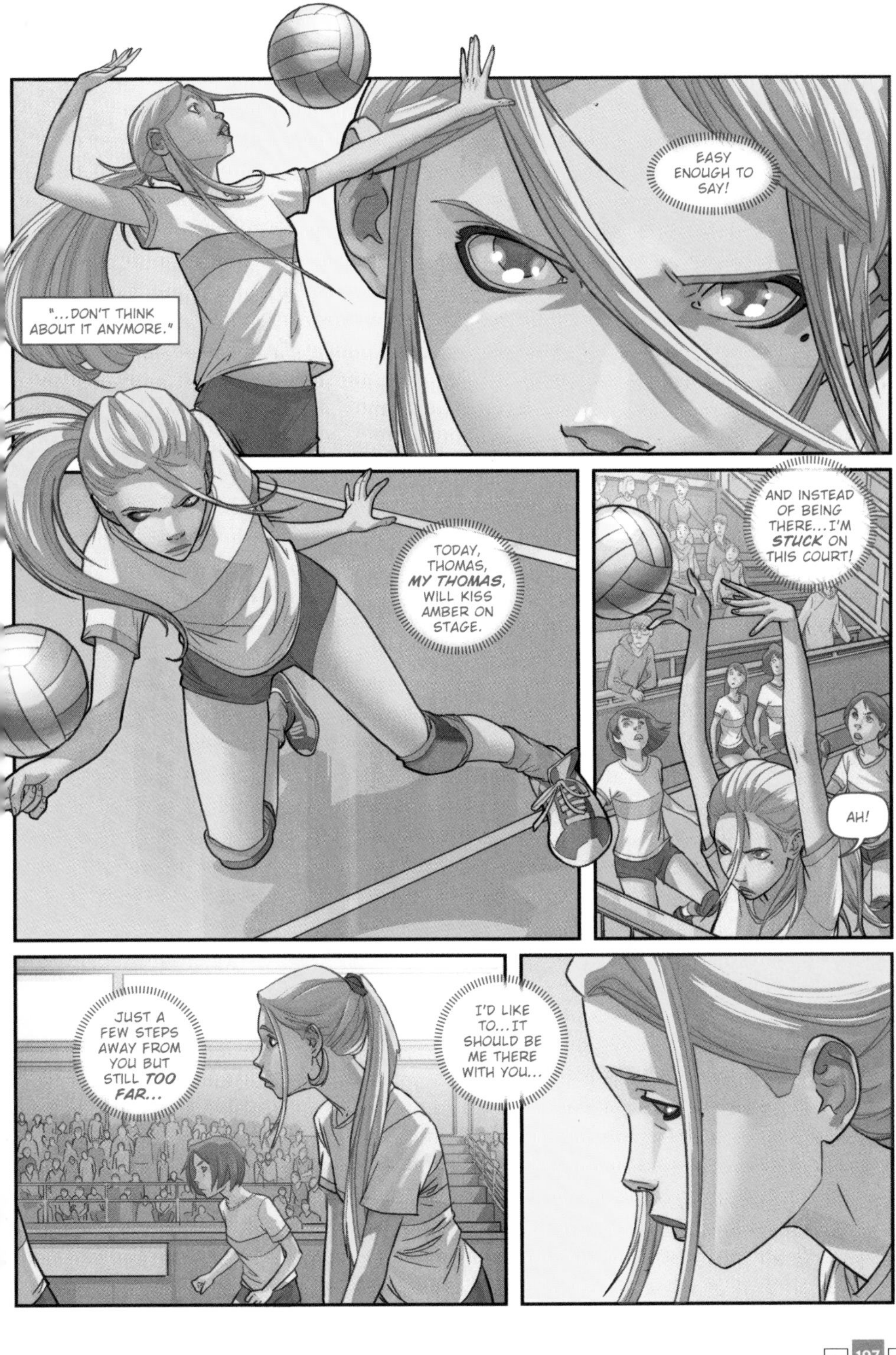
"...DON'T THINK ABOUT IT ANYMORE."
EASY ENOUGH TO SAY!
TODAY, THOMAS, MY THOMAS, WILL KISS AMBER ON STAGE.
AND INSTEAD OF BEING THERE...I'M STUCK ON THIS COURT!
AH!
JUST A FEW STEPS AWAY FROM YOU BUT STILL TOO FAR...
I'D LIKE TO...IT SHOULD BE ME THERE WITH YOU...

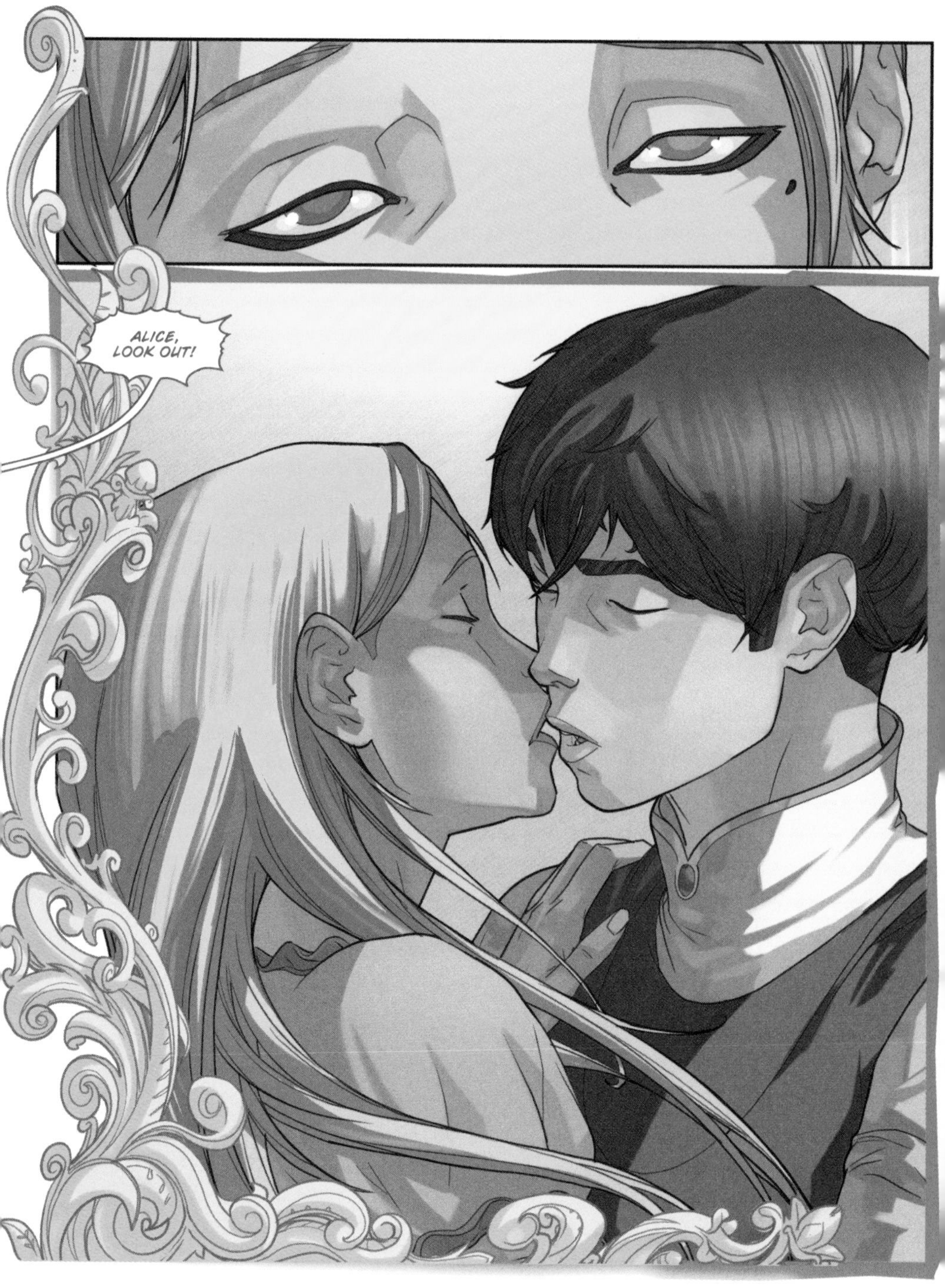
ALICE, LOOK OUT!

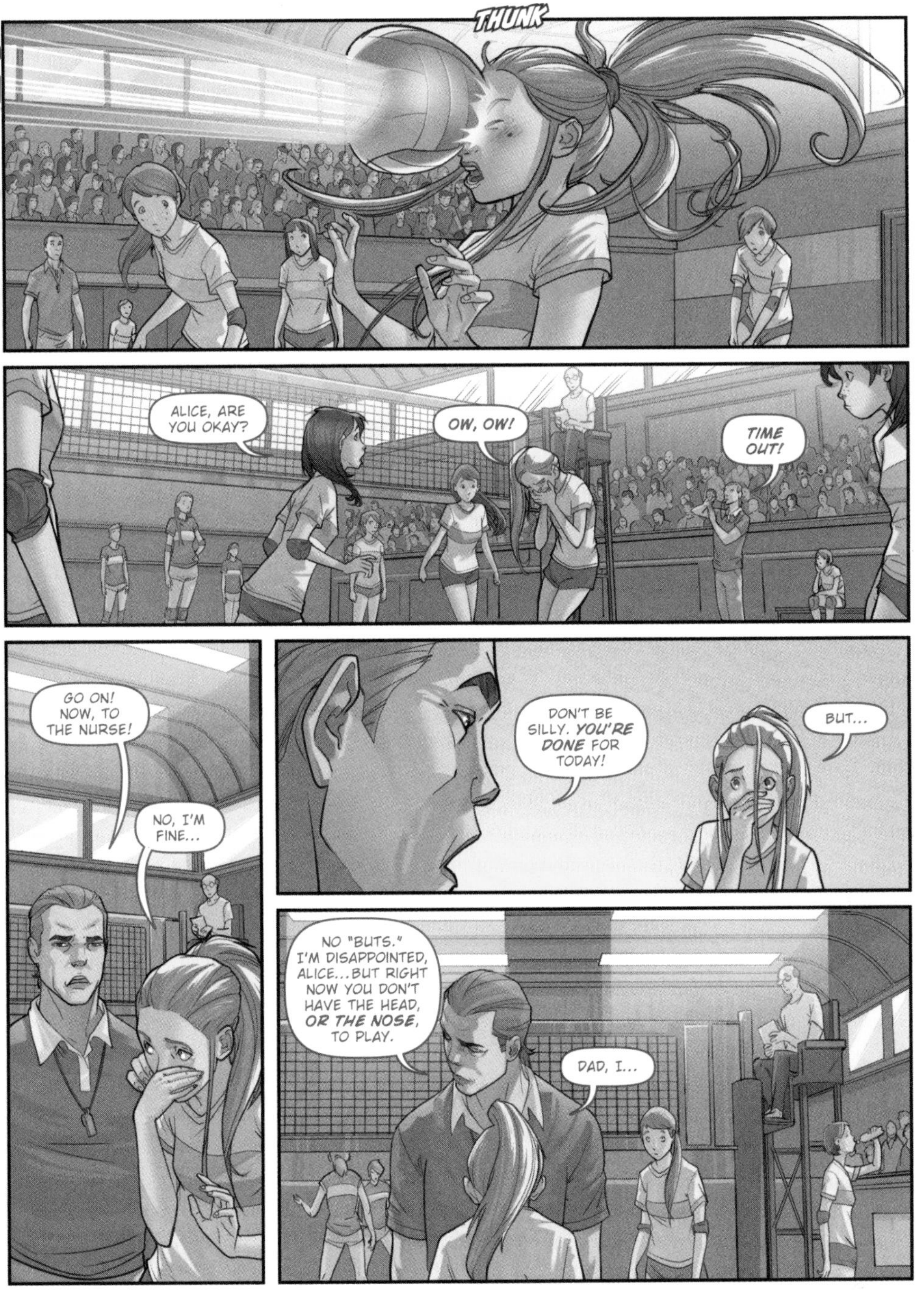
THUNK
ALICE, ARE YOU OKAY?
OW, OW!
TIME OUT!
GO ON! NOW, TO THE NURSE!
NO, I'M FINE...
DON'T BE SILLY. YOU'RE DONE FOR TODAY!
BUT...
NO "BUTS." I'M DISAPPOINTED, ALICE...BUT RIGHT NOW YOU DON'T HAVE THE HEAD, OR THE NOSE, TO PLAY.
DAD, I...

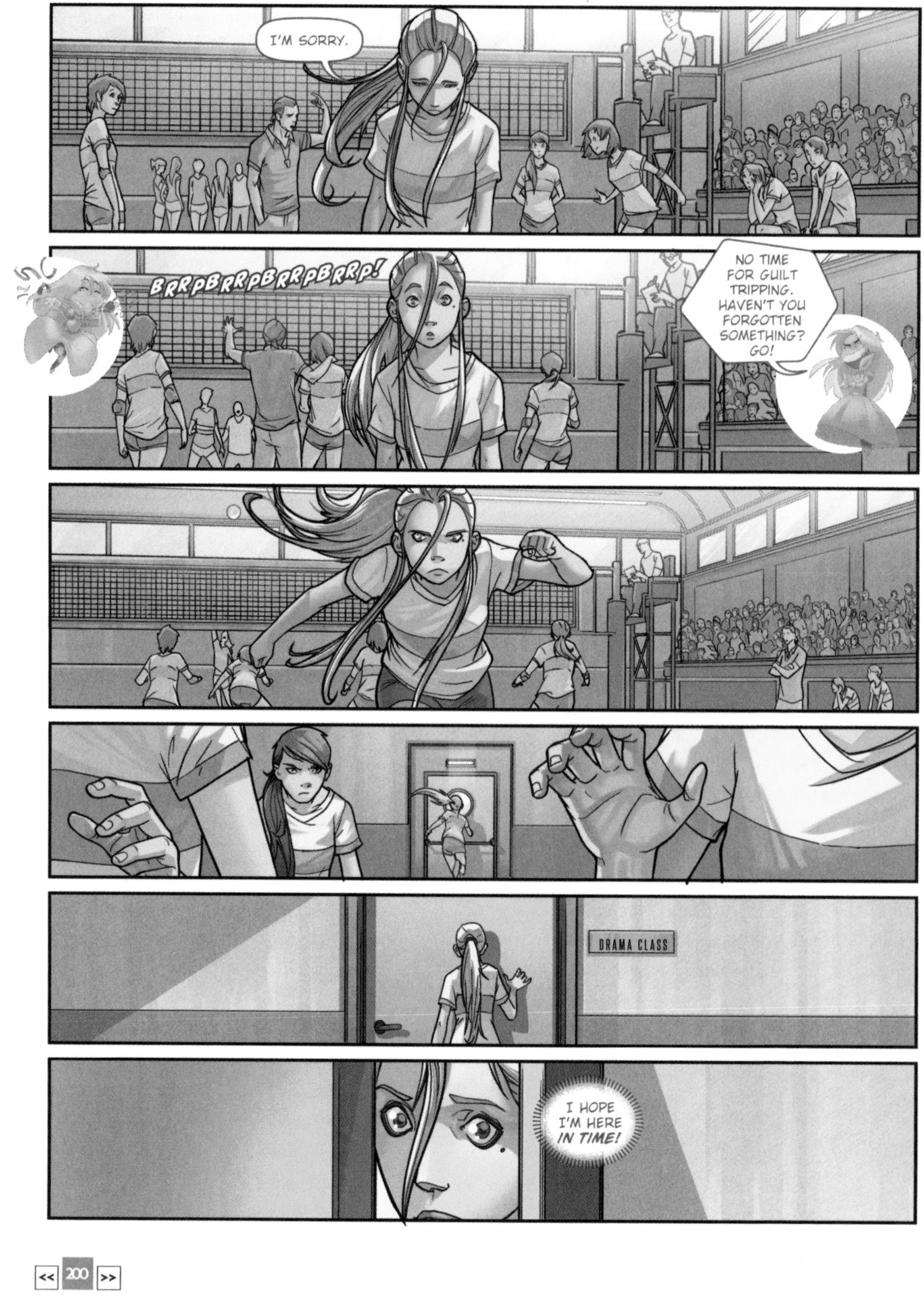
I'M SORRY.
BRRPBRRPBRRPBRRP!
NO TIME FOR GUILT TRIPPING. HAVEN'T YOU FORGOTTEN SOMETHING? GO!
DRAMA CLASS
I HOPE I'M HERE IN TIME!

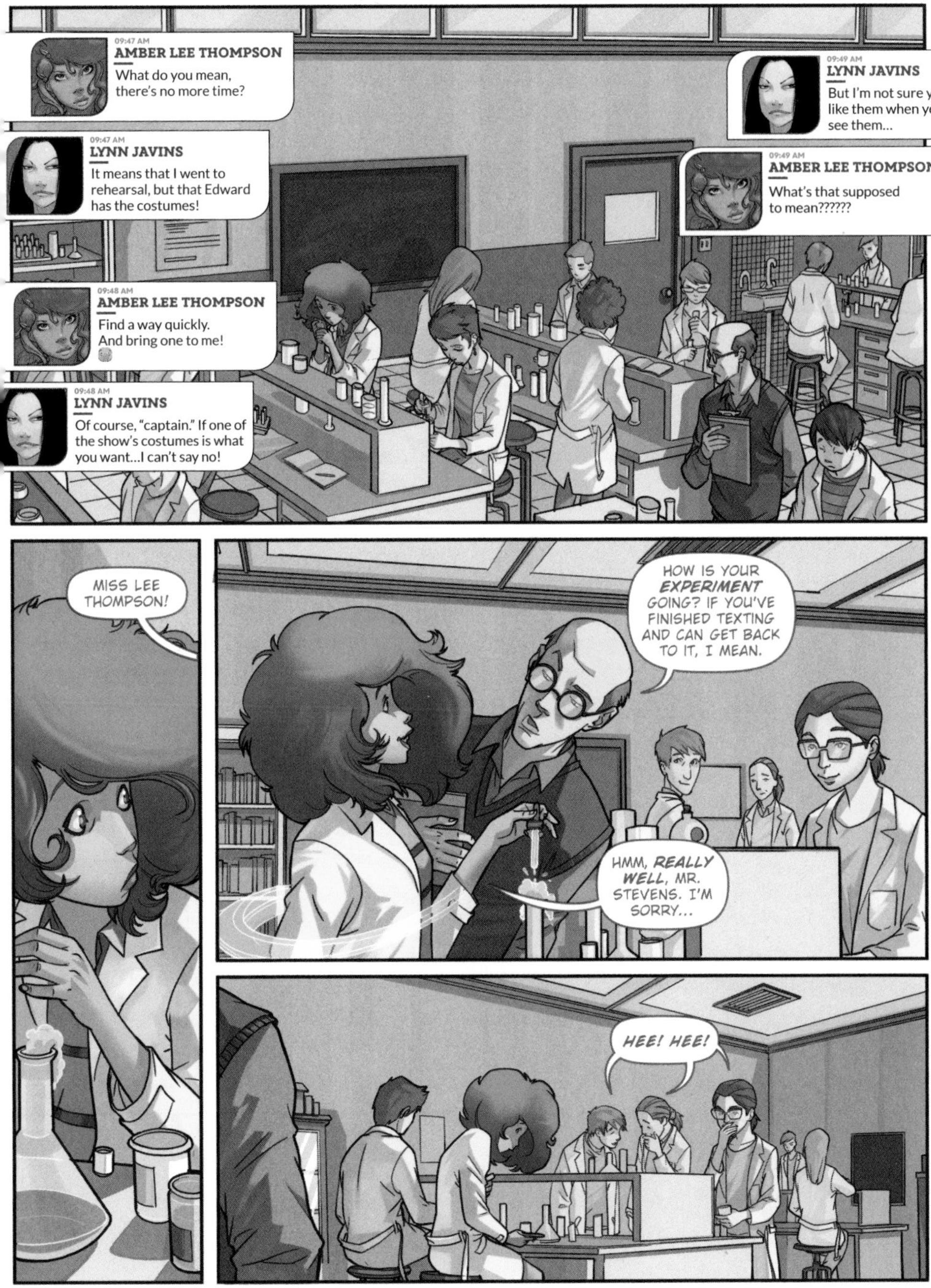
09:47 AM
AMBER LEE THOMPSON
What do you mean, there's no more time?
09:47 AM
LYNN JAVINS
It means that I went to rehearsal, but that Edward has the costumes!
09:48 AM
AMBER LEE THOMPSON
Find a way quickly. And bring one to me!
09:48 AM
LYNN JAVINS
Of course, "captain." If one of the show's costumes is what you want...I can't say no!
09:49 AM
LYNN JAVINS
But I'm not sure you'll like them when you see them...
09:49 AM
AMBER LEE THOMPSON
What's that supposed to mean??????
MISS LEE THOMPSON!
HOW IS YOUR EXPERIMENT GOING? IF YOU'VE FINISHED TEXTING AND CAN GET BACK TO IT, I MEAN.
HMM, REALLY WELL, MR. STEVENS. I'M SORRY...
HEE! HEE!

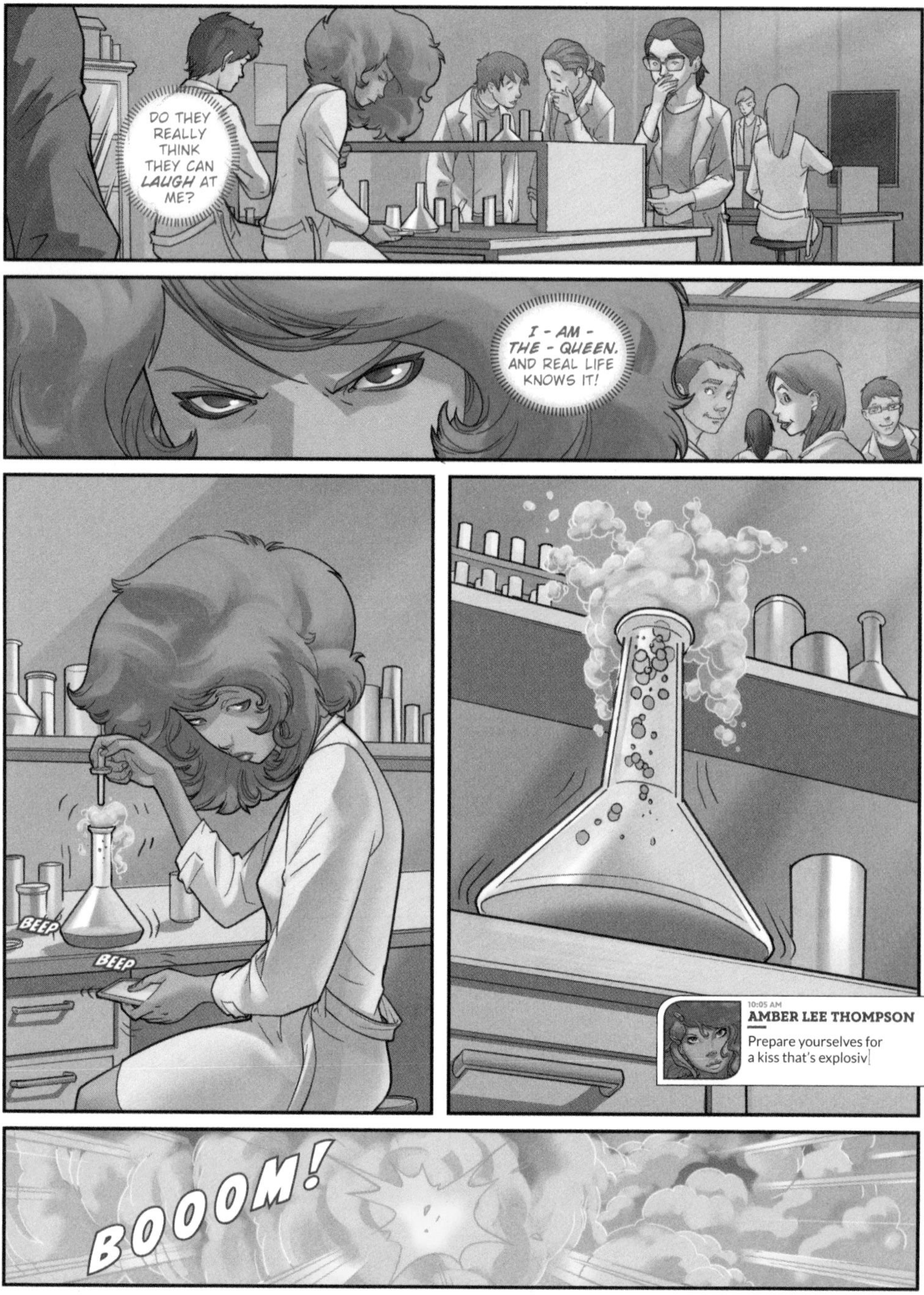
DO THEY REALLY THINK THEY CAN LAUGH AT ME?
I - AM - THE - QUEEN. AND REAL LIFE KNOWS IT!
BEEP
BEEP
10:05 AM
AMBER LEE THOMPSON
Prepare yourselves for a kiss that's explosiv
BOOOM!

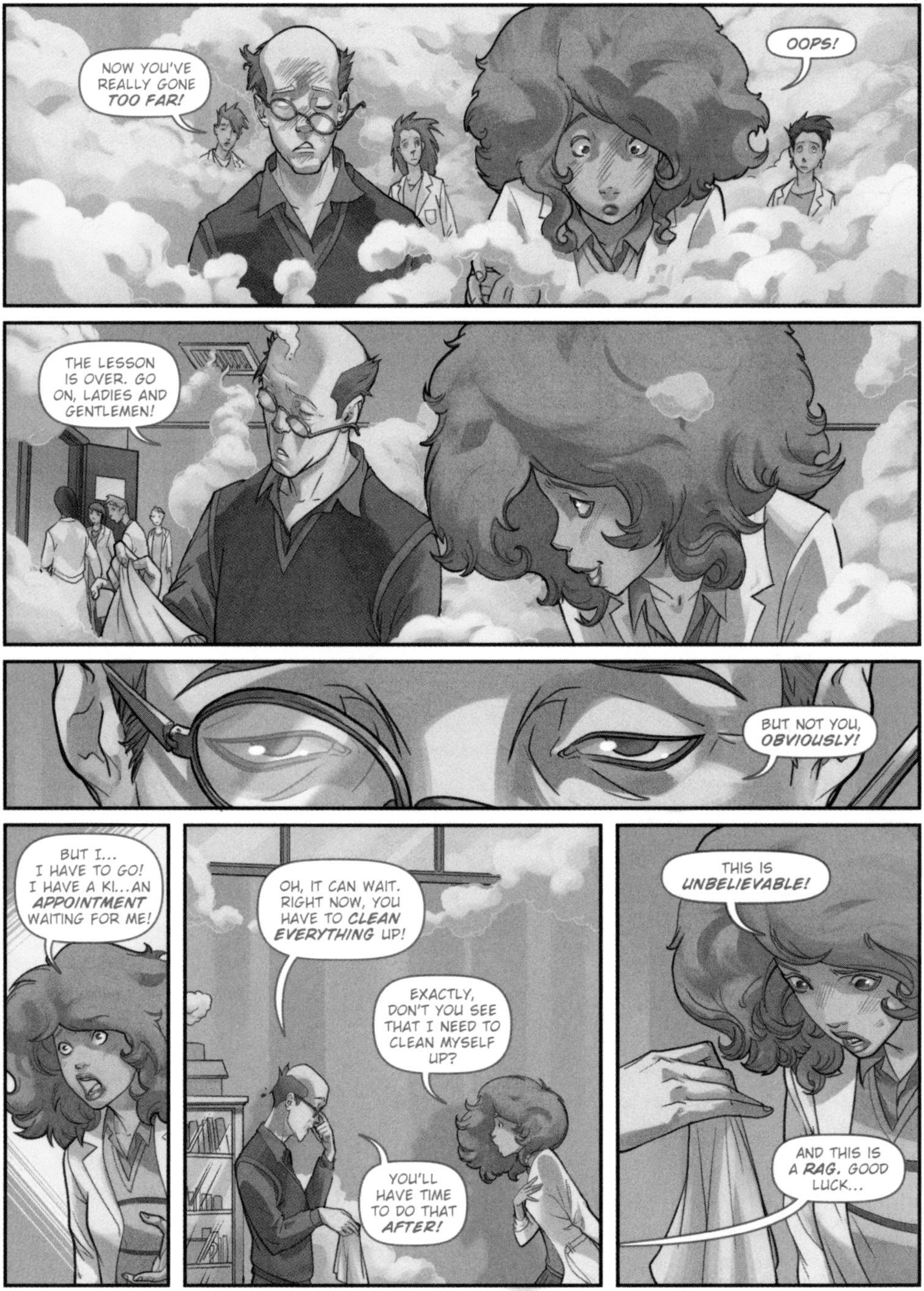
NOW YOU'VE REALLY GONE TOO FAR!
OOPS!
THE LESSON IS OVER. GO ON, LADIES AND GENTLEMEN!
BUT NOT YOU, OBVIOUSLY!
BUT I... I HAVE TO GO! I HAVE A KI...AN APPOINTMENT WAITING FOR ME!
OH, IT CAN WAIT. RIGHT NOW, YOU HAVE TO CLEAN EVERYTHING UP!
EXACTLY, DON'T YOU SEE THAT I NEED TO CLEAN MYSELF UP?
YOU'LL HAVE TIME TO DO THAT AFTER!
THIS IS UNBELIEVABLE!
AND THIS IS A RAG. GOOD LUCK...

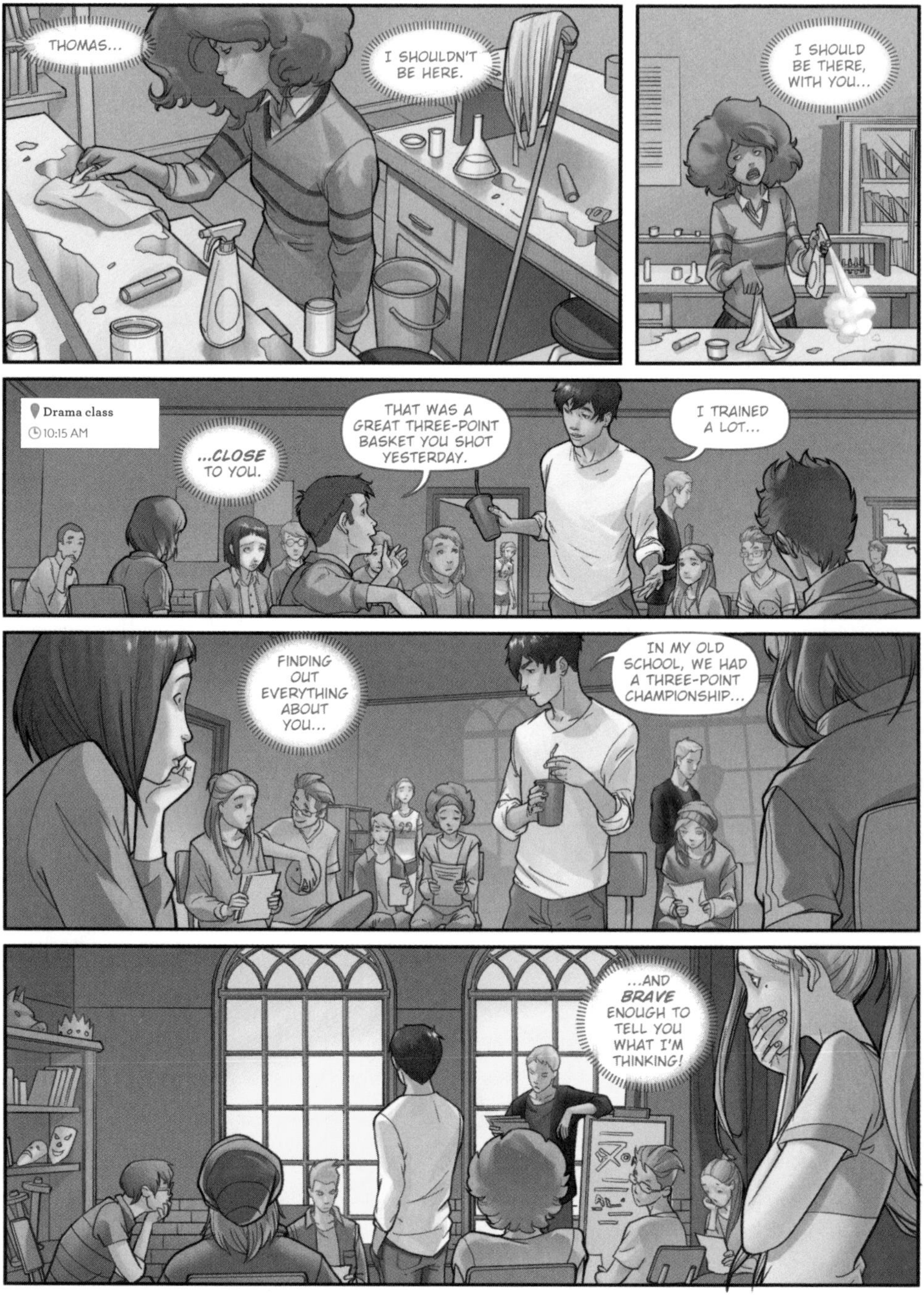
THOMAS...
I SHOULDN'T BE HERE.
I SHOULD BE THERE, WITH YOU...
Drama class
10:15 AM
...CLOSE TO YOU.
THAT WAS A GREAT THREE-POINT BASKET YOU SHOT YESTERDAY.
I TRAINED A LOT...
FINDING OUT EVERYTHING ABOUT YOU...
IN MY OLD SCHOOL, WE HAD A THREE-POINT CHAMPIONSHIP...
...AND BRAVE ENOUGH TO TELL YOU WHAT I'M THINKING!

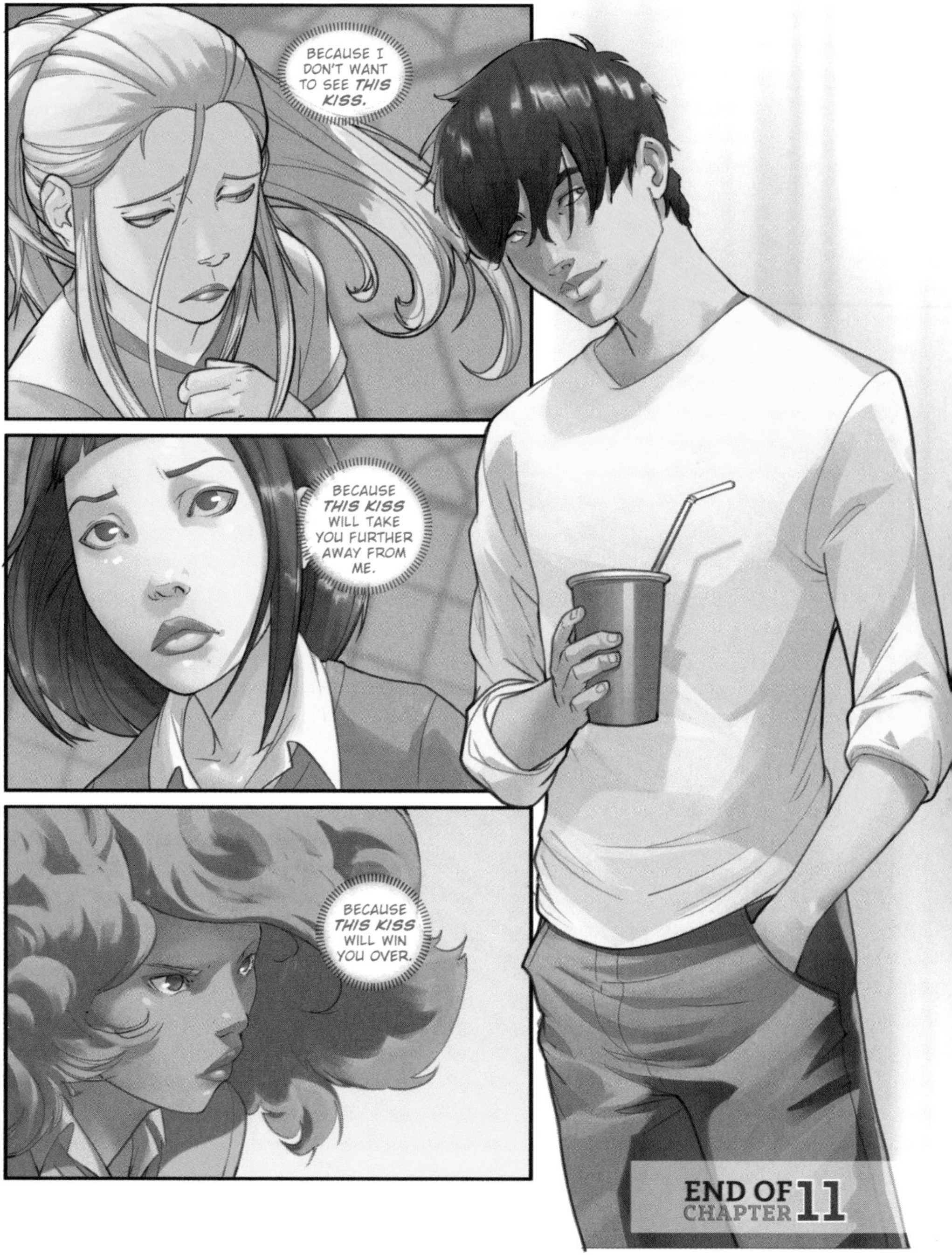
BECAUSE I DON'T WANT TO SEE THIS KISS.
BECAUSE THIS KISS WILL TAKE YOU FURTHER AWAY FROM ME.
BECAUSE THIS KISS WILL WIN YOU OVER.
END OF CHAPTER 11

CHAPTER 12

A new JULIET

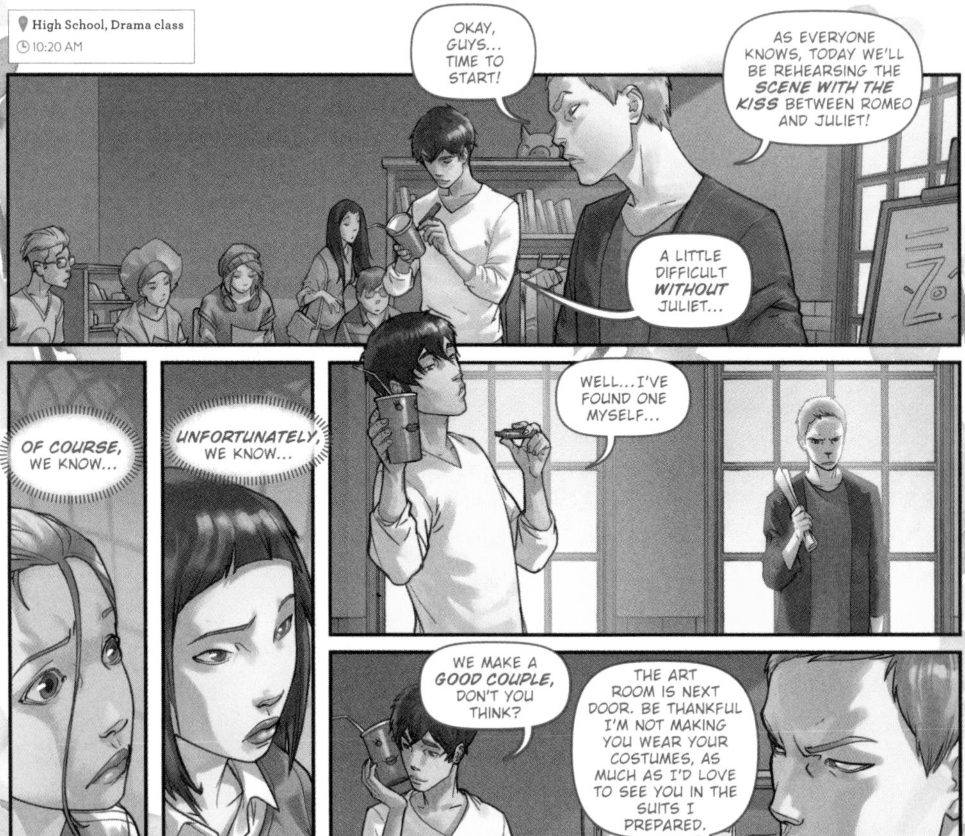
High School, Drama class
10:20 AM
OKAY, GUYS... TIME TO START!
AS EVERYONE KNOWS, TODAY WE'LL BE REHEARSING THE SCENE WITH THE KISS BETWEEN ROMEO AND JULIET!
A LITTLE DIFFICULT WITHOUT JULIET...
OF COURSE, WE KNOW...
UNFORTUNATELY, WE KNOW...
WELL...I'VE FOUND ONE MYSELF...
WE MAKE A GOOD COUPLE, DON'T YOU THINK?
THE ART ROOM IS NEXT DOOR. BE THANKFUL I'M NOT MAKING YOU WEAR YOUR COSTUMES, AS MUCH AS I'D LOVE TO SEE YOU IN THE SUITS I PREPARED.

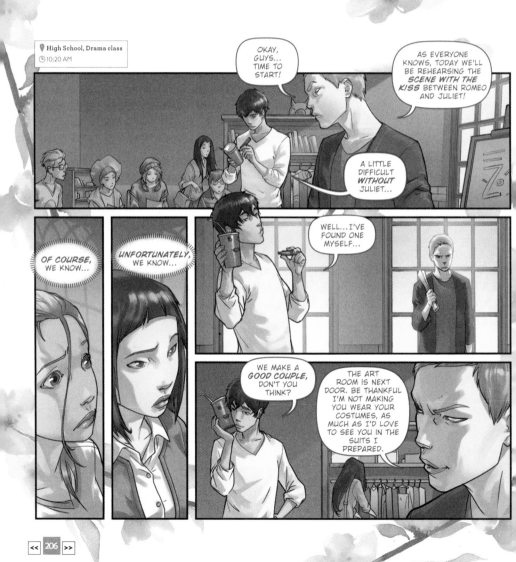

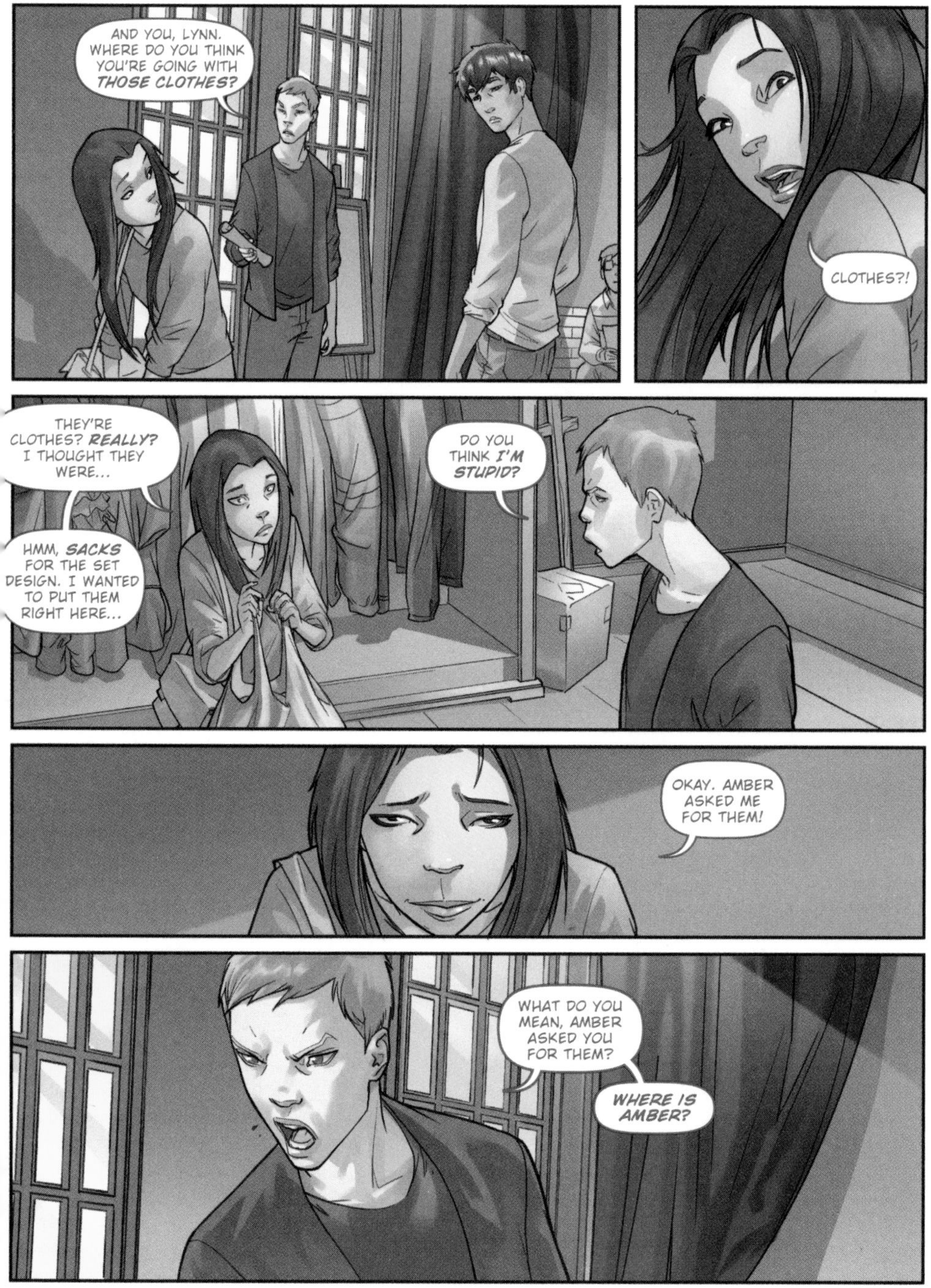
AND YOU, LYNN. WHERE DO YOU THINK YOU'RE GOING WITH THOSE CLOTHES?
CLOTHES?!
THEY'RE CLOTHES? REALLY? I THOUGHT THEY WERE...
HMM, SACKS FOR THE SET DESIGN. I WANTED TO PUT THEM RIGHT HERE...
DO YOU THINK I'M STUPID?
OKAY. AMBER ASKED ME FOR THEM!
WHAT DO YOU MEAN, AMBER ASKED YOU FOR THEM?
WHERE IS AMBER?

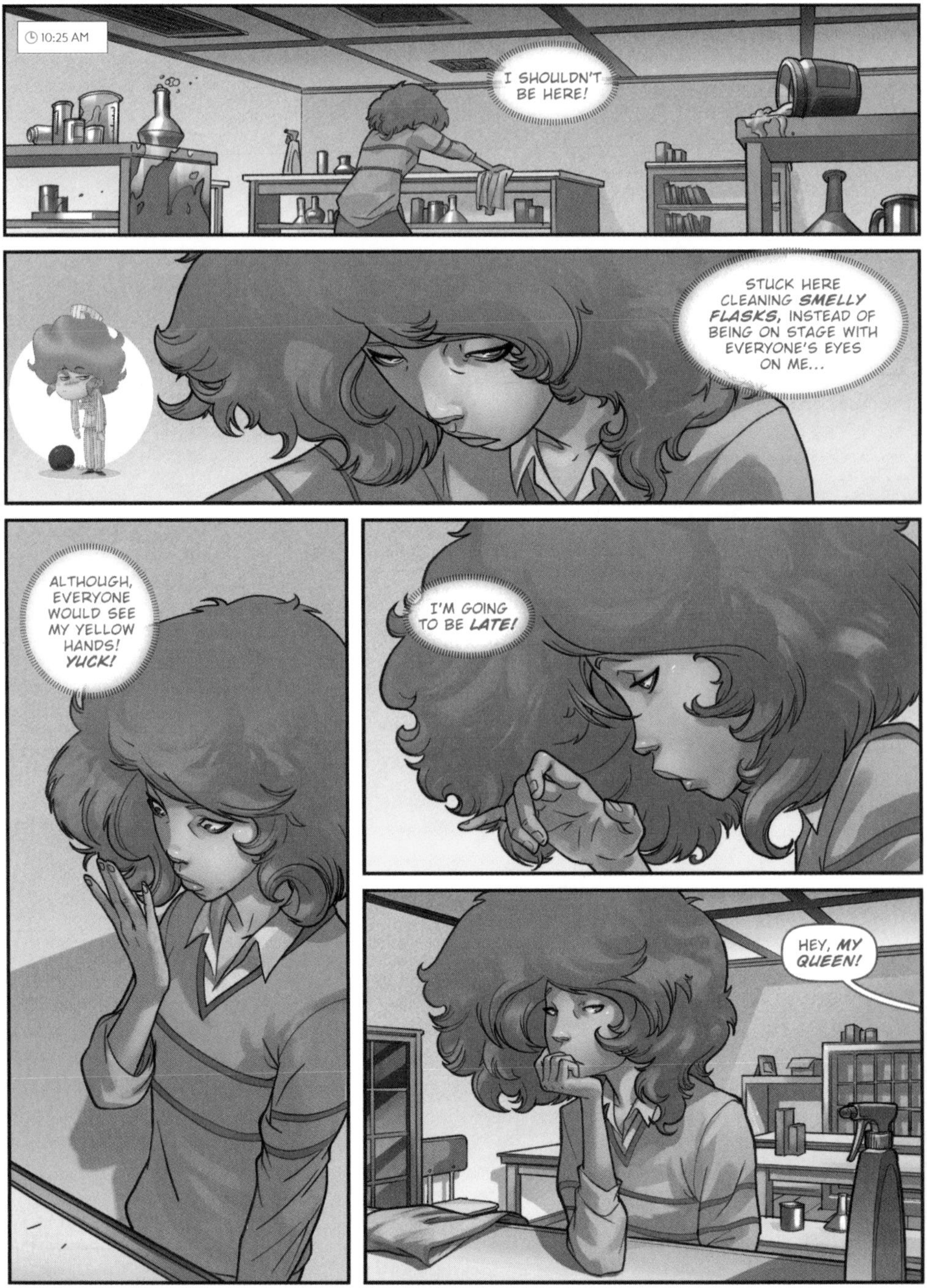
10:25 AM
I SHOULDN'T BE HERE!
STUCK HERE CLEANING SMELLY FLASKS, INSTEAD OF BEING ON STAGE WITH EVERYONE'S EYES ON ME...
ALTHOUGH, EVERYONE WOULD SEE MY YELLOW HANDS! YUCK!
I'M GOING TO BE LATE!
HEY, MY QUEEN!

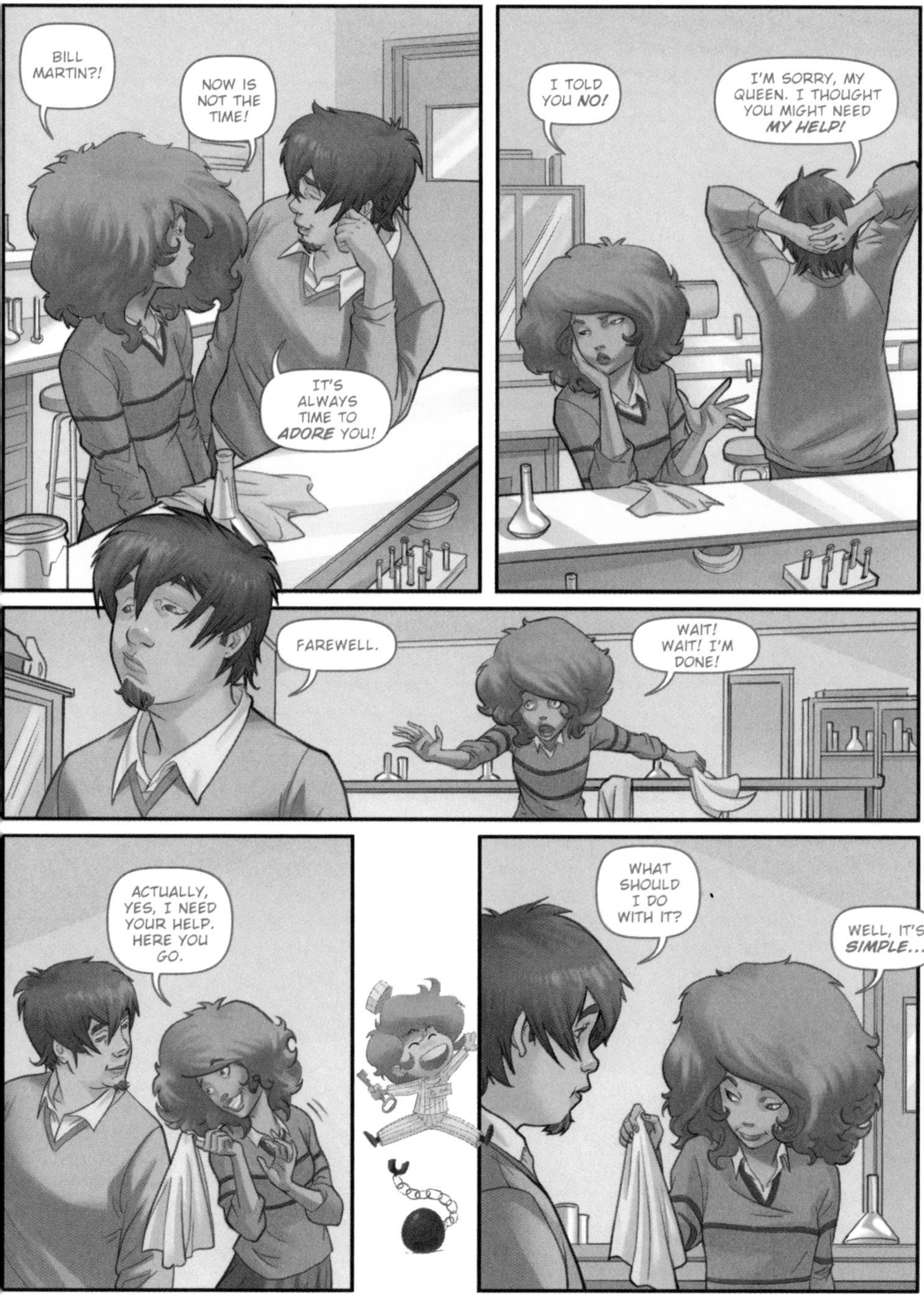
BILL MARTIN?!
NOW IS NOT THE TIME!
IT'S ALWAYS TIME TO ADORE YOU!
I TOLD YOU NO!
I'M SORRY, MY QUEEN. I THOUGHT YOU MIGHT NEED MY HELP!
FAREWELL.
WAIT! WAIT! I'M DONE!
ACTUALLY, YES, I NEED YOUR HELP. HERE YOU GO.
WHAT SHOULD I DO WITH IT?
WELL, IT'S SIMPLE...

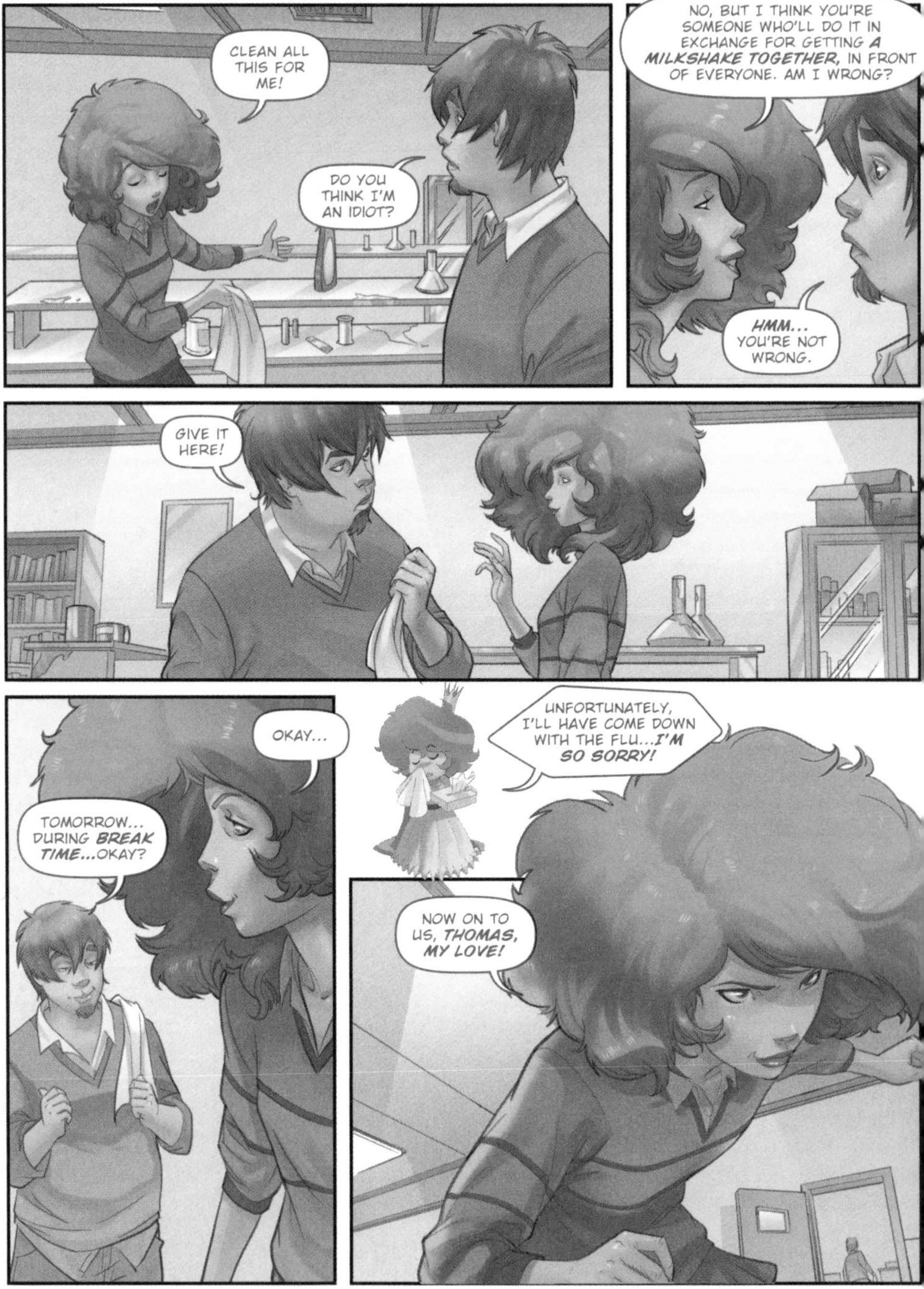

CLEAN ALL THIS FOR ME!
DO YOU THINK I'M AN IDIOT?
NO, BUT I THINK YOU'RE SOMEONE WHO'LL DO IT IN EXCHANGE FOR GETTING A MILKSHAKE TOGETHER, IN FRONT OF EVERYONE. AM I WRONG?
HMM... YOU'RE NOT WRONG.
GIVE IT HERE!
OKAY...
TOMORROW... DURING BREAK TIME...OKAY?
UNFORTUNATELY, I'LL HAVE COME DOWN WITH THE FLU...I'M SO SORRY!
NOW ON TO US, THOMAS, MY LOVE!

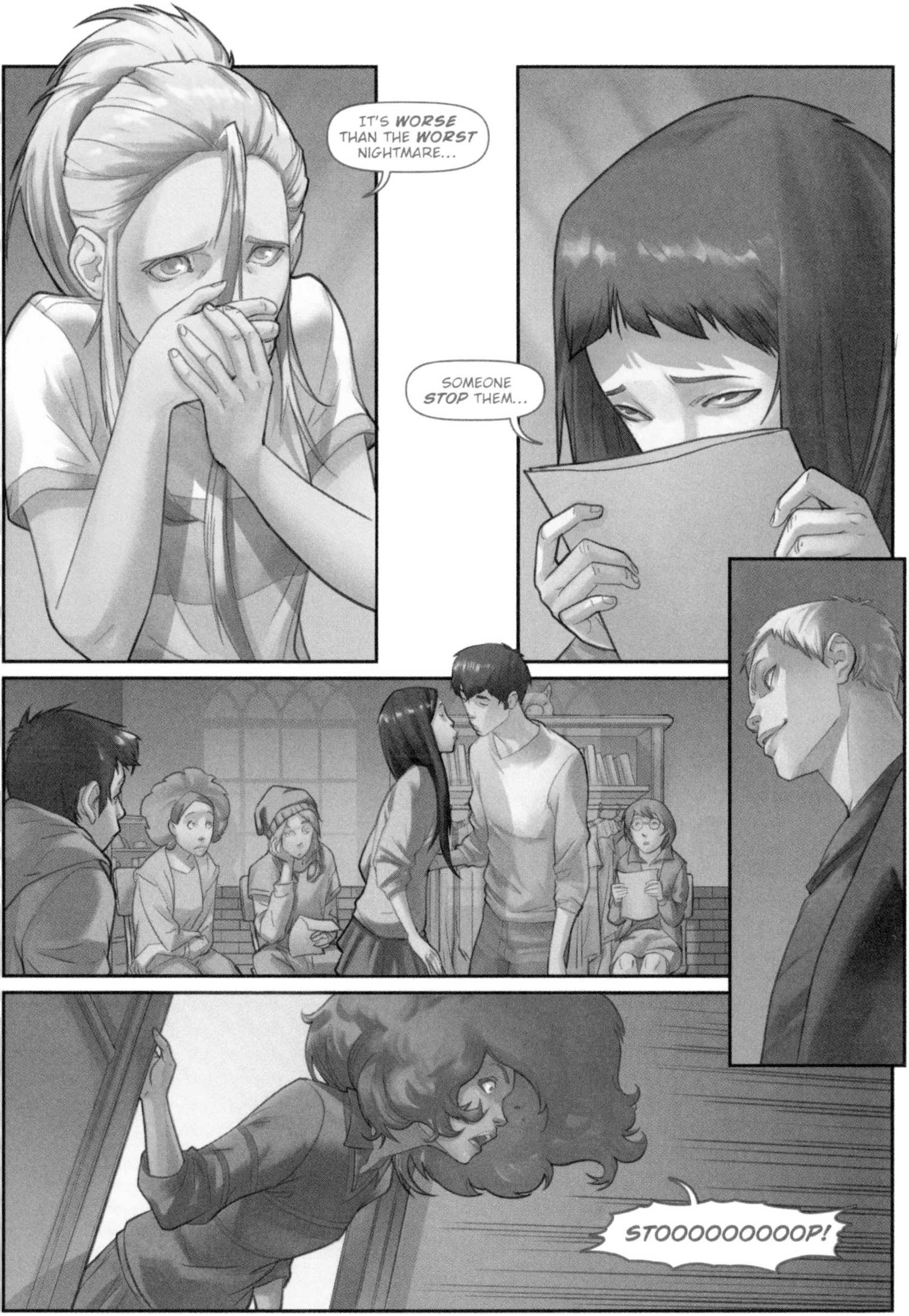
IT'S WORSE THAN THE WORST NIGHTMARE...
SOMEONE STOP THEM...
STOOOOOOOOOP!

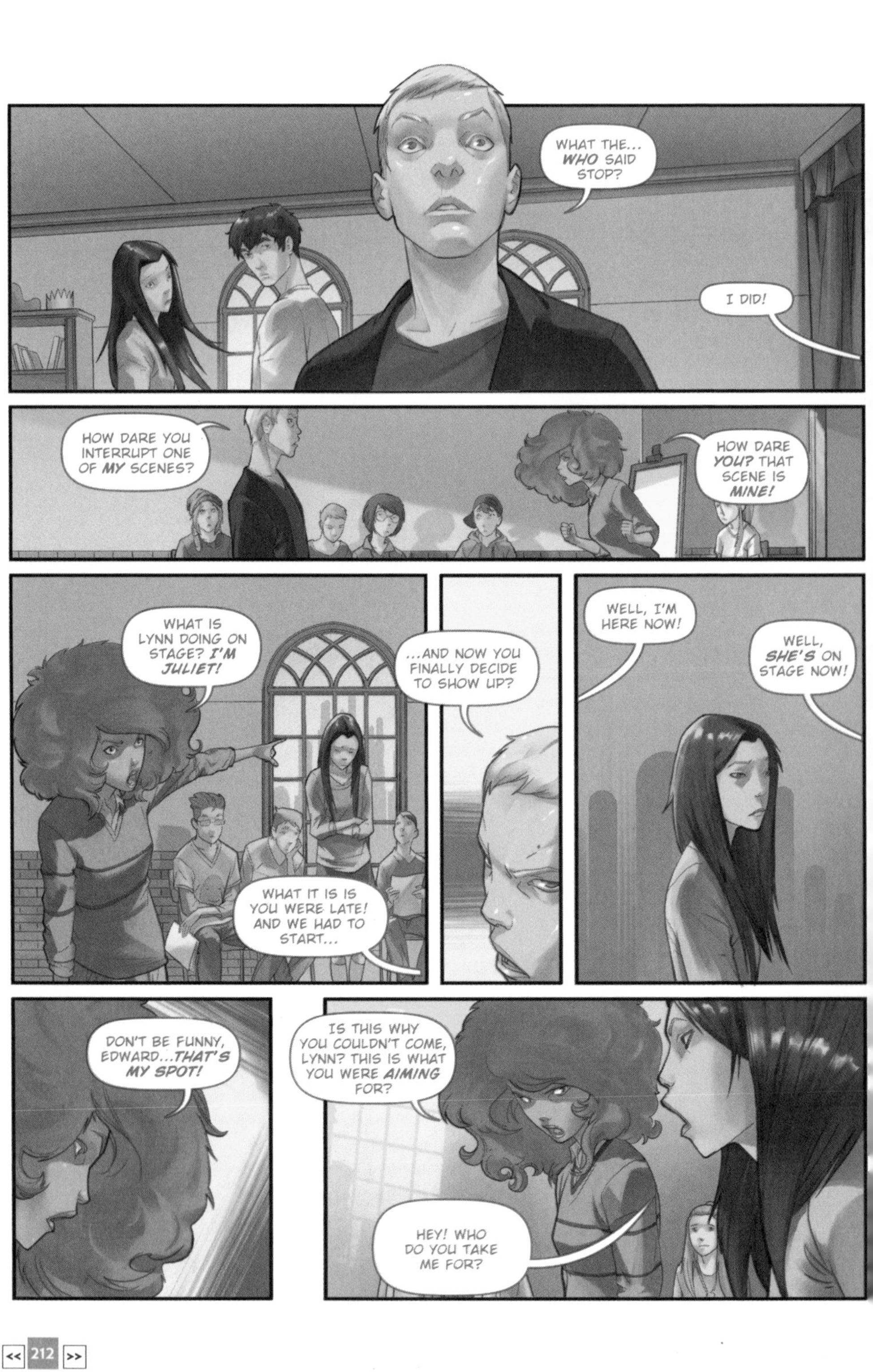
WHAT THE... WHO SAID STOP?
I DID!
HOW DARE YOU INTERRUPT ONE OF MY SCENES?
HOW DARE YOU? THAT SCENE IS MINE!
WHAT IS LYNN DOING ON STAGE? I'M JULIET!
WHAT IT IS IS YOU WERE LATE! AND WE HAD TO START...
...AND NOW YOU FINALLY DECIDE TO SHOW UP?
WELL, I'M HERE NOW!
WELL, SHE'S ON STAGE NOW!
DON'T BE FUNNY, EDWARD...THAT'S MY SPOT!
IS THIS WHY YOU COULDN'T COME, LYNN? THIS IS WHAT YOU WERE AIMING FOR?
HEY! WHO DO YOU TAKE ME FOR?

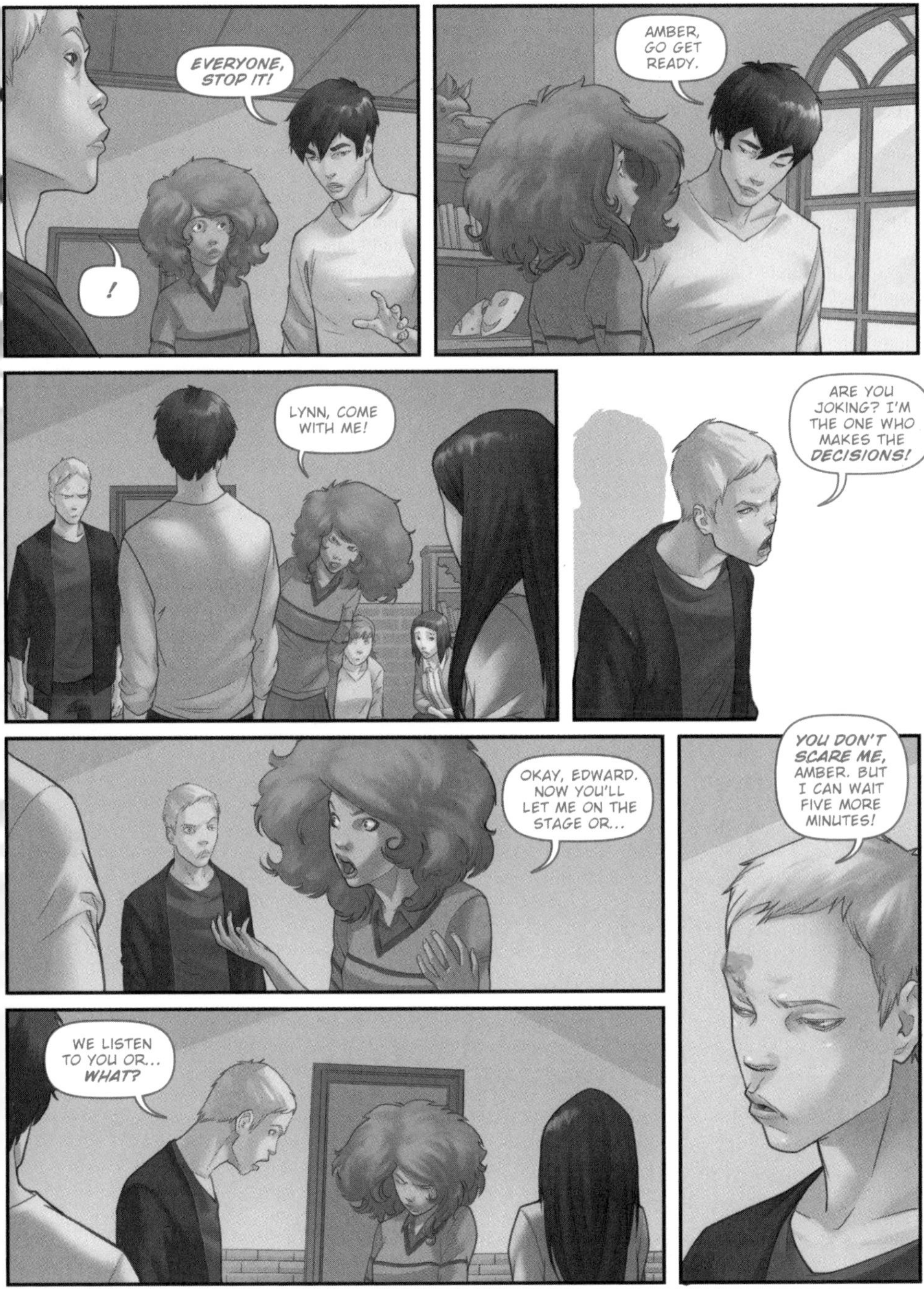
EVERYONE, STOP IT!
!
AMBER, GO GET READY.
LYNN, COME WITH ME!
ARE YOU JOKING? I'M THE ONE WHO MAKES THE DECISIONS!
OKAY, EDWARD. NOW YOU'LL LET ME ON THE STAGE OR...
WE LISTEN TO YOU OR... WHAT?
YOU DON'T SCARE ME, AMBER. BUT I CAN WAIT FIVE MORE MINUTES!

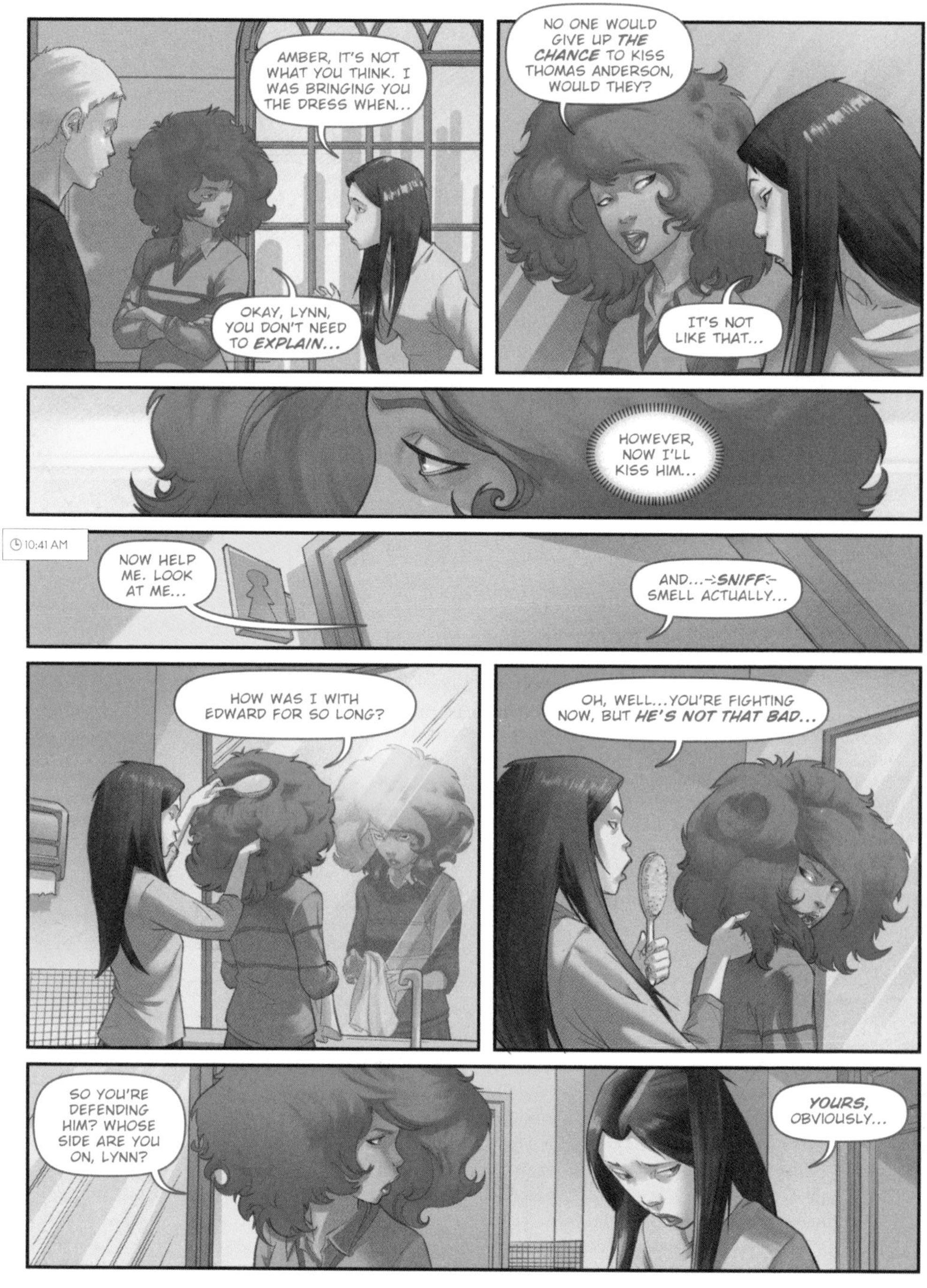
AMBER, IT'S NOT WHAT YOU THINK. I WAS BRINGING YOU THE DRESS WHEN...
OKAY, LYNN, YOU DON'T NEED TO EXPLAIN...
NO ONE WOULD GIVE UP THE CHANCE TO KISS THOMAS ANDERSON, WOULD THEY?
IT'S NOT LIKE THAT...
HOWEVER, NOW I'LL KISS HIM...
10:41 AM
NOW HELP ME. LOOK AT ME...
AND...SNIFF SMELL ACTUALLY...
HOW WAS I WITH EDWARD FOR SO LONG?
OH, WELL...YOU'RE FIGHTING NOW, BUT HE'S NOT THAT BAD...
SO YOU'RE DEFENDING HIM? WHOSE SIDE ARE YOU ON, LYNN?
YOURS, OBVIOUSLY...

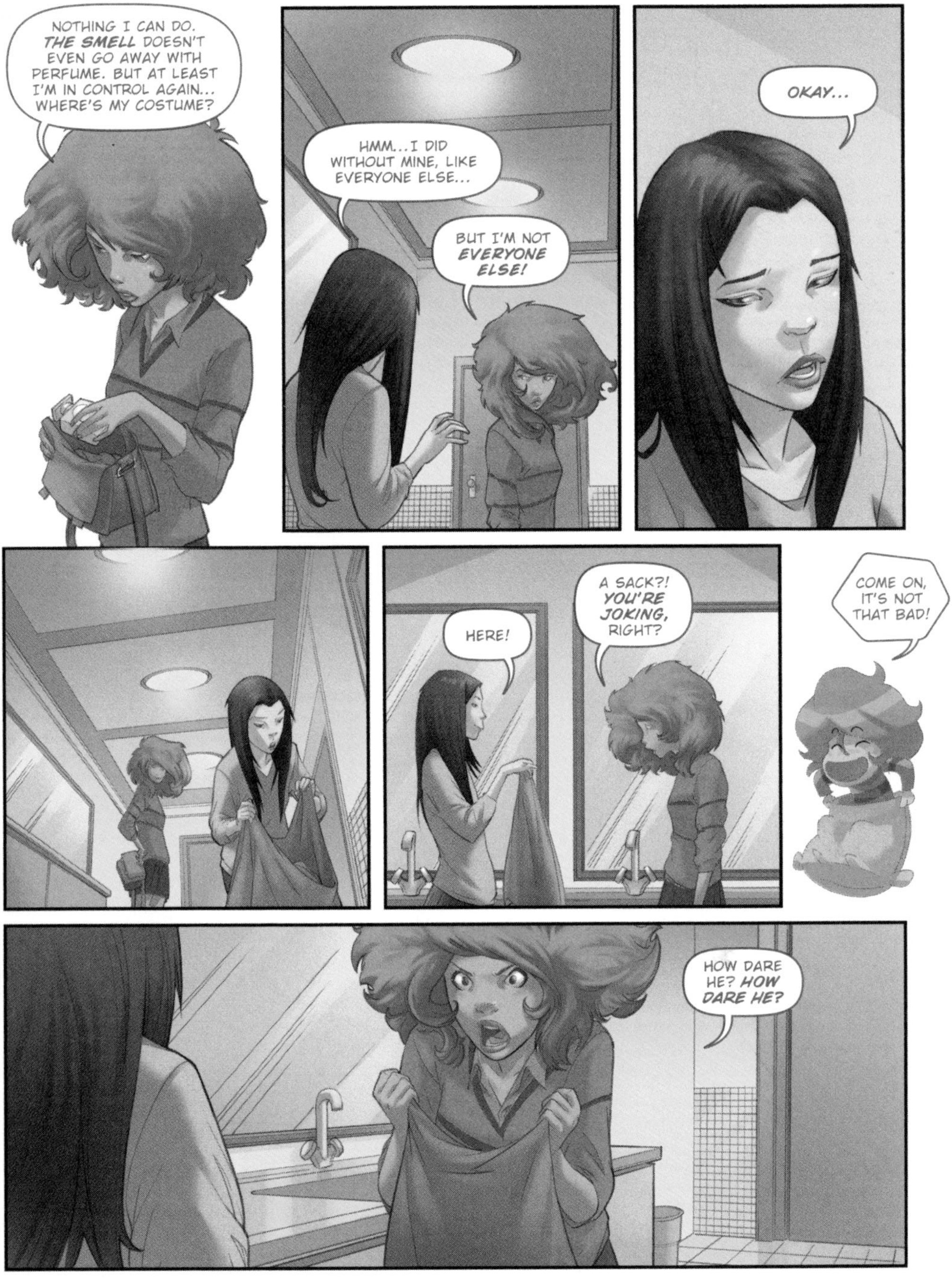
NOTHING I CAN DO. THE SMELL DOESN'T EVEN GO AWAY WITH PERFUME. BUT AT LEAST I'M IN CONTROL AGAIN... WHERE'S MY COSTUME?
HMM...I DID WITHOUT MINE, LIKE EVERYONE ELSE...
BUT I'M NOT EVERYONE ELSE!
OKAY...
HERE!
A SACK?! YOU'RE JOKING, RIGHT?
COME ON, IT'S NOT THAT BAD!
HOW DARE HE? HOW DARE HE?

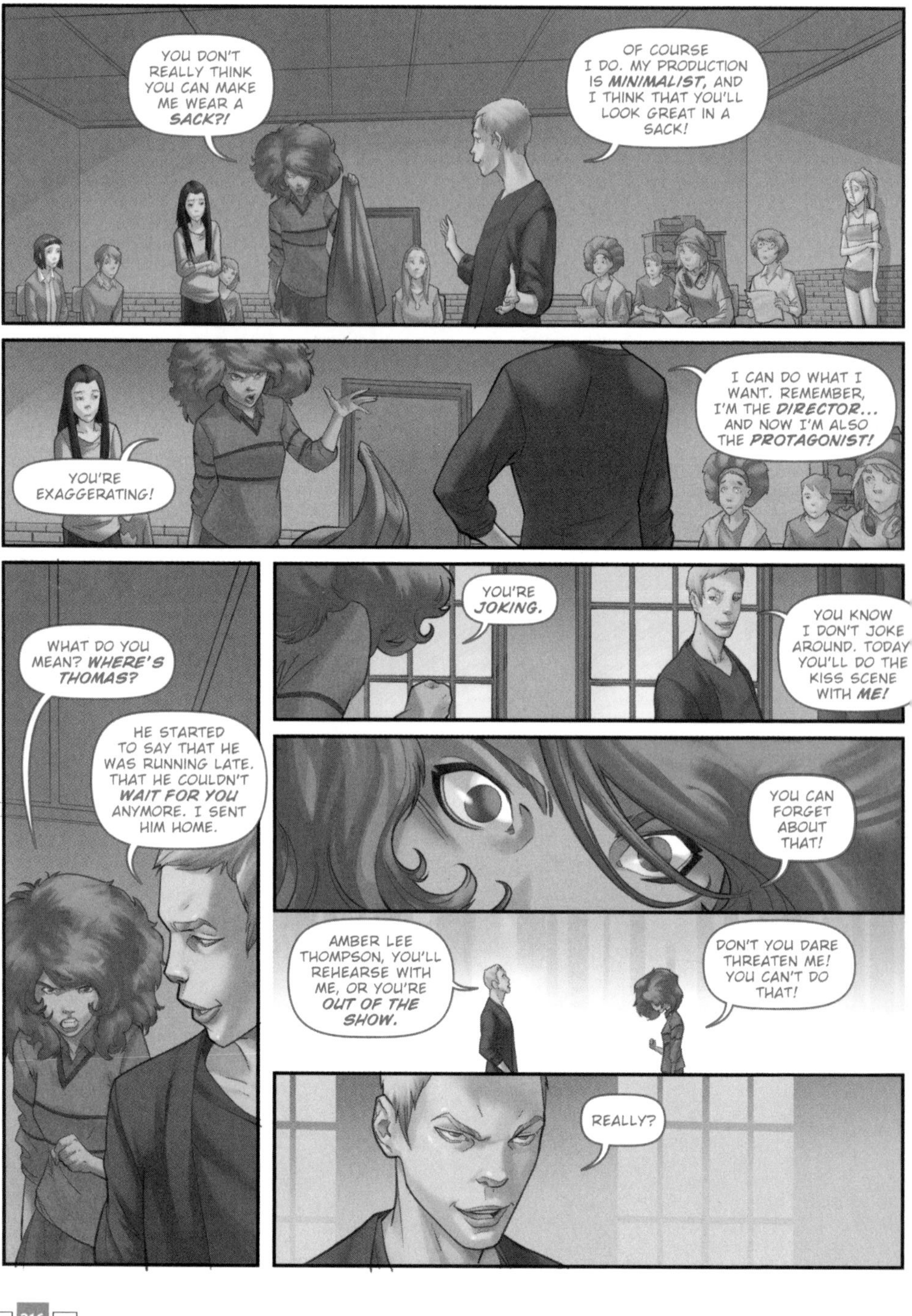
YOU DON'T REALLY THINK YOU CAN MAKE ME WEAR A SACK?!
OF COURSE I DO. MY PRODUCTION IS MINIMALIST, AND I THINK THAT YOU'LL LOOK GREAT IN A SACK!
YOU'RE EXAGGERATING!
I CAN DO WHAT I WANT. REMEMBER, I'M THE DIRECTOR... AND NOW I'M ALSO THE PROTAGONIST!
WHAT DO YOU MEAN? WHERE'S THOMAS?
HE STARTED TO SAY THAT HE WAS RUNNING LATE. THAT HE COULDN'T WAIT FOR YOU ANYMORE. I SENT HIM HOME.
YOU'RE JOKING.
YOU KNOW I DON'T JOKE AROUND. TODAY YOU'LL DO THE KISS SCENE WITH ME!
YOU CAN FORGET ABOUT THAT!
AMBER LEE THOMPSON, YOU'LL REHEARSE WITH ME, OR YOU'RE OUT OF THE SHOW.
DON'T YOU DARE THREATEN ME! YOU CAN'T DO THAT!
REALLY?

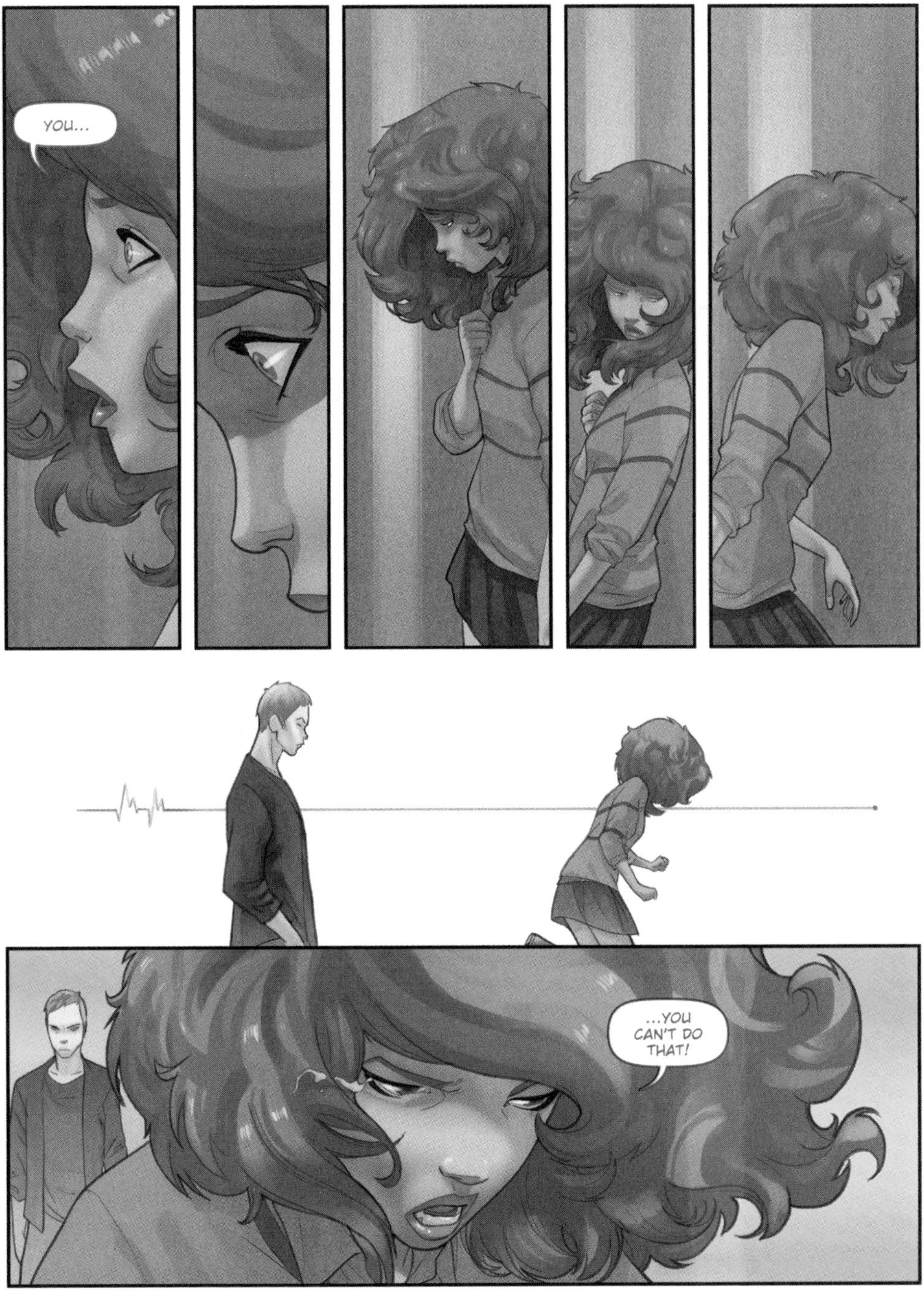
YOU...
...YOU CAN'T DO THAT!

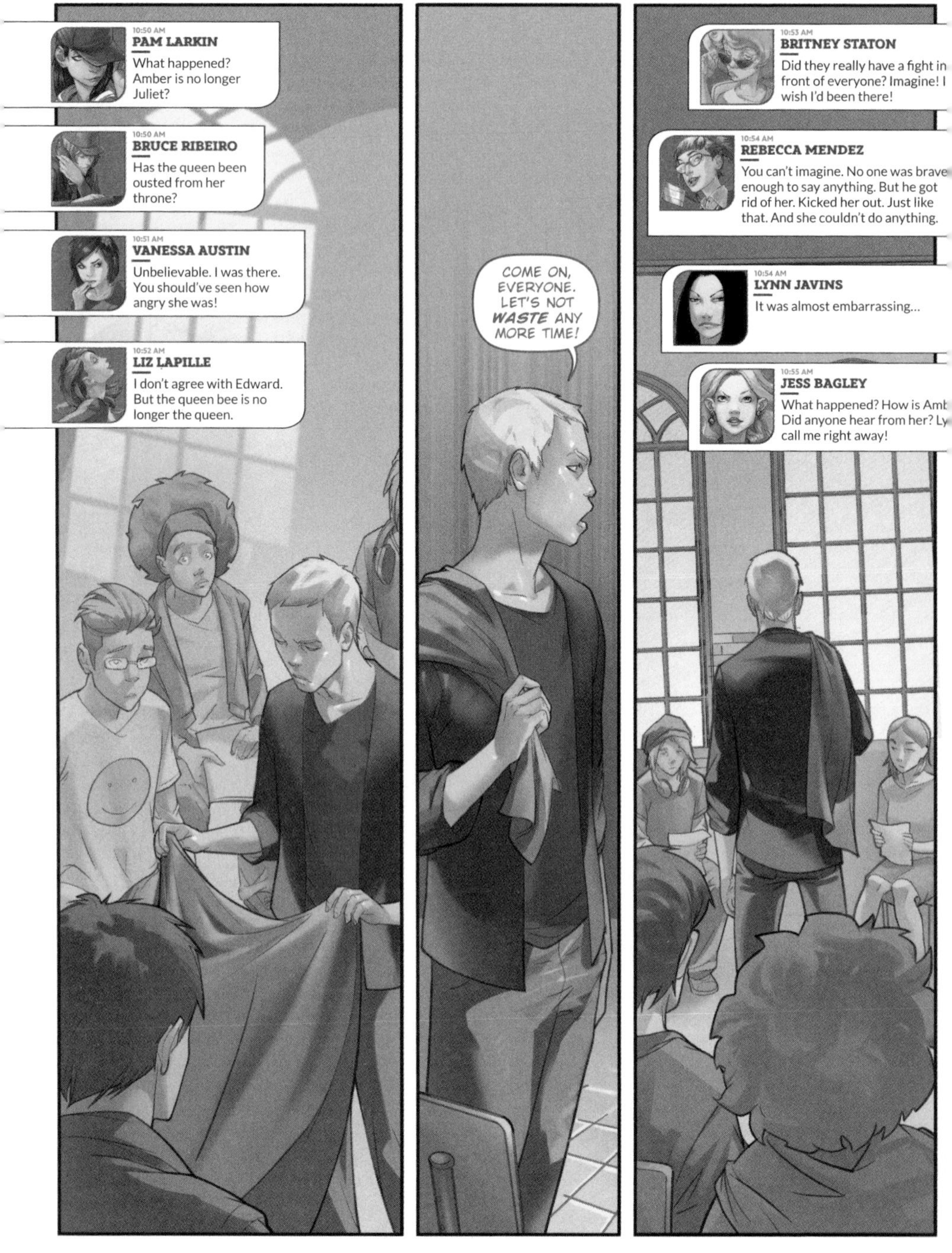

10:50 AM
PAM LARKIN
What happened? Amber is no longer Juliet?
10:50 AM
BRUCE RIBEIRO
Has the queen been ousted from her throne?
10:51 AM
VANESSA AUSTIN
Unbelievable. I was there. You should've seen how angry she was!
10:52 AM
LIZ LAPILLE
I don't agree with Edward. But the queen bee is no longer the queen.
COME ON, EVERYONE. LET'S NOT WASTE ANY MORE TIME!
10:53 AM
BRITNEY STATON
Did they really have a fight in front of everyone? Imagine! I wish I'd been there!
10:54 AM
REBECCA MENDEZ
You can't imagine. No one was brave enough to say anything. But he got rid of her. Kicked her out. Just like that. And she couldn't do anything.
10:54 AM
LYNN JAVINS
It was almost embarrassing...
10:55 AM
JESS BAGLEY
What happened? How is Amb
Did anyone hear from her? Ly
call me right away!

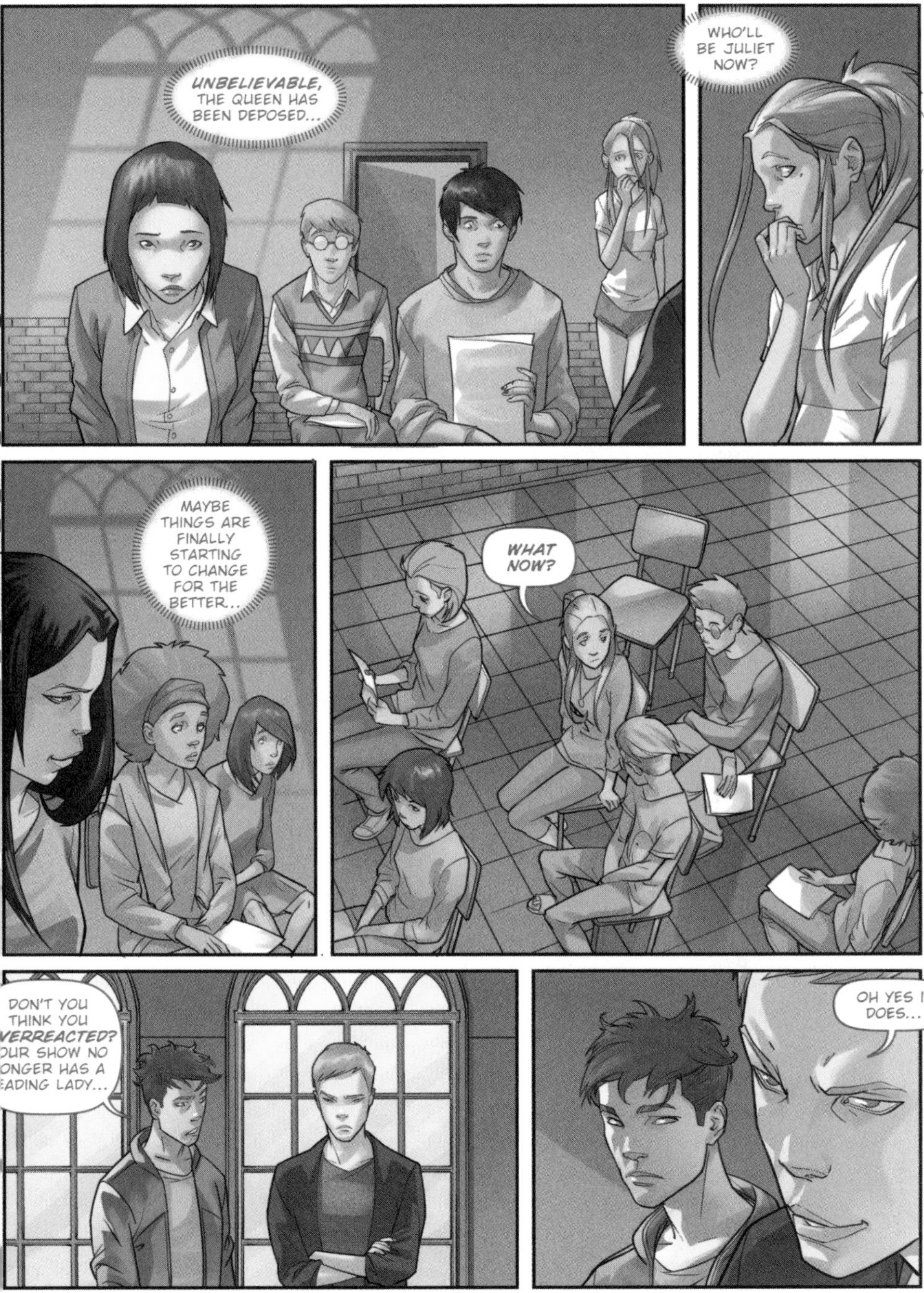
UNBELIEVABLE, THE QUEEN HAS BEEN DEPOSED...
WHO'LL BE JULIET NOW?
MAYBE THINGS ARE FINALLY STARTING TO CHANGE FOR THE BETTER...
WHAT NOW?
DON'T YOU THINK YOU VERREACTED? OUR SHOW NO ONGER HAS A EADING LADY...
OH YES IT DOES...

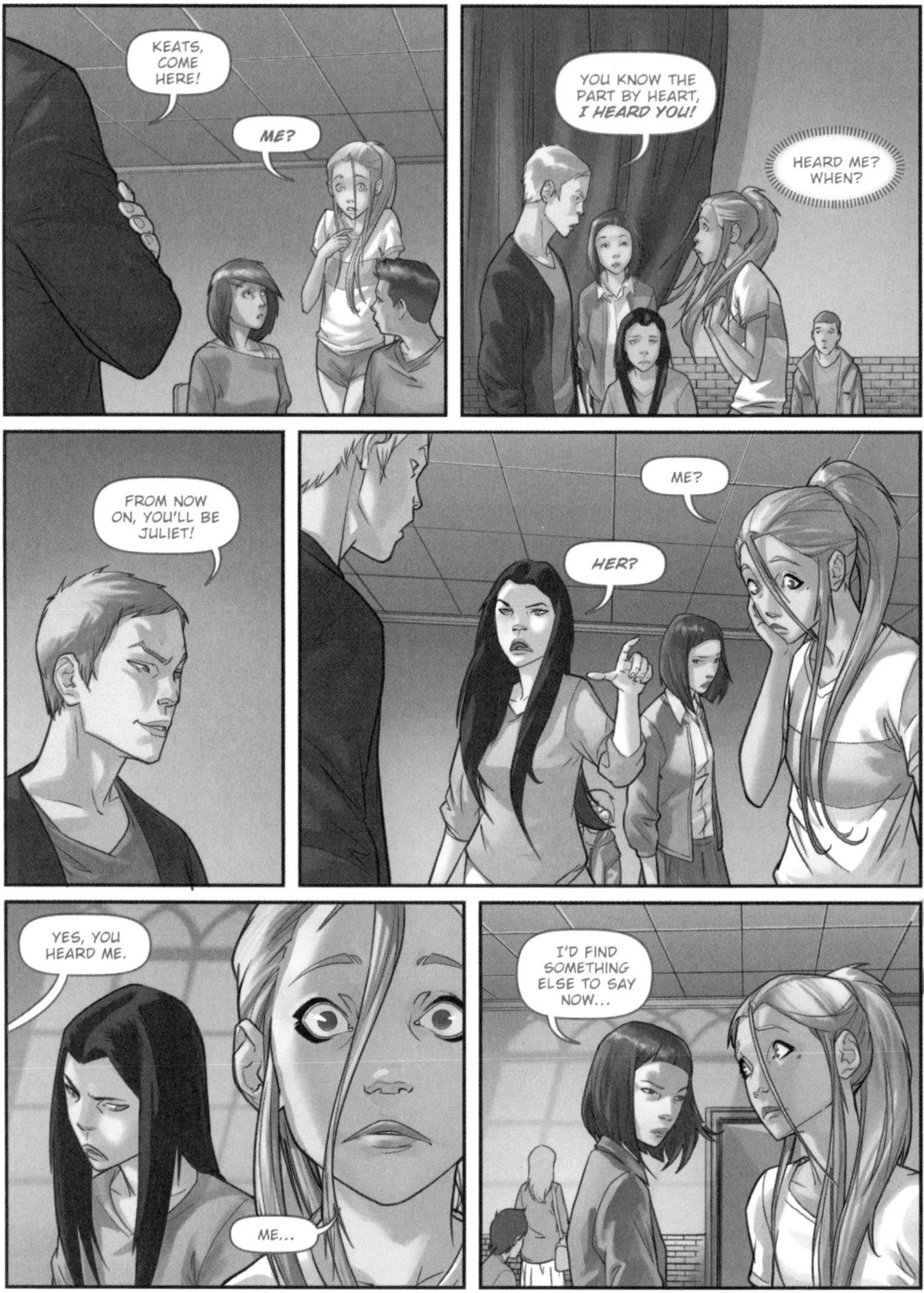
KEATS, COME HERE!
ME?
YOU KNOW THE PART BY HEART, I HEARD YOU!
HEARD ME? WHEN?
FROM NOW ON, YOU'LL BE JULIET!
ME?
HER?
YES, YOU HEARD ME.
ME...
I'D FIND SOMETHING ELSE TO SAY NOW...

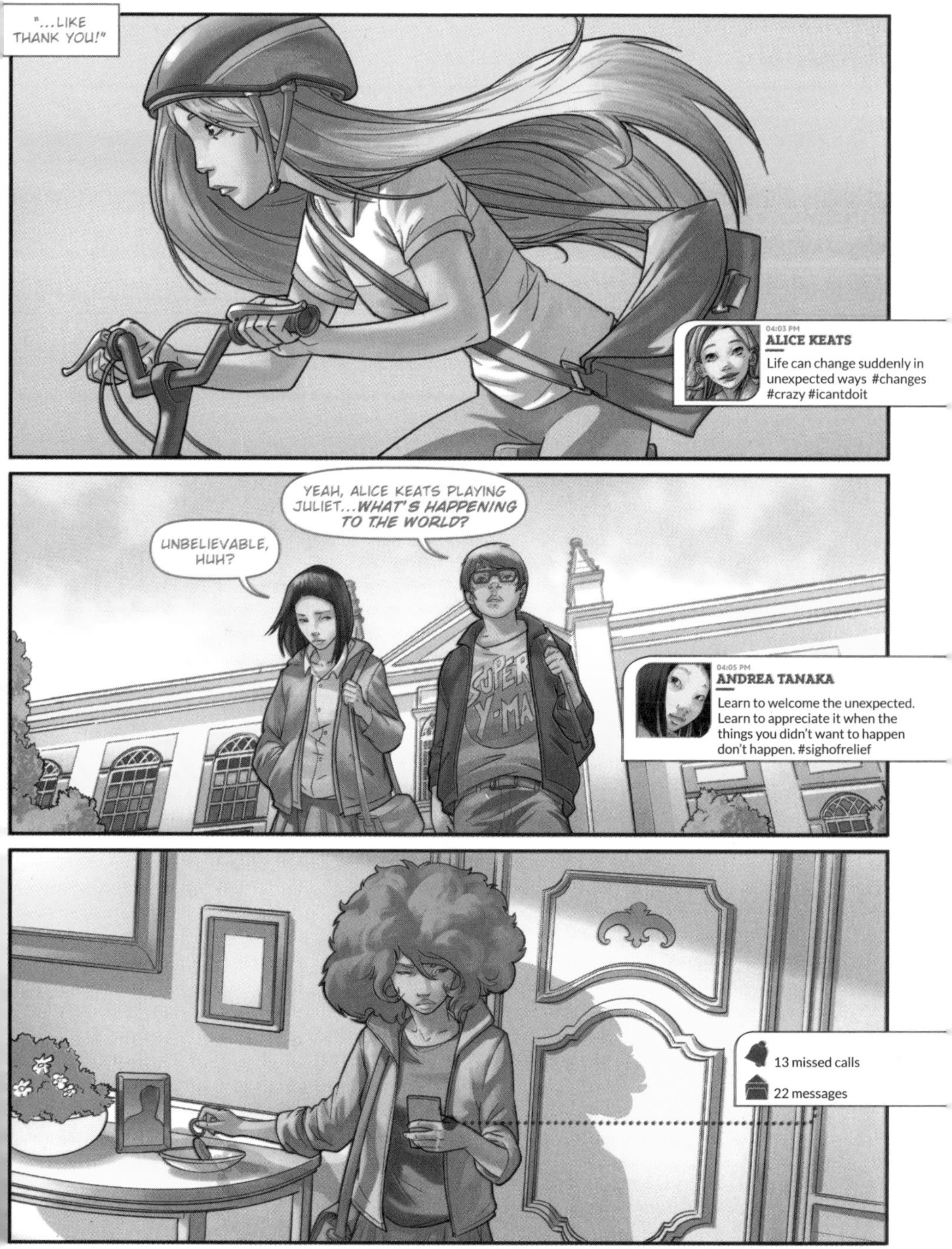
"...LIKE THANK YOU!"
04:03 PM
ALICE KEATS
Life can change suddenly in unexpected ways #changes #crazy #icantdoit
UNBELIEVABLE, HUH?
YEAH, ALICE KEATS PLAYING JULIET...WHAT'S HAPPENING TO THE WORLD?
SUPER Y-MA
04:05 PM
ANDREA TANAKA
Learn to welcome the unexpected. Learn to appreciate it when the things you didn't want to happen don't happen. #sighofrelief
13 missed calls
22 messages

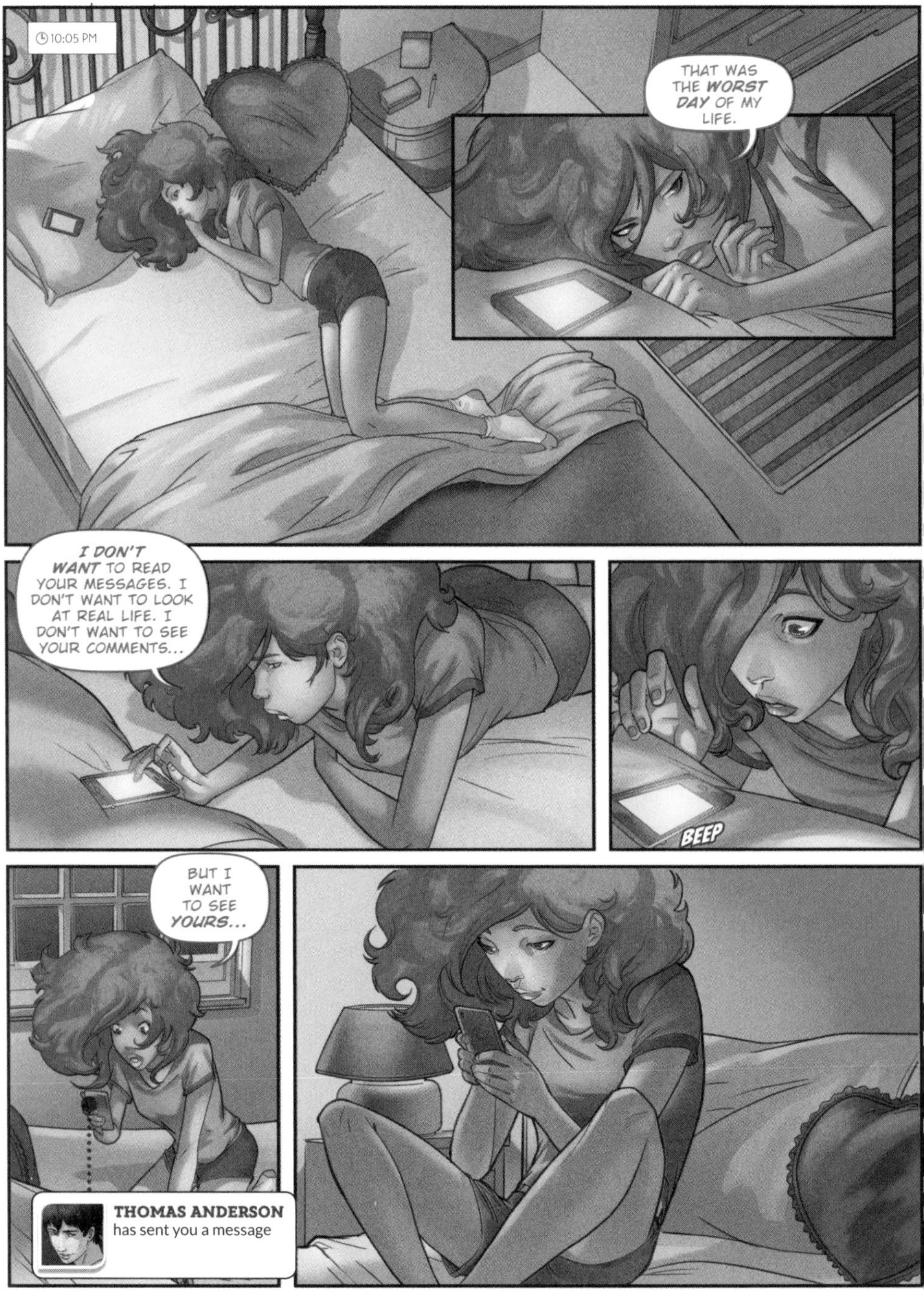
10:05 PM
THAT WAS THE WORST DAY OF MY LIFE.
I DON'T WANT TO READ YOUR MESSAGES. I DON'T WANT TO LOOK AT REAL LIFE. I DON'T WANT TO SEE YOUR COMMENTS...
BEEP
BUT I WANT TO SEE YOURS...
THOMAS ANDERSON
has sent you a message

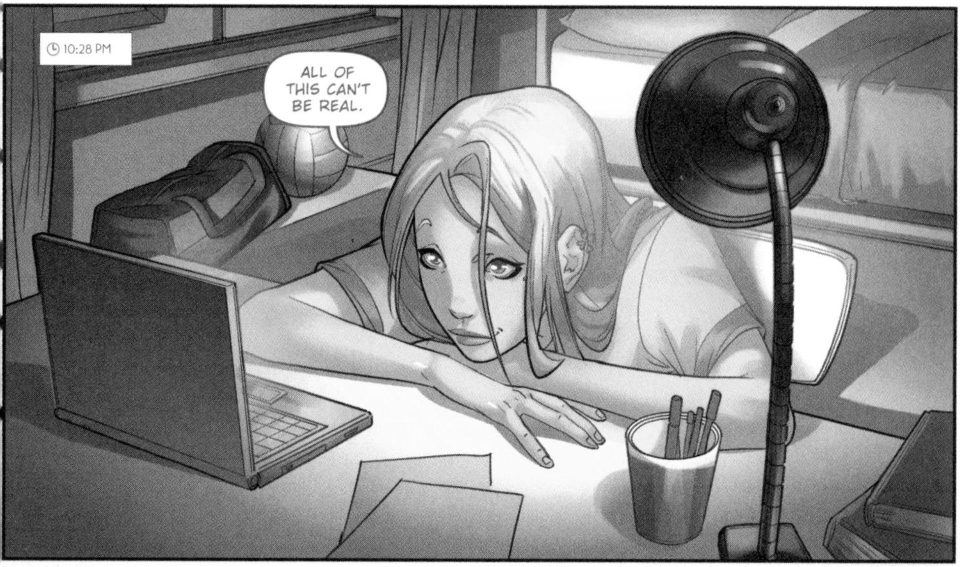
10:28 PM
ALL OF THIS CAN'T BE REAL.

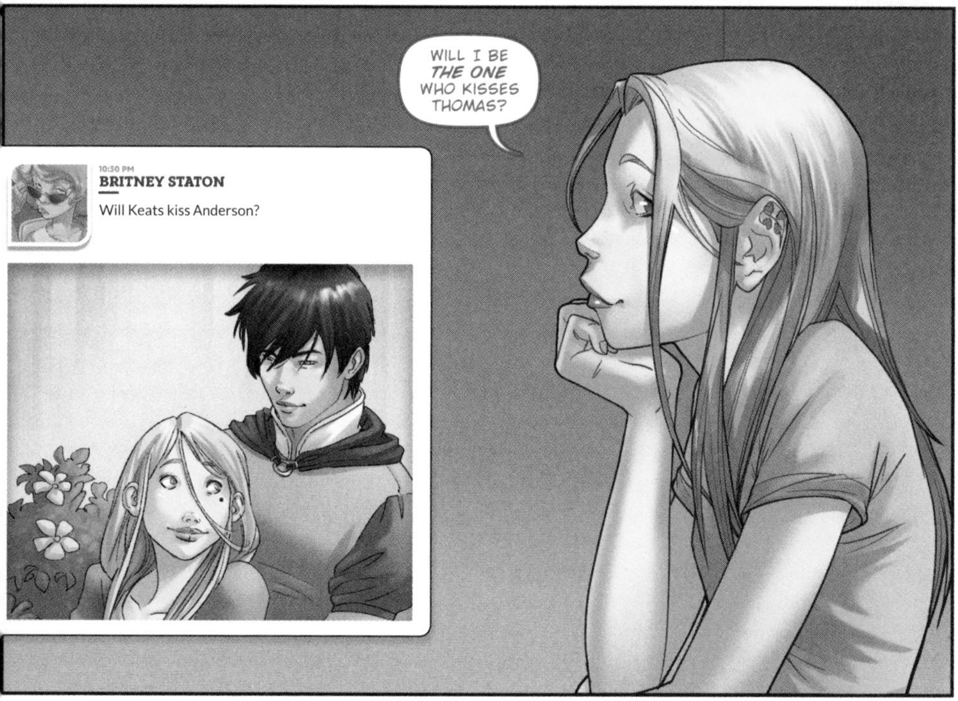
WILL I BE *THE ONE* WHO KISSES THOMAS?
10:30 PM
BRITNEY STATON
Will Keats kiss Anderson?

END OF CHAPTER 12

Disney
realife #

#The Day I'll Kiss Him

Plot: Alessandro Ferrari
Script: Silvia Gianatti
Layout: Alberto Zanon
Cleanup: Marco Failla
Emotidolls: Andrea Scoppetta
Color: Massimo Rocca, Pierluigi Casolino, Andrea Scoppetta, Mario Perrotta, Slava Panarin, Giuseppe Fontana
Watercolor backgrounds: Valeria Turati
Translation: Edizioni BD and Erin Brady
Lettering and Infographic: Edizioni BD

COVER
Layout and cleanup: Alberto Zanon
Color: Slava Panarin

CONTRIBUTORS
Tomatofarm

Original project developed by Disney Publishing with the contribution of Barbar Baraldi, Paola Barbato, Micol Beltramini and Diana Tomatozombie

#5

#I'm Sorry I Can't

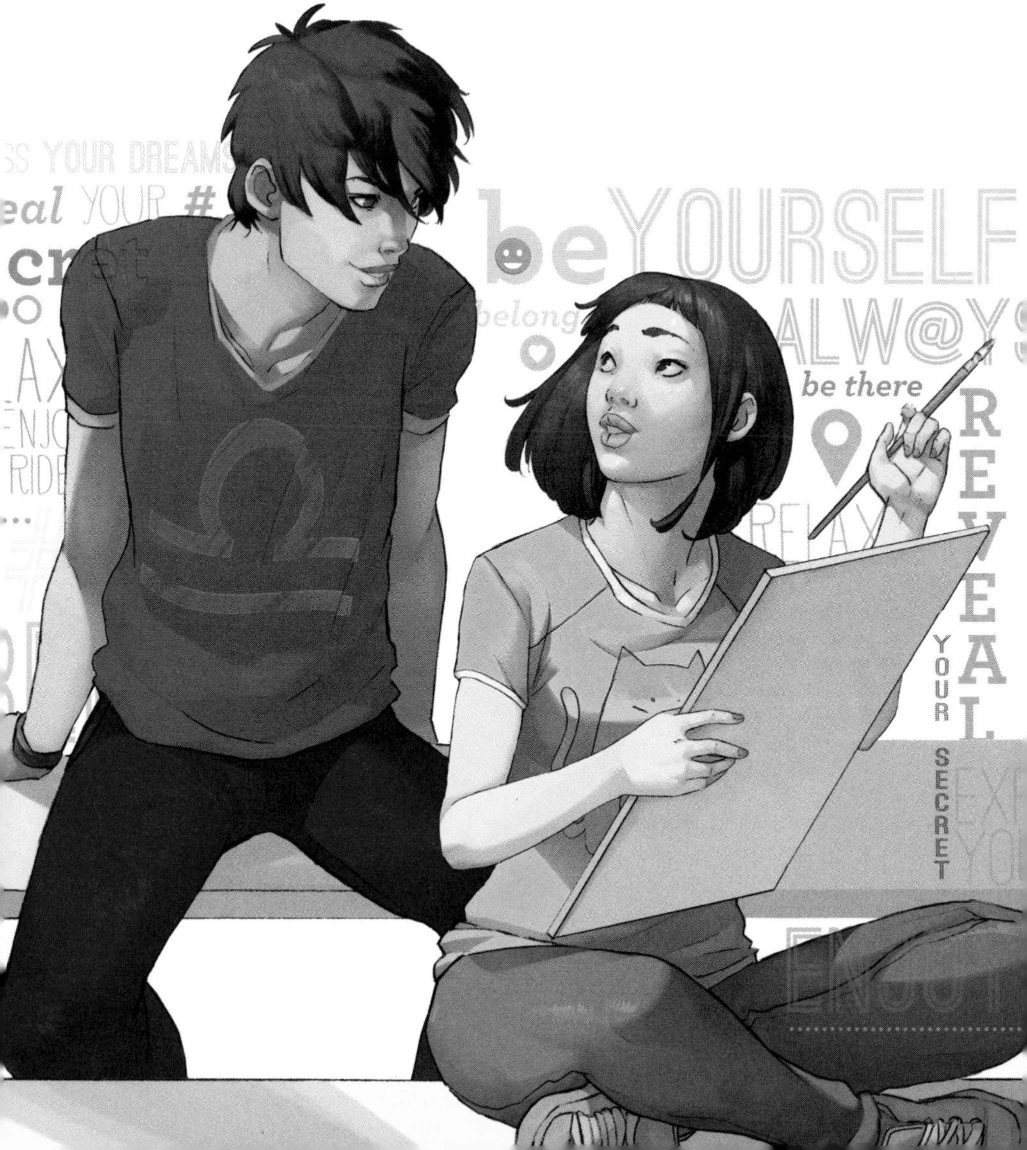

be YOURSELF
belong
be there
REVEAL
YOUR SECRET

CHAPTER 13

OFFLINE

London International High School
Marylebone,
Thursday
08:30 AM

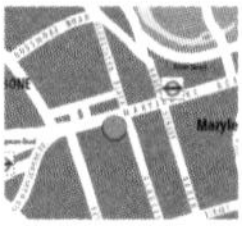

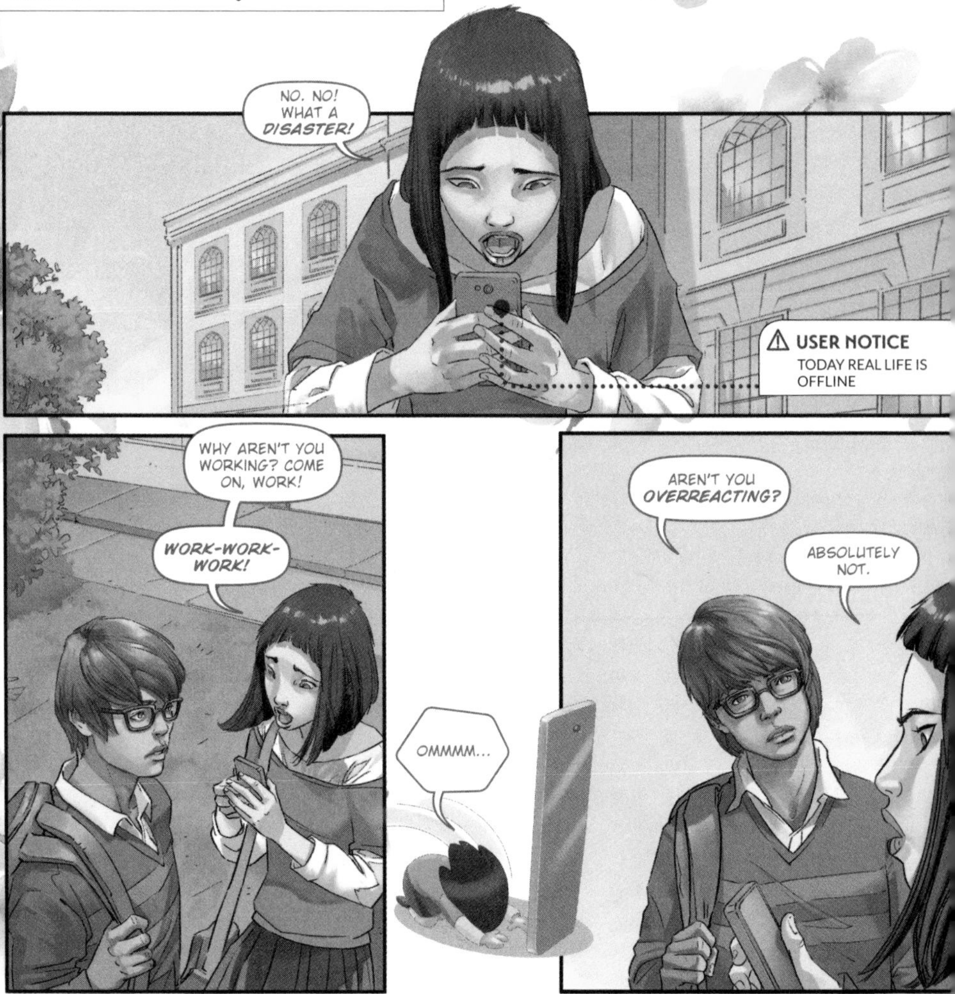
NO. NO! WHAT A DISASTER!
USER NOTICE
TODAY REAL LIFE IS OFFLINE
WHY AREN'T YOU WORKING? COME ON, WORK!
WORK-WORK-WORK!
OMMMM...
AREN'T YOU OVERREACTING?
ABSOLUTELY NOT.

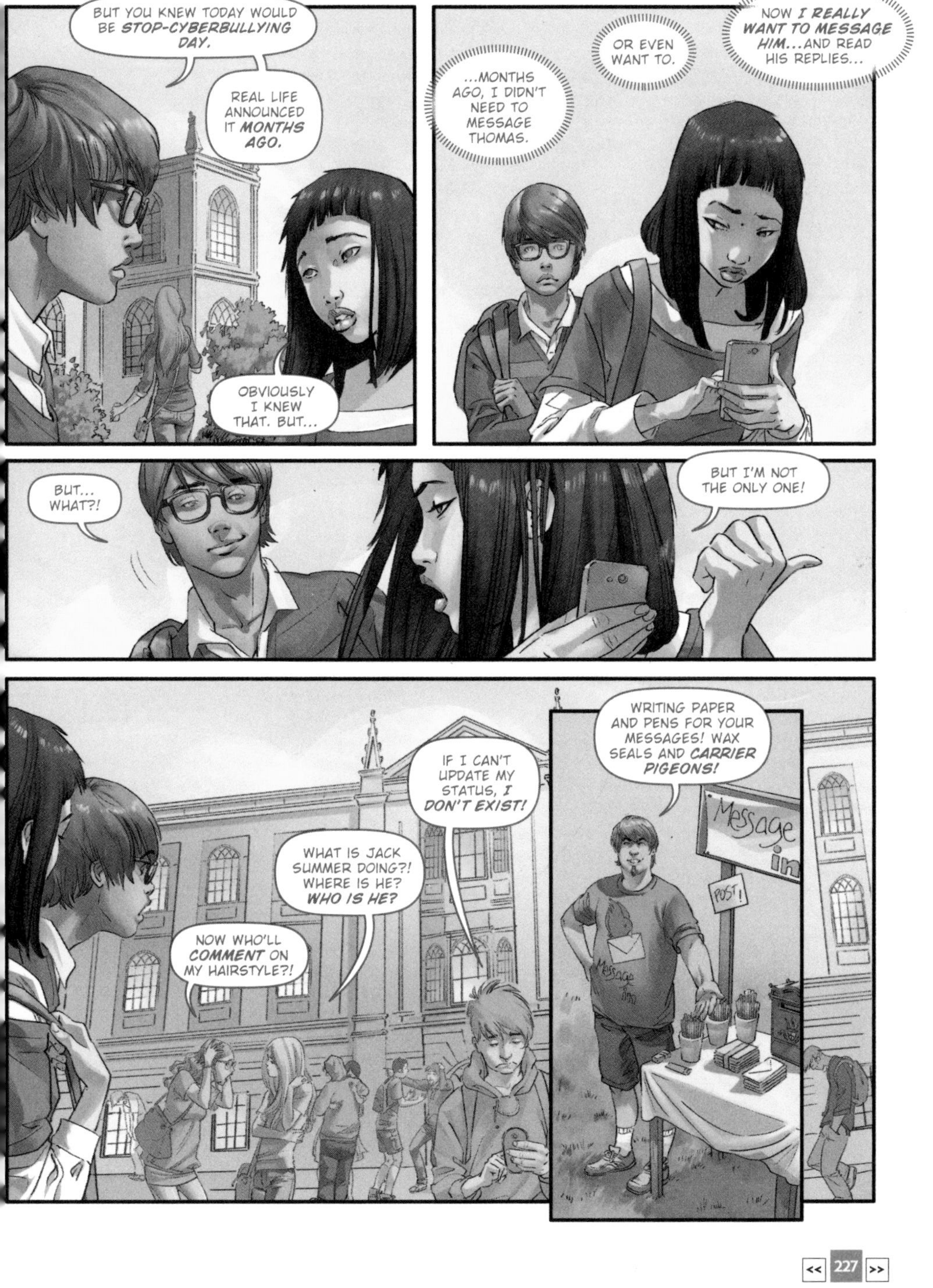
BUT YOU KNEW TODAY WOULD BE STOP-CYBERBULLYING DAY.
REAL LIFE ANNOUNCED IT MONTHS AGO.
OBVIOUSLY I KNEW THAT. BUT...
...MONTHS AGO, I DIDN'T NEED TO MESSAGE THOMAS.
OR EVEN WANT TO.
NOW I REALLY WANT TO MESSAGE HIM...AND READ HIS REPLIES...
BUT... WHAT?!
BUT I'M NOT THE ONLY ONE!
NOW WHO'LL COMMENT ON MY HAIRSTYLE?!
WHAT IS JACK SUMMER DOING?! WHERE IS HE? WHO IS HE?
IF I CAN'T UPDATE MY STATUS, I DON'T EXIST!
WRITING PAPER AND PENS FOR YOUR MESSAGES! WAX SEALS AND CARRIER PIGEONS!
Message in
POST!

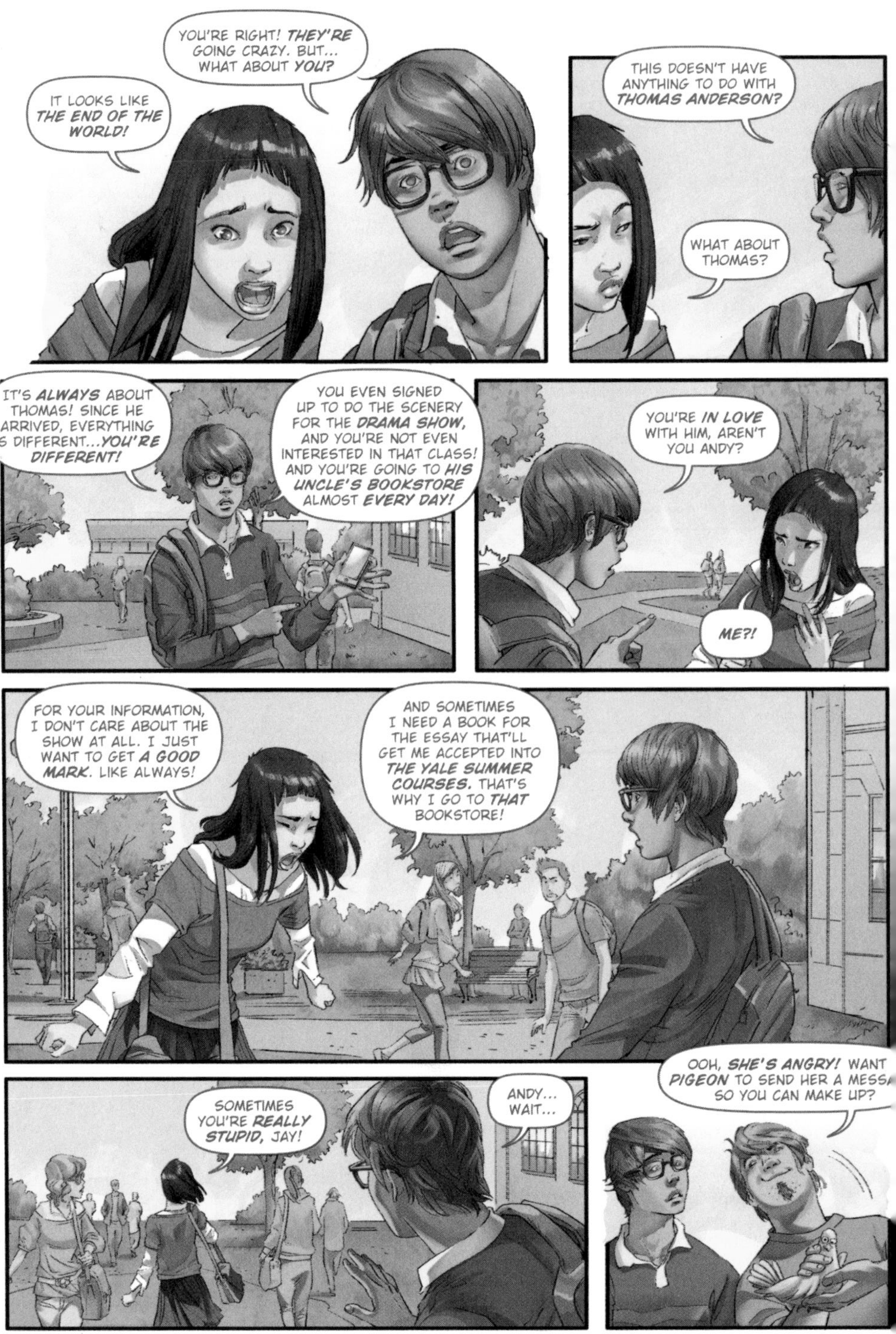
IT LOOKS LIKE THE END OF THE WORLD!
YOU'RE RIGHT! THEY'RE GOING CRAZY. BUT... WHAT ABOUT YOU?
THIS DOESN'T HAVE ANYTHING TO DO WITH THOMAS ANDERSON?
WHAT ABOUT THOMAS?
IT'S ALWAYS ABOUT THOMAS! SINCE HE ARRIVED, EVERYTHING IS DIFFERENT...YOU'RE DIFFERENT!
YOU EVEN SIGNED UP TO DO THE SCENERY FOR THE DRAMA SHOW, AND YOU'RE NOT EVEN INTERESTED IN THAT CLASS! AND YOU'RE GOING TO HIS UNCLE'S BOOKSTORE ALMOST EVERY DAY!
YOU'RE IN LOVE WITH HIM, AREN'T YOU ANDY?
ME?!
FOR YOUR INFORMATION, I DON'T CARE ABOUT THE SHOW AT ALL. I JUST WANT TO GET A GOOD MARK. LIKE ALWAYS!
AND SOMETIMES I NEED A BOOK FOR THE ESSAY THAT'LL GET ME ACCEPTED INTO THE YALE SUMMER COURSES. THAT'S WHY I GO TO THAT BOOKSTORE!
SOMETIMES YOU'RE REALLY STUPID, JAY!
ANDY... WAIT...
OOH, SHE'S ANGRY! WANT PIGEON TO SEND HER A MESS
SO YOU CAN MAKE UP?

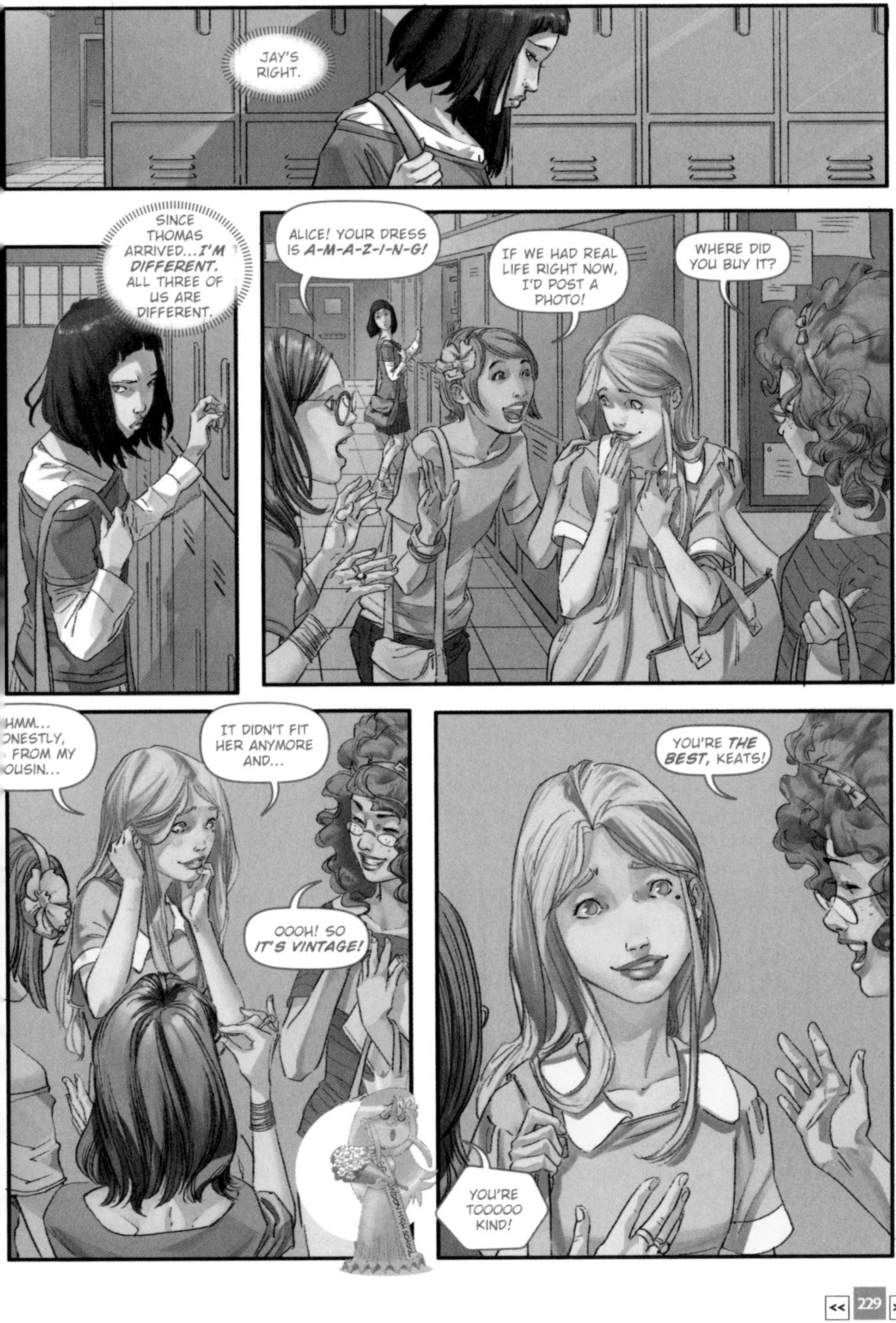
JAY'S RIGHT.
SINCE THOMAS ARRIVED... I'M DIFFERENT. ALL THREE OF US ARE DIFFERENT.
ALICE! YOUR DRESS IS A-M-A-Z-I-N-G!
IF WE HAD REAL LIFE RIGHT NOW, I'D POST A PHOTO!
WHERE DID YOU BUY IT?
HMM... ONESTLY, FROM MY OUSIN...
IT DIDN'T FIT HER ANYMORE AND...
OOOH! SO IT'S VINTAGE!
YOU'RE THE BEST, KEATS!
YOU'RE TOOOOO KIND!

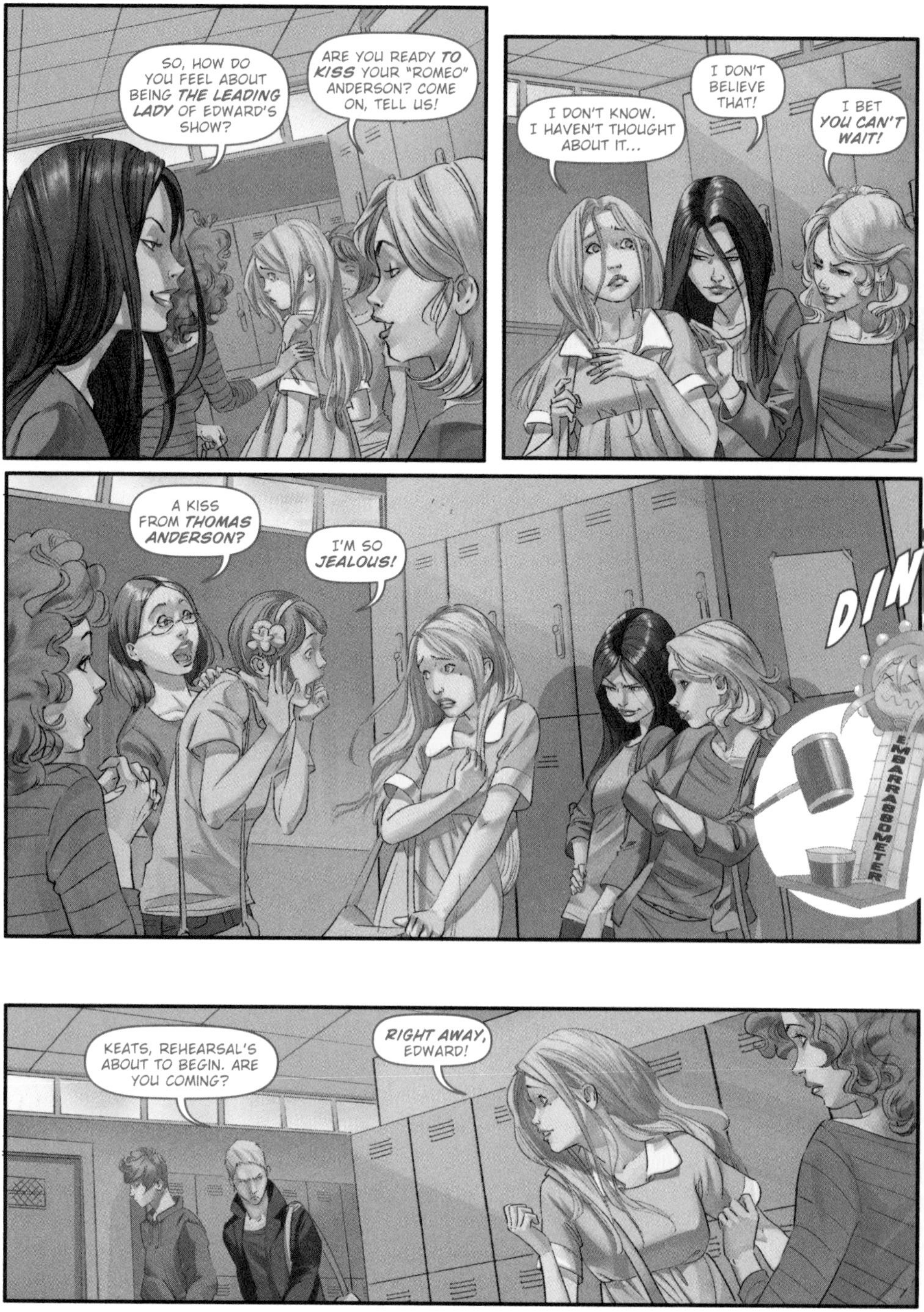
SO, HOW DO YOU FEEL ABOUT BEING THE LEADING LADY OF EDWARD'S SHOW?
ARE YOU READY TO KISS YOUR "ROMEO" ANDERSON? COME ON, TELL US!
I DON'T KNOW. I HAVEN'T THOUGHT ABOUT IT...
I DON'T BELIEVE THAT!
I BET YOU CAN'T WAIT!
A KISS FROM THOMAS ANDERSON?
I'M SO JEALOUS!
DIN
EMBARRASSOMETER
KEATS, REHEARSAL'S ABOUT TO BEGIN. ARE YOU COMING?
RIGHT AWAY, EDWARD!

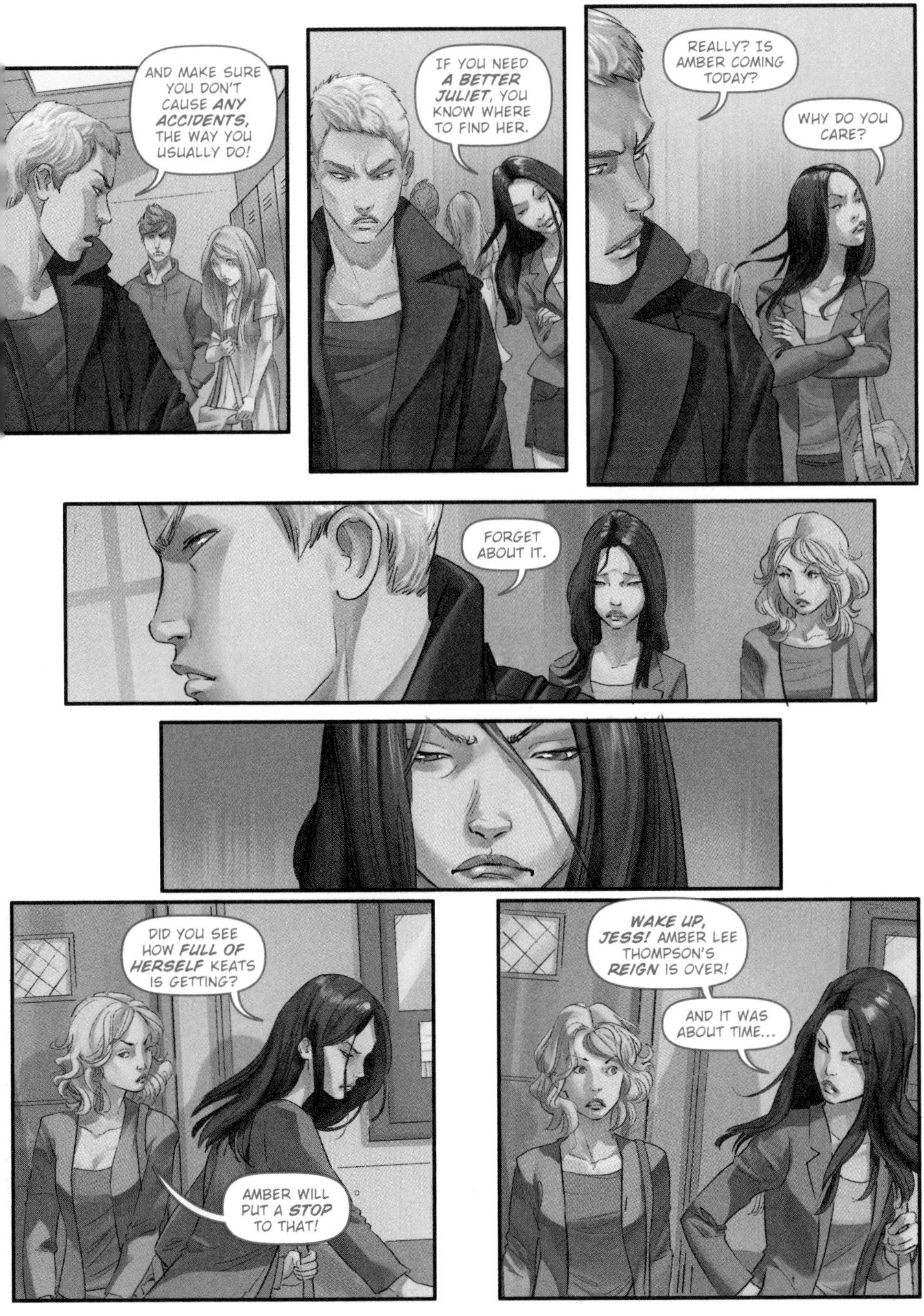
AND MAKE SURE YOU DON'T CAUSE ANY ACCIDENTS, THE WAY YOU USUALLY DO!
IF YOU NEED A BETTER JULIET, YOU KNOW WHERE TO FIND HER.
REALLY? IS AMBER COMING TODAY?
WHY DO YOU CARE?
FORGET ABOUT IT.
DID YOU SEE HOW FULL OF HERSELF KEATS IS GETTING?
AMBER WILL PUT A STOP TO THAT!
WAKE UP, JESS! AMBER LEE THOMPSON'S REIGN IS OVER!
AND IT WAS ABOUT TIME...

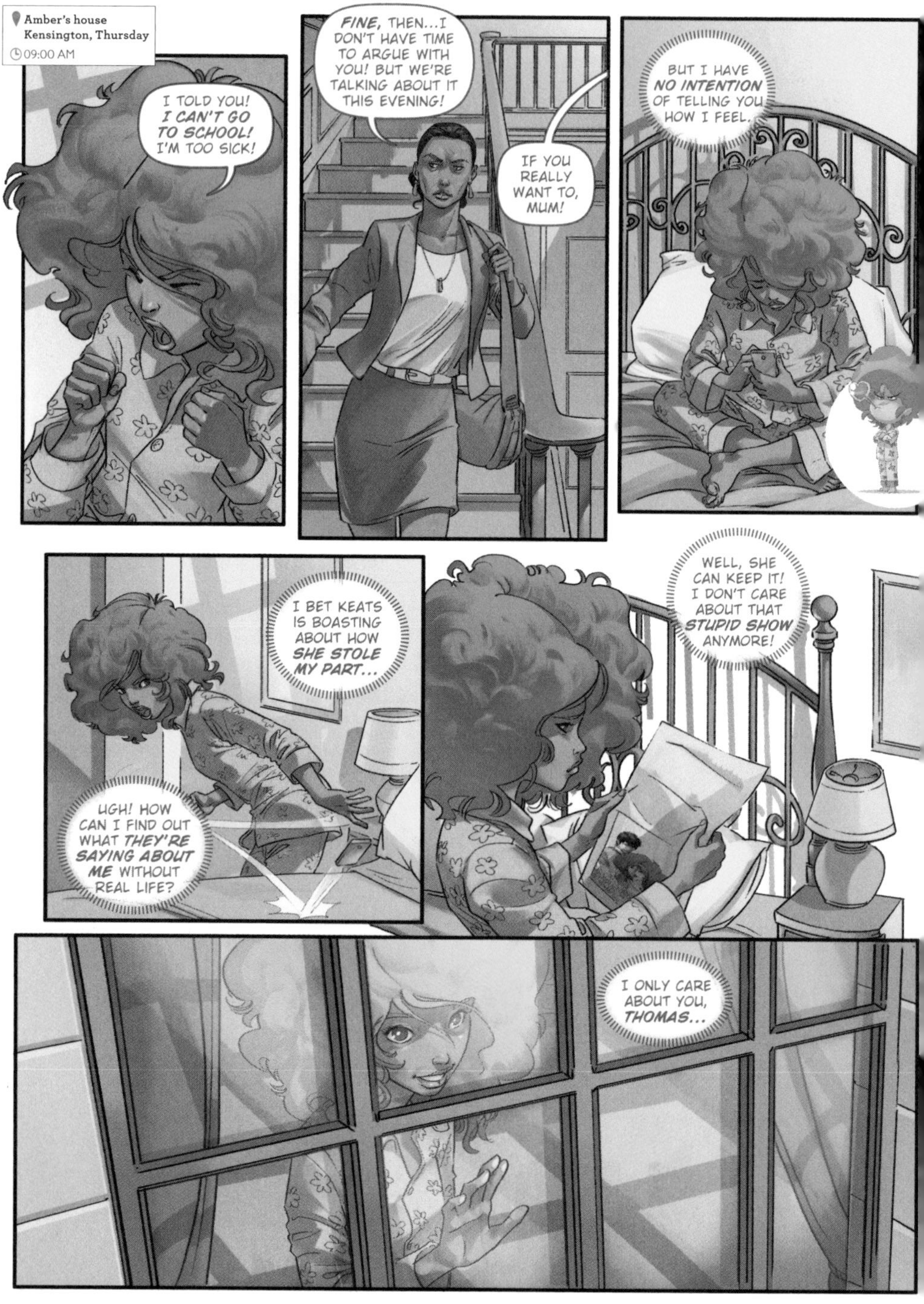
Amber's house
Kensington, Thursday
09:00 AM
I TOLD YOU! I CAN'T GO TO SCHOOL! I'M TOO SICK!
FINE, THEN...I DON'T HAVE TIME TO ARGUE WITH YOU! BUT WE'RE TALKING ABOUT IT THIS EVENING!
IF YOU REALLY WANT TO, MUM!
BUT I HAVE NO INTENTION OF TELLING YOU HOW I FEEL.
I BET KEATS IS BOASTING ABOUT HOW SHE STOLE MY PART...
UGH! HOW CAN I FIND OUT WHAT THEY'RE SAYING ABOUT ME WITHOUT REAL LIFE?
WELL, SHE CAN KEEP IT! I DON'T CARE ABOUT THAT STUPID SHOW ANYMORE!
I ONLY CARE ABOUT YOU, THOMAS...

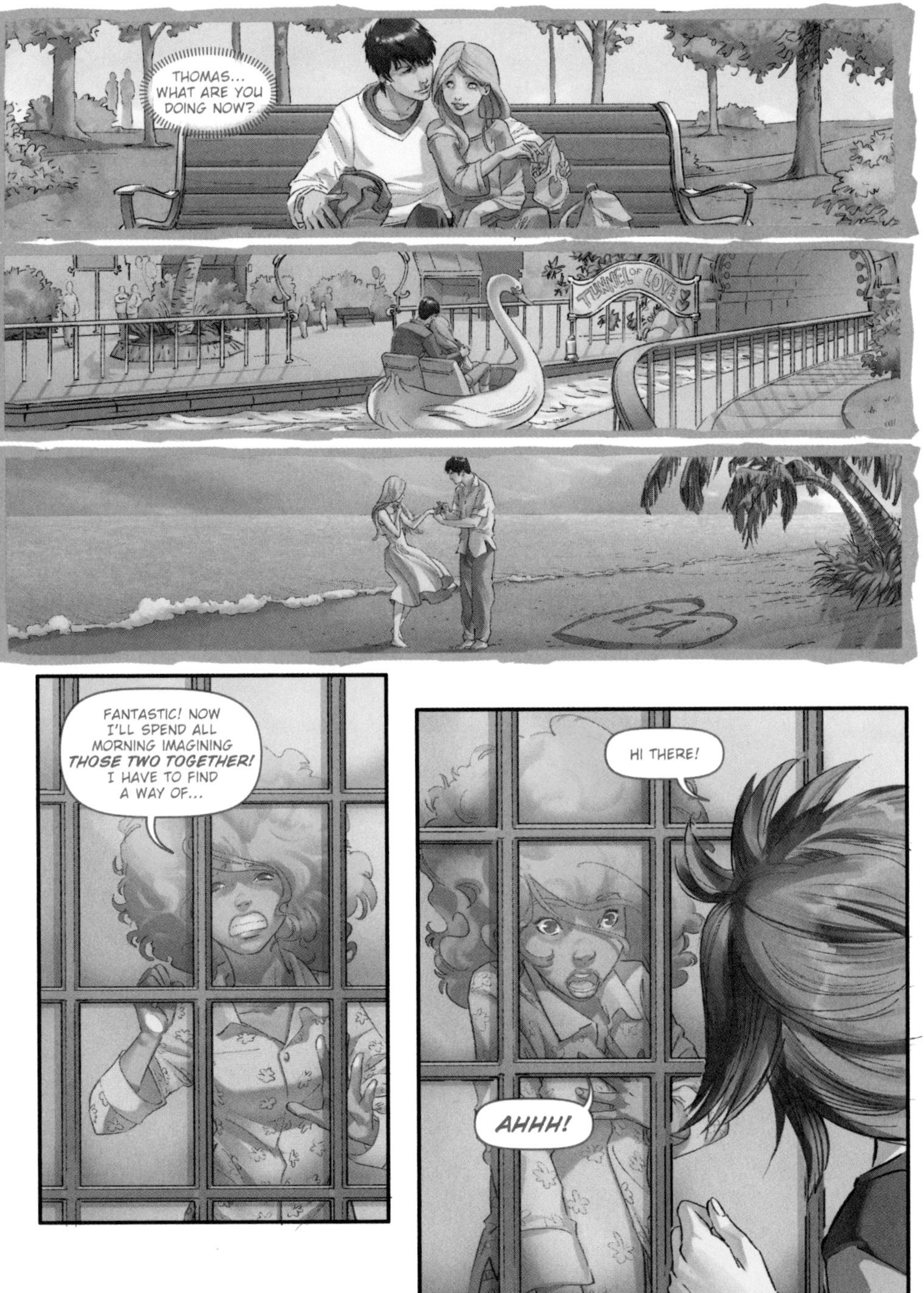
THOMAS... WHAT ARE YOU DOING NOW?
TUNNEL OF LOVE
FANTASTIC! NOW I'LL SPEND ALL MORNING IMAGINING **THOSE TWO TOGETHER!** I HAVE TO FIND A WAY OF...
HI THERE!
AHHH!

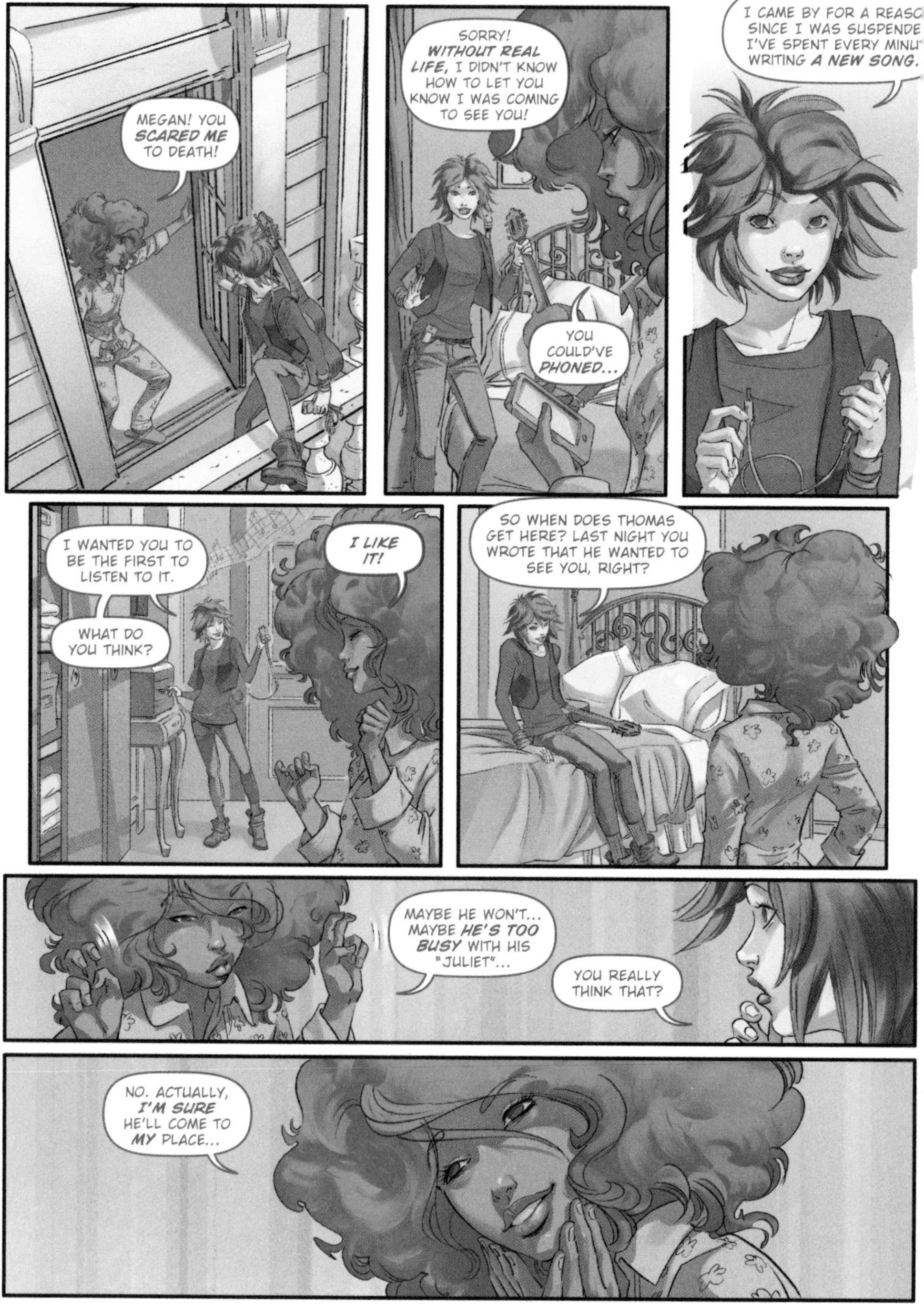
MEGAN! YOU SCARED ME TO DEATH!
SORRY! WITHOUT REAL LIFE, I DIDN'T KNOW HOW TO LET YOU KNOW I WAS COMING TO SEE YOU!
YOU COULD'VE PHONED...
I CAME BY FOR A REASO SINCE I WAS SUSPENDE I'VE SPENT EVERY MINU WRITING A NEW SONG.
I WANTED YOU TO BE THE FIRST TO LISTEN TO IT.
WHAT DO YOU THINK?
I LIKE IT!
SO WHEN DOES THOMAS GET HERE? LAST NIGHT YOU WROTE THAT HE WANTED TO SEE YOU, RIGHT?
MAYBE HE WON'T... MAYBE HE'S TOO BUSY WITH HIS "JULIET"...
YOU REALLY THINK THAT?
NO. ACTUALLY, I'M SURE HE'LL COME TO MY PLACE...

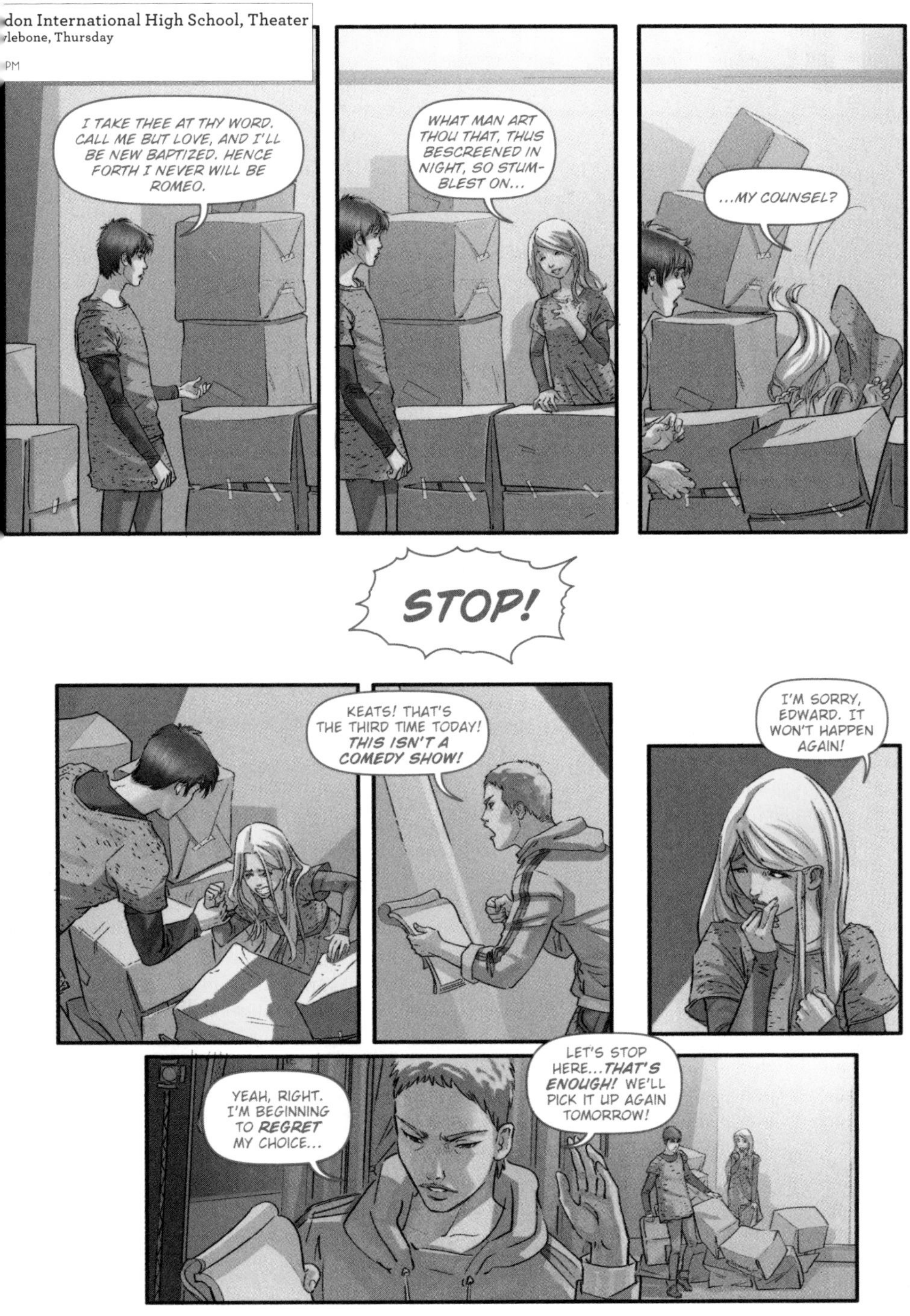
don International High School, Theater
lebone, Thursday
PM
I TAKE THEE AT THY WORD. CALL ME BUT LOVE, AND I'LL BE NEW BAPTIZED. HENCE FORTH I NEVER WILL BE ROMEO.
WHAT MAN ART THOU THAT, THUS BESCREENED IN NIGHT, SO STUMBLEST ON...
...MY COUNSEL?
STOP!
KEATS! THAT'S THE THIRD TIME TODAY! THIS ISN'T A COMEDY SHOW!
I'M SORRY, EDWARD. IT WON'T HAPPEN AGAIN!
YEAH, RIGHT. I'M BEGINNING TO REGRET MY CHOICE...
LET'S STOP HERE...THAT'S ENOUGH! WE'LL PICK IT UP AGAIN TOMORROW!

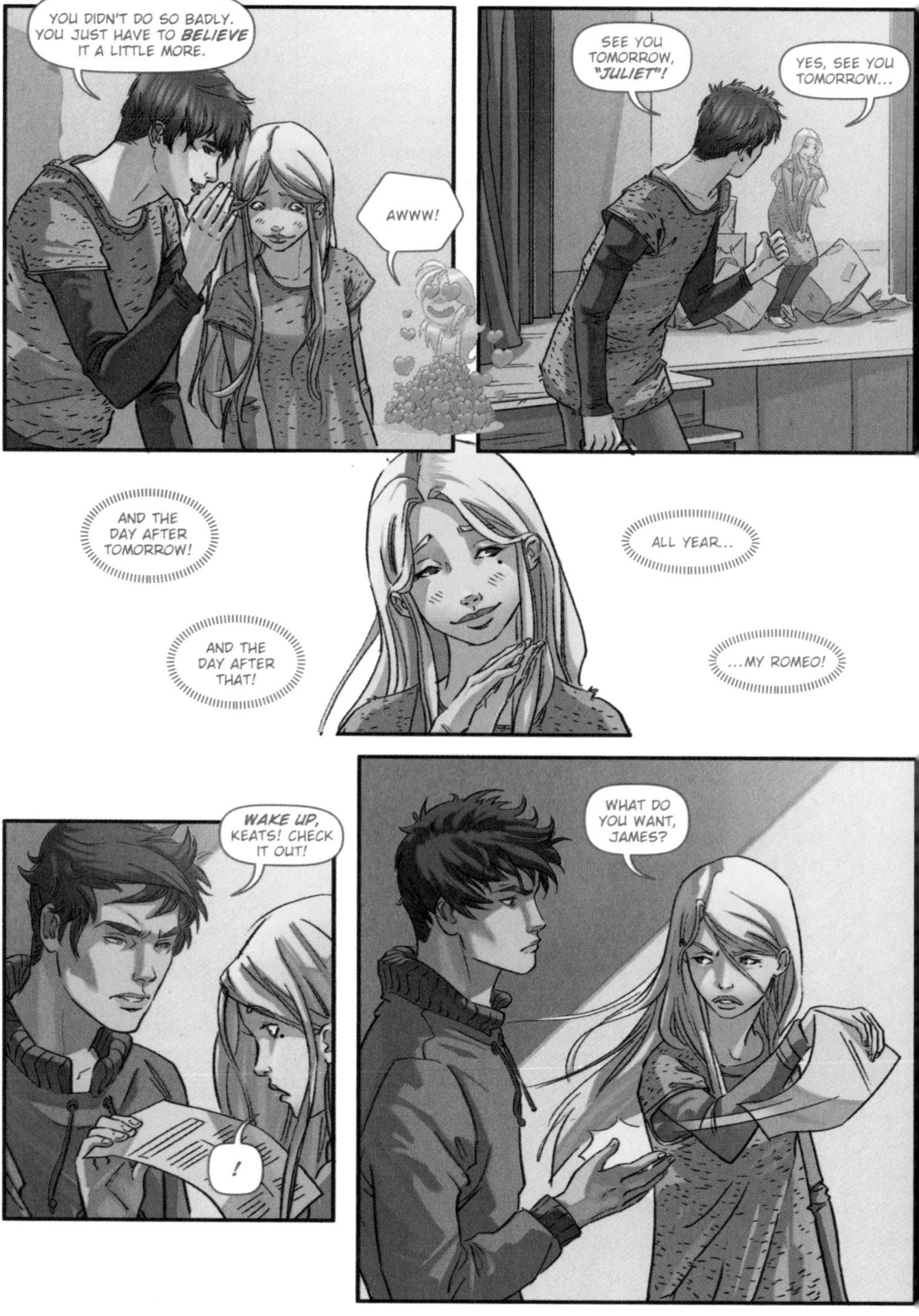
YOU DIDN'T DO SO BADLY. YOU JUST HAVE TO BELIEVE IT A LITTLE MORE.
AWWW!
SEE YOU TOMORROW, "JULIET"!
YES, SEE YOU TOMORROW...
AND THE DAY AFTER TOMORROW!
AND THE DAY AFTER THAT!
ALL YEAR...
...MY ROMEO!
WAKE UP, KEATS! CHECK IT OUT!
!
WHAT DO YOU WANT, JAMES?

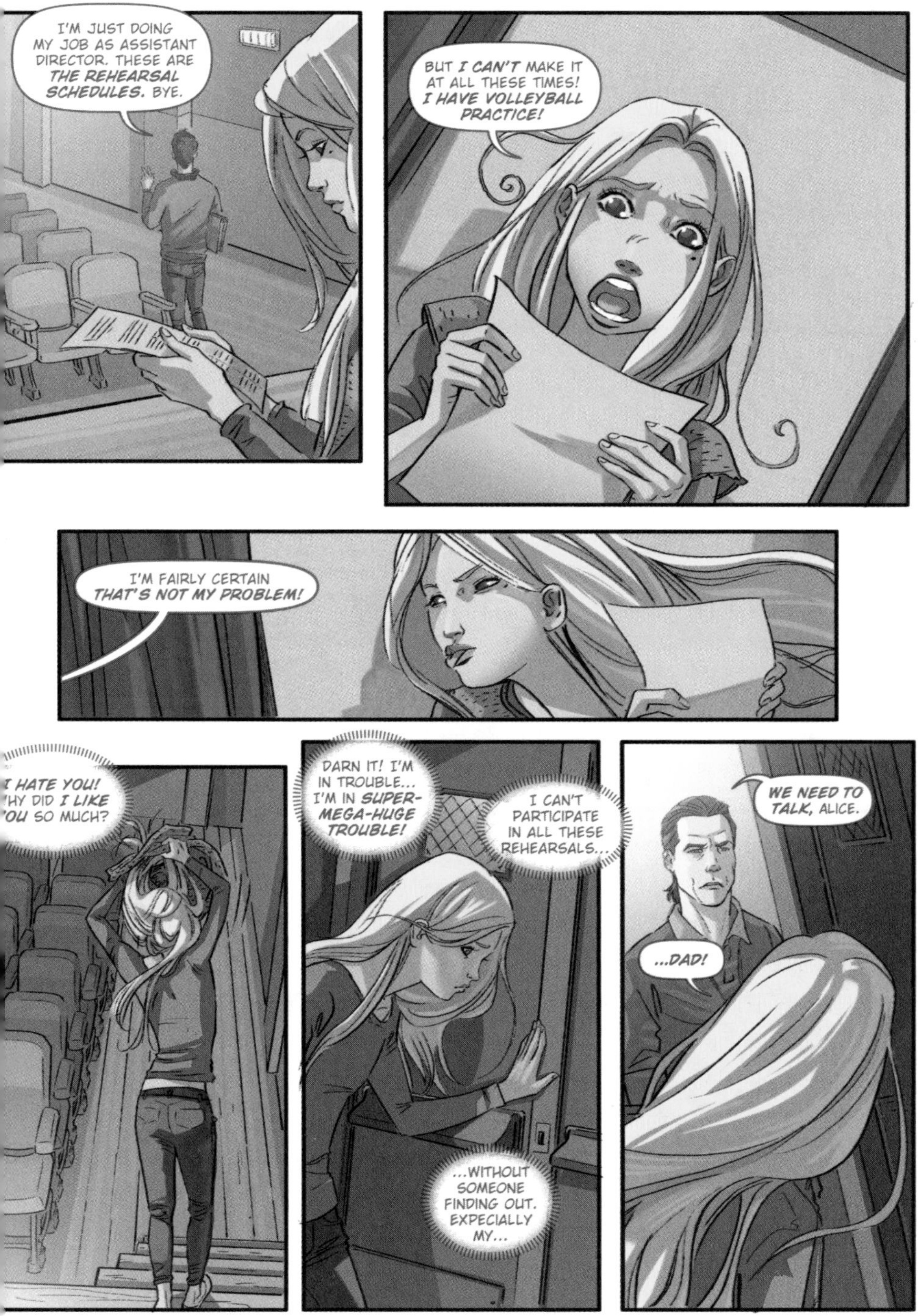
I'M JUST DOING MY JOB AS ASSISTANT DIRECTOR. THESE ARE THE REHEARSAL SCHEDULES. BYE.
BUT I CAN'T MAKE IT AT ALL THESE TIMES! I HAVE VOLLEYBALL PRACTICE!
I'M FAIRLY CERTAIN THAT'S NOT MY PROBLEM!
I HATE YOU! WHY DID I LIKE YOU SO MUCH?
DARN IT! I'M IN TROUBLE... I'M IN SUPER-MEGA-HUGE TROUBLE!
I CAN'T PARTICIPATE IN ALL THESE REHEARSALS...
...WITHOUT SOMEONE FINDING OUT. EXPECIALLY MY...
WE NEED TO TALK, ALICE.
...DAD!

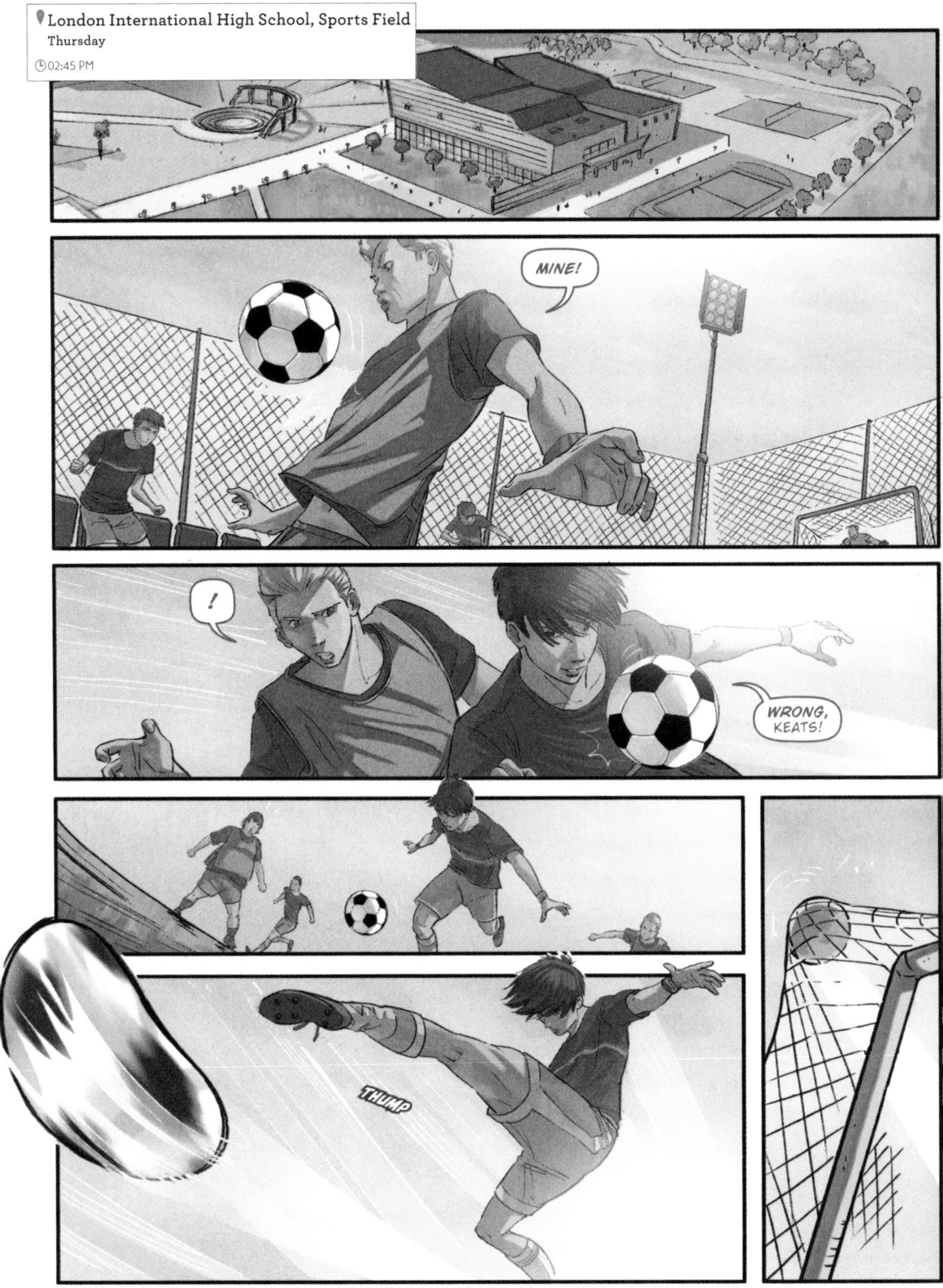
London International High School, Sports Field
Thursday
02:45 PM
MINE!
!
WRONG, KEATS!
THUMP

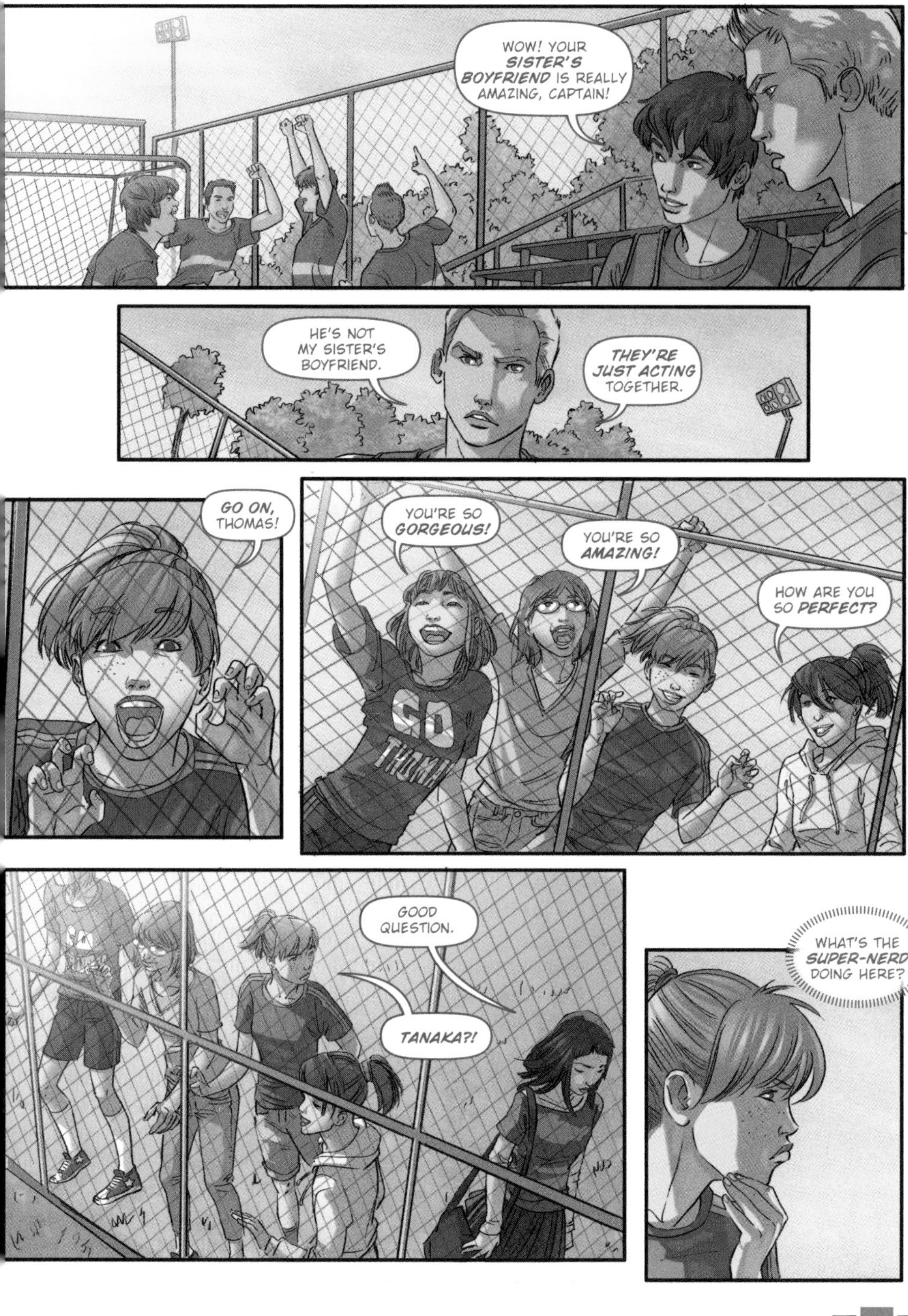
WOW! YOUR SISTER'S BOYFRIEND IS REALLY AMAZING, CAPTAIN!
HE'S NOT MY SISTER'S BOYFRIEND.
THEY'RE JUST ACTING TOGETHER.
GO ON, THOMAS!
YOU'RE SO GORGEOUS!
YOU'RE SO AMAZING!
HOW ARE YOU SO PERFECT?
GO THOMA
GOOD QUESTION.
TANAKA?!
WHAT'S THE SUPER-NERD DOING HERE?

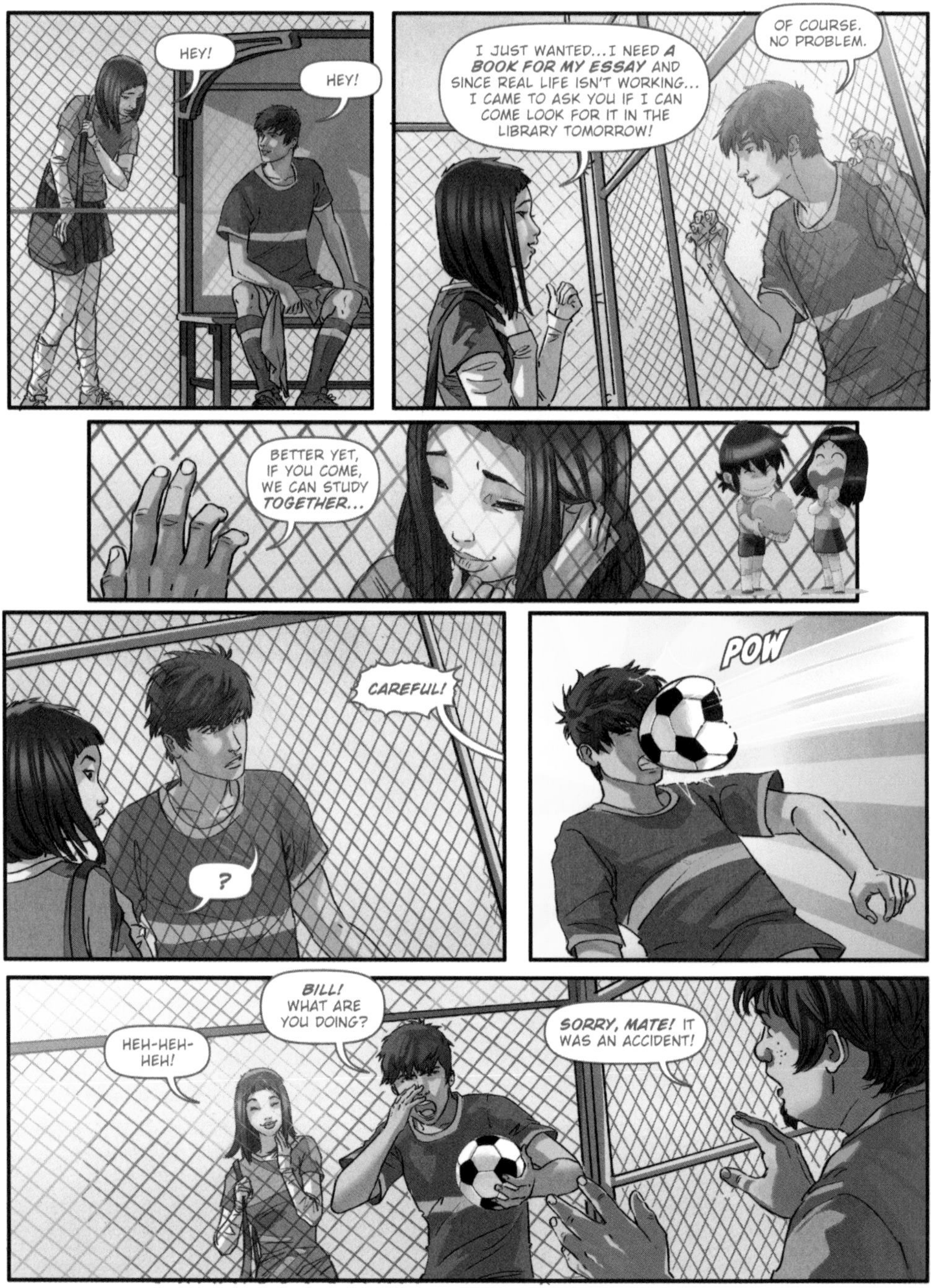
HEY!
HEY!
I JUST WANTED... I NEED A BOOK FOR MY ESSAY AND SINCE REAL LIFE ISN'T WORKING... I CAME TO ASK YOU IF I CAN COME LOOK FOR IT IN THE LIBRARY TOMORROW!
OF COURSE. NO PROBLEM.
BETTER YET, IF YOU COME, WE CAN STUDY TOGETHER...
CAREFUL!
?
POW
BILL! WHAT ARE YOU DOING?
HEH-HEH-HEH!
SORRY, MATE! IT WAS AN ACCIDENT!

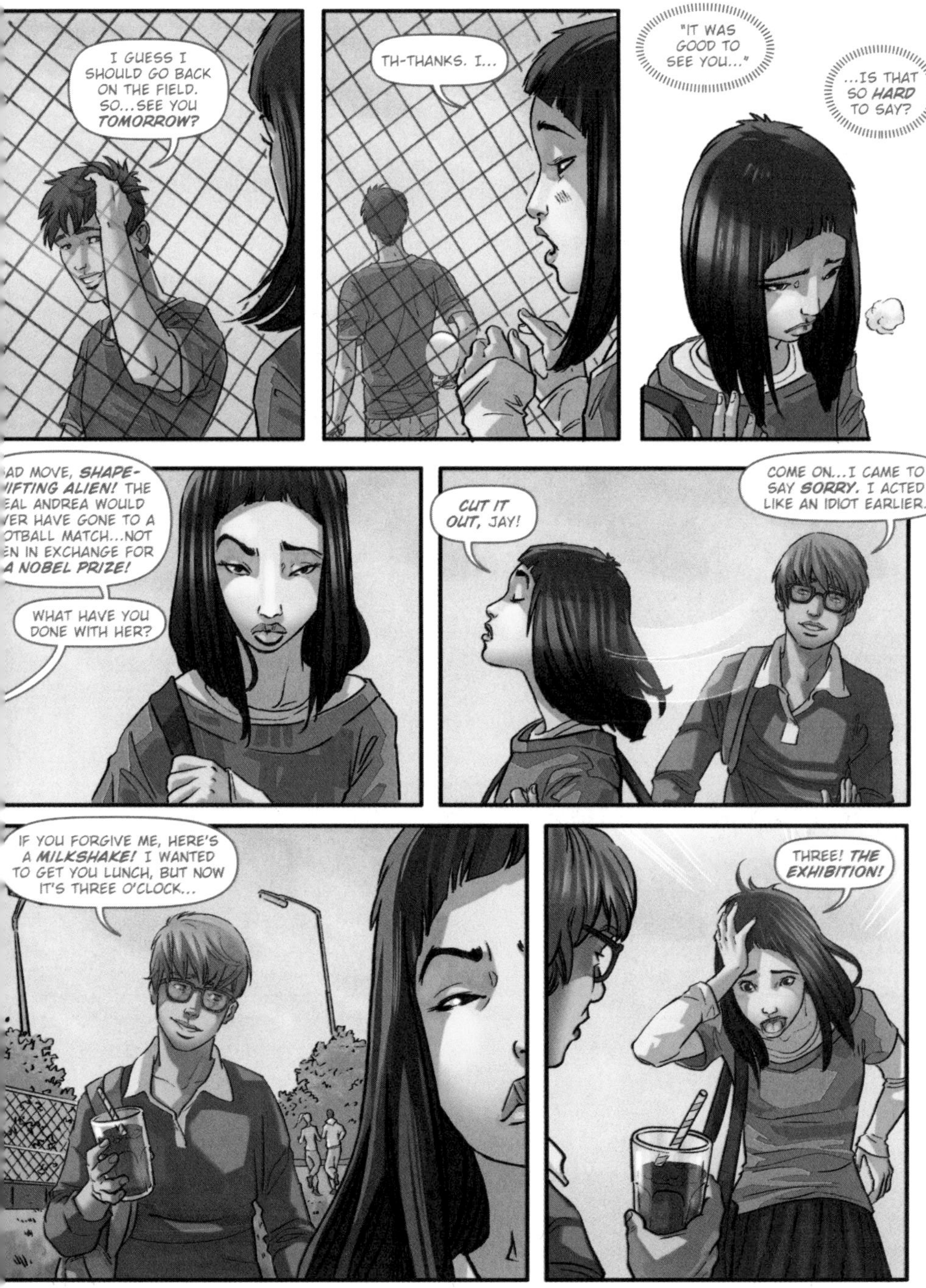
I GUESS I SHOULD GO BACK ON THE FIELD. SO...SEE YOU TOMORROW?
TH-THANKS. I...
"IT WAS GOOD TO SEE YOU..."
...IS THAT SO HARD TO SAY?
AD MOVE, SHAPE-IFTING ALIEN! THE EAL ANDREA WOULD VER HAVE GONE TO A OTBALL MATCH...NOT EN IN EXCHANGE FOR A NOBEL PRIZE!
WHAT HAVE YOU DONE WITH HER?
COME ON...I CAME TO SAY SORRY. I ACTED LIKE AN IDIOT EARLIER.
CUT IT OUT, JAY!
IF YOU FORGIVE ME, HERE'S A MILKSHAKE! I WANTED TO GET YOU LUNCH, BUT NOW IT'S THREE O'CLOCK...
THREE! THE EXHIBITION!

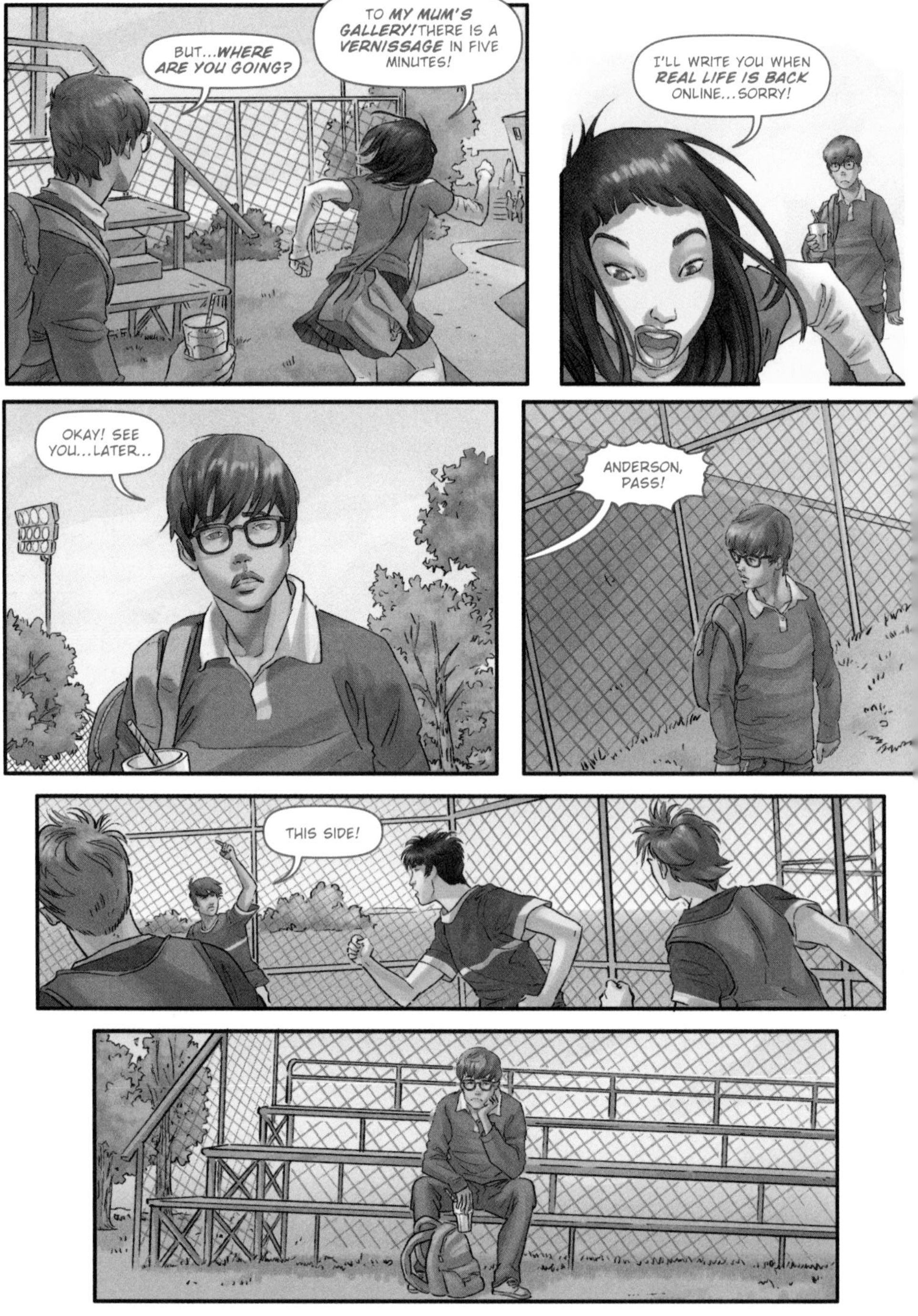
BUT...WHERE ARE YOU GOING?
TO MY MUM'S GALLERY! THERE IS A VERNISSAGE IN FIVE MINUTES!
I'LL WRITE YOU WHEN REAL LIFE IS BACK ONLINE... SORRY!
OKAY! SEE YOU...LATER...
ANDERSON, PASS!
THIS SIDE!

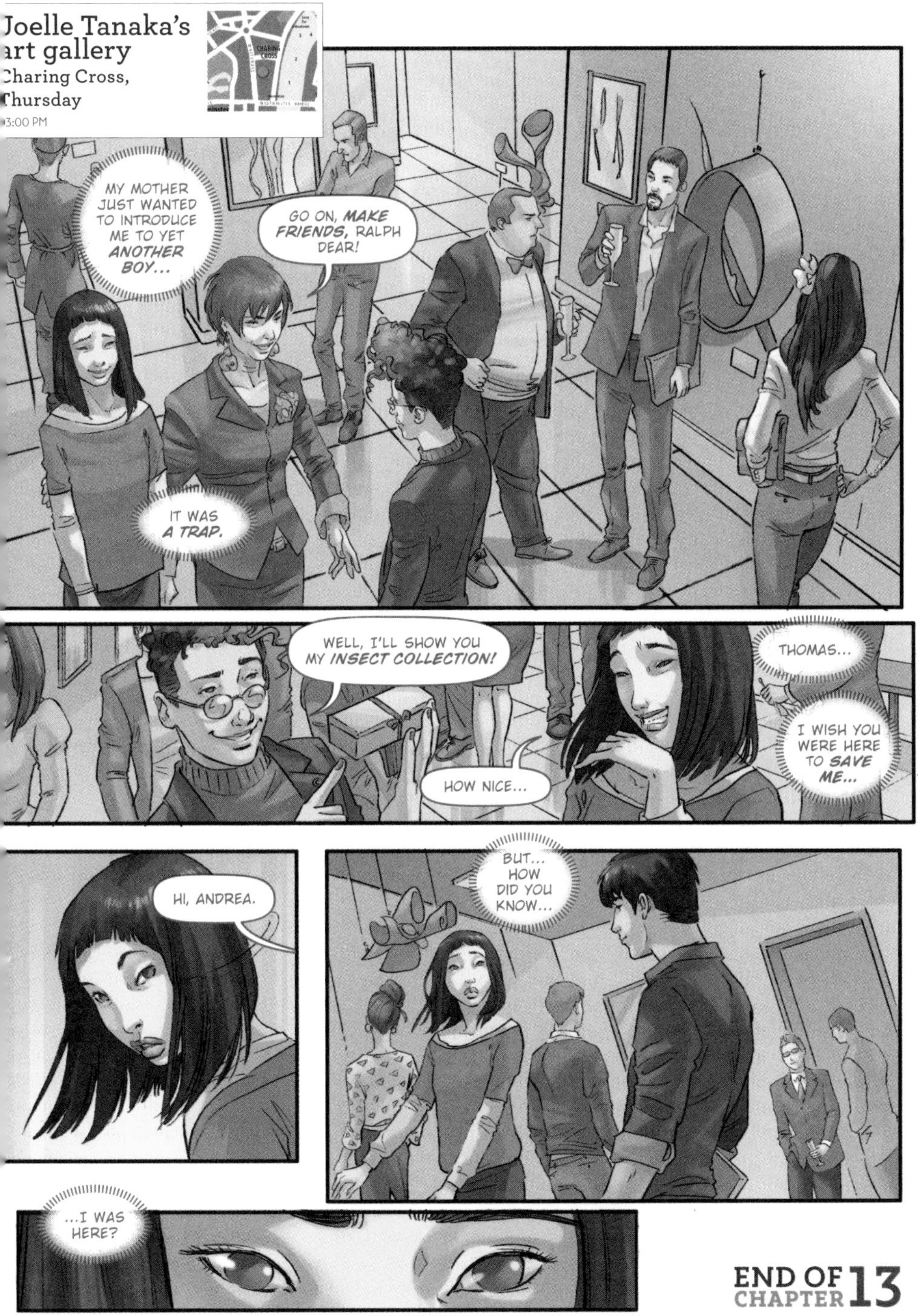
Joelle Tanaka's
art gallery
Charing Cross,
Thursday
3:00 PM
CHARING CROSS
MY MOTHER JUST WANTED TO INTRODUCE ME TO YET ANOTHER BOY...
GO ON, MAKE FRIENDS, RALPH DEAR!
IT WAS A TRAP.
WELL, I'LL SHOW YOU MY INSECT COLLECTION!
HOW NICE...
THOMAS...
I WISH YOU WERE HERE TO SAVE ME...
HI, ANDREA.
BUT... HOW DID YOU KNOW...
...I WAS HERE?
END OF CHAPTER 13

CHAPTER 14

ALMOST a DATE

East London
Thursday
03:00 PM

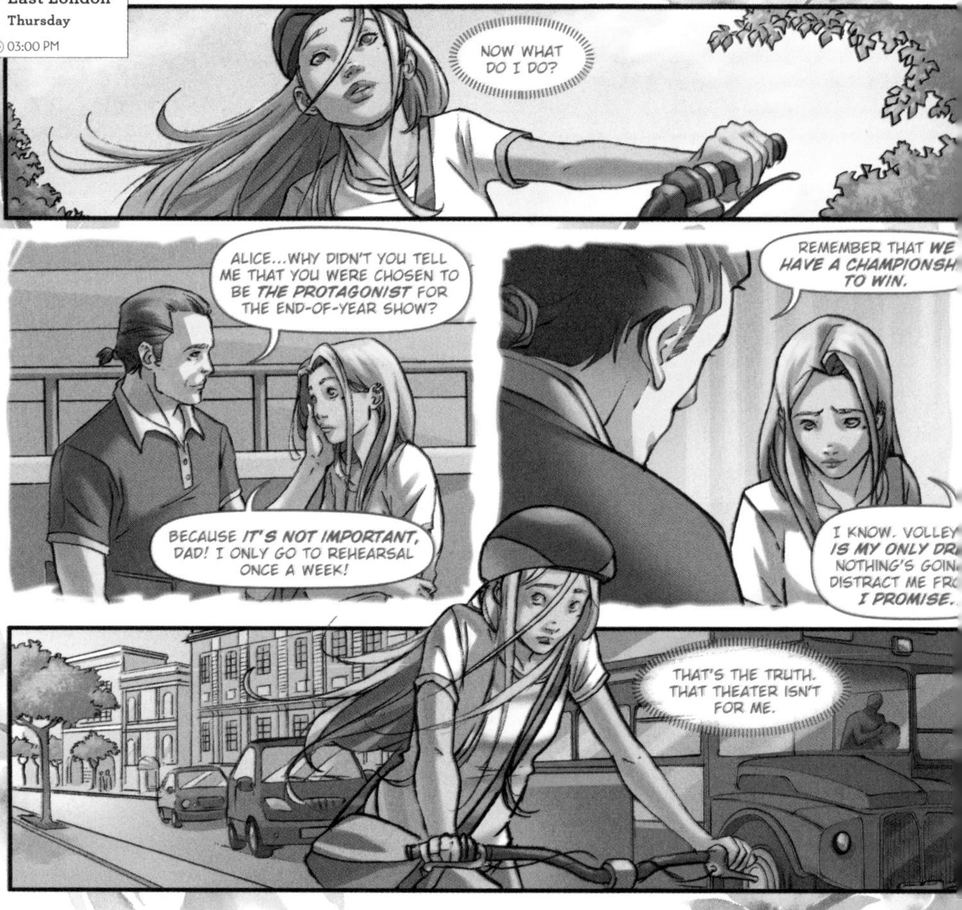
NOW WHAT DO I DO?
ALICE...WHY DIDN'T YOU TELL ME THAT YOU WERE CHOSEN TO BE THE PROTAGONIST FOR THE END-OF-YEAR SHOW?
BECAUSE IT'S NOT IMPORTANT, DAD! I ONLY GO TO REHEARSAL ONCE A WEEK!
REMEMBER THAT WE HAVE A CHAMPIONSH TO WIN.
I KNOW. VOLLEY IS MY ONLY DR NOTHING'S GOIN DISTRACT ME FRO I PROMISE.
THAT'S THE TRUTH. THAT THEATER ISN'T FOR ME.

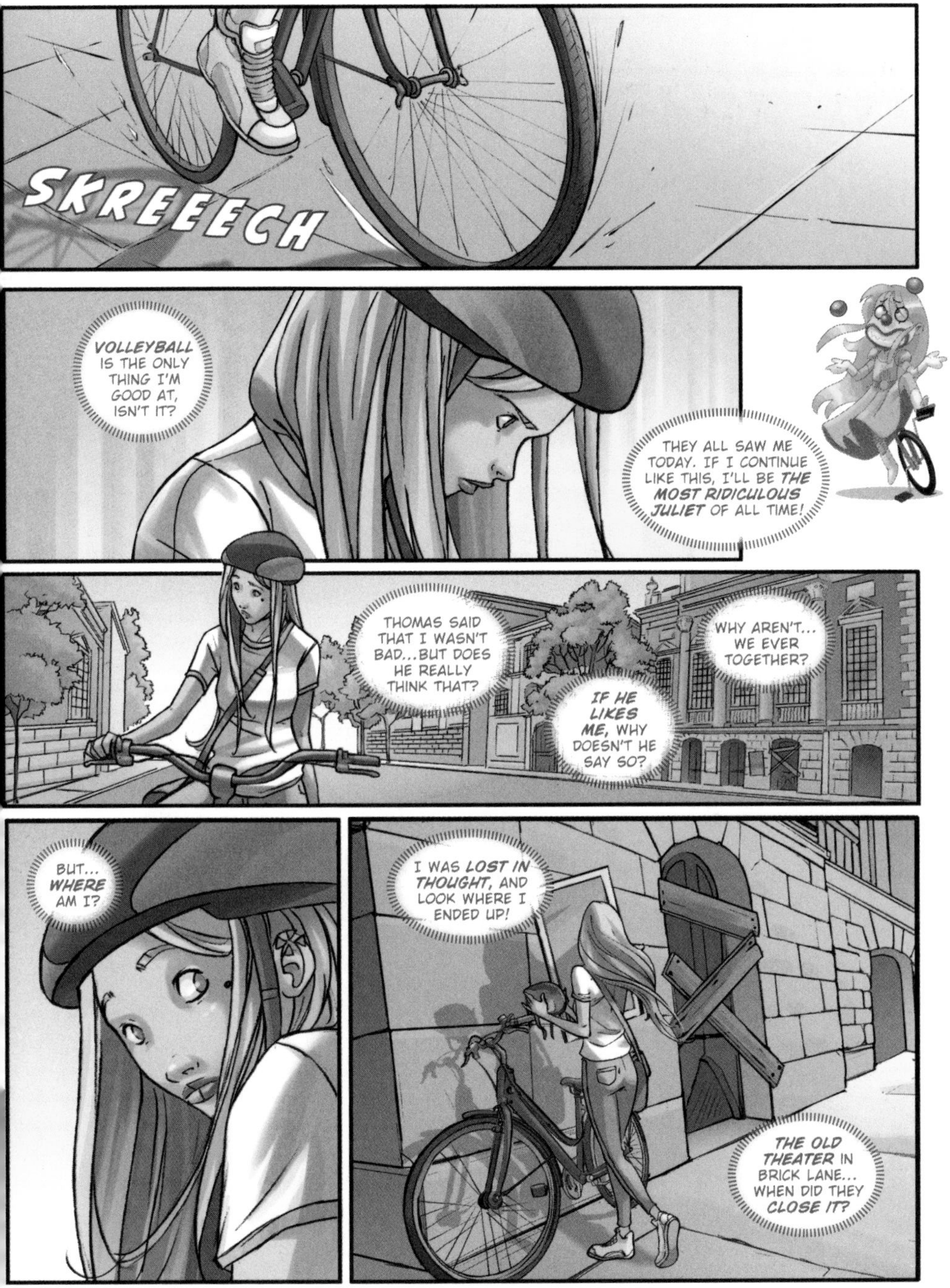
SKREEECH
VOLLEYBALL IS THE ONLY THING I'M GOOD AT, ISN'T IT?
THEY ALL SAW ME TODAY. IF I CONTINUE LIKE THIS, I'LL BE THE MOST RIDICULOUS JULIET OF ALL TIME!
THOMAS SAID THAT I WASN'T BAD...BUT DOES HE REALLY THINK THAT?
IF HE LIKES ME, WHY DOESN'T HE SAY SO?
WHY AREN'T... WE EVER TOGETHER?
BUT... WHERE AM I?
I WAS LOST IN THOUGHT, AND LOOK WHERE I ENDED UP!
THE OLD THEATER IN BRICK LANE... WHEN DID THEY CLOSE IT?

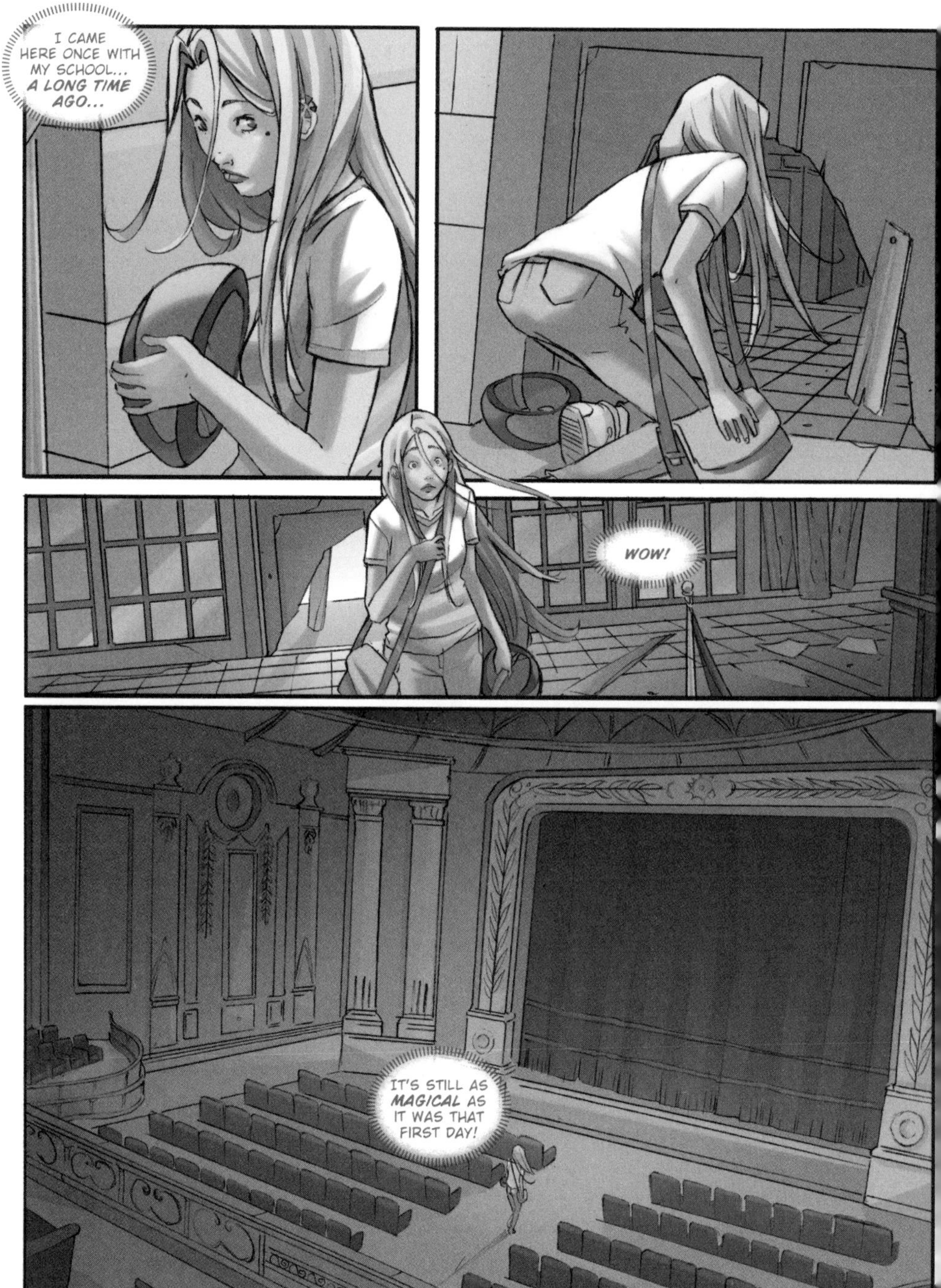
I CAME HERE ONCE WITH MY SCHOOL... A LONG TIME AGO...
WOW!
IT'S STILL AS MAGICAL AS IT WAS THAT FIRST DAY!

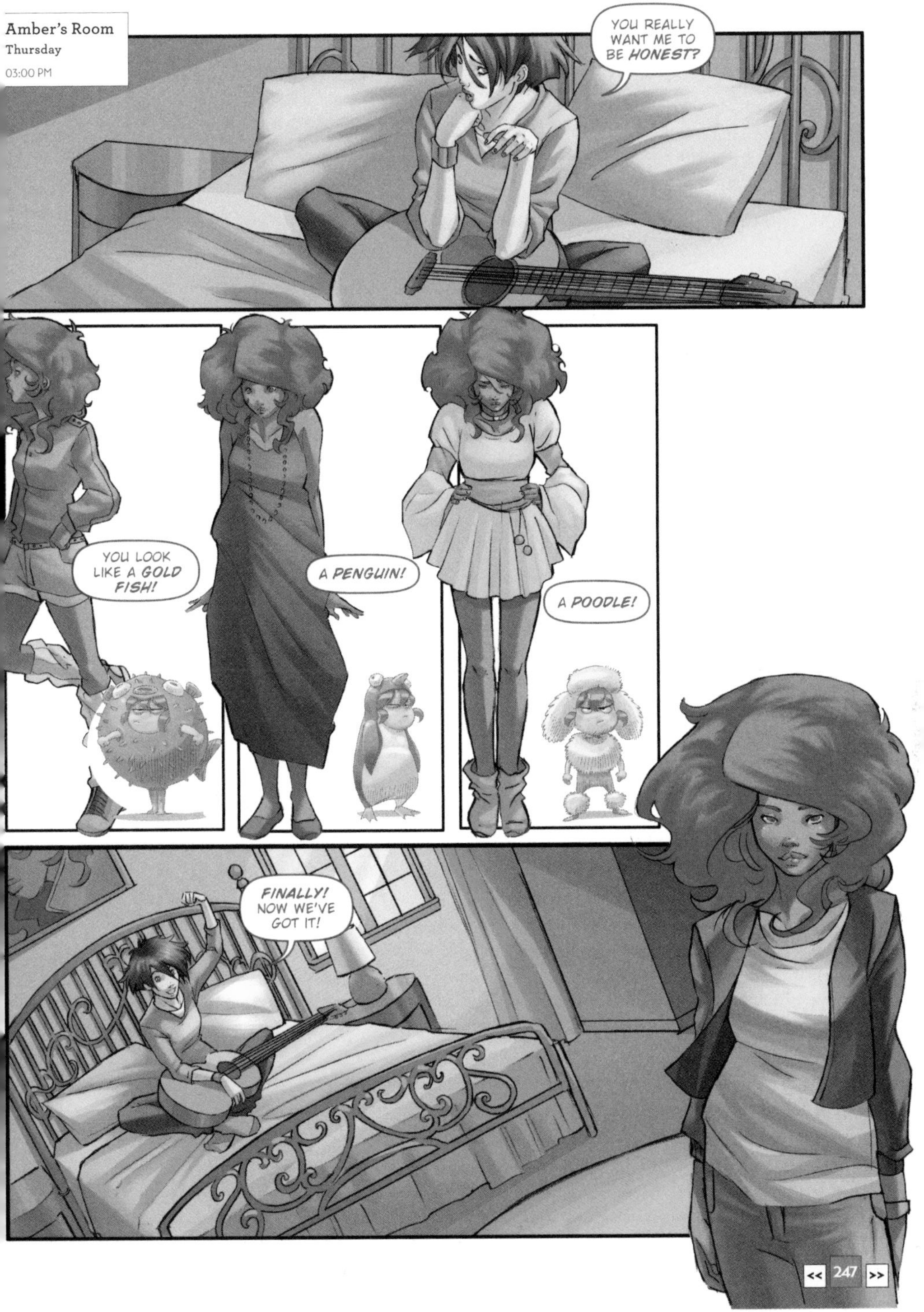
Amber's Room
Thursday
03:00 PM
YOU REALLY WANT ME TO BE HONEST?
YOU LOOK LIKE A GOLD FISH!
A PENGUIN!
A POODLE!
FINALLY! NOW WE'VE GOT IT!

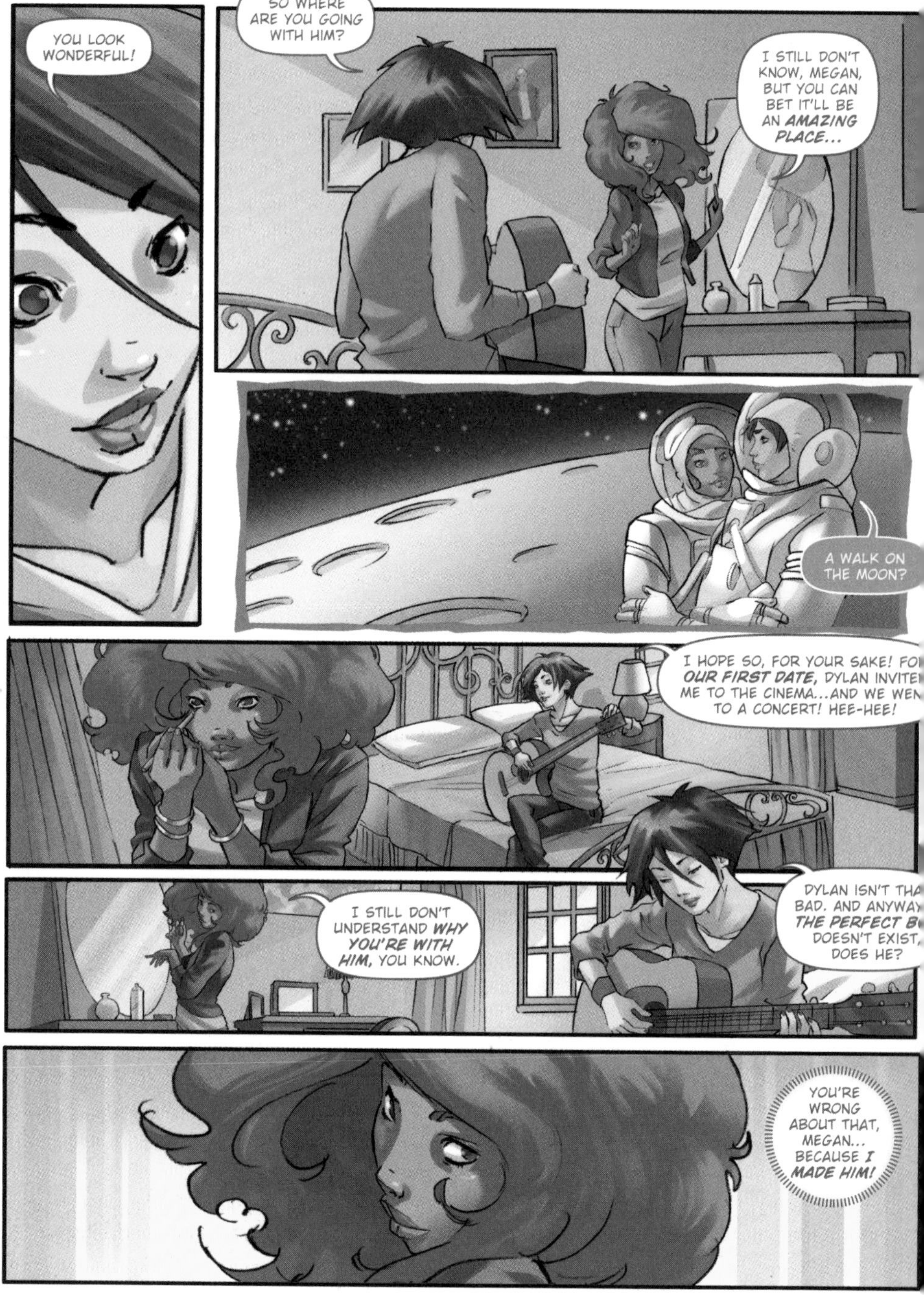
YOU LOOK WONDERFUL!
SO WHERE ARE YOU GOING WITH HIM?
I STILL DON'T KNOW, MEGAN, BUT YOU CAN BET IT'LL BE AN AMAZING PLACE...
A WALK ON THE MOON?
I HOPE SO, FOR YOUR SAKE! FO OUR FIRST DATE, DYLAN INVITE ME TO THE CINEMA...AND WE WEN TO A CONCERT! HEE-HEE!
I STILL DON'T UNDERSTAND WHY YOU'RE WITH HIM, YOU KNOW.
DYLAN ISN'T THA BAD. AND ANYWA THE PERFECT B DOESN'T EXIST, DOES HE?
YOU'RE WRONG ABOUT THAT, MEGAN... BECAUSE I MADE HIM!

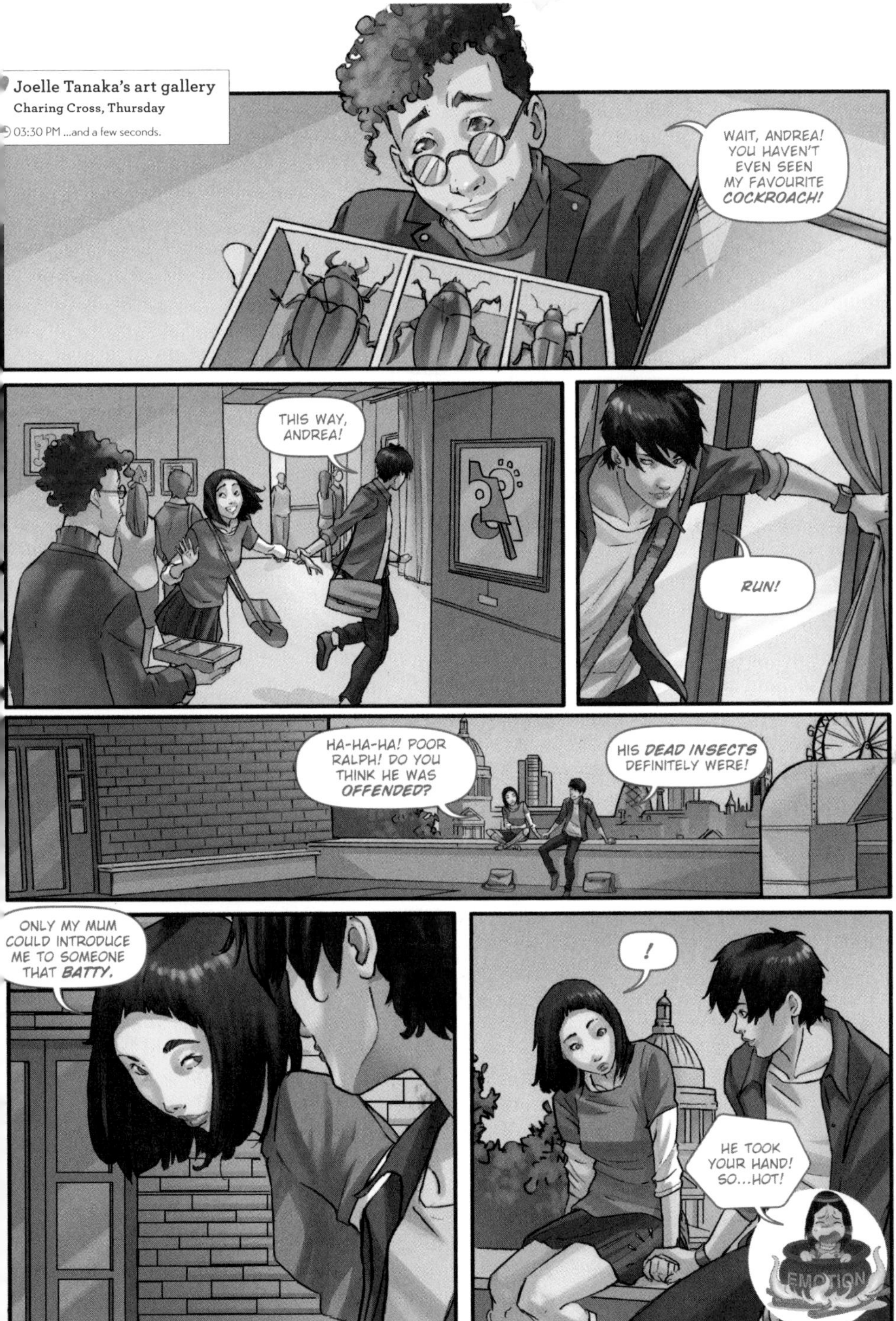
Joelle Tanaka's art gallery
Charing Cross, Thursday
03:30 PM ...and a few seconds.
WAIT, ANDREA! YOU HAVEN'T EVEN SEEN MY FAVOURITE COCKROACH!
THIS WAY, ANDREA!
RUN!
HA-HA-HA! POOR RALPH! DO YOU THINK HE WAS OFFENDED?
HIS DEAD INSECTS DEFINITELY WERE!
ONLY MY MUM COULD INTRODUCE ME TO SOMEONE THAT BATTY.
!
HE TOOK YOUR HAND! SO...HOT!
EMOTION

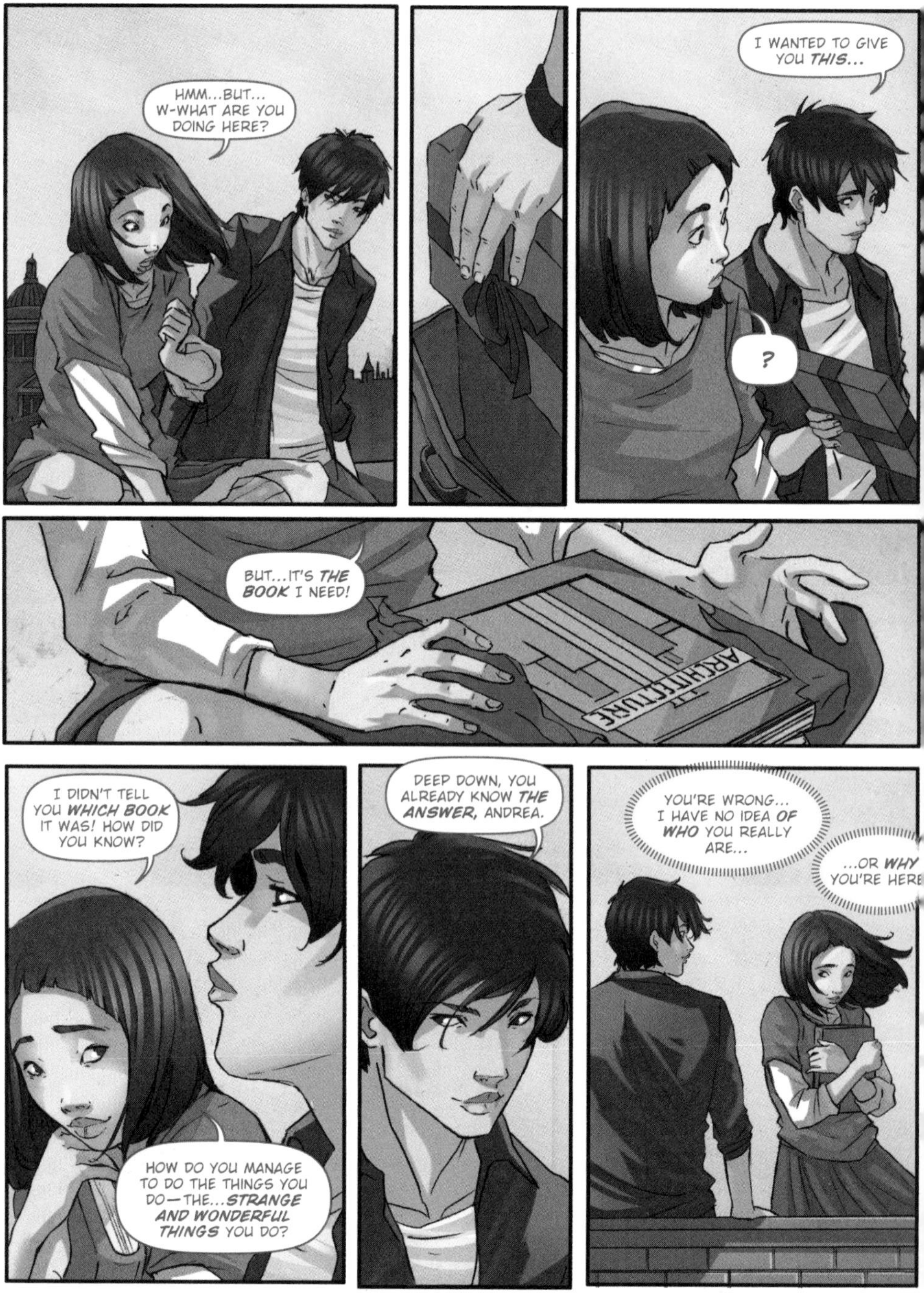
HMM...BUT...
W-WHAT ARE YOU
DOING HERE?
I WANTED TO GIVE
YOU THIS...
?
BUT...IT'S THE
BOOK I NEED!
ARCHITECTURE
I DIDN'T TELL
YOU WHICH BOOK
IT WAS! HOW DID
YOU KNOW?
HOW DO YOU MANAGE
TO DO THE THINGS YOU
DO—THE...STRANGE
AND WONDERFUL
THINGS YOU DO?
DEEP DOWN, YOU
ALREADY KNOW THE
ANSWER, ANDREA.
YOU'RE WRONG...
I HAVE NO IDEA OF
WHO YOU REALLY
ARE...
...OR WHY
YOU'RE HERE

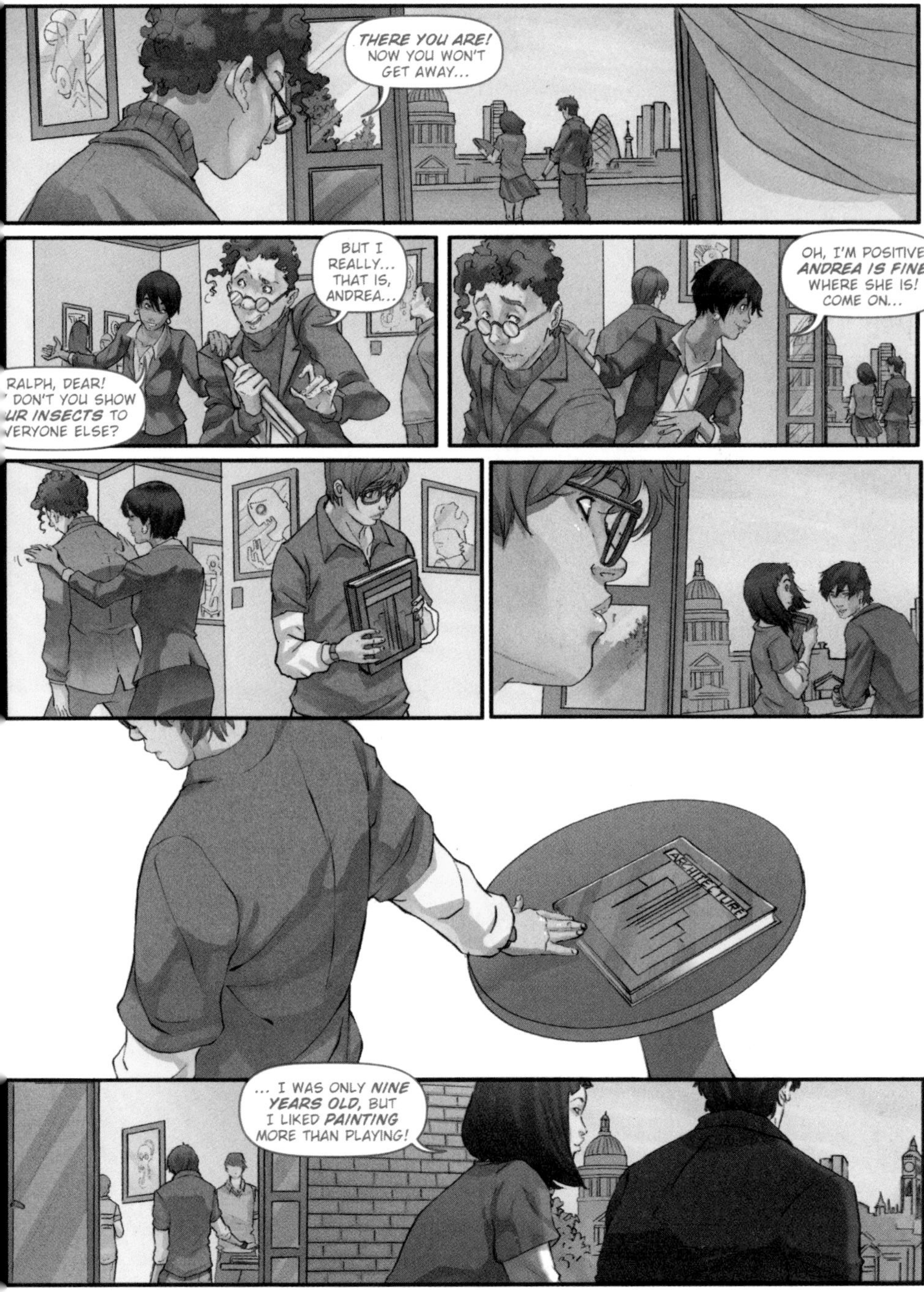
THERE YOU ARE! NOW YOU WON'T GET AWAY...
BUT I REALLY... THAT IS, ANDREA...
RALPH, DEAR! DON'T YOU SHOW UR INSECTS TO VERYONE ELSE?
OH, I'M POSITIVE ANDREA IS FINE WHERE SHE IS! COME ON...
... I WAS ONLY NINE YEARS OLD, BUT I LIKED PAINTING MORE THAN PLAYING!

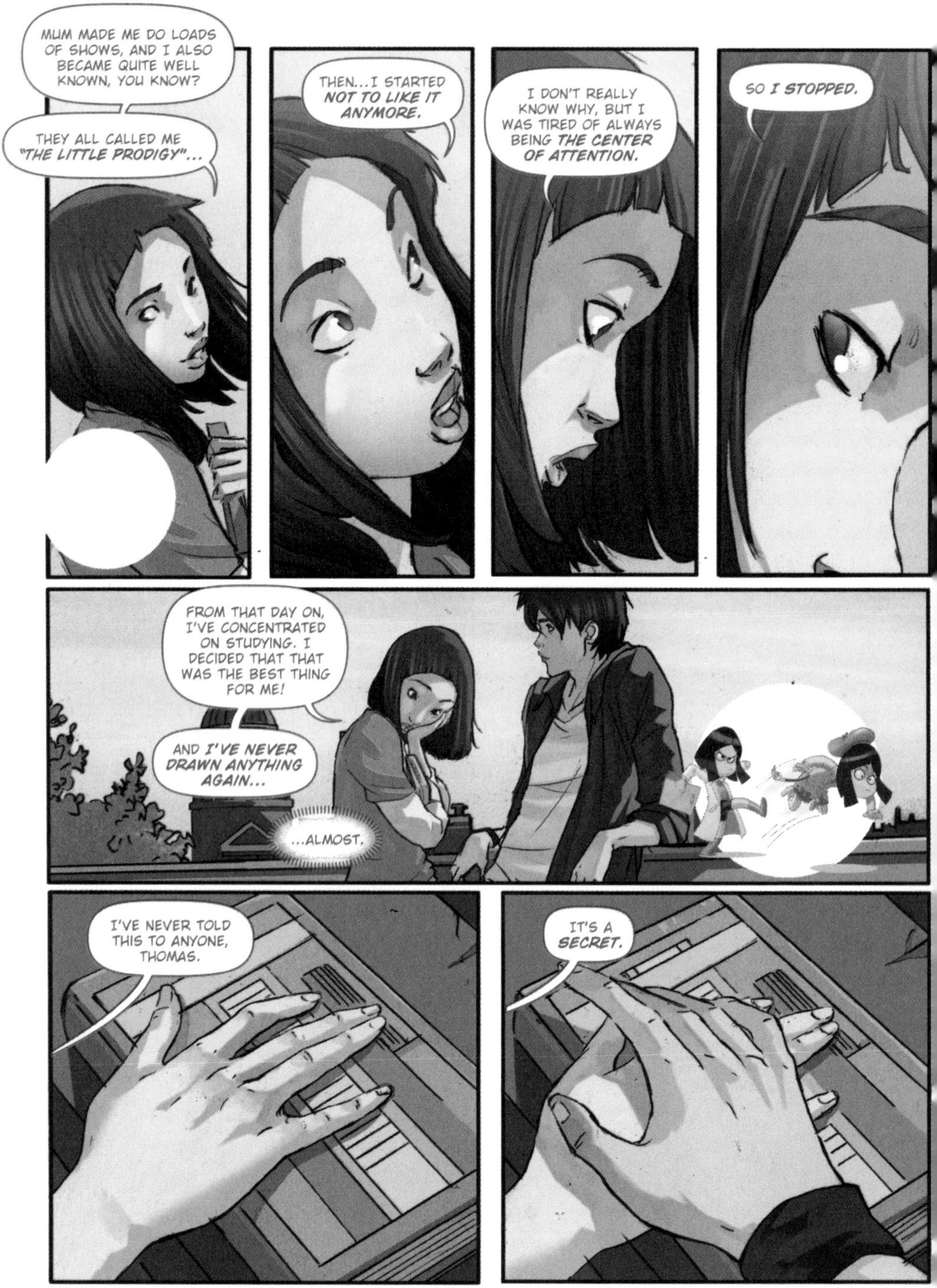
MUM MADE ME DO LOADS OF SHOWS, AND I ALSO BECAME QUITE WELL KNOWN, YOU KNOW?
THEY ALL CALLED ME "THE LITTLE PRODIGY"...
THEN...I STARTED NOT TO LIKE IT ANYMORE.
I DON'T REALLY KNOW WHY, BUT I WAS TIRED OF ALWAYS BEING THE CENTER OF ATTENTION.
SO I STOPPED.
FROM THAT DAY ON, I'VE CONCENTRATED ON STUDYING. I DECIDED THAT THAT WAS THE BEST THING FOR ME!
AND I'VE NEVER DRAWN ANYTHING AGAIN...
...ALMOST.
I'VE NEVER TOLD THIS TO ANYONE, THOMAS.
IT'S A SECRET.

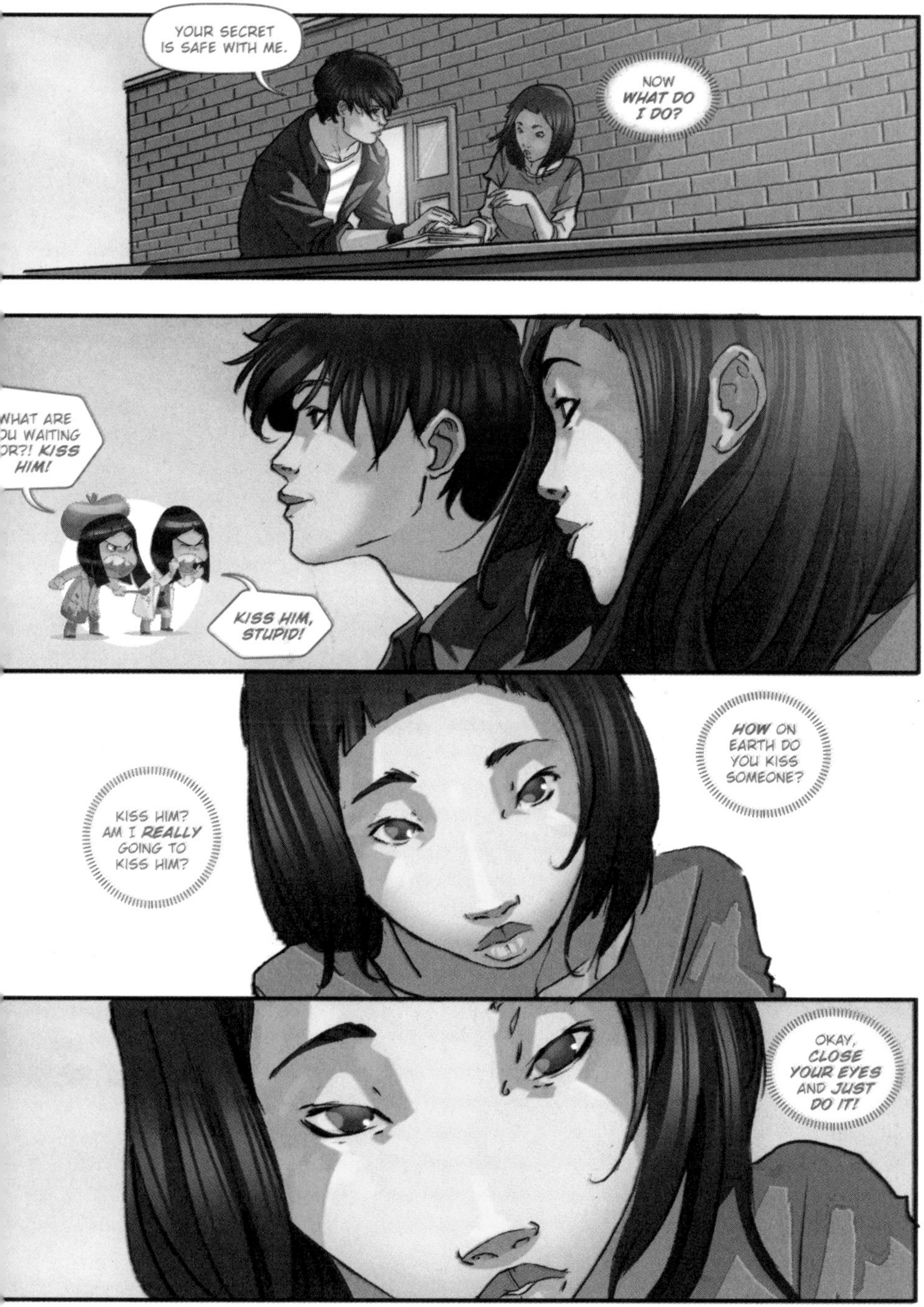
YOUR SECRET IS SAFE WITH ME.
NOW WHAT DO I DO?
WHAT ARE OU WAITING OR?! KISS HIM!
KISS HIM, STUPID!
HOW ON EARTH DO YOU KISS SOMEONE?
KISS HIM? AM I REALLY GOING TO KISS HIM?
OKAY, CLOSE YOUR EYES AND JUST DO IT!

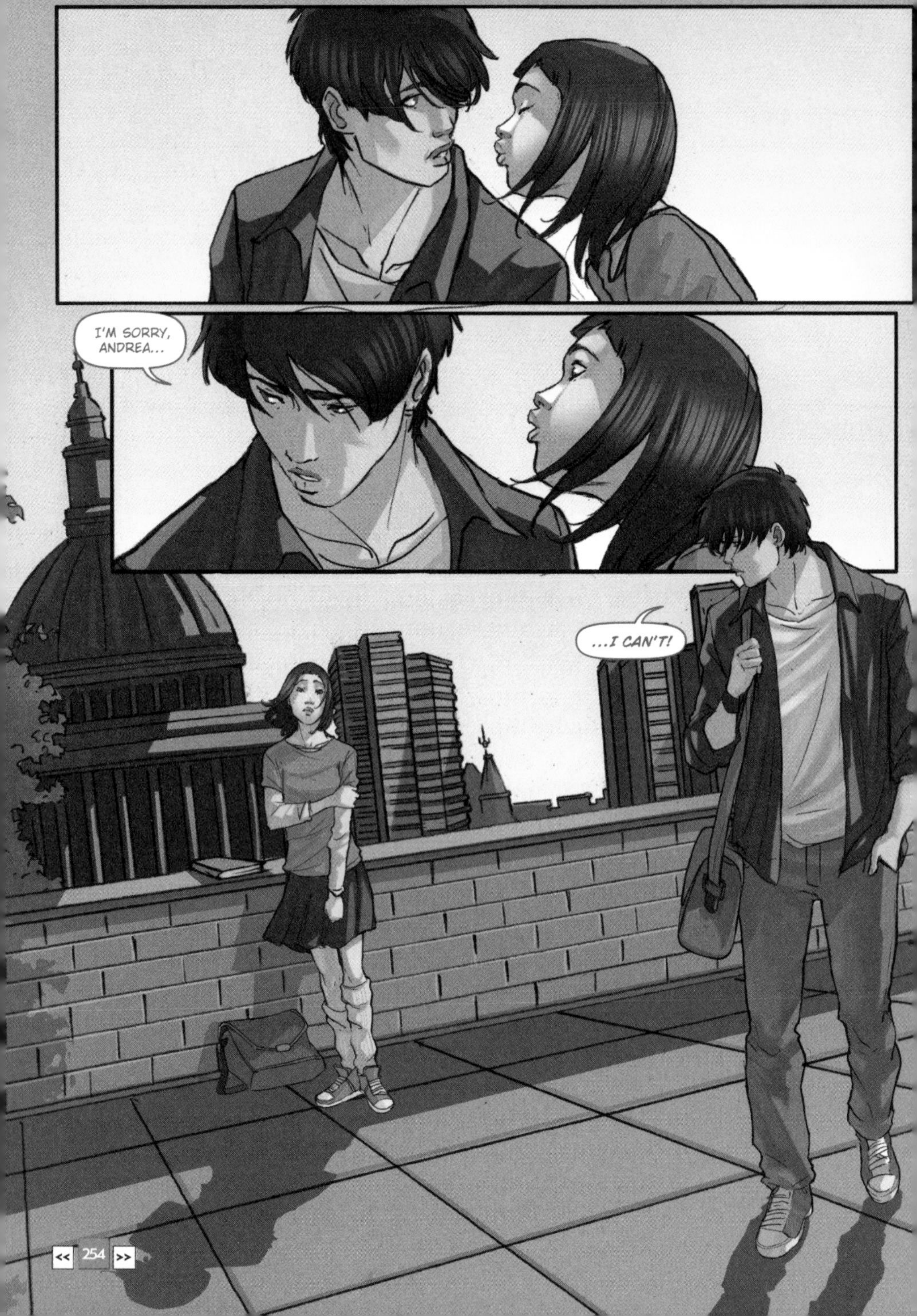
I'M SORRY, ANDREA...
...I CAN'T!

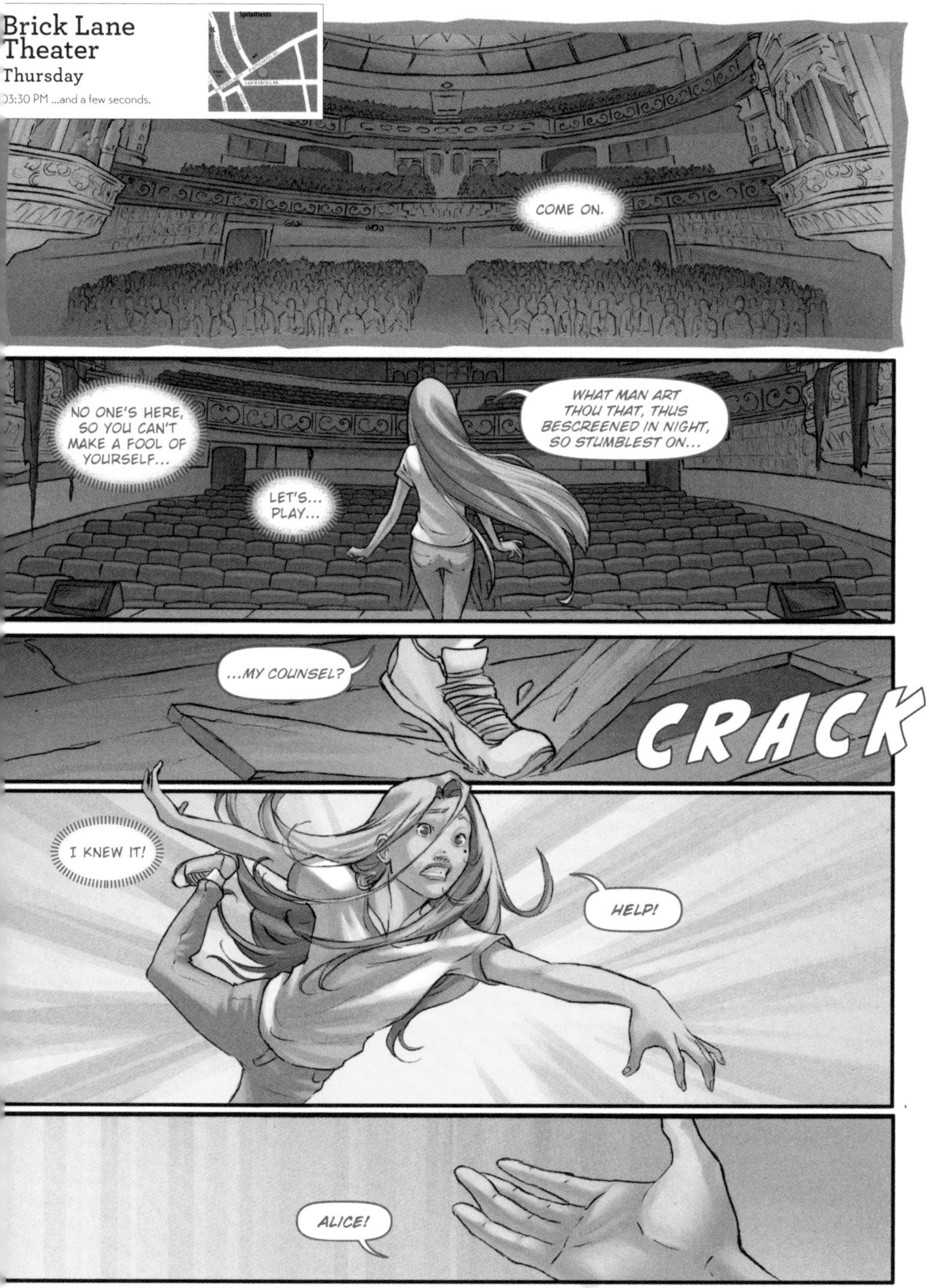
Brick Lane Theater
Thursday
03:30 PM ...and a few seconds.
COME ON.
NO ONE'S HERE, SO YOU CAN'T MAKE A FOOL OF YOURSELF...
LET'S... PLAY...
WHAT MAN ART THOU THAT, THUS BESCREENED IN NIGHT, SO STUMBLEST ON...
...MY COUNSEL?
CRACK
I KNEW IT!
HELP!
ALICE!

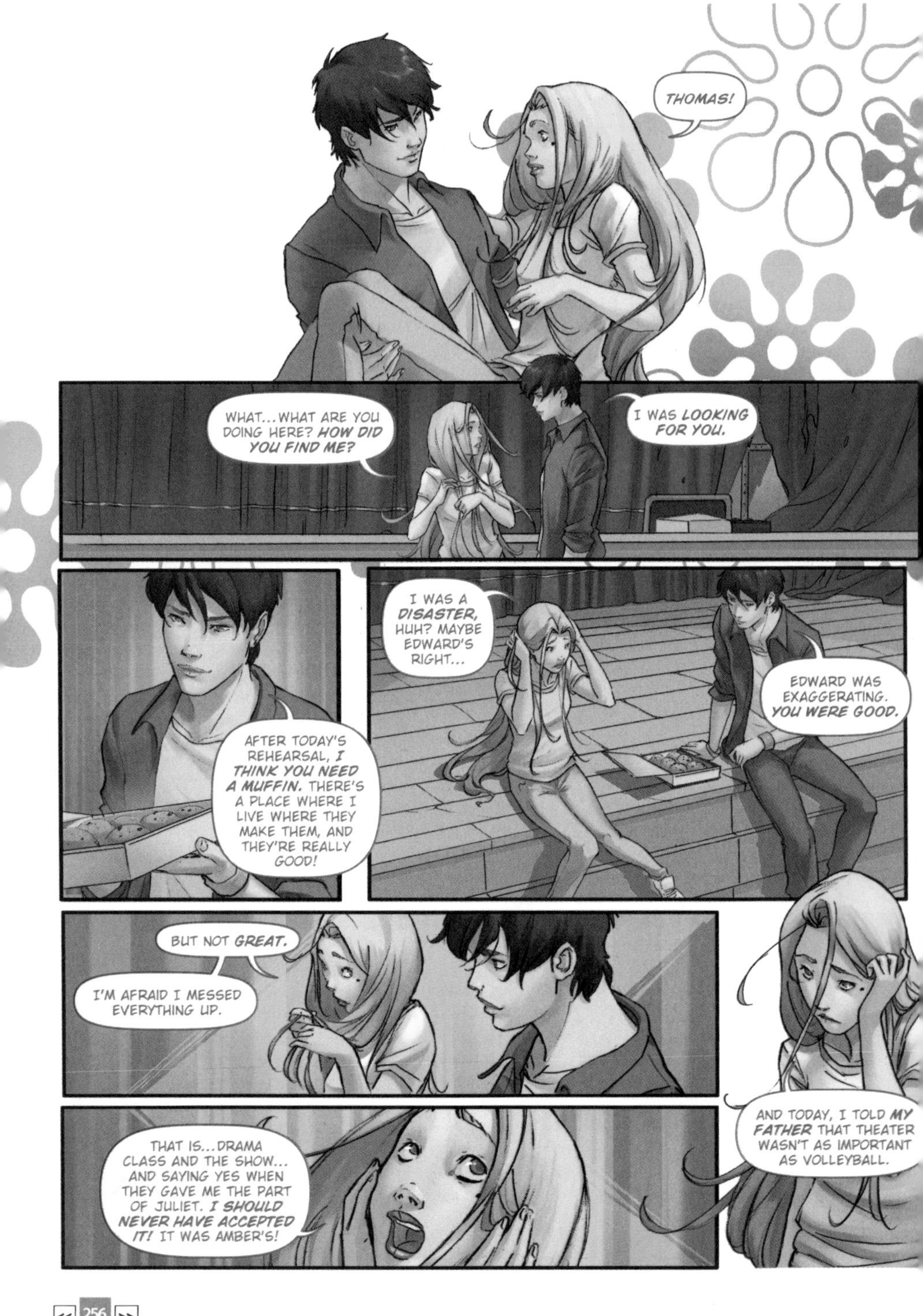
THOMAS!
WHAT...WHAT ARE YOU DOING HERE? HOW DID YOU FIND ME?
I WAS LOOKING FOR YOU.
AFTER TODAY'S REHEARSAL, I THINK YOU NEED A MUFFIN. THERE'S A PLACE WHERE I LIVE WHERE THEY MAKE THEM, AND THEY'RE REALLY GOOD!
I WAS A DISASTER, HUH? MAYBE EDWARD'S RIGHT...
EDWARD WAS EXAGGERATING. YOU WERE GOOD.
BUT NOT GREAT.
I'M AFRAID I MESSED EVERYTHING UP.
AND TODAY, I TOLD MY FATHER THAT THEATER WASN'T AS IMPORTANT AS VOLLEYBALL.
THAT IS...DRAMA CLASS AND THE SHOW... AND SAYING YES WHEN THEY GAVE ME THE PART OF JULIET. I SHOULD NEVER HAVE ACCEPTED IT! IT WAS AMBER'S!

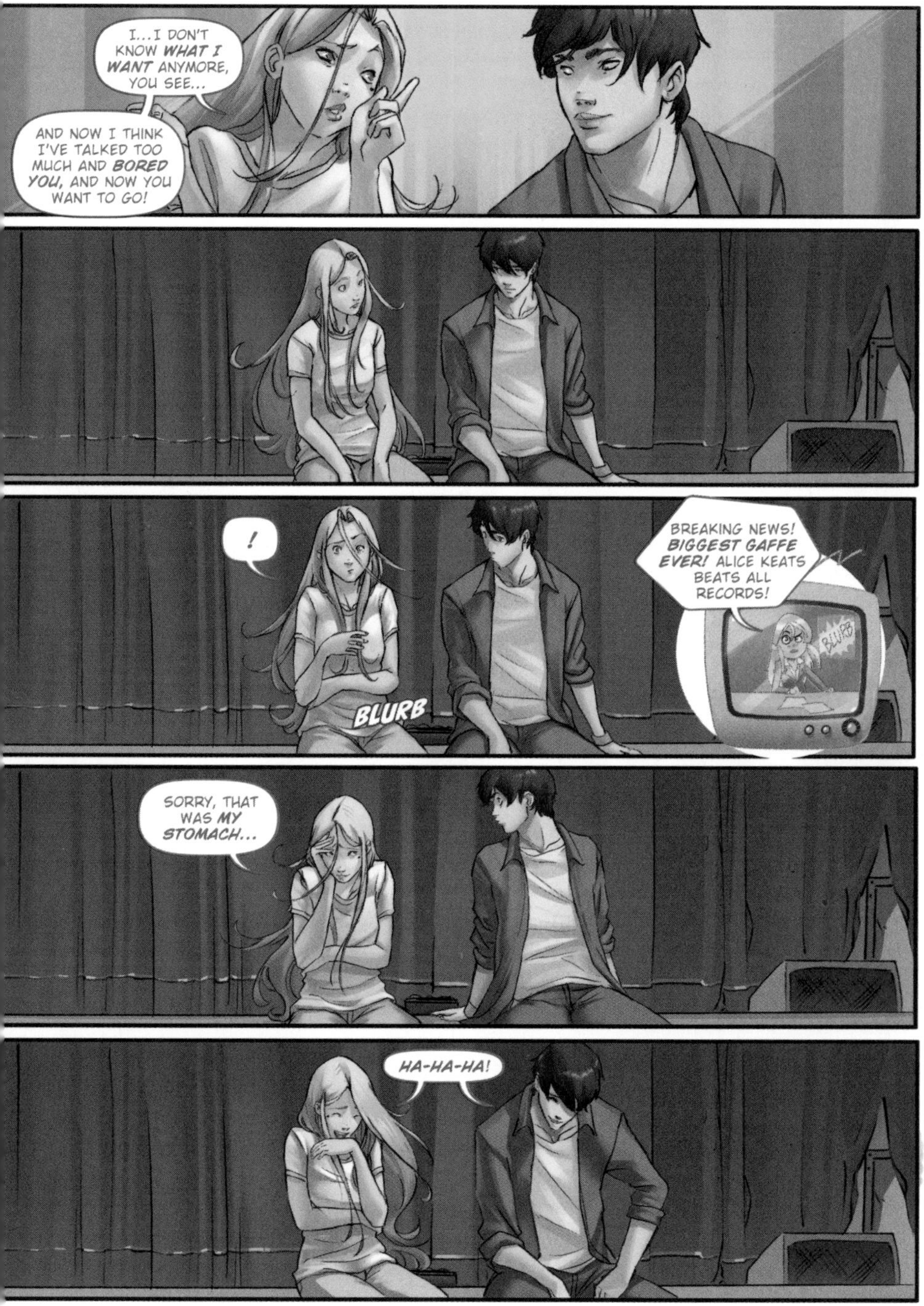
I...I DON'T KNOW WHAT I WANT ANYMORE, YOU SEE...
AND NOW I THINK I'VE TALKED TOO MUCH AND BORED YOU, AND NOW YOU WANT TO GO!
!
BREAKING NEWS! BIGGEST GAFFE EVER! ALICE KEATS BEATS ALL RECORDS!
BLURB
BLURB
SORRY, THAT WAS MY STOMACH...
HA-HA-HA!

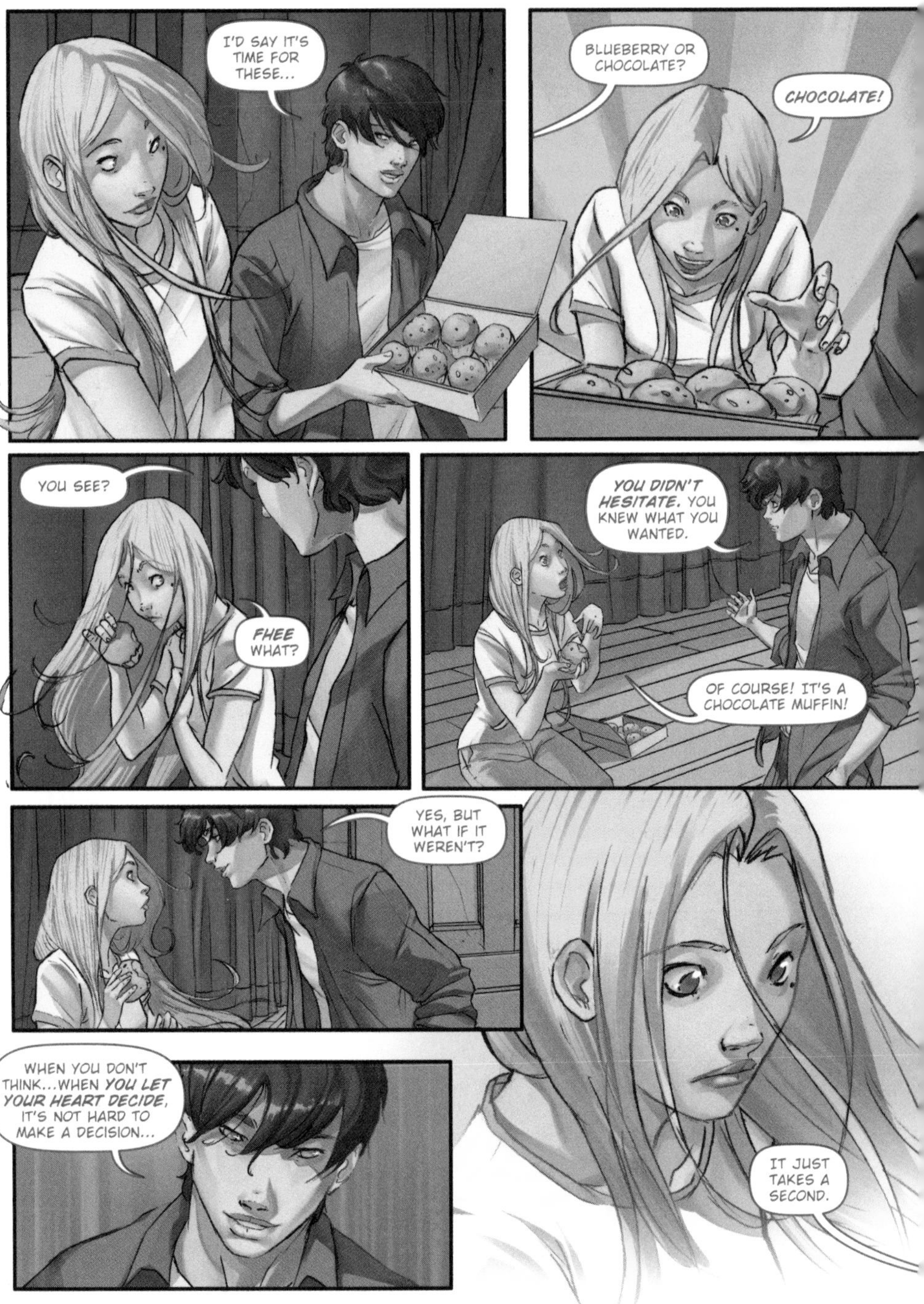
I'D SAY IT'S TIME FOR THESE...
BLUEBERRY OR CHOCOLATE?
CHOCOLATE!
YOU SEE?
FHEE WHAT?
YOU DIDN'T HESITATE. YOU KNEW WHAT YOU WANTED.
OF COURSE! IT'S A CHOCOLATE MUFFIN!
YES, BUT WHAT IF IT WEREN'T?
WHEN YOU DON'T THINK...WHEN YOU LET YOUR HEART DECIDE, IT'S NOT HARD TO MAKE A DECISION...
IT JUST TAKES A SECOND.

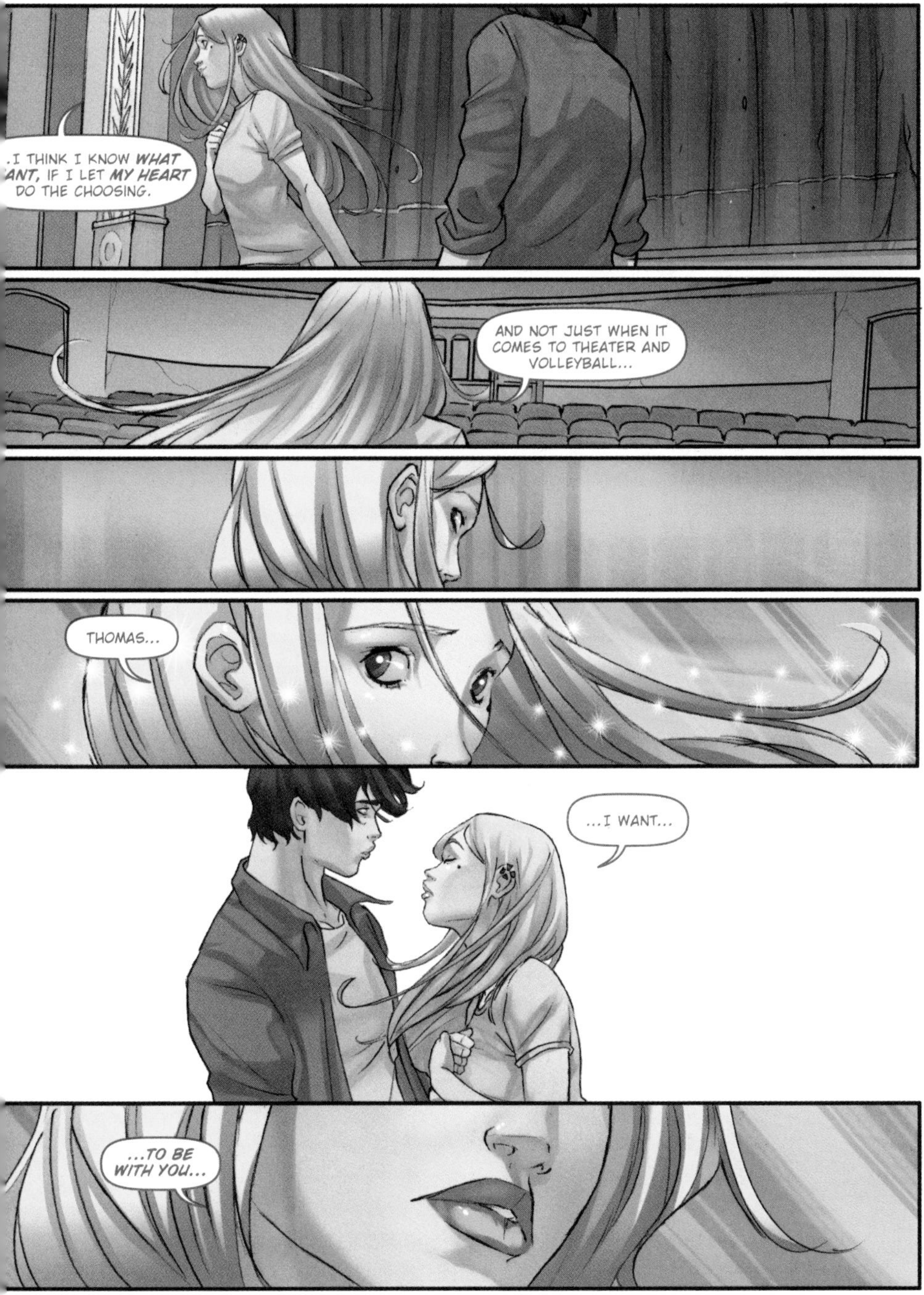

.I THINK I KNOW WHAT
ANT, IF I LET MY HEART
DO THE CHOOSING.
AND NOT JUST WHEN IT COMES TO THEATER AND VOLLEYBALL...
THOMAS...
...I WANT...
...TO BE WITH YOU...

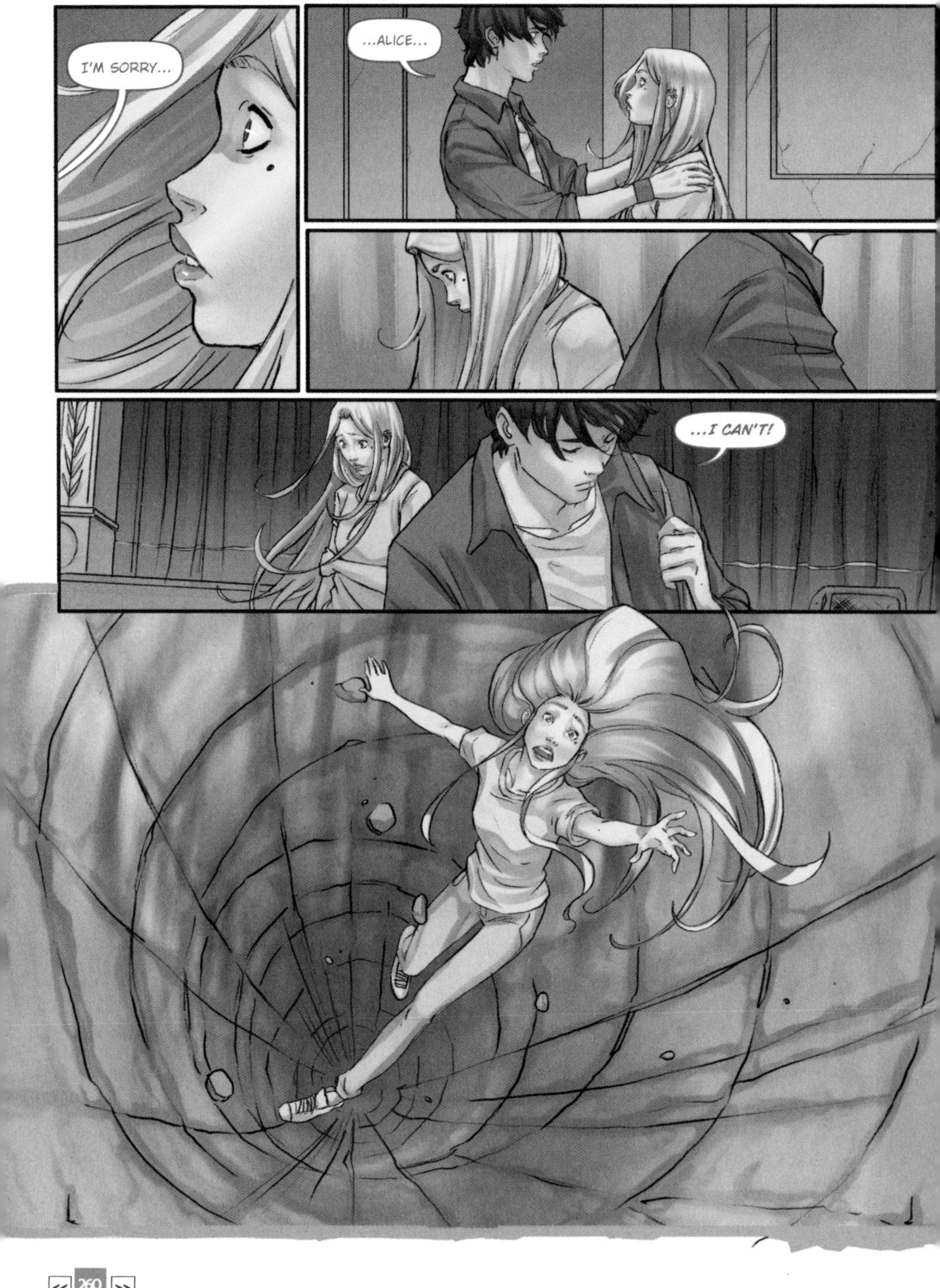
I'M SORRY...
...ALICE...
...I CAN'T!

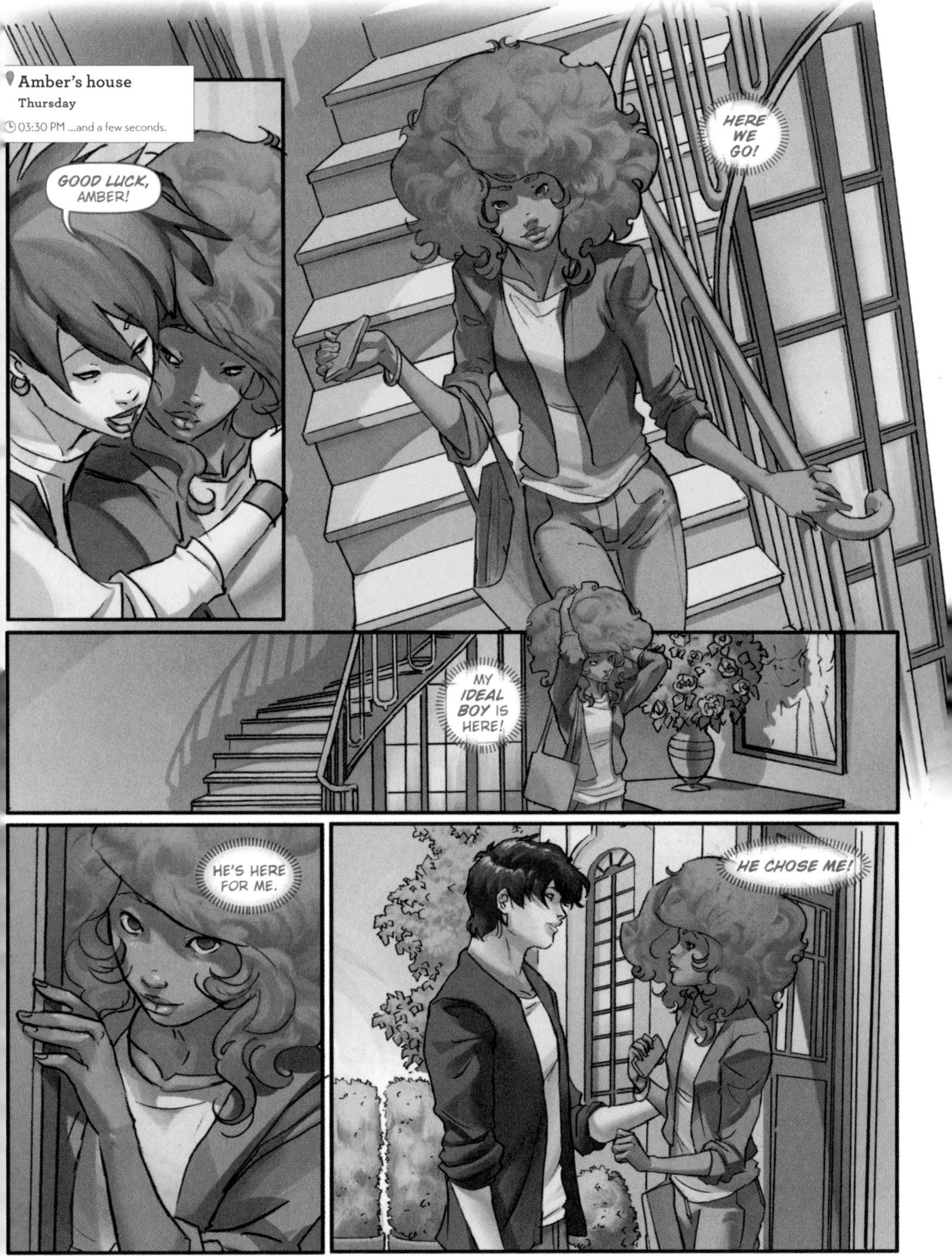
Amber's house
Thursday
03:30 PM ...and a few seconds.
GOOD LUCK, AMBER!
HERE WE GO!
MY IDEAL BOY IS HERE!
HE'S HERE FOR ME.
HE CHOSE ME!

END OF CHAPTER 14

CHAPTER 15

the UNEXPECTED CHOICE

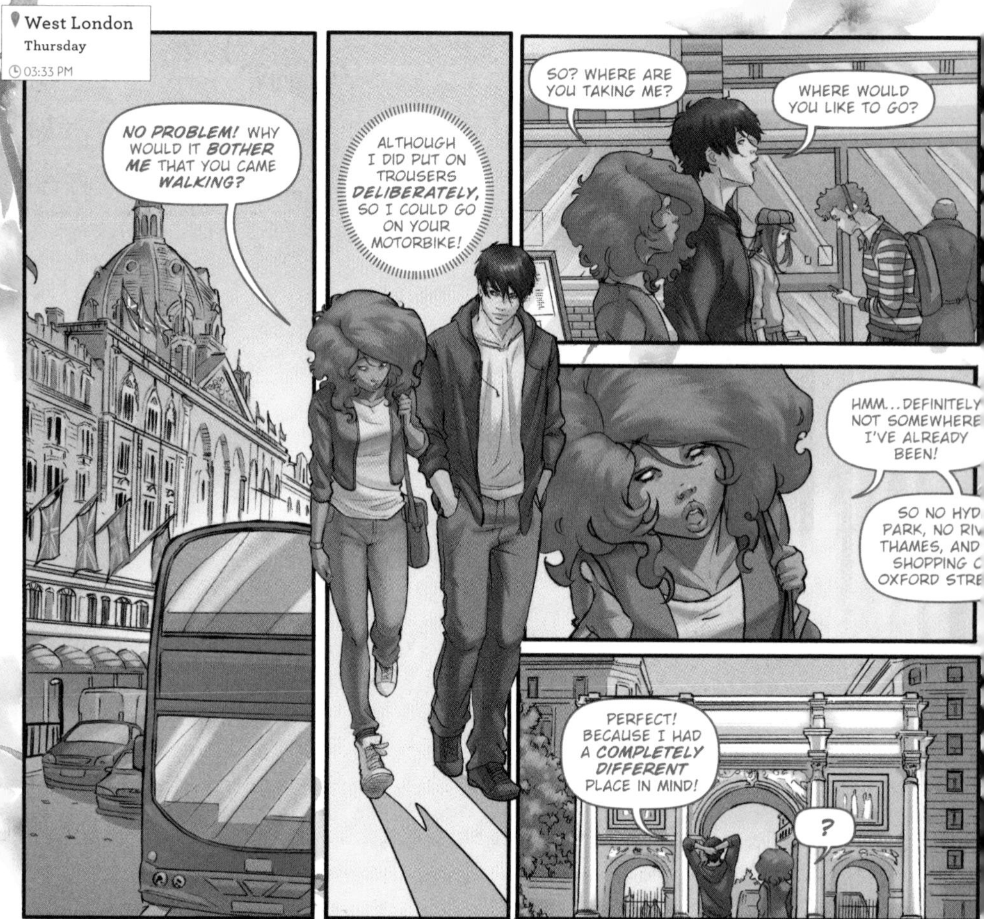
West London
Thursday
03:33 PM
NO PROBLEM! WHY WOULD IT BOTHER ME THAT YOU CAME WALKING?
ALTHOUGH I DID PUT ON TROUSERS DELIBERATELY, SO I COULD GO ON YOUR MOTORBIKE!
SO? WHERE ARE YOU TAKING ME?
WHERE WOULD YOU LIKE TO GO?
HMM...DEFINITELY NOT SOMEWHERE I'VE ALREADY BEEN!
SO NO HYD PARK, NO RIV THAMES, AND SHOPPING C OXFORD STRE
PERFECT! BECAUSE I HAD A COMPLETELY DIFFERENT PLACE IN MIND!
?

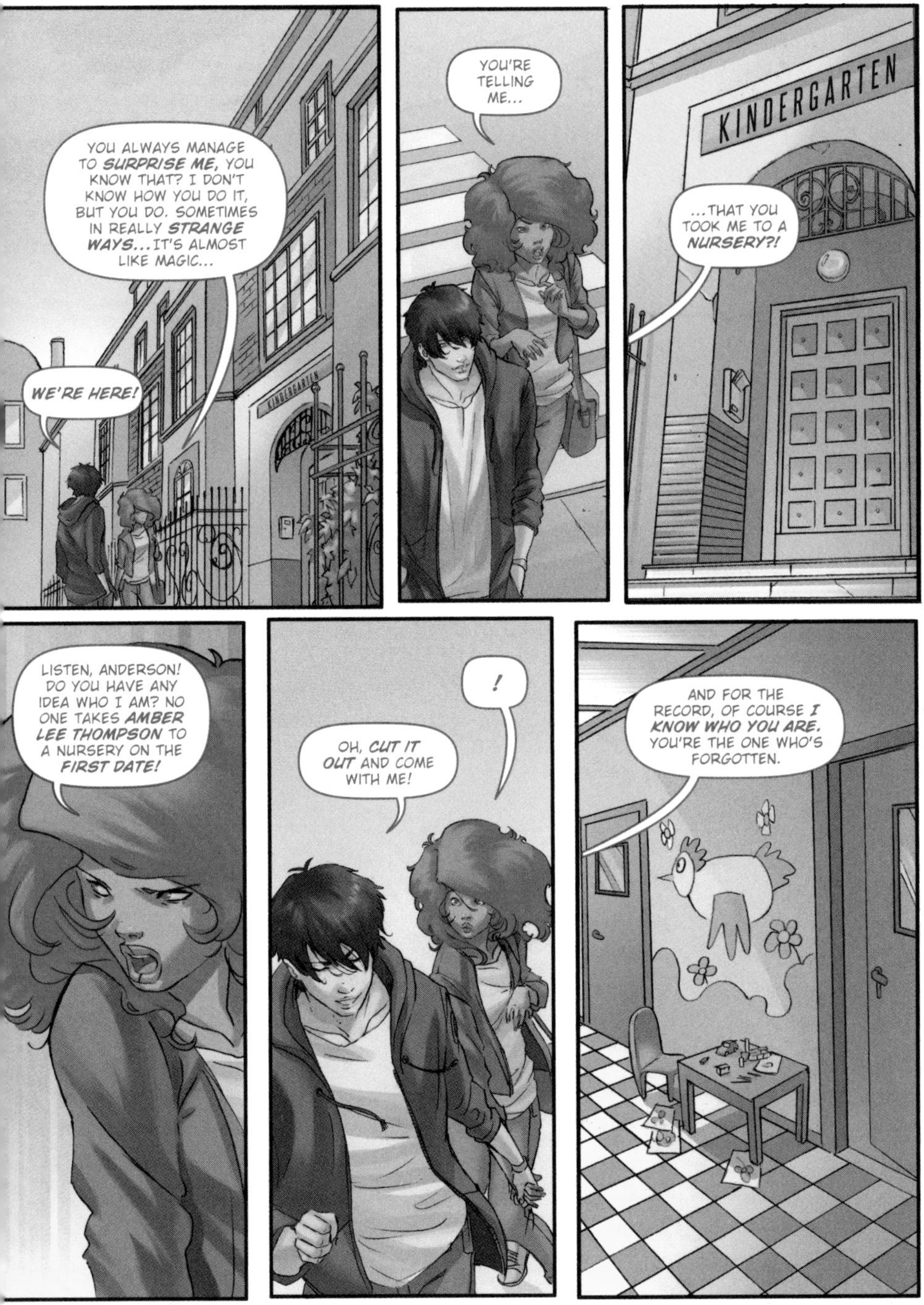
YOU ALWAYS MANAGE TO SURPRISE ME, YOU KNOW THAT? I DON'T KNOW HOW YOU DO IT, BUT YOU DO. SOMETIMES IN REALLY STRANGE WAYS... IT'S ALMOST LIKE MAGIC...
WE'RE HERE!
KINDERGARTEN
YOU'RE TELLING ME...
KINDERGARTEN
...THAT YOU TOOK ME TO A NURSERY?!
LISTEN, ANDERSON! DO YOU HAVE ANY IDEA WHO I AM? NO ONE TAKES AMBER LEE THOMPSON TO A NURSERY ON THE FIRST DATE!
OH, CUT IT OUT AND COME WITH ME!
!
AND FOR THE RECORD, OF COURSE I KNOW WHO YOU ARE. YOU'RE THE ONE WHO'S FORGOTTEN.

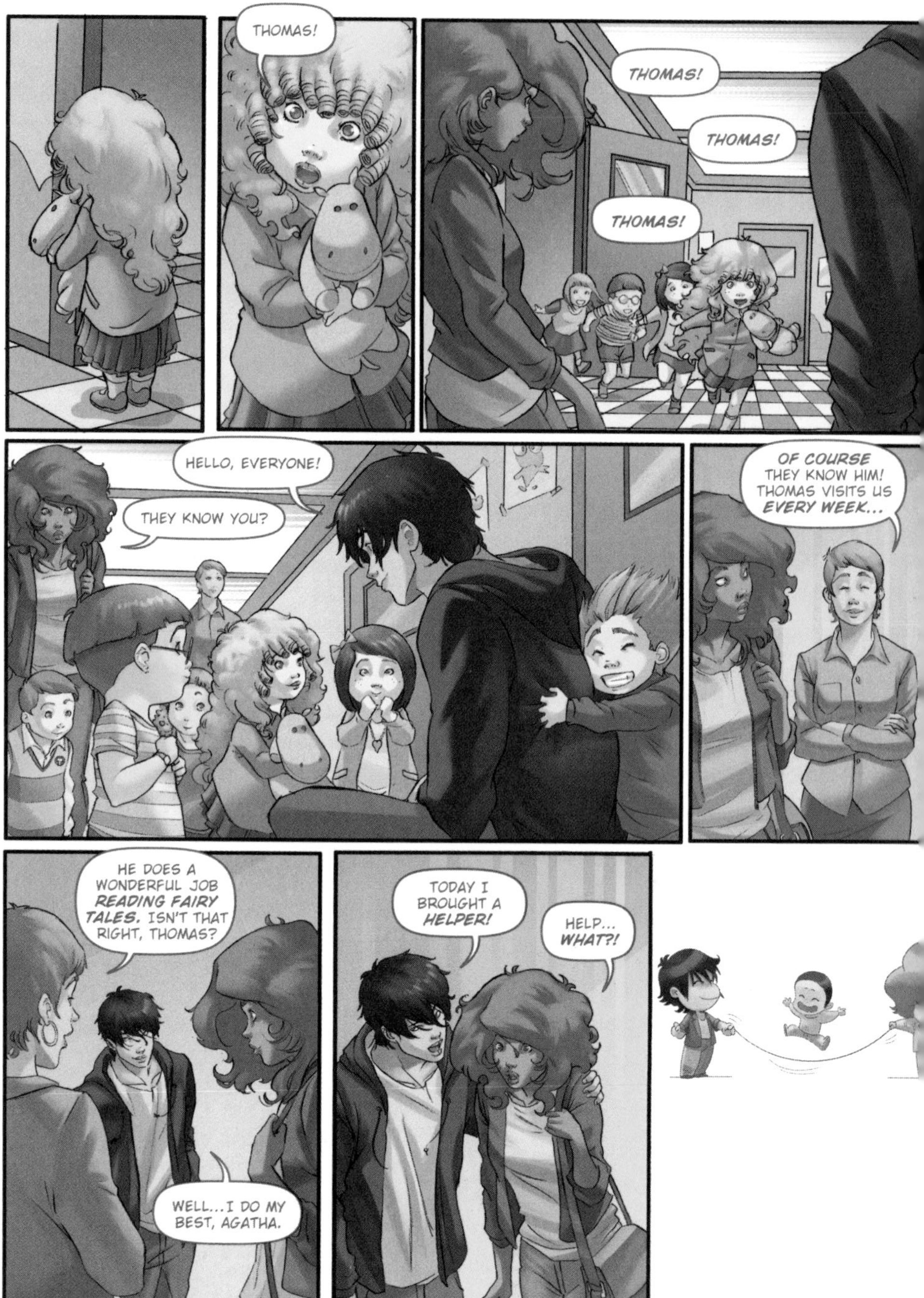
THOMAS!
THOMAS!
THOMAS!
THOMAS!
HELLO, EVERYONE!
THEY KNOW YOU?
OF COURSE THEY KNOW HIM! THOMAS VISITS US EVERY WEEK...
HE DOES A WONDERFUL JOB READING FAIRY TALES. ISN'T THAT RIGHT, THOMAS?
WELL...I DO MY BEST, AGATHA.
TODAY I BROUGHT A HELPER!
HELP... WHAT?!

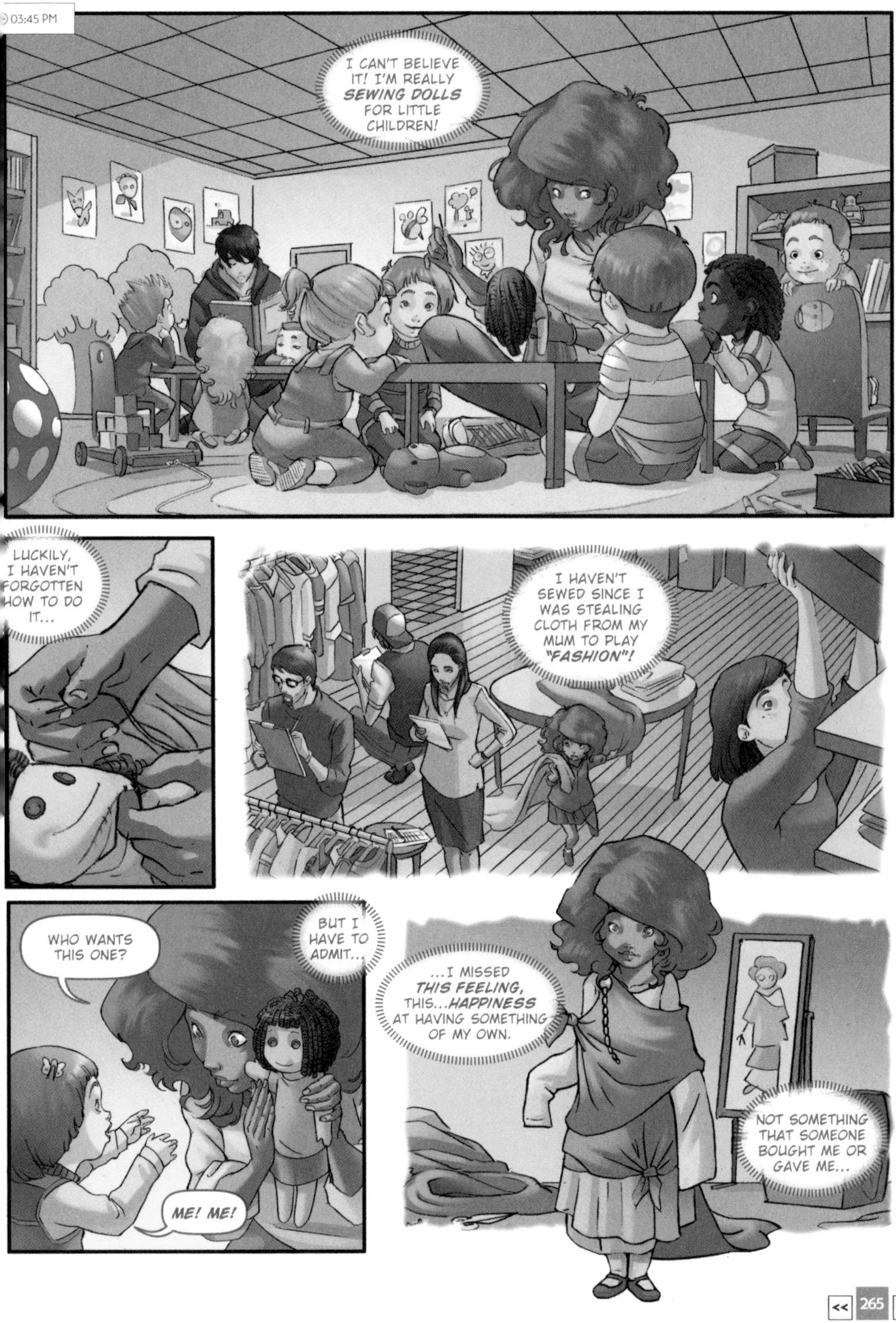
I CAN'T BELIEVE IT! I'M REALLY SEWING DOLLS FOR LITTLE CHILDREN!
LUCKILY, I HAVEN'T FORGOTTEN HOW TO DO IT...
I HAVEN'T SEWED SINCE I WAS STEALING CLOTH FROM MY MUM TO PLAY "FASHION"!
WHO WANTS THIS ONE?
BUT I HAVE TO ADMIT...
ME! ME!
...I MISSED THIS FEELING, THIS...HAPPINESS AT HAVING SOMETHING OF MY OWN.
NOT SOMETHING THAT SOMEONE BOUGHT ME OR GAVE ME...

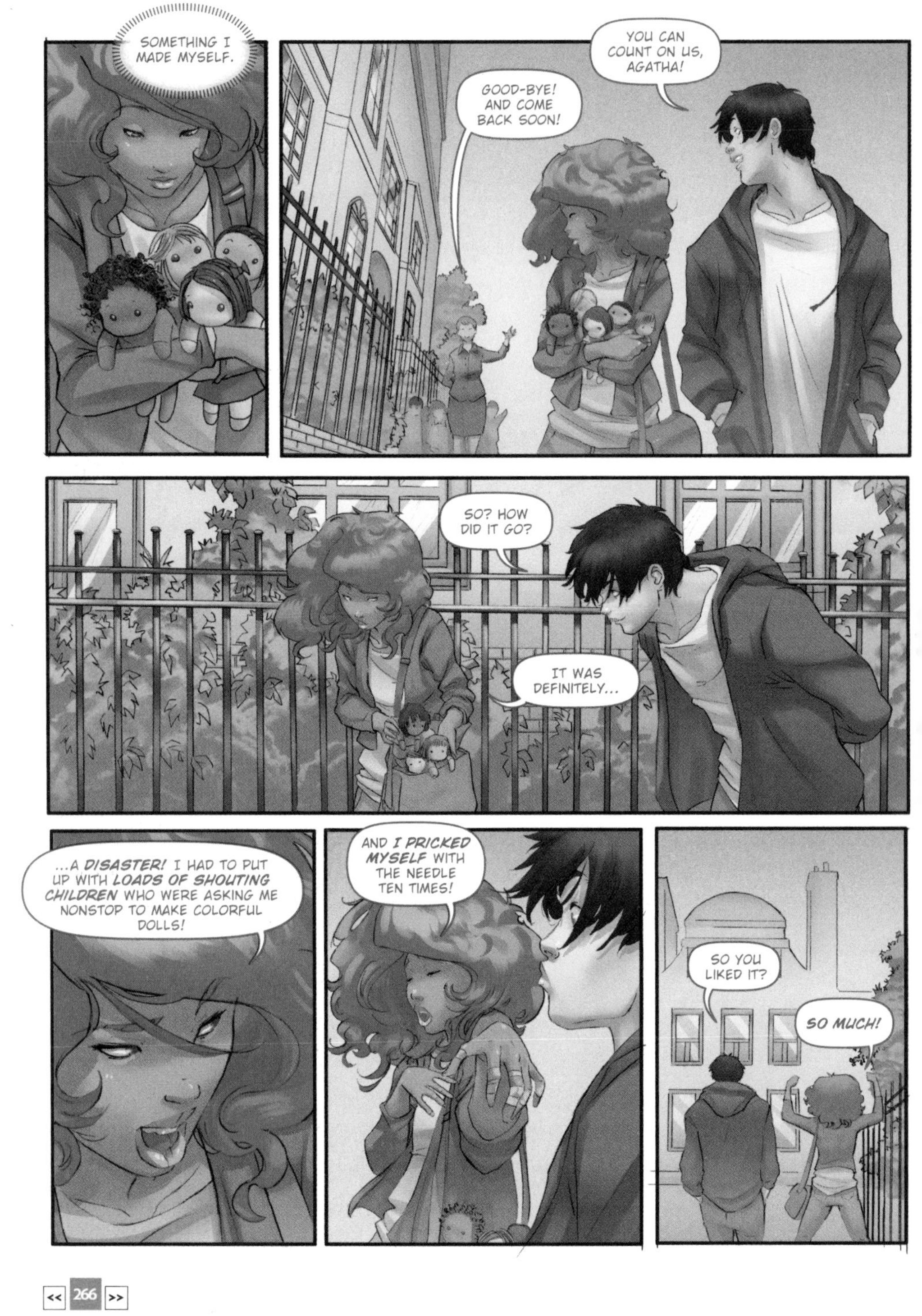
SOMETHING I MADE MYSELF.
GOOD-BYE! AND COME BACK SOON!
YOU CAN COUNT ON US, AGATHA!
SO? HOW DID IT GO?
IT WAS DEFINITELY...
...A *DISASTER!* I HAD TO PUT UP WITH *LOADS OF SHOUTING CHILDREN* WHO WERE ASKING ME NONSTOP TO MAKE COLORFUL DOLLS!
AND *I PRICKED MYSELF* WITH THE NEEDLE TEN TIMES!
SO YOU LIKED IT?
SO MUCH!

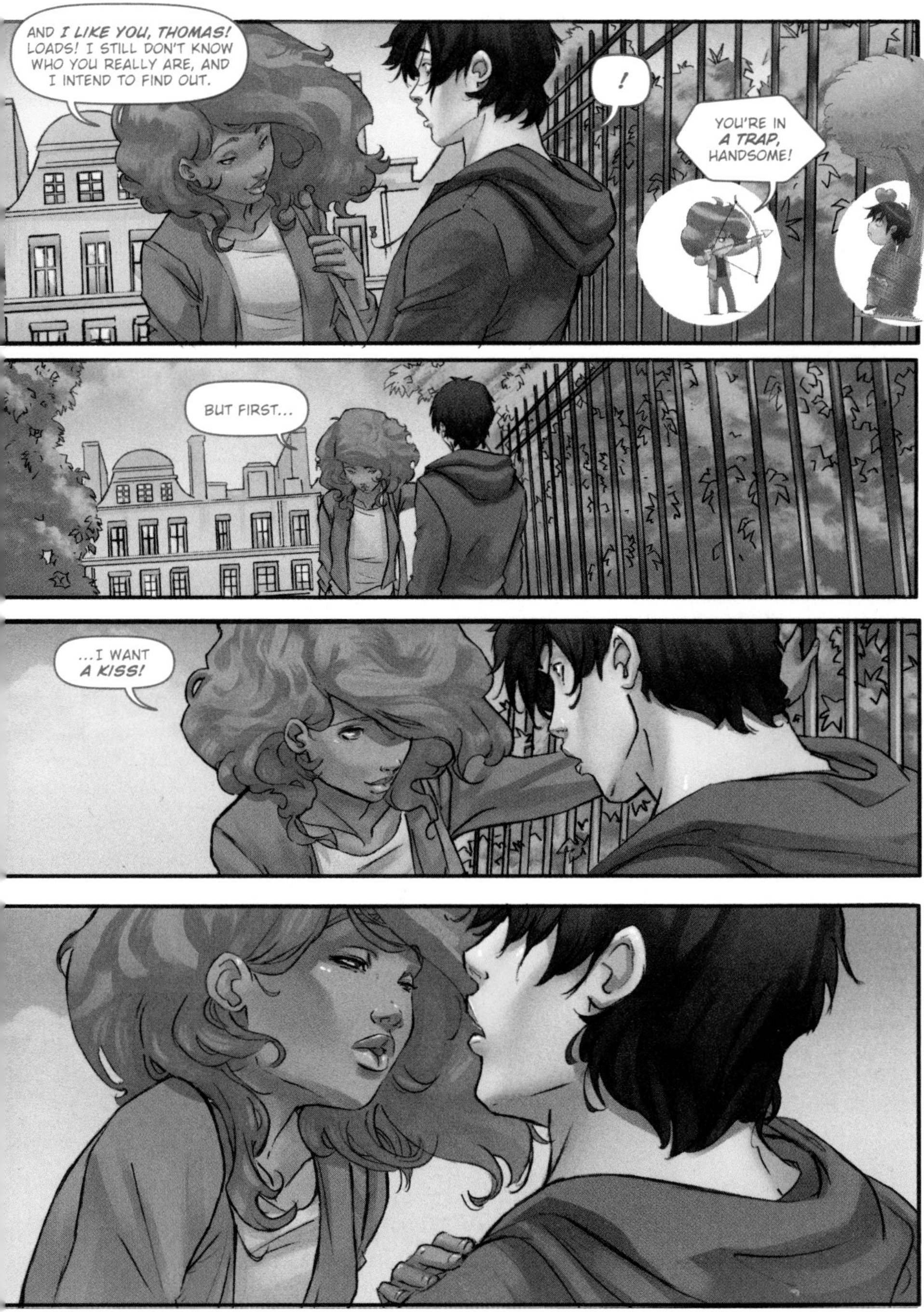
AND I LIKE YOU, THOMAS! LOADS! I STILL DON'T KNOW WHO YOU REALLY ARE, AND I INTEND TO FIND OUT.
!
YOU'RE IN A TRAP, HANDSOME!
BUT FIRST...
...I WANT A KISS!

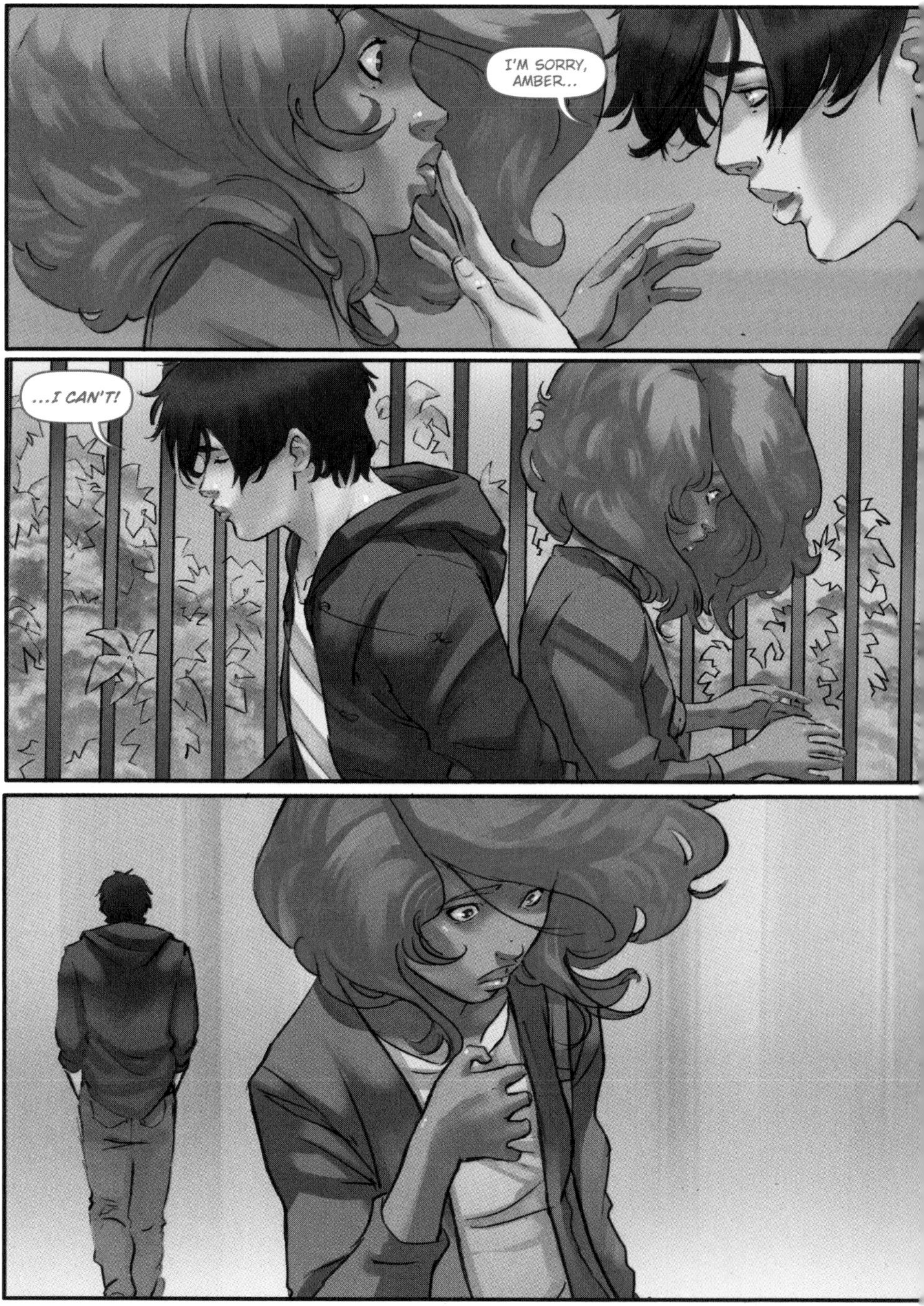
I'M SORRY, AMBER...
...I CAN'T!

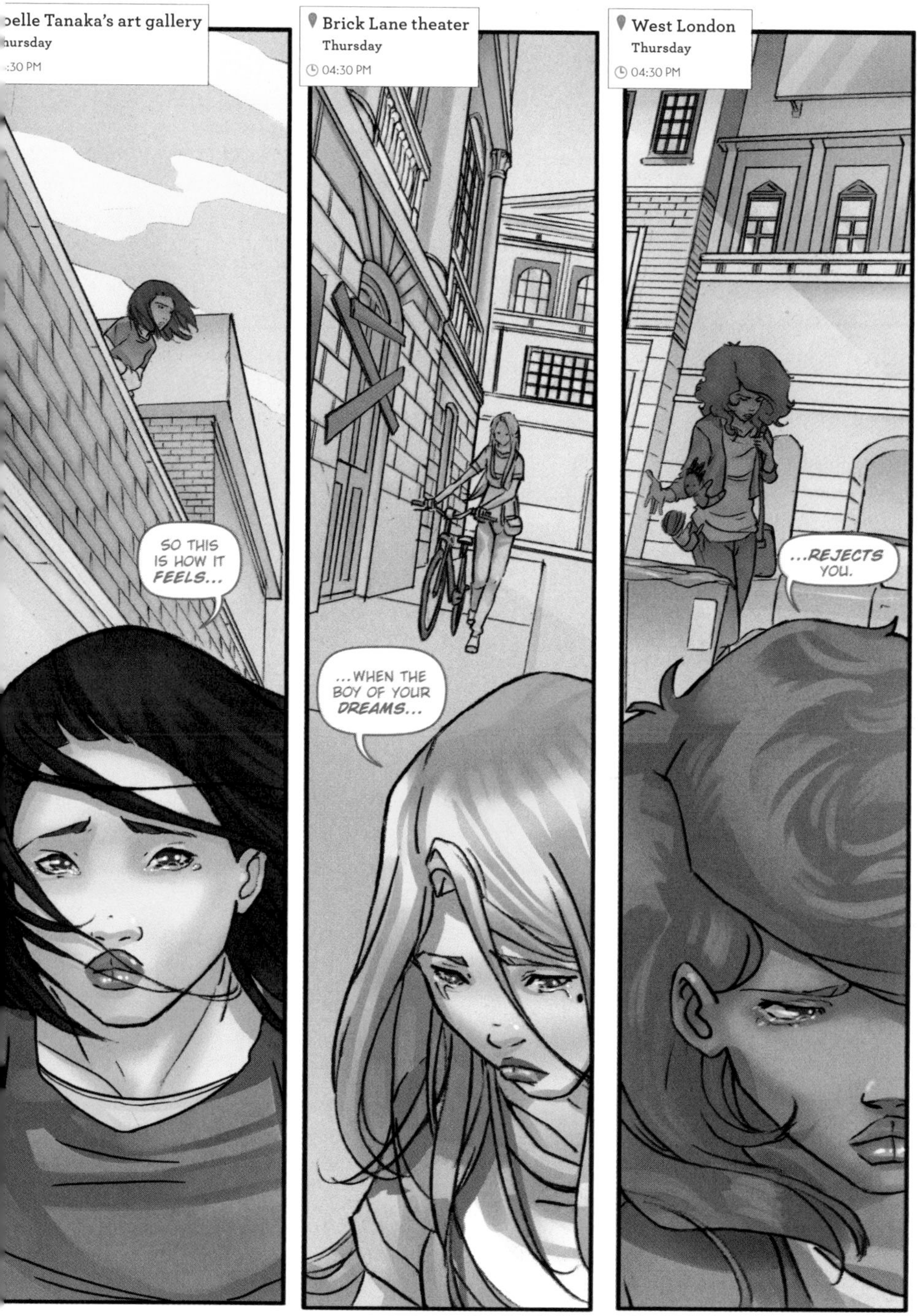

belle Tanaka's art gallery
hursday
:30 PM
SO THIS IS HOW IT FEELS...
Brick Lane theater
Thursday
04:30 PM
...WHEN THE BOY OF YOUR DREAMS...
West London
Thursday
04:30 PM
...REJECTS YOU.

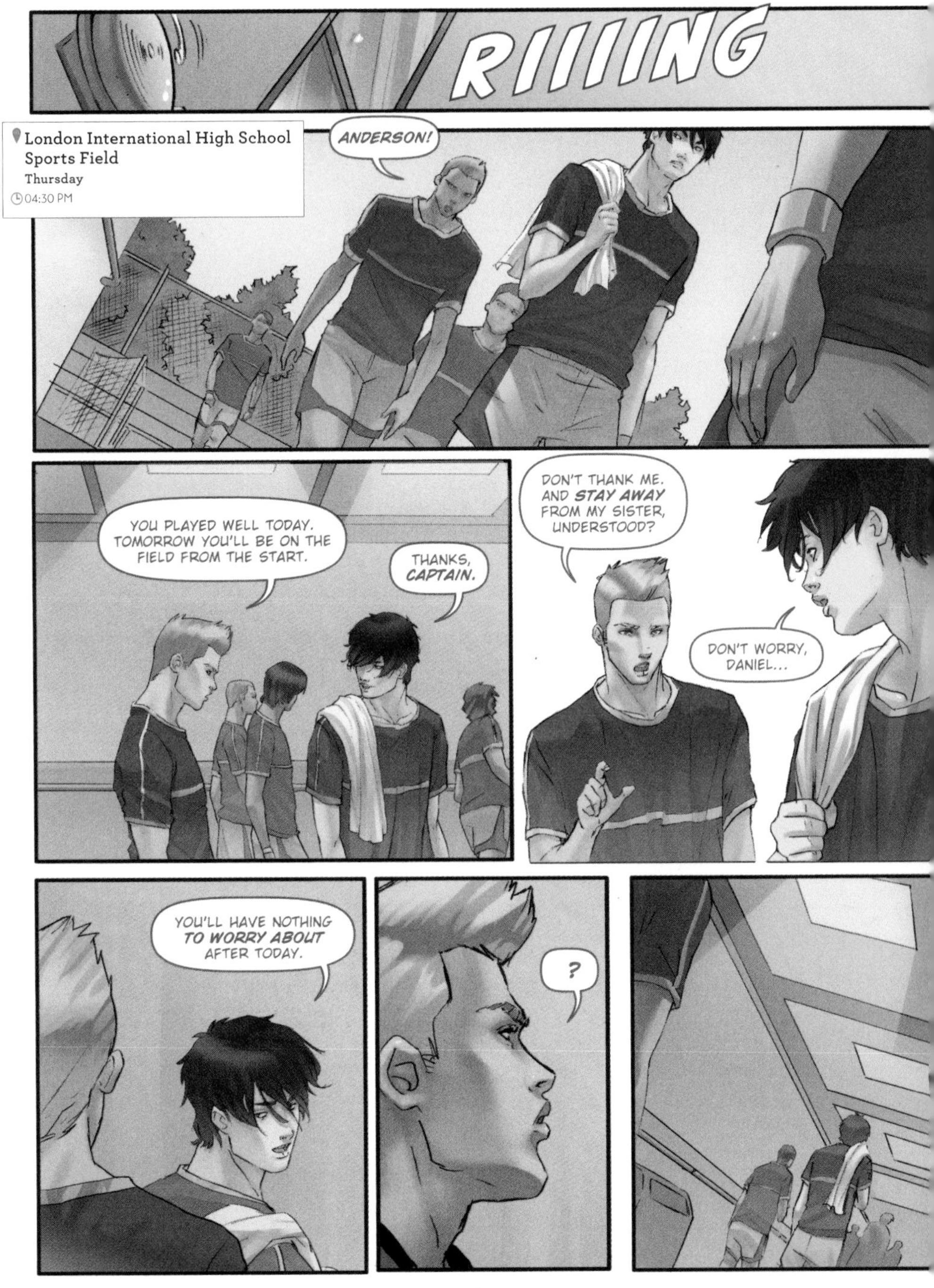
RIIIING
London International High School Sports Field
Thursday
04:30 PM
ANDERSON!
YOU PLAYED WELL TODAY. TOMORROW YOU'LL BE ON THE FIELD FROM THE START.
THANKS, CAPTAIN.
DON'T THANK ME. AND STAY AWAY FROM MY SISTER, UNDERSTOOD?
DON'T WORRY, DANIEL...
YOU'LL HAVE NOTHING TO WORRY ABOUT AFTER TODAY.
?

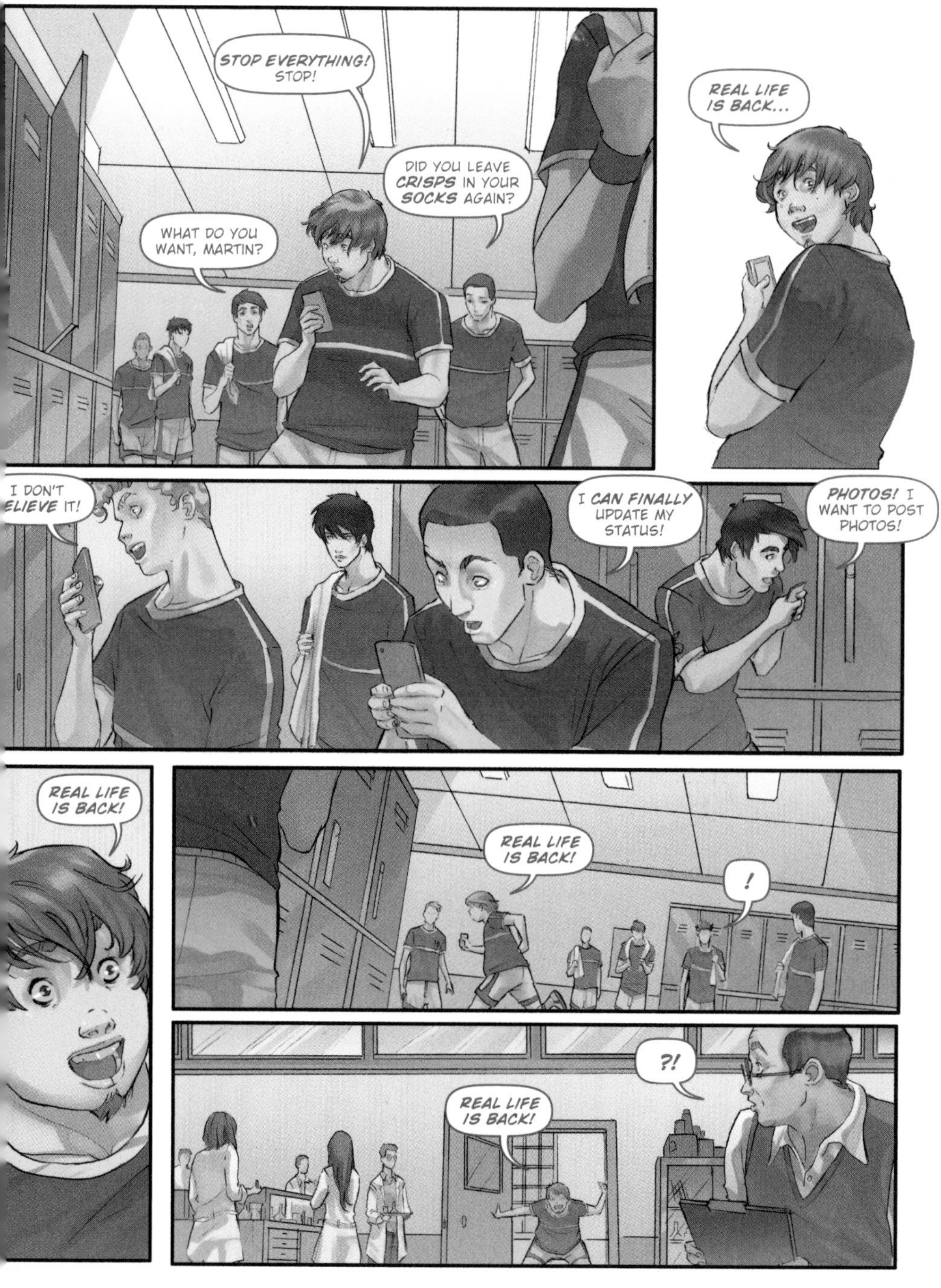
STOP EVERYTHING! STOP!
DID YOU LEAVE CRISPS IN YOUR SOCKS AGAIN?
WHAT DO YOU WANT, MARTIN?
REAL LIFE IS BACK...
I DON'T ELIEVE IT!
I CAN FINALLY UPDATE MY STATUS!
PHOTOS! I WANT TO POST PHOTOS!
REAL LIFE IS BACK!
REAL LIFE IS BACK!
!
?!
REAL LIFE IS BACK!

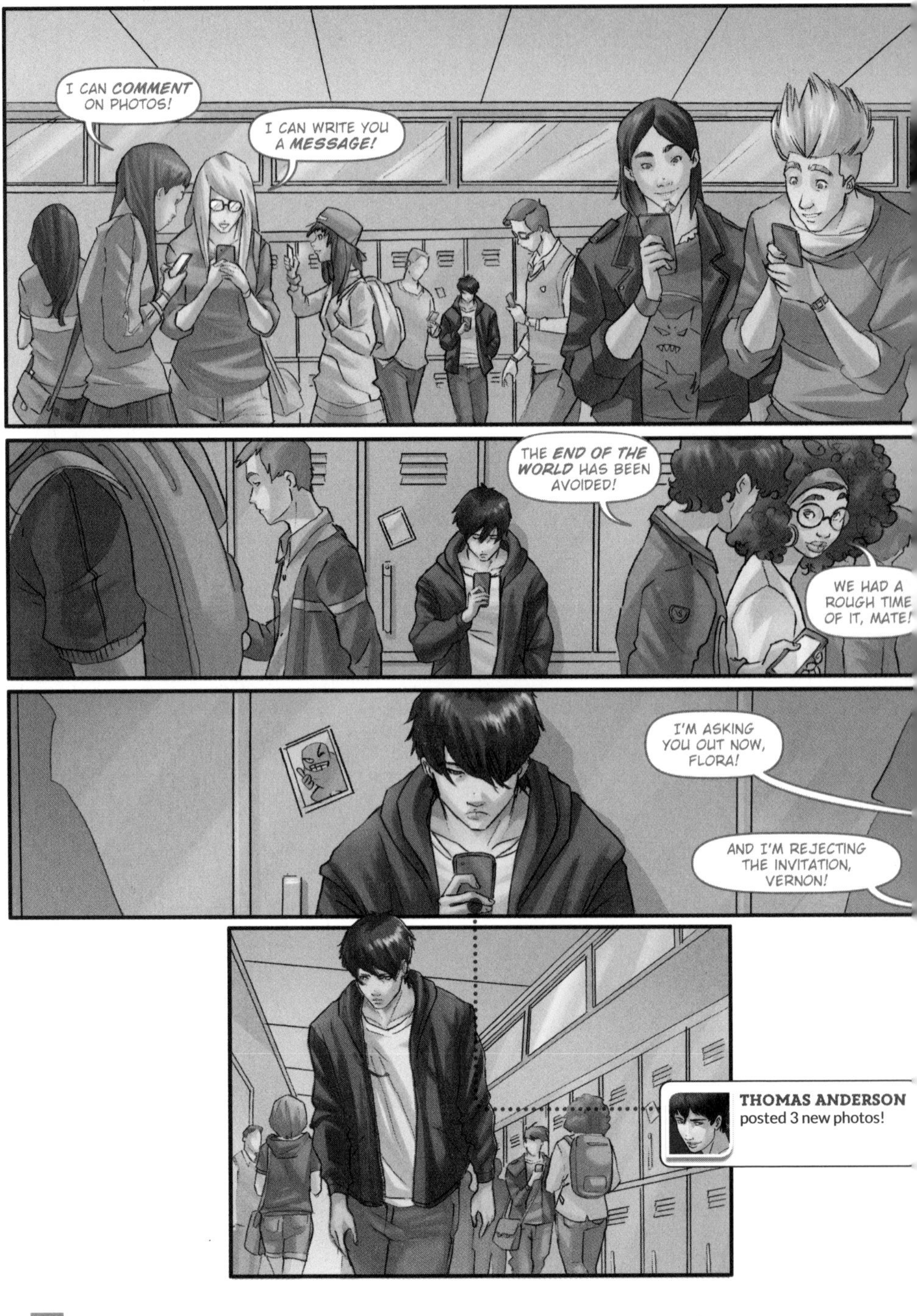

I CAN COMMENT ON PHOTOS!
I CAN WRITE YOU A MESSAGE!
THE END OF THE WORLD HAS BEEN AVOIDED!
WE HAD A ROUGH TIME OF IT, MATE!
I'M ASKING YOU OUT NOW, FLORA!
AND I'M REJECTING THE INVITATION, VERNON!
THOMAS ANDERSON
posted 3 new photos!

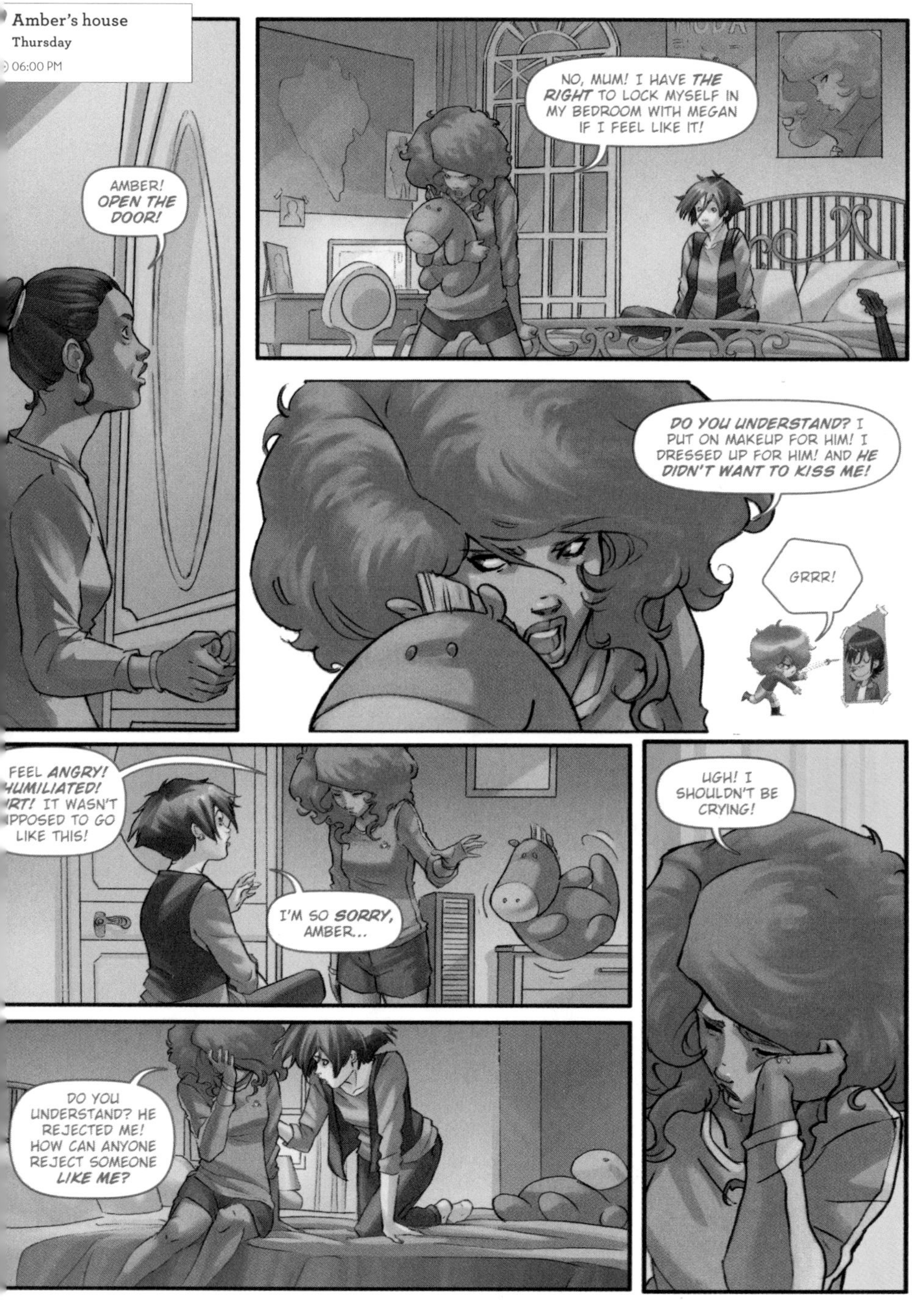
Amber's house
Thursday
06:00 PM
AMBER! OPEN THE DOOR!
NO, MUM! I HAVE THE RIGHT TO LOCK MYSELF IN MY BEDROOM WITH MEGAN IF I FEEL LIKE IT!
DO YOU UNDERSTAND? I PUT ON MAKEUP FOR HIM! I DRESSED UP FOR HIM! AND HE DIDN'T WANT TO KISS ME!
GRRR!
FEEL ANGRY! HUMILIATED! RT! IT WASN'T PPOSED TO GO LIKE THIS!
I'M SO SORRY, AMBER...
UGH! I SHOULDN'T BE CRYING!
DO YOU UNDERSTAND? HE REJECTED ME! HOW CAN ANYONE REJECT SOMEONE LIKE ME?

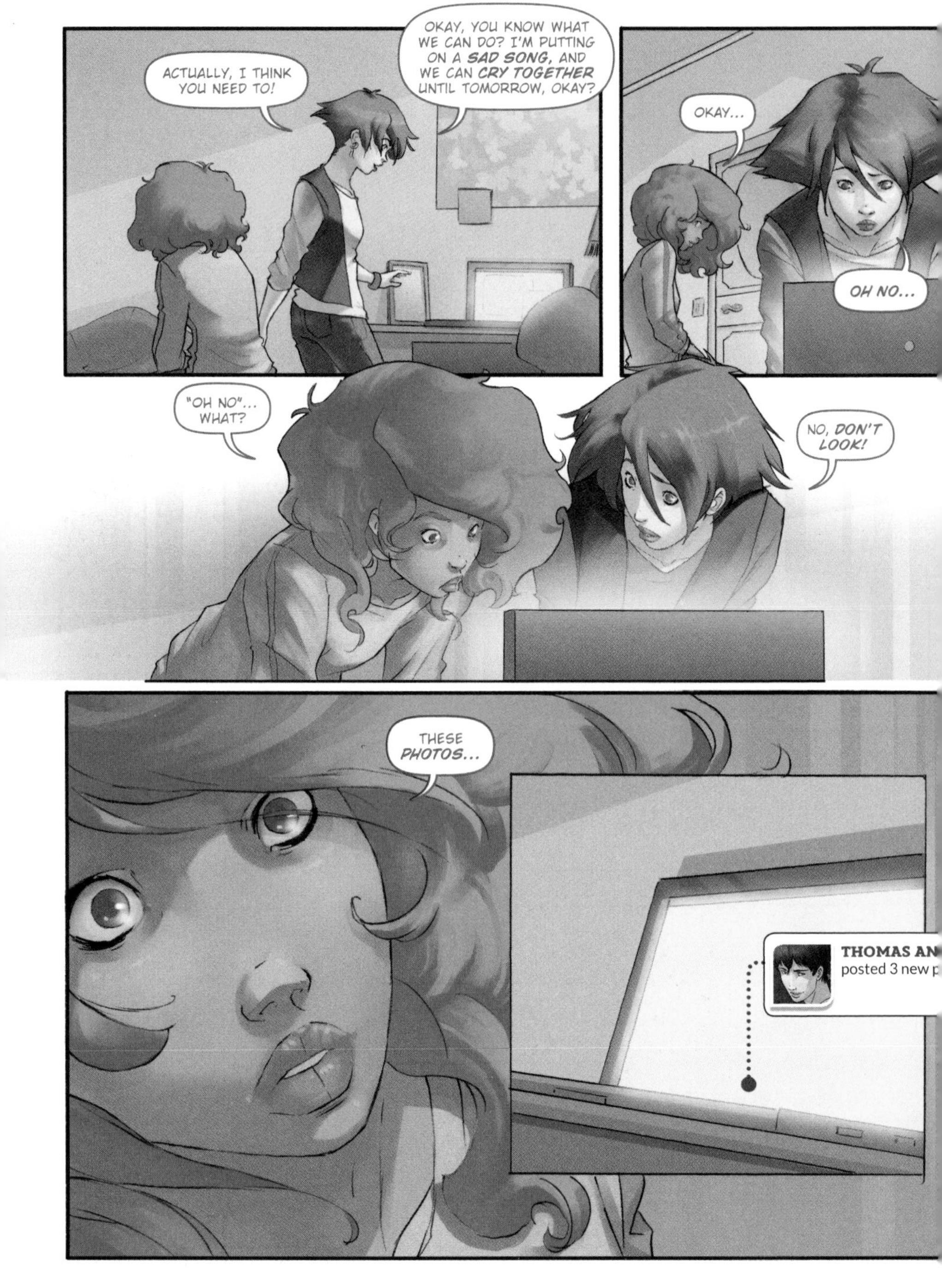
ACTUALLY, I THINK YOU NEED TO!
OKAY, YOU KNOW WHAT WE CAN DO? I'M PUTTING ON A SAD SONG, AND WE CAN CRY TOGETHER UNTIL TOMORROW, OKAY?
OKAY...
OH NO...
"OH NO"... WHAT?
NO, DON'T LOOK!
THESE PHOTOS...
THOMAS AN
posted 3 new p

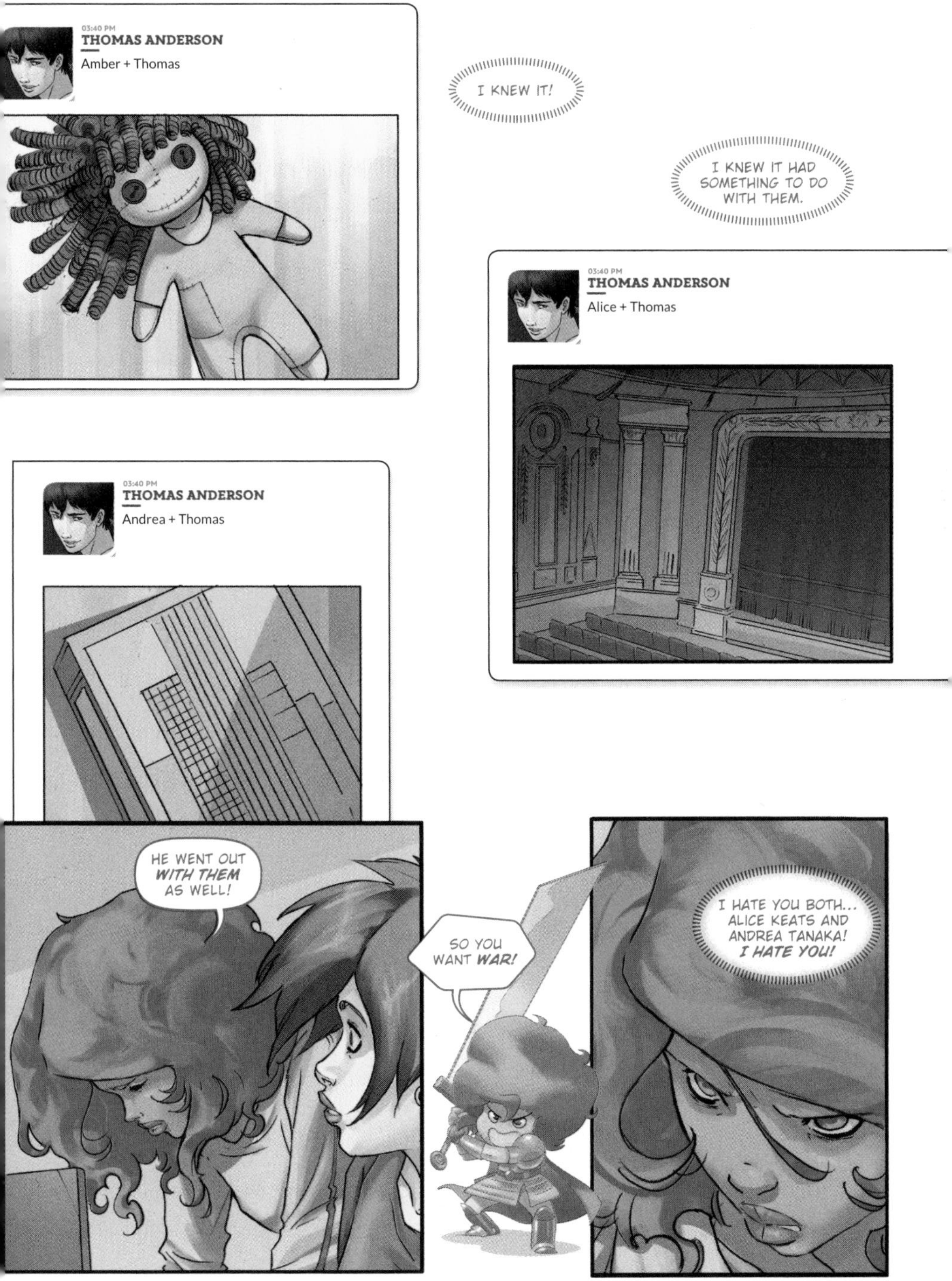
03:40 PM
THOMAS ANDERSON
Amber + Thomas
I KNEW IT!
I KNEW IT HAD SOMETHING TO DO WITH THEM.
03:40 PM
THOMAS ANDERSON
Alice + Thomas
03:40 PM
THOMAS ANDERSON
Andrea + Thomas
HE WENT OUT WITH THEM AS WELL!
SO YOU WANT WAR!
I HATE YOU BOTH... ALICE KEATS AND ANDREA TANAKA! I HATE YOU!

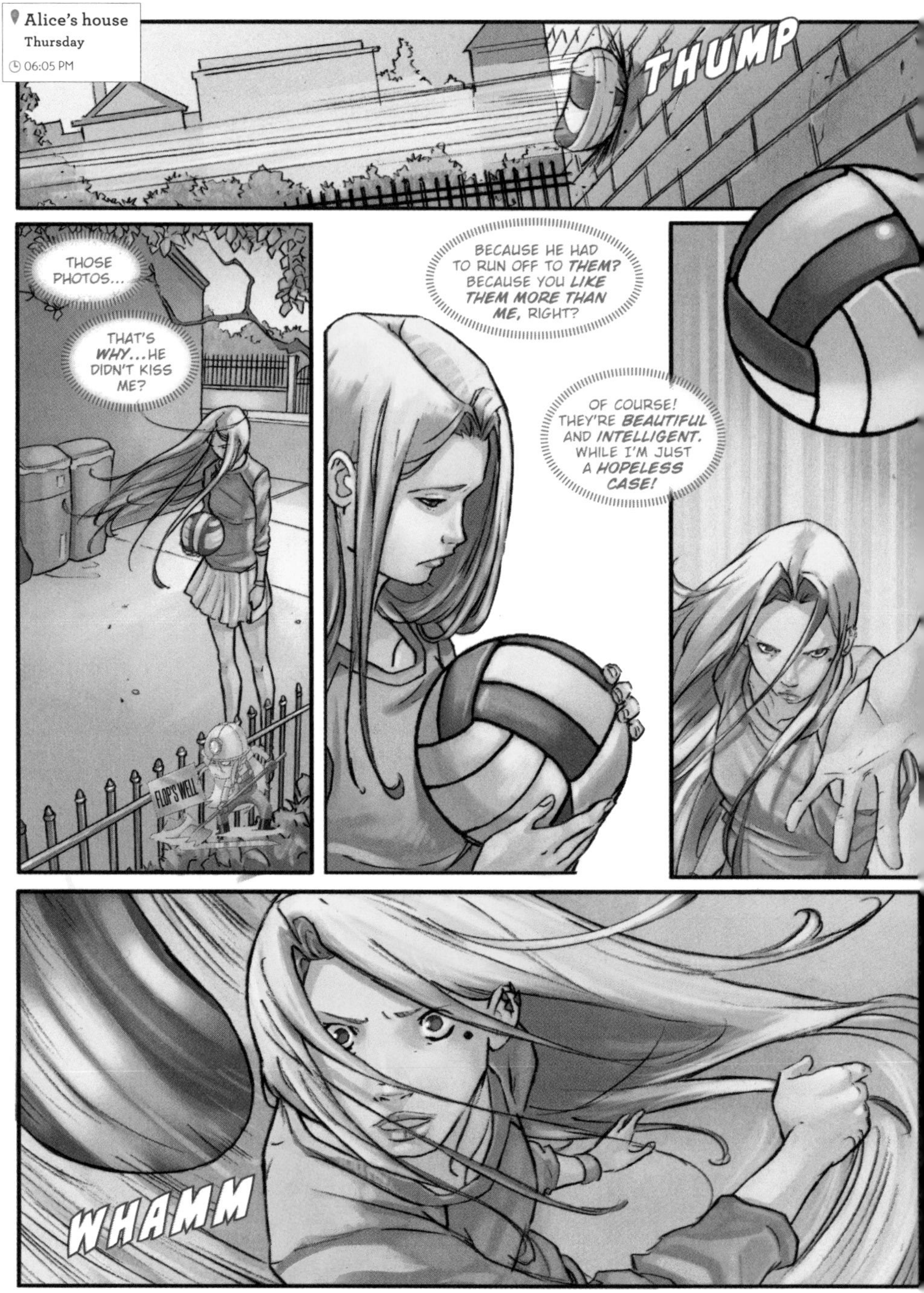
Alice's house
Thursday
06:05 PM
THUMP
THOSE PHOTOS...
THAT'S WHY...HE DIDN'T KISS ME?
FLOP'S WELL
BECAUSE HE HAD TO RUN OFF TO THEM? BECAUSE YOU LIKE THEM MORE THAN ME, RIGHT?
OF COURSE! THEY'RE BEAUTIFUL AND INTELLIGENT. WHILE I'M JUST A HOPELESS CASE!
WHAMM

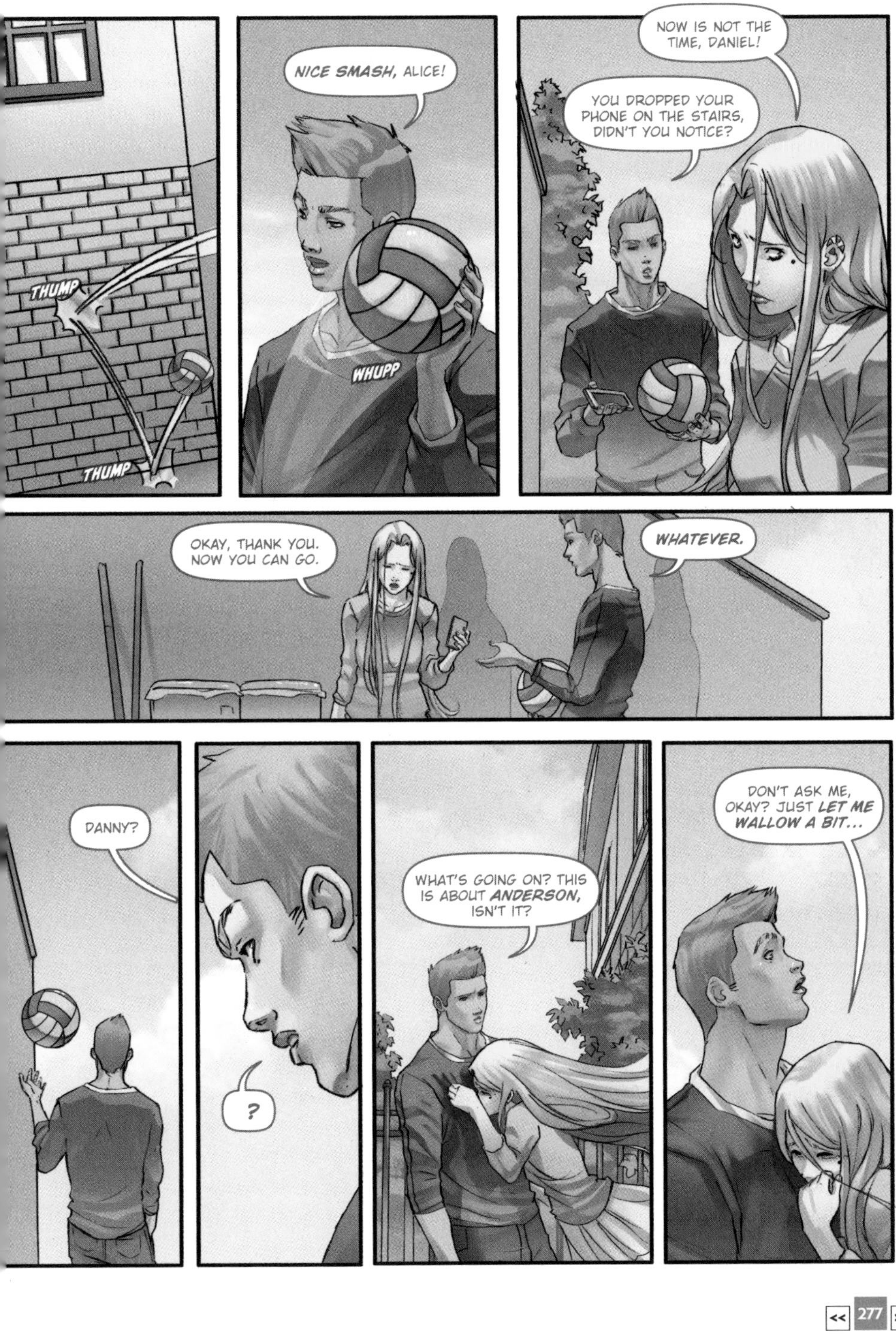
THUMP
THUMP
NICE SMASH, ALICE!
WHUPP
NOW IS NOT THE TIME, DANIEL!
YOU DROPPED YOUR PHONE ON THE STAIRS, DIDN'T YOU NOTICE?
OKAY, THANK YOU. NOW YOU CAN GO.
WHATEVER.
DANNY?
?
WHAT'S GOING ON? THIS IS ABOUT ANDERSON, ISN'T IT?
DON'T ASK ME, OKAY? JUST LET ME WALLOW A BIT...

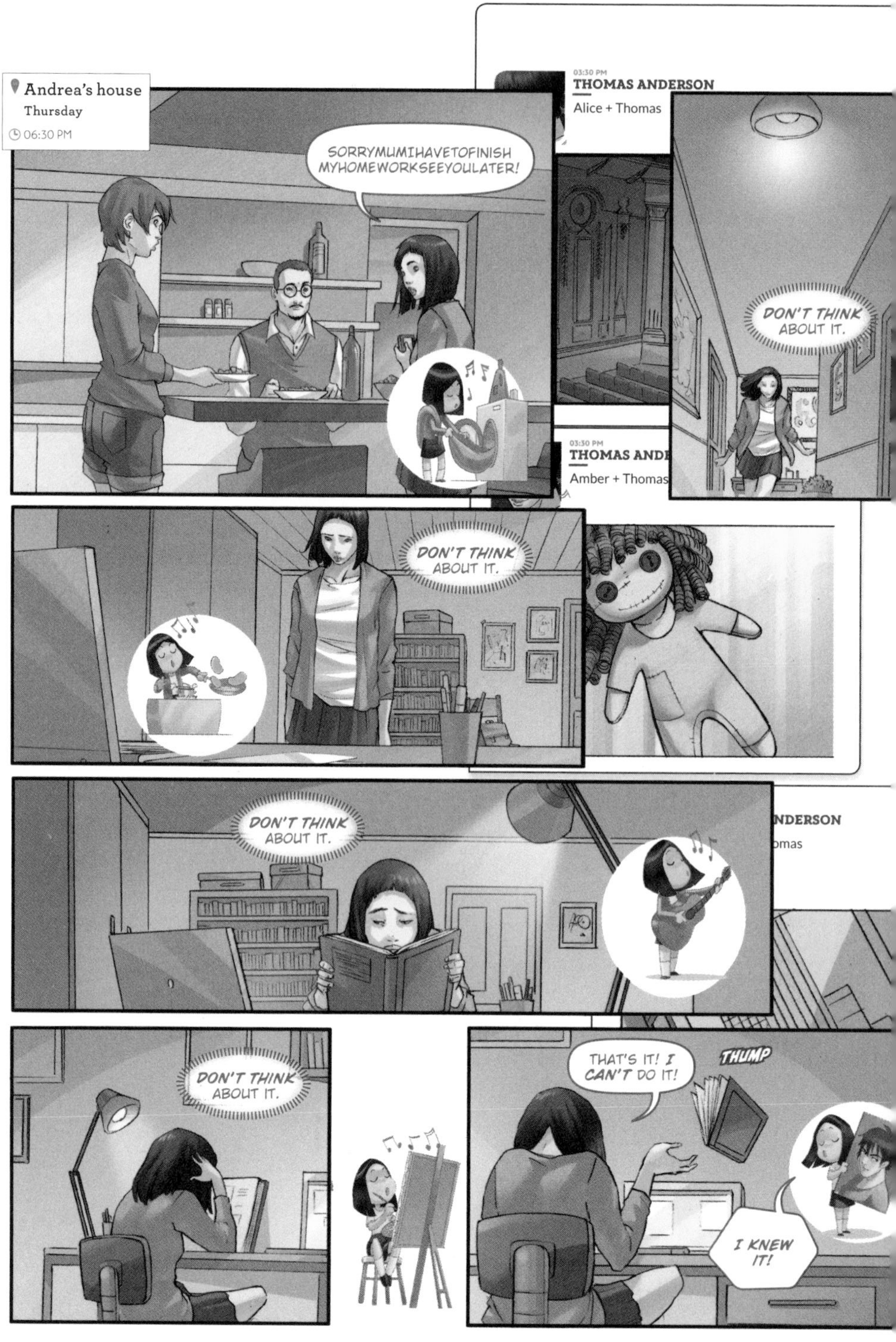
Andrea's house
Thursday
06:30 PM
SORRYMUMIHAVETOFINISH MYHOMEWORKSEEYOULATER!
03:30 PM
THOMAS ANDERSON
Alice + Thomas
03:30 PM
THOMAS ANDE
Amber + Thomas
DON'T THINK ABOUT IT.
DON'T THINK ABOUT IT.
DON'T THINK ABOUT IT.
NDERSON
omas
DON'T THINK ABOUT IT.
THAT'S IT! I CAN'T DO IT!
THUMP
I KNEW IT!

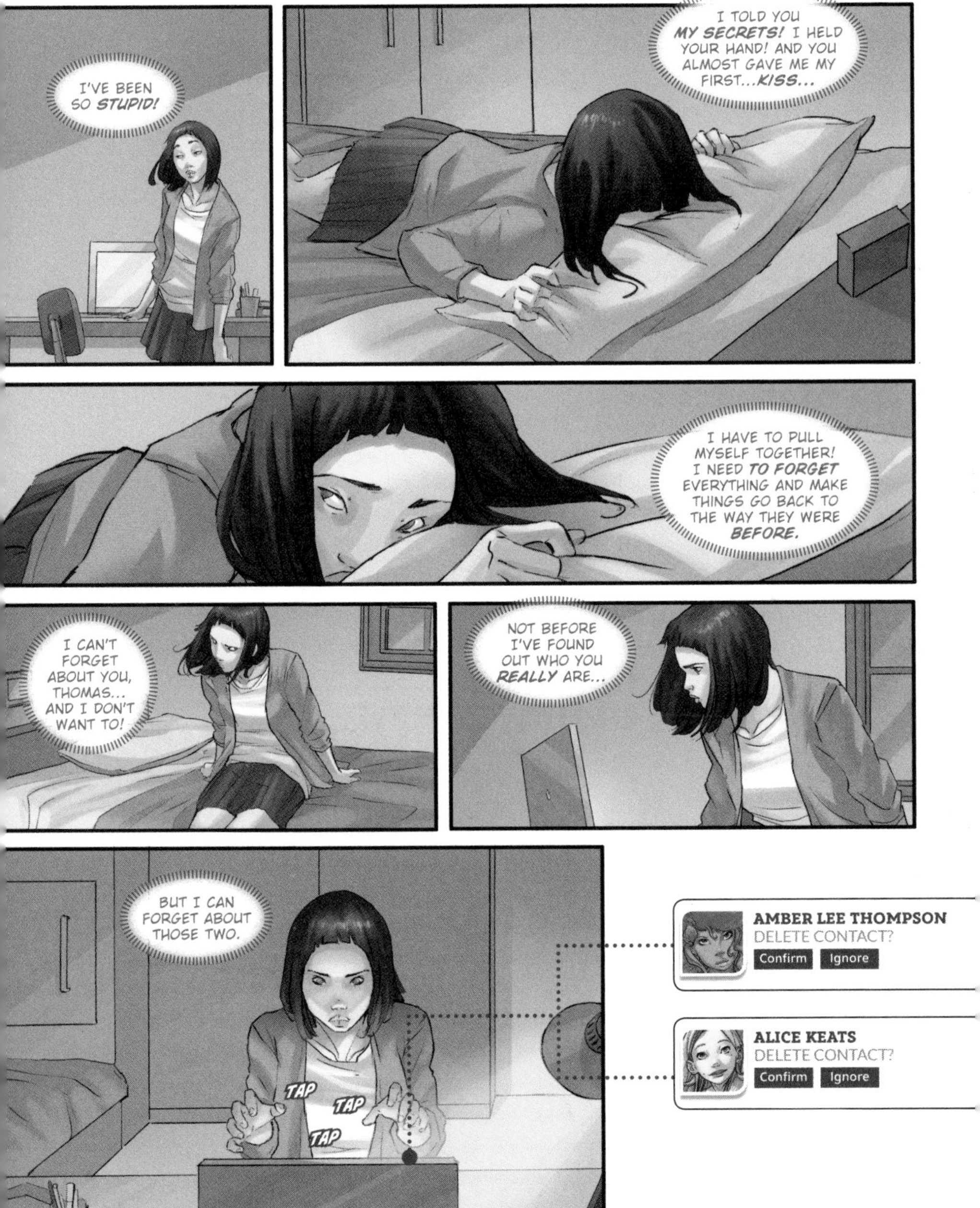
I'VE BEEN SO STUPID!
I TOLD YOU MY SECRETS! I HELD YOUR HAND! AND YOU ALMOST GAVE ME MY FIRST...KISS...
I HAVE TO PULL MYSELF TOGETHER! I NEED TO FORGET EVERYTHING AND MAKE THINGS GO BACK TO THE WAY THEY WERE BEFORE.
I CAN'T FORGET ABOUT YOU, THOMAS... AND I DON'T WANT TO!
NOT BEFORE I'VE FOUND OUT WHO YOU REALLY ARE...
BUT I CAN FORGET ABOUT THOSE TWO.
TAP
TAP
TAP
AMBER LEE THOMPSON
DELETE CONTACT?
Confirm Ignore
ALICE KEATS
DELETE CONTACT?
Confirm Ignore

END OF CHAPTER 15

#I'm Sorry I Can't

Script: Alessandro Ferrari
Layout: Simone Buonfantino, Elena Pianta, and Alberto Zanon
Cleanup: Elena Pianta and Alberto Zanon
Emotidolls: Andrea Scoppetta
Color: Massimo Rocca, Pierluigi Casolino, Andrea Scoppetta, Mario Perrotta, Slava Panarin, Giuseppe Fontana, Gianluca Barone
Watercolor backgrounds: Valeria Turati
Translation: Edizioni BD and Erin Brady
Lettering and Infographic: Edizioni BD

COVER
Layout and cleanup: Alberto Zanon
Color: Slava Panarin

CONTRIBUTORS
Tomatofarm

Original project developed by Disney Publishing with the contribution of Barbara Baraldi, Paola Barbato, Micol Beltramini and Diana Tomatozombie

#6 #Together or Not?

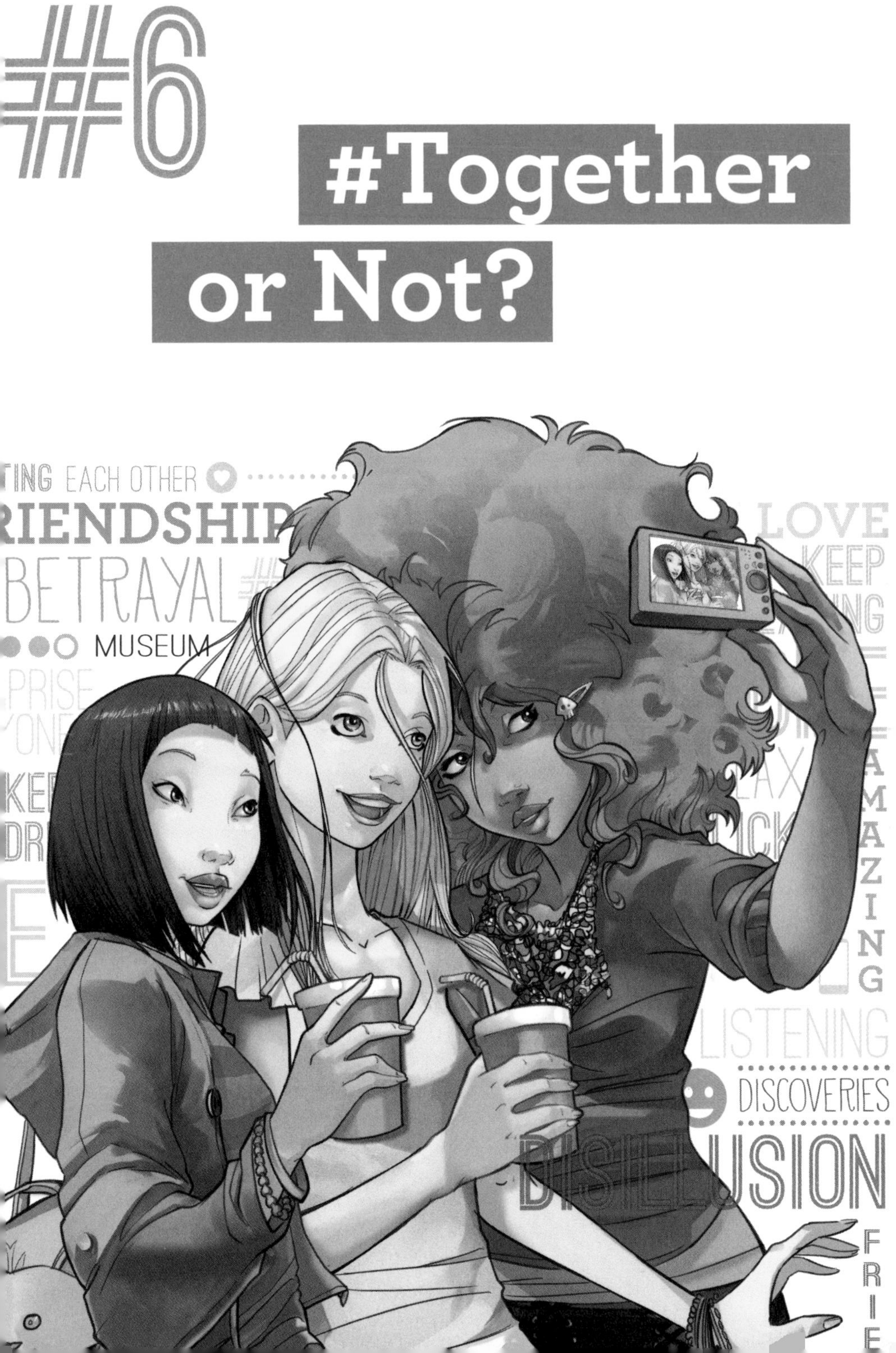
EACH OTHER
BETRAYAL
MUSEUM
LOVE
KEEP
AMAZING
LISTENING
DISCOVERIES
DISILLUSION

CHAPTER 16

a DAY at the MUSEUM

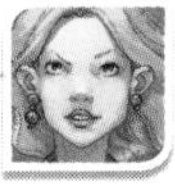

09:00 AM
JESS BAGLEY
Field triiiip!!! So happy!!!
#bestmondayever #noschool

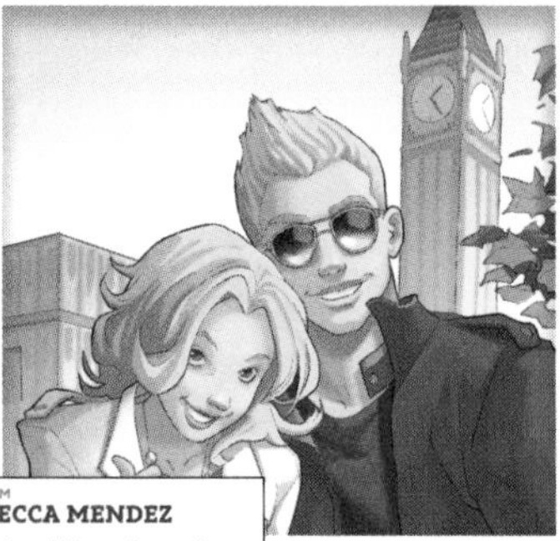

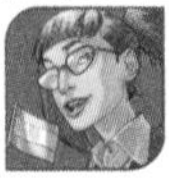

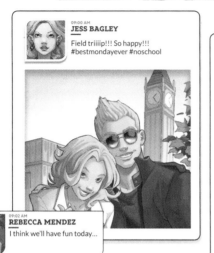

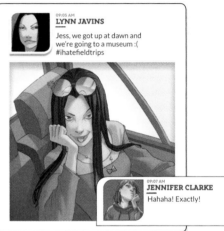

09:02 AM
REBECCA MENDEZ
I think we'll have fun today...

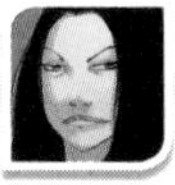

09:05 AM
LYNN JAVINS
Jess, we got up at dawn and we're going to a museum :(
#ihatefieldtrips

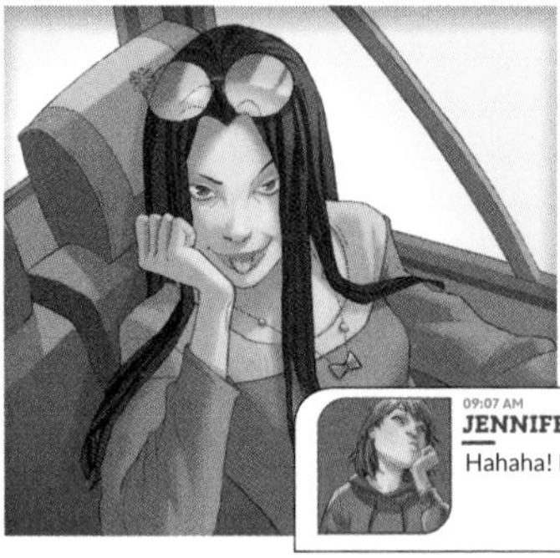

09:07 AM
JENNIFER CLARKE
Hahaha! Exactly!

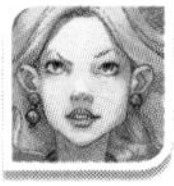

09:12 AM
JESS BAGLEY
Natural History Museum! :)))
No class today!

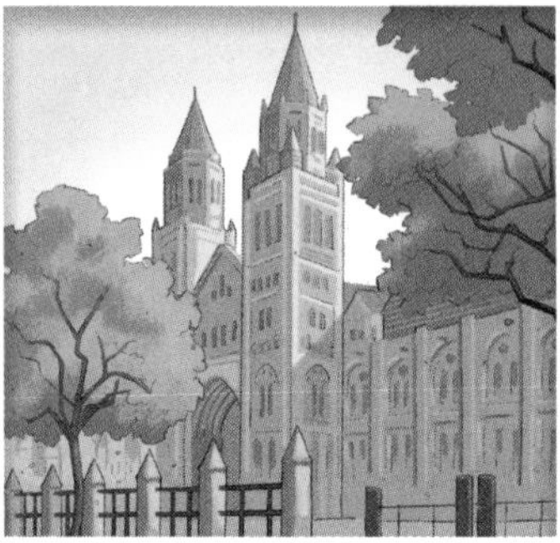

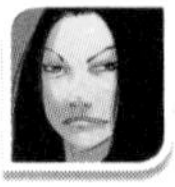

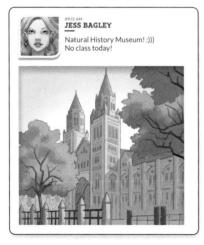

09:15 AM
LYNN JAVINS
That's why there's the party tonight!

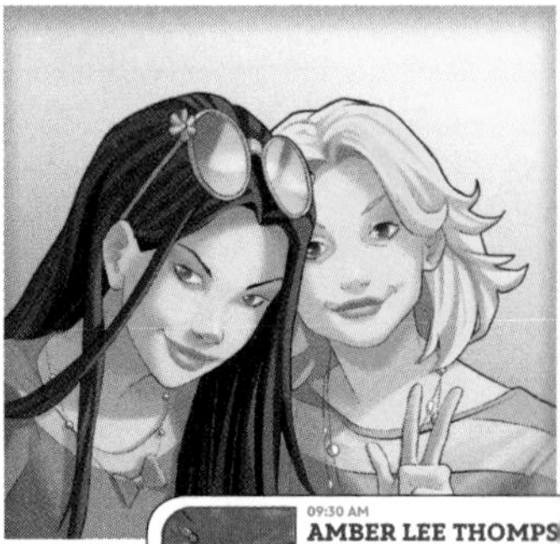

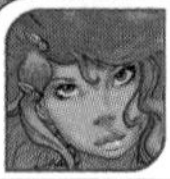

09:30 AM
AMBER LEE THOMPS
Party?

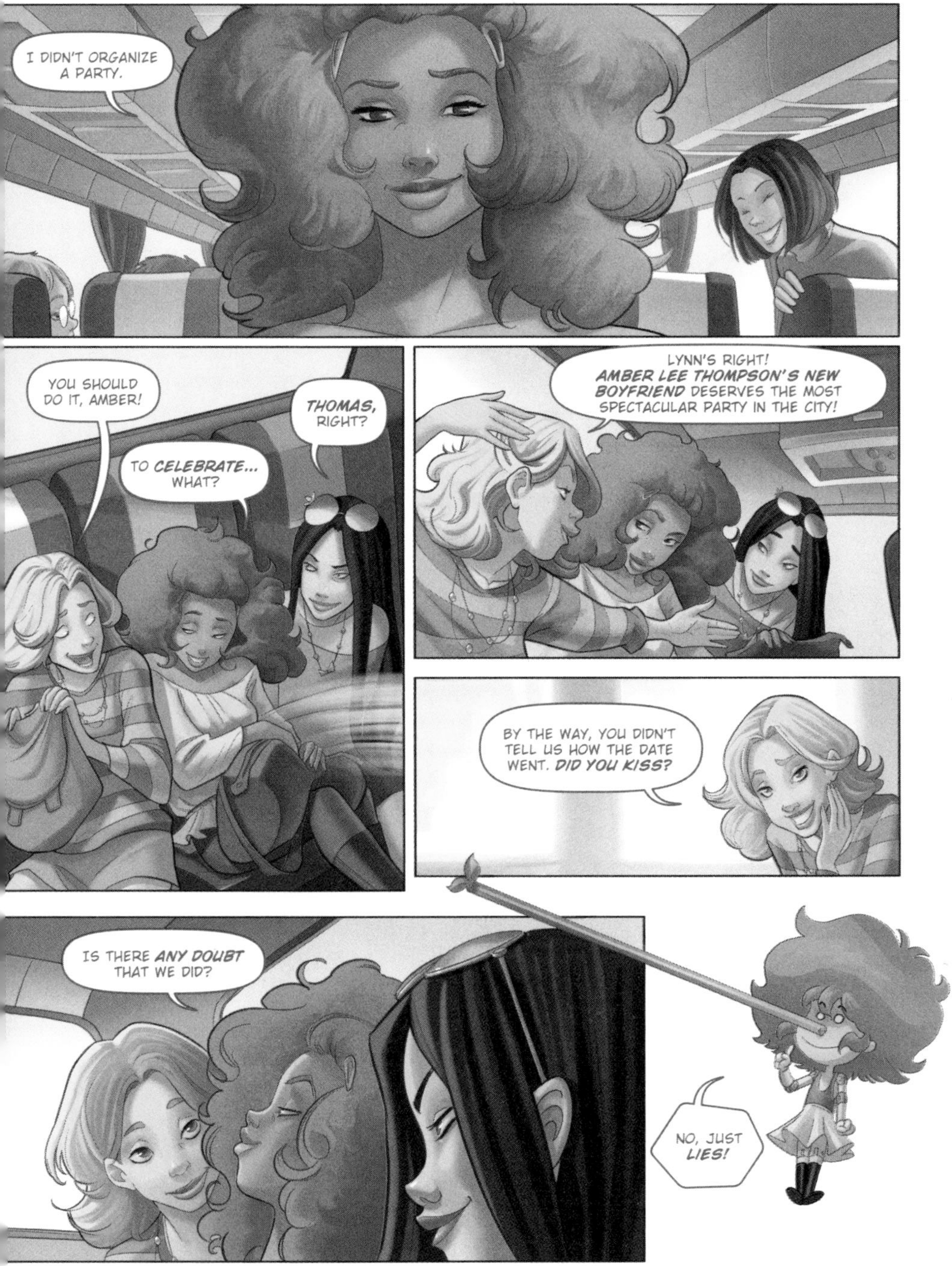
I DIDN'T ORGANIZE A PARTY.
YOU SHOULD DO IT, AMBER!
TO CELEBRATE... WHAT?
THOMAS, RIGHT?
LYNN'S RIGHT! AMBER LEE THOMPSON'S NEW BOYFRIEND DESERVES THE MOST SPECTACULAR PARTY IN THE CITY!
BY THE WAY, YOU DIDN'T TELL US HOW THE DATE WENT. DID YOU KISS?
IS THERE ANY DOUBT THAT WE DID?
NO, JUST LIES!

WE WERE SITTING ON A BENCH IN HYDE PARK...

DIDN'T YOU SAY THAT *IT WAS RAINING?*

HMM...YES. BUT THOMAS WAS COVERING US WITH *HIS UMBRELLA!*

OH, *HOW ROMANTIC!*

COME ON, *DETAILS!* WHAT DID HE SAY TO YOU?

HE WANTS US *TO GET TOGETHER.* OBVIOUSLY, I TOLD HIM I *HAVE TO THINK ABOUT IT.*

09:35 AM
LYNN JAVINS
Do you hear her? Everyone kn Thomas went out with Tanaka Keats as well!

09:35 AM
JESS BAGLEY
Imagine being dumped for those two losers! Yuck!

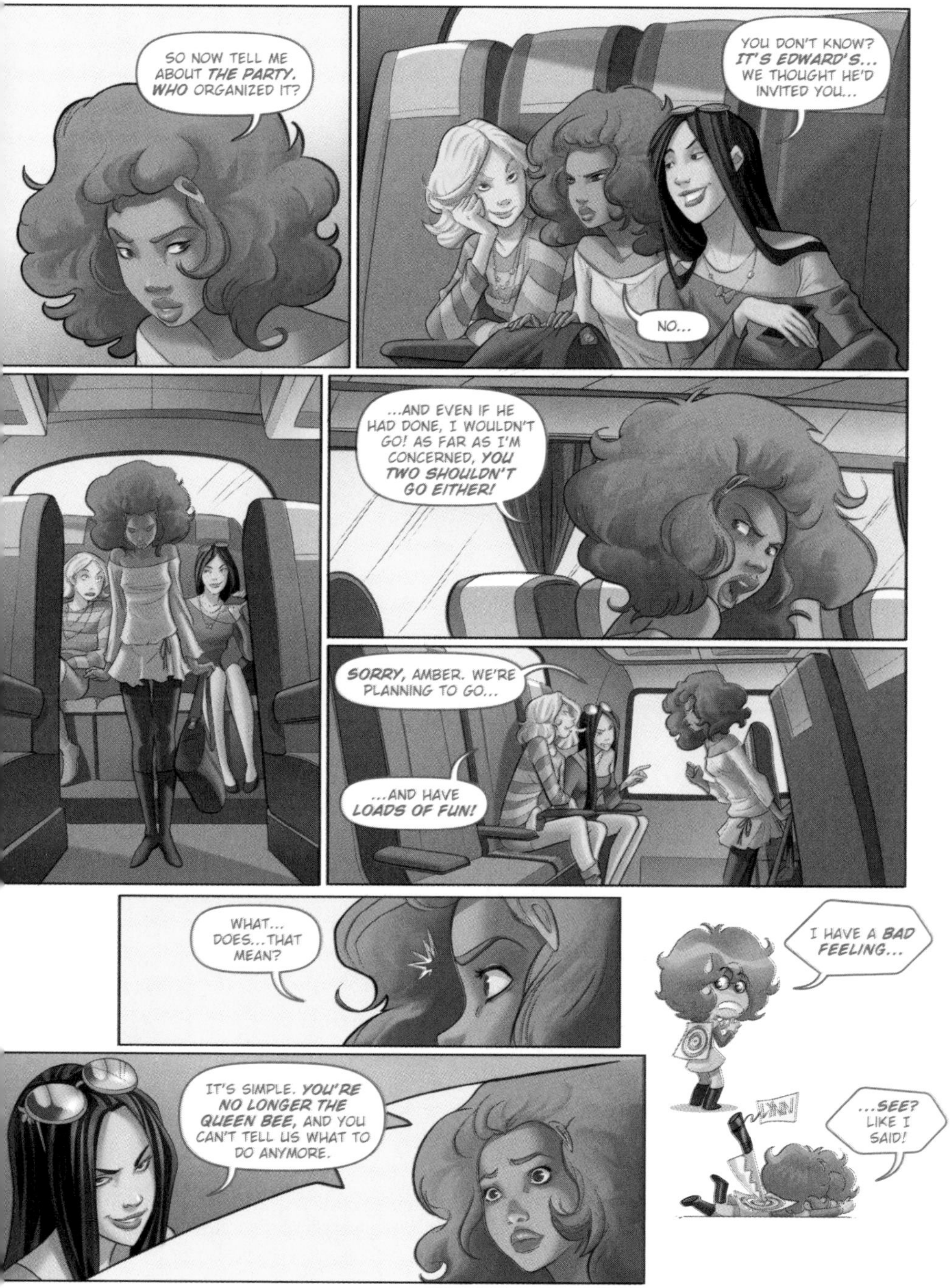
SO NOW TELL ME ABOUT THE PARTY. WHO ORGANIZED IT?
YOU DON'T KNOW? IT'S EDWARD'S... WE THOUGHT HE'D INVITED YOU...
NO...
...AND EVEN IF HE HAD DONE, I WOULDN'T GO! AS FAR AS I'M CONCERNED, YOU TWO SHOULDN'T GO EITHER!
SORRY, AMBER. WE'RE PLANNING TO GO...
...AND HAVE LOADS OF FUN!
WHAT... DOES...THAT MEAN?
IT'S SIMPLE. YOU'RE NO LONGER THE QUEEN BEE, AND YOU CAN'T TELL US WHAT TO DO ANYMORE.
I HAVE A BAD FEELING...
...SEE? LIKE I SAID!

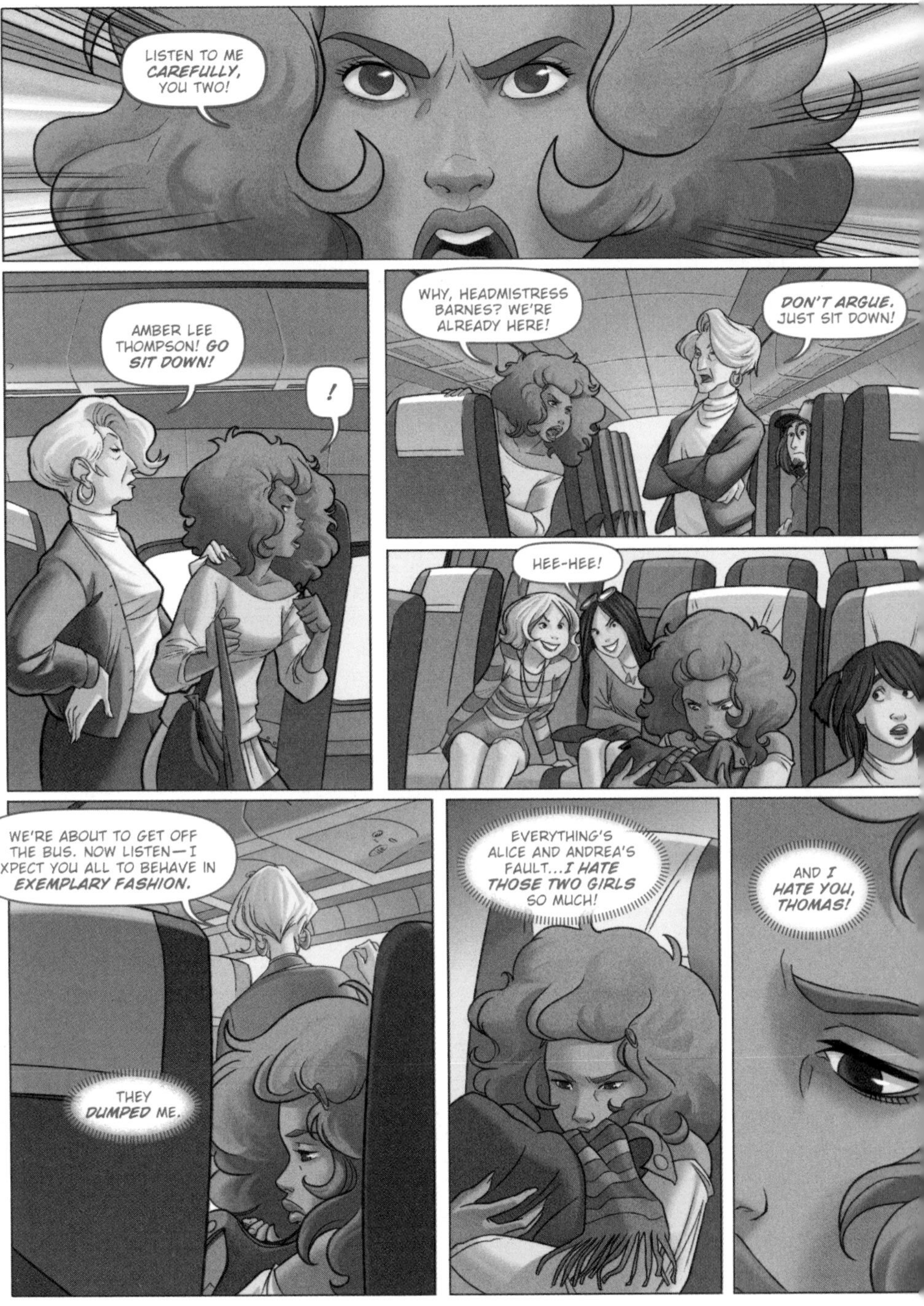
LISTEN TO ME CAREFULLY, YOU TWO!
AMBER LEE THOMPSON! GO SIT DOWN!
!
WHY, HEADMISTRESS BARNES? WE'RE ALREADY HERE!
DON'T ARGUE. JUST SIT DOWN!
HEE-HEE!
WE'RE ABOUT TO GET OFF THE BUS. NOW LISTEN—I EXPECT YOU ALL TO BEHAVE IN EXEMPLARY FASHION.
THEY DUMPED ME.
EVERYTHING'S ALICE AND ANDREA'S FAULT...I HATE THOSE TWO GIRLS SO MUCH!
AND I HATE YOU, THOMAS!

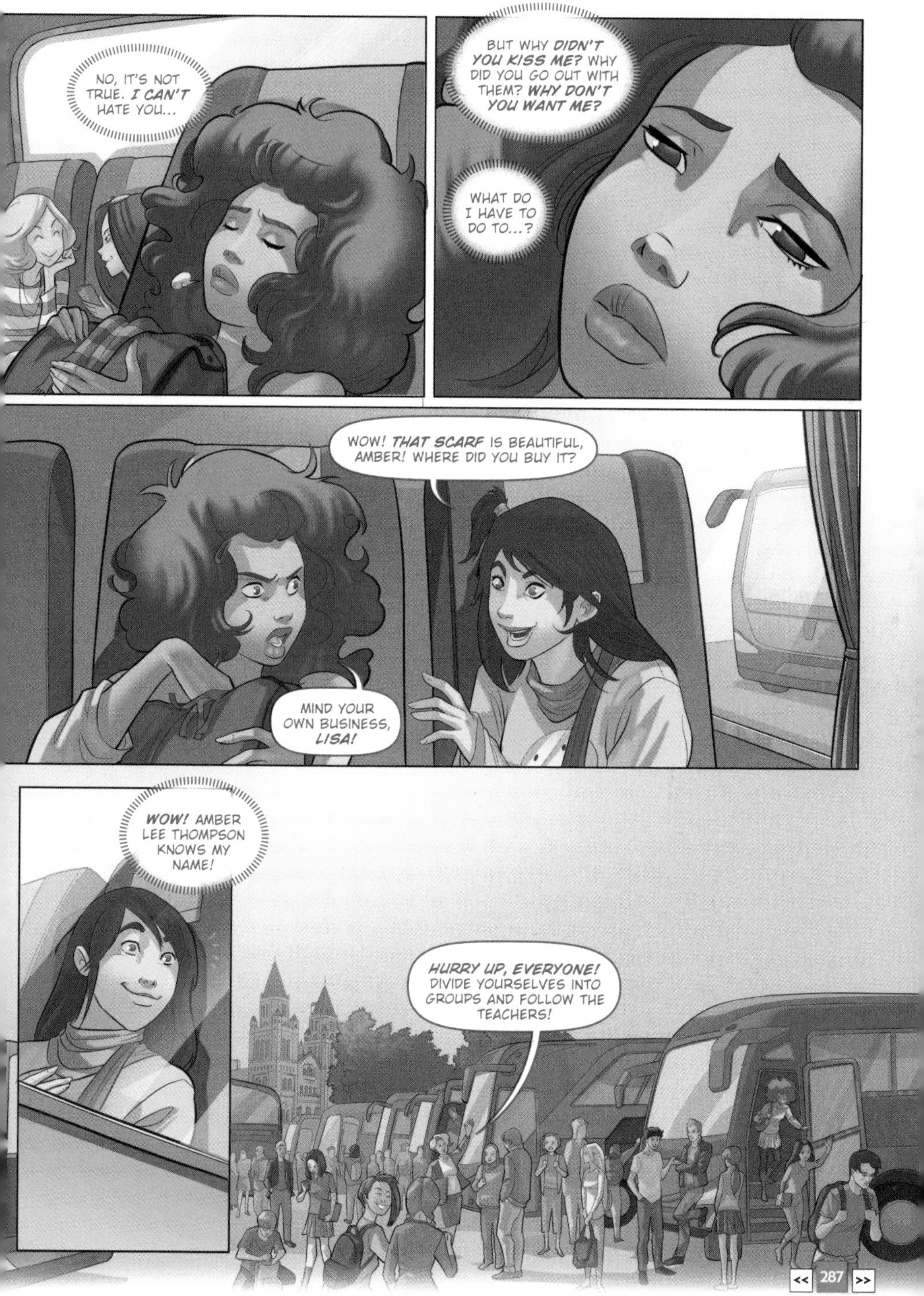
NO, IT'S NOT TRUE. I CAN'T HATE YOU...
BUT WHY DIDN'T YOU KISS ME? WHY DID YOU GO OUT WITH THEM? WHY DON'T YOU WANT ME?
WHAT DO I HAVE TO DO TO...?
WOW! THAT SCARF IS BEAUTIFUL, AMBER! WHERE DID YOU BUY IT?
MIND YOUR OWN BUSINESS, LISA!
WOW! AMBER LEE THOMPSON KNOWS MY NAME!
HURRY UP, EVERYONE! DIVIDE YOURSELVES INTO GROUPS AND FOLLOW THE TEACHERS!

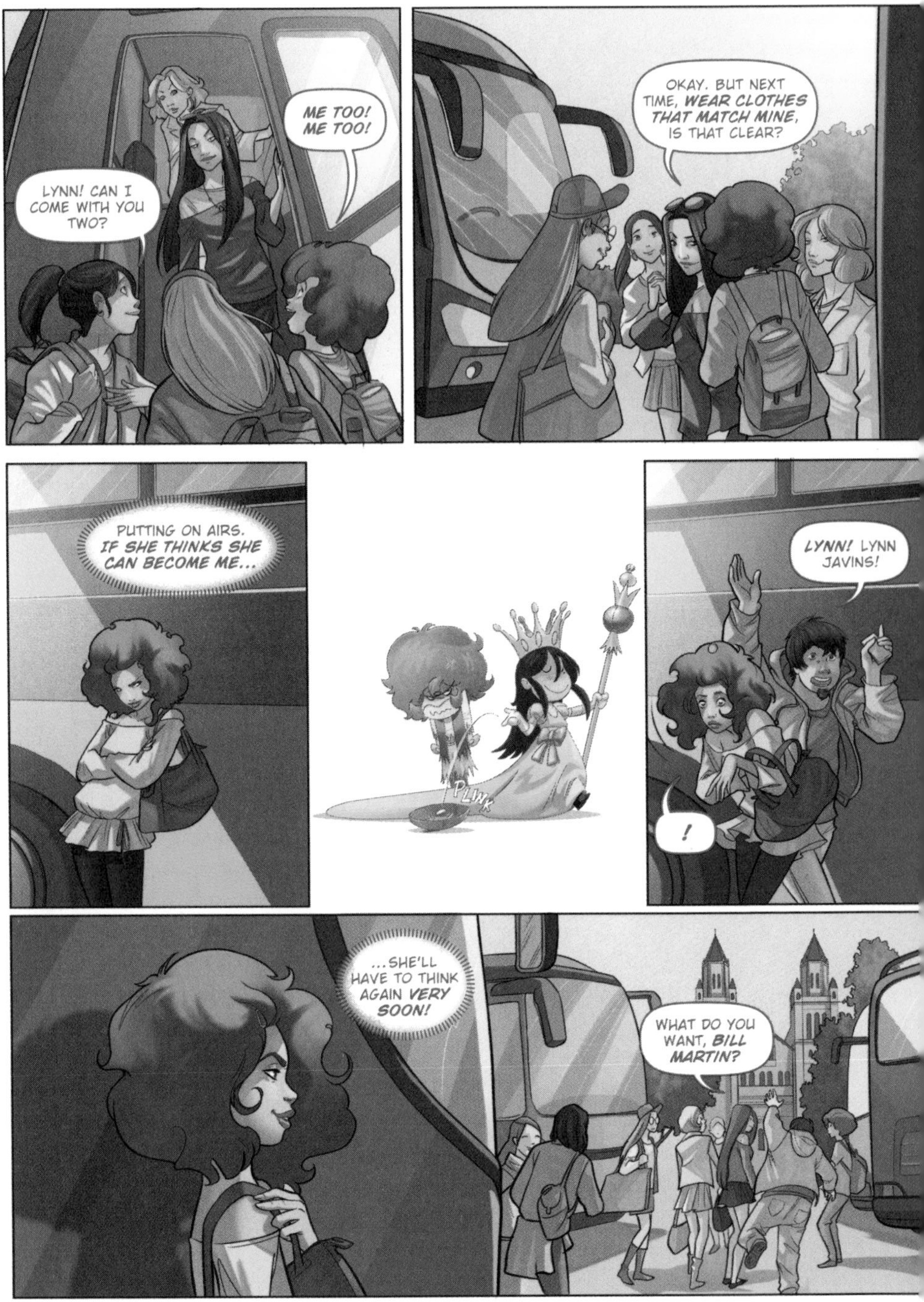
ME TOO! ME TOO!
LYNN! CAN I COME WITH YOU TWO?
OKAY. BUT NEXT TIME, WEAR CLOTHES THAT MATCH MINE, IS THAT CLEAR?
PUTTING ON AIRS. IF SHE THINKS SHE CAN BECOME ME...
PLWK
LYNN! LYNN JAVINS!
!
...SHE'LL HAVE TO THINK AGAIN VERY SOON!
WHAT DO YOU WANT, BILL MARTIN?

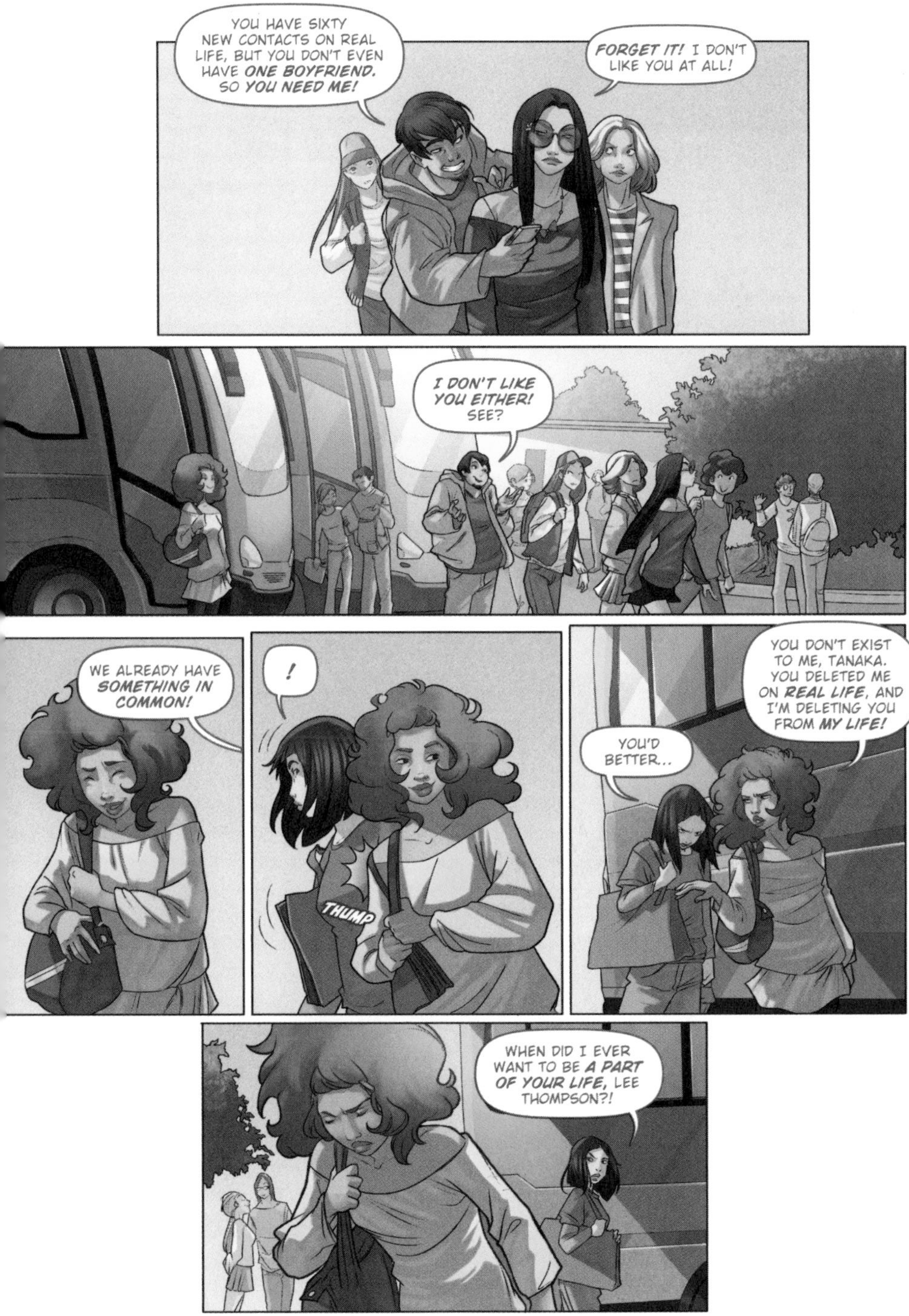
YOU HAVE SIXTY NEW CONTACTS ON REAL LIFE, BUT YOU DON'T EVEN HAVE ONE BOYFRIEND. SO YOU NEED ME!
FORGET IT! I DON'T LIKE YOU AT ALL!
I DON'T LIKE YOU EITHER! SEE?
WE ALREADY HAVE SOMETHING IN COMMON!
!
THUMP
YOU DON'T EXIST TO ME, TANAKA. YOU DELETED ME ON REAL LIFE, AND I'M DELETING YOU FROM MY LIFE!
YOU'D BETTER...
WHEN DID I EVER WANT TO BE A PART OF YOUR LIFE, LEE THOMPSON?!

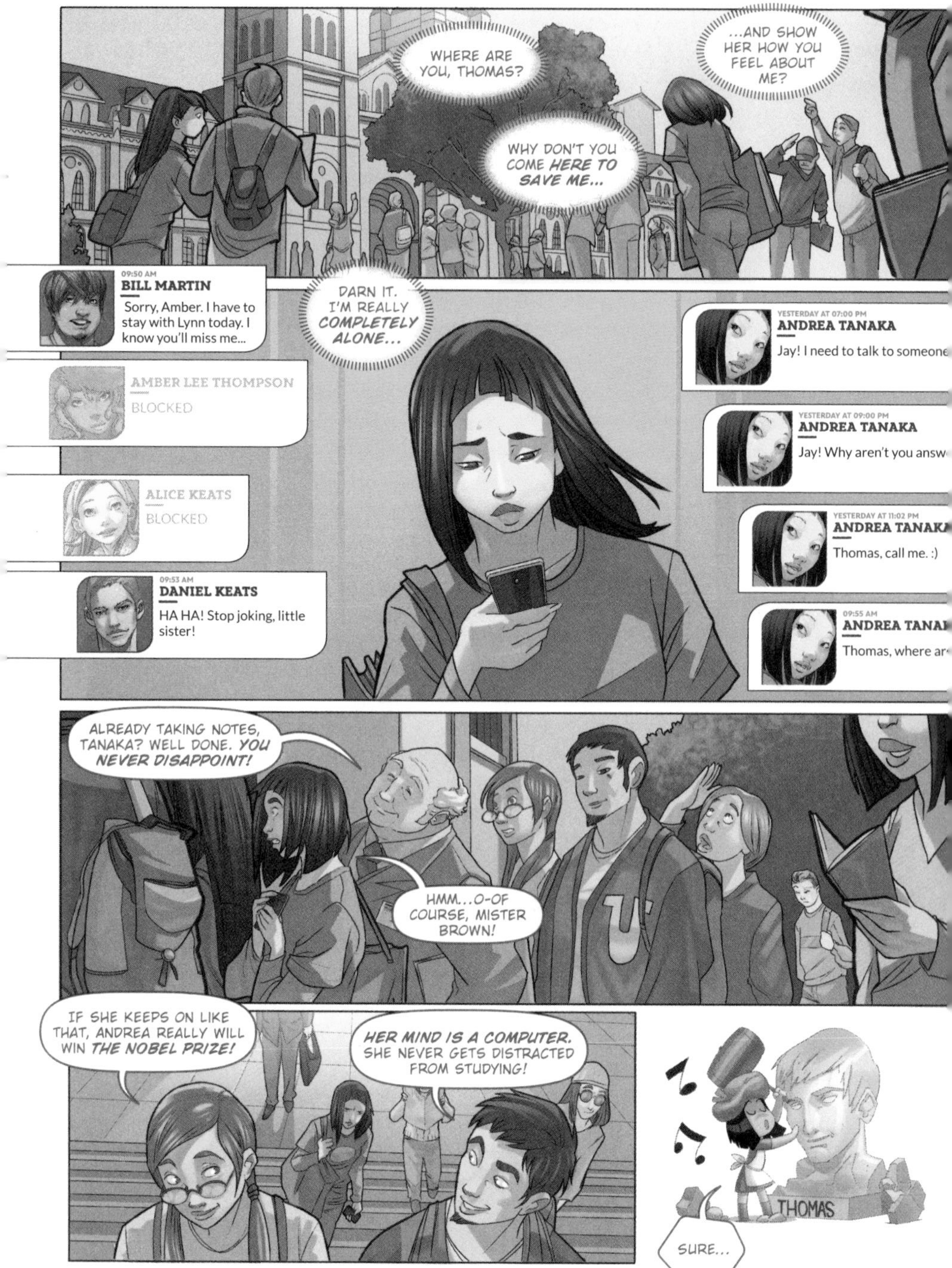
WHERE ARE YOU, THOMAS?
WHY DON'T YOU COME HERE TO SAVE ME...
...AND SHOW HER HOW YOU FEEL ABOUT ME?
09:50 AM
BILL MARTIN
Sorry, Amber. I have to stay with Lynn today. I know you'll miss me...
AMBER LEE THOMPSON
BLOCKED
ALICE KEATS
BLOCKED
09:53 AM
DANIEL KEATS
HA HA! Stop joking, little sister!
DARN IT. I'M REALLY COMPLETELY ALONE...
YESTERDAY AT 07:00 PM
ANDREA TANAKA
Jay! I need to talk to someone
YESTERDAY AT 09:00 PM
ANDREA TANAKA
Jay! Why aren't you answ
YESTERDAY AT 11:02 PM
ANDREA TANAKA
Thomas, call me. :)
09:55 AM
ANDREA TANA
Thomas, where ar
ALREADY TAKING NOTES, TANAKA? WELL DONE. YOU NEVER DISAPPOINT!
HMM...O-OF COURSE, MISTER BROWN!
IF SHE KEEPS ON LIKE THAT, ANDREA REALLY WILL WIN THE NOBEL PRIZE!
HER MIND IS A COMPUTER. SHE NEVER GETS DISTRACTED FROM STUDYING!
THOMAS
SURE...

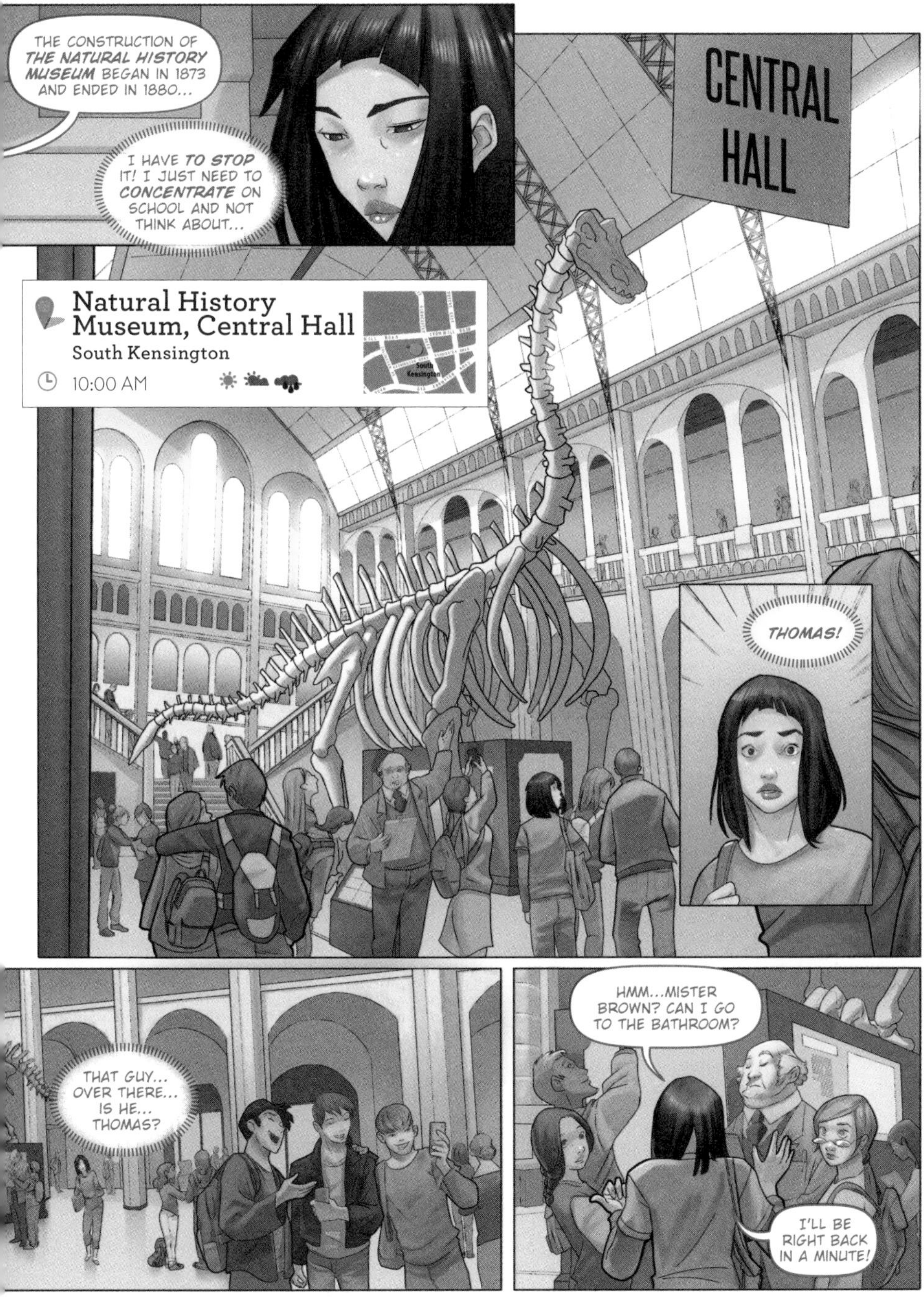
THE CONSTRUCTION OF THE NATURAL HISTORY MUSEUM BEGAN IN 1873 AND ENDED IN 1880...
I HAVE TO STOP IT! I JUST NEED TO CONCENTRATE ON SCHOOL AND NOT THINK ABOUT...
CENTRAL HALL
Natural History Museum, Central Hall
South Kensington
10:00 AM
THOMAS!
THAT GUY... OVER THERE... IS HE... THOMAS?
HMM...MISTER BROWN? CAN I GO TO THE BATHROOM?
I'LL BE RIGHT BACK IN A MINUTE!

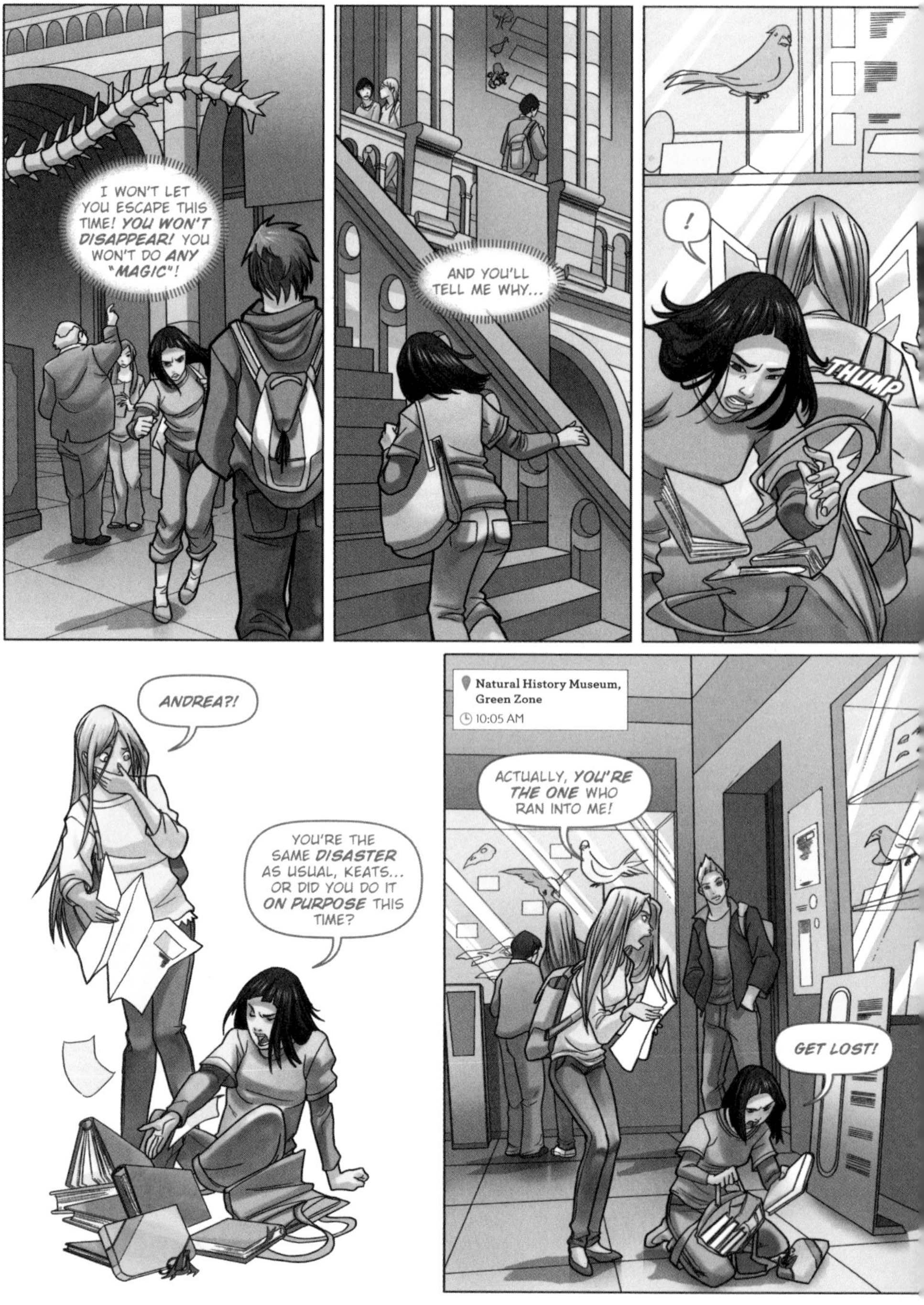
I WON'T LET YOU ESCAPE THIS TIME! YOU WON'T DISAPPEAR! YOU WON'T DO ANY "MAGIC"!
AND YOU'LL TELL ME WHY...
!
THUMP
Natural History Museum, Green Zone
10:05 AM
ANDREA?!
YOU'RE THE SAME DISASTER AS USUAL, KEATS... OR DID YOU DO IT ON PURPOSE THIS TIME?
ACTUALLY, YOU'RE THE ONE WHO RAN INTO ME!
GET LOST!

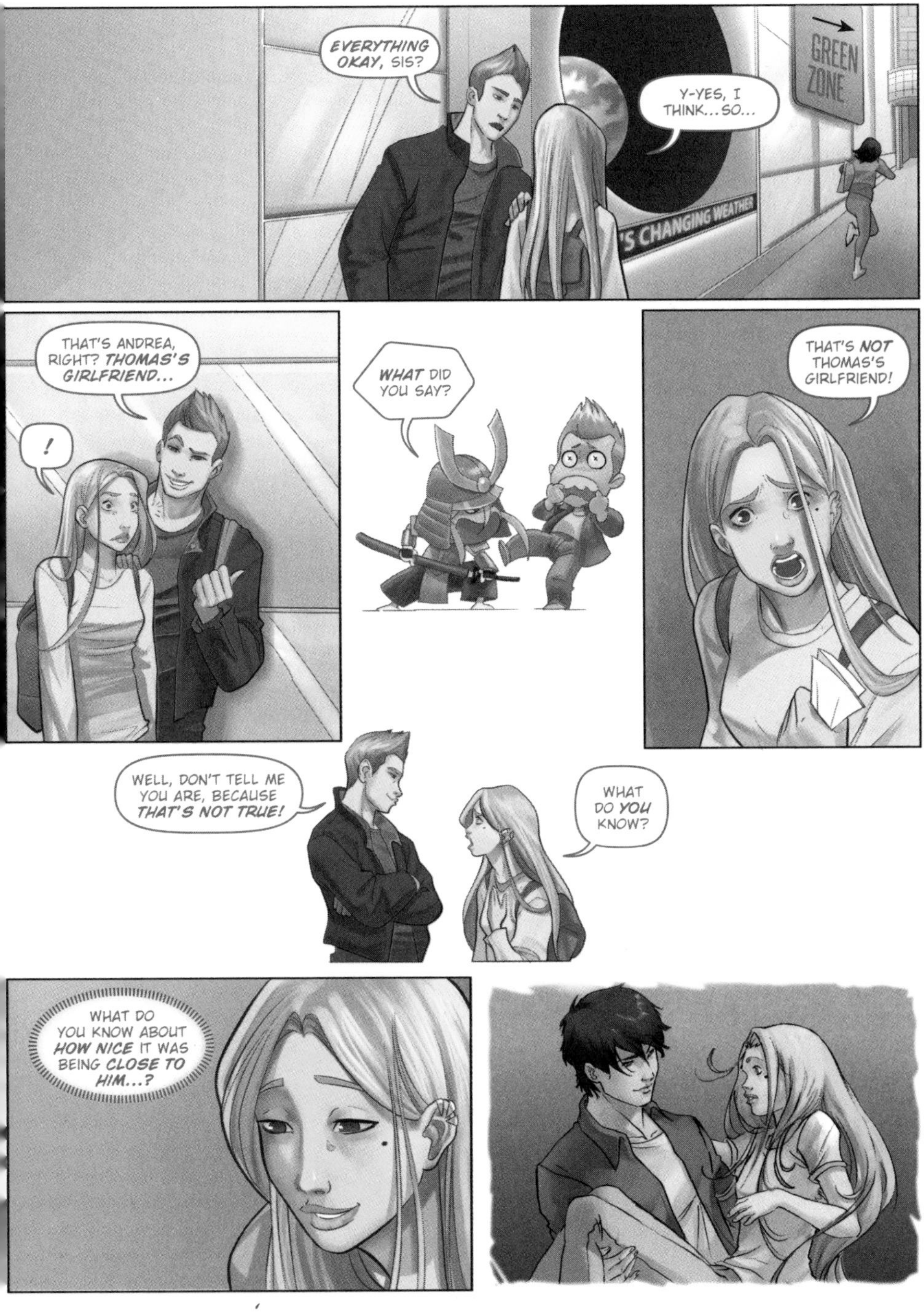
EVERYTHING OKAY, SIS?
Y-YES, I THINK... SO...
GREEN ZONE
'S CHANGING WEATHER
THAT'S ANDREA, RIGHT? THOMAS'S GIRLFRIEND...
!
WHAT DID YOU SAY?
THAT'S NOT THOMAS'S GIRLFRIEND!
WELL, DON'T TELL ME YOU ARE, BECAUSE THAT'S NOT TRUE!
WHAT DO YOU KNOW?
WHAT DO YOU KNOW ABOUT HOW NICE IT WAS BEING CLOSE TO HIM...?

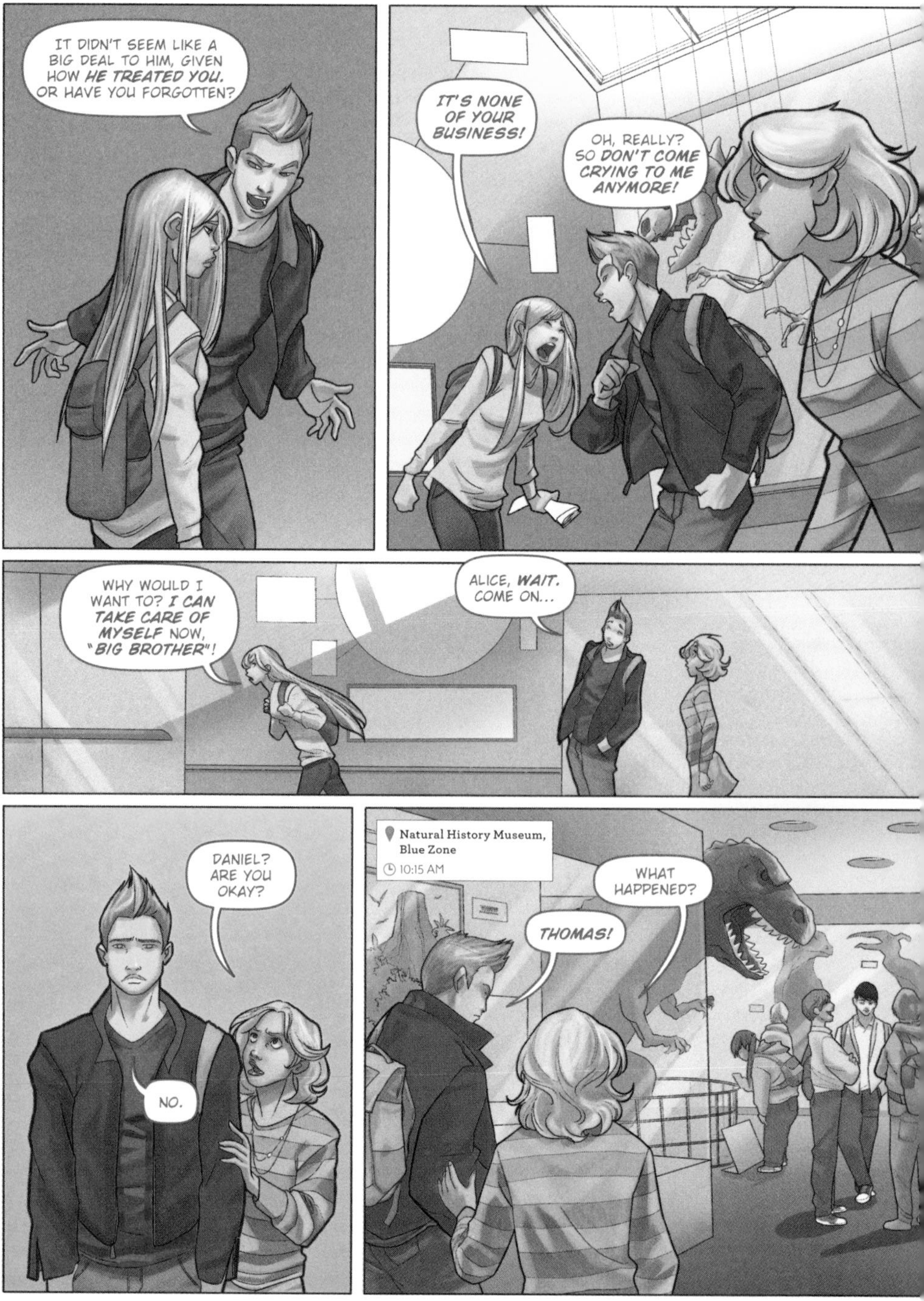
IT DIDN'T SEEM LIKE A BIG DEAL TO HIM, GIVEN HOW HE TREATED YOU. OR HAVE YOU FORGOTTEN?
IT'S NONE OF YOUR BUSINESS!
OH, REALLY? SO DON'T COME CRYING TO ME ANYMORE!
WHY WOULD I WANT TO? I CAN TAKE CARE OF MYSELF NOW, "BIG BROTHER"!
ALICE, WAIT. COME ON...
DANIEL? ARE YOU OKAY?
NO.
Natural History Museum, Blue Zone
10:15 AM
WHAT HAPPENED?
THOMAS!

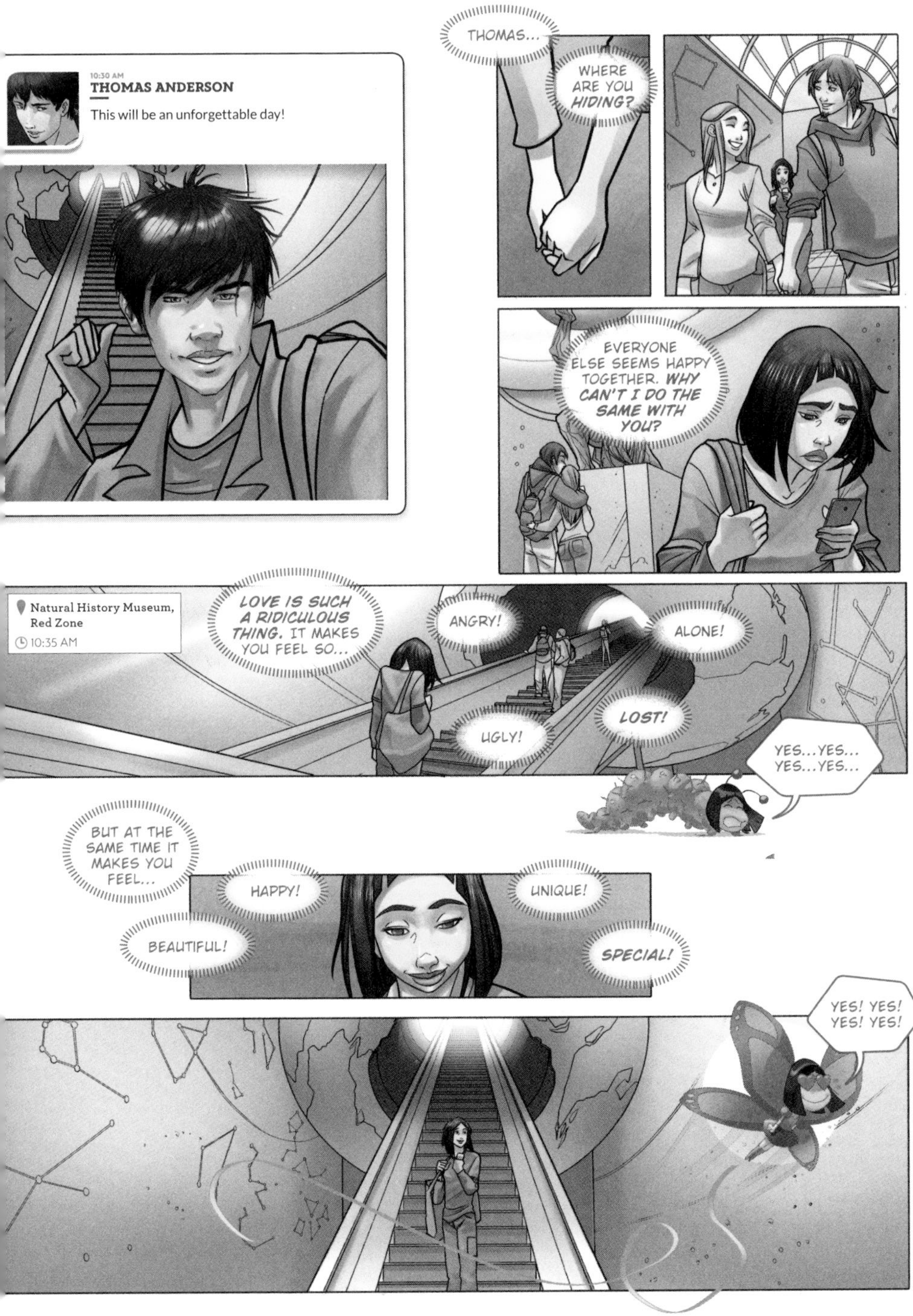
10:30 AM
THOMAS ANDERSON
This will be an unforgettable day!
THOMAS...
WHERE ARE YOU HIDING?
EVERYONE ELSE SEEMS HAPPY TOGETHER. WHY CAN'T I DO THE SAME WITH YOU?
Natural History Museum, Red Zone
10:35 AM
LOVE IS SUCH A RIDICULOUS THING. IT MAKES YOU FEEL SO...
ANGRY!
ALONE!
UGLY!
LOST!
YES...YES... YES...YES...
BUT AT THE SAME TIME IT MAKES YOU FEEL...
HAPPY!
UNIQUE!
BEAUTIFUL!
SPECIAL!
YES! YES! YES! YES!

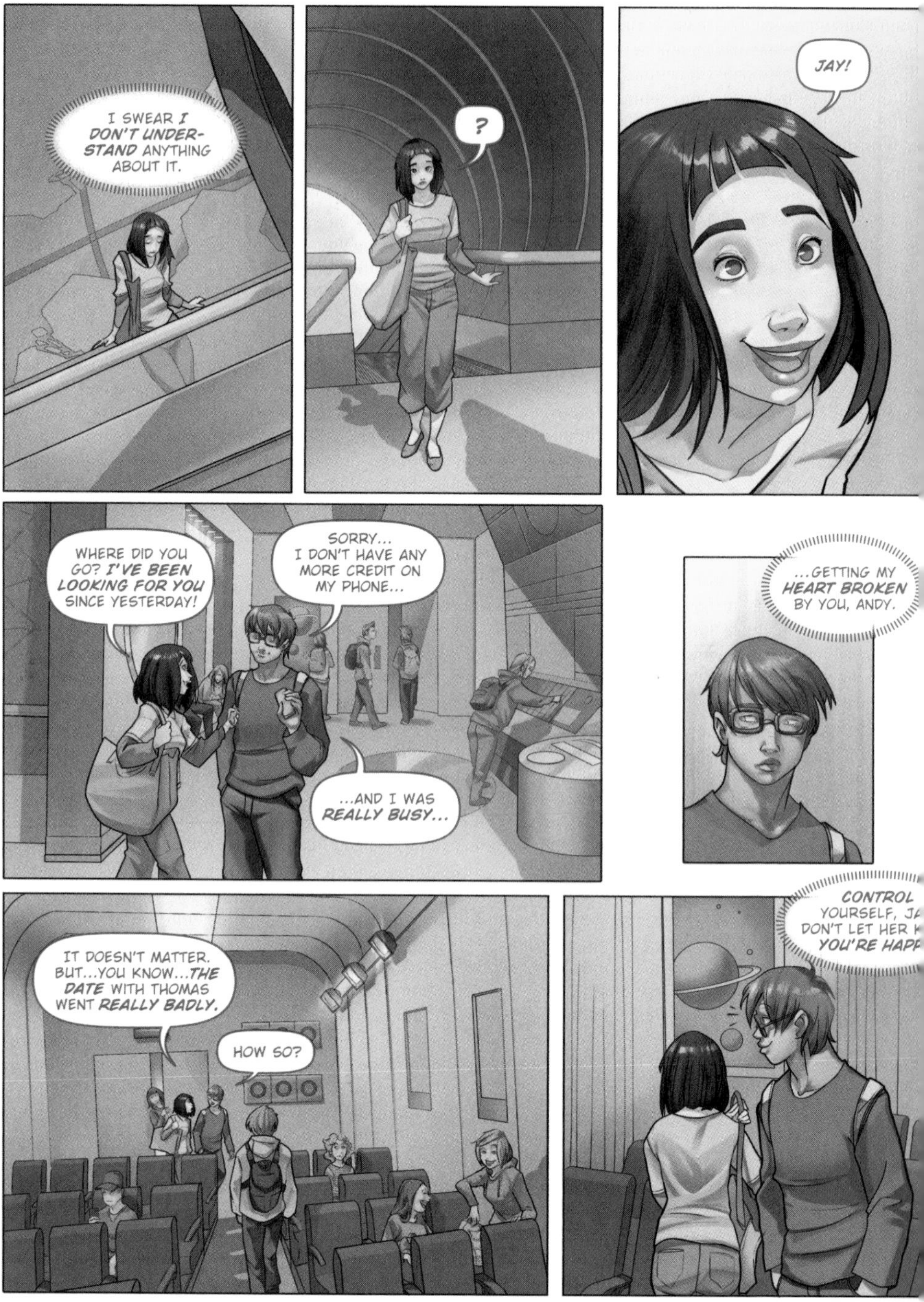
I SWEAR I DON'T UNDERSTAND ANYTHING ABOUT IT.
?
JAY!
WHERE DID YOU GO? I'VE BEEN LOOKING FOR YOU SINCE YESTERDAY!
SORRY... I DON'T HAVE ANY MORE CREDIT ON MY PHONE...
...AND I WAS REALLY BUSY...
...GETTING MY HEART BROKEN BY YOU, ANDY.
IT DOESN'T MATTER. BUT...YOU KNOW...THE DATE WITH THOMAS WENT REALLY BADLY.
HOW SO?
CONTROL YOURSELF, JA
DON'T LET HER K
YOU'RE HAPP

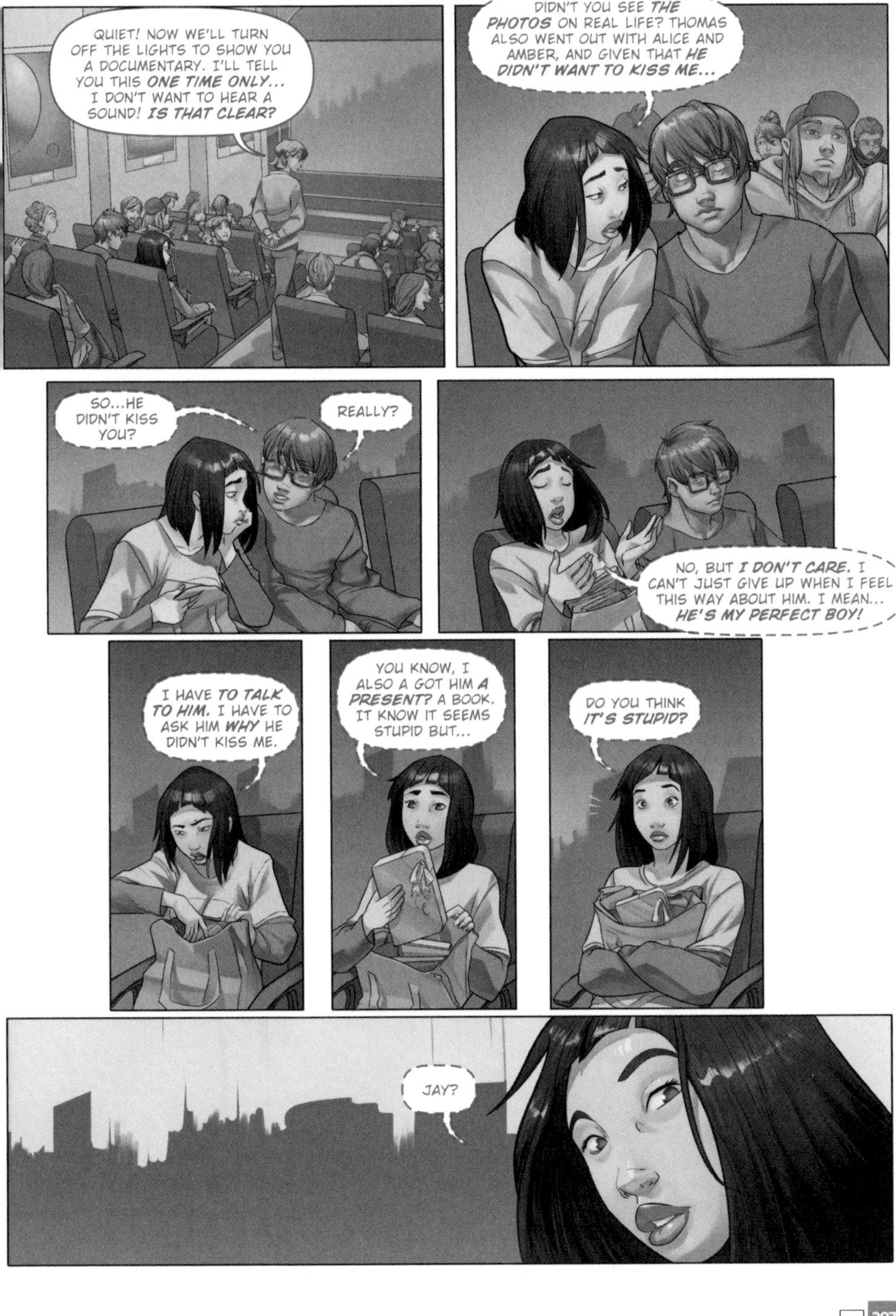
QUIET! NOW WE'LL TURN OFF THE LIGHTS TO SHOW YOU A DOCUMENTARY. I'LL TELL YOU THIS ONE TIME ONLY... I DON'T WANT TO HEAR A SOUND! IS THAT CLEAR?
DIDN'T YOU SEE THE PHOTOS ON REAL LIFE? THOMAS ALSO WENT OUT WITH ALICE AND AMBER, AND GIVEN THAT HE DIDN'T WANT TO KISS ME...
SO...HE DIDN'T KISS YOU?
REALLY?
NO, BUT I DON'T CARE. I CAN'T JUST GIVE UP WHEN I FEEL THIS WAY ABOUT HIM. I MEAN... HE'S MY PERFECT BOY!
I HAVE TO TALK TO HIM. I HAVE TO ASK HIM WHY HE DIDN'T KISS ME.
YOU KNOW, I ALSO A GOT HIM A PRESENT? A BOOK. IT KNOW IT SEEMS STUPID BUT...
DO YOU THINK IT'S STUPID?
JAY?

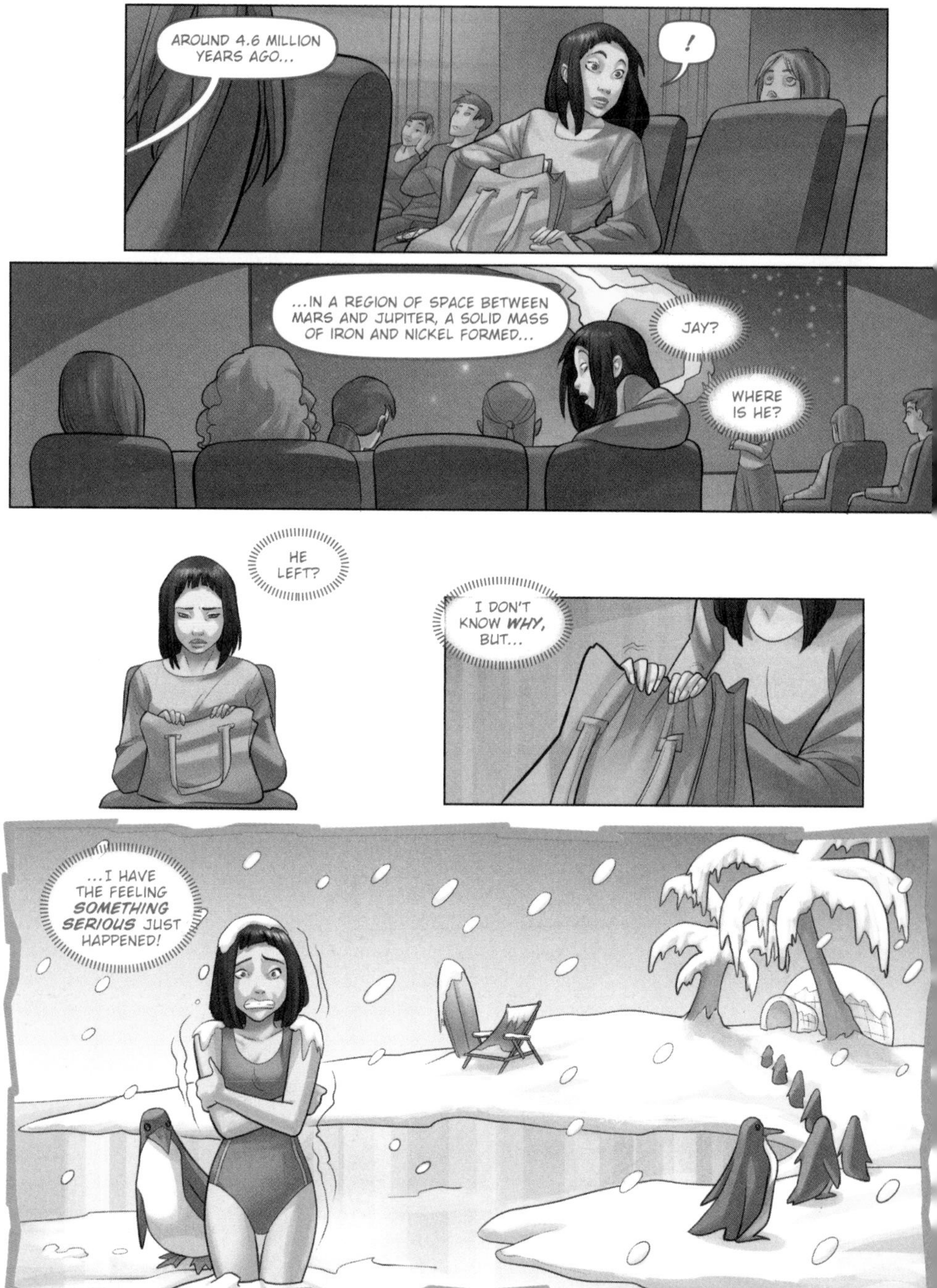
AROUND 4.6 MILLION YEARS AGO...
!
...IN A REGION OF SPACE BETWEEN MARS AND JUPITER, A SOLID MASS OF IRON AND NICKEL FORMED...
JAY?
WHERE IS HE?
HE LEFT?
I DON'T KNOW **WHY**, BUT...
...I HAVE THE FEELING **SOMETHING SERIOUS** JUST HAPPENED!

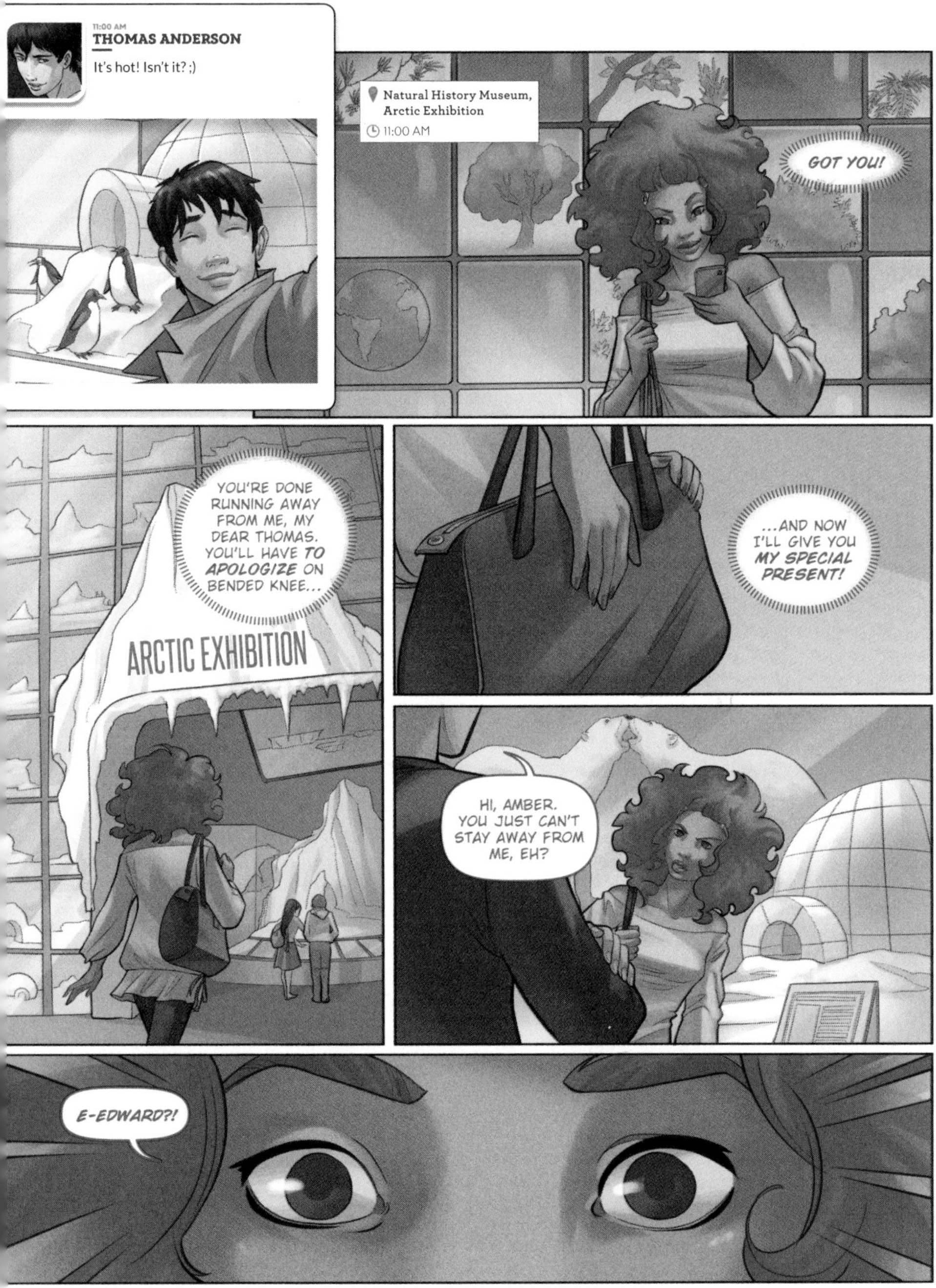
11:00 AM
THOMAS ANDERSON
It's hot! Isn't it? ;)
Natural History Museum, Arctic Exhibition
11:00 AM
GOT YOU!
YOU'RE DONE RUNNING AWAY FROM ME, MY DEAR THOMAS. YOU'LL HAVE TO APOLOGIZE ON BENDED KNEE...
ARCTIC EXHIBITION
...AND NOW I'LL GIVE YOU MY SPECIAL PRESENT!
HI, AMBER. YOU JUST CAN'T STAY AWAY FROM ME, EH?
E-EDWARD?!

END OF CHAPTER 16

CHAPTER 17

INTO the MAZE

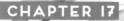

Natural History Museum, Green Zone
South Kensington
11:05 AM

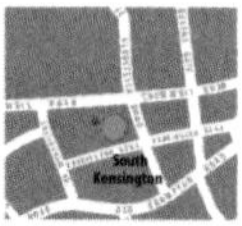
South
Kensington

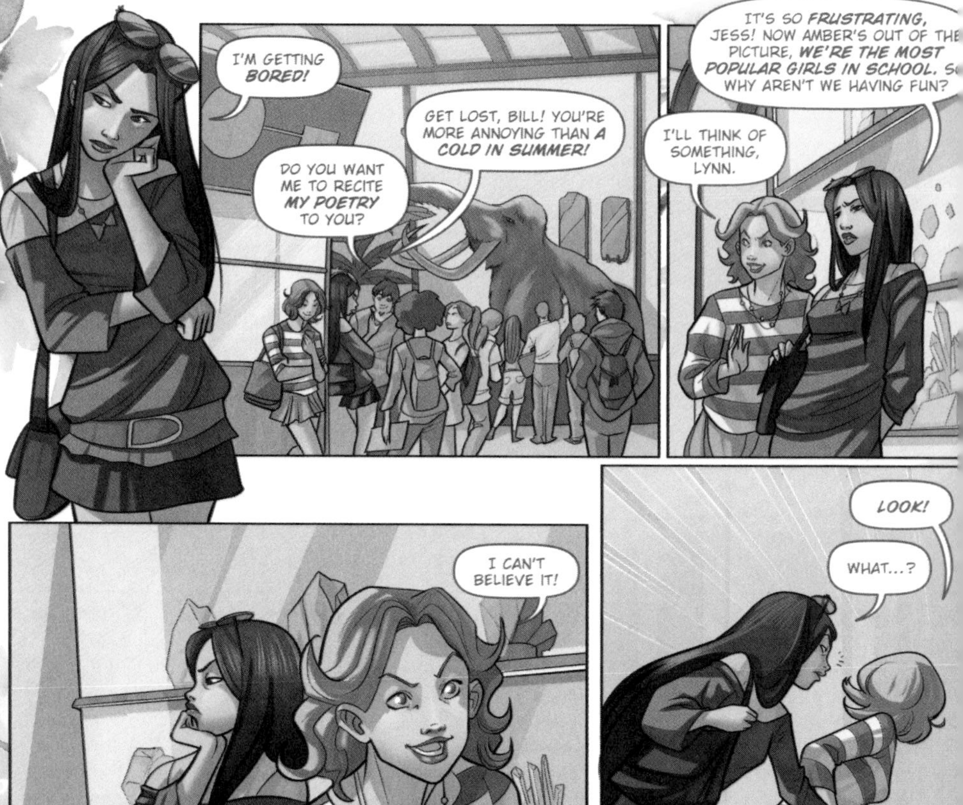
I'M GETTING BORED!
GET LOST, BILL! YOU'RE MORE ANNOYING THAN A COLD IN SUMMER!
DO YOU WANT ME TO RECITE MY POETRY TO YOU?
IT'S SO FRUSTRATING, JESS! NOW AMBER'S OUT OF THE PICTURE, WE'RE THE MOST POPULAR GIRLS IN SCHOOL. S WHY AREN'T WE HAVING FUN?
I'LL THINK OF SOMETHING, LYNN.
I CAN'T BELIEVE IT!
LOOK!
WHAT...?

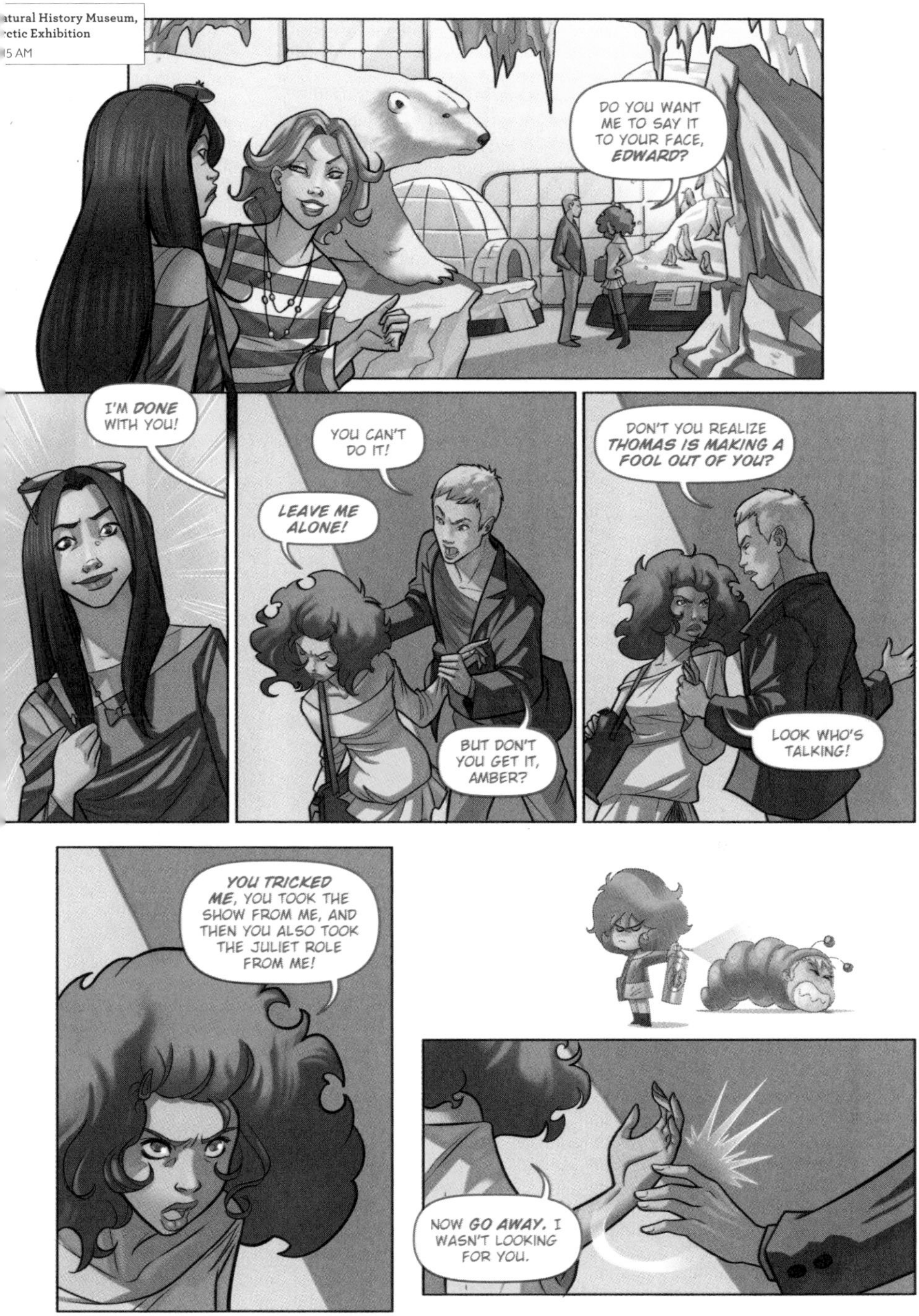
atural History Museum,
rctic Exhibition
5 AM
DO YOU WANT ME TO SAY IT TO YOUR FACE, EDWARD?
I'M DONE WITH YOU!
YOU CAN'T DO IT!
LEAVE ME ALONE!
BUT DON'T YOU GET IT, AMBER?
DON'T YOU REALIZE THOMAS IS MAKING A FOOL OUT OF YOU?
LOOK WHO'S TALKING!
YOU TRICKED ME, YOU TOOK THE SHOW FROM ME, AND THEN YOU ALSO TOOK THE JULIET ROLE FROM ME!
NOW GO AWAY. I WASN'T LOOKING FOR YOU.

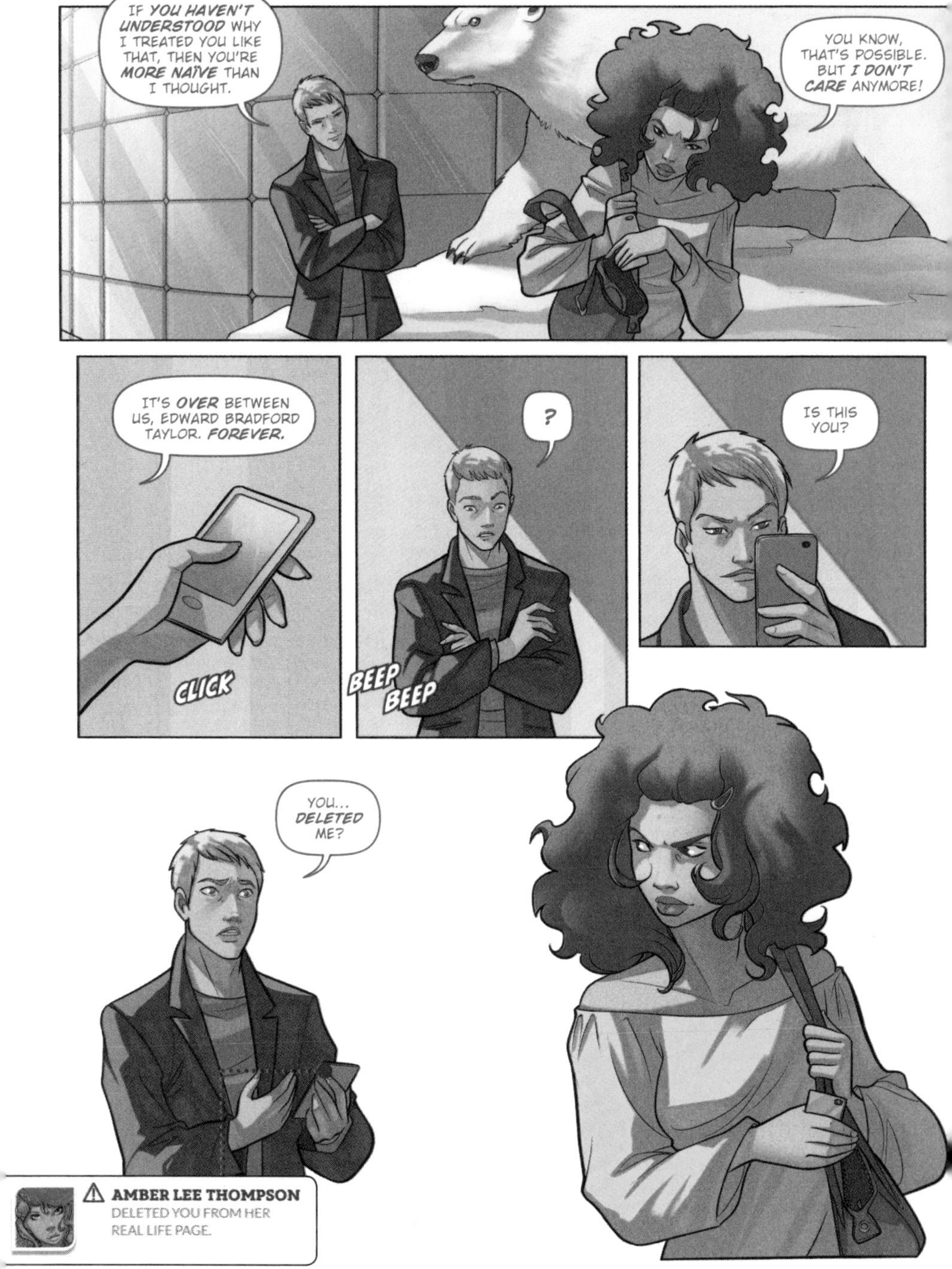

IF YOU HAVEN'T UNDERSTOOD WHY I TREATED YOU LIKE THAT, THEN YOU'RE MORE NAÏVE THAN I THOUGHT.
YOU KNOW, THAT'S POSSIBLE. BUT I DON'T CARE ANYMORE!
IT'S OVER BETWEEN US, EDWARD BRADFORD TAYLOR. FOREVER.
CLICK
?
BEEP BEEP
IS THIS YOU?
YOU... DELETED ME?
AMBER LEE THOMPSON
DELETED YOU FROM HER REAL LIFE PAGE.

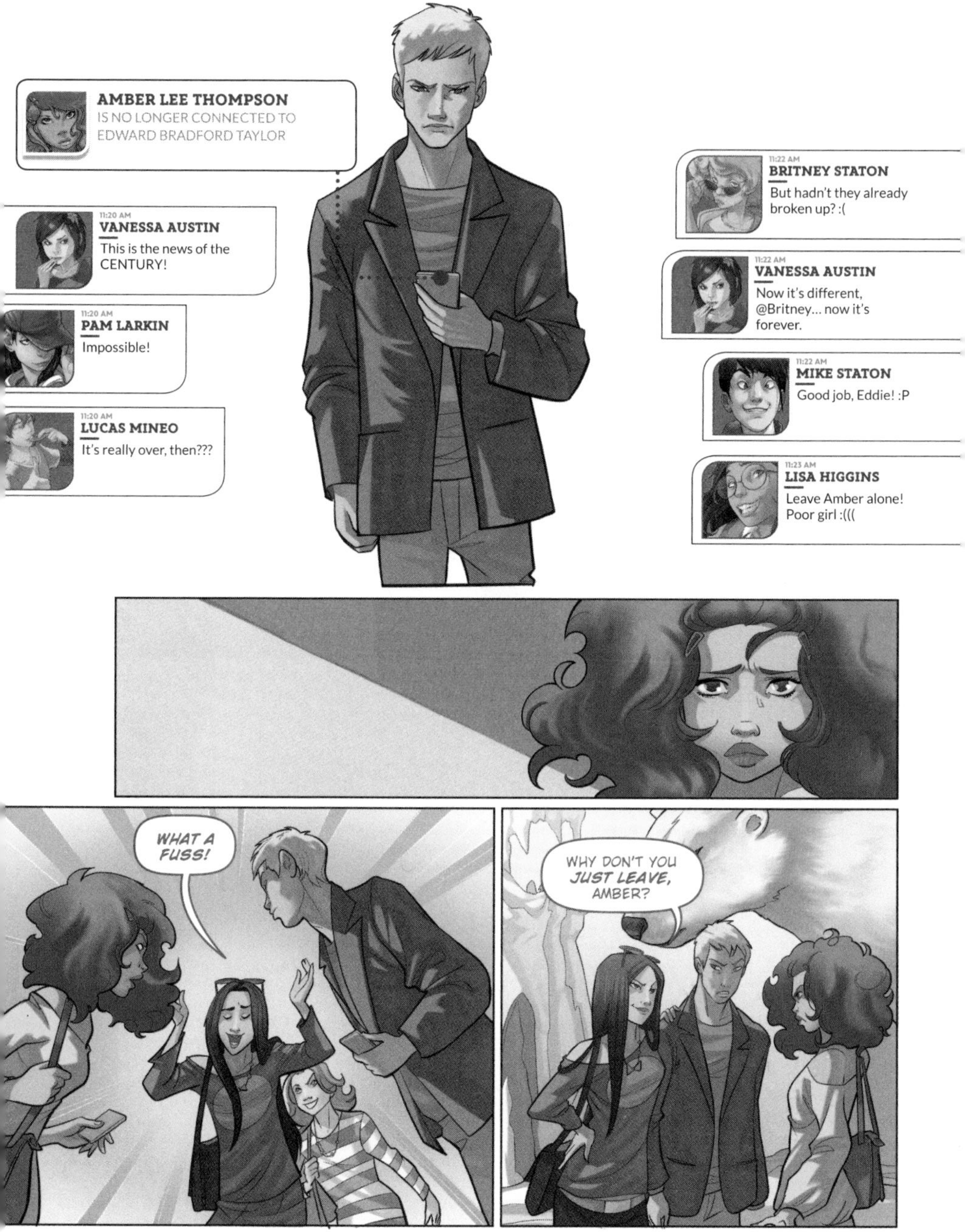

AMBER LEE THOMPSON
IS NO LONGER CONNECTED TO
EDWARD BRADFORD TAYLOR
11:20 AM
VANESSA AUSTIN
This is the news of the CENTURY!
11:20 AM
PAM LARKIN
Impossible!
11:20 AM
LUCAS MINEO
It's really over, then???
11:22 AM
BRITNEY STATON
But hadn't they already broken up? :(
11:22 AM
VANESSA AUSTIN
Now it's different, @Britney… now it's forever.
11:22 AM
MIKE STATON
Good job, Eddie! :P
11:23 AM
LISA HIGGINS
Leave Amber alone! Poor girl :(((
WHAT A FUSS!
WHY DON'T YOU JUST LEAVE, AMBER?

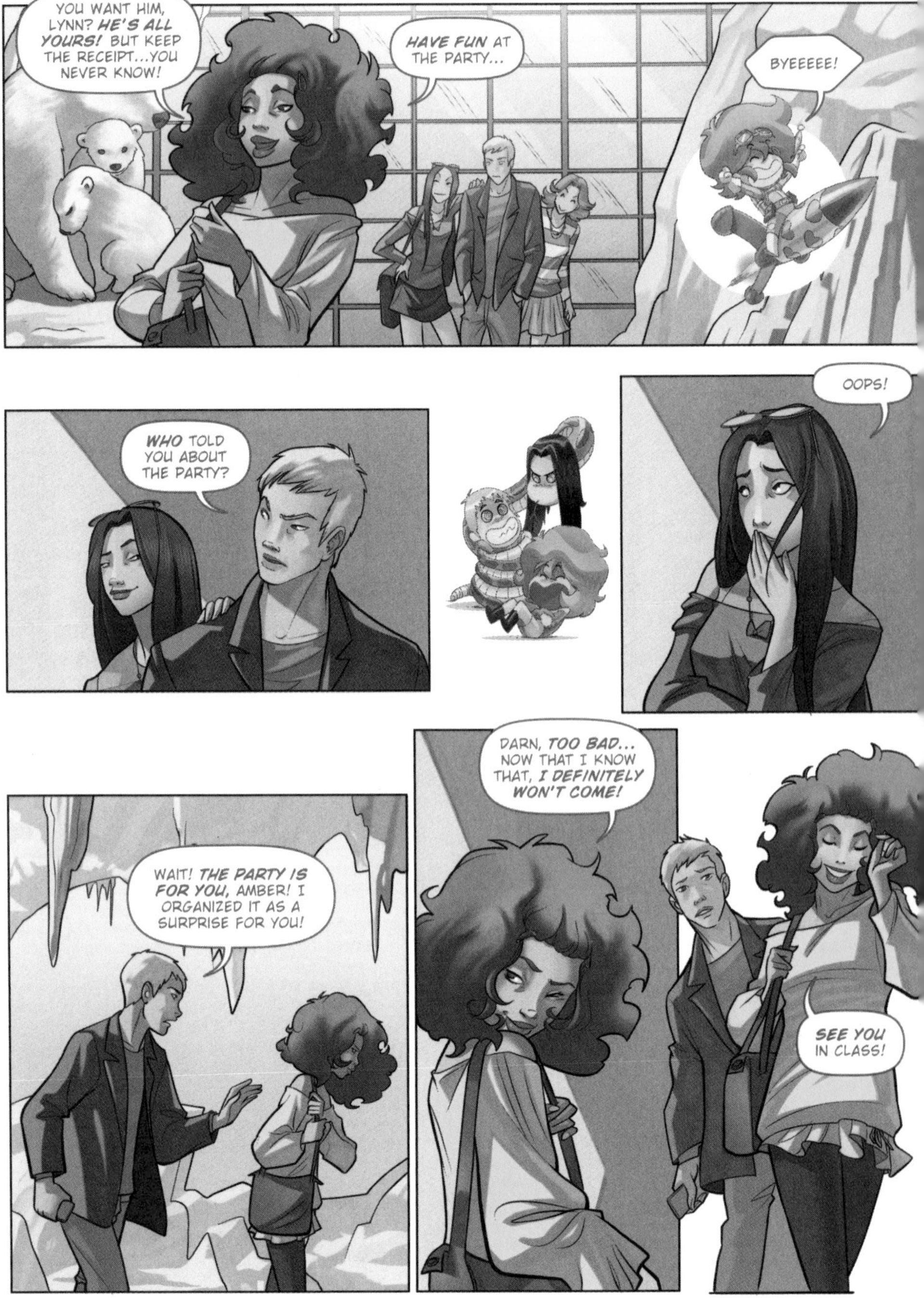
YOU WANT HIM, LYNN? HE'S ALL YOURS! BUT KEEP THE RECEIPT...YOU NEVER KNOW!
HAVE FUN AT THE PARTY...
BYEEEEE!
WHO TOLD YOU ABOUT THE PARTY?
OOPS!
WAIT! THE PARTY IS FOR YOU, AMBER! I ORGANIZED IT AS A SURPRISE FOR YOU!
DARN, TOO BAD... NOW THAT I KNOW THAT, I DEFINITELY WON'T COME!
SEE YOU IN CLASS!

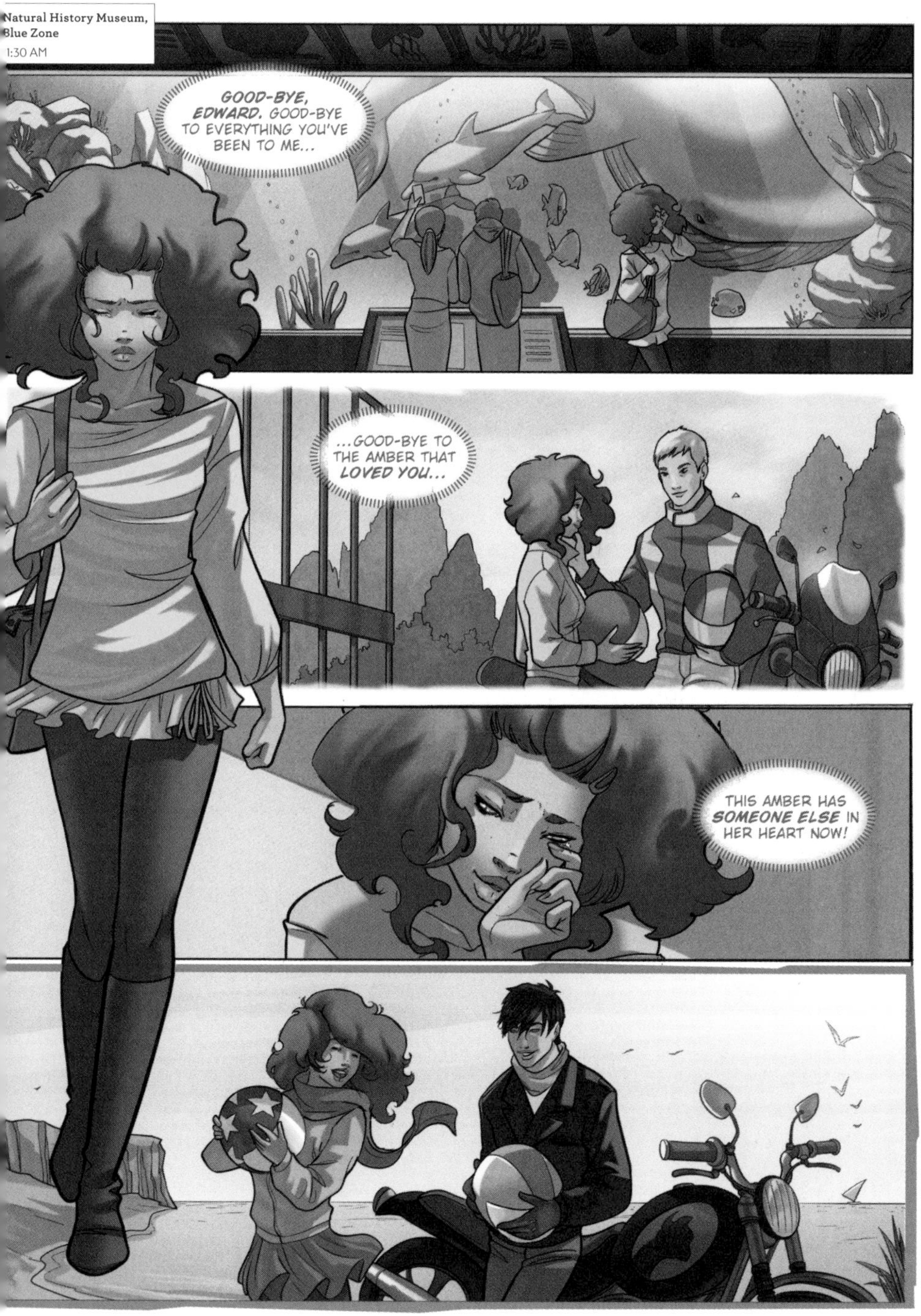
Natural History Museum, Blue Zone
1:30 AM
GOOD-BYE, EDWARD. GOOD-BYE TO EVERYTHING YOU'VE BEEN TO ME...
...GOOD-BYE TO THE AMBER THAT LOVED YOU...
THIS AMBER HAS SOMEONE ELSE IN HER HEART NOW!

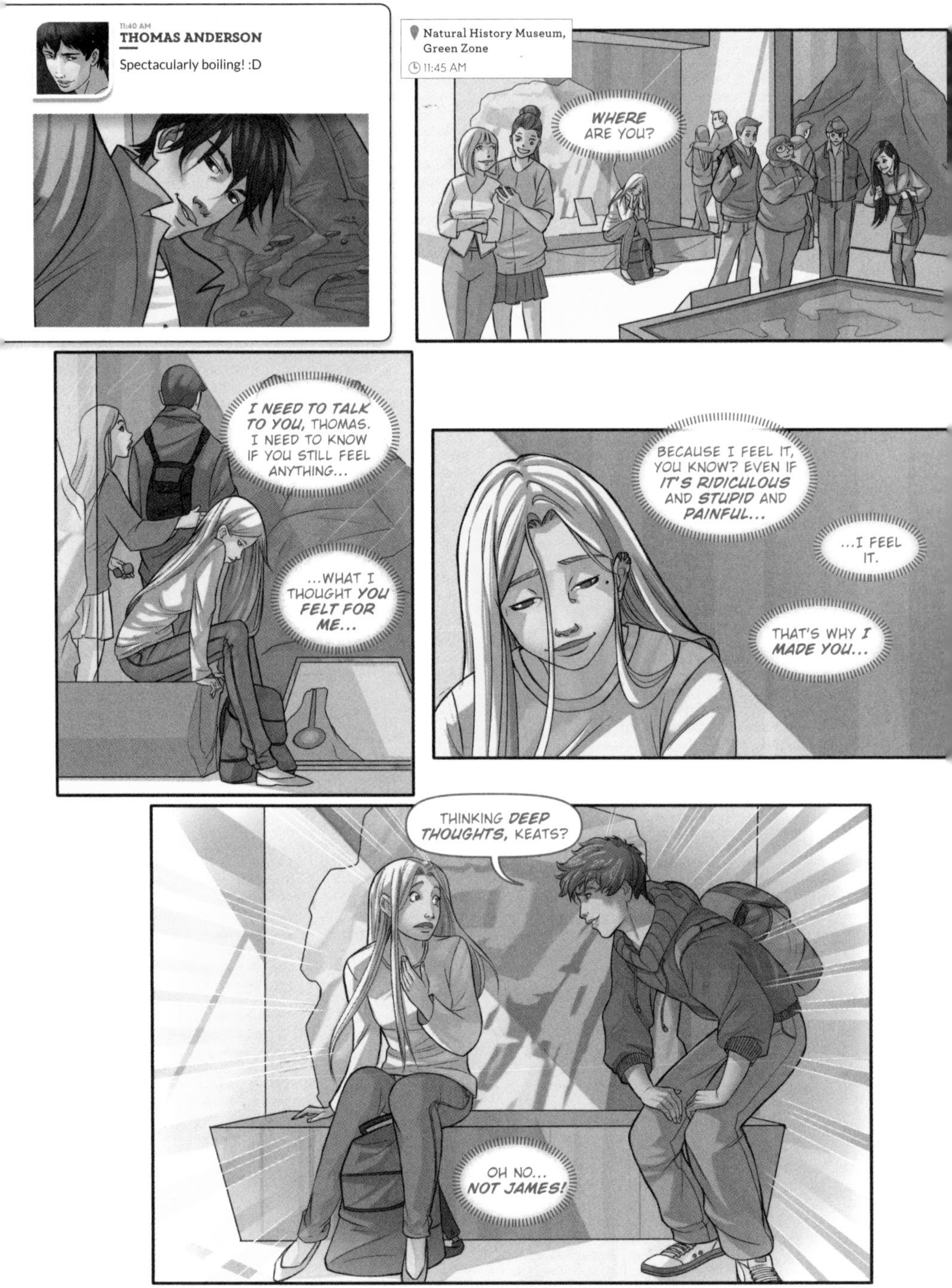
11:40 AM
THOMAS ANDERSON
Spectacularly boiling! :D
Natural History Museum, Green Zone
11:45 AM
WHERE ARE YOU?
I NEED TO TALK TO YOU, THOMAS. I NEED TO KNOW IF YOU STILL FEEL ANYTHING...
...WHAT I THOUGHT YOU FELT FOR ME...
BECAUSE I FEEL IT, YOU KNOW? EVEN IF IT'S RIDICULOUS AND STUPID AND PAINFUL...
...I FEEL IT.
THAT'S WHY I MADE YOU...
THINKING DEEP THOUGHTS, KEATS?
OH NO... NOT JAMES!

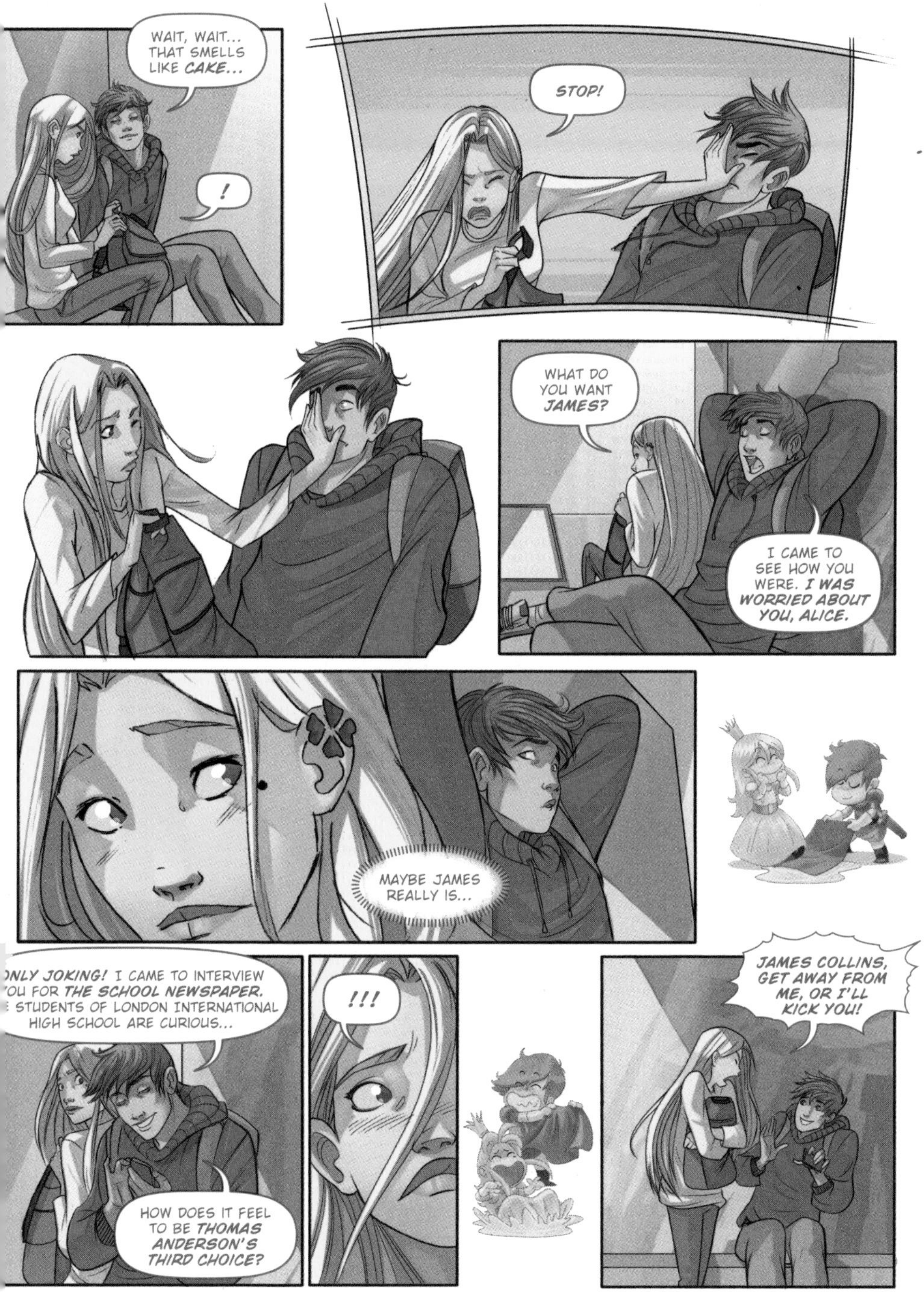

WAIT, WAIT... THAT SMELLS LIKE CAKE...
!
STOP!
WHAT DO YOU WANT JAMES?
I CAME TO SEE HOW YOU WERE. I WAS WORRIED ABOUT YOU, ALICE.
MAYBE JAMES REALLY IS...
ONLY JOKING! I CAME TO INTERVIEW YOU FOR THE SCHOOL NEWSPAPER. STUDENTS OF LONDON INTERNATIONAL HIGH SCHOOL ARE CURIOUS...
HOW DOES IT FEEL TO BE THOMAS ANDERSON'S THIRD CHOICE?
!!!
JAMES COLLINS, GET AWAY FROM ME, OR I'LL KICK YOU!

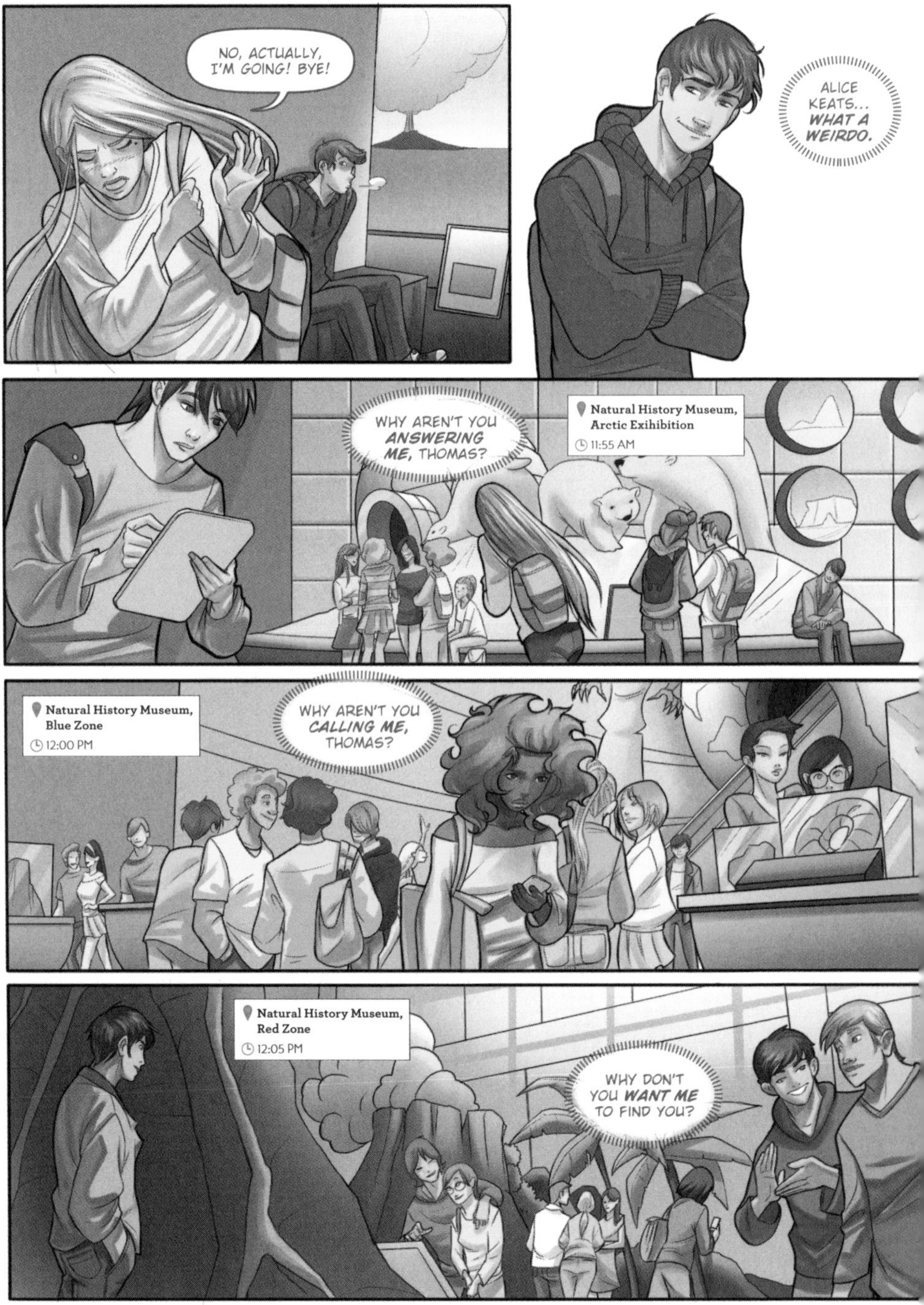

NO, ACTUALLY, I'M GOING! BYE!
ALICE KEATS... WHAT A WEIRDO.
WHY AREN'T YOU ANSWERING ME, THOMAS?
Natural History Museum, Arctic Exihibition
11:55 AM
Natural History Museum, Blue Zone
12:00 PM
WHY AREN'T YOU CALLING ME, THOMAS?
Natural History Museum, Red Zone
12:05 PM
WHY DON'T YOU WANT ME TO FIND YOU?

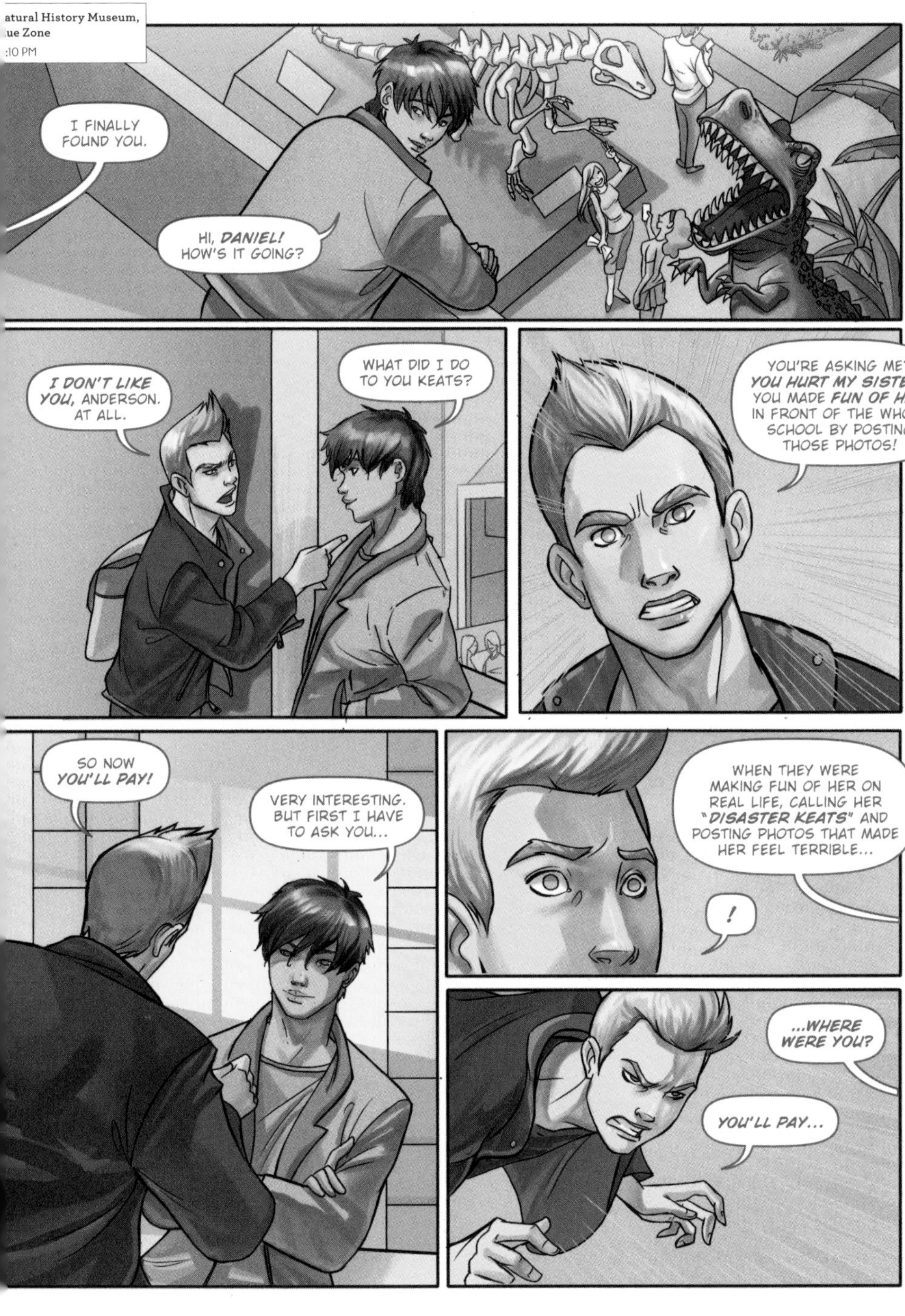
atural History Museum,
ue Zone
:10 PM
I FINALLY FOUND YOU.
HI, DANIEL! HOW'S IT GOING?
I DON'T LIKE YOU, ANDERSON. AT ALL.
WHAT DID I DO TO YOU KEATS?
YOU'RE ASKING ME? YOU HURT MY SISTER! YOU MADE FUN OF HER IN FRONT OF THE WHOLE SCHOOL BY POSTING THOSE PHOTOS!
SO NOW YOU'LL PAY!
VERY INTERESTING. BUT FIRST I HAVE TO ASK YOU...
WHEN THEY WERE MAKING FUN OF HER ON REAL LIFE, CALLING HER "DISASTER KEATS" AND POSTING PHOTOS THAT MADE HER FEEL TERRIBLE...
!
...WHERE WERE YOU?
YOU'LL PAY...

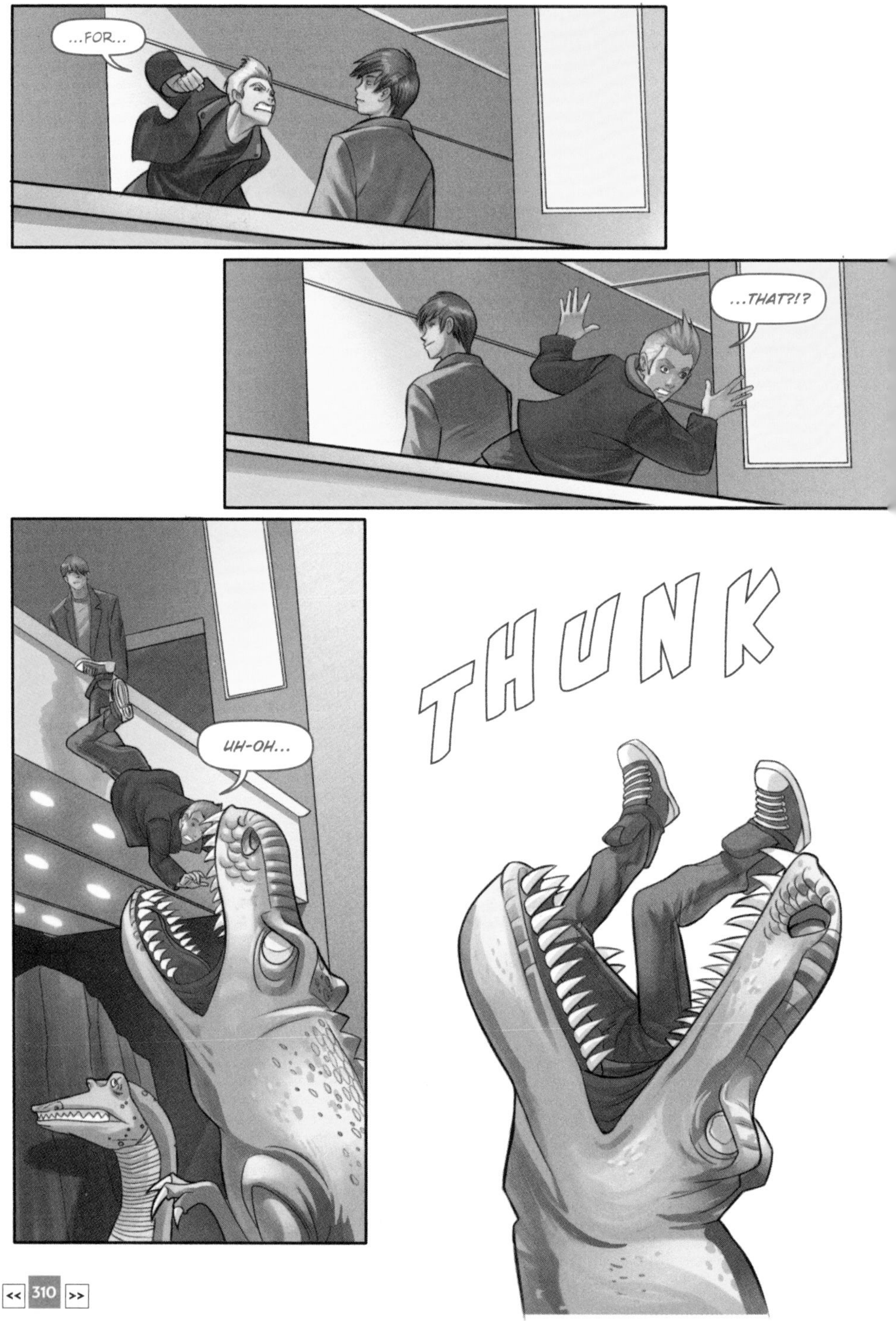
...FOR...
...THAT?!?
UH-OH...
THUNK

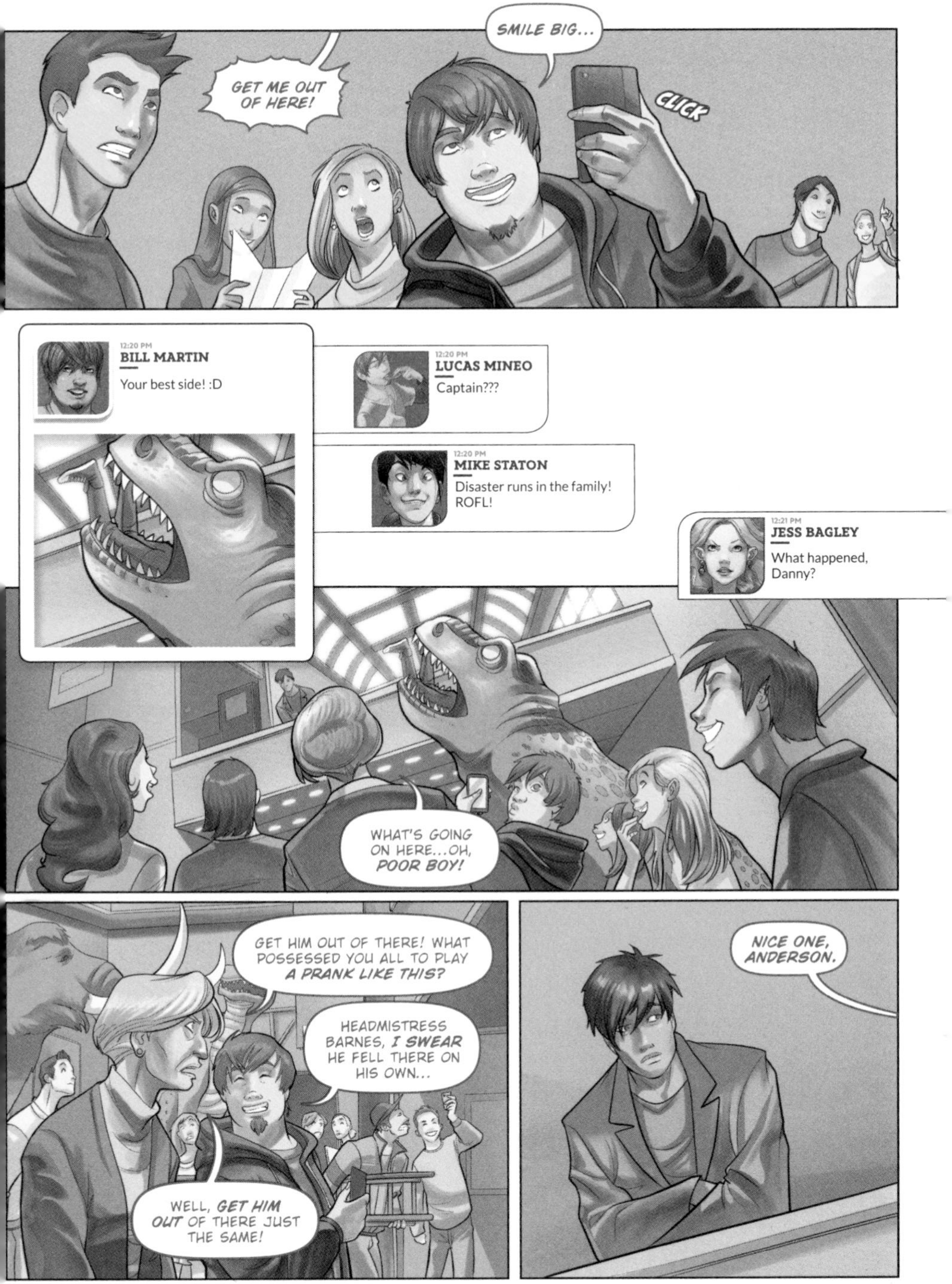
GET ME OUT OF HERE!
SMILE BIG...
CLICK
12:20 PM
BILL MARTIN
Your best side! :D
12:20 PM
LUCAS MINEO
Captain???
12:20 PM
MIKE STATON
Disaster runs in the family! ROFL!
12:21 PM
JESS BAGLEY
What happened, Danny?
WHAT'S GOING ON HERE...OH, POOR BOY!
GET HIM OUT OF THERE! WHAT POSSESSED YOU ALL TO PLAY A PRANK LIKE THIS?
HEADMISTRESS BARNES, I SWEAR HE FELL THERE ON HIS OWN...
WELL, GET HIM OUT OF THERE JUST THE SAME!
NICE ONE, ANDERSON.

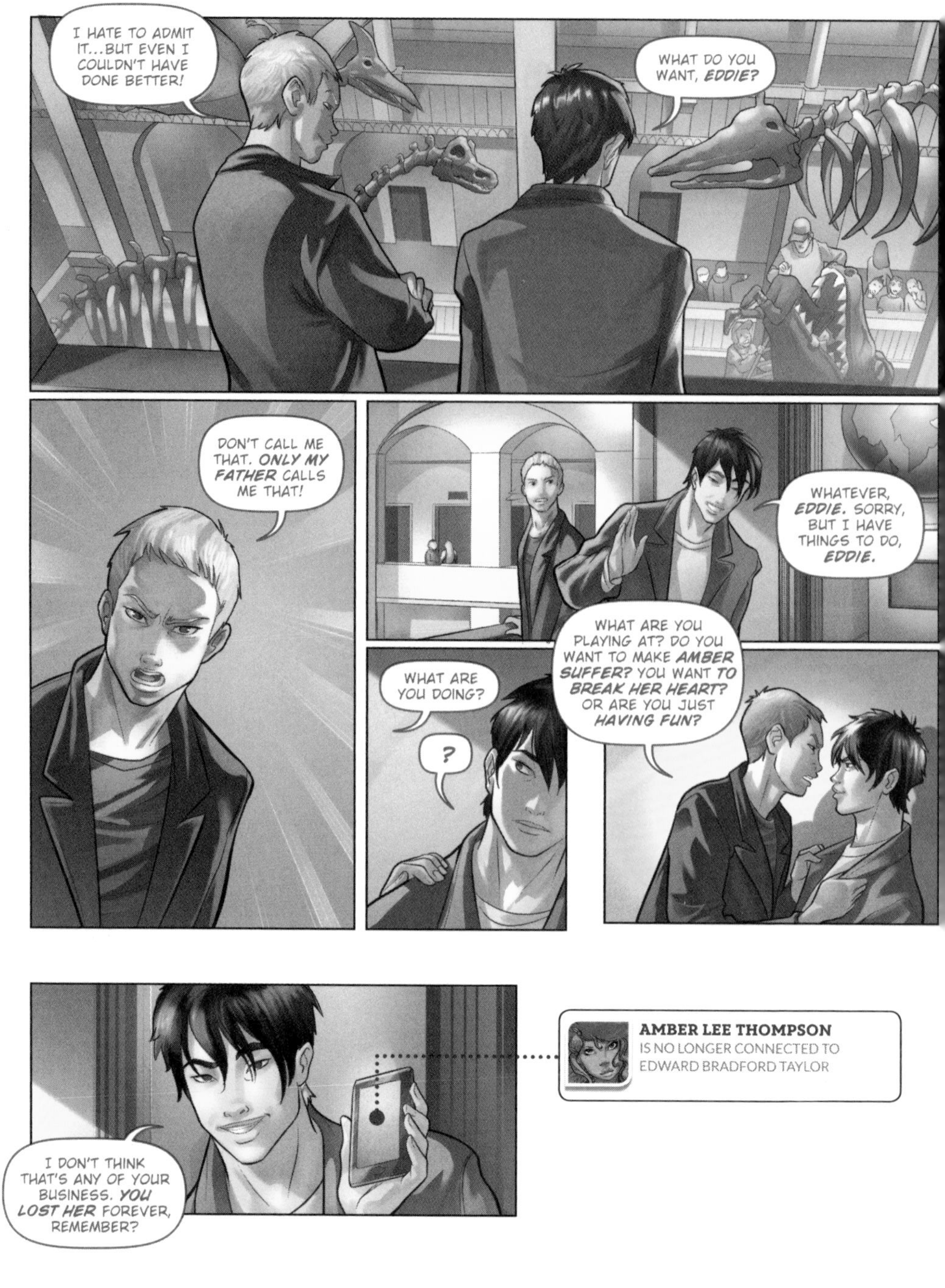
I HATE TO ADMIT IT...BUT EVEN I COULDN'T HAVE DONE BETTER!
WHAT DO YOU WANT, EDDIE?
DON'T CALL ME THAT. ONLY MY FATHER CALLS ME THAT!
WHATEVER, EDDIE. SORRY, BUT I HAVE THINGS TO DO, EDDIE.
WHAT ARE YOU DOING?
?
WHAT ARE YOU PLAYING AT? DO YOU WANT TO MAKE AMBER SUFFER? YOU WANT TO BREAK HER HEART? OR ARE YOU JUST HAVING FUN?
I DON'T THINK THAT'S ANY OF YOUR BUSINESS. YOU LOST HER FOREVER, REMEMBER?
AMBER LEE THOMPSON
IS NO LONGER CONNECTED TO
EDWARD BRADFORD TAYLOR

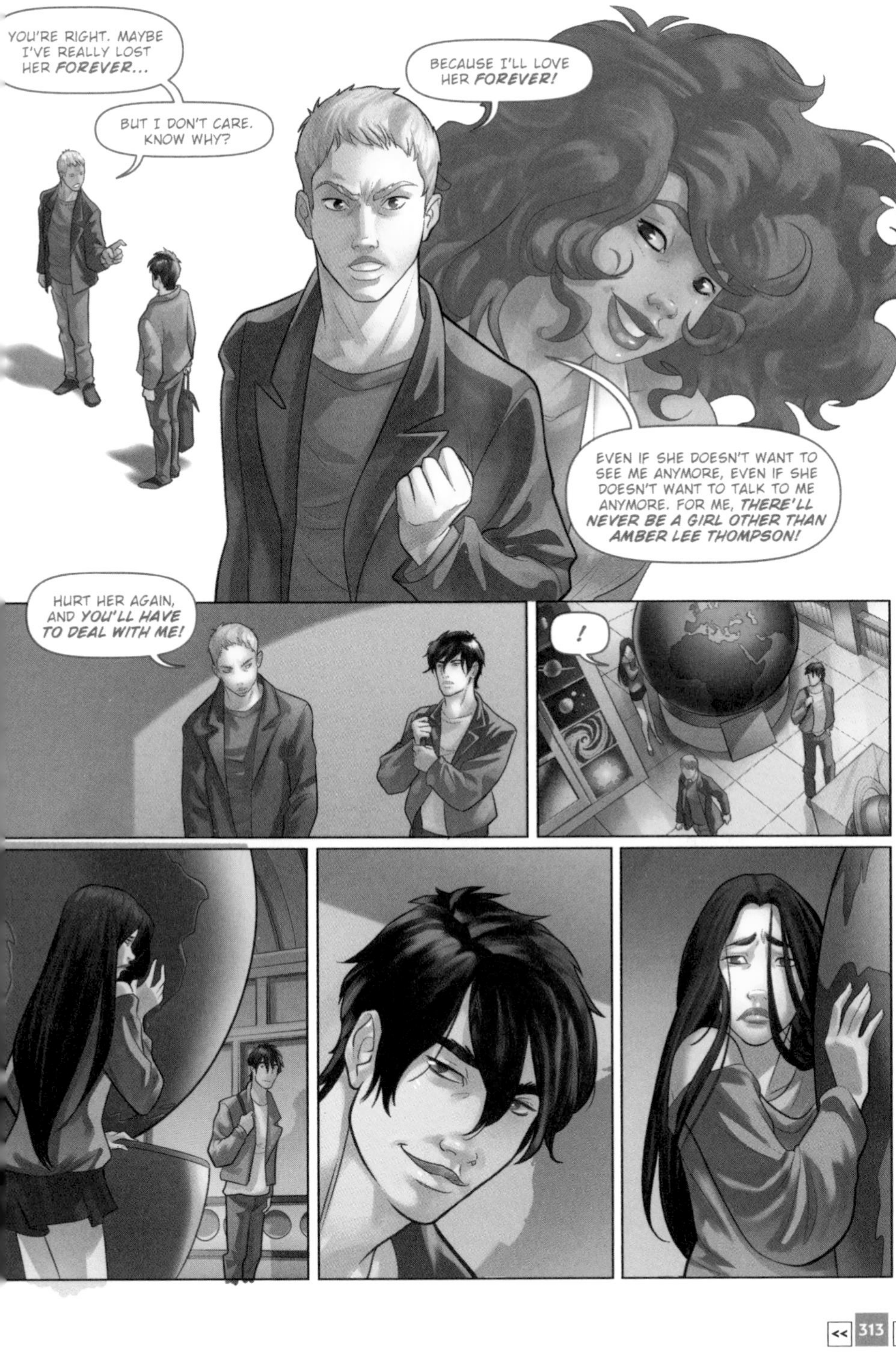
YOU'RE RIGHT. MAYBE I'VE REALLY LOST HER FOREVER...
BUT I DON'T CARE. KNOW WHY?
BECAUSE I'LL LOVE HER FOREVER!
EVEN IF SHE DOESN'T WANT TO SEE ME ANYMORE, EVEN IF SHE DOESN'T WANT TO TALK TO ME ANYMORE. FOR ME, THERE'LL NEVER BE A GIRL OTHER THAN AMBER LEE THOMPSON!
HURT HER AGAIN, AND YOU'LL HAVE TO DEAL WITH ME!
!

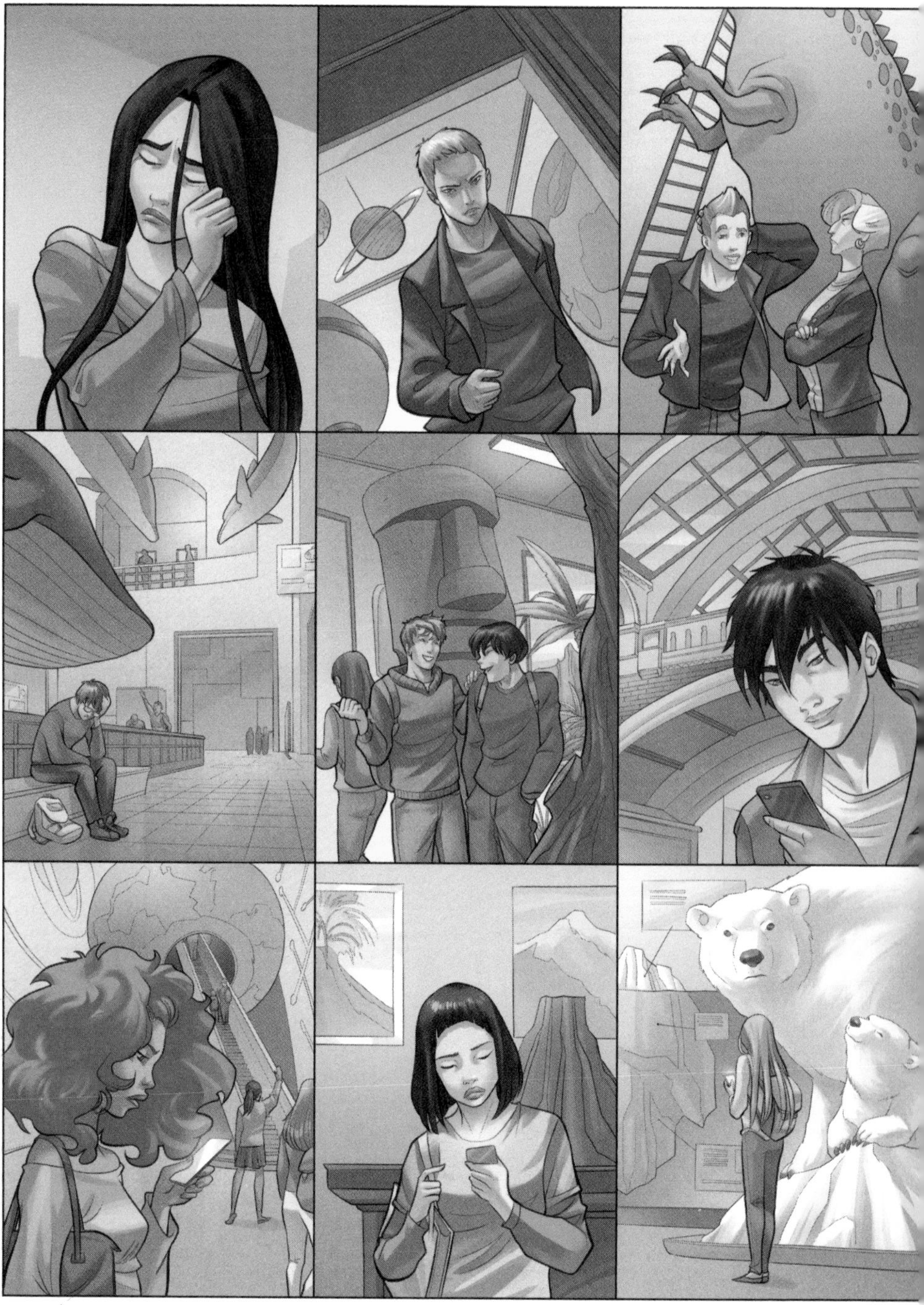

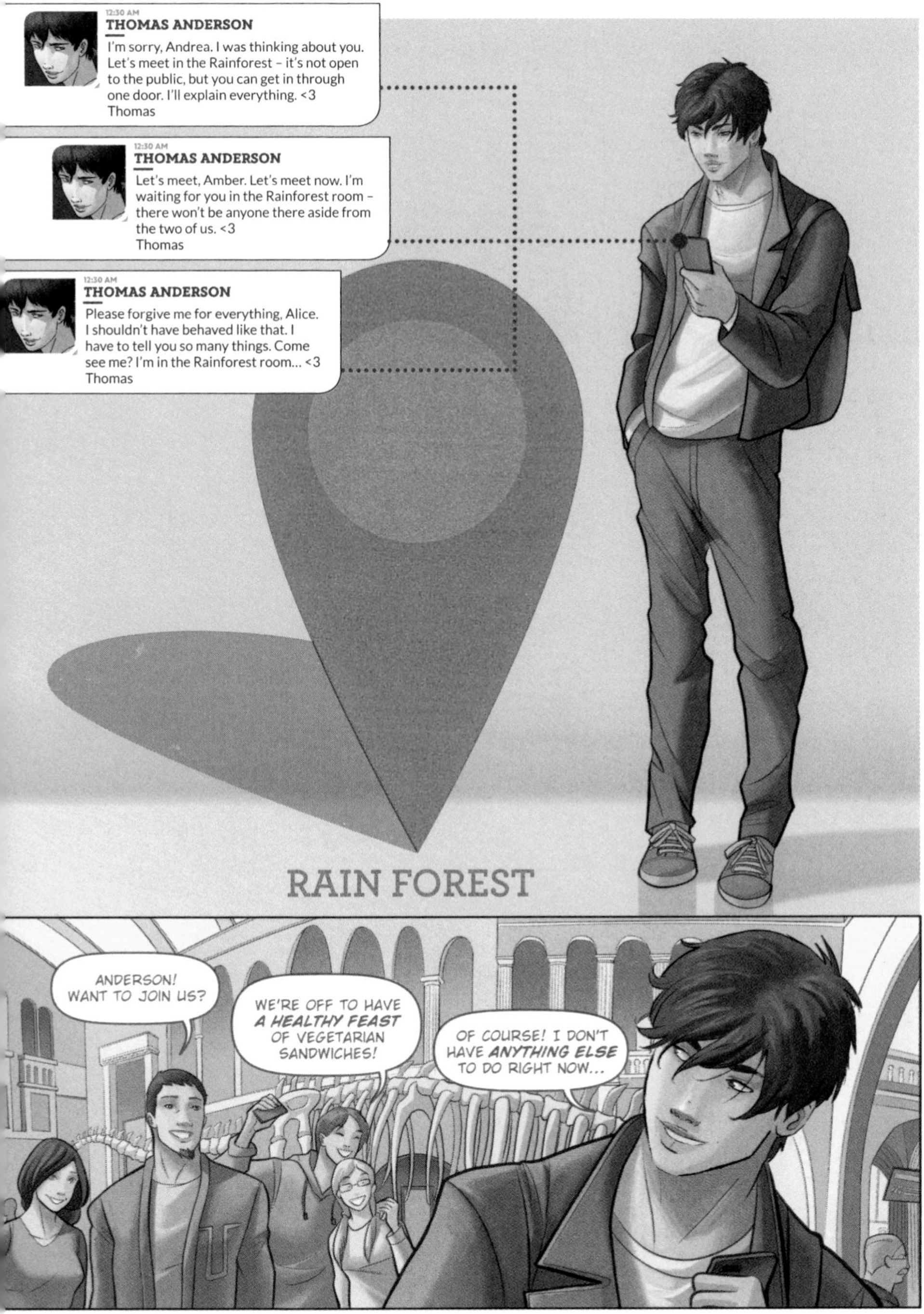
12:30 AM
THOMAS ANDERSON
I'm sorry, Andrea. I was thinking about you. Let's meet in the Rainforest – it's not open to the public, but you can get in through one door. I'll explain everything. <3
Thomas
12:30 AM
THOMAS ANDERSON
Let's meet, Amber. Let's meet now. I'm waiting for you in the Rainforest room – there won't be anyone there aside from the two of us. <3
Thomas
12:30 AM
THOMAS ANDERSON
Please forgive me for everything, Alice. I shouldn't have behaved like that. I have to tell you so many things. Come see me? I'm in the Rainforest room… <3
Thomas
RAIN FOREST
ANDERSON! WANT TO JOIN US?
WE'RE OFF TO HAVE ***A HEALTHY FEAST*** OF VEGETARIAN SANDWICHES!
OF COURSE! I DON'T HAVE ***ANYTHING ELSE*** TO DO RIGHT NOW...

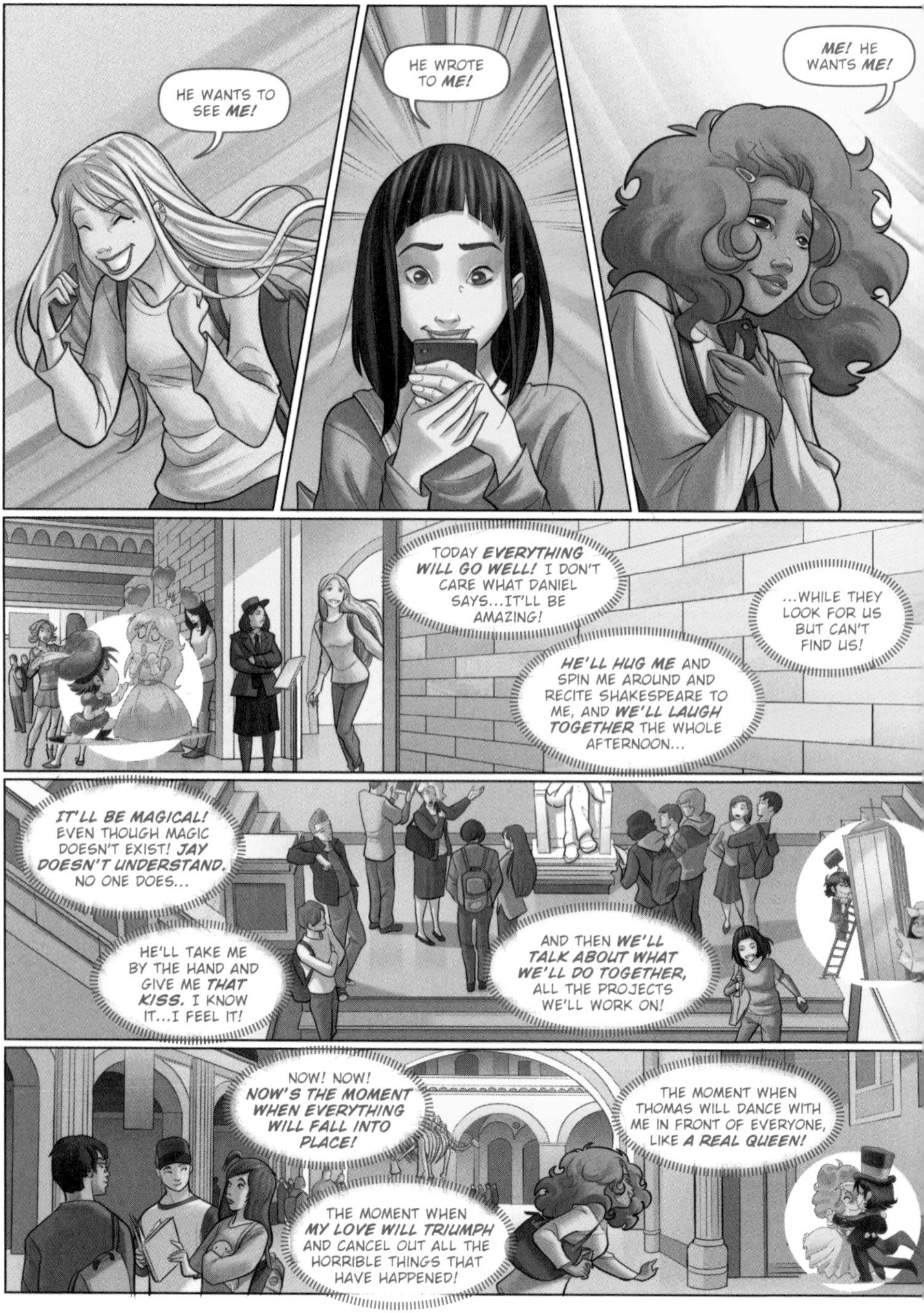
HE WANTS TO SEE ME!
HE WROTE TO ME!
ME! HE WANTS ME!
TODAY EVERYTHING WILL GO WELL! I DON'T CARE WHAT DANIEL SAYS...IT'LL BE AMAZING!
HE'LL HUG ME AND SPIN ME AROUND AND RECITE SHAKESPEARE TO ME, AND WE'LL LAUGH TOGETHER THE WHOLE AFTERNOON...
...WHILE THEY LOOK FOR US BUT CAN'T FIND US!
IT'LL BE MAGICAL! EVEN THOUGH MAGIC DOESN'T EXIST! JAY DOESN'T UNDERSTAND. NO ONE DOES...
HE'LL TAKE ME BY THE HAND AND GIVE ME THAT KISS. I KNOW IT...I FEEL IT!
AND THEN WE'LL TALK ABOUT WHAT WE'LL DO TOGETHER, ALL THE PROJECTS WE'LL WORK ON!
NOW! NOW! NOW'S THE MOMENT WHEN EVERYTHING WILL FALL INTO PLACE!
THE MOMENT WHEN MY LOVE WILL TRIUMPH AND CANCEL OUT ALL THE HORRIBLE THINGS THAT HAVE HAPPENED!
THE MOMENT WHEN THOMAS WILL DANCE WITH ME IN FRONT OF EVERYONE, LIKE A REAL QUEEN!

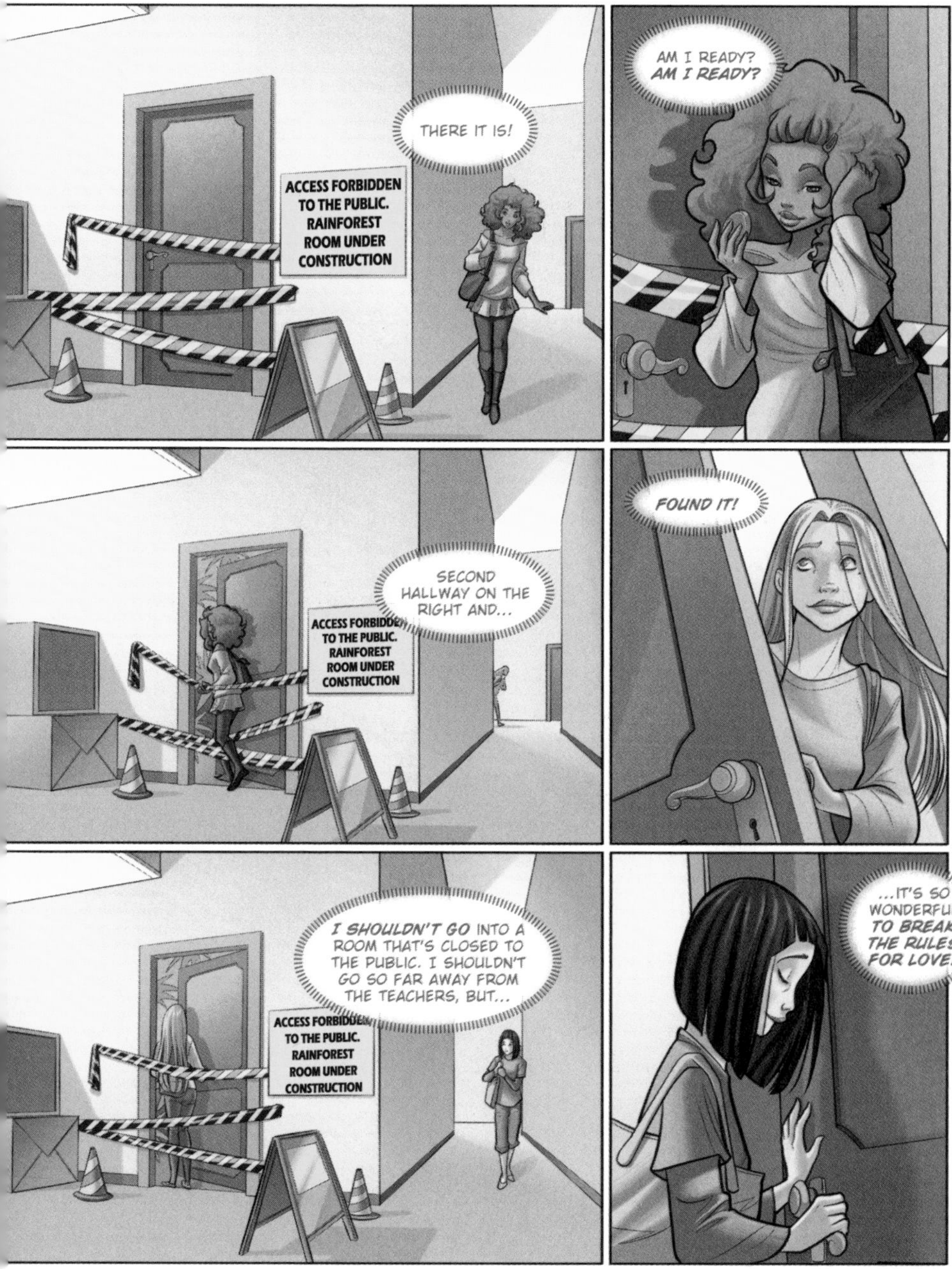
THERE IT IS!
ACCESS FORBIDDEN TO THE PUBLIC. RAINFOREST ROOM UNDER CONSTRUCTION
AM I READY? AM I READY?
SECOND HALLWAY ON THE RIGHT AND...
ACCESS FORBIDDEN TO THE PUBLIC. RAINFOREST ROOM UNDER CONSTRUCTION
FOUND IT!
I SHOULDN'T GO INTO A ROOM THAT'S CLOSED TO THE PUBLIC. I SHOULDN'T GO SO FAR AWAY FROM THE TEACHERS, BUT...
ACCESS FORBIDDEN TO THE PUBLIC. RAINFOREST ROOM UNDER CONSTRUCTION
...IT'S SO WONDERFUL TO BREAK THE RULES FOR LOVE!

END OF CHAPTER 17

CHAPTER 18

ALL for ONE

Natural History Museum, Rainforest
South Kensington
12:45 PM

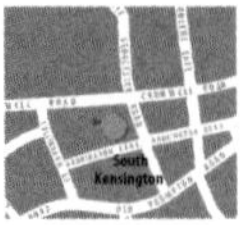
South Kensington

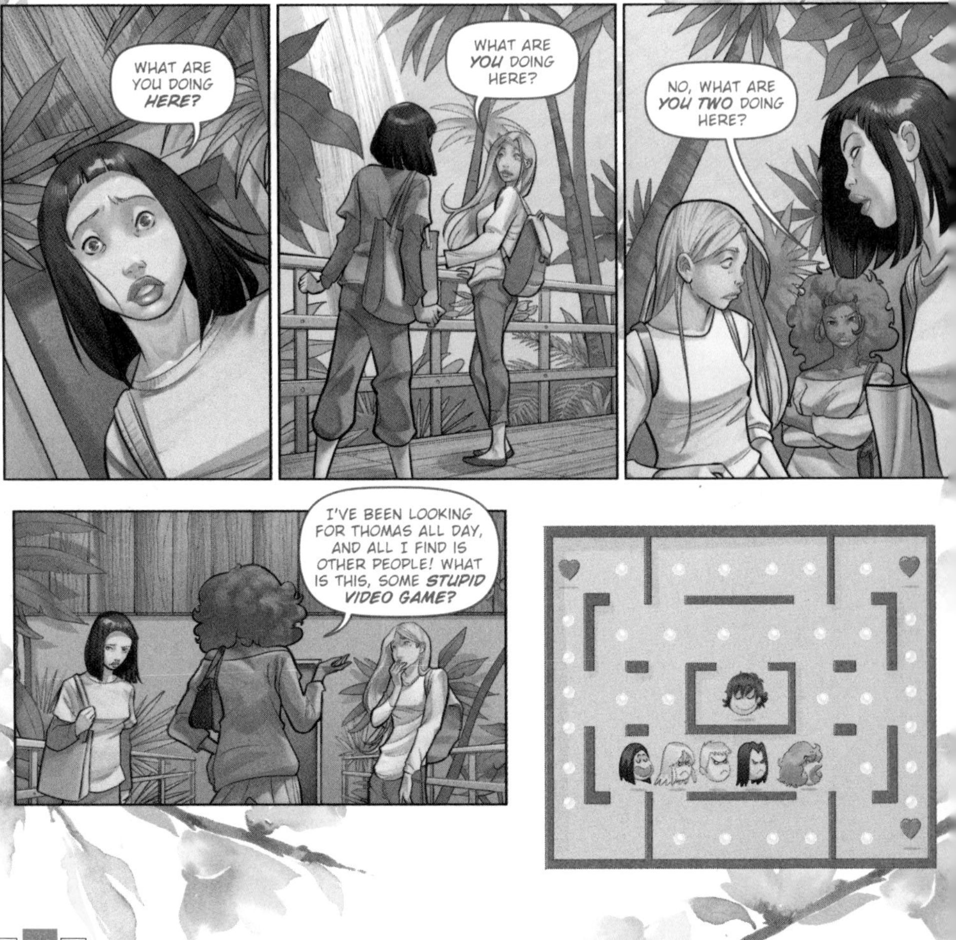
WHAT ARE YOU DOING *HERE?*
WHAT ARE *YOU* DOING HERE?
NO, WHAT ARE *YOU TWO* DOING HERE?
I'VE BEEN LOOKING FOR THOMAS ALL DAY, AND ALL I FIND IS OTHER PEOPLE! WHAT IS THIS, SOME *STUPID VIDEO GAME?*

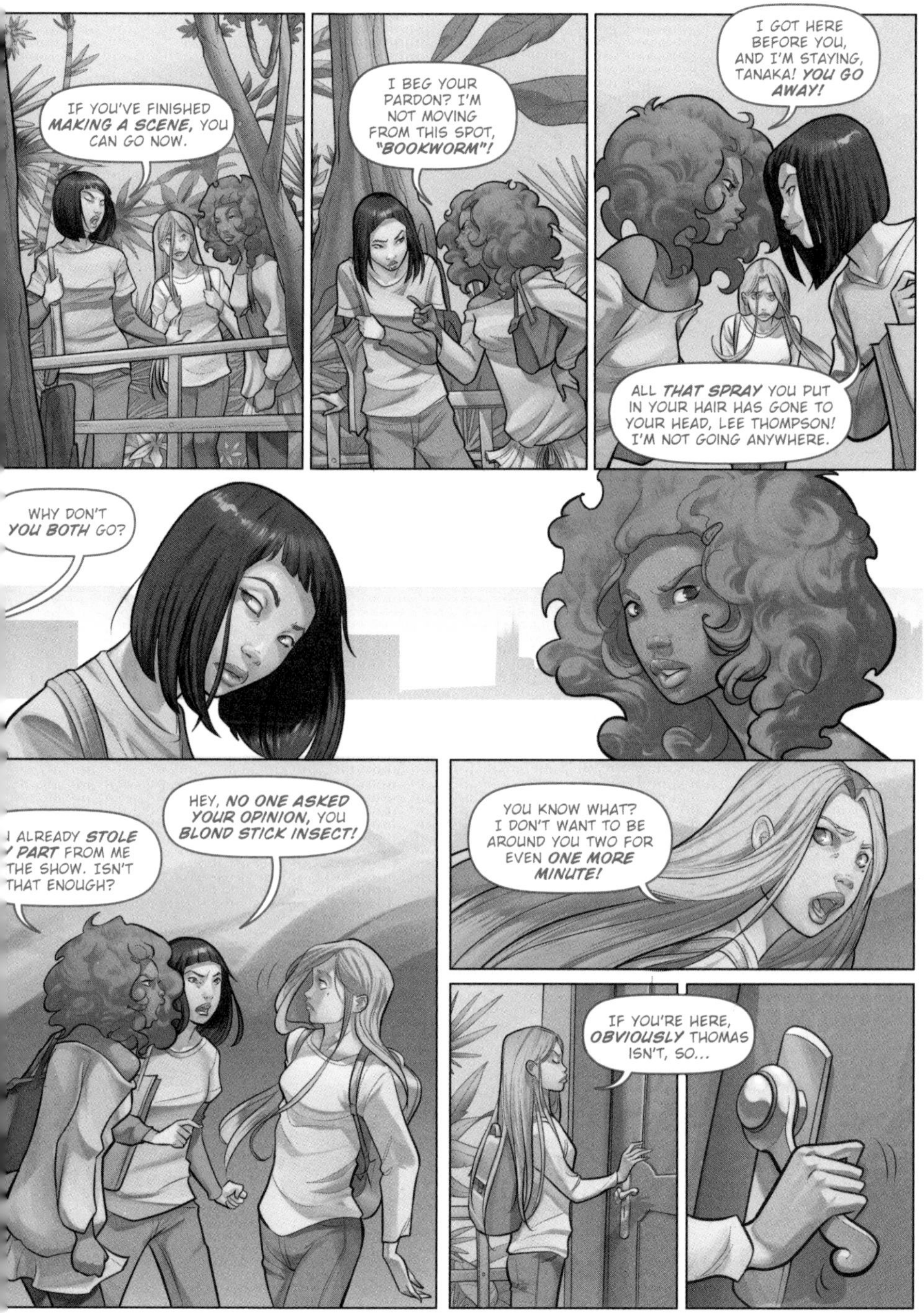
IF YOU'VE FINISHED MAKING A SCENE, YOU CAN GO NOW.
I BEG YOUR PARDON? I'M NOT MOVING FROM THIS SPOT, "BOOKWORM"!
I GOT HERE BEFORE YOU, AND I'M STAYING, TANAKA! YOU GO AWAY!
ALL THAT SPRAY YOU PUT IN YOUR HAIR HAS GONE TO YOUR HEAD, LEE THOMPSON! I'M NOT GOING ANYWHERE.
WHY DON'T YOU BOTH GO?
I ALREADY STOLE PART FROM ME THE SHOW. ISN'T THAT ENOUGH?
HEY, NO ONE ASKED YOUR OPINION, YOU BLOND STICK INSECT!
YOU KNOW WHAT? I DON'T WANT TO BE AROUND YOU TWO FOR EVEN ONE MORE MINUTE!
IF YOU'RE HERE, OBVIOUSLY THOMAS ISN'T, SO...

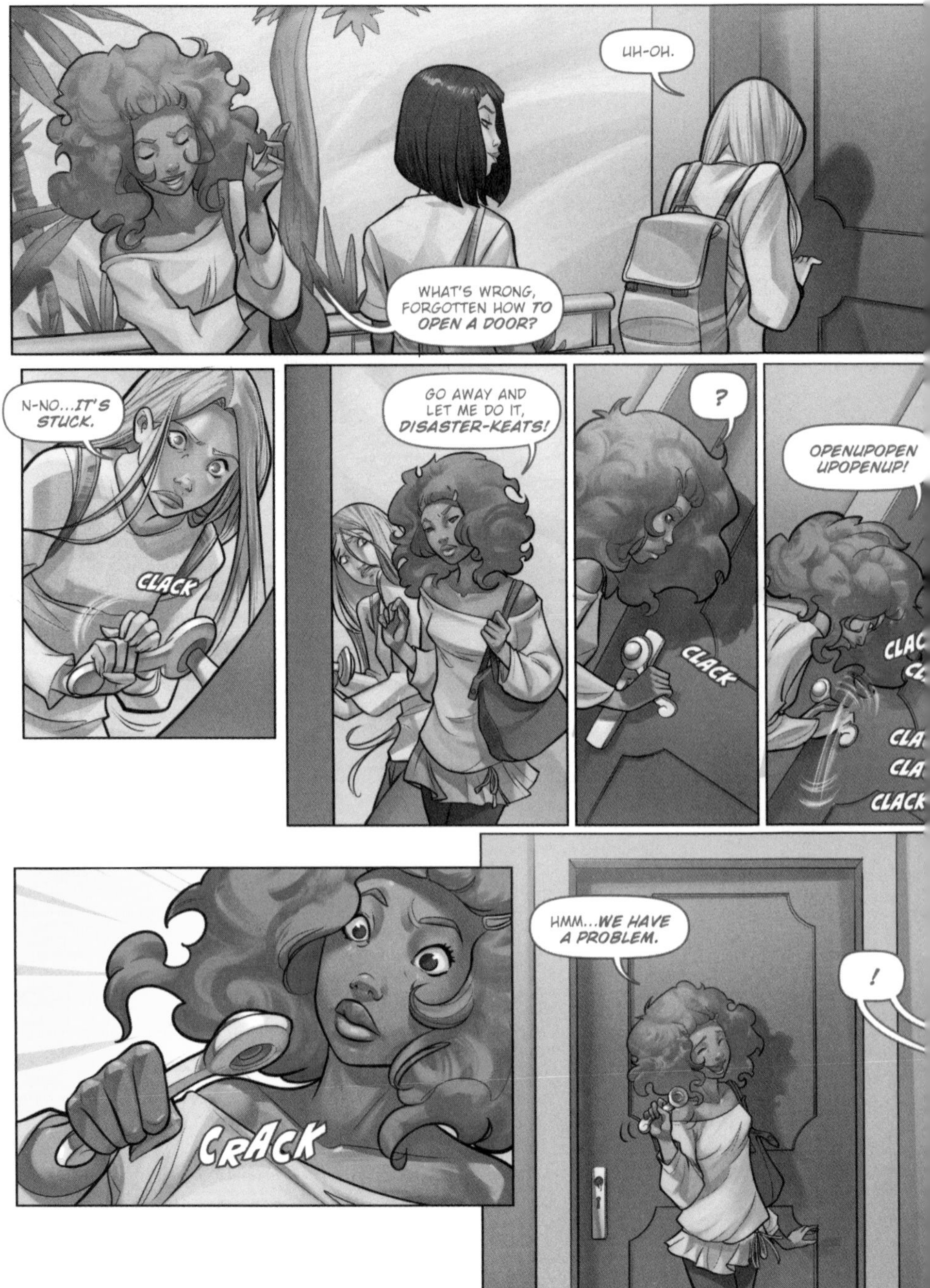
UH-OH.
WHAT'S WRONG, FORGOTTEN HOW TO OPEN A DOOR?
N-NO...IT'S STUCK.
CLACK
GO AWAY AND LET ME DO IT, DISASTER-KEATS!
?
CLACK
OPENUPOPEN UPOPENUP!
CLACK
CRACK
HMM...WE HAVE A PROBLEM.
!

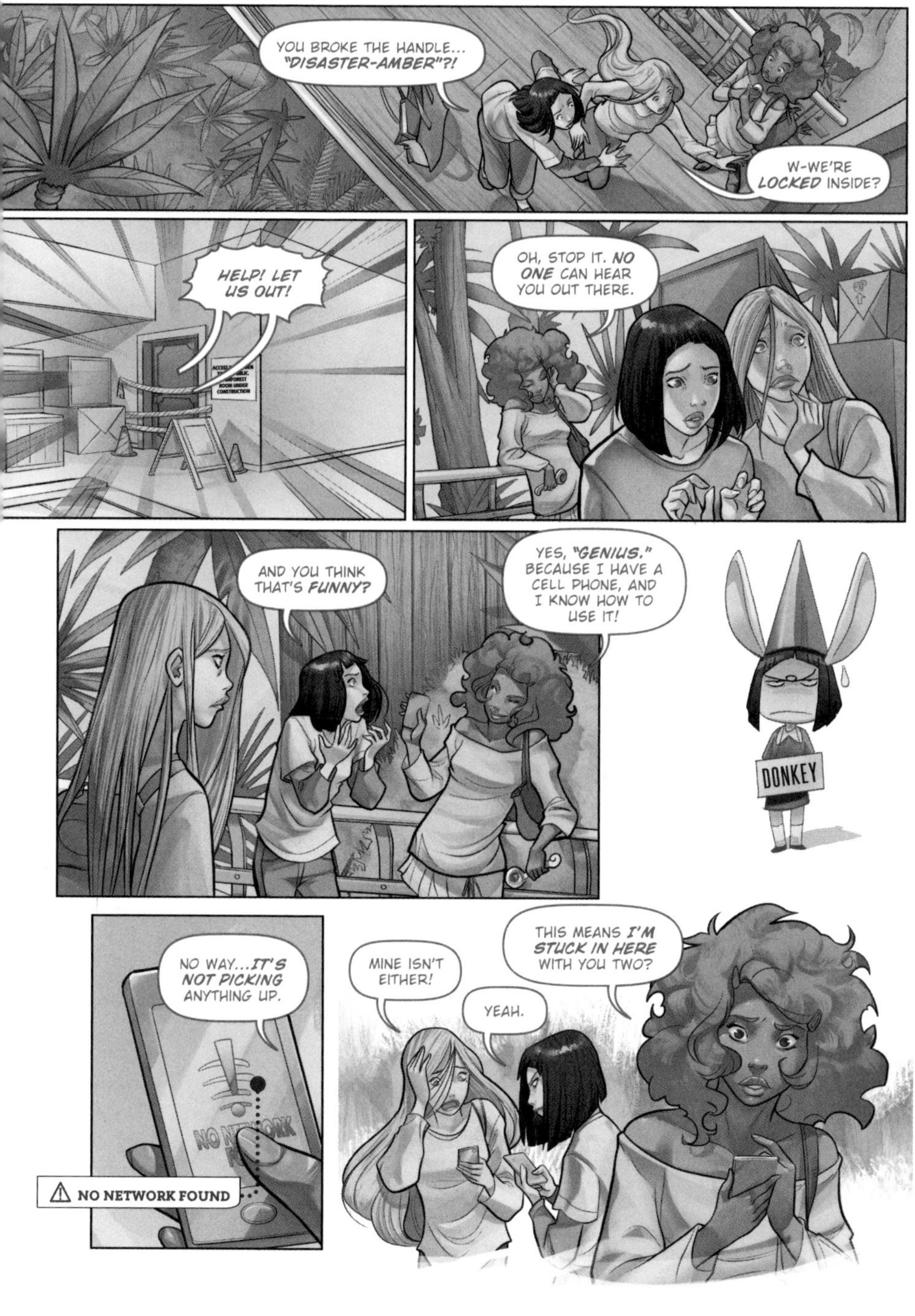
YOU BROKE THE HANDLE... "DISASTER-AMBER"?!
W-WE'RE LOCKED INSIDE?
HELP! LET US OUT!
OH, STOP IT. NO ONE CAN HEAR YOU OUT THERE.
AND YOU THINK THAT'S FUNNY?
YES, "GENIUS." BECAUSE I HAVE A CELL PHONE, AND I KNOW HOW TO USE IT!
DONKEY
NO WAY...IT'S NOT PICKING ANYTHING UP.
NO NETWORK FOUND
MINE ISN'T EITHER!
YEAH.
THIS MEANS I'M STUCK IN HERE WITH YOU TWO?

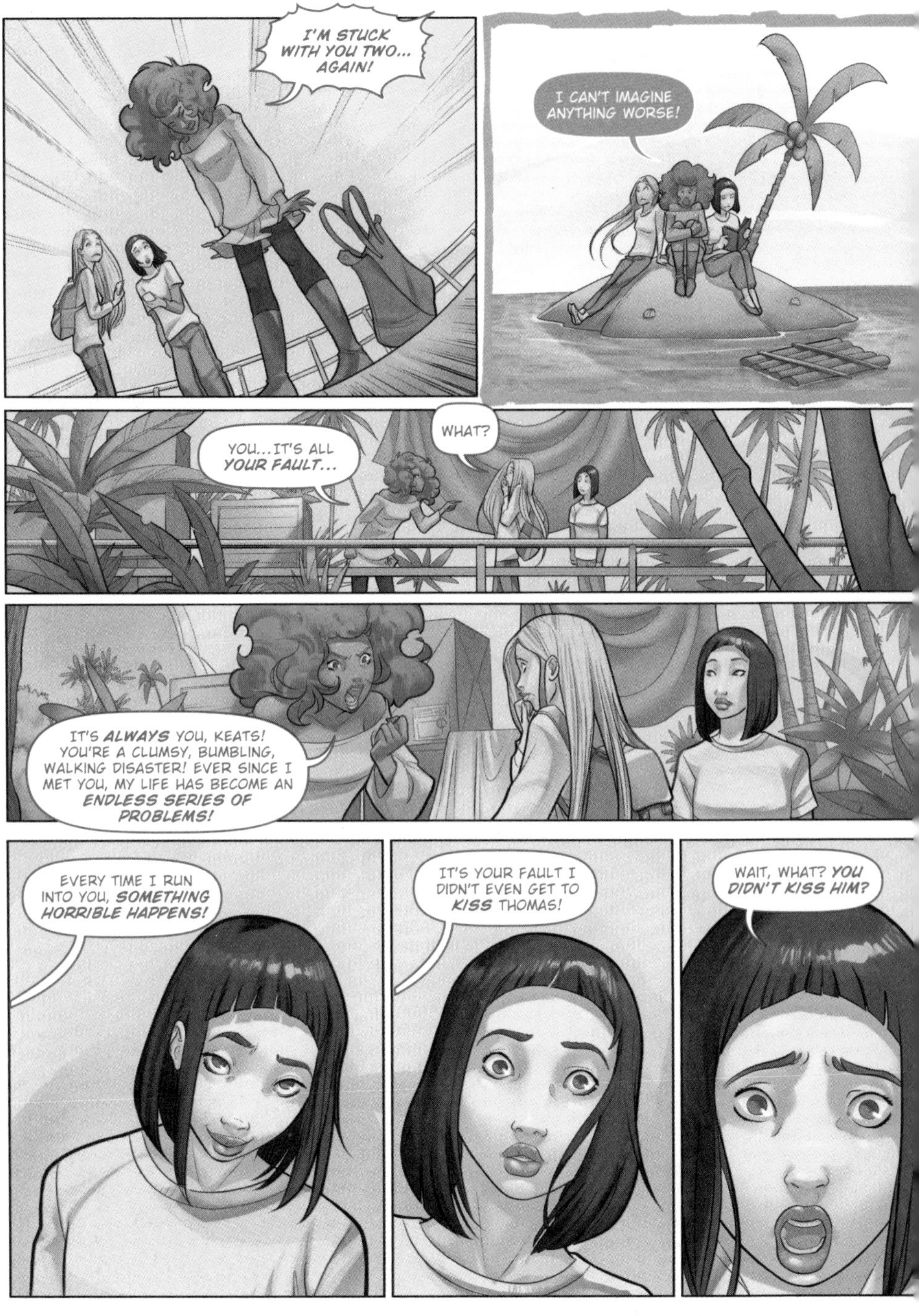
I'M STUCK WITH YOU TWO... AGAIN!
I CAN'T IMAGINE ANYTHING WORSE!
YOU...IT'S ALL YOUR FAULT...
WHAT?
IT'S ALWAYS YOU, KEATS! YOU'RE A CLUMSY, BUMBLING, WALKING DISASTER! EVER SINCE I MET YOU, MY LIFE HAS BECOME AN ENDLESS SERIES OF PROBLEMS!
EVERY TIME I RUN INTO YOU, SOMETHING HORRIBLE HAPPENS!
IT'S YOUR FAULT I DIDN'T EVEN GET TO KISS THOMAS!
WAIT, WHAT? YOU DIDN'T KISS HIM?

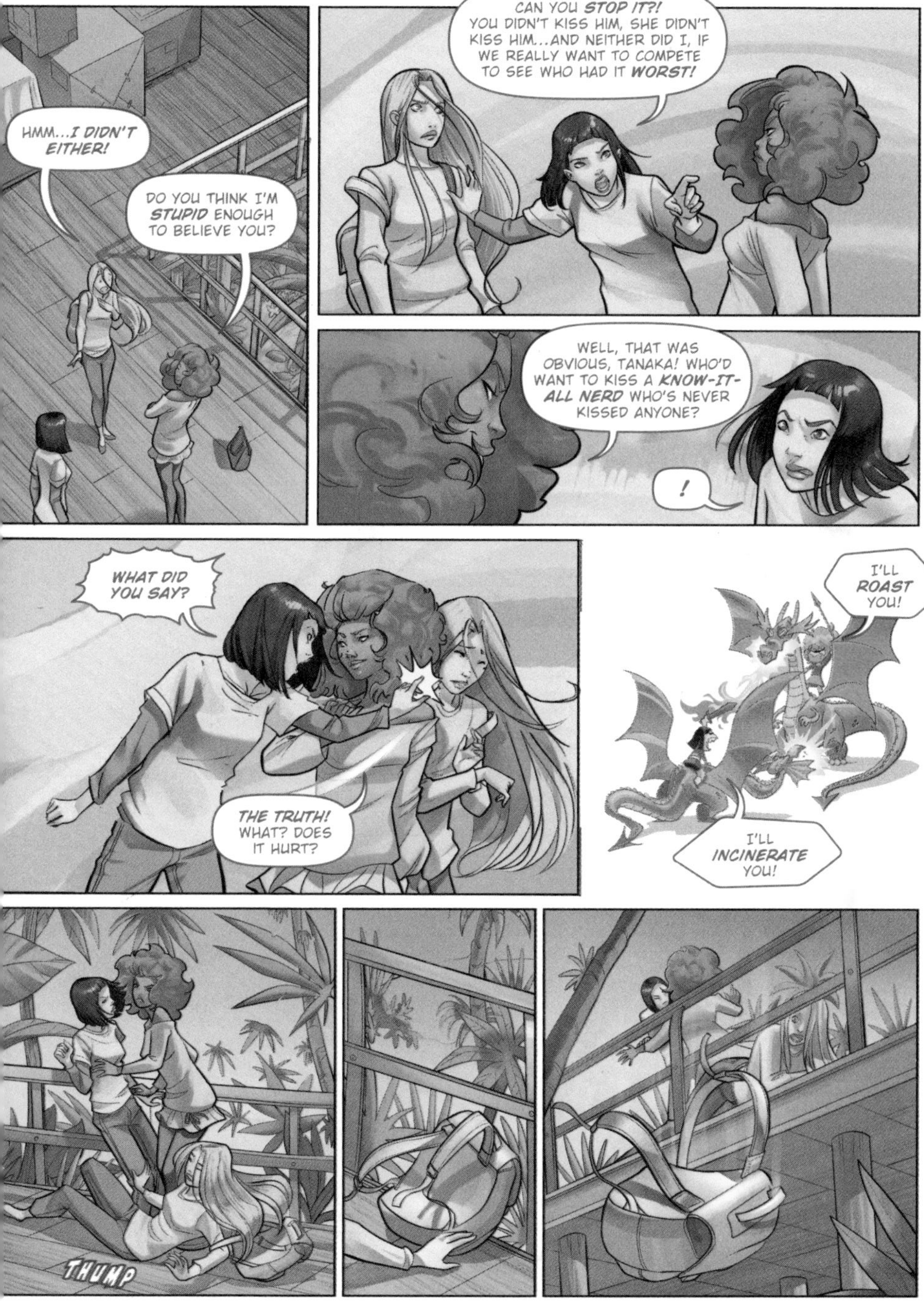
HMM...I DIDN'T EITHER!
DO YOU THINK I'M STUPID ENOUGH TO BELIEVE YOU?
CAN YOU STOP IT?! YOU DIDN'T KISS HIM, SHE DIDN'T KISS HIM...AND NEITHER DID I, IF WE REALLY WANT TO COMPETE TO SEE WHO HAD IT WORST!
WELL, THAT WAS OBVIOUS, TANAKA! WHO'D WANT TO KISS A KNOW-IT-ALL NERD WHO'S NEVER KISSED ANYONE?
!
WHAT DID YOU SAY?
THE TRUTH! WHAT? DOES IT HURT?
I'LL ROAST YOU!
I'LL INCINERATE YOU!
THUMP

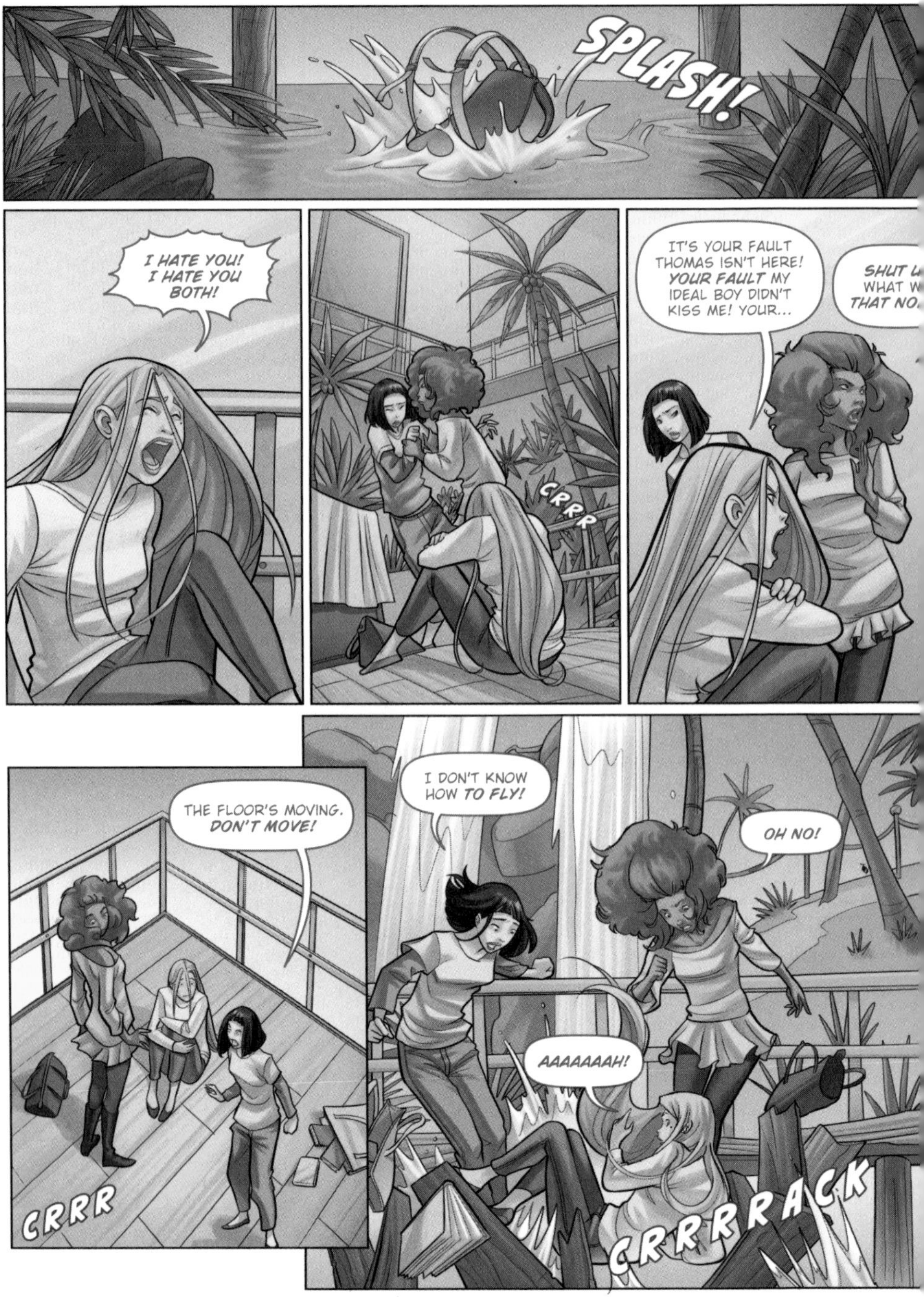
SPLASH!
I HATE YOU! I HATE YOU BOTH!
CRRR
IT'S YOUR FAULT THOMAS ISN'T HERE! YOUR FAULT MY IDEAL BOY DIDN'T KISS ME! YOUR...
THE FLOOR'S MOVING. DON'T MOVE!
CRRR
I DON'T KNOW HOW TO FLY!
OH NO!
AAAAAAAH!
CRRRRACK

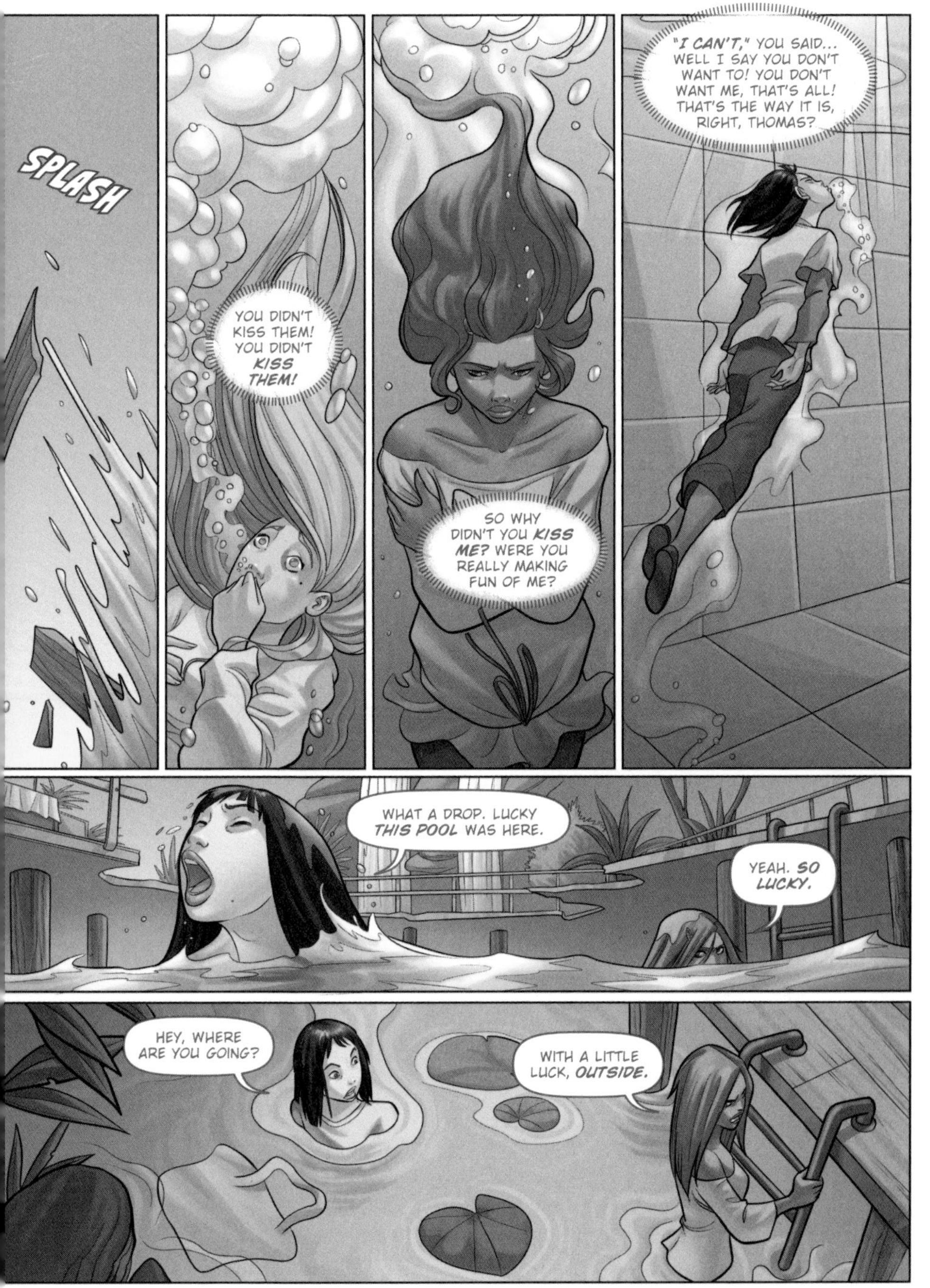
SPLASH
YOU DIDN'T KISS THEM! YOU DIDN'T KISS THEM!
SO WHY DIDN'T YOU KISS ME? WERE YOU REALLY MAKING FUN OF ME?
"I CAN'T," YOU SAID... WELL I SAY YOU DON'T WANT TO! YOU DON'T WANT ME, THAT'S ALL! THAT'S THE WAY IT IS, RIGHT, THOMAS?
WHAT A DROP. LUCKY THIS POOL WAS HERE.
YEAH. SO LUCKY.
HEY, WHERE ARE YOU GOING?
WITH A LITTLE LUCK, OUTSIDE.

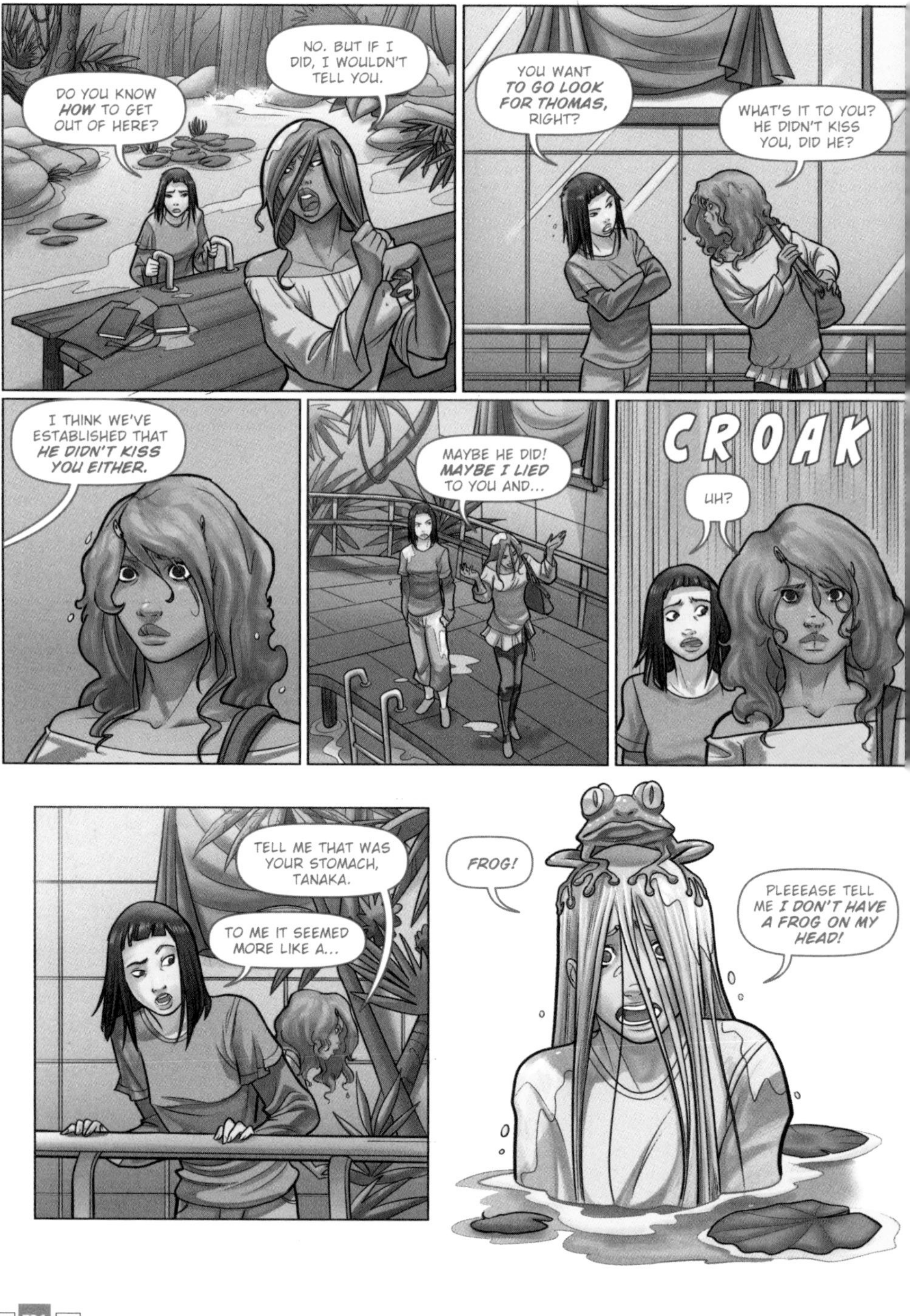
DO YOU KNOW HOW TO GET OUT OF HERE?
NO. BUT IF I DID, I WOULDN'T TELL YOU.
YOU WANT TO GO LOOK FOR THOMAS, RIGHT?
WHAT'S IT TO YOU? HE DIDN'T KISS YOU, DID HE?
I THINK WE'VE ESTABLISHED THAT HE DIDN'T KISS YOU EITHER.
MAYBE HE DID! MAYBE I LIED TO YOU AND...
CROAK
UH?
TELL ME THAT WAS YOUR STOMACH, TANAKA.
TO ME IT SEEMED MORE LIKE A...
FROG!
PLEEEASE TELL ME I DON'T HAVE A FROG ON MY HEAD!

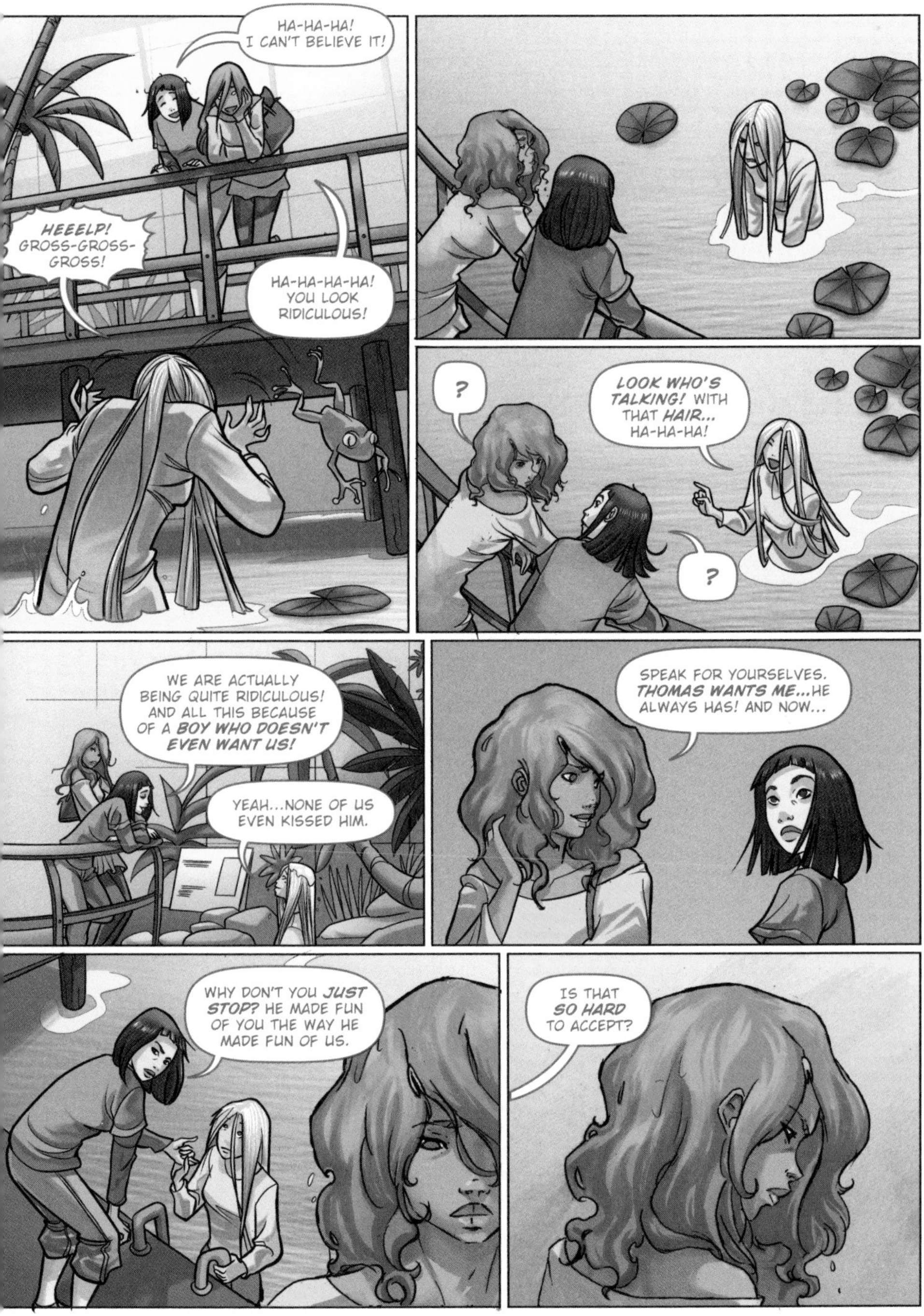
HA-HA-HA! I CAN'T BELIEVE IT!
HEEELP! GROSS-GROSS-GROSS!
HA-HA-HA-HA! YOU LOOK RIDICULOUS!
?
LOOK WHO'S TALKING! WITH THAT HAIR... HA-HA-HA!
?
WE ARE ACTUALLY BEING QUITE RIDICULOUS! AND ALL THIS BECAUSE OF A BOY WHO DOESN'T EVEN WANT US!
YEAH...NONE OF US EVEN KISSED HIM.
SPEAK FOR YOURSELVES. THOMAS WANTS ME...HE ALWAYS HAS! AND NOW...
WHY DON'T YOU JUST STOP? HE MADE FUN OF YOU THE WAY HE MADE FUN OF US.
IS THAT SO HARD TO ACCEPT?

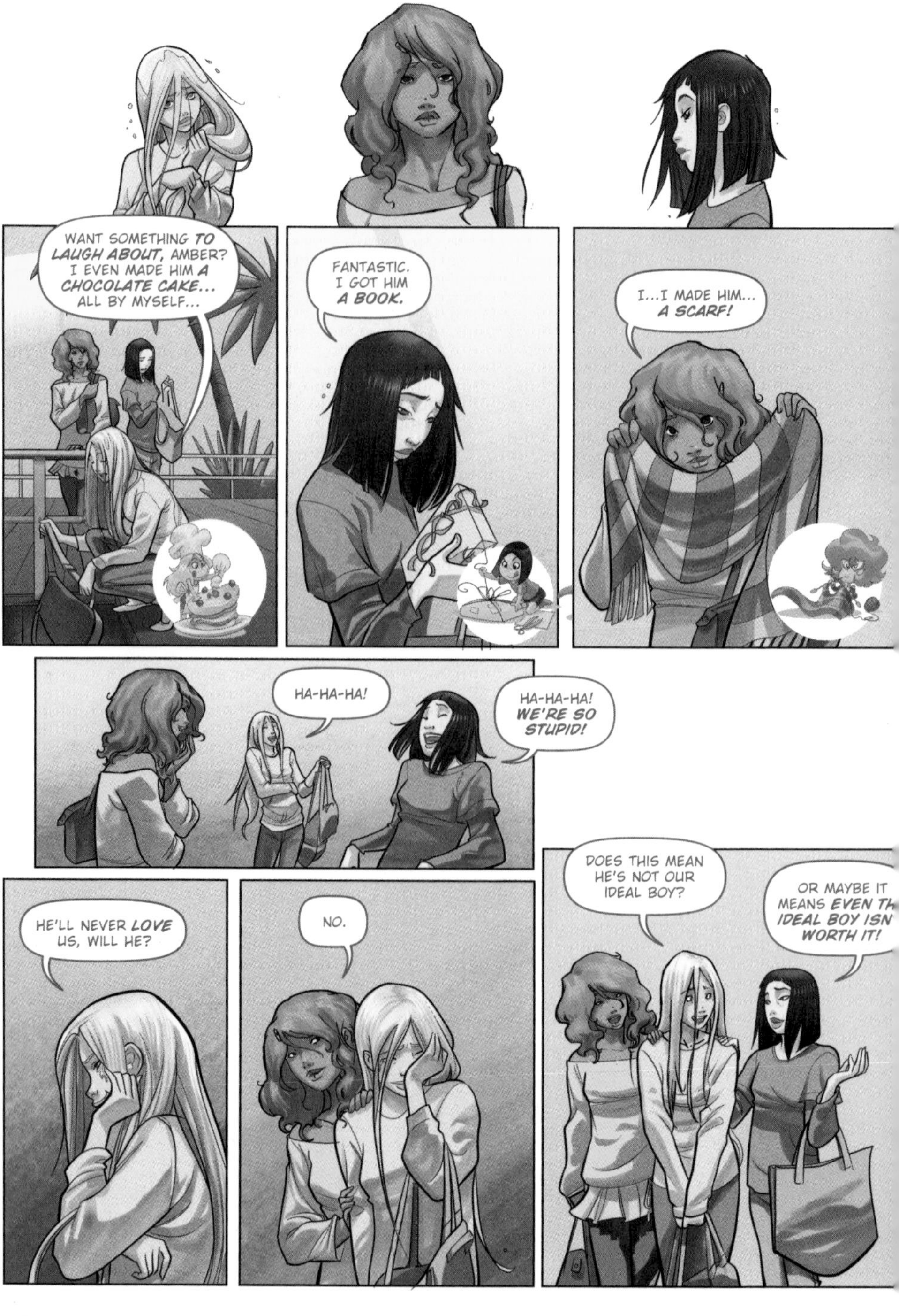
WANT SOMETHING TO LAUGH ABOUT, AMBER? I EVEN MADE HIM A CHOCOLATE CAKE... ALL BY MYSELF...
FANTASTIC. I GOT HIM A BOOK.
I...I MADE HIM... A SCARF!
HA-HA-HA!
HA-HA-HA! WE'RE SO STUPID!
HE'LL NEVER LOVE US, WILL HE?
NO.
DOES THIS MEAN HE'S NOT OUR IDEAL BOY?
OR MAYBE IT MEANS EVEN TH IDEAL BOY ISN WORTH IT!

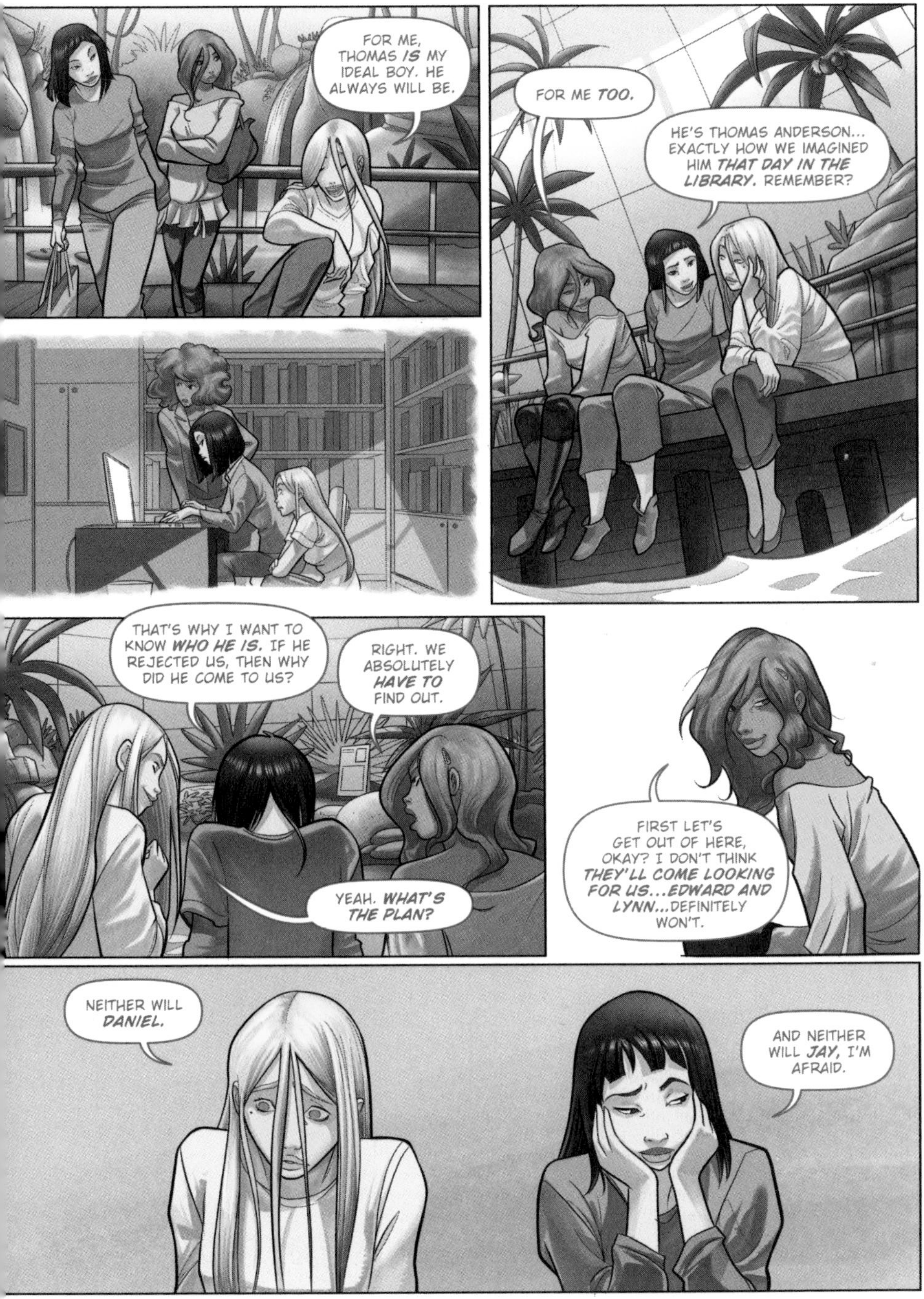
FOR ME, THOMAS IS MY IDEAL BOY. HE ALWAYS WILL BE.
FOR ME TOO.
HE'S THOMAS ANDERSON... EXACTLY HOW WE IMAGINED HIM THAT DAY IN THE LIBRARY. REMEMBER?
THAT'S WHY I WANT TO KNOW WHO HE IS. IF HE REJECTED US, THEN WHY DID HE COME TO US?
RIGHT. WE ABSOLUTELY HAVE TO FIND OUT.
YEAH. WHAT'S THE PLAN?
FIRST LET'S GET OUT OF HERE, OKAY? I DON'T THINK THEY'LL COME LOOKING FOR US...EDWARD AND LYNN...DEFINITELY WON'T.
NEITHER WILL DANIEL.
AND NEITHER WILL JAY, I'M AFRAID.

SO WE'LL DO IT *OURSELVES!*

TOGETHER, RIGHT? WE CREATED THE PERFECT BOY TOGETHER...SO WE SHOULD BE ABLE TO GET OUT OF HERE.

HOW?

WELL, WE NEED AN *IDEA* FIRST...

HMM...THERE!

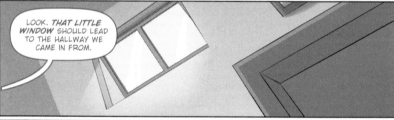

LOOK. *THAT LITTLE WINDOW* SHOULD LEAD TO THE HALLWAY WE CAME IN FROM.

IT'S A LITTLE HIGH...

I CAN DO IT!

THAT IS...IF YOU GIVE ME *A HAND...*

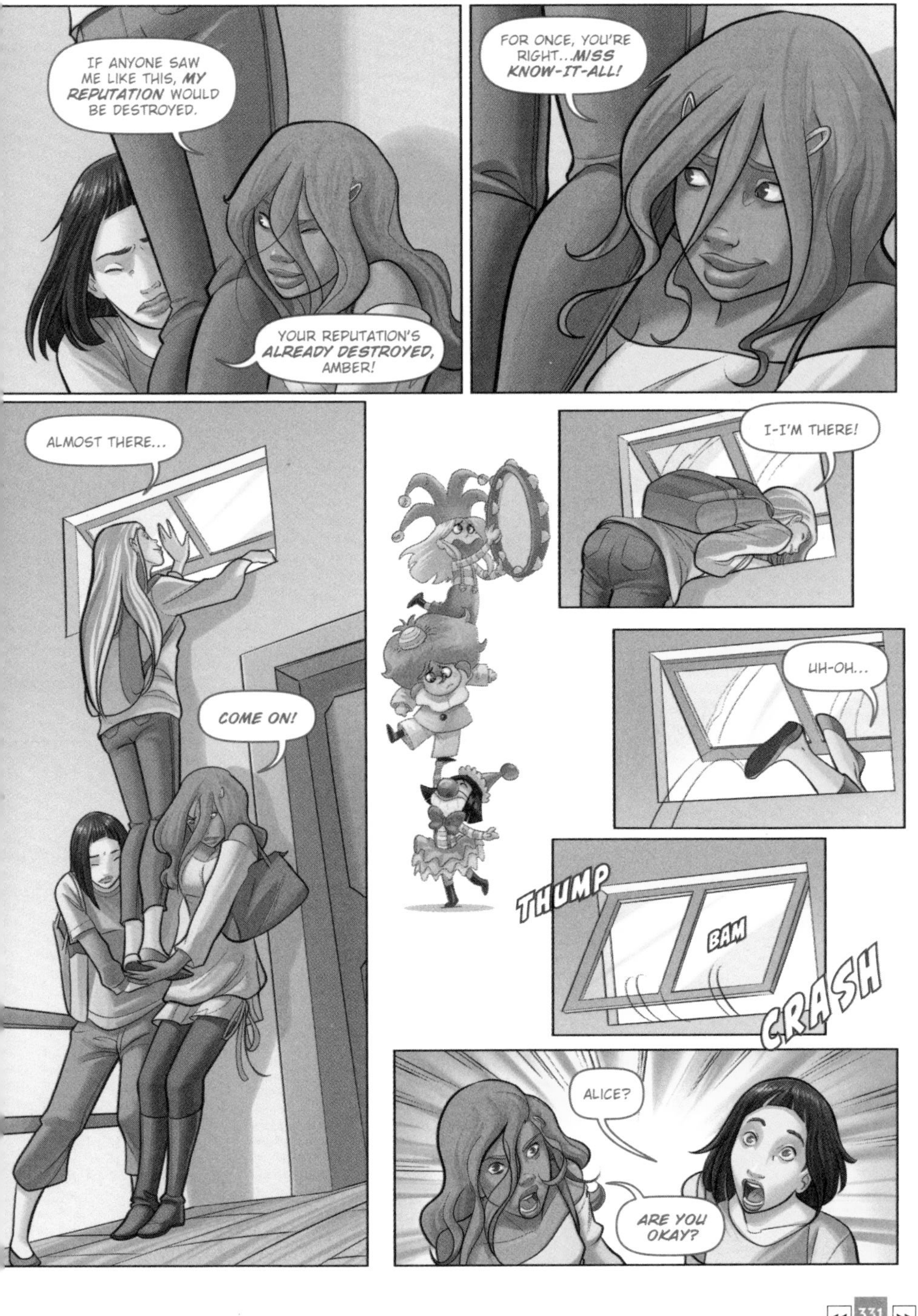
IF ANYONE SAW ME LIKE THIS, MY REPUTATION WOULD BE DESTROYED.
YOUR REPUTATION'S ALREADY DESTROYED, AMBER!
FOR ONCE, YOU'RE RIGHT...MISS KNOW-IT-ALL!
ALMOST THERE...
COME ON!
I-I'M THERE!
UH-OH...
THUMP
BAM
CRASH
ALICE?
ARE YOU OKAY?

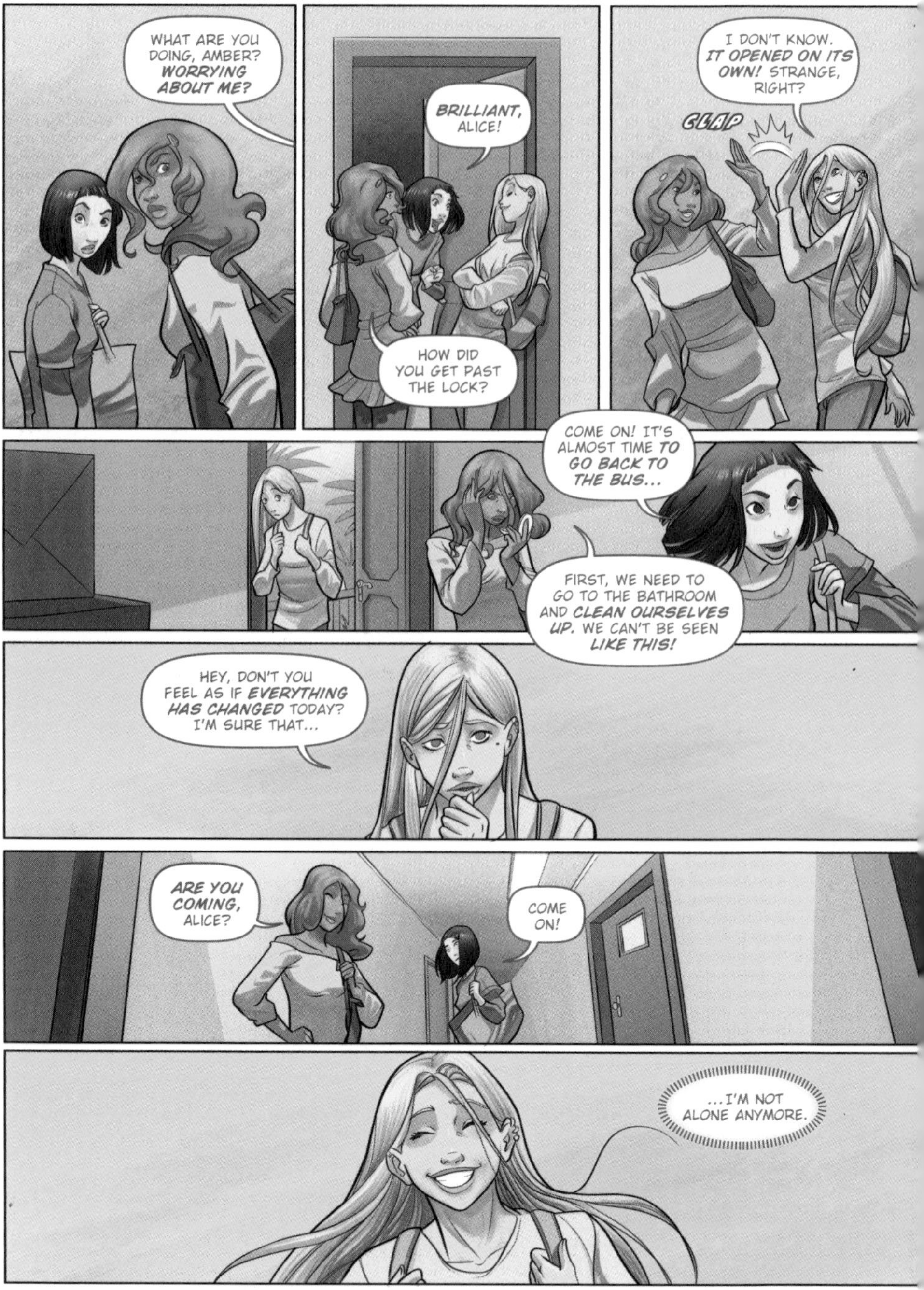

WHAT ARE YOU DOING, AMBER? WORRYING ABOUT ME?
BRILLIANT, ALICE!
HOW DID YOU GET PAST THE LOCK?
I DON'T KNOW. IT OPENED ON ITS OWN! STRANGE, RIGHT?
CLAP
COME ON! IT'S ALMOST TIME TO GO BACK TO THE BUS...
FIRST, WE NEED TO GO TO THE BATHROOM AND CLEAN OURSELVES UP. WE CAN'T BE SEEN LIKE THIS!
HEY, DON'T YOU FEEL AS IF EVERYTHING HAS CHANGED TODAY? I'M SURE THAT...
ARE YOU COMING, ALICE?
COME ON!
...I'M NOT ALONE ANYMORE.

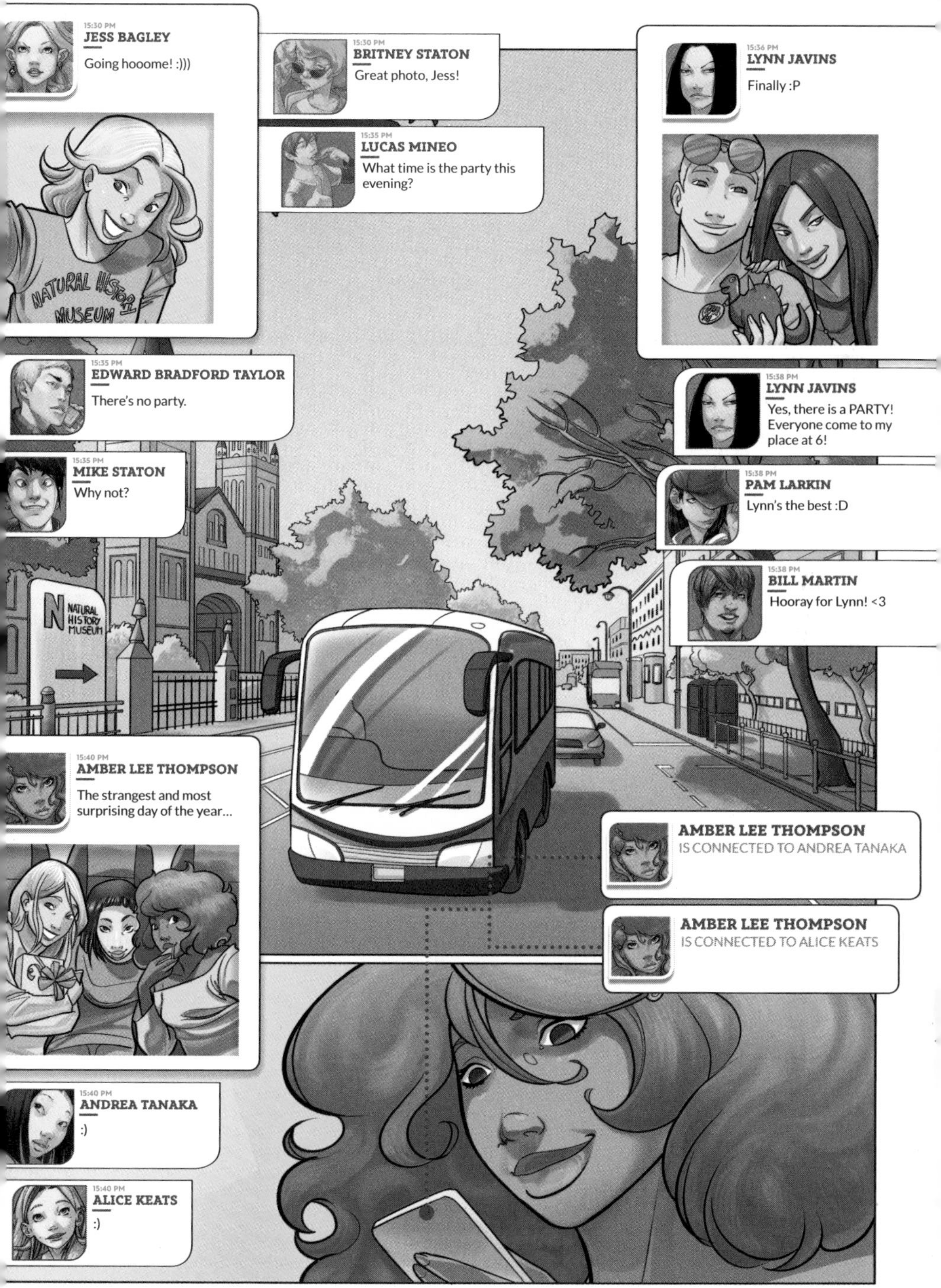
15:30 PM
JESS BAGLEY
Going hooome! :)))
NATURAL HISTORY MUSEUM
15:30 PM
BRITNEY STATON
Great photo, Jess!
15:35 PM
LUCAS MINEO
What time is the party this evening?
15:36 PM
LYNN JAVINS
Finally :P
15:35 PM
EDWARD BRADFORD TAYLOR
There's no party.
15:38 PM
LYNN JAVINS
Yes, there is a PARTY! Everyone come to my place at 6!
15:35 PM
MIKE STATON
Why not?
15:38 PM
PAM LARKIN
Lynn's the best :D
N NATURAL HISTORY MUSEUM
15:38 PM
BILL MARTIN
Hooray for Lynn! <3
15:40 PM
AMBER LEE THOMPSON
The strangest and most surprising day of the year…
AMBER LEE THOMPSON
IS CONNECTED TO ANDREA TANAKA
AMBER LEE THOMPSON
IS CONNECTED TO ALICE KEATS
15:40 PM
ANDREA TANAKA
:)
15:40 PM
ALICE KEATS
:)

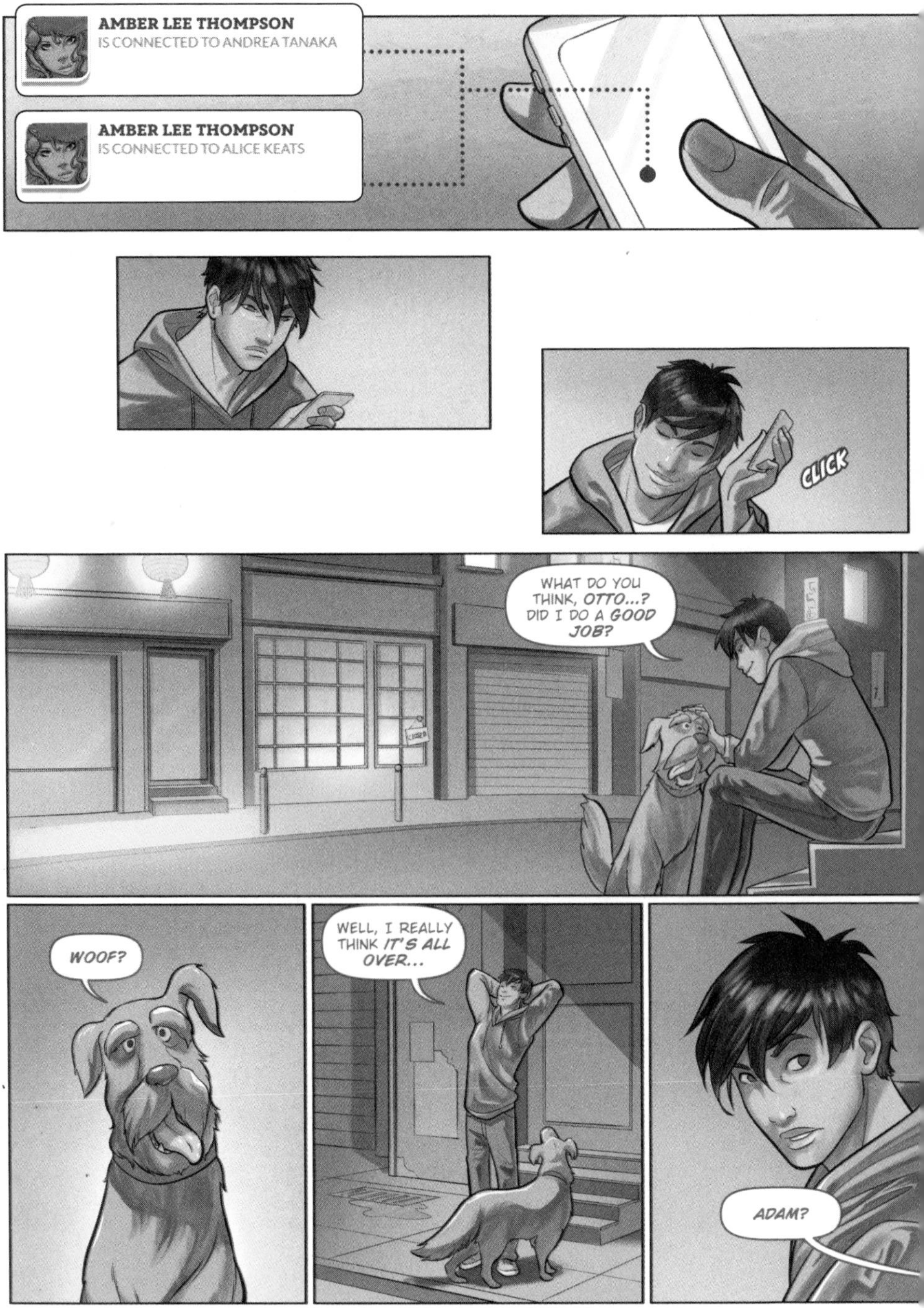
AMBER LEE THOMPSON
IS CONNECTED TO ANDREA TANAKA
AMBER LEE THOMPSON
IS CONNECTED TO ALICE KEATS
CLICK
WHAT DO YOU THINK, OTTO...? DID I DO A GOOD JOB?
WOOF?
WELL, I REALLY THINK IT'S ALL OVER...
ADAM?

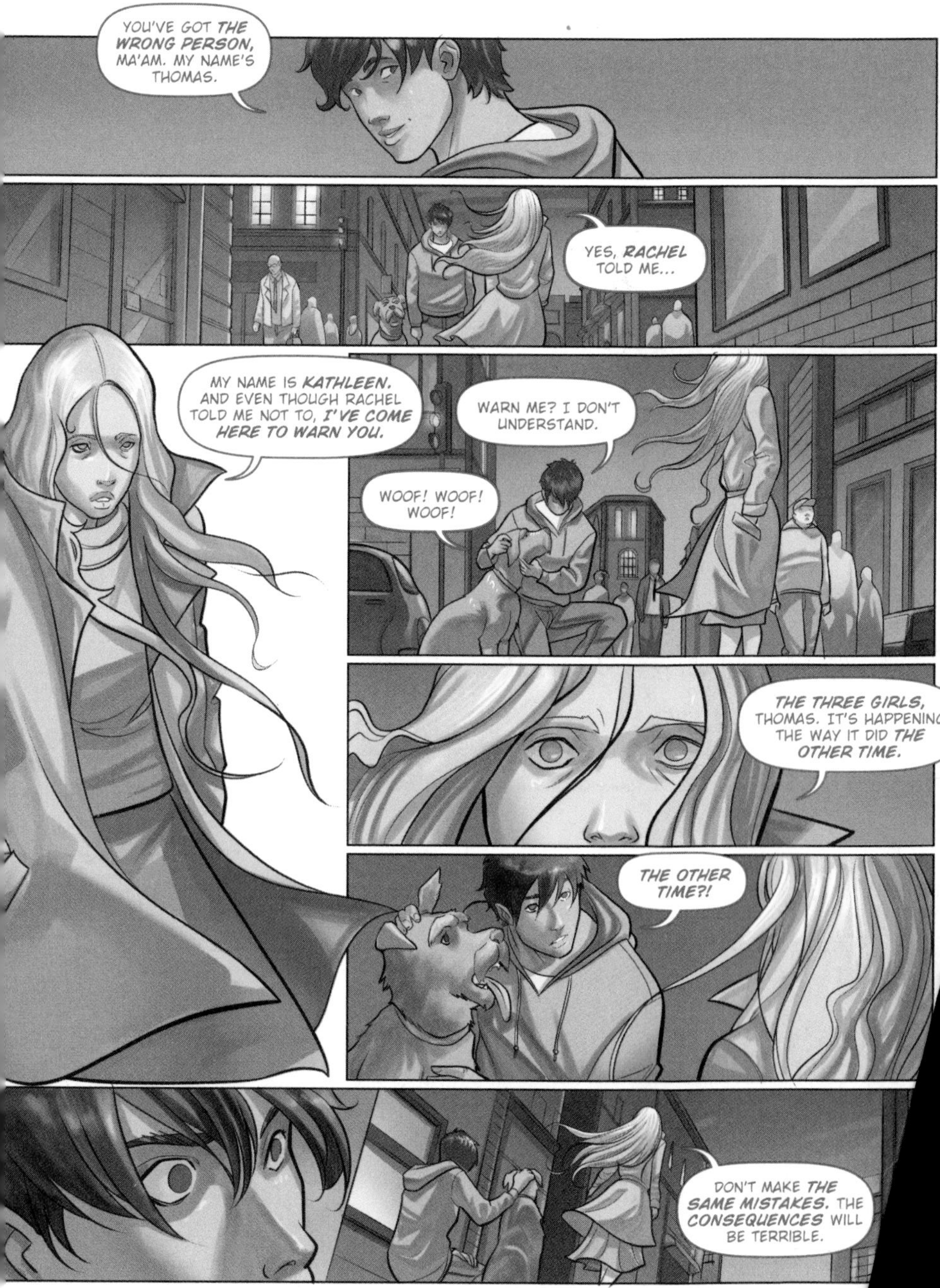
YOU'VE GOT THE WRONG PERSON, MA'AM. MY NAME'S THOMAS.
YES, RACHEL TOLD ME...
MY NAME IS KATHLEEN. AND EVEN THOUGH RACHEL TOLD ME NOT TO, I'VE COME HERE TO WARN YOU.
WARN ME? I DON'T UNDERSTAND.
WOOF! WOOF! WOOF!
THE THREE GIRLS, THOMAS. IT'S HAPPENING THE WAY IT DID THE OTHER TIME.
THE OTHER TIME?!
DON'T MAKE THE SAME MISTAKES. THE CONSEQUENCES WILL BE TERRIBLE.

END OF
CHAPTE

real life #1

#TOGETHER OR NOT?
Script: Alessandro Ferrari
Layout: Giada Perissinotto
Cleanup: Georges Duarte and Alberto Zanon
Emotidolls: Andrea Scoppetta
Color: Massimo Rocca, Pierluigi Casolino, Andrea Scoppetta, Mario Perrotta, Slava Panarin, Giuseppe Fontana, Gianluca Barone, Andrea Cagol, MADs Factory
Watercolor backgrounds: Valeria Turati
Translation: Edizioni BD and Erin Brady
Lettering and Infographic: Edizioni BD

COVER
Layout and cleanup: Simone Buonfantino and Marco Ghiglione
Color: Pierluigi Casolino

CONTRIBUTORS
Tomatofarm

DISNEY PUBLISHING WORLDWIDE
Global Magazines, Comics and Partworks

Publisher
Lynn Waggoner

Editorial Team
Bianca Coletti (Director, Magazine)
Guido Frazzini (Director, Comics)
Carlotta Quattrocolo (Executive Editor, Franchise)
Stefano Ambrosio (Executive Editor, New IP)
Julie Dorris (Senior Editor)
Behnoosh Khalili (Editor)

Design
Enrico Soave (Senior Designer)

Art
⎵ Shue (VP, Global Art), Roberto Santillo (Creative ⎵tor), Marco Ghiglione (Creative Manager), Manny ⎵s (Senior Illustration Manager, Comics), Stefano Attardi (Computer Art Designer)

Portfolio Management
Olivia Ciancarelli (Director)

Business & Marketing
⎵love (Managing Editor), Mariantonietta ⎵rketing Manager), Virpi Korhonen (Editorial Manager)

⎵ Disney Enterprises, Inc.

LETTERING ASSISTANCE FOR YEN PRESS EDITION
Rachel J. Pierce

This book is a work of fiction. Names, characters, places, and incidents are the product of the author's imagination or are used fictitiously. Any resemblance to actual events, locales, or persons, living or dead, is coincidental.

Real Life, Vol. 1 © 2018 by Disney Enterprises, Inc.

English translation © 2018 by Disney Enterprises, Inc.

YEN PRESS
1290 Avenue of the Americas
New York, NY 10104

VISIT US AT
yenpress.com
facebook.com/yenpress
twitter.com/yenpress
yenpress.tumblr.com
instagram.com/yenpress

First Yen Press Edition:
March 2018

Yen Press is an imprint of Yen Press, LLC. The Yen Press name and logo are trademarks of Yen Press, LLC.

The publisher is not responsible for websites (or their content) that are not owned by the publisher.

Library of Congress Control Number: 2018930815

ISBNs:
978-0-316-47715-4 (paperback)
978-1-9753-2758-3 (ebook)

10 9 8 7 6 5 4 3 2 1

LSC-C

Printed in the United States of America

2

18

<< 335 >>